LOVE'S GENTLE CARESS

"You don't have to be afraid anymore, Billie. I'll take care of you. . . . I'll take such good care of you. . . ."

Relaxing completely in Rand's embrace, Billie felt the touch of his lips against her hair, his warm breath against her skin. His hands moved against her back, holding her, caressing her. She felt his touch against her flesh, gentle, reassuring.

His lips touched her fluttering lids, her cheek, the bridge of her nose. He circled her mouth with light, fleeting kisses. She raised her face and he took her lips eagerly. His kiss deepened, overwhelming her, stealing her breath, making her heart race. Her mouth was his and he indulged himself freely, abandoning it at last to trail light, feathering kisses against her neck and the smooth curve of her shoulder.

"I'm so glad I found you, Billie. No one will ever hurt you again. . . ."

ELAINE BARBIERI
ECSTASY'S TRAIL

ZEBRA BOOKS
KENSINGTON PUBLISHING CORP.

ZEBRA BOOKS

are published by

Kensington Publishing Corp.
475 Park Avenue South
New York, NY 10016

First printing: January 1987

Printed in the United States of America

To Holly Anne Settineri,
the newest member of our family,
with all my love.

Chapter I

A sudden uneasiness jerked Billie awake. Cool fingers of fear trailed down her spine in the silence of the empty house. Unmoving, she strained her eyes into a darkness alleviated only by the pale shaft of moonlight filtering through the window of her room. She swallowed hard against a rapidly swelling panic that choked her throat. The ragged beat of her heart escalated to thunder in her ears as a small creak from the room beyond snapped her eyes toward the doorway.

Momentarily paralyzed by the sight of the gradually turning knob, she remained motionless for a breathless eternity as the door swung slowly open. The silent male shadow in the doorway hesitated, snapping into movement at the same moment she jerked upright to scramble toward the night table beside the bed. Her trembling fingers closed over the handle of her gun the second before it was wrested from her grasp. A blow to her face knocked her backward against the bed. Her mind registered the clatter of her gun on the floor even as a heated male body pinned her helplessly with its weight.

Still reeling from the force of the blow, Billie heard a harsh, familiar voice rasp in her ear.

"You knew I was comin' for you sooner or later, didn't you, little bitch? You was waitin' for me, but you wasn't fast enough to get away from me this time, was you? *Was you?*" A brutal hand grasped her chin, giving her head a merciless shake as the voice demanded, "Answer me! I want to hear

7

you talk now, bitch! You was never at a loss for words before . . . tellin' me what would happen if I ever tried to put my hands on you . . . tellin' me how your pa would finish me off . . . But your pa ain't alive no more, is he?"

"Let me go . . . bastard. . . ." Billie's voice was a grating whisper. "Let me go, McCulla, or I swear you'll die for this!"

"And who's goin' to do the killin', bitch? You? Hell, you ain't goin' to be in shape to do nothin' when I get done with you tonight."

McCulla's face leered into hers, startlingly clear despite the limited light of the room. There was no doubting the savage twist of his thin lips or the menace in his pale eyes. And there was no doubting the victory reflected there as she lay helpless beneath him. Her head throbbing painfully from his blow, Billie was abruptly sure that if she did not escape him now, she never would.

Panic endowing her with strength she did not realize she possessed, she was suddenly struggling fiercely. Twisting and turning, she flailed heavily at McCulla's face and neck, fists tight with fury.

Muttering a muffled curse, McCulla sought to suppress her blows, finally succeeding in pinning her wrists above her head. Holding her helpless with his superior strength, he ravaged her mouth with his as his hand tore at her nightdress, seeking her breasts.

Revulsion combined with pure terror as Billie realized she was fast succumbing to McCulla's unrelenting attack. His tongue thrust deeply into her mouth, and all but gagging under its assault, she bit down sharply in spontaneous rage. With a harsh cry of pain, her attacker jerked himself back, momentarily relieving her of his weight and allowing Billie the opportunity she sought.

Summoning all her strength, she brought up her knee in a quick, devastating blow that left him gasping. With one strong push she was free!

Billie was on her feet and running out of the bedroom when she heard the sound of McCulla's step behind her. Fear gaining control of her senses, she jerked open the front door and started across the yard, her eyes on the cover of trees that edged the narrow expanse of cleared terrain. She was running, gasping. Sharp stones on the uneven ground cut into her bare feet and she stumbled, falling painfully to her knees. The heavy footsteps behind her were drawing closer! Determination overcoming her pain, Billie picked herself up and stumbled forward once again. It was only a little farther . . . a little farther and she would be able to hide in the darkness of the woods. Just a few more yards . . .

But he was close . . . too close. In a moment of mind-consuming fear, Billie darted a look over her shoulder, her eyes meeting the furious gaze of Wes McCulla in the moment before he reached out to grasp a length of pale blond hair streaming out behind her. Jerked suddenly backward as his hand caught in the tangled mass, Billie emitted a sharp cry of pain. His labored breath hot on her face, McCulla held her helpless until her struggles trailed to a shuddering halt.

"You're goin' to be sorry you did that. I wasn't goin' to hurt you much tonight. I was plannin' on takin' it easy with you and savin' you for another day. But you changed that, bitch. 'Cause now I'm goin' to teach you a lesson. And when I'm done usin' you, I'm goin' to teach you that same lesson again. The lesson's simple. It goes like this."

Raising his arm with great deliberation, McCulla struck her a savage blow. Brilliant colors filled with pain reverberated inside Billie's head. She fought to retain her waning consciousness as a darkness unrelated to night hovered at the edge of her mind. Held upright only by McCulla's grip on her hair, she swayed weakly, the echo of his low laughter ringing in her ears.

The bitter taste of blood and bile filled her mouth. Her sight blurred. Still laughing, McCulla began dragging her back toward the house, his hand wound unmercifully in her hair. With a supreme effort, Billie regained her feet, only to have McCulla twist his grip tighter still.

Hardly conscious, Billy realized she was being thrust through the front door of the house. Stumbling, she fell to her knees. Flicking in and out of consciousness, Billie saw the shadow of McCulla's broad frame bend over her. Grasping her roughly by the hair, he jerked her up to meet

9

his eyes.

"Where's all your smart words now, Miss Wilhelmina Winslow? And who's goin' to stop me when I drag you in that room and take you? But you don't have to worry," he reassured venomously. "I ain't goin' to hit you no more . . . not now. You're havin' trouble seein' out of that one eye, ain't you? But you can see out of the other. That's good, 'cause I want you to see who's takin' you. And I'm goin' to take great pleasure in havin' you say some things I want to hear."

"You'll never make me say—"

Interrupted by her own gasp of pain as McCulla twisted his grip on her hair, Billie fought to catch her breath.

"I guess you ain't learned your lesson yet, have you? Too bad, 'cause I'm gettin' tired of teachin' you the same thing over and over. I'm beginnin' to lose my patience."

Jerking her upright, McCulla stood her unsteadily on her feet. His gaze raking her face as she swayed uncertainly, he raised his arm again. The flat of his hand crashed against the side of her head, sending her staggering backward. Grabbing her by the collar of her nightdress, McCulla pulled her around and pushed her through the bedroom door in a thrust that sent her sprawling.

Blacking out temporarily as she hit the floor, Billie opened her eyes to see McCulla towering over her. The silver moonlight glinted on the bared flesh of his chest as his hands moved to his belt.

"That's right, bitch. I'm goin' to make myself real comfortable, 'cause I'm plannin' on stayin' with you for a while tonight. And when I'm done, you an' me are goin' to talk. And you're goin' to say what I want to hear."

"Never—never—"

The pain that filled her body robbed Billie of the strength to continue. Her reeling senses reacting solely to the need for escape, she began dragging herself backward.

The low laugh sounded again. "Oh, yes, bitch . . . you'll see. . . . I'm goin' to make you tell me how much you—"

McCulla's voice went on, but Billie was no longer listening. Her palms had brushed against a hard metal object

10

as they slid against the darkness of the floor. Her heart leaping, Billie moved her hand cautiously, her shaking fingers finally closing around the familiar wooden handle of her gun. Her gun . . . the one McCulla had knocked from her hand . . . Her gun . . .

" . . . what you say then, bitch. You're goin' to beg me to—"

McCulla's voice came to an abrupt halt as moonlight glinted on the raised barrel of the gun in Billie's hand.

"B—back up, McCulla."

His body stiffening, McCulla stared at her in the dim light of the room.

"What you got there, bitch?"

"You know what I've got. Now do what I said and back up!"

Her voice wavering weakly, Billie fought the giddiness that assailed her. No, not now! She couldn't pass out now!

"Why should I back up, bitch? You ain't goin' to do nothin' with that gun. You can't even hold it steady. And you don't want to shoot me, do you? 'Cause if you did, my pa would hunt you down and find you no matter where you hid. You ain't got no place to go, so just give me that gun, bitch. And if you do your best to make me happy tonight, maybe I'll try to forget everthin' that's gone before. You'd like that, wouldn't you? I can be real good to a woman if she treats me right. I can—"

"No!"

Stopping him just as he was about to make a quick move toward her, Billie warned, in a low, emotionless voice that belied her body's violent quaking, "If you make another move, I'll shoot."

"You ain't gonna do nuthin'. But I am, bitch. I am."

McCulla lunged forward, and Billie fired. His body jerking stiffly erect as the bullet hit him, McCulla let out a low gasp.

"Bitch! I'm gonna—"

He took another step and Billie fired again. The shock of the sound jarred her reeling senses, and Billie watched as the second shot knocked McCulla backward against the wall.

11

But he did not fall . . . he did not fall! He was starting toward her again when Billie fired a third time. A low sob broke from her throat as McCulla's body jerked to a halt and fell heavily to the floor.

The room was silent except for the echo of her own gasping breath. Holding the smoking gun tightly, Billie struggled to her feet. She took a few steps to stand swaying over McCulla's lifeless form. He was dead. She had killed him and she felt nothing . . . nothing at all.

Billie shot a quick glance out the window, her eye on the night sky. In a few hours it would be dawn, and she needed to put as much distance between herself and the body in the next room as she could. She had given little thought to Wesley McCulla since she had fired that last shot, other than to cover his body with the blanket so that she might be spared the grisly sight as she dressed. Although she was certain that his destination was known to others at the Circle M, she doubted anyone would come looking for him before morning. They doubtless expected he would be spending an entertaining night and would be late to rise.

Billie gave a small involuntary shudder. Wesley McCulla, spoiled son of Daniel McCulla and heir to the largest spread in this part of Texas, had made no secret of his intentions toward her. He had not waited long after her father's death to come after her. No, just two weeks, long enough for her nightly vigilance to result in the deep sleep of exhaustion that had allowed him to gain entrance without her realization.

But her only thought now was escape. She had no choice. She was totally alone. All that was left of the Diamond W was the house and the land on which it stood. Dan McCulla would not allow the fact that she was a woman to stop him from getting his revenge. It would not matter to him that his son had deserved what he had gotten, and it would not matter how many people knew. Dan McCulla had not become the most powerful man in this section of the state without bending the law to suit his purpose.

Taking a deep breath, Billie surveyed her reflection in the

12

small mirror she had propped by the fire. The sight was startling. Looking back at her was a slender, battered youth of medium height dressed in canvas pants, loose leather boots that reached almost to the knee, homespun shirt, well-worn vest, and the inevitable bandana tied around the neck. A high-crowned, broad-brimmed hat and a much patched jacket lay on the chair.

Reaching to the bench beside her, Billie picked up her father's gunbelt and strapped it low around her hips. Yes, that was better. The only trace of femininity that remained was the long pale blond hair tied to the back of her neck and the extensive length of dark lashes visible only on her undamaged eye. Turning toward the table behind her, she picked up the scissors.

Anxiety beginning to overwhelm her at the loss of time the bathing of her bruises and the change into her disguise had taken, Billie put her scissors to the bound mane of hair. She made one cut and then another. She threw the golden locks into the fire as they fell into her hand, making certain to leave no trace on the floor. Turning back to the mirror, she leaned closer to the smooth surface and cautiously trimmed the lush, feathery lashes around her one uninjured eye until only short, dark stubs remained. Carefully, not without considerable pain, she lifted the creases of her swollen eye and repeated the process. She surveyed her image once more. Yes, she was totally unrecognizable as a woman. It was indeed fortunate that she was so tall for a woman, and so slender. Her breasts were small despite their well-rounded contours. Her father's shirt, some simple binding, and the standard underwear of the cowman had removed all trace of female curves.

She was ready to leave. Wincing as she turned to tuck the scissors into the waiting saddlebag, Billie took a short, shaken breath. The vicious beating she had withstood from Wesley McCulla was beginning to take its toll. Her head was aching fiercely, her blackened eye so painful that her good eye watered in determined sympathy. There was not a spot on her body that did not throb in protest against the vile attack, and the rapid stiffening of her abused flesh was beginning to make the simplest movement difficult. She was suddenly, frighteningly certain that if she hesitated any longer, she would not be in condition to even mount her horse.

Picking up the mirror, Billie carried it back into her room and replaced it carefully on the washstand. Her eyes drawn to the unmoving, covered body on the floor, Billie attempted to suppress the tremor that shook her. Turning quickly, she left the room. Taking only the time necessary to snatch the broad-brimmed hat from the chair and jam it on her head, and to slip her arms into the jacket that had lain beside it, she snatched up her saddlebags and walked unsteadily toward the door.

She approached her waiting horse. Mounting with considerable pain, she turned him toward the wooded trail and spurred him forward. She was determined not to look back.

Billie clutched the reins in a desperate grip, her body bent low over the saddle. She was uncertain how much longer she could go on. Despite her pain, she had maintained a steady pace northward since leaving her home the day before, certain as she was that Wesley McCulla's body would be discovered before the day was out. She had known accomplishing a good head start would be her only chance of escaping the long arm of Dan McCulla, and she was determined that the last of the Texas Winslows would not succumb to his vengeance.

She had not allowed herself to leave the saddle after departing the Diamond W, except for short intervals of necessity. She had not eaten, realizing she would be unable to keep anything down, and had finally all but fallen into her bedroll when darkness had made it impossible for her to go any farther. Mounting her horse that morning had almost been beyond her physical capability. But the second night of her flight was fast approaching, and she was only too aware that she was almost beyond the limit of her endurance. She needed to go somewhere . . . somewhere where she could rest without fear of being discovered.

San Antonio . . . It was just coming into view on the horizon. She had been there only twice before, the last time being several years ago. Surely in a town of that size a young boy could manage to find anonymity and a comfortable bed to rest his head for at least one night. She did not need to assess her appearance again to reassure herself that she was completely unrecognizable as a woman. The stiffness of her face told her only too clearly that the swelling was worse, and she had no doubt that disfiguring bruises completely disguised what little could have remained of her feminine features.

In any case, she had no choice. She needed rest and a good meal, or her journey would end right here, on the hard Texas ground. Realizing the futility of further consideration, Billie spurred her sorrel into a faster pace and bit her lips against the pain the motion incurred. Yes, she would be in San Antonio within the hour, and she would sleep.

Chapter II

Rand Pierce scowled and spurred his horse to a faster pace. Damn it all to hell, he had never seen such a motley-looking bunch as the one that had answered his advertisement! Of all the damned luck! He should've known this trail drive was jinxed from the moment Jess Williams had fallen sick and been unable to foreman the herd. With his other trail bosses already engaged in drives, it had been a matter of cancelling the contract for the Blackfoot Agency in western Montana or taking the herd there himself. He had had little choice, and he wasn't happy about it.

It had been a few years since he had personally functioned as foreman on a drive. He had been a mere boy when he had carried a musket in the ranks of the Union Army. But he had learned quickly, and when the smoke had cleared, he had seen a real future in Texas. With careful deliberation he had worked himself from drover to beef contractor until he had become well respected for his dependability and more wealthy than he had ever dreamed. So, at the age of thirty-three, he was healthy, wealthy, and had a good life. He presently had a beautiful, entertaining woman to serve his every need, and the freedom to replace her when she no longer suited him. His future looked too good to be believed, and he damned well wasn't going to let anything threaten it.

His present contract with the United States government demanded that the herd just coming into view on the horizon be delivered to the Blackfoot Indian Agent in Montana no later than mid-September. Jess Williams had received the herd of three thousand head of prime Mexican cattle at the border almost a month before. Just shortly after the trail branding had been completed, the trouble had begun.

Jess had been the first to fall sick to the fever. Then, one by one, half his crew had succumbed to the same malady that had rendered Jess unable to go on, and Rand had been left with a restless herd of prime cattle and a less than sufficient crew to drive it.

Grinding his teeth in angry frustration, Rand lifted his stained Stetson from his head and wiped the back of his arm across his forehead. He ran his free hand through his heavy black hair and jammed his hat back down on his head. The clear blue of his eyes were two brilliant sparks of color in his sun-darkened face as he squinted into the early afternoon sun. His frown deepened, the arched line of his dark brows drawing together. He grimaced at the sight of the milling cattle. He didn't like the looks of them. Pulling back on the reins, he slowed his gelding to a more modest gait. The herd had been stationary for a few days and was obviously skittish. He had no desire to come riding up like an inexperienced fool and spook them. With his limited crew, a stampede could prove disastrous.

Four mounted figures were moving carefully through the herd—four men, not including the cook, the horse wrangler, and himself, who had all been drafted into twenty-four-hour service until further notice. He had just returned from San Antonio where he had hired six new men to fill the depleted ranks of drovers. The six he had hired were the best of the dregs of humanity that had shown up in answer to the notice he had posted two days before. Most claimed to be experienced on trail drives, and he was damned if he believed them. But he had wasted enough time. The trail to Montana would take four months or more from this point on, and he had to get the herd moving.

A lone rider rode out to meet him as he approached, the weary set of his shoulders stating only too clearly his fatigue. Willie Hart was one of the most dependable men who had ever worked for him and he was grateful that the gaunt

18

Texan was not one of the men who had been stricken.

Rand nodded toward the herd as the drover drew alongside. "Looks like they're edgy, Willie. What's bothering them?"

"I ain't got an idea in the world, Rand. Maybe they sense some bad weather comin' up, or maybe this air's just layin' too heavy on their backs. All's I know is that we'd better get them movin' soon, or they're likely to take off by themselves."

"We'll have them moving by tomorrow, Willie. I just hired on six . . . drovers."

His hesitation raised Willie's sandy brows, and Rand gave a small laugh.

"They're the pick of a pretty seedy crop, and I get the feeling I'm going to have to keep a sharp eye on them. But even if they don't have the experience they claim to have, they'll have it by the time they reach Montana. In any case, I didn't have much choice. I gave them a couple of hours to settle their affairs. They'll be arriving before sunset."

Rand's voice drew to a halt as he began to work his way through the milling herd. He did not resume speaking until they had reached the cook wagon. Dismounting, he turned back to Willie, his expression thoughtful.

"I've decided that I'm going to split you and the rest of the boys into separate night guards until we can get the measure of the new men's worth." At Willie's pained expression, Rand gave a short laugh. "Sorry. I know you, Jim, and Russ work well together, but I don't have much choice. If the new boys work out, then maybe we can adjust the schedule."

Nodding without comment, Willie walked to the fire and poured himself a cup of coffee. Rand frowned and followed suit. He didn't like breaking up bunkies. His extended experience on the trail had proved a foreman did best to observe his men and allow natural companions to work together. It eliminated the occasional clash of personalities that could occur on a drive of extended duration. But he was also certain that he needed to depend on the judgment of men he respected and trusted, and he needed at least one on each watch. His eyes moving to the restless cattle, he

19

frowned more darkly. And if this night shaped up the way it appeared to be heading, he had a feeling he was going to need a full, dependable crew to keep the beeves in line.

His decision confirmed in his mind, Rand lifted the cup to his lips and tossed down the tepid coffee. Damn, even the coffee was suffering with Nate taking turns among the cattle. He knew damned well that the first thing he was going to do when the new men arrived was relieve Nate from herding duty so he could return full time to the chuck wagon. Hell, there was no point having the best trail cook in Texas if the man didn't have time to ply his trade properly.

Tossing down his cup, Rand turned, his startling eyes moving back assessingly to the restless cattle. Unconsciously flexing the muscles in his broad shoulders, he suppressed a silent groan at their stiffness. He hadn't realized he had gotten so soft. In the past two years of limited activity, he had easily maintained the lean line of his tall, well-muscled frame with the extended riding necessitated by his buying and receiving trips. An unconscious smile flicked across his lips. If he were to judge from Lucille's comments the last time they had been alone together, he'd have to say he hadn't slipped a bit. But it was now only too painfully obvious that he had come a long way from the physical condition demanded for role of trail boss.

In any case, he was certain that another week in the saddle would effectively take care of any shortcomings in that respect. And he was just as certain Lucille would be anxiously awaiting his return when this drive was over. She had left no doubt in his mind that her intentions were to change her status from daughter of a wealthy Missouri banker to wife of Randall Pierce. His outspokeness about his lack of intention in that regard had not seemed to affect her in the slightest. It appeared that Lucille had the idea she could bind him to her with her admittedly beautiful body. Despite the easy accessibility she allowed him to it, he knew she presently granted no other man such liberties and he had no doubts as to her fidelity. Only his own was in question. He supposed that was the reason why, with all the women he had known intimately, he had never been truly tempted to

20

make an arrangement permanent. To him, marriage was a firm contract that demanded complete commitment, and at the age of thirty-three years, he had come to honestly believe he was incapable of sustaining such a commitment.

Without a trace of conceit, he was fully conscious of his appeal to women. He had become aware of it early in life and accepted it as easily as he had accepted his natural leadership ability and his talent for organization. It had made his life extremely comfortable, in that he had suffered few rejections by the opposite sex in his time. But he suspected it was also proving to his disadvantage, for it allowed him almost unlimited opportunities for female companionship, which he unfortunately found himself disinclined to refuse. He didn't worry that time would lessen his appeal to the opposite sex. Truly unconscious of the fact that the maturing of his handsome features had only added another facet to his charm, he had more or less come to accept the fact that he would not make a firm commitment to a woman until age had exhausted his enthusiasm for variety. And he expected that time would be long in coming.

A small smile broke momentarily across his lips. His limited time in San Antonio had not deprived him of the opportunity to fortify himself for the long trail ahead. His brief hour with redheaded Ginger McCall had been the only bright spot in an otherwise very unsatisfactory day. And if appearances were not very deceiving, things were definitely not looking up. As a matter of fact, at this point in time, prospects for the drive and the next four months were looking distinctly unfavorable. Well, he'd just have to wait and see what sunset would bring. . . .

The bright light of afternoon against her closed lids dragged Billie awake. Startled by the intensity of the light in the small hotel room, she was instantly alert. She suffered a moment of true panic. How long had she slept?

Throwing back the coverlet, Billie attempted to stand, but her abused flesh cried out in sharp protest. Biting her lips against the pain, she forced herself to her feet and reached

21

to the night table for the pocket watch lying there. She pressed the catch, a lump tightening in her throat at the flitting memory of the many times she had seen this same watch in her father's callused palm.

It was past noon!

Alarm overcoming pain, Billie reached for her shirt and pulled it on, her movements stiff and awkward. Stepping into the baggy canvas pants posed far more difficulty, as her battered limbs battled their refusal to cooperate. Her slim female figure completely hidden in her efficient disguise, Billie slipped the stained suspenders over her shoulders and donned her vest. Picking up the gunbelt that lay on the night table, she buckled it around her flat hips and adjusted the handle of her gun.

Not bothering with the necessities of her toilette, Billie reached for her hat and saddlebags. She started stiffly toward the door, only to be stopped in her tracks by her reflection in the small wall mirror as she passed.

Oh, God, no! That hideously distorted face staring back at her could not be her own! Blinking back the heat of tears, Billie swallowed hard in horrified disbelief. The swelling originally closing her left eye had enlarged to encompass her entire cheek, as had the deep blue color of the extended bruising. The numbing puffiness had moved to include her nose and a portion of her mouth formerly unaffected. The right side of her face, only slightly less affected, bore a ragged scratch from the corner of her eye to her chin. And wincing under the surprising flash of total recall, Billie remembered the chilling sensation of Wes McCulla's heavy ring as it had raked her tender skin.

A new trembling besetting her, Billie closed her eyes and swallowed hard against the bitter taste of bile that rose in her throat. No, she was not sorry she had killed Wesley McCulla. Were she presented with the same situation, she knew she would do it again without any regret.

A semi-hysterical laugh escaping her lips, she opened her eyes and stared at her disfigured image. She supposed she had Wes McCulla to thank for the efficiency of her disguise. The skinny, bedraggled, obviously beaten boy with ragged

22

blond hair hanging limply around his face was even safer from discovery by Dan McCulla's men than he had been the day before. But she had a long journey ahead of her. Should her identity ultimately be discovered, she was certain the elder McCulla would spare neither time nor expense in pursuing her. She needed to take advantage of the time her altered appearance had granted her to put herself in a situation where she would continue to be safe once her bruises healed.

Uncertain what her next step would be, Billie was sure of one thing only. Her destination remained firm in her mind. Wes McCulla's brutal attack had forced her into taking a step she had contemplated apprehensively only days before. North . . . she was heading north. The only problem was that she had no idea how to proceed in reaching her destination. Her money was limited. She had barely enough to pay for her room. She had nothing of value to sell so she might be able to afford a train ticket. Even if she did, it would certainly be foolhardy to take such an obvious means of escape, knowing a train station would be the first place Dan McCulla's men would look for her.

The low rumble of her stomach interrupted Billie's thoughts. The sudden thought that it had been over forty-eight hours since she had eaten was startling. No doubt that accounted for her weakness and her inability to concentrate. Mentally calculating the sorry state of her finances, she came to a decision. A good meal . . . she needed a good meal. She could not afford to allow her strength to dissipate. She would be needing the full power of her endurance. She had a long way to travel.

Turning resolutely away from her unsightly reflection, Billie took a deep breath and walked painfully toward the door.

A few minutes later, assuming a confident air in sharp contrast to her inner trepidation, she entered Maggie's Cafe. Taking a moment to scan the small room, she released a short sigh of relief. Two men engrossed in consuming the large steaks before them sat nearby, with the only other customers three men conversing quietly at a table in the opposite end of the dining area. Seating herself at a small corner table that afforded her a view of the door, Billie raised her eyes to the robust middle-aged woman who bustled toward her.

Not waiting for the inevitable inquiry and steadfastly ignoring the woman's startled expression as she raised her battered face, Billie stated flatly, "Coffee and a steak, ma'am."

There was a moment's hesitation before the woman returned tentatively, "You sure you're goin' to be able to eat it, boy? Our steaks take a fair amount of chewin', and you don't look much like you're in a condition to handle it."

"I can handle it."

Her eyes moved over Billie's battered face a moment longer before the woman shrugged her ample shoulders. "Suit yourself. And take off your hat, boy. This is a respectable establishment."

Snatching off her hat, her face flushing, Billie placed it on the chair and ran a nervous hand through her ragged hair. A short time later she was attempting to sip coffee through badly lacerated lips, realizing that the whole process was going to be more difficult than she thought. Making a second attempt, she winced as the hot liquid touched the deep cut in the corner of her mouth. A sudden movement beside her jerked up her head to the waitress's noiseless appearance. Placing a plate with an enormous steak before her, the woman nodded knowingly.

"I told you it wasn't goin' to be easy. You can't even get your mouth around that cup, much less chew—"

An unexpected heat flushing her face, Billie pulled herself up stiffly, inadvertently revealing the extent of her discomfort in the short, instinctive flash of pain in her eyes.

"I said I can handle it, ma'am. And you don't have to worry. I can pay."

"I didn't ask you if you could pay, did I, boy? But since you're so quick to answer questions, answer me this curiosity, will you? How did a young fella like you get yourself in such a sorry state?"

Lowering her eyes, Billie picked up her knife and fork. She

24

began cutting her meat.

"My horse threw me."

A low, disbelieving cluck her only response, the woman turned and walked away. Her only thought that she need finish her meal and get away as soon as possible, Billie cut a miniscule piece of steak and squeezed it between her lips. Her stomach lurching at her first swallow, Billie was momentarily uncertain whether she would be able to keep it down. Taking a deep breath, she cut another piece and repeated the process, grateful that her protesting stomach accepted it with greater ease.

Glancing up, Billie saw the waitress had observed her struggle. The sympathy on the woman's lined face bringing the heat of tears to her eyes, Billie glanced away. She had no time for sympathy. She had no time for anything but escape.

Minutes later, Billie pushed herself away from the table, giving no more than a glance to the empty plate in front of her. She was already beginning to feel the benefit of a full stomach. Her battered knees giving her more trouble than she cared to acknowledge, she walked over to the counter and withdrew her money pouch. Her eyes lifting to the wall beside her caught a posted notice.

A trail herd was looking for drovers. . . . It was going north, to Montana. . . .

"No use lookin' at that notice, boy."

A now familiar voice turned Billie toward the unsmiling waitress.

"Ma'am? . . ."

"I said there's no use lookin' at that notice if you had a mind to apply for the job. Judging from the looks of the fella that posted it two days ago, I'd say he's pretty particular. And you have three things goin' against you, boy. You're young, skinny and, I expect, inexperienced in the work."

"I'm not inexperienced, ma'am."

"It don't matter, nohow. That fella hired the men he needed this mornin'. I saw him ridin' out of town a little while after, and he wasn't lookin' too pleased."

Her keen gaze seeing the disappointment that flashed in Billie's eyes, the woman hesitated. "But if you're lookin' for

25

work, the fella who helped me around here quit a couple of days ago and—"

"No. Thank you, ma'am. I'm not looking for work. I'm heading for Mexico." Lowering her eyes as she spoke the deliberate lie, Billie opened her money pouch. "How much do I owe you?"

With the feeling that the sturdy woman had not been taken in by her untruth, Billie awaited her response.

"Well, I figure a young fella like yourself will be needin' all the money he has if he wants to make it to Mexico."

"Ma'am? . . ."

"I'm sayin' I've already made a considerable profit this mornin'. You put your money right back in your pocket."

Startled by the woman's response, Billie swallowed, momentarily unable to respond. Taking a short breath, she nodded.

"Thank you, ma'am."

Unable to say more, Billie turned and walked toward the door, intensely aware that the woman's sympathetic gaze followed her.

Rand eyed the men gathered around the campfire assessingly, his gaze lingering on the new faces in his crew. He was keenly aware of the stiffness between his established hands and the newcomers, and he frowned darkly. Experienced trail drovers knew the dangers of inexperienced men in their midst, and it was obvious there were some reservations about this particular group.

Well, if anything could accomplish a mellowing of the unease between the men, Nate Straw's meal would do it. Grunts of satisfaction were already echoing around the circle and he suspected attempts at conversation would soon begin.

Listening only halfheartedly to Jim Stewart's first friendly overture to the new drover across the fire, Rand reviewed the newcomers carefully.

Bob Fogarty: Short, stocky, and barrel-chested, it was obvious he had done hard physical labor most of his life.

26

Rand had no doubt the man could handle the physical aspects of trail herding, but it was difficult for him to understand how a man of Fogarty's age would find himself unemployed this time of year unless he had been in some trouble.

Tim Cannon: Of medium height and stature and an undetermined age, he sat slightly apart from both the old and new men. He claimed to be from Louisiana and appeared to be the sort who did not make friends easily. But there was something about Cannon that had convinced him to take him on. He hoped he had made the right decision.

Cal Johnson: Tall, with a thin wiry physique, he was fresh from Alabama and the only man in the crew who was of a height to look him directly in the eye. Johnson had been honest about never working on a drive of such duration before, but he claimed to be anxious to learn. Time would tell.

Josh Hall and Seth Brothers: He grouped them together in his mind because they were obviously trail partners, claiming to have soldiered together in the war. It was also obvious they knew cattle and worked as a team. It would take him a few days to figure if that was to his advantage or not.

His gaze moving to the last of the new men, Rand suppressed a smile. Jeremy Carlisle: young, no more than twenty-two or twenty-three and the most outgoing of the entire group, he was already setting the men at ease with his friendly smile and easy manner. If he did not miss his guess, the young fellow would turn out to be a real asset to the crew.

Well, whatever the case, they would be up before dawn tomorrow. He would allow only the time for the new men to cut their allotment of ten mounts from the remuda before beginning the drive in earnest. He had no doubt there would be a few problems to iron out, but it was his intention to make his policy perfectly clear from the outset. He was going to give them only a few minutes more before calling in the men on duty with the herd and speaking to them as a group. He wanted there to be no mis—

The sound of an approaching horse pulling his attention

27

from the men ringed around the fire, Rand squinted into the deepening twilight. A lone, unfamiliar rider was approaching. Drawing himself to his feet, Rand measured the narrowness of the man's stature and the stiffness of his carriage. Waiting only until the rider had pulled his horse up into the circle of light and had dismounted, he inquired evenly, "Can I help you?"

Keeping to the edge of the light, the rider replied in a strangely thick, boyish tone, "I'm looking for work and I read your notice in San Antonio. I'm experienced in trail driving . . . worked with my pa when he drove his herd north on the Old Western Trail two years in a row."

"Sorry, boy. I don't need any more help." Interrupting the hesitant, youthful rambling, Rand shook his head firmly. Annoyed when the boy lingered in the shadows of the fire instead of advancing toward him to a point where he could see him more clearly, he continued curtly, "I hired all the men I needed this morning."

"Oh. . . ." There was a moment's more hesitation before the boy began again in a firmer tone. "I heard you have three thousand head on the hoof, and the talk is you've only got ten men. To my reckoning, that would still leave you shorthanded, and I figured you could use another experienced hand. . . ."

Hell, the damned brat was trying to tell him his job! As annoyed by the youth's presumption as he was by the fact that the boy continued to lurk in the shadows of the fire, Rand snapped, "I told you boy, I've got a full crew. And if I was looking for another hand, I wouldn't hire a boy."

Expecting that his sharp setdown would turn the fellow on his heel, Rand was surprised when the boy returned insistently, "Don't be misled by my age and size, Mr. Pierce. What I lack there, I make up for in experience. My pa depended on me as much as he did any one of his hands, and—"

But Rand was no longer listening. Hell, he had no time for this kind of annoyance tonight. He had to set the ground rules for the men and assign them to their watches. And he wanted to have an opportunity to assess their reactions to what he had to say before they all took to their bedrolls for the night.

His interruption of the boy's statement was flat and unyielding.

"Even if I believed you, boy, I told you I don't need any more help. So if that's all you got to say—"

"Rand—"

Nate Straw's deep voice cut into the silence that followed, turning Rand in his direction. A spark of censure in his eye, the graying cook continued slowly, "The boy's ridden a long way out here from San Antonio. I got a healthy helpin' of stew and a couple of biscuits left in the pot. Maybe he'd like to fill his stomach before he starts back."

Holding his cook's eye for a moment longer, Rand glanced back in the boy's direction. Leave it to Nate to remind him that his irritation had allowed him to forget the simple rules of hospitality observed on the trail.

Rand's voice was clipped. "Well, boy, are you hungry?"

The short hesitation before the boy gave a silent nod succeeding in upping his inexplicable irritation another notch, Rand snapped, "Pull yourself up to the fire then, and Nate will dish you out something to eat."

Seeming to realize that he had the attention of the entire crew, the boy lingered in the shadows a moment longer before taking an abrupt step forward into the full light of the fire. The series of spontaneous gasps that sounded around the fire echoed in his own mind as Rand's eyes fell on the boy's swollen, distorted features.

Holding out a steaming plate as the boy approached, Nate shook his head, voicing aloud the question in everyone's mind.

"What in hell happened to you, boy?"

The narrow shoulders shrugged indifferently. "I got jumped in an alley a couple nights ago."

"Don't look much like they was tryin' to rob you, whoever they was. It looks more like they was tryin' to kill you."

The boy's mumbled response was short and tinged with a note of finality.

"Well, they didn't."

29

Giving his head a short shake, Nate pointed toward the fire. "Go sit over there, boy. I'll bring you your coffee."

Rand's eyes followed the boy's limping gait. His quick appraisal of the boy's equipment had revealed a brand new rope coiled on the saddle. New chaps were tied to the bundle in the rear. Hardly the well-used gear of an experienced drover. Somebody had given him a beating, all right. The swollen condition of the boy's lips accounted for the strangely thick manner of speech that had puzzled him, and his bruises probably accounted for the youth's stiffness. He didn't have a doubt in the world the boy was lying. His smart mouth had probably gotten him into a situation he couldn't talk himself out of. If anything, the boy's battered condition made him more certain than ever he would do best to get rid of him. He didn't need a smart-mouthed troublemaker in his crew, no matter how shorthanded he was.

Smarting under the silent acknowledgment that the boy had been right in his assessment, that he could indeed do with another good hand with a herd of this size, Rand resumed his seat.

Intensely conscious that the exchange had held the full attention of the men, Rand was relieved to hear the low buzz of conversation begin around the campfire. He was not especially proud of his handling of the boy and was truly uncertain why he should still find himself so annoyed. His eyes drifted back in the boy's direction, and he frowned at the obvious difficulty the youth had in eating. It was apparent that his lips were so cut up that the kid found it difficult to slip the spoon between them, and he was certain that nothing short of raging hunger could force the boy to ignore his pain.

Unable to withdraw his eyes from the slender youth, Rand frowned more deeply. What was it about the skinny brat that made him so edgy? Hell, he was getting as bad as the damned herd.

The sound of movement at the cook fire turned Rand from his scrutiny of their unexpected visitor at the same moment the handle of the oversized coffee pot in Nate's hand snapped. The pot crashed to the stones beneath it with a loud, resounding clatter.

Instantly, the restless herd behind them rose as if one steer and in the space of a moment were off and pounding into the semidarkness on a headlong, panic-stricken course. Stampede!

On his feet in a second, Rand raced for the temporary remuda strung behind the cook wagon. He mounted his horse in a swift fluid movement, hardly aware of the scramble of activity around him as his men fought to gain control of their frightened and rearing mounts. Using quirt and rowel unsparingly, he galloped forward, urging his powerful black into the thundering stream of cattle.

The pounding of hooves a deafening roar, the choking dust adding to the opacity of the darkening twilight, Rand plunged into the herd as it ran in blind pursuit of the lead. All sound submerged by the general din in the time that followed, Rand was gradually alerted to the fact that his men had fought themselves into position around the frightened onslaught of wild-eyed beeves by the distinct flashes of their six-shooters sparking signal in the semidarkness. Aware that an attempt to check the first mad rush would be futile, Rand felt a glimmer of satisfaction in the knowledge that his crew had found their spots and were wisely attempting no more at present than to hold the herd together.

Rand spurred his horse forward. His objective to reach the lead, he pushed his gelding to the full extent of its power. Racing at the head of the pounding herd at last, Rand leaned low over his mount's back in an attempt to ease its strain. Visibility all but nil in the descending darkness, he was vaguely aware of another horse drawing close to his rear in a backup position designed to aid him in turning the herd when the time was ripe. Certain Willie Hart was again proving his dependability by positioning himself so favorably, Rand shot a quick glance over his shoulder.

A sorrel, smaller than the mount Willie had been riding, pounded bravely forward within the thundering melee, the slender figure crouched over its back stringently maintaining its line amongst the threatening crush. The boy! Damn him, he was going to get killed! The mare was too small . . .

couldn't have the endurance or strength needed to remain upright within the herd! But there was no compromise in the steady push of the horse and rider behind him, no quarter as the boy fired his six-shooter into the ground, forcing an outward surge of cattle back into the forward press.

The sudden pressure of cattle immediately to his rear demanded his attention, dragging Rand's gaze from the rider behind him. Unable to spare the boy another glance, Rand pressed his gelding onward.

Twilight had given way to a moonless night lit only by a scattering of a few stars as the herd raged on unchecked. Still in his position to the side of the lead, Rand sensed a subtle change in the runaway herd. Maintaining his position, he fired a signal shot into the air. Turning, he saw a succession of flashes like fireflies in the night around the running beeves. Position and timing would never be better.

Taking a deep breath, Rand spurred his stalwart black out to the front of the stampeding herd. Firing into the ground just short of the faces of the head steers, he began forcing them in a gradually curving path. His strategy was seeing success when Rand became aware of an unexpected forward surge of cattle from behind the lead. His mind reacting immediately to the threat of being overrun, Rand shot a quick glance behind him to gauge the strength of the thrust. Startled, he saw the small sorrel charge forward against the pressing beeves. The slender figure bent over its back fired into the ground, and when there was no change in the cattle's direction, fired again. A third, determined shot, almost into the faces of the panicking surge, was effective in forcing the curve. Taking advantage of the narrow margin he had gained, the boy pressed his small mare full against the heavy flanks of the wild-eyed steers, driving them fearlessly into line behind the lead.

Once again in full control, Rand turned the original lead back with expert skill, slowly forcing them in a circular path that led them to a gradual, regulated halt.

Realizing his black was all but spent, Rand paused within the melee of confused, exhausted cattle. His heart pounding wildly, Rand glanced over his shoulder, his eyes anxiously searching the darkness. His relief intense as his eyes touched on the small sorrel and the outline of the thin, erect figure on its back, Rand released an unconscious breath.

Spurring his horse in their direction, Rand pulled up alongside the small, winded mare. Looking down into the battered face barely discernible in the semidarkness, Rand could see little other than the fact that the boy's slender body was quaking visibly. Unable to make out the kid's expression and fully aware that the reverse was also true, Rand paused. When he spoke, his voice was gruff.

"Boy, you have yourself a job."

There was no response from the trembling youth other than a short nod of his head. Satisfied at that, Rand rode off into the darkness.

Chapter III

"I'll take the black!"

Her hand raised in a signal indicating her choice of horses as the cut again came around to her, Billie squinted into the dust-filled air of early morning. Moving at her selection Hank Casey singled out the animal she had chosen, and the round moved on to Bob Fogarty.

Billie sighed. The cattle had been restless, and it had been a long time before they had been able to bed them down the previous night. When the task had finally been accomplished, she had fallen into her bedroll in complete exhaustion. There had been little surprise exhibited within the crew when she had finally laid out her bedroll and slept as one of them, and she was thankful for the acceptance of the men.

She had awakened at daybreak to a clear spring morning, the delicious aroma of strong coffee, and Nate Straw's cooking. Remembering that her hunger of the night before had gone unsated because of the cattle's unexpected run, Billie had ignored the protest of her aching flesh and limped immediately to the cook fire. Ignoring the amused looks of the men around her, she had eaten until she had been filled to bursting. Immediately thereafter, Rand Pierce had ordered up the remuda, and the selection had begun.

Only a few more cuts remained, and each of the new men would have their quota of ten mounts chosen for the trail ahead. Ten mounts each, more than adequate to ensure a fresh horse in the event of trouble. Billie was pleased with the luxury. Her father's drives, although admittedly of a shorter duration than the one on which they were about to embark, had not been so well supplied, and they had ultimately suffered for the lack.

Her eyes moving toward the horses remaining to be selected, Billie began a slow process of elimination. She mentally discarded the two pintos left within the group as possible choices. She had learned early on that a spotted horse was a freak of color in a range-bred horse. She was well aware that more often than not the attractive coloring indicated inbreeding and the physical and mental impairment that went along with it. No, she would more happily settle for the grulla. The size of his breadbasket indicated he would be able to carry food for a long ride and would probably be a good swimmer. With the number of rivers ahead of them, there was no doubt she would . . .

A sense of uneasiness breaking through her concentration, Billie glanced over her shoulder to catch the intense perusal of Rand Pierce. Glancing away as quickly as she could free her glance, Billie felt a new tension tighten her stomach. Damn the man! He had been watching her intently since she had awakened, and she was certain his interest did not bode well for her future within the group.

But she was also certain the man had no suspicions as to her true sex. Her disguise was too complete, and she had demonstrated only too clearly her ability with cattle. Her reaction to the stampede the night before had been instinctive, and she had been mounted and scrambling for a position within the fear-crazed herd before she had had a chance for thought.

It was still a mystery to her why she had sought the dangerous position directly to the rear of the arrogant trail boss who had seemed so determined to drive her from camp. Perhaps it had been her father's training and the realization that the hard-eyed foreman had been totally unprotected in his vulnerable position at the lead of the runaways. Or perhaps it had been the desire to see respect reflected in the brilliant blue eyes that had dismissed her so carelessly. In any case, she was certain she had earned his respect, although suspicion apparently remained.

Whatever else, she felt relatively safe within this group. And most importantly of all, she was on her way north.

"Come on, boys, speed it up! We haven't got all day!"

Authority rang in the deep voice that interrupted Billie's thoughts, and she turned toward Rand Pierce with a frown. This was one foreman who would leave no doubt in the minds of his men who was boss. His overbearing attitude was a sharp departure from the quiet, soft-spoken manner in which her father had handled his men. Rod Winslow had depended on his men's respect rather than his tone of voice to enforce his orders. But in the end, respect had not been enough to keep Rod Winslow's men with him when Dan McCulla's orders had threatened their lives.

Fighting the sadness that assaulted her mind at the memory, Billie turned back to the remuda once more. Yes, she would take the sorrel and the grulla when her turns came around again, and damn Rand Pierce and his scowl!

Rand leaned back against the chuck wagon, his broad shoulder resting casually against the canvas. But his indifferent posture was deceiving. The brim of his hat, pulled low on his forehead, hid the intense scrutiny with which he was observing the cut of the remuda. His wrangler, Hank Casey, had easily driven the remuda of over a hundred horses for which he had sole responsibility into viewing distance. There was plenty of good horseflesh still to be chosen in that group, and Rand was certain silent observance would net him some insight into the experience of his new men.

So far, he had found his observations very interesting. Cal Johnson had obviously been honest about never working a trail drive before. His choice of horses appeared to be given to selecting the ones with the most appealing appearance. His first choice of the buckskin pony was a poor one. The horse was slender and was probably fleet of foot, but unless he was very wrong indeed, the animal would be lacking in stamina. It appeared Cal had a lot to learn.

The rest of the new men had made good selections with few exceptions. Josh Hall and Seth Brothers had appeared to consult on each other's cut, joining in mutual amusement at the selections of the other drovers when the men's choices did not meet with their approval. Their amusement at the expense of others was not appreciated. He'd have to keep a close watch on those two or he suspected they'd cause him trouble before the drive was done.

Jeremy Carlisle was obviously having the time of his life. He had openly declared he had never had more than one horse at his disposal in his entire life. His grin had reflected that he liked the feel of having his choice of horseflesh.

Rand's amusement dropped away as he moved his gaze to the thin figure standing slightly apart from the group. The boy had turned down all friendly overtures extended to him so far that morning. He had chosen to take his breakfast to the far side of the fire, where he had consumed it voraciously despite the obvious problem he was having in slipping the food past his swollen lips. Now, participating in the cut, he was once again standing apart from the group, his eyes studying the animals carefully with each selection.

Rand had not been surprised that the boy's choices were excellent. The youth had obviously been trained to choose a horse for durability and power. He doubtless had several good swimmers amongst his choices, animals that would serve him well in the country they were to pass. But the boy's performance the night before had shown he was as experienced as he had claimed, despite his age. It had also demonstrated he had the intelligence and courage to put his training to good use.

So . . . what was it about that kid that set his teeth on edge? It wasn't his looks. Hell, the boy had been so badly beaten he couldn't tell what the kid looked like except that his hair was blond and he was incredibly skinny. He just could not put his finger on the cause for his discomfort. He could not deny that the boy's courage during the stampede had earned him a place on the drive, but he was determined to keep his eye on him until he had resolved his negative feelings. He had learned long ago that his perceptiveness with people was usually sound, and he had no intention of allowing the undernourished pip-squeak's bruises to gain his sympathy. He didn't have Nate Straw's bleeding heart, and he had no tolerance for the boy's insolence. The gall of the kid . . . riding into camp and telling him how he should run his outfit!

Unconsciously nodding his approval of the broad-chested grulla the boy had selected, Rand unexpectedly caught the youth's glance. Hell, the kid had the nerve to look annoyed to see him observing. Rand's brow moved into a frown as he turned and started back toward the campfire. There was something about that boy. . . .

Well, wherever he came from and whatever he was doing on this drive, that kid was going to toe the line. He'd make sure of that. And he'd be watching that scrawny little twit real close . . . real close.

"I don't usually give formal instructions at the beginning of a drive, but since a number of you men haven't worked with me before, I think it best to make myself real clear."

His dark brows drawn into a frown that Billie was beginning to suspect was his normal expression, Rand Pierce scanned the faces of the men gathered around him. The remuda cut had been accomplished and it was almost mid-morning. It was obvious that the anxious trail boss was not about to allow much more time to elapse before starting the cattle on the trail. But it was also obvious that he had something to say and was not about to hesitate in saying it.

"First of all, most of you know that you would have been working under Jess Williams on this drive if the fever hadn't laid him and a good number of my other men low. And I suspect that before this drive is over, a number of you will be considering it your misfortune that I was forced to take over this herd in order to complete my government contract. But I'm telling you now, if you follow my orders and give me a good day's work, there'll be no problem from me. My first priority is getting this herd through, intact and on time to the Blackfeet.

"Those who have worked with me before know that I feel the secret of trailing cattle is never to let your herd know that they're under restraint. I consider it reasonable to allow the cattle to string out for three quarters of a mile, with you men evenly divided on each side. My two point men will ride out in front of the lead and direct the course of the herd. There'll also be two men on swing, a few on flank to ward off range cattle and see that none of the beeves wander or drop out, and two drag drivers in the rear. We'll not be driving this bunch hard. I expect we'll cover no more than fifteen to twenty miles a day. The condition of the herd and remuda demands that sacrifice.

"And I want to caution you younger men about your saddle stock." Rand's eyes scanned the faces surrounding him, seeming to rest a fraction longer on Billie's bruised features. "You're all well mounted, and the safety of the herd depends on the condition of your horses. Keep your saddle blankets dry and clean, and don't let anything that might happen to your horse be your fault. Ordinarily we might get along with six or eight horses each on this drive, but with the emergencies we're liable to face, we don't have a horse to spare. I'll hold you all personally accountable for the condition of your mounts, and the price of any horse that doesn't reach Blackfeet country for sale through personal neglect will be deducted from your wages."

Facing down the few frowns in the group, Rand waited until his words had been absorbed. "Now, are there any questions?" Silence his only response, Rand continued determinedly a few moments later.

"All right, your night watches will be as follows: First watch, eight o'clock to ten-thirty, Willie Hart, Bob Fogarty, and Seth Brothers; second watch, ten-thirty to one o'clock, Jim Stewart, Tim Cannon, Josh Hall; third watch, one o'clock to three-thirty, Russ Byrd and Cal Johnson; fourth watch, three-thirty to daybreak, Wyatt Wond, Jeremy Carlisle, and Billie Drucker."

Not batting an eyelash at the foreman's use of the name she had assumed, Billie kept her silence as Rand continued.

"The only men not pulling night watch will be Nate Straw, Hank Casey, and me."

Hesitating a moment longer, Rand unconsciously pulled his impressive frame to its full height. His squinting gaze assessed the faces around him.

"Well, then, if you've nothing to say, let's get on with it."

Smarting under Rand Pierce's dictatorial attitude, Billie had begun to follow the men to their mounts when a heavy hand on her shoulder stopped her in her tracks. Turning, she met the full force of the startlingly blue eyes that had studied her so intently. Her heart beating a rapid tattoo in her chest, Billie returned Rand's stare, her battered face showing no sign of the turmoil within.

Waiting until the other men were out of earshot, Rand offered tightly, "I want to get some things straight with you from the start, Drucker. You didn't take me in with that story about being jumped in an alley. Somebody gave you a hell of a good beating, and my thoughts are that you probably deserved it." Ignoring the flush that rose to Billie's face, Rand continued with measured arrogance, "So, I'm making myself real clear. I don't want to see any of that kind of problem starting in this group. I won't put up with a troublemaker or a smart mouth. Is that understood?"

Fighting to control her anger at the injustice of his remarks, Billie shook off Rand's restraining hand and took a deep breath. Her unspoken reaction did not go unobserved.

"I said, is that understood?"

"Yes, it's understood."

Pinning her with the unyielding blue of his eyes, Rand continued, "And another thing . . . I don't want to see you using that sorrel mare of yours."

"Ginger?" Startled, Billie shook her head. "She's completely dependable. You saw her last night . . . how well she—"

"She's too small. You're damned lucky you both didn't get trampled last night. Just because you were lucky once and that horse didn't go down, that doesn't mean it won't happen next time."

"That mare's as strong as any horse in your remuda, and

41

she has more heart."

"I don't want you using her on this drive. You can let her travel with the remuda. Casey will be responsible for her just like he is for the other horses. When the drive is over, you can ride her to kingdom come . . . I don't give a damn! But you won't sit on her back while you're working for me, is that understood?"

"I told you she's—"

"And I told you! . . ." His sudden flush matching the color in the battered face turned up to his, Rand paused to rein his anger under control. That arrogance of the little bastard . . . telling *him* what he was going to do on this drive.

His puffy lips tight, the youth continued to stare up insolently into his face and Rand felt a new rush of anger. Barely controlling his desire to shake the skinny little pup to within an inch of his life, Rand took a deep breath.

"Do you understand what I said, Drucker?"

The youth's response was short and clipped.

"I understand."

"I don't want you on that mare."

"I said I understand!"

"And I want you to understand one more thing. . . ."

"What is that, *Mr. Pierce?*"

His hands itching to close around the kid's skinny neck, Rand muttered from between tight lips, "You did a hell of a good job last night during that stampede, and that's the only reason I hired you against my better judgment. But as far as I'm concerned, you're not in the clear yet. And I want you to know I usually take the last watch with the men . . . so I'll have my eye on you. Don't think you're going to get away with anything. . . ."

"I don't expect to try."

Rand hesitated, his eyes assessing. "Well, maybe you're smarter than you look. Now get going!"

Seething, Billie turned abruptly on her heel. She stomped away, her anger overcoming the throbbing pain that resulted. The bastard . . . the nasty, arrogant bastard!

Rand's eyes burned into the narrow, retreating back.

Muttering tightly under his breath, he turned away.

Billie squinted into the afternoon sun and took an angry breath. Hours had passed since her early morning confrontation with Rand Pierce, and she was still seething. Of all the pompous, arrogant asses! And he was a bully, to boot! Shooting a quick glance forward, Billie searched the herd in front of her for a sign of his broad-shouldered outline. Her eyes stopped on the image she sought, and her lips moved spontaneously into a straight, tense line.

It hadn't taken her long to get filled in on Mr. Randall Pierce. With a fair amount of new hands in the crew, she had only to keep her silence and her ears open to learn all she wanted about him. From the brief background Willie Hart had supplied in answer to Jeremy Carlisle's inquiry, Rand Pierce was one of those fellows who had an eye to heavy profit. It seemed Pierce had come to Texas with little more than a few dollars in his pocket and the horse he was riding, and he was now one of the wealthiest men in this area of the country. He had several trail foremen working for him and he seldom took his contracted herds over the trail anymore. Willie had commented that Rand Pierce's success was such that he now traveled in influential circles and was a very important man.

Her eyes glued on the object of her thoughts, Billie flicked her quirt absentmindedly against the side of the lagging steer beside her and herded him back into the stream of beeves. Her stiff lips curled in contempt. She had met men like Rand Pierce before—Dan McCulla, to name one. . . . An eye to profits and a blank spot when it came to decency and the law could get a man far on the road to wealth. She had recognized that hardness in those brilliant blue eyes the moment she had stepped up to the campfire the night before and faced Pierce's scrutiny. There was not a spark of humanity there. He had not even had the generosity to extend the hospitality of his campfire. Instead, she had been treated like an unwanted stray until the great man had been shamed by his own cook!

And she hadn't been asking for charity. She knew damned well she could earn her way on any drive. Dan McCulla's ongoing war with her father had kept Rod Winslow's working capital so low that he had been forced to allow her to work right along with his hands at the Diamond W. And she had liked it that way. She was not much for woman's work—cooking, washing, and cleaning. Her father had found it was easier and cheaper to hire a woman to do that work so she could be free to work with him.

A familiar sadness flicked over her senses, and Billie blinked back the heat of tears that warmed her lids. She was well aware it was not only her ability and her father's need that had allowed Rod Winslow to compromise his standards and allow his daughter to ride beside him to do a man's work. Rather, it was the fact that no matter what the weight of the problems filling Rod Winslow's mind, his daughter was always foremost in his thoughts. Her father had wanted her to have a full knowledge of a working spread. He had always said he didn't have much in the world; the Diamond W was all he had to leave her, and he had wanted her to know how to handle it.

Her throat thickening uncomfortably under the weight of her thoughts, Billie took a deep breath and adjusted her position in the saddle. Pa had told her she was special— smart and good-looking, too. She had seriously considered her reflection in the mirror for the first time after her father had made that sober statement. She had come to the conclusion that her father was prejudiced and that there was nothing truly physically outstanding about her. Blond hair and black eyes—an unlikely combination, almost as unlikely as the dark brows and lashes that framed her eyes. Her features were small and pleasant enough, but there was certainly nothing womanly about her height and slenderness. But her pa had been proud of that, too, even going to the extent of taking out a stick and measuring her height in inches. Eight inches over the mark of five feet—not the petite proportions of the women most men found attractive.

It had appeared Wes McCulla had liked tall women, too. . . . She had almost stood eye to eye with him, although

44

the breadth of his powerful body had shrunk her in size. She had seemed to be a challenge to him. He had followed her with his eyes, lusting after her. He had been unwilling to accept the fact that she did not feel the same attraction to him. Her refusal of him had turned his fascination to hatred, and he had become all the more determined he would have her.

But in the end, he had been no match for her gun. . . .

Her body quaking spontaneously at the chill that moved down her spine, Billy was abruptly aware that Rand Pierce had turned in her direction. His keen eyes had caught the tremor that had shaken her, and she bristled under his scrutiny. Well, let him look! She was beginning to shake off the effects of Wes McCulla's beating. Her stiffness was lessening, and she had felt a noticeable difference in the puffiness around her mouth when she had awakened this morning. She would soon be functioning normally, but she had no illusions about her appearance. It would be a month or more before her face returned fully to normal, and she was content with that. By that time she would be a safe distance away and fully absorbed into this group. That was, if Rand Pierce did not find a reason to dismiss her before then.

Her stomach tensing, Billie suffered Rand Pierce's steady perusal for a few moments longer before he turned his mount and began to maneuver his way back toward her. Damn him, what did he want now?

Doing her best to ignore Rand Pierce's approach, Billie directed her attention to the trailing cattle. She was almost tempted to ride off to the rear in the few minutes before Rand pulled up alongside. But no, it was better to face him.

Devoting her attention to a protesting cow beside her, Billie allowed Rand Pierce to ride alongside for the space of a few moments before turning her head in his direction. His irritation at her delay in acknowledging his presence was obvious. Billie experienced a small wave of satisfaction that was immediately negated by Pierce's first words.

"What's the matter, Drucker? Having trouble keeping up?"

Smarting, Billie retorted tartly, "That'll be the day. . . ."

"You didn't look so cocky a few minutes ago. As a matter of fact, it looked to me like you were a little unsteady in the saddle."

"Looks are deceiving sometimes."

"Are they?"

Her irritation mounting, Billie exerted a stringent effort to control her tongue. It would not do to give this arrogant bastard the setdown he deserved. She did not fool herself for a moment that he was actually concerned. He had obviously taken a dislike to her and was not about to let up on his harassment. But she had stood far worse. She was bearing the marks of a physical attack that paled everything in its shadow.

"I'd say they are." Billie met Rand's intense stare with a level gaze of her own. "I admit I wasn't in the best shape last night when you took me on, and that stampede all but did me in. But I'm feeling better today, and I'll feel even better tomorrow. And no matter how I feel, you can be sure you'll get a good day's work out of me. I earn my keep . . . I always have and I always will."

"Did you earn that sweet little beating you took, too?"

His mocking retort was unexpected, and Billie's temper flared. "That's none of your damned business, Mr. Pierce!"

"It's my business if it interferes with your work."

"I just told you it won't!"

"That's something you're going to have to prove to me, Drucker."

"I'll prove it. . . ."

Billie's menacing squint and the trailing manner of her response was not wasted on Pierce.

"Don't pit yourself against me, Drucker. You're no contest. I'll beat you on all counts. If you're smart, you'll answer my questions, obey my orders, and do your job . . . nothing more. The next time I ask you if you're having a problem, just answer me yes or no. I don't need your smart mouth. And just for the record, at present you're a member of my crew. It is my business how you feel, just like the physical condition of my beeves and my remuda are my business. If I think I need to ask you that same question five more times today, I will. And you'll answer me. Is that understood?"

Her face flushing hotly, Billie clenched her teeth tightly shut against the response that sprang to her lips.

"Drucker . . . I'm warning you. . . ."

Fury obvious in her flashing gaze, Billie held Rand's eye steadily as she mumbled through tight lips.

"I understand. . . ."

"I didn't hear you. . . ."

"I said *I understand.*"

"I told you to watch your mouth. . . ."

"I was only answering you, like you ordered. Now, is there anything else?"

The tightening of angry lines on the handsome face staring into hers indicated she had gotten to Rand Pierce once more, and Billie suppressed her satisfaction as the arrogant trail boss spurred his horse forward without another word. Watching as he reassumed his position beside the lead, Billie mumbled some fitting words under her breath.

"That kind of thing ain't goin' to get you nowhere, boy."

Her eyes darting beside her, Billie frowned at the gaunt Texan who had ridden up without her realization. Staring into Willie Hart's sober, sun-darkened face, Billie felt a flicker of sadness deep inside. There was something about him, the distinctive set of his wiry frame, the concern reflected in the lines of his face, that reminded her of her father when he was disturbed. Unable to respond, she waited silently as Willie's low, drawling voice continued,

"I got to admit, I ain't never seen Rand react to nobody the way he has to you, boy, but you ain't doin' yourself no favor by angerin' him. I'll tell you now, he's a damned hard man when he's riled."

"I haven't done anything to make him angry."

"Maybe not, but you sure as hell had a smug look on your face right now when I rode up. And from the set of his shoulders, I'd say Rand didn't leave just now in too good a mood."

"I only said—"

"Look, I ain't rightly interested in what you said to Rand, or what Rand said to you, boy. It ain't none of my business,

47

and Rand wouldn't like me stickin' my nose in where it don't belong. But, well, it looks to me like you've had more than your share of knocks in the last few days." His sympathetic gaze moving over her face, Willie shook his head. "I don't know what kind of a man could beat a kid like you up so bad, and it ain't none of my concern. But since you're new to this outfit, I thought I'd say a few words which might set you back on the right foot here."

Hesitating only a moment to measure Billie's reaction to his statement, Willie continued quietly, "Rand Pierce is a hard man, but he's fair. I've been workin' for him since the time he took his first herds up this trail himself, and I ain't never knowed a better boss. He pays his men real good and treats them square. I don't know nothin' about his personal business and I don't care. I just know you can depend on a fair shake if you do your job."

His graying brows drawing together in a frown, Willie shook his head. "There's somethin' about you, boy, that's put his back up. I don't know what it is, but he ain't likely to let it go too easily. My advice to you is to bite your tongue and bear it for a week or so. Rand may be hardheaded, but he ain't above admittin' when he's been wrong about somebody. If you really want to make it in this outfit, you can. It's up to you."

Billie's eyes moved over Willie's weather-beaten face consideringly. How that stiff-necked bully had ever earned this hard-working Texan's respect, she could not understand, but there was no doubting the sincerity in Willie's expression. And she was determined not to throw the concern that had prompted his advice back in his face.

She attempted a smile that only resulted in the cracking of her cut lips and a spontaneous wince. Her embarrassment at the flicker of sympathy on Willie's face shortened her response.

"I'll keep everything you said in mind, Willie. And—and I thank you for—"

"You don't need to thank me for nothin', boy."

Pulling the brim of his hat down a little lower on his forehead, Willie gave a short nod and spurred his horse up into the flow of cattle, gone as quickly as he had appeared.

Billie followed the slight Texan for a few moments with her gaze until a nagging feeling snapped her head toward the lead to catch Rand Pierce's glance. Suspicion showed in the squint of his eyes, and Billie felt her irritation flare anew. Damn, what was the man thinking? She didn't need this kind of problem. . . . She already had enough to worry about.

The sudden separation of three steers from the column a short distance ahead interrupted her angry speculation, and Billie spurred her horse forward spontaneously. Halting their straying run with an efficient circling movement of her horse, she applied her quirt effectively and herded them back toward the main stream. Within minutes they were back in line, and Billie could not resist another short glance to the lead. Rand Pierce's back was turned to her, his attention centered on the distant horizon. Of course, he would have been watching when she had felt that momentary weakness a short time before, but now when she did her job . . .

Oh, damn! Suddenly disgusted with herself, Billie averted her head toward the brilliant afternoon landscape. Next she'd be expecting a pat on the back just for doing her job. Turning her horse, Billie spurred the responsive chestnut toward the rear of the herd, determined to think no more.

Rand lifted his broad-brimmed Stetson from his head and wiped his arm across his forehead. If this afternoon's heat was any indication of the days to come, they were in for a long, hot drive. But worrying him even more was the talk he had heard in San Antonio. When he had started this drive he had not taken into account that this area had suffered a considerable drought the previous summer. Local spring showers had been sufficient to start the grass nicely, but evidently water in quantities needed for three thousand beeves on the hoof was going to be hard to find. He did not look forward to a dry drive.

Taking a deep breath, Rand scanned the horizon. He had been relieved when they had turned the herd onto the Old Western Trail. Years of trail herds driven over the same ground had united irregular cow paths into a broad passage-way, seventy-five yards wide in some places, which was as well-defined and easy to follow as the course of a river. He was well aware that several herds had started up the trail ahead of them, and it was a relief to know that where one could go another could follow . . . if there was enough water. He had been out scouting ahead of the herd for most of the morning. It appeared they would have enough water for this night's camp.

A strange uneasiness tugged at the back of his mind and Rand sent a brief glance over his shoulder to survey the rumbling herd. Unconsciously his eyes sought out the slight figure who moved efficiently at its flank, and he felt another flicker of annoyance. He most certainly did not need the distraction of that smart-mouthed kid on this drive. Well, he had already determined that if the boy gave him any more problem, he would send him packing. He would be better off shorthanded than putting up with . . .

His eyes catching on a movement to the west of the herd, Rand was suddenly alert. Two mounted figures riding toward them. . . . Rand's expression creased into a frown. Indians. What were they doing here? It would be a few more days before the herd was in Indian country. The Army had the tribes in the area pretty well contained these days, but there were always renegades. . . .

Tension stiffening his spine, Rand continued at the lead of the herd as the two mounted figures drew closer. Unable to ignore their approach any longer, Rand turned his mount in their direction and rode toward them. Reining up, he watched carefully, his expression unrevealing, as the Indians drew their horses to a halt within conversing distance.

Rand's eyes moved in slow assessment, aware that the gazes of the men facing him did the same. They appeared to be Apaches, and if he was to judge from the bearing and demeanor of the larger of the two, the man held a position of importance within his tribe. Rand's eyes narrowed.

The first brave appeared to be tall, probably six feet or more in height when standing. Black unbound hair streamed past his shoulders, gleaming in the sun. His skin was smooth, the angled planes of his face and his classic features unmarked by age or disease. His bared chest revealed a physique of athletically trim proportions, and long legs clad in buckskin efficiently gripped his horse's sides. He was obviously in the prime of life, and Rand had to admit the man was as excellent a specimen of Plains Indian as he had ever seen.

The second man was smaller in stature, of an indiscriminate age, but obviously older than the first. He was similarly clad, but he did not appear to hold the rank of the first. He appeared content to allow the other fellow to determine the course of action to be taken.

Realizing it would be unwise to sacrifice his position of authority, yet knowing the need to progress with caution, Rand held up his hand in greeting. The signal returned, he began a cautious inquiry.

"I give you greetings, but I admit to surprise to see men of your tribe here. The lands of the Apache are many miles distant. Why do you approach our drive?"

His words were met with silence. Annoyance was just beginning to pick at his waning patience when the first Indian gestured in sign language, his hands moving in a graceful manner peculiar to those accustomed to that means of intercourse. Rand frowned. His own halting gestures were met with signals in return and a low accompaniment of guttural Spanish that was meant to clarify the signs.

Shaking his head to indicate his lack of understanding, Rand turned toward the horse approaching from within the herd. Damn it all, the only Spanish-speaking men he had in this crew had fallen prey to the fever. He hadn't taken into consideration the fact that he might find himself at a loss without an interpreter. Waiting until Willie had pulled up alongside, he spoke curtly.

"Willie, these fellows don't speak English, and they evidently have something to say. Do any of the new men speak Spanish? Hell, all I can make out is that they said something about the trail and water. . . . And if they've got something to tell me, I want to hear it."

"I don't know, but I'll find out."

Turning his horse abruptly, Willie galloped back toward the herd, and Rand felt a flash of frustration. Damn it all. . . . Signaling the two men facing him to dismount, Rand did the same.

Knowing it would be to his disadvantage to show anxiety of any kind, Rand assumed a casual stance. Barely able to keep his eyes from the sun rapidly dropping to the horizon, he mentally calculated the daylight time remaining. Whatever these men had to say, he would not have time to ride out and check their statements today. He had no desire to spend a night away from camp so early on in the drive if he could help it.

Rand's uneasiness was increasing. He was well aware that Geronimo, Juh, and Chatto were still running wild in Apache lands to the west. The unexpected appearance of an Apache of this Indian's stature so near the land of the Commanche raised the hackles on his spine. Somehow he could not make himself believe this man and his companion were wandering aimlessly, but the possible reason for their mission in these lands was beyond him.

Rand fought to maintain his unconcerned facade. He strained at his impatience and the desire to turn and follow Willie's progress through the herd. The minutes stretched into the length of hours. . . .

Her concentration intense, Billie had spent a difficult ten minutes chasing a surefooted longhorn from some ragged brush as it had attempted to make an unscheduled stop of its own. She had been aware of little else but the animal's determination to escape her. She had finally succeeded in flushing it from its cover, having just accomplished returning it to the herd when Willie's rapid approach snapped her eyes in his direction.

Scanning the landscape in front of her with a quick glance, Billie's eyes narrowed as they touched on Rand Pierce's stiff figure where he dismounted to the side of the moving herd. Two Indians stood opposite him. There appeared to be no effort at conversation between them.

52

Maintaining a firm grip on her mount's reins as Willie drew to an abrupt halt beside her, she shot him an anxious look.

"What's wrong, Willie? What do those Apaches want?"

"That's what Rand would like to find out. Do you speak Spanish?"

Billie shot another glance toward Rand's uncompromising expression. Oh, no. . . . She didn't want any part of getting in the middle of the situation. She avoided a direct answer.

"What about the other men? Did you ask them?"

Willie was beginning to look impatient. "None of the old hands speak Spanish. As for the new men, you don't think I'd be askin' you if any of them was able to interpret. Hell, I'm not fool enough to put you anywhere near Rand for anythin' short of an emergency."

Billie hesitated. She spoke Spanish well enough. As a matter of fact, Juanita had told her that she spoke as well as a native. But having grown up in an area where the two languages were a necessity, she had not considered it such a novel achievement until this very moment.

Billie shook her head, the negative gesture belying the look of assent in her dark eyes.

"What in hell is that supposed to mean?" His patience all but lost, Willie directed a sharp look into her eyes. "This is no time for bein' bashful. Do you speak Spanish or not?"

Hot color stained Billie's cheeks.

"I'm not bashful. But I don't see why I should go up there and interpret for Rand Pierce. To my way of thinking, the best thing I can do is stay away from him."

"Look here, Billie! You ain't got no choice. If you don't go up there and help Rand out, and he finds out later that you do speak Spanish, you'll be out on your ear so fast you won't know what hit you." His brown eyes showing the first sign of disapproval, Willie continued tightly, "Now, what's it goin' to be? Are you goin' to prove to Rand that you're a part of this outfit in spite of the sparks that fly between you, or are you goin' to hold out?"

Billie frowned. She disliked seeing Willie look at her that

53

way. Somehow, the weathered Texan's approval had come to be important to her. Her mouth twitched in annoyance. She also knew she would never forgive herself if something happened to the men or the herd as a result of her refusal to cooperate. Willie was right. She had no choice.

Her expression was begrudging.

"I speak Spanish, but the trail boss isn't going to like it."

"You let me handle that. Come on."

Turning to follow Willie's lead, Billie edged her horse past the trailing herd. Her own words were ringing in her ears. . . .

"The trail boss isn't going to like it. . . ."

His eyes casually scanning the horizon in an attitude that contrasted sharply with the tension squeezing tighter inside his stomach with each minute, Rand kept his back to the passing beeves. He did not want to give his eyes the chance they sought—to follow Willie's progress through the herd. How long did it take to ask a few men if they spoke Spanish? His mind supplying the answer he sought to avoid, he dropped his eyes momentarily closed. Too long . . . when the answer was no.

Hell, it was going to be a long, hard session trying to find out what these two braves had to say if he couldn't . . .

The sound of approaching hooves broke into his thoughts, and Rand felt the responsive leap of his senses. Two horses! He should've realized he could count on Willie to find . . .

Turning toward the sound of approaching hooves, Rand felt his expectant expression drop from his face. Waiting only until the two horses had drawn up, he snapped sharply, "Willie, what in hell are you doing with the kid?"

"You said you wanted somebody who spoke Spanish. Well, he's the only drover you got who does."

His expression noncommittal, Willie watched a host of emotions cross Rand's face. The kid had been right. The trail boss sure enough didn't like bein' dependent on him. For the life of him, he couldn't understand what had made the boss

54

take such a dislike to the boy.

Doing his best to control his annoyance, Rand looked into the boy's bruised face.

"Is it true what Willie said? Do you speak Spanish?"

"I speak it well enough."

"Well enough to translate?"

"What do you think?"

Willie's low cough to the side of her calling her attention to the fact that she had again allowed Rand Pierce to push her into an uncautious response, Billie took a deep breath and pulled the brim of her hat a little lower on her forehead. She shot a quick glance toward the two braves who stood observing the exchange between Rand and herself.

Making an effort at a more conciliatory tone, she turned back to meet the startling azure gaze that pinned her.

"What do you want me to tell them?"

Rand hesitated as he made an attempt to draw his flaring anger under control. "Let's get one thing clear. I want you to tell them exactly what I say. . . . *Exactly,* do you understand?"

"I understand."

Mentally noting that she spent most of her time repeating those same two words to the hard-nosed trail boss, Billie watched as Rand turned to face the waiting Apaches.

His voice firm, Rand instructed, "Tell them my name is Rand Pierce and that I'm taking this herd to Montana. Tell them I want to know who they are and the reason for their visit. Tell them that I am surprised to find Apaches in this country and to have them approach our herd."

Her attention moving fully to the Indians for the first time, Billie had no problem in ascertaining the leader of the two. Her eyes caught and held the gaze of the taller Apache, and Billie felt a responsive tug in the pit of her stomach. There was pride in the way he held his tall, well-muscled frame and in the air with which he waited to hear her speak. His brilliant black eyes assessed her bruised face openly and moved freely over her person. Billie's mind registered the Apache's blatant virility even as she began in unhesitant Spanish.

55

"Esta hombre es el Señor Rand Pierce. Esta viajando con el hato hasta Montana. Quiere saber sus nombres, señores, y la necesidad de su visita. El Señor Pierce tiene sorpresa que hay Apaches aqui, tan lejos de su tribu y tan cerca de este ganado."

An almost undetectable flicker moving in the depths of the dark eyes returning her gaze, the Apache responded in Spanish, the fluid timbre of his voice startling.

"My name is White Hand. Long Hair and I come from the land of the Apache to speak with the great chief of the Commanche. We have watched the plight of men driving cattle on this trail ahead of you. We fell back to give you warning of that which is to come."

A flicker of uncertainty moving across her face, Billie turned to Rand's expectant expression. Her translation of White Hand's words was met with an immediate response.

"What do you mean, 'what is to come'?"

White Hand's gaze was direct and unblinking at Billie's rapid translations.

"Four trail herds have gone ahead of you. The first two traveled the trail you travel, the second two turned off in the direction of the setting sun after reaching the seven lakes."

Rand's reaction to White Hand's statement was guarded. "What is that supposed to mean? The last two herds could have been stock cattle, looking for better range."

"It was not search of better range that induced the white men to turn their cattle. It was the search for water."

"You're saying the land is dry after the seven lakes?"

"Three, maybe four days' travel for your animals without water."

"Three or four days! You're saying at least sixty miles of arid land. . . ."

White Hand's response was a short nod, which did nothing to alleviate the suspicion growing in Rand's eyes.

"And why is this a concern of yours, White Hand? Why do you come to warn of this danger to white man's cattle?"

Hesitating for the first time in translation, Billie shot

Rand a warning glance. Rand's response to her caution was immediate and predictable as anger flared anew in his eyes.

"Ask him the question exactly as I stated it."

"But—"

"Exactly."

His keen gaze expectant after their brief exchange, White Hand listened intently as Billie spoke in translation. His first words were surprisingly directed to her as a spark lit his dark eyes.

"You challenge this man when it is obvious he is in a position of strength here. Only a fool or a person of great courage speaks his mind in the face of overwhelming odds. I think you are the latter, and your actions speak well of you in facing this man. But do not concern yourself for his suspicions. Distrust runs deep within him. I am not adverse to answering his question."

Turning, White Hand directed his reponse to Rand's considering gaze.

"Your question is not without merit, Rand Pierce. You do well to wonder at my concern for white man's cattle. But in truth, your cattle are not truly those of the white man. They go to my brothers, the Blackfeet."

Rand's surprise as Billie turned to interpret was obvious. White Hand continued.

"My ears are tuned to whispers in the wind. There are few secrets in this land, and these days of the white man have made all Indian brothers. I would not see my brothers, the Blackfeet, pass the winter without sufficient beef to replace the buffalo that is no more."

The suspicion had not left Rand's eyes.

"So, this is merely a mission of concern for your brothers . . . with nothing in it for you?"

White Hand's gaze held Rand's unblinkingly.

"No. I have a service to offer you, and when you have judged its worth, I will ask to be paid according to its merit."

"A service?"

"A service. But I will not expect you to accept my word. I am no stranger to the white man's distrust. I would ask you to leave your cattle to travel at their own pace so I may take you ahead to prove the truth of all I have said."

"I could scout the land by myself. I don't need you for that."

"When you have satisfied yourself that I have spoken in truth, I will guide you on a trail that, while lengthening your journey by a few days, will offer you enough water for your cattle to travel without threat."

Rand hesitated, his expression unrevealing. "What payment would you expect for this service?"

"Long Hair and I travel to the Commanche. We would bring our brothers gifts . . . twenty-five head of cattle."

Rand's reaction was spontaneous.

"You expect me to give you twenty-five head of cattle on the basis of what you say now? You must be crazy!"

Billie could not restrain another warning glance, which netted her Rand's sharp admonition.

"I said, tell him *exactly* what I said!"

White Hand's response was undisturbed.

"I would not have the twenty-five head before but *after* you have made it safely into the land of the Commanche. When you are satisfied as to my honesty, I will claim what I have earned."

Rand studied White Hand intently, and Billie felt a tremor of nervousness as his silence stretched on. But White Hand appeared to bear the time with amazing calm. His brilliant eyes narrowed into slender slits, Rand began cautiously.

"We will start out at dawn to verify the truth of all you have said, White Hand. When that has been done, we will go from there to find the safer route for my cattle . . ."

White Hand nodded in agreement.

" . . . on the condition that you spend this night in my camp."

A flicker of annoyance flashed in White Hand's eyes at Rand's unrelenting distrust. The silence stretched into long minutes before White Hand responded with a short nod.

"Agreed. But I, also, have a condition."

At Rand's raised brow he continued smoothly, "You must allow this one to come with us."

His gesture toward Billie was met with a spontaneous

shake of her head as she refused translation. The irritation in his dark eyes fading, White Hand directed his next words to her.

"I, too, ask that you tell Rand Pierce exactly what I say."

Beginning to believe the enigmatic Apache understood far more than he was willing to allow them to believe, Billie turned and followed his instructions. Rand's reaction was immediate. The tightening of his facial muscles more explicit than words, Billie awaited Rand's refusal, only to be surprised as he uttered an abrupt, "Agreed."

The bargain struck, Billie turned back to her horse without another word. She had had enough of Rand Pierce's surliness . . . more than enough. . . .

The flickering shadows of the campfire played against Billie's face, but she was unconscious of its graceful dance. The day had been long and wearying. More aware than ever that she had not yet recovered from the affects of Wes McCulla's savage beating, she spooned up her stew and slid it between her lips.

Darkness had fallen and she knew a deep sense of relief that the cattle had been successfully bedded for the night. Obviously anxious not to repeat the experience of the night before, Rand had ordered the cattle well grazed before sundown, and when they had come to the bedding ground he had chosen, there had not been a hungry or thirsty animal in the lot. There had been obvious relief on Rand's face when the steers had gradually closed in and begun circling. Within the course of a half hour, all had been bedded on five or six acres. The first guard had remained while the others had returned to the wagon and the mouth-watering smell of Nate's cooking.

A low buzz of conversation moved around the campfire, punctuated by Jeremy Carlisle's frequent laugh. It seemed the fair-haired young fellow's good spirits were unsuppressable. In direct contrast to some of the other men, he seemed completely unaffected by the presence of the two Apaches in camp.

As for herself, Billie truly regretted agreeing to act as interpreter between Rand Pierce and his unwelcome visitors. She was now forced into the position of traveling in close contact with the surly trail boss for the next few days, when her most fervent desire was to stay as far away as possible.

Cautiously spooning up another mouthful of stew, Billie slid the spoon between her lips. She had deliberately situated herself at the opposite side of the campfire from Rand Pierce, making sure to allow just enough distance between herself and the other men to indicate her desire to be left alone. She had no intention of becoming drawn into casual conversation that might result in probing questions. She had set a strict strategy for herself on this drive, which included keeping herself a step removed from the men in her free time so that she might maintain her privacy without problem. She was well aware that the men were conscious of Rand's antagonism toward her, and she intended to use that antagonism as a wedge between herself and the rest of the men. At present it appeared her plan was working well. No one, with the exception of Willie Hart, appeared willing to draw Pierce's attention to himself by striking up a hard, fast friendship with her.

The situation was ironic. It seemed she was almost as much of an outsider to this little group as the two Indians who stood to the far side of the campfire. A sudden loneliness assailing her as White Hand exchanged a comment with the smaller Indian at his side, Billie returned her eyes to her plate. No, she was wrong in that observation. At least White Hand and Long Hair had each other to turn to for conversation. And their situation here was temporary. While she . . .

Suddenly unable to finish her thought, Billie concentrated on finishing the food on her plate. Putting it down as soon as it was emptied, she stood abruptly and took a quick glance around the campfire. She needed something familiar, something that would assuage her loneliness, if only for a little while.

Without her realization, Billie was walking toward the remuda. It was dark, but darkness would not prove a handicap to her purpose. Standing at the edge of the area Hank Casey had roped off, Billie whistled softly. When there was no response, she whistled again, her heart lifting as a soft whinny responded from the darkness. A third whistle brought the sound of movement from within the enclosure, and within minutes a familiar muzzle was thrust under her raised hand.

"Ginger—"

Billie's throat tightened with tears as she swallowed hard.

"Did you miss me today, girl? I missed you." She was stroking Ginger's neck, a consoling warmth pervading her with the animal's obvious delight in seeing her, when the sudden appearance of moccasined feet at her side caused a low gasp to escape her lips. Her eyes snapped to the shadowed, unexpected figure, her heart beginning an accelerated beat as she was abruptly engulfed in the power of White Hand's gaze. With a supreme effort she freed herself from his dark-eyed scrutiny and addressed him in faultless Spanish.

"White Hand, what are you doing here? You startled me."

White Hand's expression was unreadable, and Billie's heart skipped a beat.

"I wished to speak to you."

Striving to hide the apprehension that was beginning to edge her senses, Billie took a deep breath. "I am sorry. I can answer no questions without instructions from Rand Pierce."

"I wish to speak to you, not Rand Pierce." White Hand's deep voice was momentarily hesitant. "You are not pleased with the thought of becoming a part of the scouting party tomorrow."

"No, I am not."

The moon had come out from behind a cover of clouds. The effect was to illuminate the night so clearly that White Hand's image was distinctly outlined against the night sky, each feature of his handsome countenance defined. Billie swallowed convulsively. She was intensely conscious of the sharp, clear angles of his face, the strength of his profile, the obsidian eyes that assessed her so openly. The skin of his cheeks was smooth, unmarked by the stubble of the white man's beard. His lips were full but finely drawn, and she found her eyes gravitating to them when he spoke. Feeling extremely vulnerable, she was suddenly grateful that her face was shielded in the shadows of her broad-brimmed hat, for she feared her uncertainty was reflected only too openly in her expression.

White Hand's gaze strove to penetrate the shadows that obscured her face. His low voice was soft, mesmerizing.

"It is my thought that Rand Pierce has not easily accepted the fact that you will accompany the scouting party tomorrow. He looks at you in anger. He is uncomfortable with a woman in camp."

Her mind freezing with shock, Billie held the Indian's gaze for long moments without responding. Finally regaining control of her speech, she shook her head in silent denial. "Rand Pierce does not know I am a woman. No one knows."

"You are wrong. I know, as does Long Hair. I have known from the first." White Hand continued to hold her gaze unrelentingly.

"I—I ask that you do not betray the fact that I am a woman. If I am found out, I will not be allowed to remain with the drive."

"Was it Rand Pierce who beat you?"

"No, it was another man."

"Where is he now?"

"He's dead. I killed him."

There was a moment's hesitation while White Hand assessed her expression.

"That is good."

Billie took a deep breath. "Why do you ask these questions? I am not one of your people and not of your concern."

White Hand frowned, and Billie felt a moment's trepidation. She did not want to alienate this man. His presence was a threat she could not ignore. But instead of anger, her question was met with a probing gaze that seemed to look within himself as well as to search the bruised planes of her face.

62

"My answer to your question is not clear in my own thoughts. I can only tell you that I sensed in you a kindred spirit when first I saw you. Your voice raised a familiar echo in my mind which I still cannot name, and your words rang true in my heart. I knew then as I know now that you are possessed of a great courage which allows fear no place in your breast. Your heart is just, and your purpose strong. Your face is bruised, your features have been distorted by blows from a heavy hand, but your true beauty seeps through. Your warmth reaches out to me."

White Hand raised his hand to touch the jagged path of the cut that marred her cheek.

"It is good that you killed the man, Brave One, for I would have not rested while he lived."

Billie's breathing was shallow as White Hand trailed his finger down her cheek. Her reply was halting.

"I—I had no choice."

"If choice was taken from you, no guilt remains. Why do you hide in the guise of a man and run away?"

"The law could not protect me from the men who would seek to take my life for what I did."

"White man's law . . ." Contempt curled White Hand's lip. "There is little justice for the whites, and none at all for the Indian under its precepts. You do well to seek escape in the land of the Blackfeet."

"It was not my thought to go there, but to go to—"

"What in hell are you doing here, Drucker?"

A familiar voice sounding from behind startled Billie, jerking her head toward Rand Pierce's unexpected appearance. The suspicion on his face was apparent as his gaze moved to White Hand. "What are you telling this Indian?"

Her nerves jarred to the ragged edge by the events of the last few minutes, Billie snapped tightly, "White Hand and I were having a conversation that had nothing to do with you or the drive."

"You're a damned liar, Drucker! I heard both of you say my name more than once."

"You were listening to our conversation?"

"For all the good it did. I didn't understand a word you

said other than that you were talking about the law."

"So I guess you'll have to believe me when I tell you we didn't say anything that concerned you."

Billie's smug expression was wiped away by the threat in Rand's eye and the tone of his voice as he drew closer.

"That's where you're wrong, Drucker. If you want to continue working for me, you'll tell me just what this Indian said to you and what you're doing talking so secretively with him out here."

Shooting a quick glance to White Hand, Billie took a deep breath.

"I—I came out here to see Ginger." As if in confirmation, the small mare gave a soft whinny and Rand's expression tightened. "White Hand asked me a question about the drive and I told him I could not speak for you in any way."

"And his reference to the law?"

"White Hand said he has little respect for the white man's law. He says it gives little protection to the white man and none at all to the Indian."

Rand's eyes moved with silent contemplation between White Hand and herself. Appearing to finally accept her explanation, he nodded toward the mare standing silently under Billie's hand.

"Well, I hope you've finished visiting your pet. We're going to be getting up before dawn to check out White Hand's story, and unless you want to be left behind, I would suggest you turn in.

"I'd just as soon remain behind with the herd."

Something in White Hand's eyes struck a warning note in Billie's mind. She glanced up into his face. He understood! He understood every word she had spoken to Rand Pierce!

"But it just so happens it doesn't suit me to let you stay behind, Drucker. I've already agreed to take you along as interpreter, and I'm not going to let you force me into breaking my word to this savage. So get back to camp, now!"

"Yes, sir!"

Furious at Pierce's autocratic tone, Billie turned without another word and walked stiffly back to camp. Using her saddle for a pillow, she was just pulling her blanket over her back against the damp night air when she caught White Hand's gaze across the campfire. His keen eyes missed nothing, and she was truly uncertain what to expect from him at this point. But somehow, instinctively, she felt less threatened by him than she did by the arrogant trail boss who had seemed to make it his mission in life to make hers miserable.

Managing to sneak a short glance over her shoulder, she saw Pierce was following his own advice and was turning in for the night. Unexpectedly, his gaze raised and caught hers, and Billie was shaken by the heat contained in that short contact.

Damn that Rand Pierce! What did he have against her? She had done nothing to warrant the intense dislike he obviously felt for her. Groaning instinctively against the thought of the next few days, Billie pulled her blanket tight around her and closed her eyes. She had a feeling the worst was yet to come.

The heat of late afternoon was oppressive. His eyes moving to the uneven terrain extending as far as he could see, Rand took an unconscious breath at the sheer vastness of the land they had yet to cover. Spring had advanced to the point where the prairies were swathed in grass and flowers, but Rand was aware that the verdant picture before his eyes was deceiving. Almost a full day's travel had only served to corroborate the story White Hand had related to him. He had seen signs of the drives that had already covered this ground. White Hand had carefully pointed out the points where the last trail herd had changed direction and headed west. They had more ground to cover, but he was certain time would only serve to bear out the truth of everything White Hand had related.

It was apparent White Hand had a definite plan in mind. The Apache obviously intended to have the trail bear out the truth of his statements so that Rand would be willing to bargain firmly for the twenty-five head of cattle before White Hand showed him the well-watered trail on which to take his herd. Well, Rand had no argument with that. The only condition he had put on that bargain was that they cover ground quickly. His herd was still traveling in their direction, and he intended to get back to it in time to turn it onto the right trail without any backtracking involved.

In any event, he had no desire to be away from his herd any longer than three days at most. Willie was a competent segundo, but too many of his men were new. He would not feel safe until he was in charge of the herd again.

Aware of the toll the heat was taking on his weary mount, Rand forced aside the impatience that drove him and allowed his horse to set his own pace. Darting a look to his side, he saw that Drucker automatically followed suit. He knew instinctively the two Apaches traveling beside him could be depended upon to spare their animals. Indians had a healthy respect for all animal life and doubtlessly knew the dangers of being afoot in this country.

He gave a low snort. In any case, these Apaches did not suffer the same sense of urgency driving them that he experienced. No, damn them, they had little to lose. Their responsibilities were all but nil, while he had the worry of getting over three thousand head of cattle across a country which, it was beginning to appear, did not have the water to support a herd half its size.

They had been on the trail before dawn had fully broken through the night sky. Rand could not suppress a smile at the memory that crossed his mind. Drucker, for all his cocky talk, was just a kid after all. The two Apaches were already stirring in their blankets when he had opened his eyes for the first time, but Drucker had been sound asleep. He had given the boy ample time to awaken by himself and, finally disgusted, had walked to his bedroll and given the kid a hearty shake. But the boy had awakened slowly, his battered features pulling into a tight frown that had snapped into a startled, truly comical expression when he had realized who was bending over him.

His view of Drucker's face had been unhindered by the boy's broad-brimmed hat for the first time, and the full extent of the youth's battered condition had registered fully in his mind. The bruising was obviously healing. The deep blue and purple marks were fading to a paler color, and the swelling that had all but closed his eye had lessened. The puffiness around the boy's mouth had flattened to reveal surprisingly fine lips and white straight teeth beneath that had apparently been unaffected by the severe blows to the face he had sustained. The cut that marked the unbruised side of his face was still ugly, and his forehead was swollen in a way that indicated he had probably struck his head on the floor when he had fallen under the weighty blows.

But the fact that had struck him most keenly as he had looked down into Drucker's sleep-drugged face was amazement that a boy of such a young age could have snapped back so quickly after having faced such a harsh experience. It was obvious that the boy had indeed been fortunate to escape with his life after such an attack. There was not a portion of exposed skin on his body that was not marked in some way. The instinctive groans with which the boy had reacted when he had shaken him had indicated that there was also extensive bruising that was not visible, and Rand had begun to realize the supreme effort the boy must have exerted in just managing to mount his horse after his ordeal.

He had no doubt that the contest between Drucker and his unknown assailant had been grossly uneven, because if there was anything of which he was certain, it was that Drucker would be able to hold his own under normal conditions. Even now, shamed by the obvious marks of the attack, the kid wasn't about to let himself be pushed around. And as much as the kid irritated him, he had to admit to a certain amount of admiration for the boy's spunk.

But even if he was still suspicious of the Apache's motives, he had laid his suspicions about the bond that seemed to have sprung up between White Hand and the boy to rest. It was obvious the Indian admired the boy's spunk as well. He had even taken to referring to the boy as "Valerosa," and if he wasn't mistaken, that translated to something like "Brave One."

His eyes moving to the youth beside him, Rand felt a flicker of remorse. He had been damned hard on the boy. His eyes followed the weary turn of the boy's head as he responded to White Hand's comment. His narrow shoulders were slumped with fatigue, but he had not complained.

Unexpectedly, as if sensing his perusal, the boy turned toward Rand. Instant animosity shone in Drucker's dark eyes. His tone was belligerent.

"I suppose you want to know what White Hand just said. He said he's going to rest his horse for a while . . . over there in that clump of trees. I told him you would probably object, that you like to give the orders, but he said he wasn't going to push his horse any farther. He said there's water over there and—"

But Rand was no longer listening as irritation turned to full-fledged anger. The damned nasty twit! It was no wonder somebody had beaten him to within an inch of his life!

Not waiting for the boy to complete his statement, Rand interrupted in a low growl, "I know there's water over there, Drucker. I'm not blind or an idiot. And I'll thank you to confine your comments to translating what White Hand has to say. I don't need you to answer for me! Now tell him I agree with what he says. The horses need rest. We'll stop for a little while and then we'll travel right through until dark."

"Yes, sir, Mr. Pierce. Anything you say!"

Turning sharply to the two Indians at her side, Billie translated in rapid Spanish. It was beginning to become more ridiculous to her by the hour, this senseless duty she performed. She was now more certain than ever that White Hand understood English perfectly. What was more, she was also quite certain that White Hand knew she knew. But they both had secrets, and she was not about to reveal White Hand's if her silence guaranteed the Apache's silence as well.

Nodding as she completed her statement, White Hand signaled to the Indian at his side and the small party urged their horses forward.

The moon was high and they were still traveling. Rand had indicated his intention to travel as far as they could at night in order to cover as much ground as possible. There had been no objection registered to his stated intentions earlier in the day. Billie shot a furtive glance toward the trail boss's erect carriage. Of course, the man showed not a single sign of fatigue! Her eyes turned toward the two Indians who rode at her side. Long Hair's eyes were scanning the line of brush in the shadowed distance. His face was stoic, showing neither emotion nor physical distress. He had maintained complete silence for the major portion of the day. The only words he had spoken had been in the Apache tongue, for White Hand's ears alone.

Billie's eyes flicked in White Hand's direction. The glow of the moon's silver rays reflected in the black hair that lay against his shoulders and on the smooth, unmarked flesh of his bared chest. So well did his image fit the primitive land through which they traveled that, in the pale light, he appeared almost an integral part of the magnificent landscape. Billie mused silently that in other times his was an image that might have inspired fear in her heart, but she was strangely unaffected in that way by this particular Indian.

She was truly bemused by the strange sense of camaraderie that had developed between White Hand and herself. An unexpected bond, it grew stronger each hour. She was strangely affected by the concern in the Apache's gaze when he looked at her. But perhaps it was merely that she was becoming giddy from exhaustion. Whatever it was, she realized she was less than alert at the moment. She had no doubt her mind was beginning to play tricks on her. That had to be so, because a short time before she had almost convinced herself she had seen concern on Rand Pierce's face as well when he had looked in her direction.

But his concern could only bode ill for her future with the outfit. She had no doubt what would happen if she could not keep up. He obviously felt he owed her a chance because of her quick action during the stampede, but it was also obvious that he was looking for the first excuse to get rid of her. A small spark of amusement began to bubble inside her, and a smile curved her stiff lips. But instead, the arrogant Mr. Rand Pierce found himself more dependent upon her than before. She began to laugh. If he only knew White

Hand was playing him for a fool, that White Hand understood every word he spoke to her, that White Hand had doubtless employed the ruse of his ignorance of English so that Pierce would feel free to talk in front of him. Rand Pierce, the clever man of the world and wealthy businessman, was being taken by a man most of his business associates would term an ignorant savage!

Oh, it was a joke, all right! It was funny . . . oh, so funny. She could not help laughing. The humor of the situation seeming to seize control, she was suddenly unable to restrain the laughter escaping her lips. But laughter was a release, a relief that dulled the excruciating pain of her stiff, bruised body. She was laughing harder, almost doubled over her saddle as she felt restraint slipping away. Oh, God, what was wrong with her? No longer amused by the situation, she was beginning to become frightened by the runaway emotions that were overwhelming her.

A sharp admonition in Spanish tore into her thoughts, and she shot a short glance toward White Hand's stern countenance. The helplessness in her expression turned his sharpness to concern, but she was no longer in the slightest control of her actions. She was laughing harder when she felt a rough hand on her arm turn her toward Rand Pierce's dark scrutiny.

"What's the matter, Drucker?"

The annoyance in Rand Pierce's eyes had the effect of halting her unreasonable laughter with an abruptness that left her breathless. Suddenly Billie was gasping, her head reeling. A strange pounding had started in her brain and she was unable to hold her balance. She felt so strange . . . so strange . . .

"Drucker! Get hold of yourself!"

Rand's hand squeezed tighter on her arm as he sought to hold her upright. The pain of his grip cut through the weakness that had assumed control, and Billie swallowed tightly. She took a deep breath, aware of the fact that Rand's hand still gripped her arm tightly. She took another breath and forced herself erect in the saddle. The giddiness was gone, and all that was left was the deep exhaustion she strove

70

to keep out of her voice.

"I'm—I'm all right. Let go—" Grateful for the shadows that hindered Rand's clear assessment of her face, Billie attempted to shake off his grip. "I said I'm all right."

"You're not all right! And what's more, you're stupid!" At the tightening of Billie's expression, Rand continued hotly, "Stupid, that's right! It was stupid to attempt to keep up when you knew you couldn't go any farther! You should have said something. I would have—"

"I told you, I'm all right! You don't have to stop for me! If you want to rest, don't use me for an excuse. I can travel all night, and then I can—"

"Shut up, Drucker. Save your breath." Finally relinquishing his hold on her arm, Rand shot a quick glance to the two Indians who remained silent at their side. "Tell these two we're going to make camp for a few hours . . . here, right here. And then get off your horse, Drucker, before you fall off. And go to sleep."

"You're not stopping to rest because of me! I can go on. If you're stopping, it's because *you're* the one who's tired and wants to rest."

A voice in the back of her mind nagged warningly. She was pushing Rand Pierce too far, but she was unable to force herself to back down. Damn him, she hated the man—his arrogance, his sense of superiority. What cruel twist of fate had forced her to finally set herself free from the clutches of one man, only to put her at the mercy of another, equally relentless? No matter what was at risk, she wasn't going to back down. She'd go on until she dropped before she'd give Rand Pierce the satisfaction of admitting her weakness.

Rand's eyes were steady, unyielding. Strange, the penetrating blueness of their color was obvious even in the limited light of the moonlit night. He sought to pierce her resistance with their mesmerizing quality, to bend her to his will. Never . . . she would never give in to him.

"All right, Drucker." Rand's voice was low, even. *"I'm* tired. *I* can't go any farther tonight. *I* want to rest for a few hours. And I want to rest here . . . now. So get off that damned horse! And get some sleep, damn it, because we've

71

got a full day's traveling ahead of us tomorrow, and it begins at dawn!"

Her lips moving into a tight line, Billie turned to White Hand's enigmatic expression. Her gaze held a contempt clearly not meant for him as she continued with the pretense of translation.

"El gran jefe manda que descansamos aqui."

Her sarcastic reference to Rand Pierce as "The Big Chief" brought about a small quirk of White Hand's lips that was almost undiscernible in the meager light, but it gave a necessary lift to her spirits. How this silent savage had become her ally, she was uncertain, but she was extremely grateful for his presence. She became more grateful with each passing minute.

Holding her back erect with the sheerest strength of will, Billie dismounted, and within minutes she had hobbled her horse and was curled up in her bedroll. She was unaware that keen light eyes considered her sleeping form for long minutes before they, too, closed to rest. She was also unconscious of the fact that watchful almond-shaped eyes observed all in silence.

Chapter IV

Maggie O'Malley's full lips curled in concentration for long moments before she shook her head in a firm negative response.

"No, I ain't seen a girl fittin' that description in San Antonio in the past week. As a matter of fact, I ain't seen a girl fittin' that description in San Antonio in the past year or more. And you can be sure I'd have known if somebody like that was travelin' through, especially if she was alone. The boys in this town would have had this place buzzin'."

"You're sure, Maggie?"

"Yes sir, I'm sure."

Dan McCulla stared into Maggie's face unblinkingly, and Maggie suppressed a shudder. She didn't like the look of the man. There was something about the lines of his florid face and the coldness in his pale eyes. . . . The cut of the suit that covered his short, rather stocky body was a bold declaration of his wealth and the prominence he had gained farther south, despite the trail dust marking it, but she wasn't taken in one bit. She didn't much like Dan McCulla. She had to admit that she was glad he wasn't a frequent visitor to San Antonio or her cafe. To her mind, there was nothing worse than an opportunist who had taken advantage of the war and had built his fortune on the misfortune of others. The talk was that he now had a firm hand in local government and was able to twist the law to suit his purpose.

And there was no doubt Dan McCulla was a man with a

purpose today. He had entered San Antonio just after daybreak with a group of ten men or more. It was the talk of the town the way he had his men systematically covering every restaurant, bar, and hotel, looking for a young woman whom they described as about seventeen, with light blond hair and dark eyes. He claimed she was a runaway, the daughter of a friend who had asked him to find her. He hadn't given her name, saying the girl would probably think up another to use, but Maggie had determined long before he had approached her that she wouldn't give him any information, even if she had some to give. She didn't trust Dan McCulla, and one look into his eyes had been sufficient to prove to her that her suspicions were correct. Contrary to his protestations, he meant the girl no good, of that she was sure.

Removing the cloth tucked in at her broad waistline, Maggie dusted a few crumbs from the table. Her voice was brisk, her glance touching on each of the five men seated there.

"So, what'll you have, boys? Maggie's Cafe don't have much variety, but the food is fresh and hearty. I just cooked up a batch of beef stew and biscuits, and Matthew cut up some steaks this mornin' that the boys said just melt in your mouth. I don't expect you'll get a better meal in all of San Antonio."

Aware of a familiar step behind her, Maggie turned to her hired hand's openly curious expression as he came to stand beside her. She should have realized nothing in the world would keep lazy Matthew Filmore in the kitchen with the whole town buzzin' about the search Dan McCulla was conductin'. He was too nosey for his own good and one excuse was as good as any for him to sneak a few minutes away from work.

Turning, she flicked a disapproving glance over Matthew's skinny frame, her eyes taking in the greasy stains on the makeshift apron tied around his waist. The man hadn't even had the sense to change the apron he had used when he had been butchering earlier in the day before coming into the restaurant. The fool was hopeless.

Her face reflecting her distaste, she questioned sharply, "What're you doin' out front, Matthew? You can't be done with all the chores I left you, yet. I don't need you out here. And unless I miss my guess, these fellas are goin' to be wantin' you to put on five thick steaks."

"No, Maggie, wait a minute." Dan McCulla's smile was forced. "Don't chase the man back to the kitchen. I'm committed to findin' that girl, and I haven't had any luck so far today. What about you, Matthew? Have you seen a young woman in San Antonio . . . travelin' alone . . . about seventeen, a good-lookin' young thing with blond hair and big dark eyes? I'd be real appreciative if you could give me some information about her. Her daddy's fair to losin' his mind with worry over the girl, and since I said I'd be comin' to San Antonio today, he made me promise to inquire about her."

Flicking a casual glance between the two facing him, McCulla added casually, "I'm thinkin' that the girl wouldn't be hard to recognize. Other than the fact that she's real tall for a woman and has the kind of blond hair that's so pale it's almost silver, my friend admitted to me that he lost his temper in an argument he had with the girl just before she left. He dealt with her pretty harshly, I'm afraid, and he confessed he marked the girl. That's one of the main reasons he's so anxious to find her . . . so that he can make it all up to her."

Maggie had all she could do not to laugh aloud. So, desperation was forcin' the truth out into the open. There *was* more to this search than met the eye. . . . Some poor young girl was wanderin' somewhere around in San Antonio, all beat up and lost, tryin' to escape this lecher. . . .

Abrupt realization hit Maggie a stunning blow! She had all she could do to maintain her casual facade. The boy . . . the poor kid who had come in a couple of days ago! Yes, he had had pale blond hair. She remembered how the boy had touched it self-consciously when she had told him to remove his hat. Yeah, she'd say the kid had been dealt with harshly! He had been so beat up he had had to struggle to chew each bite.

75

A picture of the boy's horrendously distorted face returned to Maggie's mind's eye, and she felt an urge to smack the lyin' smile from McCulla's face. It was no wonder she had not recognized the youth as a girl. It would doubtless be days, maybe even weeks before the poor child was recognizable as a woman. And this bastard wanted to get his hands on her again.

But Matthew was obviously completely taken in. Openly flattered by McCulla's attention, he screwed up his grizzled old face thoughtfully.

"No, Mr. McCulla, I can't rightly say I seen a girl like you described in this here place."

Annoyance gained control of Maggie's tongue.

"Well, since you can't help Mr. McCulla, Matthew, I'd say you'd best go back to the kitchen and put on those steaks like I said. Mr. McCulla's in a hurry and he don't want to waste—"

Efficiently ignoring her, determined to enjoy his moment in the sun, Matthew addressed himself directly to Dan McCulla's taunt smile.

"No, I ain't seen no girl like you described, Mr. McCulla. The only young'un I seen comin' through San Antonio alone in the past week was a boy who stopped in here a few days back. Hell, he was in sad shape, I'll tell you that. Seems his horse threw him. Must'a dragged him a ways, too, considerin' the way he looked. Damn frightenin' to look at, he was."

All but groaning at her hired man's stupidity, Maggie watched as a round of knowing looks moved around the table.

"Where was the boy headin', Matthew? It might be worth seein' if we can find the boy. For all we know, he might know somethin' about the girl."

"Well, if you want to find the boy, Mr. McCulla, you're headin' in the wrong direction." Acknowledging Maggie's presence for the first time, Matthew cocked an unruly brow. "What was it you said the boy told you, Maggie . . . that he was headin' for Mexico?"

"Mexico!"

76

McCulla's head snapped toward Maggie in confirmation.

"Yes, that's what the boy said." Her assent spontaneous, Maggie nodded heartily. "And he was in a hurry, too. He took off right after eatin'. He was kinda short of cash. I suppose he figured he'd do better goin' south instead of north as he originally intended. I don't blame the boy. He could live a lot cheaper south of the border than he could here. Anyway, that's what he said."

McCulla's thick lips spread into a wide, self-satisfied smile as he turned to acknowledge the nods of the men around the table. There was a new look in his eye as he turned back toward Maggie.

"Well, I do thank you for talkin' to us, Maggie. And you, too, Matthew. You've been right helpful, and we won't forget it, will we, boys? Now, you can bring on those steaks you were talkin' about, and some of your fine biscuits. It looks like we have some backtrackin' to do today after we leave San Antonio."

"It'll be my pleasure, Mr. McCulla."

Her smile so false she was sure it would crack, Maggie turned and gave Matthew's boney arm a firm poke.

"You heard the man, Matthew. Five steaks . . . pronto! We don't want to keep Mr. McCulla waitin', do we?"

"No, ma'am."

Firmly tucking a strand of graying hair back into the bun at the back of her neck, Maggie turned her ample form toward the kitchen with a pleased smile. No, she didn't want to keep Mr. McCulla from goin' after that poor child, especially when she was certain he was goin' to be racin' in the wrong direction. No, she wouldn't want to do that, not for a minute. . . .

White Hand was riding firmly in the lead of their small party, Long Hair at his side. Rand shot a quick look to the slender figure riding to his left. The kid appeared to be holding up well, despite the unexpected heat and the extended ground they had covered in the last three days. Suddenly annoyed at his own concern for the youth, Rand gave a low, disgusted snort. What in hell was wrong with him, anyway? He must be getting soft. He had always been a hard taskmaster, demanding the same of his men that he demanded of himself. Those who weren't willing or able to keep up had been replaced by others.

But, whether he wanted to admit it or not, the situation was different with this kid. Despite their clash of personalities, he had developed a healthy respect for the boy over the past few days. It had been apparent from the first that Drucker wasn't physically up to the hard riding they had done. Besides the fact that the kid had been badly beaten, he was damned frail. Rand remembered only too clearly the almost fragile feel to Drucker's arm when he had grasped it to prevent him from falling from his horse that first night. That brief touch had impressed even more firmly on his mind the sheer strength of will the boy had employed to keep up as long as he had.

But the kid had asked no quarter in the days that had followed, and despite his concern, Rand had been unable to grant any. It had been essential that he determine White Hand's reliability before he was forced to waste valuable time in turning the herd. He was now convinced his effort had not been wasted.

It was obvious that all White Hand had said was true. He had swung them in a wide circuitous route, which had shown only too clearly that the last two trail herds had turned west to avoid the drought conditions they would experience after reaching Indian Lakes. That same sweep had also demonstrated that however limited the water supply had been in the approach to the lakes, after reaching them, the drive could be completely dry for as much as six days if he continued on the trail as planned.

There had been no doubt White Hand's unexpected appearance could save him much time and hardship on his herd if the Indian could produce an alternative, well-watered trail. Time had also served to eliminate Rand's suspicions as to White Hand's motives. The Indian had doubtless considered twenty-five head of cattle a sufficient gift to guarantee himself a place of honor at the campfire of his brothers, the Commanche. Renegade or not, he obviously thought it important to earn the beeves so he might present them unchallenged to the Commanche chief.

Rand had awakened at dawn that morning to the realization that the time had come for White Hand to complete the second part of the bargain by showing him the alternate route for his cattle. He had become immediately alert to the fact that White Hand and Long Hair were engaged in a whispered conversation. His own quick glance toward Drucker's bedroll had shown that the boy, too, was awake, but the consternation evident on the kid's face had demonstrated only too clearly that he could not understand a word of the conversation progressing between the two Indians in their native tongue.

Rising immediately, his disposition suffering from annoyance, Rand had signaled Drucker to do the same. They had eaten a meager breakfast of boiled coffee and dried beef, after which White Hand had approached them formally. Shooting a quick glance toward Drucker, White Hand had begun in unhesitant Spanish, pausing periodically in order to affect translation.

"It is my wish to know if you are satisfied with the truth of all I have stated about the conditions of the trail you were to follow." Rand's brief nod had allowed White Hand to continue. "Then I would confirm our bargain and the conditions which apply." Ignoring Rand's raised brow at the use of the word "conditions," White Hand continued unperturbed.

"Long Hair and I will lead you along a trail long used by my brothers, the Commanche. It has many small river beds. Watering spots are limited in size but sufficient for your cattle if you will water them carefully. You would do well to raise your cattle before dawn each day on this route, while the grass is still moist, and allow them to graze while they might use this method to further slake their thirst. In any event, Long Hair and I will show you the trail, and then we will depart. Other matters have waited too long while we have made this journey with you. These matters will not allow us the time needed to meet your herd and follow it on the route we have marked. But we will return when the ground has been satisfactorily covered and your cattle's well-being secured. We will take payment at that time. It is our wish to hear confirmation of that bargain from your lips."

Rand's affirmative response had been unhesitant. White Hand had assumed the lead from that point on, speaking little and maintaining a tight pace.

There had been little relenting even as the heat of the day had burned wearingly into their backs and exhaustion had begun to stiffen their bones. Satisfied that White Hand was indeed fulfilling his part of the bargain, his major concern had been for the slender youth at his side. Despite the boy's continued animosity toward him, Rand had begun to find his eyes stealing toward the boy with growing frequency to assess his physical state. He was only too aware that the boy would rather drop than admit fatigue, and he had no desire to cause the youth unnecessary hardship.

Unexpectedly White Hand drew his horse to a halt. Signaling the others to follow suit, he waited until Rand and Drucker had drawn up alongside before extending his hand to point toward the first of the Indian Lakes in the distance.

"You see, Rand Pierce, the first of the seven lakes. I have brought you in a great circle back to the point where the true danger for your herd begins. By continuing on toward the lakes, you will meet your cattle in sufficient time to prepare both them and your men for the hardship which is to come. Long Hair and I will leave you now. There is much ground we must cover before nightfall. We will be back to receive the payment promised."

Waiting only until Rand had acknowledged his statement, the Indian turned toward Drucker, and Rand felt his stomach tighten. He didn't quite like the manner in which White Hand looked at the boy. It wouldn't really surprise him if he tried to convince the boy to join him. White Hand did not have the look of a reservation Indian, and he had no doubt the Apache was a man with a mission. But he was convinced the time for renegades was limited, and he had no desire to see the boy become part of whatever ill-fated venture White Hand was planning to affect with the Commanche.

White Hand began to speak. His manner of addressing the boy and the low, mesmerizing tone of his voice brought a small frown to the youth's face. The boy shot a quick look toward Rand. The trail boss could see the youth was discomforted by the Indian's words. Obviously satisfied that Rand was unable to follow the Indian's soft statement, the boy turned his full attention back to White Hand, and Rand knew a swelling frustration. Damn the savage! If he thought he was going to lure the boy away with wild promises . . .

Billie suppressed the twinge of anxiety White Hand's words had inspired. One glance in Rand Pierce's direction had revealed a consternation in his gaze that could only indicate frustration. No, Pierce did not understand what White Hand was saying, and Billie was vastly relieved. Turning back to White Hand, Billie saw confirmation in his gaze.

"No, Brave One, this man does not understand what I say to you. He suspects that I seek to lure you from him, but he is not sure. He has come to respect you, although his dislike has remained strong. But his dislike does not affect his desire to keep you at his side."

A hint of a smile touched White Hand's lips, and the warmth it exuded touched a subtle response deep inside. Panic stabbed at her senses and Billie fought the urge to check Rand Pierce's expression again. Surely Pierce knew enough Spanish to realize he was being discussed. She could not afford to raise the trail boss's anger or suspicions. In a short time they would be back with the herd and she would no longer be so close to him as to be a constant thorn in his side. From that point on she had determined she would stay out of his way, keep her silence, and do her job. Her body was healing, but her mind still fought savage memories that would allow her little peace. She wanted only to return to the herd, to be lost in its vastness, and to remain safe in anonymity until she reached her destination. She had been lucky so far in not being followed. She wanted to do nothing to put herself at further risk.

But White Hand had not finished speaking, and she waited patiently for him to continue.

"You need not worry, Brave One. The angry man does not understand my words. His mind is too filled with thoughts of the cattle which follow us to suspect my true reason for speaking to you. He is unconscious of the beauty which surfaces more clearly each day on your face. He sees only the boy he wishes to see, while I see the woman."

Billie shook her head in spontaneous refutation of the words White Hand spoke. She had not suspected the handsome Apache of such feelings for her. She fought the desire to speak her mind clearly. But she dared not extend the conversation.

His keen eyes reading her shock and the frustration that followed, White Hand allayed her fears with a short motion of his hand.

"No, I will speak no more of this now, Brave One. I leave to perform a duty long left undone because of my delay here. But it was my desire to leave you with the declaration of my admiration for you and the thought that I know the pain you suffered was not confined to the body. The white man's law has failed you and put you in a jeopardy. I do not know the full extent of that jeopardy, but know only that its threat hangs heavy on your heart. I would share that burden with you, Brave One, and in sharing make it lighter. I ask that you think on this, consider it. We will speak again when I return."

Taking a short breath, unwilling to allow Rand's eyes to determine how deeply White Hand's words had affected her, Billie nodded.

"You are right in saying we cannot speak now, White Hand." Her eyes holding White Hand's intense gaze, Billie experienced again the warmth extended so freely from their depths. It reached out to her, and she fought to hold herself aloof from its attraction even as her heart swelled with the generosity of spirit it extended.

"But . . . I thank you for the friendship and warmth in

your heart. It touches me deeply."

A flicker of another emotion moved across White Hand's handsome face in the second before he turned to direct a clipped phrase to the Indian at his side.

Within moments White Hand had wheeled his horse around and spurred him toward the horizon. Billie was watching the two horsemen move into the distance when Rand Pierce's harsh voice broke into her wandering thoughts.

"What did White Hand say to you?"

Billie's eyes darted to Rand Pierce's face. She met his frown with one of her own.

"He said good-bye . . . that he would return soon."

"He used a hell of a lot of words to say that one sentence."

"That's all he said that concerned you."

"Everything he said concerns me."

Rand Pierce's gaze was moving intensely over her face. Uncomfortable under his steady scrutiny, Billie dropped her head a fraction lower, effectively using the broad brim of her hat as a shield against his perusal.

The boy's quick defensive posture touched Rand unexpectedly. Hell, he didn't know what Drucker had been through, but it was obvious the boy was afraid to trust anybody but himself. He certainly wasn't making it any easier for the kid with his short temper. Rand shook his head. He usually handled people quite well. What was it about this kid that knocked him so off balance? He tried again.

"Look, Drucker, you're only a kid, and I feel kind of responsible for you, so I—"

Anger flushed Billie's face a deep red. "You don't have to feel responsible or sorry for me. I can take care of myself. And I don't need anybody to look after me, so you can keep your . . ."

Rand heard no more as a surge of righteous pride pushed all other thoughts from his mind. If that didn't beat all! The damned twit was throwing his concern back in his face! That's what he got for feeling sorry for the puny little brat. Well, he'd be damned before he'd let the pip-squeak get away with talking to him like that!

"Wait a minute, Drucker. Let's get some things straight. I took you on and you're one of my drovers. Like it or not, that makes me the boss here. Your responsibility is to do your job, and mine is to tell you the best way to handle yourself when you do it. So far, you've been doing your job real well—even if you do have a big mouth—but it's time for some plain talk.

"That Indian's up to no good where you're concerned. He's got his eye on you. Hell, he's done nothing but puff you up with flattery from the first day. Valerosa . . . that mean's 'Brave One,' doesn't it? I've seen this kind of thing before. He's trying to talk you into coming along with him, isn't he . . . joining whatever plans he has in the works. Well, boy, he hasn't got anything to offer you. The government's cracking down on the Indians in these parts, and no matter what that fellow has in mind with the Commanche, it's not going to get him anything but a lot of grief."

"I told you, I don't need your advice. I—"

"Well, you're going to get it anyway." Frustration edged into Rand's annoyance. He was getting nowhere with this approach, but he was damned if he knew how else to get to the boy. And somehow, it was important to him that he did.

"Look, kid, do yourself a favor and tell that Indian you don't want a part of anything he's offering. It looks to me like you've had enough trouble. If you're smart, you'll steer clear of him, do your job, and use your pay at the end of the drive to start yourself off on the right foot. You've got plenty of time to think things over. We won't be reaching Montana for another couple of months and—"

Billie was beginning to shake with anger. White Hand was an Indian and that meant he couldn't be trusted. . . . She had been exposed to that kind of thinking before. Well, she didn't know much about Indians, but she knew she'd trust White Hand before she'd trust Rand Pierce any day of the week. She had heard enough . . .

"While we're getting things straight, Mr. Pierce, I've got some things to say, too." Struggling to keep her voice level, Billie continued determinedly, "You're my boss on this drive, and I follow your orders when it comes to driving cattle and doing my job. But as far as the rest goes, I can take care of myself. I don't need you or anybody else to stand up for me. And I don't need *anybody* to tell me how to think. I've made my own judgment of White Hand. He's a brave and honorable man."

The penetrating blue of Rand Pierce's eyes raked her adamant expression and Billie held herself stiffly erect. Every muscle in her body protesting her stiff posture, she allowed him to absorb her words fully before continuing in an unrelenting tone, "So, if that's all you've got to say, I suppose you'll want to be starting toward the lakes. The herd ought to be reaching the first one soon, and we—"

"Like you said, Drucker, *I* give the orders here, and I don't need you to remind me about my herd." Pausing, Rand shook his head. A note of frustrated resignation entered his voice. "If you're too damned hardheaded to listen to reason, you can do as you damned well please. But remember one thing. You signed on to this drive, and to my way of thinking, that means you signed on to drive cattle from San Antonio to Montana. I expect you to keep your bargain. I'm warning you now, you won't get a damned cent out of me if you take off before the drive is done." His eyes holding hers, he pressed unrelentingly. "Do we understand each other?"

Taking a firm hold on her temper, Billie nodded.

"What's the matter, Drucker? Cat got your tongue?"

"You couldn't be so lucky."

"That sure as hell is the truth. But if you don't mind, I want to hear you—"

"All right. I understand what you said. I stay with the herd all the way or I don't get paid."

Stiff-necked, Billie bore Rand's silent scrutiny a few minutes longer before the trail boss abruptly turned his horse and spurred him in the direction of the first lake. Hesitating only a moment, Billie urged her bay to follow. She was more certain than ever that it was going to be a long, hard drive to Montana.

*　　*　　*

The aroma of roasting meat permeated the air, and Rand's stomach gurgled in anticipation. They were camped for the night at the second of the seven lakes. Natural reservoirs with rocky bottoms, the lakes were stretched out in a line with approximately a mile between each, and pushing on to the second had given them an edge in their journey for the next day. He had been satisfied with their progress.

Whatever the case, one look at Drucker had convinced him it would be unwise to press on any farther. The heat of spring had become unrelenting in the last few days, with the air far more heavy than normal. Perspiration had ringed the boy's forehead and upper lip, liberally staining his clothing by the time they had reined up at the lake. Rand had been aware that he was in much the same shape, but he had not felt the fatigue that was demonstrated only too clearly in the boy's posture and the weary tilt of his head. They had been up before dawn that morning and had had a full day. And they would be up before dawn the next. Yes, despite the fact that he would have kept on had he been alone, it had been time to take a well-deserved break.

It had been several days since they had eaten a cooked meal, and Rand was certain his appetite was going to do justice to the prairie bird turning a light golden brown over the fire. The sound of an approaching step snapped Rand's face up just as Drucker hit the circle of light from the campfire.

He motioned to the small pot the boy carried.

"The coffee's over there."

The boy dumped an unmeasured amount of the fragrant ground beans into the water and turned to place the pot on the fire. Rand's eyes moved across the boy's back and he shook his head. The kid was a reasonable height all right, but he was the skinniest damned boy he had ever seen! He was beginning to have his doubts that those narrow shoulders would ever broaden and those frail arms would ever begin to show a bit of muscle.

Small as the boy was, he was a prime target. He'd probably end up being the first choice of the bully in every town they hit from here to Montana. The boy had spunk, but spunk wasn't always enough. It looked like he was going to have to keep an eye on the kid for the duration of the drive. One thing for sure. Drucker wouldn't survive another beating like the one he had suffered.

The boy sat silently beside the fire, his small hands working at turning the bird. How long had it been since Drucker had first appeared in camp? Six days? As far as he could see with that damned hat in the way, it looked as if his facial bruises were healing pretty well. At least the boy had two good eyes to see out of again. And they were damned big eyes . . . taking up most of his small face.

Rand surveyed the boy's profile etched against the fire, unconsciously remarking at its fine line. It was amazing his nose had escaped being broken, considering the extent of the beating he had taken. The puffiness around his mouth had gone down, and Rand had noted a day or so before that the boy no longer experienced difficulty in eating. His mouth was well drawn, the fullness of the bottom lip giving it a slightly pouting quality. Funny, he couldn't remember ever seeing the kid smile. As a matter of fact, he couldn't remember ever seeing the kid without his hat pulled down tight on his forehead, except for the time he spent in his bedroll.

He remembered the night before. Their scouting party had settled down for the night in the usual manner, with the two Indians on one side of the fire and Drucker and himself on the other. Drucker had fallen asleep as soon as his head had hit the makeshift pillow. The rays of the full moon had caught on his pale hair, giving it an almost incandescent glow. It had near to fascinated him. He had never seen the like of its color. Then the boy had turned in his sleep, and he had gotten a glimpse of an innocence and vulnerability that was completely hidden by the youth's normally guarded expression.

A second sense had snapped his eyes across the fire at that moment to see White Hand observing the boy as well. There was no doubting the Indian's virility. It was written in his manner of speech, in every movement of his agile, well-formed body. His cool, unshakable demeanor declared his manhood and his pride. He had no doubt White Hand had several wives and numerous children who awaited his return and the outcome of his mission to the Commanche. But there was also no doubting White Hand's interest in the boy . . . and he didn't like it.

Whatever it was, there was something about the damned arrogant little twit that seemed to have touched White Hand as deeply as it had touched him. Irritation began to color Rand's wandering thoughts. No matter what Drucker had said, White Hand had not confined his comments to a simple good-bye when he had spoken so boldly to the boy in his presence. And, if he wasn't mistaken, the Indian had truly enjoyed the advantage Rand's ignorance of the language had allowed him. Well, if he had, it was the last time that Indian was going to enjoy such an advantage. When White Hand and his silent partner returned for payment, he would see to it that the twenty-five head were cut out immediately and the two of them sent on their way. He fully intended to keep Drucker away from that Indian's influence if he had to tie the kid to his side.

Abruptly annoyed with the line his mind had taken, Rand drew himself to his feet.

"I'm going to take a walk down by the lake. Give me a call if that bird is done before I come back, Drucker."

Nodding his assent, the boy did not bother to turn in his direction. Turning toward the narrow path to the lake, Rand felt his irritation grow. Six days, and the kid hadn't said more than three words to him that weren't said in anger. But he didn't seem to find it at all hard to talk to that damned savage! Unwilling to ponder the reason for his mounting annoyance, Rand continued on toward the lake. He had had just about all he could take for the time being.

Sorely tempted to rip off the small wing of the golden brown bird to sample its juicy meat, Billie took a deep breath. She was so hungry she could barely stand it. What was keeping Rand Pierce so long? He had gone down to the lake more than half an hour before. The coffee was brewed and fragrant, and the bird was doubtless done to perfection . . . or as close as it could be to that state under the primitive conditions of their campfire. She had heard Rand's stomach sound vocally just prior to his leaving. He had been hungry, too.

Damn, where was he? She didn't much like the thought of leaving the bird over the fire and going to find him. If some hungry animal was lingering out there in the darkness and took the opportunity to come and snatch it away, she didn't think she'd be able to stand it. She was already salivating.

Popping a few of the berries she had picked into her mouth, Billie drew herself wearily to her feet. She could not wait to fall into her bedroll. Dawn would come early, and her body was crying for rest. It had been a hard few days, and she was just beginning to realize how fortunate she had been to be taken on as part of Pierce's crew. The country was extremely difficult and she had no doubt she would have been unable to make it to her destination by herself.

But she would be truly relieved when she was no longer in such close contact with Rand Pierce. She had felt the weight of his eyes studying her when she had crouched by the fire. His scrutiny had been difficult to bear when there had been others to distract his attention, but now . . .

Grateful that the full moon was unobstructed by clouds, Billie walked cautiously down the well-lit path to the lake. Slowing her pace as she reached the edge, Billie scanned the area. Rand was nowhere to be seen. A tremor of nervousness moved up her spine. He had said . . .

Even as her eyes searched the shadows, Billie was startled by a sudden splash on the placid surface of the lake. She had only to turn her eyes in the direction of the sound to see that Rand had surfaced and was swimming toward her. Billie's eyes darted to the shadows at water's edge, her gaze touching on clothing tossed in a careless pile. Rand had seen her and raised his hand. He was calling out to her, but she was unable to hear . . . to think.

Her heart pounding, Billie stood rooted to the spot as Rand stroked evenly into the shallow depths and finally stood up.

89

The silver glow of the moon glinted on the broad stretch of his shoulders as Rand brushed back the ebony hair plastered to his forehead. He was walking briskly despite the pull of the water, obviously invigorated by his brief swim. His startling eyes were amazingly vivid in the limited light, and he was smiling. She didn't remember ever having seen him smile before. The transformation was unsettling. The harsh planes of his face softened as the grooves in mid-cheek sank into unexpected dimples. His lips stretched wide across teeth that were amazingly white against the darkness of his face. He raised his hand to brush the few remaining droplets from his forehead and his grin broadened.

Billie watched his approach, intensely conscious of the ever-dropping level of the water as it moved steadily down his muscular length. It had exposed a broad heaving chest, peppered by a fine mat of dark hair. She swallowed tightly as the water dropped to his waist, past his slim, masculine hips, her eyes snapping back up to his face as he emerged fully from the water. Stopping to scoop up his clothes, Rand walked to within a few feet of Billie and stopped. He grinned at her silence.

The naked breadth of him was intimidating in the pale silver light, and Billie swallowed convulsively. A few drops of water clung to the dark curling hairs on his chest and, fascinated, she found her mind wondering if his skin were really as firm and smooth as it appeared . . . if it were cool or warm to the touch. She was startled by her own thoughts. She had never truly looked at Rand Pierce as a man before, but she was presently too tensely aware of his maleness.

"Why didn't you come in when I called you? The water's great. I haven't felt this good in a week."

When she did not respond, Rand shook his head. "It's the last chance you'll get for a while, you know. When we catch up with the herd we won't have time for anything, and you know what the country's like after we leave these lakes. Hell, we'll be lucky to have enough water to drink, much less wash."

When she still did not respond, Rand took another step forward, halting as she took a corresponding step backward.

His expression held a quality she had never seen there before, a hesitation that sincerely sought to define the cause of her obvious distress.

"What's wrong, Drucker?"

"I—I can't swim."

He hesitated, pursuing his questioning in a cautious manner. "You don't have to swim to cool off." He gave a small uncertain laugh. "If you're worried that I'll sneak back to the fire and leave you with nothing to eat, you can put your mind at rest. My conscience is a little stronger than my appetite."

"No." Having trouble catching her breath, Billie shook her head. "No, I—I don't want to."

His gaze studied her, moving to her hands, noting the defensive way they had sprung to the buttons on her shirt. A flutter of apprehension quickened the beat of her heart, but instead of suspicion, sympathy flickered momentarily in the depths of Rand's eyes. His voice held an unexpected gentleness.

"Look, Drucker, I've seen bruises before, if that's what you're worried about. I've had plenty of fights in my day, and I haven't won them all. I can remember a time when I looked a hell of a lot worse than you probably do. But if you'd rather I leave so you can—"

"I told you, I don't want to go in the water." Able to bear neither his closeness nor his sympathy a moment longer, Billie took a shaky breath. "I'm hungry, and I'm tired of waiting to eat. So if you don't hurry up, you're going to have to eat what's left over."

Turning, Billie walked shakily back toward the campfire. Her stomach was so tight that she was uncertain she would be able to get a single morsel past her lips. She was back at the campfire for a few minutes and had taken the bird from the fire when she heard the sound of a step behind her. Not bothering to turn around, she tore off a leg and forced herself to take the first bite. She was startled when Rand's voice broke the silence between them.

"Drucker, I'm sorry. The water felt so damned good, I was just trying to— I didn't mean to press you."

91

Unable to avoid responding, Billie turned to meet Rand's sober expression. His hair was still wet and his clothes clung damply to his body, but he was no longer smiling. She felt the loss of his smile intensely and a momentary thickness choked her throat.

"That's all right. It's just that—"

"Look, Drucker, you don't owe me any explanations." A smile flicked across his lips. "You just owe me a good day's work, and I'm sure to get that out of you tomorrow. So let's eat and get to sleep."

Nodding, Billie forced herself to take another bite, but she was no longer hungry.

Chapter V

A blood rage deepened the color on Dan McCulla's already florid face. He eyed the men facing him across the desk in the opulent library of his home, giving each a taste of the menace in his gaze. Finally settling his attention on a shifty-eyed cowboy who moved uncomfortably under his scrutiny, he assaulted him in a loud, accusing tone.

"You call yourself my foreman, Whitley. I'm the richest man in this part of Texas, and I got the best spread around. That should mean that I'm employin' the best wranglers money can buy. Well, I'll tell you, I don't like it much findin' out *ten* of my men ain't no match for *one* girl! What in hell do you mean you can't find that Winslow bitch?"

Bushy brows meeting over his thin, hawklike nose, Carl Whitley shook his head in silent refutation of Dan McCulla's statement. His fingers twitched nervously on the brim of the hat he held in his hand.

"It's just like I said, Mr. McCulla. That Winslow girl ain't no place around here. Me and the boys covered every bit of trail from San Antonio to the border, and nobody seen her, dressed up like a boy or a girl. We hit every border town for miles around. No matter what that Maggie O'Malley says, I'm tellin' you there ain't no sign of that gal headin' for Mexico."

"And I'm tellin' you that Matthew Filmore is too stupid to tell anythin' but the truth. If he says that girl said she was headin' for Mexico, she was headin' for Mexico! You boys are goin' to find her, and she's goin' to pay for what she did to my son."

Blinking under the heat of Dan McCulla's unrelenting stare, Whitley shot a quick look to the men beside him. Visibly gathering up his courage, he glanced back to McCulla's livid face.

"Maybe what you said is true, Mr. McCulla. Maybe that Matthew Filmore is too stupid to lie about what the girl told him, but that girl ain't stupid. She probably knew that old man wouldn't be able to keep his mouth shut. She probably just let him overhear what she wanted him to hear."

Obviously relieved when McCulla appeared to study his response, Whitley shifted his wiry frame. He licked his lips nervously as McCulla's eyes narrowed with thought.

"There might be somethin' to what you say, Whitley. One thing I know for sure. That old woman and her hired man wouldn't have the nerve to lie to Dan McCulla. They sure as hell know what would happen to them if they did. No, that Winslow girl must've taken them in just the way she took in everybody else."

Suddenly drawing himself to his feet, Dan McCulla walked around the desk. A sinister smile stretched across his thick lips as he came to stand directly in front of his nervous foreman.

"All right, Whitley. You've got another chance to prove you're not goin' to let a snippy little bitch get the best of you. You're goin' to take five men with you and go back to San Antonio. And you're goin' to cover that whole town until you find out where that 'boy' headed after he left."

His eyes shifting unexpectedly to the short fellow standing silently at Whitley's side, McCulla barked, "And you, Carter, you're goin' to take three boys and ride back toward Mexico. You're goin' to make sure you didn't miss nothin' when you searched for that 'boy' the first time."

"Mr. McCulla—" Whitley swallowed tightly as McCulla's eyes snapped back in his direction, but he was determined to speak his piece. "It appears to me that you're forgettin' that we're not even sure that 'boy' Maggie O'Malley was talkin'

94

about is really the Winslow girl. Hell, it appears to me a girl in her spot would be too scared to be able to come up with a plan to escape. And I can't believe a female could outsmart—"

"Seems like that was Wes's mistake, too, Whitley." His coarse features tightening, McCulla pulled his bull-like frame to its full height. A small muscle twitched in his cheek. "All Wes could see was that light yellow hair and smooth white skin. He was pantin' after her so heavy that he couldn't think of nothin' else. He underestimated that bitch, and I ain't goin' to make the same mistake!"

Reaching into the pocket of the brocade vest stretched tight over his barrel chest, McCulla drew out an ornately carved gold watch and flicked open the cover. His large, protruding eyes flicked momentarily in its direction before returning to scan his men's faces.

"Well, boys, looks like you got just enough time to get yourselves a hot meal before you get back on the road again."

"Mr. McCulla, me and the boys were kinda lookin' forward to spendin' tonight in our bunks. We figured we could start out again in the mornin'."

"Well, you figured wrong, Whitley."

The adamance apparent in McCulla's gaze effectively halted his foreman's protest.

"You're goin' to start out again tonight, and you're goin' to find that Winslow girl. She's not goin' to get away with what she done. She's goin' to pay . . . do you hear me, boys? She's goin' to pay. . . ."

Carefully surveying the faces in front of him for their affirmative response, McCulla hesitated only a moment before his harsh voice cracked in the silence of the room.

"What're you waitin' for? Get movin'!"

Turning as the last of the men shuffled through the doorway into the hall, McCulla walked back to his desk. He seated himself heavily, staring unseeingly at the closing door for a few silent seconds before slamming a beefy fist against the smooth surface of his desk in furious frustration. The sound precipitated an exchange of tense glances between the men in the hallway the moment before they turned and moved, as if one, for the door.

Rand slowed his horse to a halt and looked upward toward the blue cloudless sky. There was not a whisper of a breeze, and the unprecedented heat had not relented. From the look of things, there was no relief in sight.

He stared into the distance, his position on a slight rise of ground a short ride from the chain of Indian Lakes providing him a glimpse of his approaching herd. Three thousand beeves moved in a long, snaking line over the flat, dusty terrain stretching out almost a mile into the distance. His concentration intense, he straightened his broad shoulders unconsciously as the herd continued its steady approach.

The animals were moving well. Willie, out in front with Jim Stewart and Russ Byrd, lifted his hand in a salute. Rand smiled and returned the greeting. He had become far too removed from the reality of trail driving in the past few years. He had almost forgotten the sheer vastness of the country, the challenge of the drive, the satisfaction felt deep inside in meeting and conquering that challenge. Had the fever not stricken his foreman and his men, this herd, too, would have been viewed purely on the pages of a ledger. He would probably be in another trail town right now, contracting for his next herd or lolling between the sheets of Lucille Bascombe's delicately scented bed.

He frowned. He had given little thought to Lucille during the last week—or women of Ginger McCall's persuasion either, for that matter. He winced as Ginger was recalled to mind, remembering the coincidence of the young whore having the same name as the sorrel Drucker had ridden into camp. Somehow that similarity had tarnished the memory of that hour in San Antonio, which had been so effective in relieving his frustration. But then, he had found much of his thinking affected since the advent of that irritating kid.

Rand glanced to the horse at his side, frowning as his eyes

touched on the boy's painfully erect shoulders. If the heat and the pressure of the last few days were affecting the boy, he knew damned well the kid would die before he'd allow him to know it. Rand felt another sharp pang of regret. He had the feeling the situation between himself and the boy was past repairing, and that was unfortunate. He only hoped the kid didn't do anything foolish. He had not forgotten White Hand's scrutiny of the boy and the sense of camaraderie that had seemed to spring up between them. He had not truly sorted out his feelings, but he knew he didn't want anything to happen to the kid. As far as he was concerned, the boy had proved himself and was a full-fledged member of his crew. That probably accounted for the puzzlingly protective instinct that seemed to have pervaded his mind where the kid was concerned.

Firmly dismissing his confusing thoughts, Rand turned to more pressing matters. He was relieved to be back with the herd again and felt a heartwarming gratification in knowing the scouting he had done with the two Apaches had not been in vain. He had made contact with the herd at just the right time. Refusing to grant White Hand complete credit for that, he allowed himself a healthy portion of self-satisfaction. He would water the herd thoroughly tonight and start them on the trail White Hand had pointed out early in the morning. He was well aware that the route would add at least a hundred miles to their journey. But the safety of his herd would be guaranteed, and that fact took precedence over all.

Rand shot another quick glance to his side, his dark brows knotting into a frown. Not a word had passed Drucker's lips since they had broken camp this morning. Every statement or comment he had made had been received with a short nod or shake of the boy's head. Suddenly irritated by the fact that even now the kid refused comment about the approaching herd, Rand spurred his horse forward, impatient to meet up with a friendly face. His ear tuned to the sound of hoofbeats following in his wake, Rand glanced behind him in time to see Drucker branch off to take his former position to the right flank of the herd. The kid was obviously relieved to be out of his company. Well, that was all right with him.

Swallowing his annoyance, Rand spurred his horse toward Willie's approaching figure, apprehension overcoming his fleeting annoyance at the sight of his segundo's expression. Turning his horse so they rode side by side in the lead, Rand did not mince words.

"I know that look, Willie, and I can't say it makes me feel too secure. The herd looks good to me. What's the problem?"

"Hell, them beeves was as well behaved as pussycats while you were gone. I only wish I could say the same for them drovers you hired. For the most part, you got yourself a pretty good crew, but those two fellas, Hall and Brothers, has been busy gripin' up a storm."

"What have they got to gripe about? You said the beeves haven't caused any trouble, and I know damned well you boys have been eating better than I have in the past few days."

"They don't like ridin' drag."

Rand's brows raised in surprise. "Well, that's just too bad, isn't it, Willie? Everybody knows new men have to take turns eating dust."

"They say they're experienced men, that they ain't goin' to ride drag no more."

"That's what they think. If they want to stay with this outfit, they're going to ride the position I assign them."

Willie raised his narrow shoulders in a short shrug. "Maybe they'll take that from you, but they wasn't about to take it from me."

"We'll see about that, Willie, we'll see. . . ."

His eyes shooting back to the herd, Rand assessed the positions of his men. His gaze jerked back in Willie's direction.

"Brothers and Hall are riding flank."

"I told you, Rand. They said they wasn't goin' to ride drag no more. Cannon and Carlisle are ridin' drag, and I don't mind tellin' you, I didn't much like puttin' them there and seein' the satisfaction on those two rowdies' faces."

"Well, you aren't goin' to see it there for long, you can take my word for that. We're going to have a short discussion around the campfire tonight that's going to settle this once and for all. We've got too many important things to worry about for the next few days. I'm not about to let those two set themselves up as prima donnas."

Taking a few minutes to reign his anger under control, Rand turned to glance back into Willie's concerned face. Rand's abrupt smile was unexpected.

"Anyway, I'm damned glad to be back with the herd again, Willie. You did a real good job getting these beeves here on time. I won't forget it."

Wheeling his horse around just as unexpectedly, Rand turned back toward the herd. He was determined to make a thorough inspection. He had a feeling it was going to be a long time until night camp.

"I said Josh and me rode drag for two days, and we ain't ridin' drag no more, that's what I said!"

His expression surly, Seth Brothers punctuated his emphatic statement with sharp nods of his head. "We ain't inexperienced hands like the rest of the loafers you picked up in San Antonio. We've ridden trail before."

"If you're so damned good and experienced, what were you doing looking for a job in San Antonio when trail foremen were crying for good help?" Rand's sharp retort was instantaneous.

"We wasn't sure we wanted to sign on a trail drive again, but—"

"But you were running out of money and San Antonio's an expensive place to entertain yourself, is that it?"

"Yeah, somethin' like that."

"Well, you aren't going to get a free ride in my outfit, Brothers—you or your partner."

"We ain't askin' for a free ride."

"It's a good thing. And while we're at it, let's get something straight. You fellows signed on for the drive, and I expect you to keep your bargain. I'm not about to pay anybody unless they fulfill the terms of their agreement, is that understood?"

99

"What do you mean by that?"

"I mean I pay at the end of the drive. If you finish, you get paid. If you want to leave before the end of the drive, you don't get your time until we get to Montana . . . if you want to show up to collect then."

His gaze moving around the campfire, Rand touched on each of the men seated there. Brothers and Hall were mumbling, but the others returned his stare soberly, with the exception of Drucker. The boy was staring into the fire, his hat pulled down on his head, looking as if he had not heard a word that had been spoken.

Pausing a few moments longer for effect, Rand continued in a low, even voice. "As for tomorrow, from what Willie tells me the round has come again to Brothers and Hall for drag, so—"

"Wait a minute!" Hall's interruption was explosive as he turned maliciously toward Drucker. "What about the kid? He ain't had no turn at drag since he signed on. Talk about havin' a free ride, he ain't even been drovin', just interpretin' for that redskin and ridin' with the boss."

The sudden rise of fury snapped Rand to his feet. He didn't need to glance around the fire to see the tension that suddenly edged the group, or to know that Drucker was abruptly alert. Halting his own lurching step forward, Rand took a deep breath. His voice was low, barely controlled when he finally spoke.

"Nobody tells me how to run my outfit, Hall. If you have any objections to my orders, you can clear out right now." When neither Hall or Brothers responded, he continued. "My orders stand. Brothers and Hall on drag tomorrow, and the round starts again: Fogarty and Cannon, Johnson and Carlisle. When I feel like putting Drucker on drag, *I'll* be the one to let you know. Until then he rides flank."

The silence that met Rand's adamant statement was tense, finally broken by an unexpected voice.

"I'll take my turn on drag, just like everybody else."

His head snapping toward the dark eyes riveted on him from beneath the brim of Drucker's hat, Rand growled warningly, "I said *I* give the orders around here, Drucker.

You'll ride drag when *I* say you ride drag. The same goes for you as it does for the others. If you don't like my orders, you can clear out . . . now."

Drucker's eyes held his in sharp challenge, and Rand felt a perverse urge to twist the kid's skinny neck. The damned obnoxious twit! Anybody with an ounce of sense would realize a day on drag would just about finish the kid in his condition. He had seen fully grown men after riding drag for a day in dry country like were heading through go to the water barrel at night with an inch of dust on them, choking and coughing. . . . No, the kid wasn't up to that job yet, and he wasn't about to be the one who beat the proud little bastard into the dust . . . whether the kid liked it or not!

"You got that straight, Drucker?"

Feeling the heat emanating from those dark eyes, Rand repeated with added emphasis, *"You* ride flank."

"Yes, *sir."*

Snapping to his feet, Drucker turned on his heel and walked stiffly away from the fire. His departure seeming to signal the end of the discussion, the men remaining turned to each other in low comment before reaching for their bedrolls.

His gaze moving to the darkness into which the boy had disappeared, Rand suppressed the urge to follow the brat and shake him to within an inch of his life. Instead, he turned to Willie's assessing gaze.

"Come on, Willie. I'll map the route that Apache marked out for us. If we play it smart, we'll get these beeves through in perfect shape."

Within minutes Rand was deeply engrossed in conversation his mind almost free of the dark-eyed stare that badgered him.

Seething, Billie made her way to the temporary corral strung from the hind wheel of the cook wagon. Pausing, she attempted to spot her mount among the shadowed animals standing there, but blind fury hindered her concentration.

Damn the man! Was Pierce determined to set every man

in the crew against her? And why his objection to her riding drag, even after she willingly agreed to take her turn? He had made it only too clear that she could clear out if she didn't like taking his orders. His orders . . . Yes, that was it. He was using her to demonstrate his authority . . . the fact that *he* had the last word on this drive. The arrogant bastard! And last night she had begun to think that he . . . Well, that had been her first mistake! She wasn't about to make another.

She needed some time away from this whole bunch . . . some time by herself. Suddenly spotting her bay in the shadows, Billie was about to duck under the rope and start in his direction when a voice from behind snapped her tensely in its direction.

"Wait a minute, Drucker."

Startled by the unexpected voice behind her, Billie turned to Jeremy Carlisle's tentative smile. She stiffened, her mouth retaining its straight, angry line, and Carlisle's smile dropped away.

"Look, Drucker, you don't have to go gettin' all defensive with me. I'm not tryin' to stick my nose in your business, in case that's what you're thinkin'. I'm smart enough to know when somebody wants to be left alone. I just wanted to set things straight, for the record. Them two Brothers and Hall, they don't speak for me or for any of the other new hands. It ain't hard for any of us to see that you had a rough time of it before you hit this outfit."

"I don't need your sympathy."

"And you ain't gettin' it. But my ma bred enough good sense into my head to know when a fella needs a little time. You need it now, and the boss knows it, too. He ain't about to let those two bastards push him into puttin' you where you shouldn't be for a while."

"I can handle drag just as well as any man!"

"Yeah? At what cost? The boss wants a hand he can depend on, not a fella who's too damned beat to meet an emergency when it comes. Pierce is smart holdin' you off drag for a while, and you can bet your bottom dollar he'll put you in the schedule the minute he feels you're up to par again."

"I don't need any special treatment. I can hold my own."

"Look, I ain't goin' to argue with you." Flashing her a patient smile, Jeremy Carlisle shook his head. "You remind me of my little brother, Jim . . . always the cockiest of the lot because he was the puniest."

Carlisle gave an amused snort as Billie stiffened at his comment. "So, now I really made you mad, didn't I? Well, Drucker, it's the truth." The crinkles around his eyes and the freckles on the short bridge of his nose surprisingly clear in the limited light of the moon, Carlisle continued to smile, ignoring Billie's attempt to avoid his gaze.

"I just wanted to let you know, Drucker, that you got a friend here if you ever need one."

When Billie still refused a response, Carlisle shook his head.

"You sure are a hard-nose, Drucker. But that's your business. I'm goin' to turn in now. That bedroll is callin' me, and watch has a way of sneakin' up on a fella."

Not expecting a response, Carlisle turned and walked back toward the campfire. Billie watched the slow retreat of Carlisle's compact frame. Her eyes filling unexpectedly with tears, she swallowed with difficulty as she recalled the expression on the young man's friendly face. Under other circumstances she would gratefully have accepted the friendship he extended, but she could not afford to allow anyone to get close . . . not anyone.

Turning back toward her horse, Billie hesitated. Jeremy Carlisle was right. Her shift on watch came early. She had a feeling a lot of eyes would be on her for the next few days, and she'd be damned if she'd give anyone cause to pick on her work. She'd do her job better than any man in the outfit, and she'd make those two loafers, Hall and Brothers, eat their words.

Making a quick decision, Billie turned back toward the campfire and within minutes was unrolling her blankets. She pulled off her boots and slid into her bedroll, her bruised flesh crying out its protest at the simple exertion. She turned her face away from the fire. It was all temporary: the discomfort, the inconvenience, the secrecy. In a few months she'd be in Montana, and then . . .

Her mind consoling itself with the thoughts that followed, Billie drifted off to sleep.

The early morning heat was oppressive. Carefully supervising the cattle since the early watch, Rand had been conscious of the gradually intensifying temperature and humidity. It was going to be a hell of a drive for the next week, and he did not look forward to the prospect of three thousand thirsty beeves.

Turning his eyes to the herd, Rand scanned the drovers moving on the outskirts of the milling cattle. It appeared all the men were in position to start the first push of the day. He had to smile. Nate had given the boys one of the best breakfasts he had ever tasted on the trail. How the man managed to make biscuits that damned good under these conditions, he'd never know. His coffee was already legend on the trail, and he had even managed to come up with jam. Rand had the feeling Nate was preparing the men for the long ordeal to come, knowing that there were no limits to what a good drover could take when his stomach was full and satisfied. Rand snickered under his breath. If Nate didn't take care, they'd all reach Montana overweight.

His eyes touching on a slender figure moving outside the herd, Rand's smile slowly dropped from his face. Well, there was no risk of that happening with Drucker. While everyone else had been consuming Nate's breakfast with abandon, Drucker had consumed no more than two biscuits and a cup of coffee. Feeling a nudge of irritation at his own covert surveillance of the kid, Rand frowned. What difference did it make to him if the kid starved himself?

His peculiar irritation persisting, Rand perused Drucker's slight frame. The kid was so damned skinny. He'd never put any flesh on those bones if he started picking at his meals. And it was obvious Drucker wasn't about to spare himself any of the hard work, either. He had been the first one up for the 3:30 watch. Despite the ordeal of the last few days, he had pulled on his boots and been out to relieve the earlier watch before the other fellows were fully awake. It was obvious the kid was trying to prove something, and he wasn't going to spare himself in doing it.

Rand steadied his impatient mount. His eyes shot to the rear of the herd. Hall and Brothers were in drag position. He gave a low snort. They'd better be. It wasn't his custom to keep his men there, eating dust for the better part of the day. Rather, he allowed the men in that position to ride flank, leaving it to their discretion to fall back to pick up stragglers when the need arose. Willie had told him that he had followed the same policy while he had functioned as segundo, but evidently Hall and Brothers had shown little appreciation of that consideration, almost viewing the concession as a sign of weakness. And if he didn't realize that by punishing them he'd be punishing his other new men as well, he would have insisted that they maintain drag position for the entire day, just to show them who was boss.

His eyes darting back to Drucker again, Rand took a deep, determined breath. And if Drucker thought he was going to dictate policy to him on this drive, he had another thing coming. The kid was obviously feeling immensely better each day. He had watched the boy mount this morning, and his movements had been much more fluid. A few more days, maybe a week, and Drucker would almost be himself again . . . whatever that meant. Hell, if returning health made the boy any more ornery than he was now, there'd be no talking to the kid.

Suddenly bemused by his own line of thinking, Rand shook his head. What in hell did he care if Drucker never spoke another word on this drive?

Damn, he was going to be glad when they reached Dodge! With any luck, Jess Williams would be on hand by then to take the drive the rest of the way into Montana, and he'd be able to kiss this group good-bye. Then Lucille and he could take up where they left off. Now . . . where was that exactly? . . . Oh, yes, that had been with Lucille's full, lush body stretched out underneath his.

The memory working erotically on his senses, Rand felt the responsive rise of his body. He smiled despite his annoyance. There was nothing wrong with him that a little dose of Lucille couldn't cure . . . or Ginger. . . . One woman was as good as another.

His spirits considerably lighter, Rand raised his hand and signaled the men to start the cattle moving. The sooner he started the herd on the trail, the sooner they'd be in Dodge and the sooner he'd be rid of this whole crew. It couldn't be soon enough.

Lucille Bascombe sighed and stretched a long slender arm over her head. Relaxing back again against the soft white pillow under her head, she stared for long moments at the lace-bedecked ruffle hanging from the canopy of her bed. But the exquisite bed linens made exclusively to her specifications were the farthest thing from her thoughts at that particular moment in time. Instead, memory was returning to her mind the picture of Rand Pierce's handsome face as he had moved to cover her body with his the last night they had been together. A spontaneous flush suffused her. Rand was so handsome . . . so virile. She knew she would never tire of his strong masculine features, the startling contrast of his peculiarly brilliant eyes against his sun-darkened skin. His profile was so strong, his jaw so determined, his smile so dazzling. Her heart beat faster just thinking about him.

She could still remember the feel of his heavy black hair against her palm, the texture of his skin as she had clutched him to her naked flesh. The passion in his light-eyed gaze had been undeniable. So what if that spark had cooled the moment he had sated his desire? She was certain she would be able to overcome the indifference that had replaced it. His declaration that he was not interested in a long-term association did not bother her. She had been successful so far in her quest for his passion. She had but to brush his body with hers, to slip her tongue between his lips in a kiss. And when the situation demanded more stringent methods, a subtle stroking of the manly bulge between his thighs had never failed her.

Yes, she had decided the first night she had met Randall Pierce that he was the man whom she would marry. It mattered little to her that rumor had it he was a confirmed bachelor. She had decided to ignore talk that he still had other women in his life, despite the close association they maintained. She knew what she wanted, and she would have it. No man other than Randall Pierce was a fit match for her. In addition to the fact that the handsome cattle entrepreneur was the only man who could match her physical beauty, he was also intelligent, witty, charming. . . . All other men paled in his wake.

She had deliberated long and hard before deciding to take Rand to her bed. She had been well aware that he was not interested in a relationship free of physical intimacy. She knew that she would only be able to get him into the position she wanted by allowing him free access to her body, and she had not regretted her decision to do so. Not that she had been a virgin before he had taken her. Lucille gave a low, annoyed snort. Rand had made certain he had commented on that fact. But she had not been intimate with another man since Rand had first made love to her, and she had no intention of breaking that unspoken commitment to him.

For the truth was, she had been blind to all other men since she had first set eyes on Randall Pierce. His commanding presence left her breathless. She remembered only too well the first time she had seen the sheer power of his naked body. She remembered his expanse of shoulder and chest, his flat waist, his narrow hips. She remembered his long, well-muscled legs, his ready, impressive manhood. She also remembered the amused quirk of his brow when she had finished reviewing his physical attributes. It had been only then that she had realized she had been staring. Oh, yes, he was a truly beautiful man. He was the man she wanted. And she always got what she wanted, didn't she?

A note of annoyance penetrating her thoughts, Lucille frowned. That damned trail drive! She had just about had Rand where she wanted him when he had been called to foreman that herd of cattle. She now realized she had made a mistake when she had lost her patience and told Rand how she truly felt—that it was demeaning for a man of his importance to participate in such a common endeavor. She recalled the expression that had flicked across his face when she had told him that he had earned a position far above the men who worked for him—that he should not lower himself back to the ranks of such degrading work.

Had it been contempt she had glimpsed in his glance? She was still uncertain, but whatever it had been, he had calmly told her that she was wrong. His voice low and even, he had stated that he was a cowman at heart and always would be. He had also declared with a smile that the only thing that separated him from the men who worked for him was the fact that he had been able to accumulate more money than they. And he had smilingly asked if she thought money was the criterion for manhood.

When she had stammered her reply, Rand had told her that if she was so far above the common man, then she was indeed far above him and he would no longer bother her with his attentions. It had taken some firm persuasion to stop Rand from walking out on her there and then. It had been an extremely close call, and she was determined never to repeat her mistake. Rather, she had decided she would wait until they were married to change some of his plebeian tastes and ways.

She had been more certain than ever in the few days prior to Rand's leaving that she would one day bear the name Mrs. Randall Pierce. Just prior to Rand's leaving for San Antonio, it had been a bit of daring to take him to bed in her own room in the St. Louis mansion where she lived with her father. She was well aware that Horace Bascombe considered Rand a thorough rake and poor husband material, but she knew her father would not protest for long if she put the full force of her persuasive abilities into play and declared her intentions. Her father had long ago surrendered fully to her, openly declaring there was nothing he would deny his lovely daughter. She had found him to be a man of his word and had accepted everything he had given her as her due. It would be no different with Rand Pierce.

Suddenly bored with indolence, Lucille shot a quick glance to the gold clock on her dresser. Handcrafted in France, it was worth a small fortune and was representative of the opulence with which she was surrounded. But she did not see its beauty. Indeed, she had taken it for granted long ago. Instead, she felt merely a momentary irritation that it was only half past the hour of ten, and a long, boring day stretched ahead of her.

Throwing back the covers, petulance obvious on her lovely face, Lucille drew herself to her feet and stalked to the mirror. The lovely red-haired, blue-eyed creature that stared back at her brought a smile to her lips. Yes, how would Rand Pierce be able to resist her? Fiery red hair, clear milk-white skin, dark brows and lashes, a perfect nose, and a smile that could melt stone . . . or so she had been told many times. And her body was perfection, with full firm breasts, small waist, and well-rounded hips. She had received adulation from so many men, but never from Rand. But she would change all that, and when she was firmly ensconced as his wife, she would see that he paid for the discomforts he had given her. Of course, it would be subtle payment, but payment, nevertheless.

But in the meantime, she missed him! What was it he had said? He would probably be about five hundred miles into his journey in May and drawing into Abilene around that time? Abilene . . . From what she had heard, it was a true trail town, encouraging every manner of vice and dissipation. She truly did not care for the idea of Rand becoming involved with the common whores he would find there.

Her eyes suddenly coming to life with an idea, Lucille beamed. She would meet him there! She would go to Abilene and renew her claim over Rand's passions. She would promise him more, much more, so he would be eager to return to her when the damned trail drive was over. Yes, that was what she would do! Her father would arrange everything for her. He always did.

Unable to contain her enthusiasm, Lucille ran to the doorway, snatching up her lace wrapper on the way as she headed down the steps for the library. Arriving at the doorway breathless, she swept into the room without knocking. Ignoring the slender young man standing beside the desk, she approached her father with a glowing smile.

"Father, dear, I'm desperately in need of your help. . . ."

Chapter VI

Ignoring the growing heat of afternoon, Rand stood in his stirrups and surveyed the lush country surrounding him. For the past week they had been traveling over the immense tableland skirting arid western Texas. A few days before they had passed the blue mountains, southern sentinel in the chain marking the headwaters of the Concho River, and then they had come to their first glimpse of the hills.

Rand felt a long forgotten stirring deep inside him at the sheer grandeur spread out before his eyes. As primitive in appearance as the day of creation, the country was generous, supplying every want for sustenance of horses and cattle. The grass was well matured, and the steers had begun to take on flesh. And despite the rocky country they had passed, lame and sore-footed cattle had as yet caused no serious problem. It was May, and they were nearly five hundred miles into their journey. Rand's sense of satisfaction was immense.

Rand flicked his gaze back to the well-moving herd, his eyes automatically seeking out the positioning of his men. Not encountering the figure he sought on right flank, Rand darted a quick glance to the rear. A familiar knot tightened in his stomach. If Drucker had let Hall's snide remarks force him back into drag position despite his direct orders to the contrary, there would be hell to pay!

Spurring his black back toward the herd, Rand caught Willie's frown. It had only been his long association with the

111

lank Texan that had again forced him to listen to the man's well-meaning advice the night before. He hadn't needed anyone to tell him that he was handling the situation with Brothers and Hall poorly. But he had determined that he would be damned before he'd allow those two bullies the upper hand. The louder their grumblings had become, the firmer he had stood in refusing to allow Drucker to pull drag position with the rest of the new men.

If he were to be honest, he would admit he couldn't quite understand his own refusal. The kid had obviously recuperated adequately from the beating he had taken. Unconsciously measuring the improvement in Drucker each day, he had noted that the slight limp marking the boy's step had disappeared along with the stiffness of his movements.

But if Drucker's physical wounds had all but healed, he was certain the boy's emotional wounds were just as raw as before. Drucker's sleep was still restless, obviously filled with dreams in which he relieved the pain he had suffered when he had been attacked. He continued to remain aloof from the men. It appeared the only person the boy spoke to was Jeremy Carlisle, and he suspected the boy only spoke to Carlisle because they shared the same watch. Whatever the case, there was something about the kid, something that stirred a protective instinct deep inside him that he found impossible to ignore.

But if that damned kid was riding drag . . .

His expression tightening, Rand dug his heels deeper into his horse's flanks, momentarily gratified when the animal shot forward in sharp response. Drucker had actually had the nerve to approach him the night before and demand that he be placed in rotation for drag position. Realizing Brothers's grumbling and Hall's deprecating snickers during the evening camp had gotten to the boy, Rand had felt his irritation rise. The result had been another angry confrontation with the kid and a further tensing of relations between them.

But, right or wrong, *he* was boss of this drive, and *he* made the decisions. And no one was going to make him put the stress of drag position on that skinny runt of a kid . . . not even the kid himself! And if Drucker had disobeyed his orders . . .

His eyes suddenly catching on movement to the far right of the herd, Rand turned his horse in its direction in time to see Drucker emerge from behind some tumbled boulders, driving several harassed-looking steers in front of him. Rand's quick assessment determined that the animals were moving with considerable discomfort, which was probably the reason they had attempted to escape the steady pace of the herd. But they obviously hadn't been able to escape the kid's quick eye.

Drawing his horse to a halt, Rand felt the stirring of an emotion closely akin to pride as the boy expertly herded the protesting cattle back on stream. The kid was a damned good drover, even if he was surly and hard-headed. It had been a true gift of fate that had brought the boy into camp, despite the aggravation involved. One drover like him was worth three drovers of Hall and Brothers's caliber. He had half a mind to . . .

But his sense of well-being was fleeting, deftly wiped away as Drucker's angry, dark-eyed glance caught his. His expression partially shielded by the broad brim of his hat, the boy boldly spurred his horse in Rand's direction. He drew up alongside a few moments later. His words were terse.

"Checking on me, Mr. Pierce? Don't worry, I got your message loud and clear last night. You don't have to follow me around to make sure I follow your orders."

Anger stiffened the planes of Rand's face. Holding the boy's gaze, Rand barely suppressed the urge to lean over and knock that damned hat the boy hid behind off his head. Instead, he gritted from between tightly clamped teeth, "Look, kid, I'm not going to tell you again. I run this drive as I see fit . . . as *I* see fit! So, do yourself a favor and close that big mouth of yours before it gets you in trouble."

There was a moment's hesitation before Drucker's lips curved into a sarcastic smile. The small dimple that flicked in his cheek caused a confusing flutter in Rand's stomach as the boy returned acidly, "Yes, *sir,* Mr. Pierce."

Rand watched in tight-lipped silence as the boy wheeled his horse around and rode away. His emotions fluctuating between anger, frustration, and an almost overpowering desire to wring Drucker's puny neck, Rand waited for long moments before spurring his horse past the boy's stiff-necked figure and into position beside the lead.

The afternoon sun was setting as Rand cast a hungry eye to the sight of Nate Straw's campfire a short distance away. The cattle had been well grazed, and there was not a thirsty or hungry animal in the lot. The weary beeves had already begun circling, anxious to lie down, and he was well aware that in the course of a half hour, all would be securely bedded. His eyes moved to the muleys waiting on the outskirts, knowing the hornless cows would not venture into the herd until the others had lain down. It would only be a little longer.

Managing to restrain his impatience until the herd had been settled for the night, Rand set the guard and motioned the other men to the wagon. Noting that Josh Hall muttered a leering word to Drucker that snapped the youth's head sharply in his direction, Rand felt the rise of anger. Neither Hall nor Brothers seemed content to let the situation lie. He had been right from the beginning. Troublemakers . . . If he wasn't so damned shorthanded, he would send them packing so fast. . . .

An unexpected silhouette suddenly appearing on the horizon broke Rand's trend of thought. His frown darkened as another figure joined the approaching horseman. There was no mistaking the distinctive outlines of White Hand and Long Hair against the darkening sky, and Rand jerked a quick, spontaneous glance in Drucker's direction. The boy had spotted the Indians' approach and stood riveted to the spot where he had dismounted beside the wagon.

Not quite understanding the resentment he experienced at the boy's intensity, Rand guided his horse carefully into camp and dismounted. Straining to evaluate Drucker's expression as the boy continued to stare at the approaching

114

Indians, Rand's frustration flared anew. Damn the boy! What was going on in the hard head under that oversized hat? There was no mistaking the tension that had stiffened his skinny frame. If that Indian thought he was going to get away with anything . . .

"Drucker—"

Startled, the boy snapped a frown in his direction. Drucker's small show of irritation was effective in adding a ring of command to Rand's voice as he continued steadily.

"It looks like the Apaches have returned for payment. Make sure you stick close to my side. I don't want any misunderstandings in the event they try anything."

Drucker's gaze was hard with contempt.

"White Hand is an honorable man. He's fulfilled his part of the bargain. As long as you fulfill yours, there won't be any trouble."

"Just because you can communicate with those savages, don't think you're an expert on the Apache." His expression tightening, Rand shook his head. "You've got a lot to learn, Drucker. What do you think those two Apaches are doing off the reservation? Most of White Hand's people have contented themselves to stay in the territory the government marked out for them, but some die-hard braves are raising hell on the border. Pretty soon we'll be coming into Commanche territory. It wouldn't surprise me if those two Apaches are looking to gather as many hot-blooded braves as they can to join Juh, Chatto, or Nachee when they cross the border. The twenty-five beeves they're getting from us will probably buy them a lot of respect when they approach the Commanche campfire."

"If they were the kind of men you think they are, they'd have stolen those beeves, not *earned* them!"

"No, I don't think so. I'd say that White Hand is a little too smart for that. He wouldn't want to start trouble here, so far from the main body of his men. I think it suits his purpose far better to travel without causing any undue attention, so he can gather braves quietly and return without interference. It's too bad those poor bastards don't realize they can't win, that it's only a matter of time before the Army—"

The flush of anger that suffused Drucker's face precipitated his heated interjection.

"And I suppose you can't wait to see the Army put an end to the Apaches! I suppose you subscribe to the motto, 'The only good Indian is a dead Indian!'"

Aware that the attention of the milling drovers was now focused on their heated exchange, Rand took a firm hold on his temper and a step closer to the boy's thin, bristling figure.

"Look, I don't have to defend myself to you, Drucker. Whether you agree with me or not doesn't matter one damned bit to me, just as long as you do what I tell you. And I'm telling you to stick close to my side until White Hand and Long Hair leave this camp. I don't want any misunderstandings between myself and those two."

"I don't think—"

"I'm not asking you to think, Drucker, just translate. Is that und—"

"Understood?" His small face twitching with anger, Drucker jerked his head in a brief nod. "Yeah, it's understood."

"And I don't want you out of my sight for a minute!"

Staring wordlessly into his face for a few silent moments, Drucker turned abruptly on his heel and started toward the campfire. Rand's response to the low mumble that drifted from behind Drucker's turned back came from between tightly clenched teeth.

"What did you say, Drucker?"

Drucker turned around unexpectedly, his eyes sparking with fury.

"Nothing. I didn't say a damned thing. . . ."

"Bienvenidos, White Hand. El Señor Rand Pierce has instructed me to tell you that you have earned the twenty-five cows promised to you. He has stated that they will be cut from the herd the first thing tomorrow morning so that you may take them."

Billie's glance did not miss the small flicker that passed

over White Hand's expression as she concluded her translation. She was only too aware that White Hand's gaze remained unmoving on her face as he contemplated his response. His dark eyes seemed to read the tumult that assaulted her under his gaze and she swallowed hard in an effort to maintain her composure.

"I see concern in your eyes, Brave One, but it is needless. Long Hair and I have returned to collect our payment, and then our business here will be done. We are aware that el Gran Jefe does not trust us."

A flicker of a smile passed over White Hand's lips at his use of the term she had used before to describe Rand Pierce. Rand's reaction was immediate.

"What did he say, Drucker?"

"White Hand said they will leave as soon as the cattle are ready."

Rand gave a short nod. "I suppose that means they'll have to spend the night in camp." His reaction to that thought only too obvious, Rand took a short breath. "Tell them they're welcome to eat with us. Nate will dish them up a meal. And, Drucker, remember what I said."

Turning back to White Hand, Billie rattled in rapid Spanish, "You heard what he said, White Hand. And you're right. He doesn't trust either of you."

White Hand's affirmative nod eliminated the need for further translation. Grateful she did not have to continue the farce of translation any longer that night, Billie turned toward the campfire. Within minutes she was consuming her meal with an appetite sorely affected by the tension that had suddenly overcome the entire group.

Aware that Rand Pierce's gaze followed her intently, Billie drew herself to her feet and walked slowly into the darkness beyond the wagon. The brilliant blue of his eyes seemed to burn into her back, and Billie fought the spontaneous fluttering that always began inside her stomach each time she felt the weight of his perusal. What was wrong with her, anyway? She detested Rand Pierce and everything he stood

117

for. Arrogant, puffed up with conceit and the conviction that he could do no wrong, he was the antithesis of everything she had ever admired in a man. He possessed not a shred of understanding or concern in his entire body. All that was important to him was the herd and the money he was going to earn when he met his contract. For a short time that night by the lake, she had almost begun to believe she had read compassion in his gaze, but she had since come to the conclusion that she had allowed herself to be influenced by the sheer physical power of his masculinity.

There was no denying the fact that Rand Pierce was one of the handsomest men she had ever seen. And there was also no denying that he was well aware of his effect on women. Men talked easily around a campfire, and Willie had mentioned the name of a beautiful wealthy woman who was reputedly at Rand Pierce's beck and call. She didn't doubt it was true. Rand Pierce liked to give orders and enjoyed having people snap to his command. Hadn't his treatment of her been adequate proof of that?

But even Rand Pierce couldn't object to her answering nature's call, damn him! Her sojourn in that pursuit brief, Billie took a quick glance toward the campfire a few moments later. She was reluctant to return to the stiff atmosphere that pervaded the silent circle. Considering darkness adequate protection against prying eyes, Billie removed her hat and ran her fingers through her hair. The light night breeze lifted the moist tendrils from her scalp, and Billie released a short sigh at the simple pleasure it afforded.

She had not glimpsed her reflection since leaving San Antonio, but the stiffness of swelling had left her face. She could only assume that most of the bruising had disappeared as well. But she was certain the ragged, boyish cut of her hair and the oversized hat she wore were more than adequate in maintaining her disguise if she continued to conduct herself with care. Perversely, Billie suddenly decided to allow herself a few more moments of the freedom darkness afforded her. Carrying her hat in her hand, she walked slowly to the remuda.

The horses were startled by her unexpected approach and

skittered in the opposite direction, but a low whistle brought a familiar whinny. Within minutes a wet muzzle was in her hand and Billie dropped her hat to the ground to coo softly into Ginger's appreciative ear.

"This animal is an old friend who gives you consolation, Brave One. But it is a poor substitute for the emptiness in your heart."

Billie's head snapped up at the unexpected voice at her side. She had not heard White Hand's approach. Remembering Rand Pierce's explicit orders, she darted a quick look back toward the campfire.

"You are uneasy. El Jefe does not want us to speak."

"N—no." Hesitant as her eyes moved over White Hand's stoical expression faintly visible in the semidarkness of the moonlit night, Billie shook her head. "He doesn't trust you or Long Hair, and I'm beginning to think he doesn't trust me, either."

"El Jefe's actions do not reflect his mistrust of you . . . merely his jealousy."

"Jealousy!"

White Hand's eyes moved slowly over her face. The intensity of his gaze raised an unexpected color in her cheeks.

"You have been in my thoughts since I have been gone from your side, Brave One. The beauty I saw hidden by marks of a heavy hand haunted me. Now I have returned, only to find my mind did not assess fully the beauty which had lain hidden there."

"White Hand, I—"

"Rand Pierce sees that beauty too, Brave One."

"El Jefe sees nothing but his cattle . . . knows nothing but the need to get them delivered on time. He uses me to suit his purpose, to show the other men that *his* word is law. He knows no emotion but greed and a lust for power."

White Hand's hand moved to Billie's shoulder. The touch was unexpected against its curve, and it was at that moment that Billie realized how truly alone she had been. She returned White Hand's sober gaze in silence, her body soaking up the inexplicable trust and warmth that flowed

119

between them.

"Rand Pierce senses those things he does not clearly recognize and he is confused into anger. He feels your warmth, as do I. He perceives your need but does not acknowledge his own response. He is drawn to you, the beauty of your spirit, the grace of your body, the softness slowly returning, looking back at him more clearly each day. But I do not feel his confusion, Brave One."

Billie's heart began a slow pounding. The low, even throb of White Hand's voice seemed to assume control of her mind and body. Innately certain she should end their meeting without delay, she was unable to make herself turn away from the perception and understanding that glowed in White Hand's gaze. Perversely, she experienced a deep longing to feel the warmth he exuded enfold her, provide a buffer against her fears, against her backward surveillance of a horizon that carried the constant possibility of threat. She did not want to be alone.

White Hand paused, carefully assessing the effect of his words. Raising his other hand, he touched the surface of her hair, and she felt the tremor that shook him. "Your hair gleams in the moonlight like the wing of a dove. It is bright, a silver-gold unlike any I have seen before. In the darkness of night while we were apart, I saw its glow and longed to see your beauty clearly, as I do now. In my heart and mind you replaced many times thoughts of the mission on which I journey, and in the dark world of dreams, you rode beside me."

The gradually deepening of White Hand's voice and the slow heaving of his smooth, hairless chest were subtle signs of the Apache's deep commitment to the words he spoke. Somewhere in the back of her mind a warning bell sounded, but Billie was helpless to respond to its appeal. The harshly sculpted lines of White Hand's face, the savage splendor of his shadowed form, were no longer foreign to her. Instead, his aura called to her, to be drawn in. . . .

"When the sun rises and payment is made, Long Hair and I will leave to complete our mission. We will enter

Commanche lands and take the cattle as a gift to our Commanche brothers. We will stay there until we receive the decision of those who would join our cause. When it is time to return to the land of our fathers, I would take you with me, Valerosa. It is my desire to take you to the land of my people. There I would protect you from the white man's law and from those who would use it against you. I would take you to me, make you a part of me. It is that thought which now fills my mind—has indeed been with me since the first moment our glances touched. I would keep you with me always, would have your body bear the fruit of my seed. Your courage and beauty would give to my sons—"

The unexpected sound of a step in the darkness jerked White Hand's words to a halt. His hands dropping to his sides, the Apache stiffened and turned toward the sound of Rand Pierce's low growl.

"Drucker . . . What in hell are you doing here with this Indian?"

Abruptly shaken from her mesmerized state, Billie was momentarily unable to respond. Bending to retrieve her hat from the darkness of the ground, she turned slowly back toward Rand Pierce's scrutiny, making good use of the time involved to regain control of her ragged emotions. Anger flared to her rescue at the first glimpse of Pierce's livid face.

"Checking up on me again, Mr. Pierce?"

"I wouldn't have to check up on you if you followed my orders!" He paused to dart a quick look in White Hand's direction. "Get back to camp, Drucker. I told you I didn't want you out of my sight while this Indian was in camp, and I meant every word I said."

"White Hand was just—"

"I don't give a damn about White Hand. He's not my concern after he takes those beeves tomorrow and rides out of here. I'm not paying *him* to take my orders." His voice dropping another notch, Rand continued with significant deliberation. "And my orders to you are to get back to camp . . . right now. Whatever discussion you were having with White Hand is finished."

121

Glaring purposefully into her eyes, Rand Pierce stared down the heated retort that rose to Billie's lips. Snapping a short look in White Hand's direction, Billie turned and walked stiffly back to the campfire. She ignored the curious looks that greeted her and busied herself with her bedroll. She had been turned in for several minutes when the sound of moccasined feet and heavy boots returned to the fire. Refusing to turn and assess the climate between the two protagonists in the unexpected drama, she closed her eyes in a vain attempt at sleep.

Carl Whitley shifted his thin, wiry frame impatiently, his eyes on the frowning cowboy who approached him from the opposite side of the busy San Antonio street. He lifted his hat from his head and wiped the flat of his hand across a forehead beaded with perspiration. He slanted a quick glance upwards to gauge the position of the sun and gave a low grunt of irritation.

He and the boys had arrived in San Antonio late the night before. With firm determination, he had lead them to the nearest bar and together they had downed a quantity of Jim Crow and beer calculated to erase all memory of Dan McCulla's livid face. And the plan had worked . . . temporarily. The only problem had been that the whole lot of them had awakened this morning with pounding heads and a supreme lack of patience for the job that awaited them.

Carl shook his head, regretting the action immediately as the heavy pounding that had stopped only an hour before began anew. That Dan McCulla was like a bulldog once he sank his teeth into somethin', and that somethin' this time was the old man's determination to find Billie Winslow.

Carl sent another absentminded glance up the now familiar street. Hell, he had no doubt Wes McCulla had only gotten what he deserved. Everybody knew what Wes had in mind for that girl after she turned him down flat and had her pa warn him to keep off their spread. It hadn't made any difference to Dan McCulla, and it hadn't made any difference to him what Wes McCulla did to that snippy little bitch until it had turned into something that affected him and the rest of the hands on the ranch. As far as Carl was concerned, he was as used to turning his back on those things the McCullas didn't care to have seen as he was used to doin' Dan McCulla's dirty work. After all, he wasn't one of the highest paid hands in this part of the country for nothin'. The other boys felt the same way, too.

But he had just about had it with this useless search. They were never goin' to find that girl. No woman could disappear so completely in this country unless somethin' had happened to her. Travelin' alone the way she was—and so close to the border—she had probably been snatched up and was in a Mexican crib right now, servicin' some randy Mexican soldiers. Dan McCulla didn't have to worry about gettin' his revenge if that was the case.

But it was goin' to be a long time before he'd be able to approach McCulla with that idea. The old man was fumin', achin' to get his hands on that little tart, and he had learned long ago that when the boss was in that kind of state, the only thing to do was keep his mouth shut and do what he was told.

But they were gettin' nowhere. Marty, Larry, Jim, Stan, and he had been lookin' and askin' questions around town all day and they hadn't learned nothin' new. He'd even gone back to Maggie O'Malley's restaurant and talked to that old fool, Filmore. Nothin'. . . .

His eyes scanning the dusty street, Carl looked toward the general store. His gaze settling unconsciously on a fellow loading some travelin' supplies on his horse, he felt the sudden glimmer of an idea. Starting forward in a brisk step, he met Marty halfway across the street and motioned him to follow behind.

Standing before the clerk at the counter a few minutes later, Carl did his best to strike a friendly smile. His yellowed teeth shining from beneath his ragged mustache, he began casually, "I was askin' about a young fella a little while ago, Harry. . . ."

The short, balding clerk raised his eyes with obviously strained patience. "Look, Carl, I told you once and I told

123

you twice, I ain't seen no young boy or girl like you described here in my store in the last two months . . . or the last year for that matter. You're wastin' my time and yours askin' the same questions over and over."

"Yeah, I know, but that's what Dan McCulla pays me for and—"

"Well, he don't pay me to answer your dumb questions, so—"

"Wait a minute, Harry." His smile beginning to show signs of strain, Carl took a firmer hold on his temper. That fat little clerk was askin' for trouble with his big mouth, but he wasn't goin' to get McCulla down on his neck by turnin' the townsfolk against him now. "It just occurred to me that you get old Mrs. Henning in here sometimes to take care of the counter when you're doin' your inventory or somethin', don't you?"

"Sure, but Sarah Henning ain't been here for over two weeks."

"I ain't really interested in who she saw in the last two weeks, Harry."

His small nose twitching in annoyance, Harry Bannister shook his head. "All right, all right. If you want to talk to her, Sarah'll be in here tomorrow mornin'."

"Tomorrow mornin'!"

"Yeah, unless you want to ride out to her place now and see her. It's a damned long ride. That's why she only works when she's goin' to stay with her sister in town for a while. If she wasn't so damned good at figures, I'd get somebody else to take her place instead of—"

But Carl was no longer listening. Another night in town. . . . Well, he had no objection to that, and McCulla wouldn't have much to say about it if he came back with a lead on the whereabouts of that Winslow girl.

"All right, Harry. We'll be back in here tomorrow mornin'."

His round face screwing up in annoyance at being interrupted, Harry Bannister raised his brows above his small, wire-rimmed glasses.

"It's too bad I ain't sellin' information. I'd be doin' a real

124

brisk business today."

Carl sneered. "Yeah, it's too bad, ain't it." Turning, he shot Marty a short, satisfied look and started back toward the door.

"Looks like we're stuck another night in town. Too bad, ain't it?"

Marty's broken-toothed leer spoke louder than words.

"Yeah, ain't it. . . ."

Lucille's gaze snapped toward the slender young man who stood beside her father's desk. Her eyes widened in horror.

"No, I absolutely refuse! I don't need a—a bodyguard to travel to Abilene!"

Horace Bascombe's heavy gray brows pulled together in open disapproval of his daughter's outburst, his eyes moving to the young man who stood silently at his side. Wallace Patterson's expression was noncommittal, reflecting the same stoicism that was his trademark in the boardroom. He had often thought the multi-talented young man was probably an excellent poker player with his supreme ability to mask the workings of his quick mind with an impenetrable facade when the situation demanded. That talent was one of the many facets of "Pat" Patterson's personality that Horace admired so immensely.

His eyes darting back to his daughter's outraged expression, Horace frowned more darkly. He could not allow Lucille to sense the weakening of purpose he suffered even now. She was so beautiful, his only child, her glorious, blazing mane and fine features so like her mother's. There was not a single day that he looked into her great blue eyes when he did not remember and yearn desperately for the return of the love Honor and he had shared.

Even now, knowing it had been a mistake to give in to Lucille's every whim, he suffered the same desire to reverse his own statement of a few moments before so that he might see Honor's smile reflected on his daughter's lips. But he had submitted to this failing too often. The result had been the development of a side of Lucille's character of which he was

125

abjectly ashamed. No, not this time.

Lifting his chin with a new firmness of purpose, Horace advanced toward his daughter, unsmiling. Stopping within a few feet of her, he looked directly into her eyes, steeling himself against her silent appeal.

"I'm sorry, dear. It's unsafe for you to travel alone. You will allow Mr. Patterson to accompany you to Abilene as my representative, or you will not go at all."

Horace Bascombe's adamance was unexpected. Sensing a change in her father that she was suddenly unwilling to challenge, Lucille made an instantaneous decision to affect another tactic. Closing the distance between her father and herself, the outrage in her face changing to a smile, she placed her palm against his handsomely suited chest and raised her eyes to his.

"Oh, Father, you worry unnecessarily. Abilene is now the terminus of the Texas and Pacific Railroad! Surely that distinction has brought civilization along with it." Realizing her protest had had no effect on her father's determination, Lucille continued with a sigh of resolution and a flutter of her heavily lashed lids intended to affect an air of compromise. "But if it will give you peace of mind, darling, I'll take Aunt Jessica along with me."

Lucille waited until her father had had a moment to digest her offer. Aunt Jessica was a distant relation for whom the term "aunt" was merely courtesy, and she was well aware her father was fond of the good-natured middle-aged woman. Aunt Jessica was also a respectable widow, and the fact that she was hard of hearing and possessed of a strong propensity to doze at the slightest opportunity made her the ideal traveling companion in this case. Those particular talents had served Lucille well in the past, freeing her for long hours of entertainment that would not have been sanctioned had the unsuspecting woman been aware of what was going on while she slept. But all inclination toward a smile gradually slipped away as Horace Bascombe remained surprisingly unaffected by her ploy.

"I'm sorry, dear, I've made my decision. I've given the matter considerable thought since you first proposed the idea of traveling to Abilene a few days ago. I can fully understand your desire to surprise Rand by meeting him there. I'm sure he'll be delighted to see you, but I am not about to allow you to suffer for your naivete, darling."

"My naivete!" Lucille fought to suppress her amusement. Naive . . . Her father was the one who was naive, at least as far as she was concerned. Lucille, herself, hadn't been naive since Freddie Fox and she had spent a weekend together at his country estate. But if her father chose to consider her his innocent little darling, she would allow him his illusions. She did love him dearly.

"Lucille, dear, Abilene is a trail town. The men there are less than . . . couth. I'm afraid the arrival of a woman of your beauty would cause quite a stir. You'd be downright unsafe there, and I'm afraid Aunt Jessica's presence would guarantee me very little of that peace of mind you're talking about."

"But, Father, a bodyguard? Really!" Her eyes shooting to the slender young man who stood in silence a short distance from them, Lucille gave a small, dismissing sniff. She was particularly unimpressed by . . . what was his name? Willis Patterson? Of medium height, fair, with pale green eyes, he had not the appearance of a man who would easily intimidate a drunken cowboy. No, he looked far too civilized with his dark banker's suit, carefully cut hair, and fine, well-trimmed brown mustache.

"Pat isn't a bodyguard, dear." His lips twitching in suppressed amusement, Horace Bascombe turned his distinguished countenance toward the young man to whom he referred. "I have introduced you to him several times, you know. As a matter of fact, Pat was here in this room with me when you first swept in with this idea of visiting Abilene next week. But in the event you don't recall, I'd like you to meet Mr. Wallace Patterson. He is the youngest vice president at our bank. He has proved himself a valuable asset to our organization, and he has earned my complete trust. It just so happens that Pat needs to travel to Abilene on bank business, and I have persuaded him to time his trip so that it coincides with your visit. He has graciously agreed to extend his protection to you for the duration of that time, and I think we should both be very grateful to him, dear."

"I'm pleased to meet you again, Miss Bascombe. It has—"

Rudely interrupting the young man's polite response, Lucille turned the full power of her blue-eyed gaze on her father.

"But, Father, surely you see how awkward it will be for me to arrive with this fellow. Have you given no thought at all to what people will think . . . what *Rand* will think seeing me traveling with him? I'll have such a short time with Rand in Abilene as it is, probably no more than a single evening. Surely you see that I can't afford to risk angering him. . . ."

His eyes moving lovingly over his daughter's beautiful face, Horace hesitated. A regretful smile finally curved his lips.

"Darling, you know how difficult it is for me to refuse you anything, but this time I must, for your own sake. Aunt Jessica just will not do in a wild trail town like Abilene. I'm afraid my decision must remain firm. You will travel with Pat, or you will not travel at all. . . ."

All semblance of civility leaving her faultless features, Lucille tossed her red curls angrily. The glance she cast in Wallace Patterson's direction was filled with open contempt.

"And you think *he* will protect me! Father, I think you give this fellow more credit than is due him. You're right. You have introduced me to Mr. Patterson several times, and on not one of those occasions has he impressed me strongly enough to have me even remember his name! Surely *that* should tell you the effect he would have on one of those rough cowboys in that wild cow town you're talking about. They'd walk all over his 'protection.'"

"Lucille!"

A light flush suffusing Horace Bascombe's lined face, he shot the silent young banker an apologetic glance.

"Pat, I really must apologize for my daughter. She is not usually so ill-mannered. I'm afraid she wasn't expecting this particular turn of events and—"

"Don't apologize for me, Father! I said exactly what I meant, and I meant what I said. I will *not* go to Abilene with a bodyguard . . . this bodyguard in particular. Aunt Jessica will be more than adequate as a traveling companion."

"Lucille, I don't usually like to repeat myself, but I can see in this case it will be necessary. The fact is, you will travel to Abilene with Pat, or you will not go. That is my final word."

Unable to comprehend the rigidness of her father's attitude, Lucille shot a quick look toward the blond young man's unrevealing expression before exploding heatedly, "Father! You can't mean—"

"Lucille, I mean every word I said."

"Ohhhh—"

Her creamy complexion turning a furious red, Lucille turned on her delicate heel and stomped toward the doorway. The angry sound of the slamming door was still reverberating in the room when the fair-haired young man turned to Horace Bascombe and shook his head.

"Horace, it's just not going to work. Your daughter is an extremely spoiled young woman who is far too accustomed to having her way. She doesn't want me to chaperone her trip to Abilene."

"Pat, please." A small smile flicking across his lips, Horace Bascombe raised his hand and placed it wearily on the obviously annoyed young man's shoulder. "You're the only person who could get away with facing me with the truth about Lucille, and in the privacy of this room, I'll grant you the truth of your words. She is an arrogant, spoiled, conceited little— Well, I guess that's enough. But the fact of the matter is that I made her that way. I loved Lucille's mother dearly, Pat, and when she was killed unexpectedly, Lucille was all I had left to love. I spoiled her shamelessly. It was a terrible disservice to her, I'm afraid. Lucille has always had everything she's ever wanted, and the only problem with that is that she's now decided she wants Rand Pierce."

Pausing, Horace Bascombe took a deep breath. Obviously upset, he shook his head, the sudden weariness overcoming him in both posture and expression adding the weight of years to his distinguished appearance.

"The only problem with that, Pat, is that Rand Pierce doesn't want her . . . not the way Lucille wants him to want

129

her, at any rate. Lucille has set her sights on the wrong man. Rand is a confirmed bachelor. She's openly admitted to me that Rand's told her he's not looking for a long-term association, but she just doesn't believe him. In truth, she believes no man would be able to turn her down. I'm afraid she's in for a rude awakening, and I don't want her to get hurt any more deeply than necessary. This trip to Abilene . . . it's a mistake, but I'd never be able to convince her of that. Instead, I'm depending on you to keep an eye on her, so she won't make a fool of herself or do anything she'll be sorry for. I want you to protect her from herself, Pat. You're the only man I'd trust with the job."

"Horace, I don't know—"

"If anyone can do it, you can. You're the only man I know who's a match for Lucille when she really digs her heels into something. I have faith in you."

Pat Patterson shook his head. A smile began to stretch across his lips. The warmth of his unexpected grin added a sparkle to his pale eyes and a true magnetism to youthful features carefully schooled to present an impassive facade. It also revealed the true affection he felt for the aristocratic gentleman petitioning his aid.

"Horace, a little warning bell begins to ring inside my head when you start complimenting me. As far as your daughter is concerned, if you'll excuse my candor, I'd say the best thing you could do for her would be to take her across your knee and let your strong right hand do the reasoning. She's a determined little bitch who won't take easily to interference in her plans."

"Pat, that's my only daughter you're talking about."

Pat's smile widened. "All right, she's a *beautiful,* determined little bitch."

There was a brief moment before Horace responded with a small nod.

"You're right, of course. Will you help me?"

Pat held his gaze. "Will you give me one good reason why I should take on that virago of yours?"

"Because I ask you to."

A small, spontaneous laugh escaped Pat's lips, the warmth

of the sound returning the spark to Horace Bascombe's still sober gaze. He waited patiently as Pat appeared to consider his answer.

"Well, I guess that's as good a reason as any. All right, you have yourself a watchdog for your darling daughter, and I have myself a big headache . . . a very big headache."

Visibly relieved, Horace Bascombe laughed freely for the first time that evening and extended his hand in Pat's direction. "Pat, I have a feeling you don't know how prophetic those words will truly prove to be. You have my deepest gratitude . . . and my sympathy."

Billie watched as Rand Pierce carefully counted the beeves that Brothers, Jeremy, and she had just cut from the main herd. Holding his impatient bay on a tight rein, Rand jerked his head in a quick positive motion.

"All right, twenty-five."

He turned back to Willie Hart who had seconded the count, waiting only for the segundo's nod of concurrence before allowing his eyes to move back to the two mounted Apaches who waited nearby. Billie felt a nudge of apprehension. She wanted to talk to White Hand. The conversation Pierce had interrupted the night before needed to be completed. She needed to tell White Hand how close she felt to him, but she needed to make clear that her feelings did not transcend friendship and appreciation for the understanding he had shown her. She needed to tell him she had a purpose that overshadowed all other considerations in her mind, and it was this purpose that had given her the strength to escape those who pursued her, despite the extent of her pain. She needed to explain to him it was this purpose that drove her relentlessly northward and would allow no deviation in her course. She needed to tell him his words had warmed her heart and she would treasure them always.

"Brothers, Carlisle, drive those beeves away from the main herd. We have to get this herd moving." His deep voice cutting across the sound of restless cattle, Rand shot a short look in her direction. "Drucker, get back to the herd."

131

Her eyes snapping back to Pierce's frown, Billie was momentarily startled. She had expected to assist in the final separation of the beeves so she might use the opportunity to speak a few words to White Hand. It would be the only opportunity she would have to speak inconspicuously to him, and she was certain if she did not make the attempt, White Hand would move openly toward her. She had no desire for the attention his action would bring to her.

"But I—"

"I told you to get back to the herd, Drucker. Carlisle and Brothers can handle those beeves."

"Aw, let Drucker be, boss." Brothers's sarcastic tone entered the momentary void. The color on his sweaty face high, he continued with a meaningful leer, "Can't you see he wants to say good-bye to his friend? Or didn't you know you had a no-good damned Indian lover in your crew?"

The flush of fury that rushed to Billie's face was instantaneous, but not as quick as the sudden movement she caught out of the corner of her eye as White Hand flashed into action. Within a moment the Apache's horse was at Brothers's side, his grip on the startled drover's hair holding him immobile as his knife moved to his throat.

"White Hand! No!"

At her gasped plea, the gleaming knife stopped short, causing only a small trickle of blood to run down Brothers's throat as White Hand trembled with his supreme effort at restraint. The silence that reigned at the breathless tableau was broken by the sound of White Hand's low, guttural tone as he spat in clear, perfect English.

"It is the word of my 'friend,' whom you deride, that saves you from the fate you deserve, white man. Will you die bravely, or do you choose to live?"

Swallowing with obvious difficulty, Brothers's rheumy eyes bulged in their sockets.

"Live . . . I want to live."

Contempt apparent in his fierce gaze as his captive shuddered visibly under his power, White Hand pressed his knife closer still.

"Then you will withdraw your words . . . now!"

When there was no response from Brothers's gaping mouth, White Hand turned the tip of his blade inward, causing a fresh flow of blood to stream from the nick at his throat. The result was a low gurgle and Brothers's gasping response.

"I—I take it back . . . everything I said."

White Hand's gaze slowly rising caught and held Billie's, and she gasped at the savage heat reflected there. Reverting to Spanish, he offered in a low tone that carried clearly in the silence.

"The choice is yours, Brave One. Only at your word would I deprive my blade of the satisfaction it demands. If it is your choice, I will allow this man to live."

Trembling, hardly able to reply, Billie nodded, finally finding her voice to respond haltingly, "Yes, let—let him live."

Releasing Brothers with a sudden thrust that almost knocked the shaken drover from the saddle, White Hand dug his heels into his pony's sides. Still quivering with rage, his gaze blazing with the excitement of the moment, White Hand guided his pony to Long Hair's side. His abundant ebony locks draping his ample shoulders, the proud, indomitable spirit of the Apache war chief clearly reflected in his narrowed gaze, White Hand pulled himself erect, his impressive form outlined against the morning sky.

With a growing feeling that White Hand's outrage had forced him to reveal his true self far more clearly than he had planned, Billie fought to catch her breath. She was keenly aware that both White Hand and Long Hair stood poised for any retribution that was to follow. Her eyes shot to Rand Pierce's livid face.

Rand's broad frame was stiff, his expression frozen in a mask of fury. His voice cracked in command.

"Take your beeves and get out of here, White Hand! And the next time I see your face around here, you won't *ride* away!" Turning to flick a deadly look in Billie's direction, Rand hissed, "And don't bother to wait for a translation you don't need. That damned fool joke is over, and you can be sure I won't be taken in by you again. Now, get out of here."

Her heart pounding so wildly that she was uncertain if she would be able to maintain her seat, Billie strained for breath.

Slowly turning in her direction, White Hand addressed her in quick, clipped Spanish.

"This is not the time for us to speak, Brave One. I leave this place now, but I will return when my mission is completed."

"No, White Hand. You must not. . . ."

"I will return. . . ."

Turning, White Hand snapped a command to the Apache at his side and within moments they had started the cattle into movement. Their postures erect and proud, they drove them steadfastly into the distance without a backward glance.

Conscious of the weight of her fellow drovers' stares, Billie was about to turn back to the herd when Rand's voice cracked sharply into the silence.

"All right, let's get those beeves moving."

"You—you mean you're not goin' to do nothin' about this Apache lover here?" Blood seeping through the stubby fingers he clutched at his throat, Brothers croaked incredulously, "You ain't—"

Interrupting him coldly, Rand shot the shaken drover a menacing stare.

"Haven't you learned your lesson yet, Brothers? Get back to work!" Pausing, Pierce caught Billie's eye, the intensity of his piercing gaze shaking her down to her toes. "That means you, too, Drucker."

Not waiting for another word, Billie spurred her black into action and within minutes was in position on right flank. Keeping her eyes on the cattle surrounding her, she voided her mind of thought.

Chapter VII

Carl squirmed uncomfortably under Sarah Henning's unrelenting stare, shooting a quick look at the men standing slightly to his rear. He did not enjoy having Marty and Stan see how the small, gray-haired little bird of a woman discomforted him. But the fact was, for the first time he was conscious that it had been a week since the clothes he was wearing had left his back. The heat of the day was reflected on the large dark stains that ringed his armpits, and the dubious odor that ensued doubtlessly caused the woman's small nose to twitch in a particularly distracting way.

Aware that he had lost control of the situation the moment Mrs. Henning had pinned him with her narrowed gaze, Carl shot a quick, nervous glance around the small general store. Luckily the first influx of customers for the day had waned, and aside from Marty, Stan, and himself, the store was empty. He was not too anxious to have any more people than necessary witness the manner in which, with a disapproving raising of her brow and an expressive flare of her nostrils, the woman had managed to reduce him to a fumbling, inept boy.

His eyes darting to the counter and the large ledger on which she had obviously been working, Carl swallowed nervously. It was apparent Sarah Henning was willing to waste little time on questions when she felt she had things of much greater importance to occupy her. He also sensed a caution in the woman's attitude, which bordered on outright suspicion and was not making matters any easier in getting the answers he was looking for.

Damn that McCulla and his bulldog ways. If he weren't so sure that McCulla would just send him right back here if he returned with nothing new about the whereabouts of that Winslow girl, he'd walk out of this store right now. Instead, Carl removed his hat in a gesture of respect he had neglected before and made a greater effort at a smile.

"I'd really appreciate it, ma'am, if you'd try again to remember if you saw a girl like I described in this store a while back. Mr. McCulla's right anxious to find her. He ain't—"

A flicker of annoyance crossing her face, Sarah Henning raised her chin in response.

"There ain't nothin' wrong with my memory, young fella. If I told you I didn't see no girl like you described in this store, I didn't see none." Her gray brows again registering her disapproval with a short upward swipe, she added, "Doesn't seem likely I'd forget seein' a young woman travelin' alone, especially if she was bruised about the face like you said she was."

"I told you, ma'am, it was her pa who laid a heavy hand on her, and it's her pa's true regret for what he did that made Mr. McCulla send us out to try to find her. Her pa wants to find her and make it up to her before somethin' happens."

"I heard you the first time, Mr. Whitley. You don't have to go repeatin' that story like I'm too feebleminded to remember what you said. But just in case *you* can't remember what *I* said, I ain't seen no girl."

"Yes, ma'am, I remember what you said."

"Is that so? Well, if you don't have nothin' you want to buy—"

"Well, ma'am, the fact is, it's come to our attention while tryin' to find this here young lady I've been askin' about that a young 'boy' was seen around town about that same time. We was kinda interested in findin' him, just in case—"

"A young boy?"

The abrupt change in the old woman's attitude caused Carl to feel the first surge of hope since he had entered the

136

small, dimly lit emporium a short time before. If he wasn't mistaken, he had finally hit pay dirt. Taking a firm hold on his patience, Carl put on his most sincere expression.

"Just in case the girl thought it woud be better to travel dressed like a boy, ma'am. You see, she's a real resourceful girl with a real mind of her own. Seems like that was what made her pa so angry with her in the first place. Anyhow, I know she'd be on her way back to him right now if she knew how sick her ma is with grievin' for her. Why, Mr. McCulla said he believes the woman won't last another month in her state if that girl ain't found right away. That's why Mr. McCulla sent us out to find her. He says the girl's pa ain't got the wherewithal to look for her, and he wouldn't want her old mother's life on his conscience, knowin' he could've helped find her and didn't. Mr. McCulla said a bad conscience is a powerful weight, ma'am."

"Truly. . . ."

"Truly, ma'am."

Sarah Henning shook her gray head, and Carl felt a surge of triumph. He had hit on just the right note to turn the old woman's sympathies in McCulla's favor. He sure enough was goin' to let McCulla know how he had outsmarted the sharp-eyed old witch . . . he sure enough was.

Still shaking her head, Sarah Henning began hesitantly.

"Seems—seems like there *was* a 'boy' like you described in here a few weeks ago. It wasn't too hard to remember him, beat up like he was."

Carl carefully ignored the last remnants of suspicion in the old woman's eyes.

"I'd be real appreciative if you'd try to remember if he said anythin' about where he was goin'. Seems like nobody seen hide nor hair of him after he left this town, and if the boy is really the person we're lookin' for, we're thinkin' she might be needin' some help."

"It ain't a matter of me tryin' to remember, young fella." An edge of irritation returning to her tone, Sarah Henning sniffed impatiently. "The boy didn't do much talkin'. He just bought a new rope and the last pair of chaps Harry had in stock. I told him they was old and made for a much bigger

137

man than he was, but the boy said he wanted them anyway. I got the feelin' he was expectin' to do some heavy ridin' through country with thorny brush and wasn't goin' to risk gettin' cut up any worse than he was. Anyways, the boy didn't say nothin' else. He just paid for the things he bought and left. I ain't seen him since."

Certain he had finally gotten the information he needed, Carl could hardly contain his glee. Damn fool old woman! He had her eatin' out of his hand with his sob story, and he sure enough was goin' to milk the old fool for all she was worth.

"Well, I sure do thank you for what you did tell us, ma'am. Mr. McCulla and his friend are goin' to be right grateful to you for your help. And if you could kinda keep us in mind in case you see that 'boy' again, I know Mr. McCulla would appreciate it even more. You have a right good day now."

Turning at the old woman's short nod, Carl shot his men a triumphant look. The doors of the store had barely closed behind them when a broad smile creased the stubble on his cheeks.

"Well, what do you think, boys? Think we finally got a lead to findin' that Winslow girl?"

Digging dirty fingernails into his damp armpit in an unconscious effort at relief from a naggingly suspicious bite, Marty returned Carl's smile with a puzzled expression.

"I don't know what you're so happy about. All's you know is that boy bought a brand new rope and chaps. You don't know where he went or why."

Grimacing in mocking reaction to the man's statement, Carl signaled the two men to fall behind him as he headed toward the livery stable. "Ain't you got no sense at all? Why would the boy be buyin' brand new rope and chaps? Since he was on the run, seems to me he figured he'd be havin' a need for both of them or he wouldn't have taken the time to buy them. Now, what would a fella be needin' chaps and a new rope for?"

"Hell, that ain't hard to figure out. I always pack my chaps and check my rope when I'm goin' to be trail drivin'. . . ."

"And didn't the bartender at the hotel mention there was a

138

couple of trail herds outside town about that time when the 'boy' was here? What does that tell you?"

"You mean you think that Winslow girl might've joined a trail drive? Hell, it ain't likely she'd be able to keep up. . . ."

"You got a short memory, Marty. You remember last year when that feisty little bitch worked right alongside her pa in the roundup and trail drive? Remember how fit to be tied Wes was when he found out she wasn't goin' to be left behind where he could get at her while her pa was away? You remember Winslow's hands talkin' when they got back, sayin' she worked as hard as any one of them on the trail? And you remember how Wes could hardly take his eyes off her when she showed up in town a little while after the drive, her skin all kinda honey-colored from the sun and that hair of hers long and shiny and bleached to a silverlike gold from being on the trail?"

"Yeah, I remember."

"Well? All we got to do now is talk to Bart at the livery stable and find out what herds was passin' through about that time and—"

His toothless grin flashing, Marty shook his head. "McCulla's goin' to be right happy with the news we're comin' back with this time."

"Not as happy as he's goin' to be when he gets his hands on that girl. Hell. . . ." His eyes reflecting not the slightest concern, Carl added offhandedly, "I'm sure glad I ain't her—"

Turning into the livery stable without another thought, Carl called out impatiently, "Bart—Bart, where are you? We're in a hurry. . . ."

Lucille adjusted the folds of her skirt and directed her attention outside the window toward the last of the boarding passengers. In a few minutes the train would be leaving the station and she would be on her way to Abilene at last. With a short sigh of exasperation, she stared at the shadow of her reflection in the window. Yes, she looked lovely. The soft green of the tailor-made traveling costume she had chosen to wear complimented her brilliant red curls, drawn so artfully behind her ears in the stylish "Cadogan" coiffure. The toque hat perched daintily on the top of her head, ornamented with white doves' wings and flowers, was the perfect accessory to her outfit. Needless to say, the jacket of her ensemble was a flawless fit, hugging her generous bosom and narrow waist like a second skin, and she was well aware that the floor-length skirt, caught up at the side, slightly trained and decorated with fringing, made the most of her enticing womanly curves.

Yes, she was taking no chances. Uncertain as she was just exactly when she would be seeing Rand for the first time, she had decided to wear her best and most expensive ensembles at every step of her journey. Her father had initiated inquiries that had resulted in the general placement of Rand's herd on the map. From that, she had been able to judge the approximate time of his arrival in Abilene, and she intended to be there and waiting when he arrived. Knowing Rand as she did, she had no doubt he would take the first opportunity to escape the boredom of the trail with a short stay in Abilene. Of course, knowing his dedication to his business commitments, she was also certain he would not spend more than one night there. But one night was all she needed. For she decided she was going to drive Rand mad with wanting her.

From the first, she had entertained no doubt that their reunion would be a loving success. Having been on the trail without women for weeks, Rand would doubtless be hungry for the taste of her flesh. And the sleeping garment she had ordered made to her measurements just for this occasion, a heavenly gown of pink satin and Chantilly lace that artfully contrived to reveal while appearing to conceal, was guaranteed to drive a man beyond even the most rudimentary caution.

She had been only too aware that while Rand's passion had doubtless been aroused on each occasion when he had made love to her in the past, he had never been driven to the point of lost control. She realized fully that this supreme control was doubtless the reason he paid no support for bastard children despite an active, healthy sexual appetite. And while she had no desire to infringe on his record there, it irked her that Rand so easily held a part of himself aloof from her despite her most stringent efforts to the contrary.

But this time would be different. She would seduce him so completely that she would drive all reasonable thought from his mind. She would give of herself, holding back only enough to whet his appetite for more . . . making him unable to think of any woman but herself. And when the drive was over, he would come running back to her. . . .

Yes, Abilene was going to be very entertaining . . . *very* entertaining. An unconscious smile slipping across her lips, Lucille flicked her eyes briefly closed against her avid anticipation.

"So, you're smiling at last! I am relieved. I had begun to think you would be making the entire journey to Abilene with a frown on your lovely face. Of course, that wouldn't do. We wouldn't want to initiate unwanted lines on that smooth, flawless skin."

Her head jerking toward the sound of the low voice in her ear, Lucille frowned into Wallace Patterson's pleasant face. The reward for his compliment was a sharp response.

"Mr. Patterson, I care very little whether you feel relieved or not. As a matter of fact, had I thought a smile from my lips might give you the slightest pleasure, I would most stringently have denied myself the inclination."

The unexpected smile that stretched across his lips adding a surprising warmth to features Lucille had considered extremely uninteresting, the young banker responded generously, "I really do think it would be best if we dispense with formality for the duration of our sojourn. My friends call me Pat, and I—"

Interrupting without concern for courtesy, Lucille directed a pointedly icy glance in his direction. Her voice dripped with hauteur.

"Just so we don't waste time laboring under a misconception, *Mr. Patterson,* I have no intention of becoming your 'friend.' You are accompanying me to Abilene at my father's insistence, and it is only because of his unreasonable attitude that I am having any contact with you at all. You are my father's employee. I ask you to remember that will be the limit of our association."

"So, we're taking off the gloves, are we?"

"I merely believe this situation calls for a little straight talk."

"Well, if that's the case, let's get a few things straight right now. I don't like this situation any more than you do. If you think I like playing nursemaid to a spoiled, pampered little bitch, you're greatly mistaken. I agreed to supervise this little trip of yours purely because your father asked me. He said I'm the only man he'd trust with the responsibility. I suppose he knows me well enough to realize that I would feel no attraction whatsoever for a haughty brat who behaves no better than a spoiled child and who thinks she's several steps above everyone else in the world.

"But just so you can be further shocked by your father's poorly advised decision to place you in my care, Miss High-And-Mighty Bascombe, I'll give you a brief rundown on my personal history. I'm the son of the town drunk and a very hard-working kitchen maid. I spent enough years warming myself in front of other people's fires when I was a child to make me determined to have a huge, roaring fireplace of my own one day. Now, at thirty-four years of age, I'm a certified member of the Missouri Bar. I have a large residence of my own which is free and clear of debt and which has a fireplace in every room. I am comfortably wealthy, and I am also the youngest vice president and member of the board of directors of your father's bank.

"I have bothered to carefully point out these things to you, not because I think you're truly interested, but just so you'll be advised that I have accomplished much more in my life than you can ever hope to attain. I also point these things out to you so you might realize that had I the inclination, I would have more reason for excessive pride than the lazy, indolent, self-indulged daughter of a rich man who spends the major portion of her day posturing in front of the mirror admiring herself! So don't look down at me. To me you're just Lucy Bascombe, a redheaded, rich snip of a girl I have to shepherd

142

around to make sure that she stays out of trouble until she's back in her father's sight again. For your own sake, I'd advise you not to try giving me a hard time, Lucy. I give you fair warning. I don't intend taking any of your guff!"

Great blue eyes, which had gradually widened into huge, indignant saucers, blinked almost comically at the conclusion of Pat Patterson's statement. A sudden flush suffusing her shocked face, Lucille choked, "Don't—don't you *dare* call me Lucy!"

Unexpectedly loud blasts of the train whistle interrupted all further attempt at a vocal exchange for the next few minutes. Maintaining a frustrated silence as the sudden jerking movement of the car signaled the start of the train, Lucille was startled to see a small smile twitching the corner of Pat Patterson's brown mustache. Waiting until the final blast had sounded and the train was moving evenly out of the station, Pat allowed his smile full rein. Reaching out unexpectedly, he curved his broad palm around Lucille's two dainty hands clasped so angrily in her lap, refusing to release them even as she struggled to escape his touch. True amusement sounded for the first time in his voice.

"Quite the contrary to what you most avidly believe, Lucy, you have a lot to learn. And it just might be that I'll enjoy teaching you some of it."

"Let go of my hands!"

"Come—come now, Lucy. Your papa has placed you in my care. You'll be entirely dependent upon my good graces for the entire time until you're back in your father's care again. And, dear Lucy, I should like to inform you now, I will expect to be accorded the respect due my position of responsibility—that is, if you expect to be extended the same courtesy in return. You do understand me, don't you, Lucy?"

Blue eyes sparking fire, Lucille jerked her hands free of Pat's grip. Her full bosom heaving angrily, she raised her dainty chin. Her fine lips parted in a soft, clipped response.

"In a pig's eye, you bastard!"

"Lucy . . . for shame!"

Unable to bear the open amusement in his expression a

moment longer, Lucille snapped her head back toward the window. Her flush darkened at the sound of the subdued laughter that sounded near her ear and the low voice that whispered in mocking reassurance.

"Oh, yes, Lucy, I think Abilene will prove to be very interesting . . . very interesting, indeed."

Rand shot a covert glance to the men riding behind him, still uncertain in his mind if he had made the right decision. As far as he was concerned, a few hours in Abilene was a necessity for both him and Nate Straw. For Nate, it was a matter of restocking some supplies; for himself, it was a matter of escaping the supreme aggravation of this drive for a few short hours. He had driven many herds over the trail in his day, but this particular drive was fraught with more tension than any ten of the others he had foremanned.

There hadn't been a sign of White Hand or Long Hair since the two Apaches had driven their beeves out of sight a few days before, but he was certain they had not left Drucker's thoughts. In the time since, he had watched the boy's careful, persistent scrutiny of the horizon. It was a habit of the youth's with which Rand was long familiar but which had seemed to intensify since the Apaches had left camp.

It had also become obvious Brothers and Hall were not about to allow the incident with White Hand to die. Sullen and silent for the most part since the Apache had gotten the best of him, Brothers seemed to spend most of his spare time around the campfire fingering his neck and sending vicious glances toward Drucker.

Taking up where Brothers was obviously reluctant, Hall had kept up a steady barrage of pointed jibes and insulting remarks directed at Drucker. The result was a volatile atmosphere that had everyone on edge.

As for Drucker, he had to give the kid credit. He obviously did not intend to give Hall the satisfaction of rising to his bait. Turning a completely deaf ear to his taunts, the boy continued to conduct himself in the same solitary manner he had in the past. Unfortunately, Rand himself had not been in such tight control of his annoyance. But his few sharp words of reprimand to Hall had only resulted in a thankless glance from Drucker and a tightening of the tension. He hadn't made that same mistake again.

Fully aware that the situation could not continue as it was, Rand had made a decision the day before. Completely contrary to his former policy of allowing no free time so early in a drive, he had decided to grant the men a night in Abilene. He had compensated for the loss of time that short respite might involve by making a long evening drive the night before, which set them ahead in their schedule. He had made it clear to the men that they would be expected to return to the herd for their watches as usual, thereby guaranteeing a guard and some time in town for all.

It was fortunate indeed that he had made the decision to split Brothers and Hall on their watch. The fact that Brothers shared the first watch and Hall the second also guaranteed that they would not be together in town and thus would not be able to join forces in possible harassment of Drucker. He was annoyed at the relief that thought allowed him and the fact that he had been unable to maintain an impersonal attitude toward Drucker. What in hell was the matter with him, anyway? It was obvious Drucker resented his interference. So why his damned obsession with the kid and his problems, and his inability to shake them from his mind?

Well, he had been right about one thing, at least. He needed a few hours away from the herd, and he was damned well going to take full advantage of it. They'd be in Abilene in a few minutes and then . . .

But the rumbling of Hall's voice from behind cut into Rand's thoughts, alerting him to the first words to break the silence of the group riding slightly to his rear.

"Well, I guess we're goin' to finally find out for sure if the boss put a boy in a man's job on this drive. What do you say, Drucker? Think you can handle a night on the town? How're you goin' to celebrate a few free hours? Drinkin' some milk and readin' a book, maybe? It'd be a big surprise to me if you was man enough to do anythin' else."

"Leave the kid alone, Hall."

Jeremy's quiet warning was answered by Hall's scornful laugh.

"Hell, I can see I did things all wrong. I should've stayed a puny little squirt instead of growin' up to be a man, and then I could've had other fellas fight my battles for me. Maybe you're smarter than I thought, Drucker. You do all right. First the boss treats you like you're made of glass, and then the Indian pulls a knife for you, and now the farm boy here puts in his two cents to stand up for you."

Breaking her silence for the first time, Billie stated flatly, "I don't need anybody to fight my battles."

"I'd like to see you prove that, pretty boy."

"That's enough, Hall!" Unable to stand more, Rand turned steely eyes in Hall's direction. "Another word out of you and you're going back to the herd . . . now!"

In the brief silence that followed, anger flared in Hall's eyes, only to be replaced by a cool look of determination.

"Sure, Mr. Pierce. Anythin' you say."

Grateful that the next turn in the road revealed the first glimpse of Abilene, Rand shot Hall a final warning glance and spurred his horse forward. He had had enough of the whole situation . . . more than enough.

Her eyes moving watchfully along the street, Billie walked cautiously within the group that approached The Oasis Saloon. Her first priority to determine if there were any familiar faces in town that might recognize her, she realized her second priority was to get away from the rest of the men as soon as possible. She had no desire to spend her few free hours leaning on a bar, playing cards, or trying to stay out of Hall's way. She was only too aware how potentially dangerous that situation could become. It was obvious Hall was spoiling for a fight, and she had no intention of accommodating him.

No, her plan was simple. She would go to the nearest hotel and rent herself a room. With the advance on salary Rand had doled out to each of the men so they might entertain themselves modestly, she then intended to hire someone to drag a tub to the room and fill it to the brim with hot water. She would then spend the rest of the time allotted soaking. Secreted at the bottom of her pants pocket was the last remains of a bar of lavender soap she had packed in her saddlebag from home. It had been far too long since she had enjoyed its lather against her skin.

Without her realization, Billie's eyes drifted to the tall man walking unofficially at the lead of their small group. Rand Pierce stood almost a head above the rest of the men in height, but that was not all that distinguished him from the average man. In her silent thoughts during quiet moments on the trail, she had come to the conclusion that Rand Pierce was almost too handsome with those dark, classic features and those breathtakingly light eyes. But it was the quality of command in his voice that more efficiently set him apart from most men and, perhaps even more effective, the keen intelligence in his watchful stare that combined with a spark of ruthlessness to leave her breathless under its assault.

She had found herself breathless under his gaze more often of late, and her patience had begun to wane at the conflicting emotions assaulting her under his scrutiny. But she was helpless to combat it. She had begun to wonder if . . .

A sudden flutter of movement on the boardwalk a short distance away caught Billie's eye, tearing her mind from her thoughts the moment before an extravagantly beautiful young woman broke away from the slender man at her side. Her great eyes glowing, she moved rapidly in their direction. She called out, her voice filled with emotion.

"Rand, darling, you've arrived at last!"

Rand's fluid stride jerked to an unexpected stop as he reacted in open surprise. Obviously not willing to waste time while he digested the fact of her appearance, the young woman raced to his side. Within moments they were wrapped in a tight embrace, their mouths meeting in a mutually passionate kiss.

The low snickering around her brought Billie back to

147

reality with a start, and she realized she had stopped short while the other men were continuing to move slowly past the deeply engrossed couple. A deadening ache, stronger than any pain she had suffered at the hands of Wes McCulla, twisted in her stomach. Her mouth went suddenly dry while an unexpected moist heat began to fill her eyes.

Unable to tear her gaze from the two beautiful people clasped tightly in each other's arms, she heard Jeremy's wistful comment.

"That must be that Lucille Bascombe Willie was tellin' us about. He said she's one of the most beautiful women in this part of the country. Can't say as I disagree with him. . . ."

"Hell, guess we ain't goin' to see much of the boss while we're in town."

The soft murmurs of their voices was starting to drift away when Billie felt a sharp jab in her side.

"Close your mouth, boy, and stop your starin'" Jim Stewart's gruff voice held a note of amusement—"or you're goin' to get left behind."

Jerking her head toward the pleasant drover's indulgent smile, Billie nodded and took up her step again. When she had reached a point where she was adjacent to the tightly entwined couple, a familiar voice sounded in her ear, snapping her face up to Josh Hall's sneer.

"What are you goin' to do now, Drucker? Looks like your protector is goin' to be busy for a while. Looks like its finally goin' to be just you and me. . . ."

The menace in Hall's stare sent a tremor of fear down her spine at the same moment Billie sensed the weight of someone's perusal. She turned, catching Rand's narrowed gaze as he observed the exchange over the bright red curls of the woman in his arms. Truly uncertain which posed the greater threat, the deep pain growing inside her or the hackles of fear Hall had raised on her spine, Billie moved abruptly against her dilemma and followed Jeremy into the saloon.

Lucille's mouth was moving against his in heated greeting.

Her arms were locked tightly around his neck while his were filled with the warmth of her lush, womanly body, but Rand was strangely distracted. Reacting physically to Lucille's stimulus, he returned her kiss while his mind raced.

Lucille. . . . What in hell was she doing here in Abilene? He had no time for her now. . . . He had too many other important problems on his mind . . . a volatile situation to supervise. . . . He couldn't afford to . . .

But even as Lucille's lips separated under his, Rand looked over her brilliant red curls to see his men as they began to file past toward The Oasis. Moving almost in single file, they glanced briefly in his direction in open curiosity. But where was . . .

His eyes suddenly touching on the object of his quest, Rand saw Drucker following a short distance behind. As he watched, Josh Hall walked up beside the boy and leaned down to whisper leeringly into his ear. A flush of color suffused Drucker's face as it snapped up to Hall, and Rand's stomach convulsed into a tight knot. He felt an almost overpowering urge to push aside Lucille's clinging arms. Seeming to sense his perusal, Drucker suddenly turned in his direction, the open vulnerability in the boy's gaze almost undoing him.

Turning away, his vulnerability seeming to fade just as suddenly as it had appeared, Drucker walked calmly into The Oasis behind the other men. In a few seconds, Hall followed, and Rand felt the pressure of panic.

Lucille had drawn her mouth from his. She was talking rapidly with great emotion, her heart fluttering against his chest. Uncertain exactly what she was saying, Rand nodded, his gaze straying to the last glimpse of Drucker as he passed through The Oasis' doors.

His eyes returning begrudgingly to Lucille, Rand realized she was stepping away from him and attempting to introduce him to a keen-eyed young man who had stood observing a few feet away.

"Rand, I'd like you to meet an employee of my father's, Wallace Patterson. He kindly consented to accompany me to Abilene so I might meet you."

149

Abjectly distracted, Rand shook the fellow's hand. It was going to be a long evening.

Releasing a deep sigh of relief, Billie closed the hotel room door and turned the lock. Jerking her hat from her head, she tossed it to the nearby chair and leaned back against the rough surface, savoring the privacy the room afforded.

She wasn't quite sure how much more of this she could stand. She had spent a tense half hour in The Oasis under Josh Hall's harassment. It had only been Jeremy Carlisle's and Jim Stewart's interference that kept him at bay until a bar girl of questionable taste had taken an unexpected liking to Hall and stepped even more efficiently between. In any case, the woman had distracted him long enough for her to slip out onto the street.

Keeping to the shadows, she had made a direct line for the hotel and rented herself a room. Her eyes jerking to the steaming copper tub further cramping its generally tight quarters, Billie gave a low grunt of satisfaction and started to pull off her clothes. Arranging for that convenience had taken every penny of the money advanced to her, but it was going to be worth it. Her eyes shooting to the small bottle on the night table, Billie amended her thought. No, not every penny. She had had enough to buy herself a bottle of brandy.

The knot that formed in the pit of her stomach when she had seen Rand Pierce's arms close around that woman in the street tightened naggingly.

"A sip of brandy is good for woman problems, darlin'."

Her father's embarrassed voice when she had reacted fearfully to the cramping at her coming of age returned to her mind with great warmth. A sip of brandy had been the cure-all for the few ailments she had suffered since. Would it be effective against the relentless ache inside that would give her no rest?

Determined to shake off her inexplicable malaise, Billie gave the tub another quick glance. She would soak away her cares, and when she emerged she would be a new woman, inside and out.

Quickly stripping away the rest of her clothes, Billie was about to step into the tub when she turned as an afterthought and transferred the brandy and glass to the table within reaching distance of the copper convenience. Yes, she would attack her problems from the inside and out, and damn Rand Pierce and his redheaded woman. She didn't need him or anyone else.

Her face set with new determination, Billie turned to the tub. Within a few seconds she was up to her shoulders in the warm, sparkling water. She released a deep sigh of contentment. How she had missed the luxury of heated water and scented soap, and the time to fully enjoy both. . . .

Her spirits rising, Billie slid beneath the surface, remaining there until her bursting lungs would allow no more. Surfacing with a short gasp, she reached for the soap. Pressing her nose to its slippery surface for long, indulged seconds, she breathed deeply of its fragrance. Temporarily sated, she rubbed it into her hair and worked up a generous lather beneath her palms.

Rinsing the last of the fragrant bubbles from her scalp a few minutes later, Billie pushed the gleaming strands back from her face, squeezed out the excess moisture, and leaned back against the rim of the tub. Yes, she was feeling better already.

Her eye catching the glimmer of the amber liquid in the small bottle beside her, Billie reached out a slender hand. Carefully uncorking the top, she poured herself a more than generous sip. Her stubborn mind returned unexpectedly to the memory of red curls pressed intimately against Rand's shoulder. Her stomach tightened further as the picture enlarged to include the memory of Rand's arms holding the woman tightly, his mouth . . .

Furious at her own helplessness against her tormenting mind, Billie raised her glass. Her voice sounded quietly in the silence of the room.

"To a new woman, inside and out."

With a determined smile, she raised the glass to her lips and drained it dry.

* * *

151

"Rand, what is wrong with you tonight?"

Lucille's tense inquiry snapped Rand back to the realization that he had done no more than nod his head accommodatingly to her steady chatter for the past hour and a half. Flicking the cover of his watch closed, Rand felt his face flush with color at his open obsession with the amount of time that had elapsed since they had entered the hotel dining room. He shot Lucille and Pat Patterson a quick, apologetic glance.

"I'm sorry, Lucille. It's just . . . well, it's been a very difficult drive. We lost considerable time at the outset while I scouted up some additional drovers. And to be very honest, some of them haven't worked out too well. I really should be at The Oasis right now checking—"

"Really, Rand!" Lucille's voice was tinged with the growing impatience evidenced on her flushed face. "If it's been so difficult and the men have been such a problem, why have you rewarded them with a night off? I admit I was surprised to see you arrive in Abilene with a whole pack of drovers at your heels. And I must agree, they appear a pretty common lot. I can't imagine how you can bear to spend your days with uneducated, unwashed men who are probably illiterate and whose only talents seem to be the fact that they can think faster than a herd of dumb animals. I should think you'd have taken the first opportunity for some time away from them instead of dragging them with you."

The stiffening of his features and the tensing of angry lines around his mouth was a clear indication of Rand's reaction to Lucille's statement. His response was slow and deliberate.

"In the first place, Lucille, there are only two in my crew whom I would characterize as troublemakers. The others are good, honest, hardworking men whom I value as employees. As for their being uneducated . . . well, I didn't attend any establishments of higher learning myself. And as for their being unwashed, conditions on the trail are hardly conducive to a daily bath. Actually, it isn't difficult being with men who are unwashed occasionally, when you're as unwashed as they are."

"You are *not* unwashed, Rand!"

152

"I have been."

"Oh, why do you stand up for those degenerates?" Raising her voice loudly enough to draw the attention of other diners, Lucille continued heatedly, "I was only agreeing with what you said."

His eyes moving slowly over Lucille's face, Rand mentally shook his head. Lucille was beautiful, all right. Heads turned when he walked with her on his arm, and she had gone out of her way to let him know that she wanted him. But damn, there was nothing in that beautiful head but an overwhelming vanity and determination to have her way. A beautiful shell and an accommodating body . . . that was Lucille Bascombe. And he'd be damned if he'd be trapped by it!

"No, Lucille, you were not agreeing with me. If you thought you were, you weren't listening. Or perhaps you didn't choose to hear. That is your custom . . . hearing only what you want to hear, isn't it?"

Her azure eyes filling with tears, Lucille raised her face to Rand appealingly. "Rand, why are you being so cruel to me? I've traveled so far to be with you tonight. I realize this meeting is less than I would like it to be for us, but—but Pat is leaving for a business appointment within the half hour, aren't you, Pat?" She did not wait for the startled young man's assent to her bold declaration but continued in a rush, realizing that she was rapidly losing ground. "And then we'll have some time to be alone and . . . sort out our differences. You would like that, wouldn't you, Rand?"

"Oh, Lucille, for God's sake, behave yourself!"

Snapping Lucille's eyes wide with his unexpected interruption, Pat took Lucille's arm and gave it a firm shake. "You're acting like an annoyingly precocious child! Instead of accusing Rand of mistreating you, you'd be far better off begging his pardon for following him to Abilene and interrupting him at an obviously inopportune time. You're so self-centered that you don't even have the good sense to be gracious and generous enough to allow him out of your sight long enough to solve the problems that are obviously weighing very heavily on his mind."

"How—how *dare* you speak to me like that, Pat

Patterson! You have no right to—"

"I have every right!" His green eyes sparking with an unexpected fire, Pat pinned her with his gaze. "Your father put you in my care for the duration of this trip, and I'll be damned if I'll allow you to behave in a manner that would be an embarrassment to him!"

"I am *not* an embarrassment to my father!"

"You most certainly would be if he were here! As it is, you're an embarrassment to me!"

Turning his agitated face in Rand's direction, Pat offered quietly, "Rand, I do apologize for Lucille. It seems to me she suffers from a severe case of being indulged. I don't think I need tell you she's a spoiled, snobbish brat who is completely lacking in—"

"Spoiled brat . . . snob! Pat Patterson, you take that back!"

His eyes moving to Lucille's face, Pat snapped tightly, "I realize being faced with the truth hurts, Lucille, but someone should have taken you in hand years ago."

"Well, if someone takes me in hand, *Mr.* Patterson, it most certainly is not going to be you! So if you will kindly leave so Rand and I might finish our conversation—"

"Lucille, I'm not going anywhere." The face she had considered bland and boringly controlled suddenly evidenced enough anger to send a surge of actual fear down Lucille's spine as Pat continued slowly. "But I do think that Rand will be going, won't you, Rand?"

His eyes moving between the formerly silent young banker and the raging heiress beside him, Rand experienced the first flicker of amusement he had felt all day. This Pat Patterson, banker or not, was all right! If there were any man who could put the high-toned Lucille Bascombe in her place, it would be he. And he was welcome to the job."

Nodding, Rand slowly drew himself to his feet. "Yes, I think I *will* be going. It was a . . . rare experience seeing you again, Lucille."

Ignoring the expression of absolute shock that moved over Lucille's indignant face, Rand turned toward the startling young man and extended his hand.

"Pat, it's been a pleasure meeting you. I do hope we meet again under more comfortable circumstances. I have a feeling it would be most pleasant."

"Thank you, Rand. I feel much the same. And don't worry about Lucille. I'll take care of her."

"You will *not* take care of me! Rand—"

"Sit down, Lucille."

"I will *not* sit down!"

"Yes, you will, damn it!" Placing the flat of his hands on her narrow white shoulders, revealed so enticingly in the low cut of her amber-colored gown, Pat exerted unexpected pressure that seated Lucille with a less than ladylike thump. Effectively ignoring the fact that Lucille's eyes were bulging with indignation, Pat offered Rand a parting smile.

"As I said, I'll take care of her, Rand. Don't worry about a thing."

"Thanks, Pat."

Turning, his anxiety allowing him no more than a moment's relief at the ease of escape the understanding young banker had afforded him, Rand made his way to the door. Stopping to drop several greenbacks with the waiter, he shot a glance to his rear. Lucille's complexion the same color as her fiery hair, she was assailing Pat with a whispered heated tirade that the fellow was obviously ignoring with great effectiveness. A flicker of a smile moved across Rand's lips. Oh, yes, that fellow was all right. . . .

Turning away, Rand made rapid, lengthy strides toward the exit. The two seated at the table behind him dropping from his mind the moment the hotel door closed behind him, he squinted into the darkening street. His eyes sought the bright, glaring lights of the building only a few short doors away. His destination was The Oasis. . . .

"What do you mean you don't know where they are? Damn it, man, weren't you curious when *both* of them disappeared?"

His lined face slightly indignant, Jim Stewart raised his graying brow.

"When did I get appointed bodyguard for that kid, Rand? I like Drucker just as much as you do, even if he is a quiet sort. And you know damned well I wouldn't let either of those two bullies take advantage of him, but that don't mean any one of us should be his keeper."

"You know damned well that bastard was just waitin' for an opportunity to get the boy alone. Hell, if I thought this was going to happen, I would've bypassed Abilene entirely." His dark brow knotted into a tight frown, Rand turned, his eyes seeking out the rest of his men standing at the bar.

"Didn't any of you see either Drucker or Hall leave?"

"I don't think you have anythin' to worry about, Mr. Pierce."

Jeremy Carlisle's unexpected response jerked Rand's intense gaze in the young man's direction. The young drover smiled a rather lopsided grin, which appeared to be the direct result of the half-filled bottle resting beside his arm.

"Drucker didn't spend no more time than was necessary at this bar. He'll probably be the only one of us who'll be back to the herd without a headache tonight. Anyways, as soon as Gracie over there sidled up to Hall and got his mind off Drucker for a few minutes, the kid took off. I don't know where he went, but he sure enough looked like he had a definite destination in mind."

"When did Hall leave?"

"A little while later, I think."

"And didn't it occur to you that Hall might've seen Drucker leave and followed him?"

Carlisle looked momentarily taken aback.

"No, Mr. Pierce, it sure enough didn't."

Momentarily too exasperated to respond, Rand held the young man's gaze.

"Looks to me like you've been leaning pretty heavy on that bottle, Carlisle. I don't care how you amuse yourself while you're in town, but I'm giving all of you fair warning. I expect you to show up back at the herd *on time* and in a shape to handle your watch. And you can pretty well depend on it that any man who doesn't won't be getting any more time off for the rest of the drive."

Ignoring the flush that colored Carlisle's face, Rand turned and headed toward the door. There were a few other bars in town. Drucker had to be somewhere. . . .

Exasperation written in the tight lines of his face, Rand walked out of the last of the Abilene bars. Night had fallen and the main street of the active cow town was ablaze with lights. Sounds of music and laughter from the abundant saloons and other establishments of dubious entertainment rolled onto the street, combining into a subtle din that would have been titillating had Rand been of another state of mind. As it was, the incessant sounds of men and women at play only succeeded in increasing his irrational distraction.

Damned if he hadn't been in and out of every one of those brightly lit dens of iniquity! He had talked to every bartender, madam, and anyone else who looked as if he might have some information to offer, but he hadn't turned up a sign of that illusive kid.

This night was turning into a nightmare. Where in hell could Drucker be? Worrying him even more was the fact that he had run into Hall at the last saloon he had visited, and the bastard had looked a little too pleased with himself. For all he knew, Hall had already caught up with the kid and left him lying in an alley somewhere, worse off than he had been when he had first shown up looking for a job.

Taking off his hat, Rand ran a nervous hand through his heavy dark hair. Of one thing, he was certain. Drucker was still in town. Out of desperation, he had gone back to check the livery stable a short time before on the off chance that Drucker might have returned to the herd. Drucker's horse, the undersized sorrel he had chosen to ride to town, was still in its stall.

He was certain of another thing, also. If anyone—*anyone* had put a hand on that kid . . .

Unwilling to allow his mind to linger on the thought, aware that the sense of panic deep inside him was rising, Rand racked his brain. He had looked for Drucker in every spot open to the public in town. Damn, he needed a drink.

He had half a mind to go back to the room he had taken at the hotel and the bottle of Jim Crow he had left there and . . .

The hotel . . . the only place he hadn't checked . . .

Taking the steps two at a time, Rand flicked his eyes down the hotel hallway. Coming to a brief standstill at the landing, he scanned the room numbers on the doors. Room sixteen . . . The damned kid had taken a room only three doors down from the rooms Lucille and Pat had taken. If he had accepted the invitation Lucille had seemed so determined to extend earlier, he probably would have run into the annoying runt on the landing!

As it was, he had spent the last two hours in a near panic with the thought that the kid might be hurt. No doubt it had been that same preoccupation that had left him so immune to the warmth of Lucille's greeting and the lush contours of her body, which she had gone to great pains to present so appealingly to his eye. Damn, if that kid was all right . . . if he was relaxed and asleep in a nice comfortable bed while he had been running all over town . . .

But then, again, if he wasn't all right . . . if Hall *had* gotten to him and he was bruised and beaten . . .

A new flush of panic all but overwhelming his mind, Rand walked rapidly down the hall, stopping abruptly as the number sixteen met his eye. His heart thumping a wild tattoo in his chest, he raised his hand and pounded on the door.

"Drucker, are you in there?"

Pausing for a response, Rand felt a new flush of fear at the silence that ensued. The clerk at the desk downstairs had said that he had not seen the boy come down. He had to be in there.

"Drucker—Drucker, it's Rand Pierce. Answer me, damn it!"

Rand paused again, his heart pounding so wildly that he was almost uncertain he had heard the soft sound from beyond the closed door. He held his breath. It was a low

158

response . . . almost a whimper. . . .

He called again. "Drucker. . . ."

The halting, labored response this time was louder.

"I—I can't let you in. Please—"

A flush of fear held Rand immobile for long seconds. Drucker *was* hurt! He could hardly speak. . . . He was calling out to him. . . .

Taking a step back, Rand looked at the hardwood door for the space of a moment before he raised his foot and directed a powerful kick in the area of the lock. When the first assault did not budge the door, he kicked it again and then a third time. Plunging forward into the gap at the same moment the door snapped open, Rand came to a sharp, shuddering halt. Startled, he took a disbelieving step backward.

Standing in a deep copper tub in the center of the room, wrapped tightly in a light cotton sheeting that clung to her slender body to reveal far more distinctly than it concealed, was the most beautiful woman he had ever seen. Silver-gold hair, still damp from her bath, curled around her face, appealingly accenting its exquisite contours. Skin, flawless and tinged with a golden glow, stretched tightly over her finely etched features, while eyes a darker and deeper black than the night sky regarded him intently. She made a small, nervous movement, clasping the sheeting more tightly over her breasts, and he swallowed tightly. The slender arch of her neck, the smooth line of her narrow shoulders, the slim, graceful movement of her arms and hands as they trembled lightly . . .

Rand's eyes moved back to her exquisite face and he took a short breath. His voice was a hoarse whisper as he came to complete realization.

"God, Drucker, is that you?" There was no response except the last resounding of his own voice in the silence of the room.

Drucker . . . A woman! Suddenly, it was all so clear: the reason for his sense of disquiet since Drucker had arrived in camp; the peculiar sense of awareness that jangled his subconscious whenever Drucker was near; his preoccupation with Drucker; his inability to separate himself from Drucker's problems; the strong protective instinct that nagged at him, causing him to seek Drucker's figure out amongst the herd time and again.

The brave, hotheaded, determined kid who had torn him up inside was a woman, a woman whose femininity had called out to him from the first, tortured him with its silent, siren call. A warm beat began to flood through Rand's veins and a long ignored joy came slowly to life inside him.

"I knew . . . it had to be . . . the way I felt . . . I knew. . . ."

Reacting spontaneously to the sound of a step in the hallway, Rand reached back and pushed the door shut behind him. The sound of the clicking lock registered in the back of his mind as he noticed for the first time that Billie was swaying weakly.

In a quick, spontaneous movement Rand moved forward, his arms encircling her, supporting her with his strength. He pulled her closer. The slender, damp length of her body was strained against his. She felt so sweet . . . so good in his arms. It was true. This was Drucker . . . the true Drucker . . . the one he had sensed beneath the surface, the one who had drawn him closer to her each day, the one who had confused and possessed his mind. He pulled her closer still, his one palm moving caressingly over her straight, smooth back while his other hand tangled in the moist curls at the base of her neck. His heart was pounding. Elation swept his mind. He lifted her to the floor. Somehow he had known this was how it would be.

Drucker looked up, but the dark-eyed gaze he had come to know so well was strangely remote. The pleasantly tangy scent of her breath reached his nostrils and his eyes jerked to the well-sampled bottle and glass on the table beside the tub. Oh, no. . . .

Rand's eyes flicked momentarily shut and he took a firm hold on his patience. A smile filled with irony curved his lips as he looked down into Drucker's eyes. His voice was an exasperated whisper.

"Drucker, you're drunk."

160

Billie lifted her chin and strained to focus her wavering gaze on the handsome face so close to hers. It was Rand Pierce . . . the same Rand she had seen kissing that redheaded woman. The memory revived the deadening ache she had been so successful in relieving only a short time before, and she felt again the heat of tears under her heavy lids. But Rand's brilliant blue eyes were moving warmly over her face. His lips were tantalizingly near. The hard lines of his face were relaxed into the strangest smile. . . . He was laughing at her!

Raising her chin, Billie attempted to shake her head in refutation of his insultingly incorrect observation, but the room reeled unexpectedly, forcing her to cling to the strong arms supporting her. Her narrow brows drawing together in annoyance, she took a deep, steadying breath.

"I am *not* drunk."

Rand's face drew closer. His smiling lips brushed hers, and he breathed a low sigh.

"Drucker, why did you do this to me? You had me tied up in knots inside. I was running around in circles, not knowing why I felt the way I did when I looked at you . . . why I could think of nothing else but you. I couldn't understand why I wanted you near me, why I wanted to take care of you, keep you safe. I've waited so damned long to find the real you. And now you're here in my arms at last, so beautiful that you make me ache . . . and you're drunk. . . ."

"I am *not* drunk."

"Oh, yes you are, darling." A deep tenderness suffusing him, Rand pressed another light kiss against her lips. The sweet taste of her mouth called for more, and he tore his lips from hers with a low curse. Keenly aware that he was trembling, Rand scooped Billie up against his chest. His voice was husky with the myriad emotions assaulting him. "You're beautiful, you're soaking wet, and you're drunk."

Taking her the few steps to the bed, Rand carefully stood Billie on her feet. He swallowed hard as she raised her face to his. Her sweet, womanly perfection, revealed so openly to him for the first time, played havoc with his senses.

Billie managed a short shake of her head, an apparent

effort to clear her mind. The slight slur to her voice and her obvious confusion brought to stirring life all the deep, protective instincts he had previously sought to suppress.

"I—I told you when you knocked that I couldn't come to the door . . . to go away . . . please. . . ."

"But I didn't, did I, darling? I came in and found you." Raising his hand, Rand trailed his fingertips along the rise of her cheek, across her warm, soft lips. He wanted so desperately to taste them again, to . . .

Abruptly dropping his hand to his side, Rand took a firm hold on his emotions. "You're going to rest for a little while, Drucker, darling. You're going to sleep off that brandy you've been drinking. And then we're going to talk."

"I don't want to talk."

Reaching over, Rand pulled the light coverlet from the bed. Taking the ends of the saturated sheet from her hands unexpectedly, he released them and allowed the sheet to drop to the floor. Her startled gasp echoed in the room at almost the same moment he slid the coverlet around her and enclosed her in its dry confines. Desire warred with his failing resolution at the memory of her sweet, womanly perfection. How could he have been so blind?

Ignoring Billie's ineffective protests, Rand lifted her into his arms again and lay her on the bed. The temptation too much for him to withstand, he covered her parted lips with his own, warmly, briefly.

"Now go to sleep. . . ."

"I—I can't sleep now. I have to go back to the herd. . . ."

"Sleep. I'll wake you in plenty of time."

"But—"

"Go to sleep, Drucker." Lifting a hand that trembled revealingly, Rand stroked the smooth skin of her cheek. Her eyelids were growing heavier, and in a last futile effort at protest, Billie attempted to speak. But her words were muffled by the warmth of Rand's kiss.

Within minutes she was breathing deeply, rhythmically.

Still disbelieving the events of the past few minutes, Rand straightened up, his eyes moving over Billie's inert figure. Without another sound, he turned toward the table a few steps away. He reached for the bottle and glass with a trembling hand. Oh, yes, he needed a drink. He needed it badly.

Abruptly aware that his glass was again empty, Rand reached for the bottle on the night table. Only an inch or so of the golden amber liquid remained at the bottom, and his brow moved into a startled frown. He couldn't have drunk all that, could he? He didn't even like brandy. He replaced the bottle on the stand and put the glass beside it. He had had enough. But he had to admit brandy was effective against what had ailed him. About three—or was it four—drinks ago, his supreme agitation had lessened. He was now able to look at Drucker with a little more objectivity.

An hour had passed and she was still sleeping. He was going to have to awaken her soon if he was going to get any answers before he had to return to the herd. But a few minutes before he had decided to wait just a little longer. He had spent the past half hour lying beside her, propped on his elbow, his hand supporting his head as he sipped his brandy and looked down into her sleeping face. He didn't think he'd ever get tired of looking at her.

Drucker . . . his lovely Drucker. How could he have been such a fool? Careful lest he disturb her, Rand touched the gleaming tendrils that edged her face, marvelling at their glow. He had never seen hair such a pale, shimmering color. It was almost the color of moonlight. And it was obvious she had cut it hurriedly to effect her disguise. But the harsh, ragged edge had softened under the effects of her bath and the swirling locks now framed her face in a pale, silky cloud. The effect was breathtaking.

Rand trailed his gaze warmly over Billie's face, again noting the long, spiky lashes that lay against her cheek, jutting out from the dark, stubbly fringe that rimmed her lids. It had taken him a few minutes to realize the reason for their uneven length. Drucker had obviously cut her lashes at the same time she had cut her hair.

Frowning at the fear that could push her to such drastic

lengths, Rand recalled to mind his first sight of the extremely disfigured youth who had turned out to be the woman lying beside him. Those beautiful eyes had been badly bruised, one puffed shut. Her face had been so swollen that it had been impossible to make out her features. Rand looked down at the fine line of Drucker's lips, his stomach tightening at the memory of the painful struggle he had witnessed as she had attempted to get food past their cut and bruised surface. Trailing his finger down her smooth cheek, Rand followed the pale line, which was all that remained of the ragged cut that had extended from the corner of her eye almost to her chin. Who had done that to her? Whoever it was, the first thing he was going to do when Drucker awakened was to tell her that she didn't have to be afraid anymore. He would take care of her.

Spontaneously, without his realization, Rand caressed the smooth white shoulder peeking out from the blanket that covered her. He slid his hand underneath the blanket to smooth the bare flesh of her back and curved her against him. He closed his eyes against the wealth of feelings assailing him. The sweet fragrance of Drucker's skin rose up into his nostrils and Rand pulled her closer still. God, how he loved holding her in his arms. He had not realized such a simple act could stir so much emotion inside him.

Releasing her just enough so he might again look into her face, Rand smiled. Brandy was an effective sedative. Drucker was barely stirring, her lips moving in a softly mumbled word of protest against his invasion of her nether world of sleep. He kissed her lips into stillness. His mouth was moving warmly against hers, savoring its sweetness, when her lips parted in a soft sigh. The unconscious invitation too much for him to ignore, Rand slipped his tongue into the sweet hollows of her mouth, gently tasting its honeyed depths.

Tormented by the supreme beauty his lovely Drucker had awakened within him, Rand covered her face with light butterfly kisses, his lips caressing her fluttering eyelids, the exquisite planes of her face. Trailing his lips to her ear, he whispered soft words of love between intermittent kisses, fondling the soft lobe lovingly with his tongue before trailing his ardent attentions down the slender column of her throat.

Drucker turned in her semiconscious state, unconsciously accommodating the line of his caresses, and Rand's heart thundered in wild acceleration. The light coverlet had loosened to reveal a small, rounded breast, and a deep tenderness overwhelmed him. Slowly lowering his head, Rand trailed his lips across the delicate swell, worshipping the tender flesh before finally covering the pink, virginal crest with his mouth.

The low gasp that escaped Drucker's lips snapped Rand's gaze up to her startled expression. Drucker stared at him. A raging panic suddenly coming alive in eyes that did not seem clearly focused, she pushed and shoved at his broad shoulders, twisting and turning in a wild attempt to break free. She was beating at his shoulders and face, kicking and fighting, her eyes growing wilder with each passing second. Unable to do anything else in the face of the hysteria that had abruptly gained control of Drucker's senses, Rand moved to cover her squirming body with his, efficiently taking control as he caught her flailing hands at the wrist and pinned them above her head with one hand.

She was shuddering violently under him even as he sought to allay her fears with soft words of reassurance. Her breasts rose and fell in deep, agitated breaths. Tears streamed down her face as she whimpered broken, frightened pleas clearly connected to another time and place, the horror of which had again seized her mind. Her struggles began anew as she fought to escape the hand he raised to stroke her cheek. Her body jumped with a start as he caught her chin securely at last, forcing her to meet his eyes. Holding her gaze, Rand flinched at the fear he saw reflected in there. His voice was a low whispered plea.

"Drucker, don't be afraid of me. I won't hurt you. I'd never hurt you."

Her eyes were wide, still not seeming to see him clearly. Her heart was pounding wildly against her chest. Her voice was a breathless whisper.

"Let—let me go."

Her fear shaking him more than he dared to admit, Rand was momentarily unable to speak. He dared not allow himself to think of the remembered horror that could inspire such fear in her valiant heart. Gently stroking her cheek with his fingertips, Rand found his voice at last.

"Drucker, please listen to me. I didn't mean to scare you. I don't want to frighten you. I want to love you, Drucker. I want to love you. . . ."

Lowering his mouth slowly, Rand brushed Drucker's trembling lips with his. Her body went rigid under his touch and a new fear rose within him. Her eyes were wide, obsidian pools, dark with the terror that overwhelmed her mind. Her words were stiff and halting, her voice so ragged that he was almost uncertain of the words she spoke.

"Let—let me go. McCulla . . . bastard . . . I'll kill you again. . . ."

"Drucker. . . ."

She was completely still beneath him and Rand began to feel a new, more overwhelming anxiety. Her breathing had gone suddenly shallow, her face pale. Her eyes were dropping closed when he abruptly released her wrists and slid from her body. Quickly wrapping the blanket tighter around her, he pulled himself to a seated position on the side of the bed and reached to the night table to pour a healthy measure of brandy into the glass. Sliding his one arm beneath her back, he raised her in his arms and held the glass to her lips.

"Drucker, drink. Come on, drink. This will make you feel better."

All trace of color had left her face. There was no response to Rand's urgent whisper. Panic raged unchecked inside him in the moment before Drucker's eyelids fluttered and began to rise. Swallowing against his fear, Rand urged again quietly, "Come on, Drucker, just a little sip. You'll feel better."

The still, colorless lips twitched and then parted, and Rand tilted the glass. The first swallow difficult, Drucker took another sip. At his urging she took another and Rand began to feel the first glimmer of hope. A flush of color rose in her cheeks and Rand felt a deep relief surge through him. Drucker's eyes slowly lifted to his. Recognition dawned in their depths and a joy that was close to delirium swept Rand's senses.

"Drucker, tell me you're all right. . . ."

The sweet taste of brandy was in her mouth as Billie shook the last remnant of terror from her mind. She swallowed the burning liquid gratefully, her mind registering an encouraging voice that urged her to drink again. She took another sip, and then another, her breath coming more freely as the healing warmth slid down her throat to overwhelm the frightening rigidity that had assailed her.

McCulla was dead. . . . She knew he was dead. It had been a frightening dream that had returned him to her room to lean over her bed once again, to imprison her with the weight of his body. She allowed her eyes to open slowly. She need have no fear. Gentle hands touched her now. The voice that whispered in her ear was filled with concern, pleading with her. Her slitted gaze touched first on full lips and then a strong, familiar chin. Her eyes slowly rose to brilliant blue eyes filled with emotion, and she made an attempt to speak.

Rand's deep, affected voice filled the void.

"Drucker, tell me you're all right. . . ."

The pain in his voice almost too much to bear, Billie whispered hoarsely, "I'm—I'm all right."

Billie's eyes moved confusedly around the room, touching first on the abandoned tub, and memory stirred in her mind. She remembered the unexpected knock on the door while she bathed, and Rand's voice. She remembered her ineffectual effort to rise from the tub as the pounding increased. She remembered struggling to her feet, wrapping the sheet around her just as the door slammed open and Rand appeared in the opening. She remembered his face . . . the look in his eyes. . . . That look was with him still.

But memory faded, returning in broken fragments Rand's smile as he carried her to the bed. She glanced down,

167

suddenly flushing at the realization that she was naked beneath the blanket in which she was wrapped.

Her heart beginning a new pounding, she remembered awakening with the weight of Wes McCulla's body pinning her against the bed. His lips were against her body, and she was screaming, fighting to be free of him. . . .

"Drucker, what's wrong? Are you feeling sick again? Drucker. . . ."

Snapping herself from the fear that had again begun to inundate her mind, she returned her gaze to Rand's face where he sat on the side of the bed. The emotion reflected there stimulated an unexpected surge of warmth inside her. Inexplicably, she raised her hand to touch Rand's cheek.

"I'm all right."

Turning his face unexpectedly, Rand held her hand against his lips, his eyes dropping momentarily closed as he pressed a kiss against her palm.

"Oh, God, Drucker. It took me so long to find you, and then I thought I had lost you again. . . ."

In a swift, facile movement, Rand lifted Billie onto his lap. His arms wrapping tightly around her, he rocked her gently. His words were a soft emotion-filled chant against the pale silk of her hair.

"You don't have to be afraid anymore, Drucker. I'll take care of you. . . . I'll take such good care of you. . . ."

Relaxing completely in his embrace, Billie felt the warm touch of Rand's lips against her hair, his breath against her skin. His hands moved warmly against her back, holding her, caressing her. She felt his touch against her flesh, gentle, reassuring.

His lips touched her fluttering lids, her cheek, the bridge of her nose. He circled her mouth with light, fleeting kisses. She raised her face and he took her lips eagerly. His kiss deepened, overwhelming her, stealing her breath, making her heart race as he invaded the moist hollows with his tongue, seeking, drawing, caressing. Her mouth was his and he indulged himself freely, abandoning it at last to trail light, feathering kisses against her neck and the smooth curve of her shoulder.

168

Her heart pounding in her breast, Billie felt the softness of the bed once again against her back. The blanket slipped from her shoulders, exposing the rounded swells of her breasts to Rand's eyes, his touch, and her heart began pounding anew. His warmth moved to cover her, but his gentle caresses stilled. Her eyes snapped up to his startling expression of concern as he cupped her face gently in his hands.

"Drucker, darling, tell me who you see."

Not quite comprehending his question, Billie shook her head. "I—I see you, Rand Pierce. . . ."

His fingers splaying, stretching into the pale silk of her hair, he pressed his mouth warmly against hers. Drawing away at last, he insisted breathlessly, "Tell me who's kissing you, Drucker."

When she hesitated, thinking his unexpected demand a joke, he grated tightly, "Tell me, Drucker. Tell me whom you see."

"Rand . . . I see you . . . Rand Pierce. . . ."

"Yes, Rand. . . . And it's Rand who's going to love you, darling. I wanted there to be no confusion in your mind."

Ignoring her questioning glance, Rand gathered her tight against him. His mouth covered hers, renewing his total conquest of a few minutes before. His hands moved gently, intimately against her body, stroking, caressing, eliciting a full range of unfamiliar, stirring emotions. His gentle mouth followed suit, caressing the trail his hands had warmed so effectively only moments before.

The blanket no longer afforded her even partial shielding, but Billie did not miss its protective warmth. Rand was there, covering her, protecting her, holding at bay the ragged fear that still hovered at the fringes of memory. The tender touch of his hands, the heady warmth of his lips, lifted her high into another sphere where only brilliant, glowing sensation prevailed. There was no fear, there was no pain, only a world where beauty and brilliant, translucent, undulating colors assaulted her mind.

She was lost to his touch as Rand's mouth followed the curve of her breast, kissing, fondling, teasing her flesh. She was breathless with a keen, unknown desire, clutching him tight against her as his mouth closed over the aching crest. She was gasping, writhing in the throes of an unknown ecstasy that drew her deep, deeper into its thrall.

She was still gasping within its grasp when Rand moved to cover her body with his. She could feel the shaft of his passion firm against her as his hands moved to cup her face.

"Look at me, Drucker. I want to be certain you know . . . you see who's possessing you."

Waiting only until her gaze touched his, Rand lifted himself, his manhood moving against her softness for a brief second before he plunged deep and clean within her. Her body arching at the unexpected pain of his entry, Billie gasped, her nails digging into his shoulders even as Rand looked up into her face in startled disbelief.

"Oh, God, Drucker, I didn't know . . ."

The brilliant blue of Rand's eyes held hers for the briefest second. The multitude of emotions reflected there registered in the recesses of her mind as he began his first, tentative thrusts. Sensing his restraint, feeling the power he held in tenuous control, Billie ran her hands across the bared breadth of Rand's shoulders. Her breath caught in her throat as his strong body took up a slowly escalating rhythm. Sliding her arms around his neck, Billie abandoned herself to the warmth that began to pervade her mind, the spontaneous urgings of her body as she rose to meet and join his deepening penetrations. There was no time for thought as the glowing ecstasy assumed control, claiming her as completely as the strong arms that held her, clasping her closer still until they rose to career high into a bright, kaleidoscopic world, soaring limitlessly, breathlessly, on the wings of total reward.

The dimly lit room was filled with a breathless silence when Rand raised his eyes to hers at last. The concern in his gaze touched a warmth deep inside her as he whispered against her lips.

"Drucker . . . are you all right, darling?"

His hand was caressing her cheek, his eyes consuming her

with a look so intense that she was momentarily unable to respond.

"Drucker. . . ."

"I'm all right."

A relieved smile moving across his lips, Rand lowered his mouth to hers in a tender kiss. Drawing himself back with a reluctance reflected in the tightening planes of his handsome face, Rand suddenly slid his arms around her. His embrace was both gentle and fierce in an abrupt display of emotion as he clutched her close.

"No one will ever hurt you again, Drucker . . . not ever again. . . ."

Lucille's eyes moved to the clock on the scarred dresser, her mind registering her complete disgust with the fact that another hour had passed and she was still unable to fall asleep. Sleep! Was that the reason she had come all the way to this godforsaken cow town? Was that the reason she was now ensconced in a shabby room in an even shabbier hotel, where the ceaseless revelry on the street outside her window made any degree of rest impossible? Was that the reason she had endured the dubious protection and the supreme agony of Mr. Wallace "Pat" Patterson's company? For sleep?

Raging against the supreme injustice of her situation, Lucille jerked herself into a sitting position in bed and darted another look at the offending clock. And damn, what was she doing here, lying in her lonely bed, chastised like an errant child, when this was the last place in the world she wanted to be? What had come over her to give in, even momentarily, to Pat Patterson's harangue?

Drawing herself to her feet, Lucille paced the limited distance between the dresser and the bed, stopping to assess her appearance in the washstand mirror as she passed. Oh, yes, she looked too good, even in this unspectacular garment, to be sleeping alone this night. She had so much to offer Rand. She had been waiting so long to see him, to be held in his arms.

Lucille darted another look at the clock on the dresser. Her gaze remained unseeingly on its face. Half past the hour of eleven . . . The night had barely begun, and she would no longer play the fool in her solitary room. She was suddenly at a loss to understand why she had remained here so long. Surely, she had not been affected by the warning in Pat's pale green eyes when he had escorted her to her door, nor had she been intimidated by his tone. He was nothing to her, and when they returned home, he would not even have the sanction of her father to back him up.

The picture of the young banker's face returned to haunt her mind, and Lucille gave her head an angry shake. A few hours ago she had come to terms with the fact that she had been wrong about Pat Patterson. He was anything but the man she had thought him to be on first impression. Medium height, mediocre looks, weak personality . . . and totally uninteresting. She could not have been more wrong. The only thing that had not changed in her original estimation was the fact that Pat Patterson was of medium height. But even that height could be threatening to an individual such as she who stood only an inch or so past the mark of five feet, especially when that person of medium height was truly enraged. And enraged Pat had been.

A new heat rising to her face just in memory, Lucille fought total recall of the argument that had arisen after Rand had taken his leave. The arrogant Mr. Patterson had retained his patience until she had arisen from the table for the third time in an attempt to pursue Rand. Then his control had snapped. She could still feel his steely grip on her shoulder, could still see the light of fury that had lit his pale eyes as he had gritted through clenched teeth, "Lucille Bascombe, you spoiled little bitch, you will *not* trail after Rand Pierce like a lovesick whore! Can't you understand? he wants no part of you! What sane, reasonable man *would* want anything to do with a conceited little snob who's concerned only with herself? Don't you realize that your beauty means nothing in the face of your totally obnoxious attitude and behavior?"

She had protested, but he had continued his soft-spoken

tirade, his pale eyes pinning her at the table in the hotel dining room until he had finished with, "Face it squarely, Lucille. You've lost Randall Pierce. You'll just have to find some other poor fellow to set your sights on. But let me give you fair warning. If he's a man of any worth at all, you'll have to change your ways. Otherwise he'll give you no more than a vigorous romp in bed and a quick pat on the backside when he says good-bye."

With that he had jerked her unceremoniously to her feet and pointed her in the direction of the door. He had not let her out of his sight until she had entered her room and locked the door behind her, and she had been pouting in the room ever since, much like the frustrated child he had described.

Yes, she most certainly had been wrong. Wallace "Pat" Patterson had anything *but* a weak personality. He was, in fact, the only man who had ever stood up to her. She had even tried a little wheedling on him and it hadn't worked! As for his looks, they weren't actually mediocre. True, he wasn't as outstandingly handsome as Rand. Rather, his serious face was pleasant with small features and an attractive mustache. His pale hair was stylishly cut and shone with cleanliness rather than the oil some men used in place of soap. And for all his modest stature, there was no denying the strength she had felt in his arm when he had ushered her so firmly out the door. And when he smiled—or more often when he was angry—a new man came to life in his face . . . attractive, vital, and most interesting. But damned irritating, too! And she was not going to let him get the best of her. . . . No, indeed!

Her mind suddenly set, Lucille stomped to the wardrobe door. Reaching inside, she pulled out the negligee she had hung there two days before with brilliant hopes. She'd be damned before she quit without giving it a decent try!

Slipping the modest gown she wore to the floor, Lucille removed the enticing garment from the hanger and raised it carefully over her head. She dropped it onto her shoulders and slipped her arms through the delicate straps that held up the sheer lace bodice. Carefully taking the matching wrapper and dropping it on the bed as she passed, she walked to the washstand mirror and faced her own image.

Well, that was more like it! Yes, the Chantilly lace bodice in a natural shade of ecru was the perfect touch, lined only enough to afford some support to her generous breasts without concealing the outline of their appealing fullness. The rest of the garment was in a pink satin that clung tenaciously to her body like a second skin. It emphasized the delicate proportions of her slender rib cage and waist, while displaying to distinct advantage the rounded curve of her hips and the delicate hollows beneath. The skirt of the garment was an absolute masterpiece, with long inserts of Chantilly lace strategically placed and sewn upward from the hem to reveal the slender length of her legs and a glimpse of the shadowed nest between.

Taking a brush to the brilliant length of curls spilling down over her shoulders, Lucille stroked the fiery strands until they gleamed. Turning, she took the wrapper from the bed and slipped it over her shoulders. She made a small grimace. It was lovely, but the fine lace sleeves that billowed to her wrists covered too much skin, and the lace bodice did not dip deeply enough into the bosom to be truly effective. Oh, she supposed it would do. Once she was in Rand's room, she would not have it on long enough for it to truly matter after all.

Pausing to slide her feet into the high-heeled satin slippers beside her bed, Lucille gave herself a last appraising look. Oh yes, Rand would not be able to resist her.

Turning, Lucille walked firmly toward the door to her room, stealth overcoming her actions as she cautiously turned the key in the lock. Slowly, with great deliberation, she twisted the doorknob and drew it open. Rand was in room number thirteen, only a few short steps down the hall. She had made certain to ascertain that small detail when Pat had allowed her a moment to herself while he had arranged for their table that night.

Slowly drawing open the door, Lucille leaned over and cast a wary glance into the hallway. It was empty. Now if it would only stay empty until she could rouse Rand. Taking the precaution to cast a quick glance in the direction of

174

Pat's room, Lucille felt a deep stab of satisfaction at the fact that there was no light coming from beneath the door. Her jailer obviously was asleep.

With extreme caution, Lucille stepped into the hallway and pulled the door shut behind her. Darting another glance up and down its narrow expanse, she walked the short distance to Rand's door in hurried steps. She had raised her hand to knock when the sound of footsteps on the staircase snapped her attention in its direction. The sound of hearty male laughter and a brittle feminine shriek froze her in her tracks. Her eyes wide with horrified anticipation at being caught in the hallway in her rather revealing costume, she listened as an annoyed voice called from the first floor. A short, angry exchange followed, resulting in the retreat of the heavy footsteps and several truly common words in comment in that same shrill feminine voice.

Releasing a deep sigh of relief as light footsteps followed the heavier ones back down the steps, Lucille turned again toward the door in front of her. Taking a moment to smooth her hand against the tresses that she was certain had truly stood momentarily on end, she raised her hand to knock when a deep voice sounded angrily in her ear.

"What're you doing out here in the hall, Lucille?"

Jumping with a start, Lucille snapped her eyes to her rear. Catching and holding the gaze of glaring green eyes, Lucille exploded angrily, "What are *you* doing out here, *Mr.* Patterson? You have all but scared me out of my wits with your damned sneaking up behind me!"

"If you weren't such a damned persistent little witch, I wouldn't find it necessary to sneak up behind you! And I take back my question." His eyes swept her attire in open deprecation. "It's only too obvious what you're doing here." Taking a deep breath and an obvious grip on his temper, Pat continued quietly, "It's just unfortunate Rand won't get the opportunity to see how lovely you've dressed . . . or should I say *undressed* yourself for him."

"Ohhhh, you beast!" Her well-manicured hands curling into talons as she stared into Pat's unyielding face, Lucille hissed venomously, "And what makes you think *you're*

175

going to stop me from talking to Rand if I wish?"

"Lucille, only a fool would conclude that you want to talk if you appeared at his door in that getup. Rand's no fool, and neither am I. So you're going back to your room like a good girl. . . ."

"Oh, no I'm not! I'm going to knock on this door, and when Rand answers, I'm going inside and you're not going to stop me!"

"I wouldn't suggest you try, Lucy. . . ."

"Lucy! That does it!"

Incensed, Lucille turned to the door. Her hand was just descending to its hard surface when she was suddenly jerked from her feet at one fell swoop and tossed over a surprisingly broad shoulder. Before she realized what was happening, she was bobbing down the hall toward her room, the world turned more upside down than she cared to believe. Within minutes, the inverted interior of her room met her vision. The sound of the door closing behind them the signal to turn her world right side up, Lucille was suddenly plopped on her feet to confront a stiff-faced Pat Patterson.

"Lucy, I'm warning you, if you try to get into Rand Pierce's room again—"

The reiteration of the nickname she despised the final straw, Lucille uttered a low, angry growl. Raising her hand, she swung with all her might, hitting Pat's cheek with a resounding crack.

His face flushing a color that almost matched the mark of her hand on his cheek, Pat muttered from between clenched teeth, "You're going to be sorry you did that, Lucy. You've gone too far, and this time you're going to get what you should've gotten years ago."

Moving so quickly that she was taken by surprise, Pat grasped Lucille's arms firmly, holding her immobile as he sat on the edge of the bed and flipped her bottom up across his lap. His hand descended, making contact with her delicately rounded derriere in a loud crack that shook the silence of the room. Before she could recover from the shock, his hand descended again and again in rapid, repeated strokes, and Lucille shrieked with indignity. Her hands beating at his legs

176

and arms in a frantic effort to break free, she was helpless against his superior strength. She was sobbing with fury as her eyes snapped wide with the final indignity of being dumped casually on the floor as Pat resumed his feet.

Fully aware that her hair was hanging in her eyes like a common kitchen maid, that her face was blotched from crying, and that her posture suffered from the painful throbbing that still heated her posterior portion as she drew herself to her feet, Lucille clenched her hands into a tight fist and made ready to swing. But the steely glint in the green eyes boring into hers froze her arm in the air.

"I wouldn't, Lucy. . . ."

Her hand was beginning to shake, and Lucille finally dropped it to her side. A deep sob inadvertently escaped her lips, and to Lucille's final humiliation she was suddenly sobbing uncontrollably, her body heaving in deep, shaking breaths that she was unable to control.

Unwilling to allow him his moment of triumph, Lucille jerked away from Pat's unyielding scrutiny, her face flaming even as she stuttered through her tears. "Get—get out of here, Pat Patterson! N—now . . . out! I don't want to see your face or—or hear your voice again. You're a beast . . . a violent beast who—"

But she did not have the opportunity to complete her halting harangue as she was suddenly turned and drawn against a hard, firm chest. Gentle arms held her close as a voice entirely void of the anger of moments before whispered in her ear.

"Don't cry, Lucy. I wasn't trying to make you cry. I just wanted to show you . . . to let you know. . . . Oh, damn, look at me!"

Pat looked down into the spotty, miserable face of the woman still sobbing in his arms and a flicker moved across his unsmiling expression. "Would you believe that beating hurt me more than it hurt you, Lucy?"

His question was met with a flicker of disbelief in the reddened eyes looking into his, and a spontaneously clutching of an aching backside. Lucille's sobs had subsided into deep hiccups that continued to shake her small frame.

Pat shook his head.

"All right, maybe it didn't, but I sure as hell know I don't feel as good as you think I do right now. As a matter of fact I feel—"

Unexpectedly lowering his head, Pat covered Lucille's trembling lips with his own, his hands slipping around her and tangling in her hair as his kiss deepened.

Abruptly coming to life under his hands, Lucille jerked herself free. Her reddened eyes narrowed into little slits, she spat furiously, "Is—is this your way of proving complete domination over me, *Mr.* Patterson? Well, if it is, it's not going to work! You're still a sneak, a bastard, and a beast, and I want you out of here right now!"

"Lucy. . . ."

"And my name is *Lucille,* damn it! *Lucille!*"

A strangely victorious feeling beginning to flood her senses at the tightening of Pat's small features, Lucille lifted a slender, trembling arm and pointed rigidly to the door.

"Out!"

His face flaming, Pat turned on his heel. But it was not before the flush of color that had rushed to his face had served to revive Lucille's lagging spirits almost to the point of delirium. The sound of the slamming door reverberated in her room, bringing a triumphant smile to her lips. So, he thought he had won out over her, did he? Well, she had just had the last word! She would always have the last word on Mr. Wallace "Pat" Patterson, or she'd die in the attempt!

Lifting her chin, her spirits considerably revived, Lucille stomped to the washstand. A low groan of disgust escaped her lips as she viewed herself in the mirror. She was a mess! How could she face Rand tomorrow with her delicate complexion all spotted from that foolish bout of crying? Oh, damn . . . damn!

Striding through the doorway of his room in a quick, angry step, Pat slammed the door behind him without a thought to the other sleeping guests.

Damn her, the little witch! She had to push him to the

limit, force him to drastic measures. He hadn't wanted to hurt her, to make her cry. But that spanking he had given her had been long overdue.

The thought giving him little consolation, Pat walked to the bed he had vacated with such haste at the sound of Lucille's closing door only a few minutes before. The memory of Lucille standing in front of Rand Pierce's room returned, and a new flush suffused his face.

Damn her. . . . Why couldn't she get it through her beautiful head that Rand wanted no part of her, that she'd be better off devoting herself to someone who really wanted her like—like—

The dawn of realization hit him a shattering blow. Taking two staggering steps toward the bed, Pat sat himself down with a thump. Oh, Lord, not like himself!

His startled green eyes stared blankly into space. No, he couldn't be that stupid. . . . He couldn't! Lucille Bascombe despised him. She hated the ground on which he walked. And, in addition to that, she thought herself above him in every way. Lucille Bascombe was a conceited, arrogant little snob who had set her mind on one man, Rand Pierce. She was also intelligent, quick-witted, possessed of more spirit than was actually wise, and the loveliest, most desirable woman he had ever met. And where did that leave him?

The memory of Lucille standing before Rand Pierce's door again returned to his mind, and his body flushed with a new, jealous heat. In a sudden flash of candor, Pat knew. It left him with the unenviable job of convincing that fiery little virago that *he,* not Rand Pierce, was the man for her. It was a fact of which he was abruptly very, very sure. The problem would be in convincing Lucille.

Pat took a deep, steadying breath. Oh, Lord, what had he done? . . .

The sound of a slamming door down the corridor echoed in the silence of the darkened room. Raising his head to peek into the small face that rested against his chest, Rand saw that Billie still slept undisturbed, and an aching tenderness

179

stirred inside him. He pulled her closer, his hand reaching up to caress her pale, silken locks.

A small smile flickered across his lips. Lucille's annoyed murmurs in the hall had been unmistakable, as had been Pat Patterson's heated replies. Then the scuffle and Lucille's sputtering protests as her voice had retreated down the hallway. He had the idea her retreat from his door had not been voluntary. The slamming of another door a few minutes later had only served to reinforce that conviction.

He also had a feeling Pat would keep Lucille out of his way for the remainder of his time in Abilene. He couldn't thank him more. There was only one woman who filled his mind now. It occurred to him he wasn't even sure who she was, but that mattered very little. She was lying in his arms now, and tomorrow she would tell him everything he wanted to know.

Lifting his head, Rand touched his lips to the pulse beating against the almost transparent skin of Drucker's temple. She was here in his arms and that was where she was going to stay. He'd see to that. . . . Oh, yes, he would.

Who was that, the shadow just disappearing behind the barn? Annoyance creasing her brow, Billie hastened her step, finally breaking into a run as a peculiar feeling of apprehension crawled up her spine. She had seen that particular shadow before, always turning out of sight, beyond her range of vision. She ran faster. Her apprehension turned into panic as she rounded the corner in time to see the figure disappear behind the trees in the nearby field. Again . . . he would not get away from her again!

She increased her speed, her booted feet barely touching the ground as she flew over the rutted yard. She could see him. . . . She could see his shadow again. He had stopped running to look back at her and she felt a flash of triumph as his hesitation gave her the advantage she sought. She was gaining on him, getting close enough to make out his image. He was . . . he was . . .

A quick jerk of pain snapped her eyes downward toward the gnarled root that had snared her, tumbling her head over heels. Over and over she rolled, the world spinning crazily around her in the second before her head crashed against the ground in a jarring halt.

She was momentarily numb, unable to move. Breathless, she raised her throbbing head, only to see the shadow was unmoving. He was close . . . so close. The sun beyond the darkened grove held his outline in dark relief, and she squinted, trying desperately to identify his face.

"Wait . . . please, wait. . . ."

He hesitated, and suddenly snapped into motion. He was running again.

She dragged herself to her feet, the pounding in her head increasing as she attempted in vain to follow him.

"Stop . . . wait, please!"

But he would not. He was drawing away from her, out of her sight. Her sense of loss overwhelming, she fought the deep, heaving sobs that shook her. She cried out once more.

"Please, wait . . . wait. . . ."

"Drucker. . . . Drucker. . . ."

A low, familiar voice penetrated the darkness that was falling around her. She tried to respond but she could not control the sobs that stole her breath. A gentle touch against her cheek, her eyes, her lips, consoled her, and she struggled to awaken.

Brilliant blue eyes met her dazed gaze and Billie experienced a moment of shock as a wide, callused hand caressed her cheek, wiping away her tears. Concern marked his face as Rand whispered against her lips, "It's all right, darling. It's all right."

Her mind suddenly clear, Billie flicked her eyes around the room. The tub . . . the bath sheet dropped conspicuously beside the bed . . . Rand lying beside her . . . What had she done?

Rand's palm was resting against her naked waist, his mouth moving gently against hers. Her eyes suddenly jerked to the window. Dawn . . . it was dawn! Her shift . . . she was late!

Her sudden movement as she attempted to draw herself to her feet took Rand momentarily by surprise. He caught her

181

arm as she threw her feet over the side of the bed.

"Oh, no, you're not going to get away from me that fast."

"Let me go. I'm late . . . late for watch. . . ."

His response was a low, husky laugh. "You don't have to worry about that. The boss won't care if you're late. . . ."

A fierce resentment stiffened Billie's face.

"But *I'll* care. . . ."

His smile fading, Rand returned her gaze in silence. His unyielding grip drew her back against the bed despite her effort to stand, and she was perversely grateful. She was all too conscious of her nakedness. To expose herself completely in the dim light of the room would have been momentarily too much to bear.

"Drucker . . . what's wrong?"

"Nothing . . . nothing's wrong."

"Was it the dream? You were crying. I tried to wake you up, but you were sleeping too deeply."

"It was nothing . . . an old dream."

His knotted brow showed Billie only too clearly what he thought of her response. Unwilling to meet his eye, Billie again looked toward the window. She took a deep breath and made an attempt at a more rational note.

"I—I'd like to get up now. I want to get dressed."

"No."

Billie's eyes snapped to Rand's face. His expression dark, he was the old Rand, formidable, unyielding. But she was more comfortable with him than the gentle, loving Rand she did not know.

"I said I want to get up."

"And I said no. We have to talk, Drucker."

A sudden panic shook Billie's mind. No, she couldn't talk to him now. She knew what that would mean. He wanted to know who she was, why she was running. She couldn't . . . couldn't tell him she had killed a man. . . .

"I don't want to talk. I want to get up."

Rand's frown darkened. He adjusted his position, turning closer. Billie was intensely aware of the fact that Rand's naked hip was pressed against hers, that his broad chest brushed her bare shoulder. She was beginning to tremble, fragments of memory returning the taste of the firm lips so close to hers, their touch against her body. She remembered his heavy, dark hair beneath her palms, the breadth of his shoulders . . .

Panic overwhelming her, Billie attempted to roll from the bed. But Rand had anticipated her reaction. In a quick motion he flipped his broad body over to pin her against the disheveled surface. His warm nakedness pressed against hers more than she could bear, Billie squirmed and twisted in an attempt to break free.

The new hoarseness in his voice as Rand held her helpless beneath him caught Billie's ear, snapping her eyes up to his as he muttered with a small smile, "Drucker, lie still, please. I only wanted to talk to you, but if you keep squirming like that we just might end up doing a bit more than talk."

Their intimate posture left no question as to his meaning, and Billie felt a new flush rising to her face. Her body went rigidly still.

But her rigidity obviously did not please him any more than her attempt to escape. Frowning once more, Rand supported himself above her, sparing her the bulk of his weight. His hand moved to her cheek, his frown darkening as she tensed at his touch.

"You don't want me to touch you, do you?"

"I told you, I just want—"

"Why? What's wrong? Was I too rough? Did I hurt you last night?"

Unable to bear the uncertainty in his gaze, Billie shook her head.

"No—no, you didn't hurt me."

"Then why are you—"

"I don't want to talk about it. I just want to go back to the herd. They'll be waiting for me, wondering where I am."

Incredulity spread slowly across Rand's face.

"You don't really expect me to let you go back to the herd just like nothing happened, do you, Drucker?" He shook his head, mumbling under his breath, "Hell, listen to me. I don't even know if that's really your name." He took a firm breath. "What is your name, Drucker? Where do you come from?

183

What happened to you to make you come looking for a job dressed as a boy?" He hesitated, his voice taking on a quality akin to menace. "And who hurt you?"

"I—I don't know. I told you. I was robbed. Whoever it was dumped me in an alley. I never saw him."

There was a moment's hesitation before Rand responded.

"You don't expect me to believe that, do you, darling?"

His unexpected endearment shaking her more than she dared admit, Billie felt a warm heat flood her eyes. Her first sign of weakness obviously more than he could bear, Rand groaned low in his throat, his arms slipping around to pull her tight against him.

"Drucker, honey, don't pull away from me. You're frightened, and you're having some regrets about last night. But I'm not. . . . And I want to help you, but you have to tell me who you're running away from . . . where you're running to . . . what happened. . . . Don't you see? That's the only way I can help you."

Drawing himself just far enough away from her so he could look into her eyes, Rand swallowed tightly. He was intensely conscious of her slender warmth against his flesh. Her small breasts were brushing his chest, her breath fanning his lips. Her eyes, a damp black velvet, shone into his, and he was breathless against their assault. He lowered his lips toward the soft, appealing mouth so close to his and brushed it softly.

"Drucker, let me help you."

There was no response. He kissed her again. This time his kiss deepened, his arms drawing her closer still. His hand was in her hair, savoring the fragrant silk. His palm was sliding down her side, the soft, naked contours of her body sending a new, more powerful current of emotion through his veins. He drew his mouth from hers, but she made no sound, her eyes a soft, unconscious appeal he could not ignore.

Following her silent urging, he covered her parted lips with his, his kiss deepening, stirring a soft whimper of protest that was smothered by his urgent quest. He was no longer thinking but was following the driving instinct deep

184

inside him.

His . . . Drucker was his. He had claimed her last night, and he was not going to give her up. He would claim her again and again and again, until she no longer denied that she belonged to him.

Lost to his passion, Rand covered her face with kisses, her throat, the warm mounds of her breasts. His hands moved over her slim, naked length, smoothing, caressing, glorying in the beauty that was his, and his alone.

He raised his gaze to Drucker's small, perfect face, his throat tightening at the passion reflected in the flush of her skin, her trembling lips.

"Drucker, I—"

But he could stand no more. His supreme need overwhelming him, Rand shifted his position. With one swift thrust he was deep inside her. Complete possession raised him to new heights of elation as her moist warmth closed around him.

"Oh, God, Drucker. . . ."

His heart too filled to say more, Rand lowered his mouth to hers. Her lips parted to welcome him, her arms slid around his neck to hold him close. His passion too far gone to indulge, Rand tore his lips from hers. Plunging deeply, powerfully, he brought her quickly, efficiently to the edge of her passion, his eyes watching her face as he trembled on a similar brink. Her body was quivering under his, small and vulnerable, his alone, only his. In a quick, loving thrust he sealed his possession, his soft cry at consummation mingling with hers to make them one in the intimate ecstasy they shared.

Still entwined, their bodies were motionless in the early morning silence of the room. Loath to separate from her, Rand lifted his head from the fragrant pillow of Billie's hair. Gently stroking the pale wisps from her cheek, he pressed a light kiss against her lips. Her heavy lids fluttered and slowly lifted to bathe him in a glow of darkly smouldering ebony. He was speechless against the tumult it raised inside him. Rand lowered his head, his mouth sinking deeply and fully into hers to indulge yet another facet of his complete ob-

185

session for the woman in his arms. Drawing himself from her at last, Rand rolled to the bed beside her. He took her small hand in his and raised it to his lips.

"We still need to talk, darling."

Her hand gave a spontaneous jerk, and Rand moved to his side, his eyes looking into hers. He curved his arm around her shoulders, turning her toward him, pulling her flush against his warmth once more. He pressed his lips to her temple, enjoying the steady throbbing of the pulse there. It occurred to him that she had suddenly become necessary to him, as necessary as the lifeblood that pumped through his veins. It was an aching certainty within him, and he was not even sure of her name.

Her voice was soft, her breath warm against his neck.

"Please, I want to get up."

Releasing her without a word, Rand watched as Billie drew herself to her feet, his eyes moving over her slender, naked length as she walked to the washstand. Aware of the soft tinge of embarrassment that colored her skin but unable to withdraw his eyes, he saw her moment of indecision as she turned toward the tub. His gaze so intense that he saw the hackles that rose on her arms as she stepped into the cooled water, Rand followed her movements as she soaped the cloth and moved it against her skin.

His eyes darted momentarily to the window. The light of early morning was now full and bright, and he was aware that the moist heat of spring would soon be overwhelming. Funny, he was oblivious to all and everything when he held Drucker in his arms. Reluctantly, he rose and walked to the washstand, his eyes straying back to Drucker even as he completed his own ablutions.

He had slipped into his trousers and was reaching for his shirt when Billie rose from the tub. Quickly snatching up the bath sheet from the floor, he walked to her side and wrapped it around her. In a quick, facile movement he lifted her from the tub. Realizing he was trembling, Rand took a firm hold on his determination. No, he would not allow his desire to deter him again. He smiled at her frowning protest as he took the few steps to the bed. Standing her briefly on the floor, he sat down abruptly and pulled her onto his lap.

Drucker's lovely face was close to his. Miniscule droplets of water still shone on her clear skin and clung to the ragged length of her lashes. Her lips were parted, her straight, slender brows in a small frown as she directed the full power of her questioning gaze into his eyes.

"Now. We're going to talk now, darling."

Her eyes going suddenly cold, Billie attempted to rise, but his firm hand on her arm stayed her.

"I'm getting your trousers wet."

"If that bothered me, I wouldn't have seated you on my lap."

"But—"

Unable to stand her growing anxiety, Rand curved his hand around the back of Billie's head and drew her mouth to his. Withdrawing reluctantly a few moments later, he said softly, "Drucker, I want there to be more than just this between us. You're shutting me out. Why won't you tell me—"

"You hired me as one of your drovers. That doesn't give you the right to pry into my private life."

"Right now I *am* your private life."

"You're not."

Anger was beginning to heat Rand's emotions.

"You're telling me that last night . . . this morning . . . they mean nothing to you. You forget, Drucker. I know you were a virgin. . . ."

"And I'm not any longer." Steeling herself against the pang her words induced, Billie raised her chin. "That doesn't give you any responsibility toward me . . . or any right to question me."

"It isn't responsibility that I feel."

"I don't intend to satisfy your curiosity. In spite of last night . . . this morning, things will go on as they have before. We—"

"You can't really mean what you're saying!" Agitation and incredulity warred inside Rand. The desire to shake the slender, tempting woman seated so intimately on his knee grew to overwhelming proportions. His hand tightened on her hip in anticipation of attempted flight. "You know I can't allow you to return to the herd . . . to continue on with us."

Unprepared for the jolt that shook her at his words, Rand slid his arms around Billie, his hand rubbing her back. The color had drained from her face and little beads of perspiration were appearing on her upper lip.

"Drucker. . . ."

"What do you mean? You—you were satisfied with my work, I know you were. I worked as hard as any of the men . . . harder than some. I did my job. . . ."

"That isn't the point."

She was trembling, and panic tinged Rand's senses.

"What *is* the point?"

"Drucker, you're a *woman*. You don't belong on a cattle drive with men."

"I've been on drives before and there's never been a problem."

"The other men will be uncomfortable knowing—"

"But they don't know I'm a woman. They don't even suspect."

Rand shook his head. "You don't think I'll allow this masquerade to continue. . . ."

"It's better that way."

"Why?" Drucker was regaining control, and Rand's anger was escalating. "And why should I do anything you ask? You tell me what's happened between us means nothing to you. You refuse to tell me who you really are, what you're running away from. For all I know, you could be a fugitive from justice!"

Billie's eyes turned bitter cold. Her words were short and halting.

"Don't be ridiculous."

Incensed, Rand took Billie's face between his palms, his eyes blue agates that burned into hers.

"If I'm ridiculous, you're the one who made me that way. Talk to me, Drucker, talk to me."

Tears suddenly springing to her eyes, Billie shook her head. "I—I can't. . . ."

His anger fading in the face of her growing distraction,

Rand pressed softly, "Don't you trust me, Drucker? Don't you believe I'll take care of you . . . protect you from whatever you're afraid of?"

"How can you protect me if you leave me behind?"

"You can wait here for me . . . or anywhere else you prefer. I'll write out a draft on the bank."

"I don't want your money."

"What do you want, Drucker? Tell me."

"I want to go on as before. I want to go to Montana with the herd."

"What's in Montana that you're so anxious to reach. Or should I ask *who's* in Montana?" A hot stab of jealousy pierced Rand's vitals as Billie avoided his gaze. He gave her a hard shake. "Who, Drucker?"

"No one!" Billie's dark eyes were suddenly blazing. Still clutching the damp sheet, she struggled to get to her feet. She was squirming and pushing at his chest but his arms wrapped tighter around her, holding her fast. Her breath was coming in deep, heaving gasps, and he was intensely conscious of the warm swells of her breasts through the saturated cloth that separated them. He clamped his legs closed, catching hers in a viselike grip as he held the back of her head in his palm.

"Drucker, stop. . . . Stop this."

"All right . . . All right." Suddenly motionless, Billie raised her chin. Her eyes were hard. "Go back to your herd. I don't need you or it. I can get to Montana by myself. But let me go now, damn you. Let me go!"

Rand stared into the beautiful, enraged face so close to his. No, he didn't want this. He didn't want her anger. He just wanted her. How had he managed to alienate her so completely?

"Drucker, don't you understand? I only want to help you."

"Help me? If you want to help me, you'll let me stay with the drive, just like before. I'll be safe. . . ."

Catching her slip, Rand snapped tightly, "Safe? Safe from what?"

Billie took a deep breath. She released it moments later in a resigned sigh. She was tired.

"Please. I don't want to argue anymore. If you can't let me

stay with the herd, I'll find my own way to—"

"No, damn it. No! You're not going to run away again."

"But you said—"

Rand's mouth tightened. "You can stay with the herd."

Billie regarded him in silence.

"But I'm putting an end to the masquerade. I'm going to tell the men you're a woman."

"No!"

"Yes, damn it!"

Billie shook her head. No, it couldn't work. Word would get around. A woman riding with a trail herd as a drover would cause too much talk, draw too much attention to her. Before she knew it, McCulla would be hot on her trail. She had no doubt Rand would feel obliged to stand up for her if McCulla showed up. No, she couldn't bring the whole situation down on his back just because he felt a responsibility toward her.

"Never mind." Her brief smile was resigned. "Let's just forget the whole thing. I'll find my own way. But—but I would appreciate it if you could pay me today for my time with the herd."

Rand's face went perfectly still. He was so close that she could see the small lines that splayed out from the corners of his eyes, that crinkled so appealingly with his grin. She could see the dark, stubby lashes that lined the azure blue of his eyes, emphasizing their outstanding color. She could see the slashes in mid-cheek, which deepened with the dazzling warmth of his smile. But he wasn't smiling now. A small muscle ticked in his cheek.

"All right. You can come back with the herd just the way you left it, if that's what you want. You win."

Rand's complete reversal took Billie by surprise. No, she didn't want to *win*. She just wanted to get to Montana, and it was suddenly clear that Rand was right. Things had gotten too complicated for her to stay with the drive.

"No, you're right. I think it would be best if I went on alone."

Anger flared in Rand's eyes, and Billie drew back spontaneously, only to feel his grip tighten almost to the point of pain.

"Oh, no, Drucker, you're not going to get away from me that easily. You wanted to go on with the herd just like before. I'm giving you what you want. We'll go back to the herd, together. I'll tell them that you were sick . . . that you couldn't make it back for your shift."

"They won't believe you."

"I don't give a damn if they believe me or not."

Her throat choking unexpectedly with emotion, Billie shook her head.

"No, I don't think—"

The muscle in Rand's cheek ticked in warning, halting her response just as he interrupted tightly, "Look, you want to get to Montana. I'll get you there safe and sound. Are we agreed?"

Hesitating only long enough to consider the unexpected urgency in his expression, Billie nodded.

Loosening his hold, Rand appeared to release his breath as well. Restraining her as she attempted to get to her feet, he pressed quietly, "Will you tell me one thing? Is your name really Drucker?"

The tightness in Billie's throat almost precluded speech.

"My—my name is Billie. That's all I can tell you."

His hand curling gently around her neck, Rand whispered huskily, "Then kiss me, Billie, because I sure as hell want to kiss you."

Rand's mouth was closing over hers. When he took her close in the circle of his arms, all thought of the damp sheet she clutched left her mind. As if of their own will, her arms encircled his neck and she heard his soft groan as her breasts pressed warmly against his chest. And then she heard no more.

Carl Whitey was beginning to sweat. Realizing his discomfort was becoming obvious as a rank odor began to rise from the stained underarms of his shirt, he faced his employer across the familiar desk in his office. Hell, whatever had made him think Dan McCulla would show some gratitude? The damned bastard didn't know the meaning of the word.

"Tell me again, Whitley. What did the old lady in the store say?"

His nose twitching with silent grievance, Carl ran his finger over his ragged mustache.

"I already told you what she said."

"Well, tell me again."

"The old lady said that she hadn't seen no girl like I described to her, but when I mentioned the boy, her eyes lit up. She remembered a boy, all right."

"And she told you . . ."

"She told me the boy was pretty well beat up. And she said he bought a new rope and some chaps."

"So, on the basis of that, you concluded the 'boy' was Billie Winslow and that she joined a trail drive."

"Look, Mr. McCulla. The old lady told me them chaps was way too big for the kid, but the kid was desperate to have them. I'm thinkin' it wasn't just a whim that pushed a kid as beat up as he was to stop and buy them chaps. I'm thinkin' that he was thinkin' he was goin' to have a real need for them. You know the average cowpoke don't even use chaps most of the time. The only thing chaps is good for is for when you're drivin' cattle through thorny brush. You know damned well thorny brush can cut up a man's legs real bad if he can't get out of its way when chasin' some steer. And I'm thinkin' the kid figured he was cut up bad enough already."

Dan McCulla remained silent. Leaning back in his high-backed chair, he kept his pale eyes trained on Carl's face, effectively raising the level of his agitation without a word. Taking McCulla's silence as an invitation to go on, Carl gripped the brim of the abused hat he held respectfully in his hand and continued.

"So me and Marty went to the livery stable. Just about every herd that comes to town stops to stable their horses there, so I figured that'd be the best place to find out just what herds was passin' through at that time."

Carl paused in the vain hope McCulla would comment about his obvious resourcefulness. When no comment was

192

forthcoming, he cleared his throat and returned to his narration.

"Like I said, me and Marty went to the livery stable and spent some time with Bart Ford. Seems like nine trail herds passed by San Antonio around the time the boy was there. They was all from down by the border. Hear tell one of them herds was all long-legged Mexican steers that can run the legs off a good horse. Anyways, Bart said that along with the cattle, them drovers brought some kind of fever back from the border with them. Seems like that fever got them drovers down so bad that the contractor for the herd had to come all the way from St. Louis to take it over himself. Bart said the fella looked to be an ornery kind of cuss for all his good looks and fine clothes."

Noting that impatience was flooding new depth of color into Dan McCulla's already florid face, Carl hastened to continue.

"Anyways, that contractor was lookin' to hire drovers to replace them that got sick."

Carl stopped and grinned into Dan McCulla's face. The abrupt explosion that erupted from McCulla's moist lips was unexpected.

"Well? Don't stop there, damn you! What else did you find out?"

Startled, Carl shook his matted head.

"I didn't find nothin' else out. Bart wasn't sure which one of them herds that contractor fella was connected to, or where it was headin'. So I figured I'd come back here and let you know what I found out."

Slowly drawing his generous bulk to his feet, Dan McCulla leaned forward on his desk, supporting himself on the palms of his hands as he glared into his foreman's perspired face.

"So, you're tellin' me I should send you on a holiday . . . ridin' trail to follow nine trail herds so you can check out the drovers. Of course, while you're at it, you'll make sure to stop in at all the cow towns on the way, just to make sure you don't miss out on any information you might pick up, isn't that right, Whitley? And all this on the vague possibility that this 'boy' you're lookin' for might be Billie Winslow."

Truly indignant, Carl lifted his stubbled chin. His eyes holding a faint glimmer of gumption, he nodded his head. "That's right, Mr. McCulla. To my mind, that's the only way that girl could've disappeared like she did." Taking a deep breath, he continued, "That is, unless she was snatched up into some Mexican crib. Pretty and fair-haired like she was, and ridin' all alone, seems to me she was askin' to get picked up by some randy Mex lookin' for a new addition to his house."

The livid color was beginning to fade from Dan McCulla's face. Drawing himself back, McCulla raised a thoughtful hand to his chin, his eyes never leaving Whitley's face. He hesitated only a minute longer before speaking.

"All right, Whitley, the job is yours. Take Marty and Larry with you, but I'm warnin' you. Don't make a party out of this trip, not if you ever want to work in this portion of the country again." A new light coming into his peculiarly pale eyes, Dan McCulla added tightly, "And if you do find her, you can depend on a real good bonus waitin' for you when you come back."

His spirits taking a quick jump at the promise of reward, Carl nodded his head with unusual vigor.

"You can depend on us, Mr. McCulla. We'll bring that bitch back here. . . ."

"Oh, no you won't, Whitley." A sinister smile moved across McCulla's lips. A thread of menace entered his voice, raising the hair on the back of Carl's neck as he continued slowly, "You'll find out where she is and where she's goin', and then you'll wire me and tell me. That bitch has a reward comin'—a personal one—and I don't want her anywhere around here when she gets it."

Carl nodded. Hell, this was better than he thought. McCulla was goin' to take care of his own dirty work for a change. Yeah, he was goin' to like this.

Carl had just turned toward the door with a satisfied smile when the boom of McCulla's voice stopped him in his tracks.

Turning back, Carl faced McCulla's squinting leer.

"One more thing. Before you come back in this house,

Whitley, you take a bath. *Comprende?*"

Whitley's ragged mustache twitched revealingly.

"Yeah, comprende."

Making as fast an exit as possible, Carl closed the door behind him with tenuous restraint. Jamming his hat back on his head, he turned and stomped down the hall, the sound of low muttered oaths trailing behind him.

Chapter VIII

His eyes trained to the west of the herd, Rand surveyed the uneven terrain. They had crossed the Clear Fork of the Brazos a few days earlier and had entered well-watered, open country. The weather had been exceptionally good. Only a few daytime showers had fallen, but they were nearing country in which rain was more frequent.

Rand ran his eyes over the surface of the rapidly flowing river in the distance. Its swollen condition was an indication of recent rains to the west. He didn't like its looks. They had passed two herds of yearlings in the past two days and had been told that the Brazos had been impassable for a week. They were nearly twenty miles below that point right now, and it was time for a decision.

He could continue on the Old Western trail and camp at the side of the regular crossing. The only problem with that idea was that he had also been advised that several herds were already waiting at that point. Beside the fact that he had no desire for an extended wait, he was well aware that all grazing for several miles around the crossing was already taken up by the water-bound herds, and to trespass on range already occupied was a violation of an unwritten law.

His other alternative was to throw the herd off the trail and head them northeast, hoping they would strike the Brazos a few miles above Round Timber ferry. Once the herd was on the way, he could then ride ahead to locate the ferry for the wagon and hunt up a crossing. And while no herd took kindly to another attempting to pass them when in traveling condition, Rand knew he had lost enough time already.

Rand shook his head. His concentration was poor and his patience was short at best. He grimaced in self-disgust. He had a herd of over three thousand steers to deliver to Montana, and all his judgments since returning from Abilene several days before had been clouded, unclear. The only thing that was clear to him was the reason for his preoccupation.

Turning, Rand surveyed the herd, his eyes settling immediately on the figure he sought. There was no mistaking Billie's slender proportions among the men. Damned if he knew how he had been fooled for so long. As it was now, all he could see when he looked at her was the warmth of the dark-eyed gaze that jutted up to his from under the brim of that oversized hat. When she rode, he saw the gentle slope of narrow shoulders—shoulders he had followed lovingly with his lips. He saw long legs gripping the sides of the horse—the same legs that had slipped around him to accommodate his loving entry of her body. He saw a stained, oversized shirt that he knew hid small perfect breasts, which were incredibly sweet against his lips. He could see it all, while to others it remained unseen, and it was driving him crazy.

Irritating him even more was the fact that Billie appeared not to suffer a single particle of the same distress. But he knew she, too, had other thoughts on her mind. He had not forgotten the men's expressions when Billie and he had made their late entrance into camp after leaving Abilene. He was well aware that the seeming preferred treatment she had received had only elevated the hard feelings still harbored by Brothers and Hall. He also had not missed the fact that Jeremy Carlisle had seemed to take it on himself to stand between the two surly drovers and Billie, and he alternated between a burning jealousy and relief that the young drover had taken on the task he could not afford to assume openly himself.

Rand's eyes followed Billie's slender form covertly. It occurred to him that she was truly the antithesis of everything he had always thought he preferred in a woman. He had always been attracted to small, full-blown, and experienced beauties, the type of which Lucille was the perfect example. He had always preferred malleable women, making it clear at the outset of each relationship that his interests were of short duration and would not be confined to polite conversation and an occasional kiss. But Billie's tall, willowy proportions stirred passions of which he had not realized himself capable, and her keen mind and provocative spirit evoked emotions within him that were so complex as to boggle his mind. It came to him with a sudden clarity that with Billie it had not been the type of woman who had attracted him, but rather the woman herself.

But bothering him far more than all these realities was the recurring thought that would give his mind no peace. God, he had almost lost her! In that small hotel room in Abilene where they had loved so completely, Billie had almost walked out of his life without a backward look. He remembered clearly the expression on her small, beautiful face as she had sat on his lap, the directness of her gaze when she told him she'd find her way to Montana alone. It had been so easy for her to give him up, while the thought of being without her had all but shattered him.

Suddenly conscious of the line his thoughts were taking, Rand gave a small shrug. He supposed this whole thing could be considered ironic justice. How many times had he gotten out of a woman's bed, turned his back, and walked away without a second thought? He had turned Lucille over to that young banker, Pat Patterson, without the slightest regret. One woman is as good as another. . . . His own words came back to haunt him, and he realized the fallacy of the statement he had made with adamance so many times before.

But however deep his own personal involvement, it was obvious Billie did not feel the same. Montana. . . . What was it that drove her so relentlessly to reach that barely civilized spot? Or should he ask, who? . . .

A burning jealousy tying his stomach into knots, Rand took a deep, firm breath. Whatever and whoever it was that drove Billie, and whoever she turned out to be, it would make no difference. With realization of the depths of his feelings had also come determination. It would be a long drive to Montana, and by the time they reached that godforsaken spot, Billie would be his, completely. He needn't panic or submit to the agitation that drove his mind to distraction. With every mile and every day that passed, he would bind her to him more closely. He would deliver the herd, and they would leave Montana together. He would teach her what it was to truly be loved. It was a task he looked forward to with great anticipation. It was a task he would devote himself to for the rest of his life.

But for now it was the immediate present that ate at him. Three days. . . . It had been three days since he had touched Billie or even looked freely into her face. He ached for her, his longing so strong that it was almost a palpable, living presence inside him. But he would not go on much longer so deprived.

With that decision made, Rand raised his hand and motioned the men riding in the lead and swing positions forward. Spurring his horse into movement, he rode toward their approach. By noon he would have the herd efficiently turned off the trail and traveling northeast. If his self-searching of the past few days had determined anything, it had been that it was a time for action in every facet of his life, and he would not wait a minute longer to implement the course he had decided to take.

Sitting to the far side of the campfire as was her custom, Billie consumed the last of her "trail chicken" and beans. The crispy fried bacon was little change from the average trail fare, but she had little thought for the variety of the meals since she had returned from Abilene. Whatever Nate Straw dished up, it was always good and in ample amounts to satisfy even the heartiest appetite. Billie put down her empty plate and picked up her cup to drain the last of her coffee.

She turned her head to Jeremy Carlisle's appreciative comments.

"Damn, Nate, if that wasn't the best 'chicken' I ever ate! I'm sure enough goin' to miss all this top rate food when this drive is over."

Slowly raising his gaze, his craggy face noncommittal as he surveyed the young drover's expression for signs of jest, Nate finally offered in a low, exaggerated drawl, "Well, boy, I'm glad to see at least one of you fellas here has an educated palate. And I do thank you, 'cause it seems like compliments and appreciation for hard work are in short supply in this here camp."

The low chorus of groans that echoed around the fire raised the first trace of a smile on Billie's lips. She had been on enough drives to know good chuck when she ate it, and also to realize that drovers were short on compliments and long on complaints in that area. But Nate's long-suffering expression elicited the reaction he had sought as the men followed their groans with comments generous enough to bring a satisfied smile to his weather-beaten face.

"Well, boys, seems to me like you've got a special treat comin' for all them kind words. I ain't promisin' nothin', but night camp tomorrow just might have a special surprise."

The speculation those words induced was responsible for a sudden glut of conversation, under cover of which Billie quietly drew herself to her feet and walked out of the fire's circle of light into the darkness beyond. She needed some time to herself . . . alone.

Once under the cover of darkness, Billie took off her hat and ran her hand through her hair. She took a deep breath, inhaling the fresh night air and delighting in the slight breeze that moved against her scalp. She revelled in that small freedom darkness allowed, as well as freedom from the weight of the varied gazes that followed her.

It had not been an easy three days since arriving back at camp. True to his word, Rand had offered a short but very convincing explanation for their late appearance. But the reaction had been inevitable. Brothers and Hall, truly one in their determination to make her pay for the favoritism they felt she enjoyed, had taken every opportunity to bait her. Determined that she could not afford to indulge her anger, she had ignored their calculated insults, offered mainly when Rand was not present, only to find that Jeremy Carlisle had taken up the cause of her champion.

Inwardly appreciative of Jeremy's unrelenting consideration and good humor, she had attempted to stop him with an accusation of interference, only to have the young man state that he was just evening the odds. He had added rather shamefacedly that he had let Drucker down in Abilene and that he was glad Pierce had had the sense to check up when she had left them. When Billie had insisted that she didn't need anyone to check up on her, Jeremy's only comment had been that he hoped somebody would have the good conscience to stand up for his younger brother if the situation demanded it while he was gone. Her heart warming at the stubborn decency displayed in Jeremy's face, Billie had not had the heart to say more.

But most disturbing of all was Rand's covert perusal. Somehow she had become acutely attuned to the touch of his glance and had found herself turning countless times to suffer his silently accusing gaze. She found herself at a loss to understand it. What did Rand want from her? He had agreed to allow her to come back to the herd in the same capacity as before. He had said he would get her to Montana . . . where she wanted to go. That was all she wanted and all that was settled between them.

It had occurred to her in the free moments when she could indulge her thoughts that she had made a greater mistake than she realized in Abilene. She could not afford the warm memories that assaulted her, or the stubborn desire of her own wandering gaze as it had returned countless times to Rand's broad-shouldered outline against the endless sky. She was only too aware that her first priority was escape and the preserving of her own life. To that end she should be dedicating her thoughts, perusing the horizon.

She was only too aware that Rand doubtlessly had had dozens of intimate encounters such as theirs. He was such a beautiful man, and his expertise in the area of lovemaking was undeniable. The touch of his hands was gentle and knowing; the caress of his lips was endlessly erotic. And for all the strength and power of his passion, he was tender, oh so heartshakingly tender. Of it all, she feared it was this tenderness that had marked her beyond redemption.

She had no doubt in her mind that Rand had but to snap his fingers and any number of desirable women would answer his call. Surely the beautiful Lucille Bascombe would be the first to respond. When the drive was over, Rand would leave the trail to other foremen. He would return to his own world of government contracts and wealth, and all that it included. The lovely Miss Bascombe, or someone like her, fit perfectly into that world. But not Billie. It was a fact she dared not allow herself to forget.

And she dared not forget that she had killed a man. No matter how justified, she had taken a life. The memory of Wes McCulla's face, so still in death, returned to her mind, and a familiar pain assaulted her. She would have to pay for that somewhere along the line. Her future was limited at best, and Rand did not hold a place in that future. She had determined she would not allow herself to . . .

The sound of a step beside her interrupted Billie's thoughts, snapping her head to the side at the same moment a strong arm snaked around her waist to draw her against a familiar warmth.

She looked up, only to feel hungry lips cover hers as anxious arms pulled her closer still. Enfolded against Rand's powerful body, she was temporarily lost to his kiss, her convictions of a moment before fading under the assault of ragged, spontaneous emotions. Tearing his mouth from hers, Rand was visibly shaken. His voice was hoarse, his breathing uneven.

"Billie, this isn't going to work."

"Rand. . . ."

"I thought it was bad before Abilene, but since. . . . Billie, it's been hell. I want to be alone with you, Billie."

"No, Rand. . . ."

But Rand wasn't listening. His one arm wrapped around her waist he was unbuttoning her shirt with shaking fingers.

"What are you doing?"

"I want to touch you."

"No, Rand, please."

But Rand's hands had already reached inside her shirt, only to come to a sudden halt.

"What in hell? . . ."

"I'm wearing a binder."

"A binder?"

"I can't take a chance that anyone will see an outline and guess."

"Billie. . . ."

"Please let me go, Rand."

Rand had gone suddenly still and Billie was about to speak when he clamped his hand over her mouth and pulled her back into the shadows It was then that Billie heard the sound of a step in the darkness. Within a few seconds, Rand's voice hissed into her ear.

"It's Carlisle. He's walking over to the remuda." Rand hesitated, his voice taking on a harsher tone. "He's looking for you, isn't he?"

Rand's hand dropped from her mouth as he waited for her to respond.

"Yes, he probably is. He's appointed himself my protector."

Rand was not amused. An unexpected parting of clouds illuminated Rand's face and Billie was startled at the anger reflected there.

"You don't need him to protect you. You have *me*."

Surprise turned to anger at Rand's tone and Billie stiffened.

"You're right, I don't need Jeremy's protection. I've already told him that, just like I've told you. I don't need your protection either, Rand. When you agreed to let me come back to work with the herd, you said it would be just like before. That doesn't mean you—"

Rand's hand clamped back over Billie's mouth, interrupting her statement. Incensed, Billie began to struggle when Rand gave her a warning shake.

"Be still. He's coming back."

Succeeding in dislodging his hand, Billie shook her head.

"Let me go. If he doesn't find me, he'll go back and get some of the men to search for me."

Rand's eyes narrowed and Billie could feel his hostility. "So, you've managed to get under his skin, too."

Too incensed to reply to his remark, Billie demanded harshly, "Let me go. . . . Let me go, damn it!"

Billie had only a second to see the angry jerk of Rand's lips before he released her unexpectedly. Buttoning her shirt as she stumbled out of the shadows, she took a few steps before she heard Jeremy's voice to her rear.

"Drucker, hey, where were you? I was lookin' for you. I was beginnin' to think—"

Her patience expired, Billie turned around with a vicious snap. "I don't need a nursemaid Carlisle. So stop following me around!"

Jeremy took the few steps to her side, his familiar grin flashing.

"Drucker, you sure are the spunkiest kid I ever did meet. You tickle me, do you know that?"

Emitting a frustrated groan, Billie began walking back toward the fire, only to feel the weight of Jeremy's arm settle companionably across her shoulders as he fell into step beside her. Directing a look of pure venom toward him, Billie was met by Jeremy's amused hoot. He gave her shoulder a short, good-natured hug.

"The good Lord shorted you in size, Drucker, but he sure didn't short you in spunk. Come on, let's have a game of cards."

Nonplussed, Billie shot an exasperated glance heavenward and turned away. She started again toward the campfire, the weight of Jeremy's arm resting comfortably around her shoulder. Oh, what was the use?

Rand was not amused. Neither could he take his eyes from Billie's outline until it had disappeared beyond the wagon. Carlisle was walking by her side, his arm slung casually around her shoulders. Rand's stomach tensed into knots. He had had enough. Billie and he had to talk—and this time he wouldn't take no for an answer.

*　　　*　　　*

"Come on, get those beeves moving!"

The agitation in his voice obvious even over the din of cattle being prodded into the first movement of the day, Rand spurred his black hard. Jerking the bridle with a heavy hand as he gained ground that would hold him far to the side of the herd, he turned his horse around and directed an unsmiling glance toward the men working efficiently to the lee.

"I'd say stay out of his way today, Drucker, if you value your hide."

Turning, Billie saw Jim Stewart riding at her side, his gray brows tight over squinting gaze.

"I've ridden a lot of trail with Rand Pierce, and I ain't never seen him so damned irritable as he is this trip. But from what I've seen so far, I'd say we're all in for it today. And bein' as he seems so fond of takin' his irritation out on you, I'd say the safest thing you could do would be to stay clear of him."

Billie's eyes shot to Rand's stiff figure where he waited to the side of the slowly moving herd. Stewart was right. The rigidness of Rand's posture in itself was enough to set her nerves on edge. Using her quirt, Billie prodded the steers into line, her eyes moving back to Stewart's face with a small, acknowledging nod.

But Stewart's attention was claimed by Willie's figure as he spurred his horse to Rand's summons. Willie's squint narrowed as Rand indicated some points in the distance. His conversation with Willie was short and intense as he gestured widely in explanation.

"Looks like Rand's givin' Willie directions on the course for the day. I expect he'll be headin' out to scout up a safe crossin' for the cattle. Well, at least we'll be spared a dose of his bad temper." Shaking his head Stewart continued companionably as the steers moved easily beside them. "When it comes to trail bosses, there ain't a better or fairer man than Rand Pierce, boy, but when that fella gets a burr under his saddle, there just ain't no pleasin' him. I'd say Rand's doin' us all a favor by takin' himself off and—"

Stewart's gravelly voice trailed to a halt as Rand motioned

Willie back to point position and spurred his horse unexpectedly in their direction. His gray brow was furrowed into a deep frown as Rand reined his horse up alongside. Rand's tone and expression precluded formalities.

"Willie will be taking the herd for the day, Jim. I'll be expecting you to back him up if anybody gives him trouble."

"Sure enough, Rand."

"Drucker. . . ." His voice sharp with command, Rand continued tersely, "Follow me."

Turning, Rand spurred his horse away from the herd without a backward look. Startled, Billie followed his departing form with her eyes, only to hear a low-voiced urging from the man beside her.

"You best get movin', Drucker. I'd say the boss ain't in no mood for wastin' time. I can't say as how you got lucky enough to draw ridin' with him today, but I sure as hell know I'm glad I ain't you."

Her hesitation instinctive, Billie turned once more in Stewart's direction, only to see the flat of his hand come down on her horse's rump as he ordered simultaneously, "Get movin', boy."

Realizing she had no choice, Billie leaned into her bay's jerking start, and within a few minutes was following Rand's lead.

They had been riding at a rapid rate for over an hour and Rand had not acknowledged her presence. Uncertain what to expect, Billie had kept her silence as well, her eyes moving only in covert appraisal of the man who rode rigidly in lead. Stewart had been right. Rand's mood was black.

Carefully scrutinizing the terrain on the far side of the quick-flowing river, Rand had continued to flick his eyes from bank to bank in obvious mental calculation over the last few miles. Appearing to reach a decision, he reined his horse unexpectedly and turned in her direction.

His blue eyes burned her as he ordered tightly, "This looks like as good a place as any I've seen in the last hour to cross. I'm going to try it. Stay here."

207

"But—"

"I said, stay here!"

Billie snapped her mouth closed against a protest at being left behind. Damn him! Nothing would give her more pleasure right now than to shatter Rand's icy reserve with her declaration that she could ford that river just as well as he. And she could, too! But it was senseless to attempt to reason with him in his state of mind.

Directing a glance into his eyes, which she hoped indicated her contempt, Billie nodded. Pausing only long enough to jerk off his boots and secure them high on the saddle, Rand spurred his horse toward the river.

Her body tensing, Billie watched as Rand's horse slowly descended into the river. He had picked a good spot to ford. The water moved gradually up the big bay's sides. There would be no threat here to the animals footing. Her gaze flicking out to the middle of the watercourse, Billie frowned and spurred her horse closer to the water's edge. The current appeared to be rapid as Rand neared the middle of the river, and Billie emitted a short gasp as the big black finally met swimming water and struck out strongly for the other side of the river. But the powerful animal was a strong swimmer, and within moments he was climbing the narrow bank on the opposite side.

Not bothering to give her more than a cursory glance as he turned his animal around, Rand trailed his eyes over the ragged terrain bordering the opposite bank. Obviously satisfied with what he saw, Rand gave his horse only the time necessary to return to normal breathing before he plunged back into the glittering currents. Within minutes he was back at Billie's side, his brilliant eyes raking her face unsmilingly.

"Let's get moving."

Billie was smarting under Rand's few words of terse command. She was at a loss to understand his reasoning for ordering her to accompany him. He had all but ignored the fact that she was there. He had not even accorded her the cordiality or conversation he would have given another drover. She distinctly disliked purposely being kept in the dark as to his intentions for the day. He had obviously found a crossing that appealed to him, and she could only surmise he was now going out in search of a ferry for the wagon.

Taking a deep breath as Rand increased his pace, Billie gritted her teeth against her frustration. Well, if he was purposely setting out to irritate her, she was not going to give him the satisfaction of realizing he had succeeded. She would follow silently in his lead if it killed her.

Billie raised her eyes to the sun and squinted in appraisal. Mid-morning . . . They had located a crossing and a ferry for the wagon, and were on their way back toward the approaching herd. She shot a covert glance toward Rand. He still had not spoken a word except to give her a few quick orders. In her judgment, the herd would probably meet the point Rand had selected to ford the river sometime around noon. It was doubtless somewhere in the area of two hours until then. That probably accounted for Rand's slackened pace.

But Rand's concentration was still intense. He was scanning the landscape, apparently not yet free of a task he had set himself for the day. His eyes suddenly settling on a small stand of trees, he turned his horse in its direction without a word. He spurred the big bay forward. Swallowing her resentment, Billie followed suit, her confusion growing as Rand rode into the stand and dismounted.

He dropped his horse's reins over a low hanging branch and turned as Billie rode her horse to a halt beside him. His voice was tight with impatience.

"Well, what are you waiting for, Drucker? Do you need me to help you down from your horse?"

A spontaneous retort jumped to her lips, but Billie suppressed it with the greatest control. No, Rand was spoiling for a fight, and she was not going to accommodate him. Her hesitation only darkened his already foul mood.

"Well?"

When she made no move to dismount, Rand took the steps to her side with surprising swiftness. Before she could make a move to elude him, Rand had reached up, his arms gripping her waist firmly as he pulled her from her horse.

Placing her on the ground so close in front of him that their bodies touched, Rand reached up and jerked her hat from her head. His voice rumbled low in his throat as he tossed it to the ground and threw his own hat down beside it. His eyes devoured her face.

"I'm tired of peeking at you around that damned thing. And I'm tired of looking at you without touching you, Billie." His arms moved around her, and Billie gasped at the hunger in his heated azure gaze. "And I'm tired of talking. . . ."

Rand was kissing her, his mouth devouring hers. His hands, fingers splayed wide in an effort to absorb each loving contour of her body, moved searchingly along her back, her buttocks, clasping her to pull her flush against the rise of his passion.

Absorbed fully into the heat of Rand's raging emotions, Billie experienced a rise of desire that was efficiently destroying all reasonable thought despite her most fervent protests. Panicking under its rapid assault, Billie began to struggle, her voice escaping in a low gasp.

"Rand, no, I don't want—"

Rand pulled back abruptly. His breathing was agitated, his expression distorted by the strength of emotions held tenuously in check.

"You don't want— I'll tell you what you *do* want. You want me to make love to you. You want that as much as I do, Billie. I can see it in your eyes, can feel it in the way your body moves against mine." His mouth descended, taking hers abruptly in a deep, shattering kiss that left them both trembling.

Tearing his mouth from hers, Rand whispered hoarsely against her mouth, "Tell me you want me to stop, Billie." His lips moved against her cheek, the line of her jaw, on the slender column of her throat. "Tell me the touch of my mouth doesn't sear you the way yours sears mine. Tell me the warmth of my body against yours doesn't make you yearn the way I yearn. Tell me my touch doesn't make you want to cry out your need . . . the same need I feel for you."

Billie was gasping under his touch, her heart pounding wildly in her breast, matching the erratic beat echoing against her own. She tried to speak, tried to gain control of the raging emotions that held her in their grasp. Her lids slitted with the liquid heat moving rapidly through her veins, she peered at Rand. Yes, she needed to tell him . . . to tell him that she did not want to be close to him, could not allow his body to absorb hers again, so completely that all reality slipped from her mind. She wanted to tell him that she could not afford to indulge the emotions he raised within her or the bond that was growing between them.

With great effort, Billie whispered in protest, the sound faint and indiscernible through barely moving lips. Rand laughed low in his throat, his lips covering hers briefly, their touch stilling the feeble movement. His one hand tight in her hair, his other arm wrapped possessively around her, he held her motionless under his husky whisper.

"This is your last chance, Billie. Tell me now . . . tell me you don't want me." His mouth drank deeply from hers, and he urged again. "Tell me—"

Her senses reeling, Billie was hardly aware of the moment when Rand scooped her up into his arms. He took a few steps and lowered her until she felt the hard ground beneath her back. The scent of damp moss reached her nostrils as Rand's body covered hers, Rand's warm scent mingling with its musky fragrance in heady assault. She was not aware of the moment when her arms slipped around Rand's neck, when her mouth opened fully under his.

His hands touched her body, and the restrictions of cloth and binding became too much to bear. His naked flesh was pressed against hers, his mouth moving in a torrid, soul-shaking path of love across her pale skin. His mouth worshipped her lips, her ears, the column of her throat. Gasping as he found the roseate tips of her breasts, Billie clasped herself to him, aiding in his ardent caresses.

The callused palm of Rand's hand smoothed her flesh. Following its curving contours lovingly, Rand's hand grazed her hips, moved across the flat expanse of her stomach. His fingers tangled in the dark curls beneath, seeking, meeting, and finding the moist bud of her pulsing desire. Entering its moistness, he stroked her gently, fondling, urging her to a higher level of the sweet ecstasy that held her in its grasp. She was shuddering under his touch, her body reacting wildly to his ardent ministrations when his hoarse whisper sounded warmly against her ear.

"Look at me, Billie. Open your eyes and look at me. I want to see your face when you give to me. I want to see your passion in your eyes, hear its gasp on your lips. I want to see it pulse through your body, making you its slave the way that same passion has enslaved me."

He was still caressing her. The unearthly sensations elicited by his knowing touch raised her higher, higher. His voice sounded, more urgently than before. His caress stilled, the sudden deprivation jerking Billie's eyes open to his heated gaze. An urgency akin to pain reflected in the startling blueness of his eyes held her fast as he rasped again.

"Billie, give to me, darling. Give to me now . . . now. . . ."

Quickly, efficiently, Rand brought to full flower the need that had blossomed inside her with his subtle intimacy. A sudden panic assailing her as she teetered on the edge of her solitary ecstasy, Billie reached out to touch the face that looked so intensely into hers. Her voice was a whispered plea.

"Rand. . . ."

"Now, darling, now. . . ."

In a moment she had plunged from the yawning precipice, her heart pounding, her lips gasping Rand's name as she shuddered and writhed in the throes of the passion he had so lovingly induced.

His heart pounding, Rand stared down into Billie's love-flushed face. His eyes absorbed the impassioned flutter of her lids, the subtle movement of her lips. He listened, his heart thrilled almost to bursting as she gasped his name, calling out to him.

Unable to bear another moment of the tender torture inflicted by his need, Rand lifted himself above her. Her body was not yet still when his manhood moved intimately against her moistness. Billie's eyes rose to his, only to have

Rand's ardent whisper respond to her silent plea.

"I must, darling. Now, I need you now. . . ."

The gentle touch of Billie's hands as she reached up to welcome him, the separation of slender thighs as she moved to accommodate his loving thrust, too much for his flaring emotions, Rand plunged deep inside her. Mindless in his hunger, dauntless in his quest, Rand thrust again and again, his passionate rhythm shared by Billie's slender, quaking form as she raised herself to meet him.

Suddenly at the brink of his raging passion, Rand clasped Billie breathlessly close, inhaling deeply of the scent that was hers and hers alone as he plunged a final time. Deep within her body, surrounded by its moist warmth, he shuddered his loving tribute, his voice rasping, calling her name.

Still sealed in the cocoon of their mutual passion, Rand lifted his head moments later, his eyes dropping to the flawless, unmoving face beneath his. Billie . . . Billie. . . . Her name resounded in his mind. Echoes of the love they had shared resounding in his heart, Rand dropped a light, fleeting kiss against her parted lips. Her heavy lids lifted, and she made an attempt to separate from him. His response was an urgent whisper.

"No, darling, not yet."

He lowered his face against her hair, his arms drawing her closer. He could not bear to allow her to draw away. Not yet . . . not yet. . . .

Billie opened her eyes, coming into contact with a brilliant cerulean gaze with a start. An amused smile curved Rand's lips as he curled his palm against her cheek.

"I thought you were never going to wake up, sleepyhead."

A sudden panic assailing her, Billie attempted to sit up, only to have Rand's restricting arm restrain her.

"No, darling. Lie with me a little longer."

Intensely aware of their nakedness, Billie shot a furtive glance around them.

"Rand, the herd . . . it'll be catching up with us before long."

"No, not for a little while."

"Rand, I don't want—"

"You're not going to tell me what you don't want again, are you, darling?"

A warm flush of color transfused her cheeks and Rand laughed aloud. He lowered his lips to hers for a light kiss.

"Now that we have that settled, we can go on to something more important." At Billie's tightening expression, Rand's expression slowly sobered.

"You know we can't go on like this, Billie. I've just made love to you. You're lying here naked in my arms, and I don't even know your real name. I want you to tell me."

"No. This is a useless conversation, Rand. It'll get us nowhere."

Billie's negative response was met with a familiar stiffening of Rand's features.

"Why can't you trust me, Billie? Haven't I proved how much I care about you?"

Billie raised her eyes in challenge.

"Why are you so curious about me, Rand? I know just about as little about you as you do about me, and I haven't asked you any questions."

"It isn't a matter of curiosity, and you know it. And I'd say you know a great deal more about me than I do about you." Rand's hand was resting on her shoulder, his fingers making little circles on the white flesh as he strove to control his rising frustration. "But if you really believe what you're saying, I'm only too happy to tell you about myself."

"Rand, please. . . ."

"My name is Randall Montgomery Pierce. I'm thirty-three years old, in good health, possessed of considerable wealth, and the only child of Helen and Jacob Pierce. I grew up on my parents' farm in Illinois. I'd probably still be there if a prairie fire hadn't destroyed it. I was the only one who got out alive, and so when the Union Army was looking for volunteers—"

But Billie wasn't listening.

"Rand, I don't want to hear anymore. The herd—"

"The herd won't be here for at least another hour." A new

harshness in his tone, Rand tilted Billie's face up to his. "I guess it would be accurate to say that the reason you haven't asked any questions about me is because you're not interested." There was a brief silence as Rand paused. "You aren't, are you?"

"No."

Her gaze still forcibly meeting his, Billie saw her response had stung him, and she fought to suppress her regret. Rand gave a low laugh, a glimmer of a suspicious brightness temporarily lighting his eyes.

"Well, you're honest, at least. And the least I can do is be honest in return. I don't care how little you really care about me, Billie, because the truth is I know how I can make you feel when you're in my arms." His eyes darkening, Rand paused as his gaze moved over her still face. "And I love the way you feel in my arms, darling. I want to keep you there. The only problem is I have a feeling you're hiding something from me that I should know."

"You know everything you need to know about me."

The warning muscle ticked in Rand's cheek.

"That's right, of course. I know your real name, where you come from, whom you're running away from"—his voice dropped another notch—"and more importantly, whom you're running to."

"I told you—"

"You've told me nothing. Why, Billie, why?"

Rand's growing agitation contagious, Billie jerked her face free of his hold.

"Because I don't want to tell you!"

Her sharp response seeming to have stopped Rand where all other efforts had failed, Billie drew herself to her feet. She reached for her underdrawers and slipped them on without turning. She was attempting to adjust the awkward binding when Rand turned her to face him. Her response had obviously shaken him. The muscle was ticking in his cheek. Seeming suddenly unable to face the coldness in her gaze, Rand jerked her tight against him, his arms encircling her in an almost desperate embrace. His breath was warm against her hair, his voice ragged.

215

"Billie, I care about you. I care a lot. You can't ask me to just ignore the fact that someone beat you up—almost killed you—and that the same person might be after you to try to finish what he started. You're afraid of something, I know that. I can help you, keep you safe. Whatever or whoever it is, I can stop them. Don't you understand what I'm saying? I want you to be safe . . . with me."

Billie closed her eyes, aware of the rapid beating of Rand's heart against her breast. She had made a terrible mistake, and if she were not so uncertain how she would otherwise get to Montana, she'd leave the drive right now and never look back. She didn't want this. She didn't want to care, and she didn't want Rand to care, either. She knew Dan McCulla. The man was relentless. He wouldn't stop until he found her, and then it would be a matter of her life or his. She had no intention of including Rand in that confrontation. After she reached Montana, she'd be able to face anything that came. But not now . . . not now. . . .

Billie took a deep breath.

"Rand, I want to get dressed. I don't want to be here with you when the herd comes."

Rand gave no response for long moments. Dropping his arms abruptly, he stepped back. The coldness in his eyes matched hers. Turning he picked up his clothes and started dressing. Making certain to keep her eyes averted until she was fully clothed, Billie turned back to see Rand fully dressed and adjusting the cinch on his saddle. A familiar ache beginning inside her at his silence, she approached her horse. Stopping as she drew opposite him, Billie addressed him quietly. The sound of her voice echoed in the silence, turning him toward her.

"I don't want to do this anymore, Rand."

"This? You mean you don't want me to touch you again, is that it?"

"Yes. It would be unwise."

"I never considered whether we were being wise, Billie. I just wanted you."

The flicker of pain in Rand's eyes seared her, and Billie turned abruptly to her horse. Her throat tight, she mounted

216

up. Turning back to find him also mounted, she shook her head.

"No more."

The herd was moving toward them, but there was not a glimmer of satisfaction inside him at their easy pace. Controlling his desire to glance to his rear to confirm the fact that Billie was riding a few steps behind, Rand swallowed against the cold, hard knot that choked his throat. Billie and he had ridden in silence after mounting in that quiet grove. There had been nothing else to say.

He was still incredulous. He had watched Billie carefully while they had made love, one part of him lost to the wonder of loving her, the other part determined to make sure she experienced at least a portion of his joy. And it had been there . . . on her face. He had seen passion color her skin, had seen it flood her senses, taking control of her body and mind. Culmination had been ecstatic, complete. He had never experienced an emotion more profound or consuming. He knew he never would. Billie was the woman he loved and wanted for the rest of his life. But the joke was on him.

No more.

There had been no mistaking the finality of those two words. Billie didn't want any part of him.

His expression grim, Rand frowned into the faces of the men riding up to meet his approach. They were just over two miles from the crossing. It was time to set strategy with the men, and he needed to clear his mind. It struck him that he had expected today to be a turning point. He had expected to be entering this portion of the drive in a far different state of mind, with Billie riding close at his side. Well, it had been a turning point, all right.

Damn her! Why was she riding behind him? He wanted to be able to look at her, to gauge her thoughts. He . . . Oh, hell, he wanted to be able to stop and ask her to reconsider . . . to let him love her.

Reining his horse to a halt as Willie, Jim, and Russ pulled up alongside, Rand noted that Billie moved to the outside of

217

the group, awaiting his instructions. A good, efficient drover to the end. Damn her!

Pulling up alongside, Willie regarded Rand's expression warily.

"Well, judgin' from the look on your face, Rand, I'd say you either didn't find no crossing, no ferry, or neither."

Rand shook his head. "I found them, all right. We'll be coming up on a good crossing in the next two miles. Tell the men to switch to their best swimming horses and get ready to take the herd across. If you held those steers off water all morning like I instructed, they'll be thirsty when they reach the river. We'll send the remuda across first. With the cattle in their rear, the horses won't have any choice but to make it to the other side as fast as possible. The river is shallow until you hit the mid-point, and then there's fifty or sixty yards of swimming water. The current is swift and the channel out of the river is narrow, with poor footing. If you allow the cattle to become congested on landing, some are going to drown."

Pausing, Rand appeared to suddenly come alert to Billie's presence.

"Don't just stand there, Drucker. Find Nate and tell him to get the wagon ready for the ferry. When we reach the fording point, you'll show him the location of the ferry. We'll meet you and the wagon on the other side."

Billie stiffened. "Nate doesn't need me at the ferry. I can get back in time to help push the cattle across."

Rand's gaze pinned her.

"I'm the boss here, Drucker, and I say you stay with the wagon. Understand?"

The brief hesitation before Billie jerked her head in a short nod raised the tension considerably. Visibly relieved at her begrudging assent, Willie turned a pacifying smile in her direction.

"Nate's been complainin' of late that he could use some help with his team. He'll be right glad to have your help, Drucker."

"I don't need anybody to justify my decisions, Willie." Rand's glance, as sharp as his words, raised the brows of the men as he shot a surly glance back toward Billie. "We won't be needing you here now, Drucker. Get back to the herd."

More aware of Billie's stiff departure than he chose to admit, Rand turned back to his men's curious stares.

"That's all for now. Tell Casey to bring up the remuda. We don't have any time to waste."

His frown darkening as the men rode back toward the herd, Rand turned to scan the horizon. He was aware he was beginning to suffer in his men's opinion, but they could think what they liked. He wasn't going to have Billie with him at the crossing. Hell, the crossing was going to be dangerous at best, and he didn't need the added worry of seeing Billie fighting her way across among all those beeves. This disguise business was difficult enough for him. If she ran into any trouble, he would be certain to reveal himself. He knew what the result would be then. Billie would leave the drive. He couldn't take the chance.

His eyes drifting slowly back to the object of his thoughts, Rand saw Billie raise her eyes to scan the horizon to their rear. He had seen her do that countless times and his thought was always the same. What was she looking for . . . or whom?

The afternoon sun glinted on the surface of the water and Rand raised his hand against the glare. He had ridden ahead of the approaching herd with a few of the men. He turned, a smile curving his lips despite his agitation. Willie, Jeremy, Russ, and Cal Johnson sat their horses at the river's edge, stripped down to their underdrawers. Volunteering to take the water as the first of the herd entered the river, they had removed their boots and clothing and were awaiting its approach. Rand shook his head. Damn if Willie hadn't gotten skinnier in the last few years, while Russ had added an inch or two around the middle.

With a touch of nostalgia, Rand remembered the many times he had been out front, stripped down to his unmentionables, awaiting a herd. He had been young and full of enthusiasm, and had shrugged off the danger involved in a crossing such as this. Over the years the countless fresh graves he had seen beside rain-swollen crossings had brought a touch of sobriety to his thoughts. Now the responsibility for the safety of the men as well as the stock was his, and Rand's approach had changed completely.

The unexpected rattle of a wagon interrupted Rand's thoughts, and he turned. Damn! What was Nate doing up this far? He had told Billie to head out toward the ferry. . . .

His eyes snapping to the figure riding to the side of the wagon, Rand saw Billie's eyes were averted from his. Or was she just looking to the river's edge? A sudden flicker of movement caught Rand's eye. Jeremy had spotted the wagon and spurred his horse into action. A wide grin on his face, he galloped on a dead run toward Billie, drawing his horse up short of her stationary position with a laugh. He was obviously in high spirits in anticipation of the crossing. He reached out and slapped Billie's shoulder good-naturedly, his low comment about her obviously poor spirits drawing her glance to his smiling face.

A familiar knot tightened in Rand's stomach. His eyes assessed Billie's expression, noting that she talked to the partially naked man without the slightest embarrassment. He didn't like it. He didn't like Billie's obvious comfort with Carlisle. He didn't like the way her eyes swept his well-proportioned body. He didn't like the fact that while the relationship between Billie and himself had deteriorated drastically, the bond between Jeremy Carlisle and her was flourishing. He didn't like it at all.

"Rand. . . ."

His head jerking toward the sound of his name, Rand realized Nate had dismounted from the wagon and stood nearby. His expression was disturbed.

Resisting the urge to return his gaze toward Carlisle, who remained in what now appeared to be a one-way conversation with the silent Drucker, Rand nodded.

"What are you doing here, Nate? The crossing is a couple of miles up the river. I told Drucker—"

"If the crossin's a couple of miles up, I'll find it without any

220

problem. I don't need no pilot to show me the way."

"I'm the boss here, Nate. I've already given Drucker his orders. . . ."

Shooting a quick look to his rear, Nate took a step closer, his tone conspiratorial.

"Look, Rand. I don't need no help findin' the crossin', and that's a fact. But more than that, Drucker's been facin' some real needlin' from those two old boys, Brothers and Hall. Appears to me they figure it's goin' to be another easy day for the kid, and they ain't too keen on seein' somebody else doin' any less than they are."

"I don't give a damn what Brothers and Hall say. And I'm not letting them run the show with their grumbling."

"Rand, the kid—"

"The kid will be safe with you. I don't want to have to worry about Drucker crossing the river. Hell, if—"

His words coming to an abrupt halt, Rand took a deep breath, allowing Nate a moment for interjection.

"The kid's a good drover. He can handle himself. He ain't—"

"Drucker makes the crossing with you, Nate." His tone uncompromising, Rand concluded flatly, "The herd's getting closer. You'd better be on your way."

Lifting his eyes as Nate made his way back toward the wagon, Rand caught Billie's perusal. Jeremy had already returned to the other men and she flicked a quick glance toward Nate as he climbed on the wagon.

At Nate's, "Okay, Drucker, let's go," she darted Rand a heated look.

Turning with calm deliberation, Rand looked back to the approaching herd.

Occupying point position, Rand kept his eyes on the gradual approach to the crossing. His concentration tightening as the remuda entered the water at a rapid pace, he darted a quick look toward the opposite bank. He was intensely aware that the narrow passageway leading out of the river held the most potential danger. His eyes glued to the

221

horses as they hit swimming water, he judged the flow of the current, his eyes moving between the opposite bank and the swimming animals as the fast-moving water carried them downstream. He had made allowance for the current's pull, having directed the remuda into the water nearly a hundred yards above the outlet on the other shore.

They were nearing the river and Rand jerked his attention from the opposite shore. A short glance behind revealed that the herd was being held tightly on its course. He took a deep breath and entered the water without hesitation. The herd followed easily at the lead and Rand felt a lessening of the tension that knotted his brow. They were soon in deeper water, moving well.

A sudden drag at his reins lifted his eyes to the opposite shore. The current was getting stronger. The remuda ahead of them was swimming well, but the unexpected swiftness in the current had carried the leaders below the passageway on the other side. His heart beginning a heavy pounding, Rand saw realization dawn on Casey's face. With an expert maneuver, Casey turned the animals as they began to flounder, guiding them to the narrow footing below the cutbank, and within a few minutes the first of the remuda had gained a successful foothold.

But the delay had been costly. Turning, Rand saw that the lead cattle were beginning to go adrift and the steady stream behind them had begun to form the shape of a large letter U as the current forced them downstream. Using his position carefully, Rand forced his powerful bay against the sides of the swimming beeves, guiding them in the slow curve that would bring them safely ashore. His eyes darting to his rear, he saw Jeremy using his bay to the same advantage, with Jim, Cal, and Russ successfully completing the curve.

The firmness of the narrow bank was beneath his bay's feet and Rand felt a flush of exhaltation as the lead cattle struggled ashore. Signaling Cal forward with the leaders, Rand turned to survey the ensuing throng. His eyes hitting on steers floundering at the river's edge, he plunged into the water again, his bay reacting with instinctive power as the current began taking them in its grasp. Nudging the panicking steers with his powerful animal's broad side, Rand guided them in the necessary curve. At a sound behind him, he turned to see Russ close at his rear, closing the gap, while Jeremy completed the line to guide the animals ashore.

His eyes lifting to the opposite bank as he was once again ashore, Rand froze. Moving into the water close beside the trailing herd, he saw a familiar slender figure. Billie. . . . Damn it, she was supposed to be with Nate! What in hell . . .

His heart throbbing rapidly in his chest, Rand realized it would be useless to call out. He would never be heard above the melee of the protesting beeves and shouting drovers. Plunging into the river again, Rand made a line for Billie's strong grulla, his mind noting unconsciously that she had chosen well, that the animal was swimming strongly without hesitation.

"Rand . . . over here!"

Turning at the urgent call, Rand spotted a line of steers that had become separated from the main herd. Vigilant drover that he was, Fogarty had not missed their separation and was attempting to turn them, but the expression on his tense face was more explanatory than words. Forcing his horse forward, Rand gained Fogarty's side at the precise moment needed to effect the turn. Within moments the animals were headed back upstream toward a successful foothold on shore.

Having gained stationary ground, Rand jerked his eyes back to the herd. Billie was safely ashore, separated from him by the steady stream of steers as they emerged from the river. Unable to cut through the beeves in their agitated progress up the bank, he could do no more than watch helplessly as Billie turned her horse. Without hesitation, she plunged back into the river to aid a few bewildered steers, in performance of the same duties he, himself, had enacted so spontaneously only moments before.

But there was no more room for thought as floundering beeves demanded his attention again and again. Intensely aware that Billie had been moving between the bank and the river as actively as he, Rand attained the shore for the final time. Watching the last few trailing beeves move ashore,

Rand shot a furious glance toward Billie's stiff figure.

Exhaustion was obvious in the trembling of Billie's hand on the reins and the rigidity of her seat. Unconscious of the fact that his own bay was blowing just as hard as Billie's valiant grulla, Rand spurred his stalwart animal forward. Jerking him to a ragged stop as he reached Billie's side, Rand barely suppressed the desire to reach out and shake the stubbornness from her weary face.

Maintaining his seat in a silence that caused a momentary flicker of an unknown emotion in Billie's dark eyes, Rand felt fury test his rigid control. When he finally spoke, his low voice was ragged.

"You want everything to be over between us. That's your choice. You've made it, and like it or not, I have to abide by it. But *I'm* still boss on the trail. *My* orders are law, and like them or not, *you'll* abide by them. Right now you're no different than any other drover here. . . ."

"Then treat me like the other drovers and I'll pull my weight just like the rest. I'll—"

"You'll do *what* I tell you, *when* I tell you, Drucker! Keep that in mind if you want to stay with the herd. You won't get another chance."

Turning, Rand spurred his horse blindly forward. He had other things to handle right now: the settling of the animals; a belated noon camp; anything and everything that would keep his mind from the thought of the ultimatum he had just given Billie, an ultimatum he desperately hoped she would not force him to carry through. . . .

Carl Whitley lifted his stained Stetson and ran his stubby fingers through his matted hair. Giving the sun-drenched landscape around him a quick glance, he adjusted his position in the saddle and arched his back against its stiffness. He gave a low groan. Hell, he and the boys had been riding since daybreak, and he was just about done in. Whitley looked toward the empty horizon. And he was damned tired of fried beef and boiled coffee. This "party" McCulla had sent him on wasn't turning out to be the fun he had expected.

In the last few days he had run into four of the nine herds that had been in San Antonio around the time the "boy" had been seen there. It was obvious that none of the men connected with those outfits had seen or heard of the girl. And this whole thing was getting to be far more complicated than he had imagined. He wouldn't be having this trouble if Bart Ford had been a little more helpful, but as it was, the old livery stable owner wasn't even sure which direction that particular herd—the one with the shortage of drovers—was headed in.

He had taken a long shot and followed the tracks of the freshest drive west. The three herds still moving on that trail had been no help at all. He had since retraced his tracks and met the Old Western Trail to go north once more. He and the boys had met up with the fourth herd just the night before last, and although they hadn't been of any help, the trail boss had extended the hospitality of his camp. The freshness of the tracks he had been following most of the day had led him to believe he and the boys would be sharing another camp this night. But so far . . .

"There she is, Carl."

Marty's comment was simultaneous with the first sight of a trailing dust cloud as they reached a rise of ground. Their view of the herd increased as they continued forward, and Carl grinned. He turned to the trail-weary men who rode at his side.

"Well, boys, looks like we'll have a nice hot meal tonight. I'm thinkin' we'll go and show ourselves, make ourselves useful. I'm thinkin' that even if the trail boss ain't too hospitable, he won't be able to get out of askin' us to join him then." His eyes taking on a crafty glow, Carl continued, "And I'm thinkin' when most of the men are sittin' around the fire at night, they'll be nice and relaxed and talkin' free and easy. Tongues always work overtime around a fire. If they seen the girl, they're sure enough goin' to tell us then."

Not getting quite the reaction to his statement he expected, Carl surveyed his men's sullen expressions. His irritation was obvious as he addressed them as a group.

"What in hell's the matter with you fellas? I'm thinkin' you should be glad we're goin' to be eatin' good tonight. And I'm thinkin'—"

Marty's low interjection carried the same tone as his expression.

"And I'm thinkin' we're on a wild-goose chase! Hell, we ain't never goin' to find that girl and you know it, Carl. She disappeared from the face of the earth. I'm tellin' you, she's either layin' in a shallow grave somewhere or sittin' in a cathouse on some Mex's knee. There ain't no way she could get away with passin' herself off as a boy on a drive. Hell, no drover I know would be stupid enough to think *that* woman was a man. Hell no, not with what that little bitch had goin' for her. . . ."

Annoyance tightening the myriad lines on his face, Carl raised his brow and ran a chipped nail across his ragged mustache. It was a gesture that warned of his rising anger, and Marty stiffened. He was well aware that despite Carl's harmless, almost comical appearance, with his scrawny frame and deceivingly benign expression the man had a vicious temper. He was also aware that Carl's scrawny frame hid a wiry strength and lightning-fast reflexes and that Whitley had a dedication to following his boss's orders which had proved a great asset in the shadier side of McCulla's enterprises. He knew the other men would not challenge Carl's position, and a nervous tremor moved up his spine.

"Well, Marty, seems as like I don't remember you was hired to think . . . just follow orders. And since Mr. McCulla sent you boys out with me, I guess that means you follow *my* orders, don't it?"

His annoyance fading as Marty nodded his assent, Carl took a quick survey of the men's faces. "Just for the record, boys, I ain't so sure we're goin' to find that Winslow girl either, but we sure as hell are goin' to give it a good try. I ain't anxious to go back to Dan McCulla and tell him we ain't been able to find her. And then again, there's the matter of that reward he promised us. . . ."

His temporary lapse forgotten in the face of Carl's

regained good spirits, Marty offered doubtfully, "You really thinkin' McCulla will come through with a 'reward'?"

Carl's lips spread in a familiar yellowed smile. "Ain't you forgettin' it was Dan McCulla's baby boy that was involved in that shootin'? Young Wes, spoiled bastard and Dan McCulla's darlin' son. You can sure enough believe Dan McCulla will come through with that reward if we find that Winslow girl for him. And we don't even have to put a hand on her, boys. Ain't that nice? Hell, this job couldn't be easier. . . ."

"Yeah, *if* we find her . . ."

"Like I said, we're goin' to give it a good try." His eyes going back to the herd that traveled a short distance ahead, Carl nodded. "Seems to me this should be the Rockin' M herd we heard about. Come on boys, time's a wastin'. . . ."

"The Rockin' M, yeah, we heard a lot about your outfit on the trail. Seems like you got a real fine herd here. Where you headin'?"

Gunther Logan's small eyes twitched as he assessed the cowpoke sitting across the fire. He had a persistent itch behind his ear that signaled no good. He had learned the dependability of that itch over the many years he had bossed beeves over the trail, and the smilin' cowpoke staring at him so innocently across the fire had set if off real well. Somehow or another, this fella and his boys were too good to be true. They had approached his herd just past noon and ridden along, just like they was a part of his crew. For a few hours they had worked even harder than his own men when strays from another herd's run had come racin' back along the trail, scattering their herd. It had only been good manners for him to invite them back to night camp to share their chuck, but something was wrong. He could sense it.

Gunther scratched his ear again and responded warily.

"We're headin' north, up to Wyomin'. We contracted to a government agency there. We've been travelin' slow under orders, allowin' our beeves maximum time to graze. The agent there is new and my boss figures he's goin' to be right

227

picky when it comes to acceptance of the herd. He wants this herd delivered in prime shape."

"Well, that's real nice, ain't it." His yellow teeth bared in a wide smile, Carl nodded companionably. Seems like travelin' like this would give you plenty of time to meet all kinds of people on the trail. You might be just the fellas me and the boys is lookin' for."

Gunther felt a short warning jab in the same area that had itched so insistently a few minutes before. His expression unrevealing, he took off his Stetson and scratched his head.

"How's that?"

"Well, me and the boys is out, kinda on a mission of mercy for a friend of my boss. You see, my boss's friend had a real bad run-in with his son. The boy is a wild young cuss, and his pa sort of let his anger get out of hand while tryin' to knock some sense into the kid. Anyways, the boy ran off, and nobody's seen him since. The kid's pa feels real bad, but worse than that, his wife got taken sick with worry. They're thinkin' she won't make it through the month if that boy ain't found and talked into comin' home where he belongs."

"That's a real sad story." Gunther took long moments to adjust his hat back on his head in an attempt to hide his reaction to the stranger's tale. He had a feeling he was going to find out real soon why these fellows had attached themselves to his drive.

"Yeah. Maybe you seen the boy. He's a skinny cuss, about medium height, with blond hair and dark eyes. Like I said, his pa let his temper get a little out of hand, and the boy might've been carrying some bruises."

"I ain't seen no kid that fits that description." Turning, Gunther looked at his men. "How about you, boys? You seen anybody like that?"

The low chorus of negative grunts that echoed round the fire faded the smile from the stranger's face. Taking advantage of the men's attention, he responded with a raised brow.

"Ain't seen him, huh? Ain't seen a young girl fittin' that same description either, have you?"

"A girl?"

Taking a chance, Carl offered offhandedly, "Yeah, well, the truth is, that boy I described is really a girl who took off from her father's spread, so you can imagine why her mama is so upset. We figure she might be travelin' dressed as a boy. . . ."

Gunther pulled his stocky frame upright, his small eyes suddenly alert. His distaste for this suspicious fellow was growing by the minute.

"No, I ain't seen no girl, neither." Failing to add that if he had, this character would be the last person he'd tell, he turned to his men. "And you ain't, either, have you boys?"

The cowpoke was surveying his drovers' expressions with a keen eye as they voiced their negative replies. His casual tone was in tight contrast to his intense gaze.

"I have to say I'm right disappointed." Turning back to Gunther, he broadened his smile. "But you might be able to help put us on the right track to make a poor, grievin' mama real happy. Seems like there was a herd of long-legged Mexican steers that passed by San Antonio about the same time as your outfit. They'd had some trouble with a fever and was lookin' to hire some drovers. To my mind, that would be the perfect opportunity for the kid. You wouldn't have happened to see that herd or meet some of the fellas drivin' it? It sure would help us to know what direction that herd was headin' in."

His quick mind recognizing the description of Randall Pierce's herd, Gunther hesitated. He had heard about Pierce's troubles and knew the herd was destined for the Blackfoot Agency in Montana, but he'd be damned before he'd tell this crafty little bugger a word. With any luck, Pierce's herd had outdistanced them so far with his long-legged stock that this Carl Whitley and his crew would give up lookin' long before they'd be able to catch up with the herd. And if the kid—boy or girl—was with them, good luck to her.

His mind set that he would be glad to see the last of this group, Gunther offered Carl a watered-down smile.

"Sorry we can't help you, Whitley, but we've been too busy with our own beeves to pay much attention to anybody

229

else's." Drawing himself abruptly to his feet, Gunther shot his men a look that guaranteed their silence.

"Well, guess I'll be turnin' in. Daybreak comes real early these days."

Realizing his visitors were startled at his sudden termination of their conversation, Gunther walked the few steps to his bedroll. He pulled off his boots, lay down, and yanked his blanket over his shoulders. Hell, he wasn't goin' to waste words on the likes of them. "A mission of mercy." The only mercy involved in this situation would be if he took that poor girl in and hid her from the likes of these fellas if he did run into her. And he just might do that if he did . . . he just might.

Turning to shoot the scrawny stranger and his silent trail partners a covert, hostile look, Gunther settled down against his blanket. Those fellas weren't gettin' no information from him or his men. Hell, no. He wasn't that much a fool.

Chapter IX

"Oh, Father, you didn't!"

"Yes, I most certainly did, Lucille. You cannot expect that I would invite business associates and their wives to my house for a dinner party and neglect to invite my youngest vice president."

"Yes, I most certainly can expect that you would *neglect* to invite Mr. Wallace 'Pat' Patterson here! Father, I told you how abominably he behaved toward me in Abilene!"

Lucille raised her small chin pridefully as she faced him within the confines of the library. She had *neglected* to relate to her father the incident outside Rand's door in Abilene and the events that had followed. Not wanting to open a Pandora's box, which might prove more detrimental to her cause than beneficial, she had elaborated effusively on the incidents that had preceded it and on Rand's unexpected abandonment of her. She had laid the blame for the complete failure of Rand's and her loving reunion at Pat's door where, in her mind, it remained still. She shook her well-coiffed head regally.

"Surely you cannot expect me to welcome that—that *boor* into my home!"

His gray brows rising, Horace Bascombe directed a surprisingly steely gaze into his daughter's outraged expression.

"Lucille, you seem to forget that this is *my* home, also. You have functioned as hostess for my dinner parties since

231

you became of age. You will continue to do so until you marry and have a home of your own. It is one of the very few duties I ask you to perform as my daughter." His gaze unfaltering, Horace Bascombe paused, his voice taking on a stronger tone. "Pat is a brilliant young man and an asset to me in every facet of his work. I like him personally and find his company extremely pleasant. I will *not* sacrifice him or your childish grievances."

"Childish grievances!"

Lucille took a stunned step backward. What had come over him, her loving, malleable father? He had not been the same since she had returned from Abilene. A new suspicion entered her mind. No, he could not! Pat Patterson could not have related to her father all that had progressed in Abilene. He could not have stripped her of her dignity in her father's eyes.

The thought almost more than she could bear, Lucille felt the rush of tears. Blinking them back with extreme firmness of will, she raised her chin a notch higher. No, she would not cry! She had not been above using tears to her advantage before with her extremely susceptible father, but not *real* tears.

The revealing flush on his beautiful daughter's face affecting him far more than she realized, Horace Bascombe took a firm hold on his control. His darling child . . . He could not bear to see her suffer even so small a disappoint-ment as his refusal to comply with her wishes, but he could not give in to her. He had the feeling more had transpired between his young vice president and Lucille than either of them had indicated on their tight-lipped return from Abilene. Lucille's extreme reaction to Pat's expected pres-ence at the dinner party due to begin within the hour was proof of his suspicions, and he could only surmise that Pat had managed to accomplish the job he had sent him out to do. It had not been an easy task, he was sure. He could not pay Pat back with the deliberate slight Lucille intended.

"Yes, dear, childish grievances." His voice taking on a more gentle tone despite his intention to the contrary, Horace resisted the impulse to reach out a reassuring hand to

232

pat his daughter's narrow shoulder. "Whatever differences you may have experienced with Pat, I'm sure he felt he was doing his job as I would have had him do it. He is a very determined man. . . ."

"Determined! Humph!" The brightness of tears fading from her eyes as her father's praise of her enemy stirred a new anger inside her, Lucille directed a haughty look into her father's concerned expression. "The man is a stiff, unyielding ass, with no more sensitivity than—than the cook's pet goldfish! And I would much more enjoy sitting at the dinner table staring at cook's fishbowl than I would enjoy another taste of Pat Patterson's pompous superiority!"

"Lucille. . . ." Managing to hide his amusement at Lucille's unexpected simile, Horace shook his head in quiet disapproval. "Lucille, dear, you exaggerate."

"I do not exaggerate my feelings, I assure you, Father." Taking a deep breath, realizing these tactics were getting her nowhere, Lucille decided on another form of attack. "But you are right as usual. I have overstepped my bounds, and I do thank you for bringing that to my attention."

Taking a few steps forward, Lucille fluttered her extravagant lashes and raised her hands to adjust the cambric bowtie of her father's impeccable evening suit. She rested her hand against the stiff shirtfront, amused at the growing wariness of expression under his elegant side whiskers and mustache. He was such a dear man, so determined to do what was right for everyone. It would not hurt to make him believe she had submitted to his wishes this time. It would, after all, prove to her advantage in the long run.

"If it will make you happy, Father, I will welcome Pat Patterson with open arms."

The corner of Horace Bascombe's mouth twitched suspiciously.

"You needn't go that far, dear."

"I will make him feel *very* welcome. . . ."

"Lucille. . . ."

"That is what you want, isn't it, Father?"

Attempting to respond in a manner that would declare his

wishes with utmost clarity so they might not be miscon-
strued, Horace paused. He was beginning to feel decidedly
uncomfortable.

"It is my wish that you show Pat the same courtesy and
attention you show our other guests . . . that you make him
feel welcome in our home and at our table."

Lucille stepped back and curtsied gracefully.

"Your wish is my command, Father."

"Lucille, dear, it is not my wish to command you."

"And it is not my wish to make you angry. So you may set
your mind at rest. Pat Patterson will be welcomed royally."
Stepping forward once again, Lucille raised herself on her
toes and kissed her father's whiskered cheek. Lowering
herself lightly back to her heels, she slipped her hand
through her father's arm.

"Our guests should be arriving soon. Shall we greet them
together?"

At her father's silent nod, Lucille smiled and turned toward
the library door. She did not see the sudden droop to her
father's expression and the manner in which his eyes rose
pleadingly to the ceiling as if in supplication of a higher
power. Her mind was filled with the evening to come and the
retribution she would reap. . . .

Pat was decidedly nervous, and he didn't like it. He had
entered the Bascombe residence only moments before. He
had settled his hat with the servant at the door and was
approaching the living room directly behind a rather buxom
matron and her husband with whom he was not acquainted,
and whom he could not care less to meet. He had had only
one thought on his mind all day. Lucille . . .

The question that had reverberated in his mind ever since
Lucille and he had returned to St. Louis and had bid each
other rather tight good byes still went unanswered.
Why? . . . Why had he set his mind on a spoiled little witch
who would run him a merry chase? There were so many
other women more than receptive to his sharp wit and loving
attentions. Why, then, had he settled on a self-centered little

rich girl whose self-indulgence had progressed to the point of fault, and who regarded everything in relation to the pleasure it would bring to her?

It had come to him in the dark hours of the night that he had never met anyone quite like Lucille Bascombe. She was more beautiful than she had a right to be. Her body was more lush and appealing than was safe for the normal male, and she was far too intelligent and quick to be taken advantage of unless she chose to be. And she obviously wanted nothing to do with a lowborn son of a kitchen maid who had made it into society and financial security on his own. Perversely, idiotically, those things only made him want her more.

Raising his hand, Pat smoothed the surface of his light hair and squared his shoulders. Lucille had left him with few illusions. She had let him know that his compact, well-muscled frame did not compare in her mind with Randall Pierce's tall, leanly muscled proportions, that his fair complexion and coloring looked faded and insignificant beside Randall Pierce's dark, compelling looks. Toward that end, he had ordered an evening suit especially for this occasion. He was well aware that Lucille's discerning eye would note that he was the ultimate in fashion without being gauche.

She had completely ignored him on the few occasions they had met socially since Abilene, frustrating each and every effort he had made to contact her. He was well aware that he was not making strides in his effort to press his suit. But if he were to be entirely candid, he would have to admit that his efforts had been so carefully disguised as to be unrecognizable toward that end. He was far too wise to give Lucille the added advantage of knowing he wanted her, and he had made stringent efforts to conceal the burning edge of longing that had begun to add a true misery to his days.

Rounding the corner of the hallway, Pat saw Lucille and Horace Bascombe standing formally by the entrance to the living room as they greeted their guests. He all but gasped at his first sight of Lucille, distinctly aware that he owed the matron walking in front of him a true debt of gratitude for

235

the generous bulk that so adequately hid his rather juvenile reaction.

But, Lord, there was no woman who compared with Lucille's extravagant beauty! Her gleaming red-gold locks were pulled back from her exquisite face, cascading in a glimmering fall to the smooth white shoulders bared in a daring décolletage. Her gown was a shimmering turquoise silk, which deepened the glow of already breathtaking eyes. The deep cut of the cuirasse bodice at Lucille's waist emphasized its minute proportions. The short puffed sleeves called attention to her slender arms as she gestured gracefully. The generous skirt, trained, flounced, drawn up at the sides entablier, and trimmed with large velvet bows in the very latest fashion, made the most of well-rounded hips.

A fine perspiration broke out above Pat's upper lip in memory of the warmth of those well-rounded lines beneath a particular pink satin negligee, and he made a strong effort to draw himself under control. Damn the little witch! She knocked the breath out of him! And she was such a vain little twit. She would recognize her advantage in a minute. No, he could not afford a second's lapse.

His emotions were under tense rein by the time the talkative matron was dragged almost forcefully away from her gracious hosts by her rather embarrassed husband. Pat extended his hand warmly in Horace Bascombe's direction.

"Horace, I'm delighted to be here."

"Pat, so good to see you."

His eyes moving from Horace Bascombe's rather tense face, Pat turned toward the slender woman at his side. Prepared for a rather sharp cut, he was astounded by Lucille's extravagant smile.

"Lucille, I do thank you for inviting me. . . ."

He was unable to finish his polite statement before Lucille raised herself on her toes to press a warm kiss against his cheek and exclaim effusively, "Dear Pat, how wonderful to see you again! I am so delighted that you were able to attend our small party. It most certainly would not be the same had you found yourself unable to come. I have so looked forward to talking to you this evening."

Shooting her father a quick, warm look, Lucille unexpectedly slipped her arm through Pat's. "You will excuse us, won't you, Father? It really has been too long since Pat and I have had an opportunity to speak."

"Uh, well, certainly, Lucille." His aristocratic face taking on an almost apologetic expression, Horace turned to Pat. "I have the feeling Lucille has been waiting for your arrival with bated breath, Pat. I hope you're up to it."

His impassive demeanor in sharp contrast with his true reaction to Lucille's assault on his senses, Pat raised his brow with a small smile.

"Aren't you the one who commented in the office this week that I'm one man who's never caught napping, Horace?"

"Yes, I suppose I am."

"Father!" Her eyes widening innocuously, Lucille shook her head. "You almost make it sound as if Pat isn't safe with me."

"I'm not so sure he is. . . ."

"Father, you wound me."

"Lucille. . . ."

Horace's warning tone going completely unheeded, Lucille turned sweetly to Pat.

"Oh, come, Pat. You must ignore Father. We have so much to discuss."

Drawing him firmly away, Lucille slanted a flirtatious glance up into Pat's eyes, and he gave a small laugh. He waited only until they were out of Horace Bascombe's earshot before speaking.

"All right, Lucille. What are you up to? Last week you couldn't spare me so much as a word, and tonight I'm number one on your priority list."

"Oh, yes, Pat dear. That you are."

Lucille was leaning slightly against his side, her full breast brushing his sleeve. In an attempt to distract his mind from the erotic contact, Pat offered lightly, "You look especially lovely tonight, Lucille. Blue is most definitely your color."

Her smile reflecting a glimmer of surprise, Lucille shook her head.

"I must say your compliment is truly unexpected. I had the feeling you saw nothing more when you looked at me than a flushed, spoiled termagant."

"A *beautiful*, flushed, spoiled termagant . . ."

Appearing determined to maintain her welcoming facade, Lucille offered with a stiff smile, "You are *so* generous. . . ."

Pat's smile broadened. "And you are *so* transparent. You want something, Lucille dear. Why don't you tell me what that 'something' is?"

"Pat darling, you are so suspicious. And even if you were correct in your assumption, why should I do you the favor of confirming your suspicions?"

Pat leaned down to smile into her face in an intimate posture that was contradicted by his keenly assessing gaze.

"Because, dear Lucille, the sooner you tell *me* what you want, the sooner I'll tell *you* what you're going to have to do to get it."

Lucille clamped her teeth tightly closed. Her lips deviated from a smile long enough for her to mutter a single word.

"Bastard."

"Now *that's* the Lucille I've come to know. . . ."

Turning, Lucille called authoritatively to the passing maid.

"Mary, do bring your tray here. Mr. Patterson and I would like some champagne."

Reaching out, Lucille disengaged her arm from Pat's only long enough to take two glasses. Offering one to Pat, she whispered as she smiled sweetly into his eyes.

"If it were not for my father, Pat dear, instead of offering you champagne, I would most happily spit in your eye. But the poor, misled gentleman that he is, my father thinks highly of you and I don't want to cause him distress. . . ."

"Well, that's a switch. . . ."

". . . at this dinner party, at any rate." Her small nose twitching with barely concealed annoyance, Lucille raised her glass to her lips and took a deep swallow.

Pat gave a small laugh.

"You drink like a sailor, Lucille."

Lucille lowered her glass. Her smile was rapidly deteriorating to a grimace.

"I know it will come as a surprise to you, Pat, but I'm not in the slightest interested in your opinion of me or anything I do. Dear fellow, you are beneath contempt, and it was my extremely poor fortune to be in a position where I was subject to your caprice for even so short a time." Taking a deep breath, Lucille restored a smile to her lips with obvious difficulty. "But you will not force me into irritating my father tonight. I've made up my mind to that."

"And in addition, you want something from me. . . ."

"Yes, and I can see now is not the time to discuss it."

"On the contrary, Lucille. I would say now is the perfect time."

Lucille's lush lashes fluttered provocatively.

"You're wrong."

"Why is that, Lucille dear?"

"Because if I stand here another minute, I will spit in your eye."

Raising her hand, Lucille tapped her fingertips lightly against Pat's cheek.

"Ta ta, darling."

With an erotic turn of her hip, Lucille was swept away. Her light touch was still warm on his cheek when a low laugh escaped Pat's lips. Oh, no, that sultry little bitch wouldn't get away so easily. His eyes followed Lucille across the room and he drained his glass. He laughed again. He'd made up his mind to have her, and have her he would. . . .

Pat was no longer laughing. The small dinner party was in full progress. Well-dressed guests moved easily within the room, chatting freely as a pianist provided a steady stream of background music from the far corner of the room. He had been indulging in pointless, inane conversation for the past hour and had even had the dubious privilege of being introduced to the rather large matron behind whom he had entered the house. Her steady stream of conversation had held him pinned in the corner for twenty minutes while she had elaborated on the merits of her lovely, unmarried daughter whom she was determined to have him meet. All the more irritating was the fact that out of the corner of his eye he was certain he had seen Lucille turn to catch his pained expression—and he was just as certain her smile had brightened.

Other than that, Lucille had reverted back to her former attitude of completely ignoring him. Several attempts to engage her in conversation had been deftly avoided, while she had turned to conduct elaborate flirtations with not one but *three* rather bemused young men. She was presently involved in a warm conversation with the third fellow, who had just had the audacity to touch her shoulder in an entirely inappropriate manner.

His temper was slightly appeased as Lucille's eyes darted to her shoulder and back up into the young fellow's face with a quick flick of her eyes that removed his hand more efficiently than a vocal reprimand. Pat snatched another glass from a passing tray and downed its contents with one gulp.

"Come now, Pat. That's champagne you're drinking, not red-eye."

Turning at the voice in his ear, Pat looked into Horace Bascombe's amused expression. His eyes returning momentarily to his empty glass, Pat shook his head.

"Earlier this evening I accused someone of drinking like a sailor. I guess I'm guilty of the same offense, Horace."

"Well, our actions are not always wise, are they, my young friend? Somehow I have the idea my lovely daughter might have something to do with your obvious frustration."

"Oh, hell, is it that obvious? I thought I was doing a better job of hiding my frustration than that."

"Only to me, Pat. You forget, I know you well. I've seen that cynical expression on your face too many times in the boardroom not to be aware of the agitation it masks. It seems to me I've done you a great disservice."

"How is that?"

"Getting you involved in my daughter's shenanigans . . ."

Pat hesitated, gauging Horace Bascombe's expression. He finally shook his head, his expression wry. "I have to admit,

240

it was a decidedly dirty trick, Horace. Because the fact is, now that I'm involved, I can't seem to get myself uninvolved."

"Are you certain you want to?"

Pat's green eyes narrowed into slits. A slow realization was beginning to dawn on his mind.

"Horace. . . ."

"Oh, I admit, I don't envy any man the chase Lucille will run him once he decides to pin her down. She has her mind set on one man. . . ."

"And she's not going to get him."

Horace shook his head, disturbed. "I know. Rand has other plans for his future. He—"

"You're right. Rand Pierce doesn't want any part of Lucille. But it wouldn't make any difference if he did."

"What are you trying to tell me, Pat?"

"You know damned well what I'm saying." Pat shook his head, his smile incredulous. "You took me in completely with that story you handed me."

"It wasn't a story, Pat. Lucille is incorrigible, unmanageable. You are the only man I know who could handle her. But she's also a warm, beautiful, loving woman who will make the right man a wonderful wife. Life will never be boring with Lucille. . . ."

"Never. . . ."

"Pat, are you patronizing me?"

"You've watched me for the past hour. Did I look like I was patronizing you?"

"Hell, no. You looked like a fellow in love."

"Oh, damn it! I *am* obvious."

"Only to me . . . Only to me."

His austere expression softening, Horace Bascombe raised his hand and clapped Pat warmly on the shoulder.

"Pat, just in case you're wondering, you have my approval and my support."

Pat's expression was wry. "Thanks."

"But don't let Lucille know it."

"Lord, no."

"I think I've finally got her to the point where she's

241

concerned about my reaction to her escapades. She never has been in the past. I consider that quite an achievement." Horace's aristocratic face reflected his pride as he added briefly, "Feel free to use that fact to your advantage if you choose. It's not that I've lost faith in you, Pat, but I think it's safe to say you're going to need all the help you can get."

Pat's eyes moved to Lucille's vivacious face. She was involved in a conversation with several handsome young couples. She outshone every woman in the group and he felt a premature pride. She made a small quip that rocked the group with laughter and Pat nodded.

"Yes, I think you're right."

"Well, go to it, Pat. Time's wasting."

Pat held the older man's gaze. He gave a short laugh.

"Thanks."

"She's worth it, Pat."

Pat raised eyes gone suddenly sober. "I know. . . ."

The announcement that dinner was served sent Pat across the room toward the laughing couple standing in the far corner.

"You will excuse us, won't you, Jerry? Lucille has promised to go in to dine with me."

The polite young man was obviously taken aback. "But Lucille just said—"

Turning to Lucille, Pat scolded lightly, "Do you see what you've done, Lucille? You've left this very nice young fellow without a dinner partner."

"I've left? . . ."

"It really is unforgivable of you to have accepted both our invitations. You do have a habit of doing that, dear."

Gritting her teeth in a travesty of a smile, Lucille offered with tight control, "Well, then we'll all have to go in to dinner together, won't we?"

Taking her arm firmly, Pat smiled. "No, we won't. I'm sorry, Jerry. Maribelle Davis seems to be free." At the young man's expression of disinterest, Pat shrugged. "Well, in any case, Lucille isn't. See you later, Jerry."

Lifting Lucille almost off her feet with his firm grip, Pat propelled her into the dining room. With hardly an eye to the sumptuous buffet, Pat took a plate and attempted to place another in Lucille's hand. She resisted.

"I don't care to eat right now."

"All right, don't. Just fill your plate and you can watch me eat. I've indulged you long enough. It's time to drop the other shoe, Lucille. You said you wanted something from me. It's time to tell me what it is."

They were making their way along the table in record time. Taking a sample from each of the tempting platters, Pat made certain to put a more than representative amount of food in Lucille's plate too.

"I told you, I'm not hungry."

Pat raised his brow. "Do you want everyone to think you're afraid to eat your own food?"

"Ohhhh . . ."

Her low groan of exasperation picking up his spirits, Pat smiled.

"Dear heart, you'll give the other guests the mistaken impression you're not enjoying my company. And you wouldn't want to upset your father, would you?"

"Give me that damned plate. . . ."

They were seated at last and Pat shot a glance around them. He had chosen the perfect spot for a little intimate conversation. Seated at a small table near the patio door, they were just far enough away from the rest of the guests to ensure privacy.

"I'd like another glass of champagne."

"I'm not sure you should have any more."

The sudden flare in Lucille's expressive eyes brought Pat to his feet. Compromise . . .

"I'll be back in a minute."

Making his way quickly to the corner of the buffet, Pat poured two glasses of champagne. Turning, he saw Horace had caught his daughter's gaze. Then, doing something entirely unexpected, Lucille opened her eyes wide. Forming her mouth into a small circle, she pulsed her lips open and closed in a rhythm decidedly reminiscent of a dainty denizen of the deep. Pat turned a quizzical gaze to Horace's face at the exact moment the older gentleman choked viciously on his champagne. Horace was still attempting to catch his breath as Pat returned to Lucille's side.

Dismissing the confusing events of a moment before, he seated himself and placed the filled glass on the table in front of Lucille. He had decided to waste no more time.

"All right. You want something more from me than a glass of champagne. I know it must be something important or you wouldn't subject yourself to a heavy dose of my authority for more than two seconds."

"Your authority?"

"Whatever you want to call it. . . . I've presently got the upper hand and you're burning. . . . So, dear heart, what can I do for you?"

"Stop calling me 'dear heart'!"

"That's a fairly reasonable request. That won't cost you much. . . ."

"Pat, you bastard, I've had enough of this!"

"Don't raise your voice, darling. Horace will get upset."

"I want to know just what you told my father about Abilene!"

"Told him? . . ."

"Did you—did you tell him—" Swallowing against the sudden emotion that filled her eyes and throat, Lucille raised her chin. "Did you tell him about that last night . . . when I went to Rand's room?"

Aghast, Pat put down his fork. When he did not answer but stared into her flushed face, she pressed tightly, "My father's attitude has changed toward me . . . as if he no longer trusts me. . . ."

Regaining his voice, his expression severe, Pat offered quietly, "Have you ever given him reason to trust you?"

"No, but that hasn't stopped him in the past. He's always trusted me because he *wanted* to trust me. If I thought that you'd done something to change that—"

Pat shook his head. "No, Lucy. I haven't told your father anything except that you gave me a damned hard time and that Rand walked out on you."

Lucille's face flushed with hot color.

"That was *your* fault! You're the reason Rand walked out of that hotel dining room and didn't come back! You're proud of yourself, aren't you?"

"Yes, reasonably so."

"And you think you've won!"

"If you mean by that that I think Rand is finished with you, yes."

"Well, you're wrong! Just because you won last time doesn't mean you'll win again. Rand will be in Dodge within a month's time. He told me before he left that he thinks his foreman will be well enough by that time to meet him in Dodge and take over the herd. He'll have the responsibility for those dirty cattle and even dirtier men off his mind and we'll have a real reunion then. We'll come back together. We'll—"

Her hand flying to her lips, Lucille stopped in mid-sentence.

"Your father didn't tell me anything about your plans to meet Rand in Dodge."

Regaining her composure, Lucille lifted her slender brows.

"Possibly that's because he doesn't know of my plans. I'm not going to tell him."

"You were going to sneak off . . . probably leave him a note. . . ."

"Yes, that's right! You're not going to get the chance to spoil things for me again."

"And you wouldn't have told me, either, if you hadn't lost your temper and slipped." Lucille refused comment, and a raging jealousy added another dimension to Pat's anger.

"But I know now. . . ."

"I don't give a damn!"

Taking her hand unexpectedly, Pat urged Lucille to her feet. With a stiff smile he drew her through the nearby doors and out onto the patio. They had just walked into the shadows when he turned. Taking her roughly by the shoulders, he growled down into her face, "You'd better give a damn! Whether you like it or not, you've made me a party

245

to your deception, and I don't like it! I won't do that to your father. He's been too good to me and, unlike you, if someone trusts me, I don't let them down."

Lucille's voice took on a choked quality. "I—I'm not letting my father down. I just—I just can't let him run my life, that's all."

"You're not going to Dodge!"

"I am!"

"You're not!"

"Damn you, Pat Patterson, I'm going to Dodge if I have to crawl, do you understand? Nobody's going to stop me, nobody!"

Their glances were forged by the heat of their passionate exchange. Taking a deep breath, Pat broke the prevailing silence with his low, sober tone.

"We'll see, Lucy, we'll see. . . ."

The heavy rain that had been incessant all day had slowed to a steady drizzle. Standing in the midst of a dismal night camp, Rand darted a quick glance skyward. He gave a low, disgusted snort and adjusted his slicker against his shoulders. Not a star was visible in the night sky, adding another facet to the gloom that had overcome his outfit. It was a well-known fact that nothing depressed drovers like falling weather, and it appeared that this drive was not going to be the exception.

Rand shot a quick look around his silent campfire. The men had consumed their meal without speaking, exhaustion and discomfort silencing normally active tongues. He frowned. Nate, in his usual dependability, had managed a hot meal and had had the foresight to keep a ready pot of coffee over a well-protected fire. The men were drinking liberally in an obvious attempt to relieve the bone-chilling dampness.

Rand's glance moved to Billie's silent, solitary figure beside the fire. Her slenderness overwhelmed by a slicker obviously meant for a much larger man, she was as protected as the rest of them against the weather, but Rand knew just how effective that protection was. He knew that her hat was saturated to the point where it was little more than an uncomfortable, soggy weight upon her head, that the rain was trickling down her neck just like it was trickling down his. He knew that the dampness was beginning to settle inside her, chilling her to the marrow. She was so slender, with so little natural protection against the elements that held them at their mercy.

Rand's eyes followed Billie's hand as she raised her cup to her lips. Her hand was trembling with a chill. The lapse of a few seconds before she settled the hot cup against her mouth betrayed the fact that her lips were quivering just as violently. His brows knit in a frown. His burning need to stride to her side and take her under his slicker to share the prevailing warmth of his body was almost overwhelming.

Forcing his gaze from Billie's shuddering figure, Rand shot an assessing glance toward the herd. Not a hoof had bedded down for the night, and he knew only too clearly what that meant. He disliked trading on exhausted men, but he had no choice.

"Stewart, Cannon, Hall . . ." Rand hesitated only until the men addressed had turned their eyes to his. "We're going to be doubling the shifts tonight. You'll be going out with the first watch. The second two watches will start at one o'clock and stay until daybreak."

The low round of groans that met his announcement was expected, and he offered a small smile.

"Sorry, boys. Tell it to the weather. If we don't keep a tight rein on this herd, we'll be chasing them to kingdom come at the first crack of lightning."

Dragging themselves to their feet, the men walked toward their mounts and Rand shook his head. They were a good group for the most part, and he knew they'd do their job no matter how tired and uncomfortable they were. Rand's eyes moved inevitably back to Billie. It was obvious she was stringently attempting to control the deep shudders that shook her frame, and Rand felt a new frustration beset him.

Hell, how much more torture was that little witch going to put him through before this drive was over? Didn't she

247

realize what she was doing to him? He ached with wanting to love her, comfort her, keep her safe and protected. Two weeks . . . It had been two weeks since he had so much as touched her, and every nerve in his body cried out in torment. But she was oblivious to his pain. It was either that or the fact that she did not care, which kept her so cold toward him. In his present state of mind, Rand was uncertain which he wanted to believe.

To outward appearances, the situation had not changed. Insistent on pulling her weight in the crew, Billie drove herself harder and longer than the other men. But it was a war of silence that prevailed between Billie and him, except for the times when his own frustration and Billie's adamance resulted in heated exchanges. He made a small, spontaneous grimace. He was still uncertain who emerged the winner from those altercations—if, indeed, there was one.

But whatever he chose to believe, he was abruptly certain of one thing. He was not going to stand the torture of seeing Billie shiver out another moment in this ceaseless drizzle. Combining the two shifts was a necessary move, which had also accomplished another important fact—Hall's and Brother's removal from camp. He only hoped that realizing their watchful eyes were no longer trained on her, Billie would respond favorably to his intended action. Whatever the case, he didn't intend to wait a moment longer. He had taken enough.

Rand drew himself to his feet as his eyes moved around the campfire. Jeremy Carlisle had walked to Billie's side and was talking softly. He was obviously trying to urge her into moving her gear under the wagon where she might find a few hours respite from the drizzle while she slept. Her eyes on Jeremy's face, Billie did not see Rand's approach. He was a few steps behind the spot where Billie still sat when he heard her response.

"I told you I'm fine. If you're cold, *you* can put *your* blankets under the wagon and get out of the rain for a few hours."

"Yeah, but I ain't shiverin' like you're shiverin'. Drucker, you keep up bein' this hardheaded, and you ain't goin' to be around to collect your pay at the end of the drive."

"Think so?" Her voice unnaturally low with hoarseness, Billie snapped into Jeremy's concerned expression. "I'll be the first one on line to get my pay when we reach Montana, and you can bet on it."

"Don't waste your breath, Carlisle."

Rand's unexpected interjection snapped both gazes in his direction as he came to stand towering over the spot where Billie sat stubbornly. Her eyes narrowing, Billie responded stiffly, "I was just about to tell him the same thing."

Rand ignored her comment. His voice was terse.

"Get up, Drucker."

"Why?"

"I said, get up."

Hesitating only a moment in responding to his command, Billie drew herself to her feet, and Rand was suddenly aware of the reason she had remained so adamantly seated. Her body shuddering so actively that she could barely stand, Billie took a deep breath in an obvious attempt to steady herself.

"That does it." His arms aching to pull her close, Rand raised his hand with tenuous control and pointed at the wagon. "Get yourself inside that wagon and tell Nate to give you a shot of Jim Crow before you shake yourself to pieces!"

"No, I don't intend—"

Not allowing her another minute for argument, Rand grabbed Billie's arm in a steely grip and ushered her toward the wagon. Holding her firm against her protests, Rand directed an unrelenting stare into Nate's questioning glance.

"Clear out a spot in that wagon for this brat before he gets sick and brings the fever down on all of us again!"

Billie's temper flared anew.

"I told you I don't want or need—"

"And *I* told you to get in that wagon or I'll put you in there myself!"

Challenging his furious gaze for long moments, Billie was about to respond when Nate turned a hard look in her direction.

"Rand's right, boy. You ain't in no shape to argue. If you

listen to what he says, you'll be fine and dandy when time comes for your shift. Otherwise you're more than likely goin' to be more a hindrance than a help when we cross the Red River in a day or so. To my mind you'll be doin' us all a favor by sacrificin' a little of that hard-nosed pride of yours right now and takin' that warm spot to sleep and that shot of whiskey like Rand says."

Her eyes falling under Nate's steady stare, Billie turned silently toward the wagon. Within minutes she had disappeared inside. Nate turned to Rand's livid face.

"Don't worry about a thing, Rand. I'll dose the kid up real fine."

Rand nodded.

"Do what you have to, and if he doesn't make it out for his shift, that's all right with me." At the further narrowing of Nate's gaze, Rand added belatedly, "I'd rather he lose a night's work now than have a sick kid on our hands later on."

"Whatever you say, Rand."

A light smile touched Rand's lips. "Hell, that's damn good to hear for a change, Nate. Maybe you can teach that kid in there who's boss of this outfit."

Nate shook his head. "I ain't a miracle worker, Rand."

Rand nodded. No response was necessary.

Billie pulled the blanket closer around her and snuggled into its warmth. She was uncertain how long she had been in the chuck wagon, but her shivering had stopped long before. Her heavy lids dropping closed, she mused silently that perhaps it was the close quarters in the crowded chuck wagon, the liberal dosage of whiskey Nate had all but forced down her throat, or maybe just the simple fact that she was finally out of the unrelenting dampness. But she felt absolutely lovely wrapped in a soft cocoon of warmth, with the soft murmur of drizzle against the canvas top of the wagon. She was trying desperately hard to keep alert, ready for her watch, but it was difficult . . . so very difficult.

A soft, compelling warmth was moving against her cheek, her forehead, her mouth. She relaxed, indulging the pleasant sensation, her lips parting in a sigh. The gentle caresses deepened, drawing her to a pleasant awareness that precluded sleep. She opened her eyes slowly, focusing with a start on brilliant blue eyes intimately close.

"Rand!"

The euphoria of a few moments before slipping away, Billie came suddenly awake to reality. The sound of drizzle had stopped and pans were clanging busily outside the wagon. A gray shaft of the first light of dawn penetrated the wagon, and she came to full realization.

"My shift . . . I missed—"

"I told you, the boss won't care."

Rand was crouched beside her in the limited space of the wagon, his eyes moving over her face with an expression that stirred dangerous emotions inside her.

"Rand, the men will guess—"

"The men in camp are asleep, and the others are on watch. Nate's too busy cooking to give either you or me a thought."

"Why didn't someone wake me up for watch?"

"Because I told them not to."

"But—"

"You were shaking so hard when Nate gave you that red-eye that he said you spilled as much of it as you drank."

"I'm all right, Rand. I could've gotten up. I—"

Rand slid his hand lightly across her lips.

"Don't say anything else, Billie. Not another word, please. We'll only end up going around in the same vicious circle. This time I want to talk to you, to say some things that need to be said."

He hesitated in an obvious effort to find the right words. Distress was apparent in the strong planes of his face, and Billie ached with his pain. But she dared not let him know. Steeling herself against the need that called out to her from Rand's troubled gaze, she nodded.

Moving his hand, Rand smoothed the fine platinum wisps from her forehead, his fingertips resting against the light pulse there.

"I've been doing a lot of thinking in the last two weeks. It occurs to me that I've handled everything badly from the

251

start between us. I have no excuses except that you were a new experience for me, Billie. I'd never met anyone who affected me so intensely. You tied me up in knots from the first moment you walked into camp that night. I was so damned frustrated and confused. I was half out of my mind worrying about you, wanting to take care of you, and I didn't know why. Then I walked into your hotel room that night in Abilene. . . . Realization hit me like a bolt of lightning, darling. I knew what I wanted. I wanted you."

Pausing briefly, Rand took a deep breath. The hand that caressed her forehead trembled, and Rand gave a short laugh. "But that's where I went wrong, isn't it? I wanted you so much that I assumed you wanted me, too. You were vulnerable and inexperienced, and it wasn't hard to make you respond to me. The only trouble was that in my enormous conceit I took for granted that you felt the same way I did, that you wanted that loving never to end. It's been damned hard to face the fact that might not be so."

Making an attempt at a smile, he continued softly, "It also occurred to me that the personal problems that started you heading north were pushing everything else from your mind. So, if that's part of the problem between us, Billie, I'd like to take care of that first. I know you're running away from somebody or something. I know someone hurt you. . . ." Rand paused again, the spontaneous tightening of his features revealing the anger that had flushed his mind at the thought. "Let me help you, Billie. I want to protect you from whatever you're afraid of. But you have to tell me who or what—"

"No."

"Billie, be reasonable. You're here in my camp. If someone is after you, threatening you, I should know."

"No."

Rand dropped his lips to her forehead. His trembling hand moved in her hair, and Billie felt a new breathlessness assail her.

"Please don't, Rand."

"Billie, I—"

"Rand, you told me I could stay with the herd. You said

you'd live with my choice about the way I wanted things to be between us."

Rand's arms had slipped around her and he was holding her close against his chest. His breath was warm against her hair. "I know what I said. All right. Just let me hold you for a few minutes more. God, I love the way you feel in my arms."

"Let me go, Rand. You're deliberately giving me away. The men will be back for breakfast soon or Nate will get suspicious or one of the men will wake up and realize how long you've been in here."

"Billie," Rand swallowed tightly, "let me take care of you. . . ."

Billie swallowed hard against the need in Rand's voice.

"Rand, nothing has changed since we last talked. You're the same, and so am I." Rand stiffened, and Billie steeled herself against the words that were to follow. "I'm a drover with this herd, Rand, and you're the trail boss. That's all there is between us and all there's going to be."

There was a breathless silence before Rand responded.

"And if I've decided I can't live with that after all?"

Billie's eyes moved slowly over Rand's face.

"Then I'll have to leave the drive."

Allowing some space between them while still refusing to release her, Rand gave a low laugh.

"Hell, I'm a thickheaded bastard, aren't I? I keep thinking that I want you so bad that you have to want me back, but it doesn't always work that way, does it?" He gave her a hard shake. "Does it?"

"No, it doesn't."

Rand stared into her face, and Billie felt his pain. His voice was a low whisper.

"You're going to have to say it, Billie. You're going to have to tell me straight out so I can't twist it around in my mind and make it come out the way I want it to be. Hell, there's no other way I'm going to get it through my head. . . ."

Billie took a deep breath and nodded.

"All right, I'll say it straight out, if that's the way you want it. I want you to leave me alone, Rand. I don't want you to touch me again."

Rand's hands dropped from her shoulders, and Billie lowered her eyes. There was nothing she wanted more than to have Rand hold her, to keep her safe in the circle of his arms. But it was too late. It was too late the moment she fired the shots that killed Wes McCulla. Nothing could change that . . . nothing.

Within a few moments Rand had stepped down from the wagon. The clanging of pans stopped momentarily. She heard Nate's voice break the silence.

"How's the kid doin', Rand?"

Rand's voice was stiff.

"He's feeling better. He's mad because nobody woke him up for his watch."

Billie could almost hear Nate shake his head. "I'm goin' to have to talk to that boy."

"Don't waste your time, Nate. It's useless."

Nate gave a small laugh. "You sound like a beaten man, Rand."

Rand's voice was devoid of mirth.

"Yeah? Maybe I am."

Carl made his way through the milling herd, his eye on the chuck wagon around which the drovers clustered. He had scanned the water-bound herds as he had come over the hill. This outfit appeared to be the best out of three, with approximately thirty-five hundred Texas cattle on the hoof, and he figured it was as good a place as any to get a noon meal. A small smile picked up the corners of his ragged mustache, and he shot a knowing glance over his shoulder to the men riding behind him. Larry and Marty flicked a smile in return. Hell, it was about time they had a good hot meal. Two days of rain and he was beginnin' to feel like he was moldin' clear through.

Realizing they had drawn the attention of the entire crew as they approached, Carl put on his most disarming smile. He had determined a few days before that he was not going to quit this job McCulla had set him on until he found that damned girl. He and the boys had had a miserable week on the trail. The weather had turned bleak, and this was the first time the sun had shone in six days. As it was now, the air was so heavy he could almost feel its weight against his skin, and he had determined that the only thing that was goin' to make this discomfort worthwhile was that reward McCulla offered. And it had better be good. Yeah, he could think of a dozen ways to spend a reward.

Deciding to put those thoughts aside for another time, Carl widened his smile as he drew up alongside the chuck wagon and dismounted. He walked toward the tall cowboy who had gotten to his feet as he approached, marking him as the trail boss of the outfit. He stifled a short laugh as he extended a practiced hand in greeting and introduced himself. He was gettin' real good at this.

Seated comfortably a short time later, Carl scraped up the last drops of gravy remaining in his dish and uttered a low sigh of contentment.

"Well, that is by far the best chuck me and the boys has had in a dog's age, and I do thank you. It sure was a piece of luck when we headed ourselves in this here direction."

Charlie Stark's wrinkled brow creased a little deeper. "On your way up north, are you?"

"Well, I don't rightly know if I can answer that question, friend." At the trail boss's inquisitive expression, Carl stifled a belch and continued cautiously, "'Cause the fact is, me and the boys don't rightly know where we're headin'."

"Sounds mighty curious to me. . . ."

"The fact is, we're trailin' somebody."

Charlie Stark stiffened. He had an aversion to bounty hunters, considering them one step down from out-and-out murderers, and he wasn't about to entertain them in his camp.

Alert to the trail boss's reaction Carl gave a small laugh. "We're kinda on a 'mission of mercy.'" Noting that the trail boss's lined face had not deviated from its stiff lines, he continued with a small shake of his head, "My boss, Dan McCulla—you probably heard of him—he's a big man in the southern part of the state. Well, he kinda took pity on a poor neighbor of his. Seems like that neighbor had a run-in with his boy, and the boy run off. Now the boy's ma is real sick. Seems like that poor old lady ain't goin' to last long if that boy don't come home real soon."

Carl had trouble maintaining his earnest expression. The story was growin' kinda stale on his tongue. He was goin' to have to think up another one before long if things kept up the way they were.

Charlie Stark was not convinced.

"A mission of mercy, huh?"

"That's right. Me and the boys been on the trail for over three weeks, and we're sure hopin' if we do find that young fella, it ain't too late to save his poor old mama."

The sharp trail boss raised his bushy brows and nodded his head.

"I expect you're wonderin' if any of us here saw this boy you're talkin' about. . . ."

"I figure if you did, you wouldn't have forgotten the kid. He's kind of a skinny fella, medium height, with real light hair—almost like a silver yellow—and dark eyes. I expect he was a little messed up, too, bein's his pa took a heavy hand to him before he left."

Charlie's expression tightened.

"A heavy hand, you say?"

"Yeah, well, Jeff Streicker never was the most patient man when it came to his boy givin' him back talk. And the boy is a real stubborn cuss with a mind of his own. But old Jeff's regrettin' his ornery behavior now, all right. He promised Mr. McCulla he won't never lay a hand on the boy again if he comes home."

"I wouldn't bet on it. A leopard don't often change his spots."

Carl gave a short shrug. "Anyways, Mr. McCulla figures the boy should know his ma is ailin' real bad. He says she's a good woman who deserves to have her son at her side when she's dyin'."

Charlie Stark shot Carl a short, disbelieving glance. "Well, I don't mean to interrupt your story, friend, but there ain't been no boy fittin' that description around this trail drive. And bein's we've been stuck here for over a week, waitin' for the river to go down, we got to know the hands with the other two herds waitin' here. I think I can safely say there ain't no boy that looks like that with them, either."

Carl shook his head. "Is that right? . . . Well, that sure enough is a disappointment. Somebody saw the boy in San Antonio just about the time your herd was passin' through, and we kinda hoped—"

"Well, like I said, all the herds headin' north on this trail is stuck here until the river gets passable. There ain't a one of them that can cross the Brazos when it's this high. Heard tell one herd did cross a little farther north at the beginnin' of the week. But that was Rand Pierce's herd, with them long-legged Mexican cattle. Hell, they can run the legs off a good horse and probably swim the fins off a fish."

His expression freezing, Carl blinked almost comically. "Mexican cattle? . . ."

"Yeah, Rand Pierce's herd. He don't usually take his herds on the trail no more. He's into contracting with the government. Heard he had some trouble with the fever and had to come all the way to San Antonio to take over this herd himself. Nice fella, that Pierce."

Straining to keep his casual facade, Carl prompted lightly, "You say he crossed the Brazos a little farther up?"

"That's what I heard. But we waited this long, and we're not goin' to take a chance on losin' any of our critters so early on. We got plenty of time to meet our schedule."

"Interestin', real interestin' . . ."

Getting slowly to his feet, Carl stifled another belch and patted his stomach contentedly.

"Well, I do thank you for the chuck, neighbor, and the friendly talk. Me and the boys have to be movin' on. It won't do no good if we find the boy and it's too late to save his old mama from dyin' from a broken heart."

Charlie's squint showed more than a trace of disbelief.

"Yeah, that would be a pity."

Charlie Stark's squint tightened as the three riders cleared his herd and started north at a rapid pace. He shook his head. Somethin' sure put a bee in that Carl Whitley's bonnet. Well, whatever it was, he sure enough hoped that boy they

257

was lookin' for had a healthy head start, because he had a feelin' them fellas was up to no good . . . no good at all.

Rand looked down at the mighty Red River as a brilliant afternoon sun glinted on its surface. He shook his head. He needed no one to tell him its reputation. Its majestic grandeur was apparent on every hand, with its red bluff banks, the sediment of its red waters marking the timber along its course. Driftwood lodged in trees high on the banks indicated what might be expected when the river was angry, and Rand felt a rush of gratitude for the present level of its swirling rapids.

His decision to cross had been made much earlier. It had been influenced heavily by the present level of the water, which while not low, was down considerably from the previous line. The fact that a ferry had been available and the wagon easily taken across had been the determining factor. Particularly sobering was the realization that this crossing was only a little over a year old, and yet five graves marked its banks. The last grave, freshly dug, weighed heavily on Rand's mind.

Rand shot a quick look across the river as the herd approached behind him, his eyes narrowing. Indian lands . . . He was familiar with the primitive country on the opposite shore and the trail that led up a divide between the Salt and North forks of the Red River. To the east lay the reservation of the Apaches, Kiowas, and Commanches, another problem soon to be faced.

Rand trailed his gaze lightly across the terrain. His eyes caught movement on a rise of land, and he squinted in perusal. An Indian . . . It was to be expected. He had been advised by a passing horseman, just a few days before, that previous herds had been giving up on the average of twenty-five, and as much as fifty head of cattle to the Commanche as an offering for safe passage through their lands. He had no intention of sacrificing a single steer, no matter how well scouted or threatened they were. He . . .

His mind wandering from his thoughts, Rand stared

harder at the outline across the river. But there was something about this Indian . . . the manner in which he sat his horse, the carriage of his broad shoulders . . . The Indian drew closer to the opposite bank and Rand jerked himself rigidly erect. Turning, he shot a quick look back toward his herd, which was just coming into sight in the distance. It was traveling at a moderate pace, the remuda out in front in their usual manner of fording.

His teeth clamping tightly shut, Rand turned his horse and spurred him abruptly in the herd's direction. His bay was blowing hard when he passed the remuda, but he had no thought for the animal's discomfort. Spurring him even more heavily, Rand made a straight line for the slender figure riding swing. He reined up sharply as he reached Billie's side. With no thought for the curiosity of his men, he pinned her with his gaze.

"Follow me, Drucker."

Billie shook her head.

"But I have to—"

"I said, follow me!"

Not waiting for further response, Rand spurred his horse away from the herd, traveling on a dead run toward the river. He reined up sharply at the bank, his chest heaving with tightly controlled anger as Billie reined up behind him. His eyes on her face, he saw her gaze flick from him to the river and across to the opposite shore. Her eyes jerked to a stop as they touched on the mounted Indian on the opposite bank.

"That's right, Billie. . . . White Hand. He's waiting for you. . . . He knows, doesn't he? He knows you're a woman."

Billie lifted her dark eyes to his.

"Rand, I—I didn't know he was going to be here."

"You didn't answer me. He knows, doesn't he?"

"Yes, he does."

A pain so deep it was almost physical penetrated Rand's vitals. His hand clenched spasmodically on the reins. "You told him, but you wouldn't tell me."

"I didn't tell him, Rand, he knew. He knew from the first."

"It was a secret you shared together. . . . Did you have a good time with your jokes while you acted as 'interpreter' for me? I played the fool real well, didn't I?"

"Rand, White Hand saw through my disguise immediately. He thought you knew I was a woman. He thought the reason there was conflict between us was because you didn't approve of a woman on the drive. I asked him to keep my secret because—"

"Because you didn't trust me. You'd still have me running around in circles if I hadn't forced my way into your room in Abilene."

Billie lifted her chin against his verbal assault. Her eyes were suddenly cold.

"Do you want the truth? You're right. I'd never have told you if you hadn't burst in on me. What good did it do for you to find out I'm a woman? It's only put more pressure on the situation, made you more angry."

"You don't really mean that, do you Billie?" Incredulous that she could dismiss the lovemaking they had shared so easily, Rand shook his head. "The night we spent together, the times I held you in my arms, they were all a big mistake, is that it?"

Her heart pounding, Billie stared into Rand's disbelieving expression. She could not give in to the torment in his eyes.

"Yes, Rand, that's what it was. A mistake. It never should've happened. It won't happen again."

Unable to bear the pain in his gaze a moment longer, Billie jerked her grulla's reins, turning him sharply. Within moments she was heading back toward the approaching herd. Passing the remuda without a backward look, she ignored Willie's curious expression and fitted herself into swing position.

She lifted her eyes to Hank Casey's lead, noting that he was whipping the remuda into a faster pace as they approached the river. The cattle were picking up a companionable speed. They were nearing the water's edge. They would soon be fording. . . .

Rand held his horse firmly at the river's edge as the remuda approached at a steady run. His eyes flicked to the

260

crossing. He had chosen a spot to put the animals into the water opposite two islands. There was no swimming water between the south shore and the first island, although the river was high enough to wet saddle skirts for a distance of nearly two hundred yards after entering. Having swum the full distance earlier, he was well aware that the herd would strike swimming water immediately after leaving the first island. The cattle would be forced to swim for approximately one hundred yards before they would reach the second island a little downstream. The distance from the second island to shore was the longest, and they would not reach solid footing until about fifty yards from shore.

Rand's eyes shot to the opposite shore as the remuda reached the river bank and entered the river. White Hand stood clearly in sight, watching the fording. He turned spontaneously and shot a quick look toward Billie. But Billie was too deeply engrossed in keeping the cattle in line to spare a glance for either him or the Indian waiting patiently on the opposite shore.

Holding back until the last of the horses had entered the river, Rand was about to spur his bay forward to assume a position beside point when a shout from behind caught his attention. Turning, he saw a scramble ensuing in the rear as Carlisle, Johnson, and Hall attempted to turn back a portion of the herd, which was attempting to break free of the main stream. Without a second thought, he spurred his horse into the melee, riding at full speed to head off the cattle leading the break. Within minutes the lead steers had been turned and were headed back toward the river.

Satisfied he was no longer needed, Rand turned his horse sharply back toward the river. He took a quick, assessing glance at the fording bank. The cattle had entered the water cleanly and were halfway toward the first island. The first of the remuda had already struck deep water and were swimming strongly toward the second island. His heart pounding loudly in his chest, Rand searched the river's surface for Billie's figure. Breathing an unconscious sigh of relief, he saw her halfway across the first channel, her horse moving confidently amidst the fording beeves.

261

His anxiety not fully relieved, Rand spurred his horse into the river. Somehow he did not feel safe allowing Billie to get so far ahead of him. Frustration gained control as the beeves around him refused to cooperate with his attempted thrust forward, and Rand raised impatient eyes again to the front of the herd.

A quick assessment showed that the saddle horses were already on the second island. Having left the first island, the cattle had struck swimming water and were breasting it strongly. His eyes moving inevitably to swing position, Rand saw Billie's horse take his first step off the island into swimming water.

But something was wrong! Billie's powerful grulla was stumbling! His heart jumping in his chest, Rand watched as Billie's mount plunged into the rapidly moving river at a painful angle, Billie still on his back. Before his horrified eyes they both sank beneath the water with incredible swiftness. Within moments the spot where Billie and her horse had disappeared was coverd by the steady stream of steers, which had been following behind them.

Blind panic assailed Rand's senses. Wild with fear, he pushed his bay forward with new urgency. Frantically, he searched the surface of the water with his eyes. His blood pounding through his veins when neither Billie nor her horse reappeared, Rand pressed his mount to the full extent of his strength in an attempt to reach the spot where she had gone under. He was still fighting the steady stream of beeves impeding his progress when he saw another mounted figure swimming strongly toward the same spot from the opposite shore. Unhindered by the swimming steers, White Hand was closing in on the area, his horse swimming cleanly. But Billie was nowhere to be seen. . . . Nowhere. . . .

The cattle had moved easily through the first hundred yards of the river and had taken a few steps on the first island when Billie heard her grulla's low snort. Pulling heavily to the left, he turned his head in her direction and Billie jerked tightly on the reins in an attempt to turn him back.

Apprehension prickled her spine. The grulla was strong, one of the most dependable of her mounts, but something was wrong. . . .

Responding to her urging, the powerful animal continued forward, pressing the anxious beeves as they prepared to descend back into the river, and Billie felt a strong surge of relief. Whatever it was that had bothered her mount temporarily appeared to be gone. Billie turned briefly to her rear. The herd's push from behind was steady, allowing no lapse in the stream of cattle that made its way toward the opposite shore. She felt a flicker of satisfaction. This crossing would be accomplished in record time at the present rate of things, and she would then . . .

A sudden jerk on the reins alerted Billie to trouble the second before her mount gave a pained snort. She attempted to pull him back, stop him before he descended into the river, but it was too late to halt his forward motion. His legs were giving way! They were plunging awkwardly into the river headfirst!

The rapidly moving surface of the water was coming up to meet her eyes with a swiftness that stole her breath. The sound of her grulla's pained whinny sounded loudly in her ears. It echoed over and again as she hit the cool surface of the river with a hard, resounding smack.

She was submerged in the cloudy water, her eyes straining to see in the red-gold mistiness that surrounded her. She fought to rise to a surface filled with flailing hooves and hide-covered bodies, but there was no room, no place for her! Held down by the steers above her as they swam relentlessly toward the opposite shore, Billie felt the rise of panic. She could not breathe. . . . She needed to reach the surface. . . . She could not hold on much longer. . . .

There was a sudden break in the surface above her and a glimmer of sun lit the murky darkness. She fought the heavy weight of her limbs, twisting under the water in an attempt to raise herself to that opening to the sky. But it was too late! Another hide-covered body, hooves moving rhythmically, closed in over the spot. It was too late . . . too late!

Her bursting lungs strained for air, but there was none.

She gasped. A sandy wetness filled her mouth and she swallowed deeply. Sand gritted between her teeth as she strove again and again for breath. Water . . . water everywhere, filling her nose . . . her mouth . . . her lungs. It was consuming her.

She was floating . . . no longer in need of breath . . . no longer in need of anything or anyone as the impending darkness closed around her.

His mind alive with panic, Rand leaned on his bay's neck, urging him forward. Billie had not yet surfaced! The last person in swing position, Billie had fallen unnoticed by the men in front of her. His shouts had alerted them to her disappearance under the water too late for them to ascertain the spot where she had gone down. Their agitation obvious, the men were swimming their horses in frantic circles in an attempt to spot her beneath the surface of the churning water. His eyes jerking to a spot farther downstream, Rand saw Billie's horse surface. His heart pounding, he held his breath awaiting her appearance beside it, but his wait was to no avail.

His approach frustrated by the cattle swimming between him and his destination, Rand saw White Hand reach the second island from the opposite shore. Without hesitation the Apache plunged into the channel between the two islands. His line straight and free of the surrounding beeves, White Hand swam his horse to the area where Billie had hit the water. His concentration intense, White Hand searched the murky depths with his eyes, and Rand felt a heartfelt prayer rise inside his mind.

God, please, let him find her. . . .

With a sudden jerk on his horse's mane, White Hand turned his buckskin in the swirling water. Within minutes the responsive animal had accomplished the desired curve and White Hand was reaching down into the water. He was pulling, jerking at something beneath the surface, and within moments he had raised an inert, light-haired figure. Stewart and Byrd, at White Hand's side in moments, helped to lift

264

Billie's limp body onto the buckskin's back, and within seconds White Hand had turned his horse toward the opposite shore.

Able to think of nothing but the lifeless color of Billie's face as she had been raised from the river, Rand pressed his horse mercilessly forward. White Hand had found her, but was it too late? . . . Too late? . . .

She was choking, coughing. She retched, her body jerking in deep, grueling spasms that left her breathless. She collapsed against the hard ground, her strength depleted. She lay there for long, motionless moments. A gentle hand stroked her forehead, and her heavy lids stirred and lifted. Her blurred gaze touched on a figure crouched beside her, and she squinted in an attempt to make out the uncertain image.

Her lips parted in a hoarse whisper.

"White Hand."

Concern marked the finely sculpted planes of his face. His gaze was intense, his voice low.

"Yes, Brave One. I returned almost in time to see the river claim you."

Billie's eyes moved to the two shadows standing behind White Hand and she blinked. Stewart and Byrd . . . Her eyes snapped to the river's edge behind them to see the cattle still emerging on the banks.

"What? . . ."

"White Hand pulled you out, Drucker." Stewart's voice was low with relief. "We couldn't find you, but the Indian saw you go down." Stewart shot a begrudging look in the Apache's direction. "I suppose you owe this fella your life."

Billie's eyes moved back to White Hand, and Stewart continued quietly, "Well, if you're all right, Russ and I will go back to the herd."

"Yes, I—I'm fine." Suddenly jerking her eyes to Stewart's face, she inquired tightly, "My horse—"

"He came up a ways down the river. He's limpin', but he's all right."

Billie nodded. She was all right, and her horse and equipment had been saved. She released a short, relieved breath and pulled herself weakly to a sitting position. She was shivering despite the warmth of the day, her body quaking in deep shudders, her lips quivering uncontrollably.

"I—I'll get another horse from the remuda and be back with the herd in a few minutes. . . ."

"Damned if you will!"

An unexpected voice from behind turned Billie's head toward Rand as he dismounted angrily. Exchanging a look, Stewart and Byrd turned back toward their horses. They were directing their mounts back toward the herd as Rand took a blanket from his saddle and crouched beside Billie to wrap it around her shoulders. His hand lingered on her back as he directed the full force of his gaze into her eyes.

"You're going to stay right here until you feel stronger. I don't want you back on horseback today. You'll ride on the wagon with Nate."

"No, I—"

"Yes, you will, damn it!" His chest heaving with emotion, Rand shook his head. "You'll do what I tell you to do!"

Not waiting for her reply, Rand turned stiffly to White Hand. He had not missed the way in which White Hand had stroked the hair from Billie's forehead, and he burned with jealousy at the intimacy of the touch. A muscle jerked in his cheek.

"You saved Billie's life, and I'm grateful to you, White Hand, but that changes very little between us. I told you I didn't want you in my camp, and I haven't changed my mind. I want you out of here."

"Rand. . . ."

Rand snapped his head toward Billie.

"I told you, *I'm* the boss here! He's leaving . . . now!

White Hand's low voice interrupted the growing heat of their exchange. He addressed Rand in perfect, unhesitant English that sent the trail boss's anger up a few notches higher.

"You need not worry, Randall Pierce. I have no desire to

remain in your camp." His obsidian gaze was cold. "I have only returned because I promised the Brave One I would."

"The 'Brave One' wasn't waiting for your return. . . ."

"Rand, I can speak for myself. . . ."

Reaching out, White Hand touched Billie's shoulder.

"Take your hand off her, White Hand."

The warmth of White Hand's touch burned into Billie's skin as he turned to Rand's menacing command.

"It was my hand that drew her from beneath the surface of the river. Were I unwilling to extend it, there would be no cause for this heated exchange. For that reason, I ask that you put aside your anger so that I might speak with the Brave One now."

His expression turning as hard as stone, Rand shook his head. "I don't owe you anything, much less time to try to talke Billie into—"

"Rand. . . ." Thoroughly depleted, Billie reached up weakly to smooth a flying wisp of hair from her face. Realizing she had Rand's full attention, she offered softly, "Please . . . I would like to talk to White Hand. Just a few minutes . . ."

Rand's azure gaze held hers for long moments. Agitation was obvious in the set of his broad shoulders, in the heaving of his broad chest, in the twitch of the small muscle in his cheek. She held her breath for his reply. She did not have the strength to fight him.

Rand jerked his head in a short nod. The intensity of his gaze seared her.

"Don't try to leave with him, Billie. You may not want me, but I'll be damned if I'll sit by and let you ruin your life by running off with this savage. He has nothing to offer you but a life of hardship and deprivation."

A flush of anger colored Billie's pale face.

"I asked for some time to talk to White Hand. . . ."

"All right!" Drawing himself to his feet, Rand looked down on them. His strong frame was stiff with anger. "But don't try leaving. . . ."

Turning toward his horse, Rand was mounted within a

second and on his way toward the spot where Nate was already set up for the noon meal.

Unready to face White Hand's keen gaze, Billie attempted to stand. Shakier than she realized, she smiled at White Hand's steadying touch as she raised herself to her feet and pulled the blanket tighter around her. She smiled shakily.

"You always seem to know what I need, White Hand."

But White Hand was not smiling. His dark eyes perused her face.

"Much has changed since the last time we were together. Rand Pierce now knows you are a woman. He has come to realize the true nature of his feelings for you. He is jealous and wishes to see me gone from camp for reasons other than the deceit practiced on him."

Unable to sustain White Hand's knowing gaze, Billie dropped her eyes.

"Yes, he knows, but he's given me his word that he won't reveal my secret."

"What have you paid for his silence?"

Billie's gaze jerked back to his.

"Nothing . . . I paid him nothing. . . ."

White Hand's hand moved to Billie's shoulder in a friendly gesture made intimate by his new depth of tone, the glimmer of pain in his eyes.

"Rand Pierce has held you in his arms as I have not yet held you. You have lain with him and taken him into your body. But in his eyes I see a joining of your spirits, which I do not see reflected in yours. His anger is born of this deficiency. His heart cries out to yours, and yours does not answer."

White Hand paused, his gaze intensifying. "My heart also cries out to yours, Brave One. You are the vision I carry in my heart, the image which allows no other to fill that space. Your courage is a spirit kindred to mine; it thrills my soul. Your eyes reflect a suffering you have met and conquered with that strength. In their depths I see an awareness of the true value of life, which I would merge with my own. Your

268

physical beauty is great, surpassed only by the matchless beauty within. It is this beauty I would treasure, keep as my own, delight to see in the hearts and faces of our children.

"We have suffered a common injustice . . . bear the censure of the white man's laws without good cause. Rand Pierce was wrong when he said I have nothing to offer you. I offer you my life and all the days that it entails to hold you with me. I will cherish no woman above you, for I am forever blinded to all other women. And there is no law, of my people or yours, that would keep me from your side. This I promise you, Brave One. It matters not to me that Rand Pierce has tasted the warmth of your body, for he has only sampled that which would be mine alone for the rest of our days. I ask you to come with me now, join your life to mine so that we both may come to know the joy that is ours to share . . . ours alone."

Her dark eyes holding White Hand's intense gaze, Billie was unable to speak for long moments. She allowed her eyes to absorb the strength reflected in the finely chiseled contours of his face, the warmth in the velvet-black of his eyes, the integrity reflected so clearly in their depths. She swallowed hard as she prepared to speak.

"White Hand, I am not worthy of your generous petition. I—I would only bring the white man's law down upon you, and I would not have you share in the punishment that it would reap. And were it not for that, my heart and mind would still be filled with a task I have set myself, from which I cannot deviate. In my heart there is no room for the total love you would offer me, or even the desire which Rand Pierce feels for me. I have seen the error of Rand's and my intimacy and decided it will be no more. I have caused him much pain by my decision, and I do not wish to cause you a similar distress. I thank you for my life, White Hand, and wish that I could give it back to you as fully as you would give yours to me. I will cherish your words and your offer of love always within my heart."

White Hand's hand dropped from her shoulder and Billie's heart filled with the sadness reflected in his eyes. His low voice was deepened with emotion.

"My heart is yours, Brave One, and yours it will remain. I see the purpose of which you speak in your eyes, and your desire to see it through. I sense the strength of its calling within you. It is a need you must satisfy. Only when that need is satiated will your heart be free, and I will wait for that time. My heart and the land of my people will remain a sanctuary for you, to which you may come in time of need. They will remain forever yours." Pausing, White Hand offered softly, "Hear my words, Brave One, and think on them in the long days to come. I give them to you in hope and consolation."

Billie nodded, her throat too tight to speak.

A sudden sound from behind lifted Billie's eyes to Rand's horse as he rode in their direction. Dismounting even as White Hand stepped back from their intimate pose, Rand took a few short steps forward to stand stiffly at Billie's side.

"All right, White Hand, you had your talk. Now, leave."

"Rand, please."

"Now, White Hand."

But White Hand needed no further urging. Mounting without another word, White Hand spurred his buckskin and within minutes the sound of his pony's hooves were fading into the distance. Her eyes bright with emotion, Billie turned to Rand. Fatigue was setting in, and she swayed slightly, only to have Rand's arm snap out to steady her. Frustration obvious in his gaze, he walked her stiffly toward the wagon.

Coming to an abrupt halt, he muttered, "Get in there, damn it! Change into the clothes Nate left out for you and go to sleep. You're going to travel with the wagon for the rest of the day."

"No, I—"

Rand's face flushed. He shook his head, obviously in far more tenuous control of his emotions than she had realized. His voice was strained.

"Do what I say, Billie. Get out of my sight for a little while so I can get a hold on myself. Do you have any idea what it was like seeing you go down under that water, thinking you might never come up? We were separated by the herd. . . . I couldn't get to you. Those few minutes were the longest of my life. All I can think about now is holding you in my arms, keeping you safe, making you mine." Rand paused. His azure gaze burned her. "Have a little mercy, damn it!"

Billie turned. She climbed into the wagon in silence. There was nothing she could say.

Chapter X

Lucille gave her aging coachman a brief, measuring glance as he helped her down from the carriage onto the busy St. Louis street. She frowned as she flicked her gaze toward the train making ready to depart the station in front of her. She winced at the resounding din of the conductor's shouted monotone, the scramble of last minute passengers as they hurried to board, and the screeching whistle of the huge black engine belching puffs of soot-filled smoke into the sultry morning air.

Turning back, she glanced at Jack's stiff jowled face. To outward appearances the short, balding family retainer of long standing was formally correct in his attitude, but Lucille knew that expression. She had seen it countless times of late. She knew that frigid mask was his manner of displaying disapproval of her actions.

Lucille gave a short sniff and tossed her flaming curls. What did it matter if everyone disapproved of her actions if she was finally successful in becoming Mrs. Randall Pierce? And today she was taking a positive step in that direction . . . whether Jack liked it or not! Lucille's well-shaped lips tightened in annoyance. Jack had followed her orders with amused tolerance when she was a child. It had only been in the last few years that he had allowed his occasionally disparaging attitude to become obvious.

And damned if the rotund little fellow didn't have the ability to make his silent censure keenly felt! Shooting him another glance, Lucille stepped up onto the walkway and adjusted the folds of her azure silk walking-out dress. She was conscious of the fact that the well-fitting jacket hugged her generous bosom and made the most of her miniscule waist. The matching skirt, caught up at the sides, was bunched provocatively at the back in a manner that accented the eye-stopping sway of her delicate derriere. With conscious deliberation, she gave that part of her anatomy an intriguing little wiggle and began walking briskly toward the train station.

Pooh on Jack's censure! Approving or not, he would wait faithfully until she had returned with the ticket that would take her to Dodge in two weeks' time.

Sniffing against the scent of ash and smoke in the air and the fine layer of the grayish residue from the train that was just clearing the station, Lucille continued purposely toward the station house. Her temporary discomfort dissipated in the face of the admiring glances her attractive figure elicited from the passengers waiting to board the next train. She smiled boldly at the heavily mustached young gentleman near the doorway, treating him to a devastating flutter of lush lashes and a flirtatious smile as he opened the door in a cavalier manner. She chuckled inwardly at his revealing flush as she brushed as close in passing him as she dared. Oh, men! What children they were, and how she enjoyed them! They were so easy to control when one had the knack. And she, most certainly, had it.

Her smile fading only slightly as she approached the ticket counter, Lucille found a familiar image invading her thoughts. She amended her frivolous thoughts. Well, *most* men were easily controlled, at any rate. There were always exceptions, and the exception in her case was Pat Patterson.

Damn if that man didn't set her teeth on edge! He had not been satisfied to irritate her immeasurably at her own dinner party only a week or so before. He had since called on her several times at her home, always when her father was there and when she had been unable to tell him what she truly thought of his visits. It seemed he had made it his vocation in life to torment her, and if that was so, he was certainly succeeding. By his inquiries as to Rand's progress on the cattle drive, he had managed to ascertain that she had heard nothing of Rand or from him, thereby appearing to lend credence to his statement that Rand was through with her. Well, that might be so, but *she* was not through with Rand, and she knew exactly what she had to do to stimulate a renewal of his interest. A little exposure of feminine flesh here . . . an erotic touch there . . . and how she would enjoy that task!

Stepping up to the counter, Lucille murmured a few soft words to the bemused clerk. Turning a few minutes later, a ticket in her hand, she walked briskly back toward the door. In two weeks' time she would be in Dodge with Rand. She had not made the mistake this time of telling her father of her intended meeting. Instead, she had expressed a desire to visit her Aunt Jennifer in a nearby town. Of course, she had told him of her intention to travel with Aunt Jessica and had even had the foresight to ask Aunt Jessica to accompany her. She would, of course, send a note to Aunt Jessica a day prior to the date and cancel the trip. She would then leave on the scheduled day for Dodge. Her father would not become aware of the last minute change in plans until it was too late to stop her. It mattered little that she would face his anger when she returned. By then she would have accomplished her mission.

Mrs. Randall Pierce. . . . Mmmm . . . How good those words sounded to her ears.

Oh, there he was again, always lurking at the perimeter of her mind, his pale green eyes laughing at her! Damn that Pat Patterson! His image had succeeded too often of late in coming between erotic daydreams of Rand and herself. How was it that his modest, unimposing frame had managed so well to supplant Rand's tall, virile figure on each occasion she recalled Rand to mind? Pat Patterson's invasion of her thoughts was as irritating as his obvious determination to take a hand in her affairs. He had no place in either area, and she was determined to oust him. She was certain the ticket she held in her hand would accomplish that fact most completely.

Shooting the same mustached gentleman a warm smile as he held the door for her sweeping exit from the station house, Lucille tucked the ticket into her bag and walked briskly back toward the carriage. A small smile picked up the corners of her lips as she caught Jack's covert observation and his quick attempt to conceal it.

Old Jack was such a dear after all! Despite her annoyance, she knew he was extremely fond of her—a fondness she returned—and was only concerned for her welfare. It was this realization that allowed her to maintain her patience with his well-meaning admonishments and to travel the city alone without concern when he was at the reins. And it was the certainty of his confidentiality that made her chance his unspoken disapproval by using him to accomplish this errand today, even if it involved such a risky procedure as informing him the day before of her intention so he might have the carriage ready first thing after her father left for the bank in the morning.

Waiting almost until she had reached the carriage, Jack dismounted from the driver's seat with surprising nimbleness for a man of his years and girth, and opened the door of the carriage. Taking the assisting hand he offered, Lucille paused with her foot on the first step, her eyes sweeping Jack's unsmiling face.

An irrepressible sadness pierced her buoyant mood, and she offered spontaneously, "Jack dear, you will quite spoil my day if you continue to scowl at me in that manner. You know how dependent I am on your good humor. Surely you can manage at least a little smirk."

"A smirk, ma'am?" His full face holding its sober lines, Jack gave her a reproving glance. "Seems to me it should be you who's smirking, ma'am. Looks like you're going to put it over on Mr. Bascombe again. When he finally discovers your plans it'll be too late to do anything to stop you from chasing after that Pierce fellow. Scandalous, that's what it is. . . ."

"Jack. . . ." Realizing the true extent of Jack's displeasure for the first time, Lucille looked tensely into his face, "You will not betray me. . . . You gave me your word years ago

276

that you would never betray me to my father . . . no matter the circumstances."

"Miss Lucille, you know that was a promise made to a repentant child caught spying where she should not be."

"It was a promise made, nevertheless, Jack. I hold you to it firmly. You will not betray me and your own honor. . . ."

Jack's full white mustache quivered as he gave a resigned sigh. That promise, made under the pressure of Lucille's childish tears, had been the bane of his existence for the last few years, but he was tied to it. He raised his full brows with a shrug.

"I haven't betrayed you to your father yet, have I, Miss Lucille? As much as I would like to sometimes . . ."

Lucille suppressed her sigh of relief and turned a suddenly coquettish grin in his direction.

"Just one little smile, Jack? . . ."

His heavy jowls reluctantly lifting in a smile, Jack shook his head.

"Miss Lucille, you could charm the birds from the trees. I expect that's your problem. . . ."

"On the contrary, my problem was that you had refused to smile for me, Jack. And now that you have, you've lifted my spirits considerably." Her relief sincere, Lucille pinched Jack's sagging cheek lovingly. "You may drive me home now, dear Jack. I have a long day ahead of me and many plans to make."

His smile of a moment before disappearing, Jack snorted. His response was a low grumble. "Plans? Hanky-panky, you mean . . ."

Turning toward him as she settled herself gracefully in the carriage, Lucille leaned forward with a small whisper.

"Yes, Jack. Glorious hanky-panky . . ."

Lucille's low laughter accompanied Jack's returned scowl as he remounted the carriage and slapped the reins sharply against the horses' backs. Oh, yes, gloriously lovely hanky-panky . . .

Watching surreptitiously from his position a few doors

277

down, Pat shook his head as Lucille's carriage pulled away. Jack was frowning, his disapproval apparent, and Lucille, the little witch that she was, was looking too entirely pleased with herself. Allowing his eyes to follow the departing carriage, Pat felt his stomach tighten spasmodically. And she was looking entirely too lovely and desirable. He had seen the attention she had garnered as she had descended from the carriage into the crowded street. Red-gold curls bouncing, her lush figure encased in a stylish walking-out dress that made the most of her feminine appeal, she had left observers breathless in her wake. And how she had enjoyed herself . . .

But she had garnered more than his eye. She had garnered his heart as well, and he'd be damned before he'd let her throw herself at a man who wanted no part of her!

Lucille's carriage was turning the busy street corner when Pat stepped out from his cover. Poor Jack . . . The old coachman had approached him the evening before as he neared the Harriman household. It had turned out to be a boring party, at which he had been frustrated time and again by Lucille's devious maneuvers in escaping him. Despite his most stringent efforts, he had been almost certain he had revealed his true feelings for her, but Lucille's departing sally had set his mind to rest in that quarter. For there was one thing of which he was certain. If Lucille knew she had the upper hand in this situation, which she most definitely did at present, she would flaunt it. As it was, she appeared to be desperate to avoid him. That desperation could only make him think that she was not as sure of herself in facing him as she would have him think.

Well, at least Jack recognized him as an ally. Pushing through the station house door, Pat called to mind their encounter of the night before. It had indeed been fortunate that his carriage had reached the Harriman household during the full crush of arrivals. Rather than wait in the drive for the guests ahead of him to disembark from their carriages, he had dismissed his vehicle at the gate and decided to walk the rest of the way. Jack had called out to him from beside the Bascombe carriage parked in the drive.

"Good evenin' to you, Mr. Patterson."

Not particularly anxious to join the crowd at the front door, he had walked conversationally to Jack's side.

"And to you, Jack. I see the Bascombes have already arrived. I trust Horace is well, and Miss Lucille is looking her radiant self."

"Yes, Mr. Bascombe is well. And Miss Lucille, well, she's her beautiful self as usual. And since you probably know her better than most of her acquaintances, I guess you'll understand what I mean when I say she has that look in her eye that says something's brewing."

Pat had come immediately alert. He had taken a few spontaneous steps that had put him in a position to speak more confidentially to the obviously concerned coachman.

"Something . . . what something is brewing, Jack?"

"Well, it's not my place to say, Mr. Patterson. . . ."

"Jack, let's put all formalities aside, shall we? You know my mother was housemaid at the Teasdale residence most of her life. I was raised in the kitchen of that house, and I think I'm a pretty good judge of the loyalties of people and servants in particular. You have a true loyalty to your young mistress, although there are times when I know you must question why. And you have a keen enough eye to see that my involvement with Miss Lucille goes farther than the original arrangements her father made for me to function as her guardian on that trip to Abilene. You're also keen enough to realize that Miss Lucille is hell-bent on becoming Mrs. Randall Pierce, whether Pierce wants her or not. Now, you obviously know something. It's apparent that you've decided not to go to Mr. Bascombe direct. . . ."

"I've given my word that I wouldn't, Mr. Patterson."

"And yet you've spoken to me?"

"I've not given my word not to tell you. . . ."

A smile quirked the corner of Pat's mouth.

"Quite right, Jack. That's reasoning worthy of Miss Lucille herself."

"Yes, it is, isn't it?" Jack's smile showed a flicker of irony.

"So?" Waiting, his brow raised, Pat had urged with a trace of impatience, "If you've made up your mind to tell me, tell

279

me, Jack."

Hesitating only a moment, Jack nodded his head.

"You're right, Mr. Patterson. I suppose it's best to come right out with it. Well, the fact is, Miss Lucille told me to have the carriage ready to take her to the train station as soon as Mr. Bascombe leaves for the bank tomorrow morning. She told me she needs to make some inquiries as to the trains traveling to Dodge."

"Dodge!"

"Yes, sir. Miss Lucille is intending to go to that lawless cow town all by herself just so she can be with that fellow Randall Pierce. I've heard bad things about that place, Mr. Patterson. It's not unusual for people to be shot dead on the street by stray bullets from a cowboy's gun. There's a real bad element there. They're not civilized like us here in St. Louis."

"Well, I wouldn't go so far as to say that, Jack."

"But Miss Lucille won't be safe. She—"

"She won't get anywhere near Dodge if I have anything to say about it."

Jack's heavily jowled face had shown distinct relief.

"I was hoping you'd say that, sir. Being's Mr. Bascombe thought highly enough of you to depend on you to take care of Miss Lucille, I figured I could, too."

Pat had patted the old coachman's rounded shoulder.

"You've done the right thing, Jack. Just take Miss Lucille to the train station as planned tomorrow morning and leave the rest to me."

Jack had nodded vigorously.

"I'll do that, Mr. Patterson."

"And don't worry. I'll take care of Miss Lucille."

"It does my heart good to hear you say that, sir."

Pat's reply had been accompanied by a weak smile.

"To tell you the truth, Jack, I'm not sure how much good it's done mine. I haven't had a peaceful day since that minx came into my life."

Jack's expression had been understanding.

"Me neither, sir."

Pat had been forced to stifle a laugh, but he wasn't laughing now. He was presently standing at a ticket counter, facing a clerk, without the slightest idea as to what to say.

"May I help you, sir?"

Pat flashed the polite young clerk a smile.

"Yes, you may. The young lady who just left is my sister. You know, the beautiful redheaded woman."

The clerk's expression showed he had not forgotten, and Pat's nose twitched with annoyance. Lucille had probably given the young man the full treatment. The poor fellow had not stopped salivating yet. Holding tight to his tenuous smile, Pat continued speaking in a hopefully casual manner.

"Yes, well, I couldn't catch her on the road in time to tell her to purchase a ticket to Dodge for me, also. So, I'm afraid I'll have to bother you to write up another. You do remember the details, don't you, the time and the date? . . ."

"Oh, yes, sir. How could I forget? I tried to tell the lady that she shouldn't be traveling alone to a place like Dodge, but she was adamant. To tell you the truth, I'm relieved she'll have someone to look out for her. She's so sweet, and innocentlike. . . ."

Pat wasn't sure how much more of this he could take. Damn that Lucille!

"I'm afraid I'm in a bit of a hurry. If you could make out the ticket . . ."

"Of course, sir."

His face still flushed as Pat counted out the required payment, the young clerk bid him a strained good-bye. Striding vigorously from the train station a few minutes later, Pat felt a new resolve rouse his senses. He pulled his tightly knit frame to its full height and took a deep breath. He mumbled distinctly to the beautiful image so clear in his mind.

"All right, Miss Lucille Bascombe, you asked for it. You're going to get everything you expected . . . and more, if I have anything to say about it. That's right, you beautiful little redheaded witch. You've met your match, and it's time you found it out. As a matter of fact, the time is long overdue. . . ."

*   *   *

They had left the crossing of the Red River behind them, but the picture of the primitive land that had met his eyes on the opposite shore was still fresh in Rand's mind. It was a sight he hoped never to forget. They had worked their way up the narrow divide of the Salt and North forks of the river to a breathtaking panorama of green-swarded plain and timber-fringed watercourse, which bore no visible sign of ever having been invaded by civilized man. Antelope had come up in bands to satisfy their curiosity at the approach of the herd, while old solitary buffalo bulls had turned tail and lumbered away to keep their own company. He had been aware that few trail herds had ever passed over this particular route through Indian lands, but buffalo trails leading downstream, deep worn by generations of travel, had been apparent on every hand.

They had not suffered the harassment by Indian bands he had been warned to expect, but he had not been surprised. His constant perusal of the horizon had revealed mounted Indians following the progress of the herd from the distance. It had taken him a few days to realize their significance. Protection . . . The Indians were affording the herd protection, and he knew who that protection was meant for.

Ever conscious of Billie's location within the herd, he had snapped his gaze in her direction at the moment of realization, only to see that her eyes followed the same distant figures. Was she looking for White Hand? He had no doubt that particular Indian was responsible for the immunity they had been granted, and he was truly uncertain if he was thankful or resentful. He wanted no favors from White Hand, no matter how they benefited him. He wanted nothing to remind Billie of that Indian in any way, but it seemed White Hand had ideas of his own. Somehow he believed Billie when she said that White Hand would not be returning. But he had no doubt that it would take no more than a single signal from Billie to bring him back on the run. His own deep-seated fear was that Billie might eventually give White Hand that signal.

He had sought little opportunity to talk with Billie since fording the Red River. He was only too keenly aware that his emotions were at such a pitch that he dared not approach her. The situation grew more intolerable for him each day, but Billie showed not a modicum of discomfort with the status of affairs between them. Instead, she seemed mainly involved in the continued resentment Brothers and Hall evidenced against her. Appearing unwilling to take any more of their pointed remarks, she had begun responding with an anger that had only escalated the heated feelings between them. Knowing his interference would intensify the situation, he had been forced to watch as Billie boldly gave them back some of their own or as Carlisle took up in her defense.

The result had been his need to absent himself from the scene of his torment. Had he not a matter to take care of in Camp Supply, he was certain he would still have ridden out without looking back that morning; he was that much in need of relief.

Rand squinted up toward the unrelenting sun. It was near noon. He had given Willie instructions as to the course he should take in the next few days. He had been determined to stay away until he was in firmer control of his emotions. He had been gone only a few hours, but it was not the hunger pangs gnawing at his belly that urged him to return to noon camp. Rand gave a short, mirthless laugh. Was he the same man who had always treated women with such casual arrogance in the past, the same man who had become bored to distraction when he had continued to see the same woman for any length of time? He had been separated from Billie for only a few hours, and he ached to see her. It was all he could do not to turn his horse around and head back in the direction of the herd, despite the frustration that he knew would ensue.

It was hard for him to realize he was the same person, but he supposed the answer to that was simple. He wasn't the same. Billie had inadvertently accomplished the metamorphosis that had taken place within him. His response to her had been instinctive, a simple physical reaction to her aura, the femininity she could not disguise. It had been there, drawing him in from the first. Then they had made love, and he had experienced a fulfillment beyond his wild-

283

est expectations. In the time since, he had grown to respect Billie's strength, her sense of commitment to a goal she would not reveal. She was like no woman he had ever met before, and along with his love for her, growing stronger each day, grew a deep, abiding respect. With Billie he was no longer satisfied with taking. He needed to give. He needed to give all that he had . . . all that he was . . . all that she had made him to be. He needed that more than he had needed anything in his life.

God, how he wanted her! He longed to take her in his arms, to hold her close, to whisper against her smooth white skin all the words of love resounding within his mind. He wanted to look freely into her solemn, beautiful face, to see the corners of her lush mouth turn up in a smile meant for him alone. He wanted to see the spark of passion light the velvet darkness of her eyes. He wanted to brush those fragile, transparent lids with his mouth, to feel those spiky lashes trail against his lips. He wanted to breathe deeply of the sweet scent of Billie's flesh, to taste it with his tongue. He wanted to drink deeply from the endless well of love that was Billie. He wanted to drink until he had taken his fill, until his body was so sated that he could look at her without desire pumping his blood to a rushing within his veins.

He wanted her, but he was bound by rash promises, made in the desperate fear that he would lose her if he didn't allow her the space she demanded. But he knew now, as he had known then, that he had had no choice. He could not let her leave him, no matter the daily torture of unfulfilled and unrequited love.

Rand's eyes snapped backward toward the dust cloud rising in the distance. His herd was progressing northward behind him. Determination snapped Rand's head forward and he spurred his horse into motion. He had to get to Camp Supply to send a telegram. He wouldn't be needing Jess Williams for this drive after all. He had no intention of abandoning the herd before he reached Montana. He needed that time—every last day of it—to find a way to convince Billie that whoever she was, whatever she was running away

284

from, he would take care of her, protect her, love her to the end of his days. Because he had come to the firm and clear realization in his mind that he truly would. . . .

He was eluding her again. Her feet were flying across the rutted ground, but she was chasing a shadow, a will-o'-the-wisp. . . . No, he was stopping, looking back! She could almost see him . . . almost! . . .

"Stop! Wait for me!"

He hesitated, and she began running faster, faster. But he was too far ahead. She could no longer see him and she cried out in despair. He was gone . . . gone. . . .

"Billie . . . Billie, wake up."

Billie came gradually awake to reality. Rand's face was above hers, and momentarily disoriented, Billie shot a brief glance around her. The crackling campfire, sleeping drovers rolled up in their blankets on the hard ground, the distant sound of Russ Byrd's lulling monotone as he rode guard among the sleeping steers . . .

Her eyes moved back to Rand. The tension of the days since the Red River crossing was absent from his gaze. In its place was a warmth that all but stole her breath. Dropping her eyes closed for the briefest second, Billie steeled herself against that warmth. His low whisper raised her gaze to his.

"You were having another nightmare. You were calling out. I thought it best that I woke you up before you woke up the men."

Billie gave a casual, dismissing nod that did not ring true in the confines of her mind. "It was the same old dream. I don't pay much attention to it anymore."

Rand made no reply. He was stroking the fine wisps at her temple, his hand sliding down to tangle in the pale golden strands as his eyes moved slowly over her face. The sternness that had made his expression an impenetrable mask in the time since the crossing was gone. In its place a loving tenderness shone to tear at her heart. She was succumbing to its potent appeal, and she felt the touch of panic.

"Whe—when did you get back? Willie said you wouldn't

be back for a few more days. He said you had something to take care of at Camp Supply."

Rand nodded. "I took care of it and started right back. I figured three days was long enough to be away from the herd . . . to be away from you."

"Rand. . . ."

"I know. . . ." Desperation flickered in his brilliant gaze. His fingers tightened spasmodically in her hair. "You're wondering how many times and how many ways you have to tell me the same thing—that you don't want any part of me. I suppose I'm trying to see if you've found them all."

"Rand, please. The men will wake up and hear. . . ."

"I know. We wouldn't want that, would we, Billie? That would spoil all your plans—the plans you won't share with me. . . ."

"Rand. . . ."

Rand's hands moved to her shoulders. His fingers tightened in a tense grip.

"Billie, if I told you I wouldn't press you for any answers, if I said I'd just take things a day at a time . . ." Rand's voice trailed away and he swallowed visibly. "I want to love you again, Billie. I want that more than I've ever wanted anything in my life. I'll make it good for you, Billie, better than it was, more beautiful than—"

"No, Rand, no." Her heart pounding, Billie fought the flood of an emotion she could not indulge. She could not afford this complication in her life. She did not want to feel the longing Rand stirred inside her. "I can't, Rand. It wouldn't work out; you know it wouldn't."

"It was my fault before. I admit that, Billie. But I won't make the same mistake again. You can keep your secrets as long as you'll let me love you. I give you my word, I won't question you again." Rand hesitated. His dark brows were drawn in a tight line, his clear eyes searching her face for a sign of relenting. "Billie, I ache for you. . . ."

Unable to stand his torment, Billie tore her eyes from his. "I'm sorry, Rand. I'm sorry about everything. It—it was a mistake for me to expect that I could continue on with the herd as if nothing had ever happened between us." Suddenly

286

realizing the futility of her words, Billie took a deep breath. "And I think the time has come to correct that mistake. I'm going to leave the drive. I'll be able to find my way north from here without any trouble. I should have realized—"

The harshness that tightened Rand's features, turning the liquid blue of his eyes to ice, froze Billie's words on her lips.

"You know I won't let you leave. . . ."

Billie's response was spontaneous.

"You won't be able to stop me."

Rand's hands dropped from her shoulders. His chest heaving with obvious agitation, he stared coldly into her frown.

"Don't try it, Billie. You won't get far. I'll come after you and drag you back if I have to. I won't turn you loose to find your way by yourself to wherever the hell it is in Montana you're going." Pausing, Rand continued tightly a moment later, "I'll get you to Montana just like I promised. And I'll leave you alone, if that's the way you want it. I won't touch you again, Christ, not if it kills me. . . ."

Pulling himself to his feet, Rand stood towering over her for endless silent seconds. When he spoke his voice was devoid of feeling.

"You'd better get up. The boys will be trailing back from the herd in a few minutes. It's almost time for your watch."

Not waiting for her response, Rand turned and walked away.

Billie averted her face from his retreating figure. She drew herself slowly to her feet as her heart cried out in silence, "Oh Rand, I ache too. . . ."

Rand was striding blindly into the darkness when a low summons turned him toward Nate Straw, standing in the shadows beside the wagon. He was in no mood to talk.

"What is it, Nate?"

"Just a word of advice from an old-timer, Rand." Nate stepped out of the shadows into the light of the campfire, his face screwed into myriad lines reflecting his concern. "If you and Drucker are intendin' keepin' your secret, you'd better be a bit more careful. The boys ain't deaf, you know, and voices travel real well at night. Now, I ain't sayin' I heard what you two was sayin', but it don't take much to see that you've upset that little girl. . . ."

Rand started with shock. "So you know. . . ."

"Hell, I ain't blind, you know, although I think the rest of the boys must be or they couldn't be fooled for so long. At first the poor mite was so bruised that her own mother wouldn't have recognized her for a female in that getup she's wearin'. But it didn't take me long to see that face wasn't no boy's face, even if that little girl is as good a drover as a man." His eyes narrowing further, Nate added in a lower tone, "And if I hadn't already guessed, the way you been lookin' at her since Abilene would've been a dead giveaway. If I was to judge from them looks, I'd say you're stuck on her real bad, Rand."

Rand's expression tightened, and Nate continued without waiting for a response.

"Drucker don't owe me no explanations as to what she's doin' here dressed like a boy, Rand, and neither do you. And I ain't askin' for any. I gotta admit I admire Drucker's spunk, and I'm thinkin' she's not the kind of woman you can try throwin' your weight against. I'd say you got yourself there about a hundred and ten pounds of real wary wildcat. If you're intendin' to make her purr, Rand, you're goin' to have to take it easy, real easy. Don't forget, she's been burned. . . . Hell, some fella did a job on her good enough to kill her, and it's not hard to see that she ain't goin' to put herself in a position where she's dependent on another man too soon. It ain't been easy on her on this drive, with them two fellas snipin' and pickin' at her all the time. If you start leanin' on her, well, I'm thinkin' if you're not careful, you're goin' to lose her, Rand."

Rand shook his head. A low, ironic laugh escaped his lips. "Looks like your advice comes a little too late, Nate. She's already told me in just about every way she can that she doesn't want any part of me."

"She's still here, though, ain't she. . . ."

"Yeah, she's still here. . . ."

"So I'd say you'd better take a mite more care if you want to fool the boys a little longer. Anybody seein' your face when you left her just now would sure as blazes take another look at her, and she's lookin' less and less like a boy every day, Rand. That light hair of hers is growin' in real smooth and silky, and it don't take much imagination to see what she'd look like with them long eyelashes flutterin' up a soulful look."

"All right, Nate. You don't have to go into detail."

"I'm just tryin' to set you straight, Rand."

Turning his face toward the herd, Rand pulled off his hat and ran a weary hand through his heavy dark hair. Damn, he was tired. He had been riding for four days straight, stopping only long enough to rest his horse. He hadn't known a moment's peace until he had set his eyes on Billie sleeping by the campfire. Her nightmare had been the perfect excuse to talk to her, to touch her. But his resistance had been too low, and he had done exactly what he had vowed he wouldn't do again. Nate was right. If he pressed her, he would lose her completely. He'd return to the herd one day and she wouldn't be there.

Panic accompanied that thought and Rand turned a quick glance back toward the campfire in search of Billie's slender figure. She wasn't there. His reaction spontaneous, he took a quick step, only to be stopped by Nate's low whispered statement.

"She took a little walk, Rand. She'll be right back."

His eyes darting back to Nate's understanding expression, Rand nodded.

"You were right in everything you said, Nate. I know you're right, and I know I've handled Billie all wrong. If I had the chance, I'd do it differently. I'd— Oh, hell, what's the use?" Rand gave a low sigh. "I'm going to get a few hours sleep, Nate." Shooting a glance back toward the fire where Billie had just emerged from the darkness, he gave Nate a small smile. "Keep an eye on her for me, Nate, just to make sure she doesn't get it in her head to take off on me. She wasn't too happy with the whole situation when I left her just now, and I don't feel too safe taking a chance."

"Don't worry about a thing, Rand. I'll be cookin' with one eye on my pots and another eye on that little girl when she goes on her watch."

Rand paused, his eyes searching Nate's face. "She doesn't want any of the men to know she's a woman, Nate."

"Hell, I ain't dumb! I know that!"

"You won't tell her you know. . . ."

"I've knowed since the time we crossed the Brazos. I seen she had a need to keep a part of her life private, and I left it that way. She's earned that much."

"Yeah, I guess that's true. Thanks, Nate."

"Ain't nothin', Rand."

"Yeah. . . ."

Within minutes Rand was stretched out in his blanket near the fire. In the back of his mind he heard the sound of returning and departing horses and joking words whispered in passing . . . the changing of shifts. He remembered how Billie had felt sleeping in his arms, her slender body pressed against his. He'd have her back in his arms again. . . . He would. . . .

A flying wisp of hair tickled her cheek. Momentarily resting her spoon on her plate, Billie tucked it absentmindedly under her hat. Her eyes glued to her food, she resumed eating. She had gone over Rand's words again and again in her mind since he had arrived back in camp. It was hours later, and the freedom of noon camp allowed her to search her mind once more, but she still could not make a decision. Things had become so complicated. . . . One part of her mind urged her to leave, to follow the trail north to Montana, while the other part of her mind urged her to stay. There was no doubt she was safer with the herd than she would be alone. And if she ran off, she wouldn't be able to collect the pay she had coming to her for her work. She couldn't make it to Montana with the money she had in her pocket.

But there was Rand. . . . Each day that she stayed with the herd he became more deeply involved in her problems. She knew where that would eventually lead if she stayed. McCulla would not give up. Even now he probably . . .

A prickle of premonition interrupted Billie's thoughts. Her eyes snapping up, she saw a small group of horsemen in the distance, approaching their camp. Three men . . . three men. . . .

A cold tremor of fear coursed down her spine. There was something about the lead horseman, something familiar. Her throat suddenly tight, Billie dropped her plate. The clatter that ensued when it struck the surface of a small rock drew the attention of the men around the campfire toward her, but she was oblivious to their inquisitive stares. Unable to take her eyes from the lead horseman, she felt a slow trembling overwhelm her.

Oh, God, it was him. There could be no one else with a pinto like that, no one else who rode with such a peculiarly awkward style. Carl Whitley . . . riding as he had done countless times at Wes McCulla's side. Wes McCulla . . .

The vivid image of Wes McCulla's face, so still in death, flashed before Billie's eyes, and she emitted a low gasp. No, she couldn't let it all end here. She had to get to Montana first. Afterwards . . . If McCulla's men found her afterwards, when she knew once and for all . . .

The three horsemen continued their steady approach. Turning in blind panic, Billie scrambled away from the campfire. Her mind barely registered the low male voice that followed her.

"Drucker, what's the matter?"

She could not answer. Her mind was flashing short, distracted warnings: Run! Hide! Don't let him see you!

She was lying flat on her stomach behind a jutting formation of rock and scrub pine. She did not feel the gritty taste of the rough soil between her teeth or its rasp against her cheek. A host of terror-filled memories was assailing her, and she was paralyzed with fear.

You knew I was comin' for you sooner or later, didn't you, little bitch?

Wes McCulla's hand was tearing at her nightdress; the confining weight of his body was crushing hers. . . . The pain

291

as he struck her again and again . . . the taste of blood and bile that choked her throat . . . She fought to control her spontaneous retching.

She could hear the horsemen reining up in camp, but she could not raise her head. She could not bear to see . . .

Rand's voice sounded in the ensuing silence. It was casual in greeting, a startling contrast to the terror that shook her. . . .

Extremely conscious of the silence from behind the natural barricade of rocks that shielded Billie from view, Rand watched calmly as the three horsemen reined up and dismounted. He darted a cursory glance around the campfire. The men continued to eat in silence, their heads held forward with stringent deliberation. Rand's gaze took in Hall's and Brothers's squinting appraisal of their visitors and he shot them a silent warning.

He turned back to the three men.

"Can I help you, boys?"

"I think you sure enough can." His small eyes squinted into slits against the noon glare, the obvious leader of the three men smiled broadly. "You look like you're the man we've been lookin' for. Yeah, we run into old Charlie Stark where he was water-bound on the Brazos with a Circle K herd a while back. He described you real clear like. You must be that Rand Pierce fella."

Rand frowned. "That's my name."

The stranger extended his hand. "My name's Carl Whitley. These two fellas is my sidekicks, Marty and Larry. We've been riding this trail for a while now. I got wind of your herd down in San Antonio, and I figured you were the fella I wanted to talk to. But damn, if it wasn't a hard crack gettin' to you fellas."

"That so?" Accepting the man's hand despite his natural inclination to the contrary, Rand waited for him to continue.

"We was only a small ways behind you when that fella put us onto your trail, but we ran into some Indians after we crossed the Red River. Seems like there's a real big encampment of Comanches and Kiowa Apaches between the Salt and North fork, and they wasn't lettin' nobody past. This big fella, an Apache he looked to be, took a real exception to us and sent us back where we come from real quick. Damn if him and his braves didn't keep their eye on us so good that we couldn't sneak back through their land. Instead we had to go along the south side of the Red and then turn north to the government trail. Felt like we was never goin' to catch up with you boys."

Rand hesitated. The hackles on the back of his spine stiffened.

"Looks like you were set on findin' us. . . ."

"Yeah." His grin broadening, the stranger shot a short glance toward the pot still bubbling over the fire. "And it looks like me and the boys couldn't have found you at a better time. We been on dried beef and beans for well onto three days now, and a good hot meal would sure hit the spot."

Rand turned briefly to the cook wagon.

"Dish up what you've got left, Nate. Looks like these boys are hungry." Turning back, he motioned them to a seat in a deliberate attempt to disguise his growing impatience.

"You were saying you were looking for me?"

"Sure enough were. Like I said, we got wind of your herd when we was down in San Antonio. Bart Ford, the fella that owns the livery stable, told us about that herd of Mexican cattle you got there. He said that you had trouble with your men bringin' the fever up from Mexico with the herd, that some of your drovers was down with it and that you was lookin' to hire drovers in San Antonio."

Looking up as Nate held out a steaming plate, Carl bobbed his head gratefully. He immediately dug in his spoon and began eating, and Rand took a firm hold on his composure. His first instinct had been to send this sleazy pack back on the trail where they came from, but he knew he dared not. Intuition told him that there was more to this situation than was obvious at first glance.

Billie had definitely recognized these men, and he knew that only a fear short of terror could make her run and hide.

293

He also had a firm suspicion that these men were not chasing Billie on their own. They had the look of hirelings . . . dangerous hirelings, for all the pleasant appearance this wily fellow went to such pains to present. And he was determined to find out once and for all what and who was frightening Billie, chasing her, keeping her from him with fear. . . .

Urging him to continue, Rand nodded his head. "Well, it looks like you did find the right man after all. I was looking for help in San Antonio, but I hired all the men I needed. I'm not looking for any more help, if that's what you—"

"Oh, no, we ain't lookin' for work. . . ." A trickle of grease ran from the corner of Carl's mouth down his chin as he lowered his spoon and shook his head. "No, the fact is, we're lookin' for somebody we think you mighta hired or seen when you was in San Antonio. You see, we kinda lost track of the kid. . . ."

"The kid?"

"Yeah, well, it's like this." Quickly spooning up the last of the stewed beef on his plate, Carl stuffed it into his mouth and chewed vigorously. Running the back of his sleeve across his lips, he continued speaking through his barely masticated food.

"You see, my boss is a fella named Dan McCulla. He hired this young fella to work for him, and he took a real likin' to the young cuss. Well, it seems like the boy was workin' in his house when a big sum of money disappeared. One of the other fellas that worked for Mr. McCulla took it for granted that the kid took it. He told the kid to give the money back, but the kid said he didn't know nothin' about it. Well, old Tom lost his patience, and he beat up on the boy pretty bad. The kid ran away, and Mr. McCulla found out later that it wasn't the kid who took the money."

Swallowing the last of his food with an audible gulp, Carl reached for the cup beside him and took a deep swallow of coffee. He belched loudly and turned back toward Rand to continue. His dirt-specked face took on a sincere expression.

"Mr. McCulla felt real bad about what happened. He kinda looked on the kid like his own son and just couldn't rest thinkin' how that boy had suffered for somethin' he hadn't done. He told me and the boys to get on the trail and see if we could find the kid and tell him that Mr. McCulla's sorry about what happened, that he'd like the kid to come back."

Rand barely suppressed his reaction to the man's obvious prevarication. He knew instinctively that a man who employed a cowboy of this Carl Whitley's caliber did not do so with the expectation of an honest day's labor in mind. No, Carl Whitley had the look of a man who took the easy way out with no questions asked. Leaning back, Rand gave Carl his full attention.

"That's a real interesting story. What did this boy look like?"

"Well, he's kind of a skinny kid, medium height. He has real pale hair, like a silver-yellow almost, and dark eyes. Like I said, you probably wouldn't have forgotten him if you seen him. We're thinkin' he might've been pretty well marked. . . ."

Pausing for effect, Rand shook his head. "No, I don't think I saw a kid that looked like that in San Antonio. And I sure enough didn't hire him. I— "

"That kid you're talkin' about . . ."

The low voice that cut into their conversation snapped Rand's attention in Josh Hall's direction. He shot Hall a meaningful look, but the drover continued without responding to his expression.

" . . . the kid, was he a feisty kid, short on small talk, ridin' a small sorrel mare?"

Carl's small eyes widened, and he shot a quick look in his sidekick's direction.

"Yeah, that's him all right. Real feisty, wouldn't let nobody push him around . . ."

"Yeah, I think I seen him in San Antonio. . . ."

Rand was getting slowly to his feet. His hands were moving cautiously toward his gunbelt, but Carl was too intent on Hall's conversation to notice.

"Yeah, you remember him, don't you, Seth?" He turned to the silent Brothers at his side. "He was in the store when we stopped to buy tobacco. . . ."

295

His expression suddenly coming to life, Brothers nodded. "Oh, yeah, he was talkin' to that old lady. . . . Seems like he said he was headin' west, with McNulty's herd or one of them others, wasn't he?"

"Yeah, that's right. . . ." Turning back to Carl Whitley, Hall took the last sip of his coffee and placed his cup on the ground. "The kid said he was goin' west. . . . Damn good thing he didn't hire onto this drive, anyhow. He was too small for the job. . . ."

Getting to his feet, Hall flicked Rand a small sneer. "Guess you didn't see him, Mr. Pierce . . . That kid, I mean. If you'd seen him, you wouldn't have forgotten him. He was a damned nasty little piece."

Rand released his breath slowly, the tension that prickled the hair on the back of his neck beginning to lessen. Hall . . . That bastard . . .

"Yeah, I guess you're right." Avoiding Carl's assessing look, Rand turned to his men. "All right, boys, hit your saddles. You've been sitting long enough. We've got a lot of miles to cover this afternoon."

Slowly drawing themselves to their feet, the boys cast uneasy glances over their shoulders at the three still seated. Aware that they intended to back him up to a man, whatever he intended to do, Rand felt a rush of gratitude. Hell, these boys were all right. . . . He addressed his next words to his unwelcome visitors.

"Well, I hate to rush you, fellas, but we haven't got time to sit and chat. We've got a tight schedule to keep."

But his visitors were already rising to their feet.

"Looks like we ain't got time to waste, either, if we're goin' to find that there kid. It's a long way back to the border. . . ."

Forcing himself to retain a casual facade, Rand watched with tenuous control as the three men slowly pulled themselves to their feet and remounted their horses. He followed their retreat with his eyes as they rode out of camp. His gaze tight on the three figures until they were a safe distance away, Rand was suddenly aware that his men had drifted back from the herd and were waiting expectantly. His eye caught Hall's amused expression. Rand's silent question was met by the drover's short laugh and a short, explanatory statement.

"I might not be too fond of that kid, but I know a tall tale when I hear one. Them fellas have the look of bounty hunters or the like, and me and Seth have been at the other end of that stick enough times to know we ain't pointin' it in nobody's direction. So you can tell the kid to come out of hidin'. There ain't nobody here in this camp who's goin' to give him away."

Not giving Rand the opportunity for a reply, Hall turned his horse and rode slowly back to the herd. Signaling the other men to do the same, Rand moved in a direct line to the rocks behind which Billie had disappeared.

The sound of Carl Whitley's voice had faded, but Billie had not stopped shaking. Pressed flat against the dusty ground, her face hidden in her hands, she was lost in the terror of memory. Wes McCulla's hot breath against her face . . . his hand in her hair, jerking her to her feet only to strike her again.

Guess you ain't learned your lesson yet, have you? Too bad, 'cause I'm gettin' tired of teachin' you the same thing over and over.

Her body rocked in vivid memory of the powerful blow that had followed.

The afternoon sun was beating into her back, but she felt none of its warmth as a new round of shuddering overcame her. She did not hear the sound of a step behind her, jerking with a start as a gentle hand touched her shoulder.

"Billie, they're gone. . . ."

She was struggling to catch her breath as her eyes came in contact with Rand's concerned gaze.

"Whitley . . . the other two . . . they're gone? . . ."

"Yes. They won't be back."

Rand's words resounded loudly in her mind. Gone . . . He was gone. . . .

Billie nodded her head in short, jerking movements. She attempted to stand, but her quaking legs refused to co-

297

operate with her effort. Rand's strong hands closed on her shoulders, drawing her to her feet. There was only a brief hesitation before he pulled her into the protective circle of his arms. His pounding heart echoed her own as he held her. His voice was filled with concern as he whispered against her hair.

"Billie, whoever they really were, they won't be back. You don't have to be afraid."

Billie shook her head, her eyes remaining closed as she absorbed Rand's strength.

"But—but they will be back."

"Billie, why did—"

Rand halted his question prematurely. When he spoke again his voice was filled with new resolution.

"No. I told you I wouldn't question you anymore, and I meant it. Whoever they are, they won't find you, Billie. I promise you that."

"I have to get away from here. . . ."

"No, damn it, no!"

Still gripping Billie's shoulders, Rand held her at arm's length. Anger touched the intense blue of his eyes.

"You're safe here now. They've satisfied themselves that you're not here. And even if they *did* come back, we'd have adequate warning. They wouldn't get near you with this outfit behind you."

Billie shook her head. "I—I don't want that, Rand, don't you see? No more bloodshed, no more—"

Rand felt a new tightness rise in his throat. Oh, God, what was she involved in, his beautiful Billie? Who was after her? Folding his arms around her once more, Rand held her tight against him. Whatever it was, she was safe with him. If he was ever sure of anything, it was that he'd die before he'd let anyone hurt her again.

But she was sagging against him, her strength depleted by the unexpected visitation from her past. In a quick, facile movement, Rand scooped her up into his arms and started walking toward the wagon.

Billie's protest was spontaneous.

"Please, put me down. I can walk. I'll be all right in a minute."

He was approaching the wagon and Billie turned to meet Nate's sober gaze.

"Nate, Billie's going to ride with you for the rest of the day." Ignoring Billie's protests, Rand continued firmly. "Give her a shot of Jim Crow and make sure she stays down. We can't be sure those fellows won't be watching."

Rand placed Billie carefully on her feet, his eyes catching the concern reflected in the depths of her eyes.

"Nate knows you're a woman, Billie. He's known since the Brazos. But nobody else has guessed and he won't give you away."

Billie's eyes flicked to Nate. The truth of Rand's statement was reflected in the sober lines of his face. Her heart filling at the understanding exhibited there, Billie nodded her thanks. Unable to speak, she turned and mounted the wagon. She was about to move inside when Rand took her hand. His gaze was unwavering, his voice filled with purpose.

"Stay out of sight until nightfall. It'll be safer that way."

Still shaken, Billie took a deep breath and nodded again. But Rand did not release her. Instead, his eyes moved over her white face. His hand tightened on hers.

"Billie, don't be afraid. We won't let anyone hurt you."

Uncertain whether his offered consolation caused her relief or concern, Billie felt Rand's hand drop away. Turning, she moved into the wagon in silence.

Chapter XI

Billie took a deep, weary breath. It had been several weeks since Carl Whitley's appearance at their camp, and they had seen or heard nothing from him since. She darted a quick look up toward the cloudless sky before returning her gaze to the wide, open country that lay before her. A trickle of perspiration slipped from under the band of her hat, and she brushed it away with her forearm, conscious of the gritty rasp of trail dust against her skin.

The unrelenting heat of late June had started early that morning. The sun had been burning more hotly into her back with every hour that crept toward noon. Damp, telltale circles of her discomfort stained her sun-bleached shirt, and the coarse material of her trousers lay moist against her thighs. The ragged length of her hair had grown without her realization to a point where it stuck uncomfortably against her neck and she chafed at the added discomfort of its weight. She was suddenly conscious of the fact that she had not seen her reflection in weeks and was unable to assess the viability of her disguise. But her uneasiness was temporary, a reflection of her knowledge that the men accepted her as Billie Drucker, fellow drover. An inch or more length to her hair would not change that acceptance.

Her physical discomfort was no more or less than the men with whom she rode and she accepted it without complaint. Her burning eyes flicked to point position and touched on Willie Hart's lean frame. Her glance moved spontaneously toward Jim Stewart, who rode swing position in front of her. A smile flicked across her lips. If there had been any change in the attitude of the men toward her since Carl Whitley's visit, it most certainly did not reflect suspicion of her gender. Instead, to a man, which surprisingly included her former undeclared enemies Josh Hall and Seth Brothers, the men appeared to have banded together in defense of her position within their group.

Willie and Stewart, as senior drovers, had become more openly protective, and Jeremy Carlisle's brotherly concern had deepened to a point of irritation, which had occasionally provoked her annoyed rebuffs. But Jeremy's smiling, good-natured solicitude could not be shaken. Strangers at their camp were now greeted by the men with a caution, which silently bespoke general concern for her welfare. Yet, not a question had been posed about the reason for Carl Whitley's inquiry. Her gratitude was unspoken but profound.

If there had been any change in attitudes within camp, it had been in Rand. True to his word, he had not questioned her about Carl Whitley, and she had not volunteered any information. But tension had become more apparent in his manner each day since the unexpected encounter with her past. He had grown increasingly moody and silent. The time he had formerly spent in conversation with the men was now apparently spent on his private thoughts. She had occasionally caught him studying her covertly, but he had made no attempts to seek her out. His attitude was watchful. She suspected his intensified surveillance of the horizon was more for her benefit than for that of the herd. She knew she was constantly in his thoughts by the manner in which his eyes sought her position within the herd, around the campfire, in her blanket at night. She read the panic in his gaze when he did not immediately find her where he had expected, and she suffered his pain. She had awakened unexpectedly in her sleep only the previous night to find him crouched beside her. The azure glow of his eyes had been intent on her face, reflecting the flickering light of the campfire close by. He had not smiled when her gaze had held his in silent inquiry. His explanation had been brief.

302

"I was with the herd. . . . I thought I heard someone cry out. I wanted to make sure you were all right."

She had not responded, and he had immediately risen to his feet and walked away. Stress . . . She was causing him unpardonable stress. She did not consider that her own body ached for his touch. She forced herself to remember that she owed him freedom from a personal involvement, which would be temporary at best, and which could bring personal disaster down upon him. She promised herself that she would free him from the burden of her presence as soon as it was possible. She knew he would be upset when she left, but she also knew there were any number of women who would willingly salve the aching need inside him—women far more worldly, more beautiful than she. She knew her own need, the ache that grew inside her each time his eyes touched her, would not be as easily salved.

But it would not be much longer. The drive was already more than half over. Camp Supply and the Canadian River lay behind them and they were well into Kansas. They would soon be reaching Dodge. Rand had called the men to conference before riding out in advance of the herd that morning. His manner had been sober and almost gruff, raising the brows of his drovers. She had been stabbed by guilt. She knew she was responsible for the change in Rand, which had left the men grumbling on more than one occasion.

Either unaware or uncaring about the men's reaction, Rand had continued in a low tone that had held the men in silence.

"We'll be passing just outside of Mulberry soon. That fact is of little importance except to note that Mulberry lies approximately ten miles south of Dodge." Allowing the men a few minutes to absorb his comment, Rand had continued, "It's my intention to stop at Dodge. I have some business to settle there. It's also my intention to stay long enough to allow each of you time in town, in accordance with shifts."

A low mumble of appreciation had moved through the men assembled, but Rand had shown little reaction.

"I'll be advancing each man half a month's salary—

303

twenty-five dollars—no more, no less. I caution you, when it's gone, it's gone. All that will be left for you to do will be to ride back to the herd, so I'd be careful what saloon or card table I laid my money on. We'll cross the Arkansas River shortly after noon tomorrow. Half the outfit will go into town. The other half is going to have to bide its time until the others return. Willie will set up the watches, and I'll be expecting every man to be back when his is due."

Rand had turned abruptly a few minutes later, and after speaking a few words to Willie, had ridden off in advance of the herd. The men had not had their full say when Willie had pushed them off their seats and into the saddle. Billie suspected noon camp would air the remainder of their complaints as well as their anticipation.

As for herself, Billie had given little thought as to how she would spend her money or her time in Dodge. Her thoughts had ridden out with Rand's tall, lean figure. It occurred to her now that Dodge might be the perfect place for her to find an alternate means of transportation to Montana, one that would save both Rand and her the mutual pain they suffered. Yes, perhaps that would be the best thing to do. . . .

A familiar knot tightened in Billie's stomach and she turned her eyes to survey the herd in an unconscious bid to escape her thoughts. Dodge . . . Yes, perhaps it was time. . . .

"I've been in Dodge every summer since '77, and I can give you boys some good points. . . ." Pausing in his oration, Willie fixed his keen eye on the men seated at noon camp. Rand had taken a supply of dried beef with him on riding out that morning and had not been expected to return until late afternoon. The general consensus of feeling was relief, and in his absence Willie had begun to evidence some fatherly spirit with some earnest talk and advice. Already anticipating the pleasures of the notorious cow town, the men listened with surprising good humor.

"Dodge is one town where the average bad man of the

West not only finds his equal, but finds himself badly handicapped. The buffalo hunters and range men have protested against the iron rule of Dodge's peace officers, and nearly every protest has cost a life. A fella can't ride his horse into a saloon or shoot out the lights in Dodge. That might go somewhere else, but it don't go there. So I want to warn you to behave yourselves. You can wear your six-shooters into town, but you'd better leave them at the first place you stop. And when you leave town, you'd better not think of ridin' out shootin'. Most cowboys think it's an infringement on their rights to give up shootin' in town, but if it is, it stands. 'Cause your six-shooters ain't no match for Winchesters and buckshot, and Dodge's officers are as game a set of men as ever faced danger."

The first to break the silence after Willie's monologue, Jeremy Carlisle flashed his irrepressible grin.

"And now that you've told us the bad things, Willie, tell us some of the good things. I heard that they got some of the best faro dealers in the West at that Long Branch saloon, and I heard they got some of the prettiest women there, too."

His eye moving warily to Carlisle's enthusiastic grin, Willie responded solemnly, "Good whiskey and bad women will be the ruin of you, young fella."

The loud guffaws that followed Willie's sage advice were interrupted by Fogarty's loud interjection.

"I suppose that's why you had a glass full of red-eye in your hand and a pretty little redhead on your knee back in Abilene . . . 'cause you was two steps behind on your way to perdition. . . ."

Rewarding him with a haughty squint, Willie replied without losing a minute in hesitation.

"I never said I was smart enough to take my own good advice."

"You're goin' to have to tell me somethin' honestly, Willie." There was a twinkle in Jim Stewart's narrowed gaze. "Did you give old Rand that same sage advice about whiskey and women before we went to Abilene? I've given the matter some serious thought, and it's been my sober deduction in the past few weeks that our fine boss is sorely missin' the comforts a woman can give him. I worked with him on many a drive, and I found him to be a rather mellow fella, easy talkin' and friendly to a man. I don't remember ever seein' him so hard on himself as he is this drive, and so caught up in himself. I'm thinkin' there's only one thing that turns a man inside himself like that. If it wasn't Rand Pierce I was talkin' about, I'd say he was pinin' for a woman."

"Oh, come on, Stewart!" Unwilling to allow that statement to pass, Carlisle shook his head. "You all seen the lady that was waitin' for him in Abilene and the welcome she gave him. I'm sayin' she was right willin' to make him happy . . . whenever he said so. . . ."

Intensely uncomfortable with the line the conversation had taken, Billie shifted in her seat. Her movement jerked Jeremy's smile in her direction.

"Now don't you say nothin', Drucker. You're too young to know anythin' about what we're sayin'. If you're smart, you'll just do some listenin' and some learnin'."

Completely ignoring Jeremy's short deviation from the subject, Stewart shook his head. "Yeah, I seen that beautiful young woman. . . . And I also seen our boss leavin' her in the hotel dinin' room with a puny blond-haired fella. And if I'm not mistakin', he was visitin' saloons up and down the street for the rest of the night . . . alone. You saw him, didn't you, Hall?"

"Yeah, I seen him. . . ."

"Well? . . ."

Stewart was adamant, but the men were unconvinced.

"The boss could get any woman he wanted! Hell, you seen the way them saloon girls was lookin' at him. . . ."

"And I seen the way he was lookin' back at them. He wasn't interested."

Stewart's logic hitting him for the first time, Carlisle nodded. "Yeah, I seen that, too. . . . So, you think maybe he had a fight with that pretty redhead lady and is pinin' away?"

"Somethin' like that."

Carlisle shook his head. The smile fell from his face for the first time. "I don't mind tellin' you, that shakes my faith a bit. I was kinda enjoyin' the legend of Rand Pierce. . . ."

Willie cocked an interested eye. "What legend was that?"

"Everybody knows Rand Pierce pulled himself up by his bootstraps and is well on his way to bein' one of the richest men in this part of the country. And everybody knows he has women followin' him around, just like that society lady in Abilene. If it wasn't for the emergency that came up with this herd, he'd be enjoyin' the good life with a pretty lady on each knee. That picture kinda gave a man somethin' to aspire to in life. . . ."

"Oh, hell, boy, you are a fool. . . ."

Stewart's quick response brought a frown to Carlisle's lightly freckled face. "What are you sayin'?"

"I'm sayin' Rand's condition is only temporary. I'm sayin' any one of them pretty ladies you was talkin' about in Dodge could put his smile right back on track with a little effort. As a matter of fact, there's a lady I remember real well—Lotta McDevitt's her name. She don't consort with the average cowboy. She's kinda special like." His eyes rising heavenward, Stewart shook his head. "Cornflower blue eyes, long blond hair, and a way about her that'd melt stone." Stewart nodded his head. "Yeah, I'd say if any woman could bring old Rand Pierce back to normal, it'd be Lotta. . . ."

"Wait a minute. Seems to me it ain't that easy. . . ." Willie broke into the conversation, his mind obviously far from his sage advice that had started the conversation. "I gotta admit I see a lot of sense to what you all been sayin'. It was a real pleasant drive until a few weeks ago when Rand started dryin' up inside. He ain't cracked a smile in all that time, and I'd like to see the old Rand back just as much as all of you. But his love life ain't none of our business."

"Hell, we got two more months on this drive yet, Willie! You goin' to be able to stand Rand's growlin' that long? He's gettin' worse every day!"

"We don't have much choice, do we? Rand is the boss. . . ."

"Oh, yeah, we got a choice, Willie." A grin growing on his narrow, lined face, Stewart turned toward the men. "Lotta can fix all. . . . But she's expensive, boys. . . ."

"Are you suggestin' we buy Rand Pierce a woman in Dodge? . . ."

"That's exactly what I'm sayin'."

Willie blinked and shook his head. "That's a damned good idea!"

"What about 'goin' to perdition'?"

Willie shrugged in answer to Carlisle's short reminder. "Hell, Rand don't listen to my advice nohow. All right, boys, ante up . . . How much you all goin' to chip in?"

The boys were all digging in their pockets and Billie shook her head in disbelief. They were serious! They were going to buy Rand a saloon woman. . . .

"What about you, Drucker?" Turning toward her with a wink, Carlisle held out his hand. "You gotta learn the facts of life sometime. Ante up."

He was serious. . . . Carlisle actually expected her to contribute to this farce. Rand would never go along with it. He wouldn't . . .

"Come on, Drucker."

Hardly believing her actions, Billie reached deep into her pocket and pulled out her leather money pouch. She slapped her money into Carlisle's waiting hand. Her eyes flicked incredulously around the circle of drovers as Carlisle turned away. To a man, each had come up with a similar amount. She shook her head. Rand would never go along with it. He wouldn't . . .

Another crack of lightning lit the early morning blackness, and Lucille jumped with a start. The deafening roll of thunder that followed sent a chill down her spine and she fought the nervousness that had begun to pervade her senses. Oh, everything was going wrong! And she had planned everything so perfectly. . . .

She shot another glance to the window and stamped an impatient foot at the deluge that trailed against the glass. Rain! It had been raining all night. She had awakened to the new day only to see an overcast sky of lead gray that promised more of the same. She had done everything just as she had planned: accumulated a stunning wardrobe of daytime and nighttime apparel that was certain to leave Rand breathless; cancelled her scheduled trip with Aunt

308

Jessica at the last minute, without informing her father of her plan; arranged secretly to have Jack take her to the train station the first thing this morning. She was packed and ready to go. The train was due to leave in an hour, but the weather was not cooperating!

She had had Millie put out one of her most beautiful traveling outfits, a stunning walking-out dress in a deep forest green that contrasted beautifully with her vivid coloring. She had even gone to the trouble of having a hat made especially for the journey, a delicate straw decorated with several nesting birds, surrounded by silk foliage in the same deep green of her dress. Millie had spent hours on her coiffure. And now it was all for naught!

Rain! Damn! She would be a mess by the time she ran from the doorway to the carriage! She had been forced to put aside the beautiful outfit she had planned on in favor of a hooded cape and dress that would more easily stand the test of the weather. Fortunately, she was certain to reach Dodge ahead of Rand, so she would be able to go straight to her hotel and freshen up. But she disliked intensely any interruption in her plans—even so unavoidable a one as the weather.

Her disposition suffering as the result of her discomfiture, Lucille shot her diligent maid an exasperated look.

"Are you still fussing with that hatbox, Millie? I must be leaving. Jack is waiting to take the cases. . . ."

"I've finished, Miss Lucille."

Millie turned her rather birdlike face in Lucille's direction, and Lucille stifled an absurd desire to laugh. Millie's expression was so like those on the faces of the two feathered creatures nesting on the hat she had intended to wear. . . .

"Very good, Millie." Swallowing hard against her ridiculous inclination, Lucille shook her hand. "Call Jack, will you? We must hurry. . . ."

"Yes, Miss Lucille."

Shaking her head, Lucille turned to don her cape. She would never be able to keep a straight face when wearing that particular hat again.

She was moving quickly down the front staircase a few

309

minutes later when she observed an unfamiliar coachman picking up her cases at the front door.

"Wait a minute!" The fine line of her brow pulling into a frown, Lucille stopped the tall dark fellow in his tracks. "Who are you, and what are you doing with my cases? Where's Jack?"

Tipping his hat, the fellow turned a subservient smile in her direction.

"Jack's a bit under the weather this morning, ma'am. My name's Harvey Bigelow, Jack's nephew. His old bones don't do too well in this kind of dampness, you know, and they was givin' him trouble, so he called me to take you to the station. He said you wouldn't want to be late in catchin' the train."

Lucille shook her head. *Everything* was going wrong. Now Jack was sick, and she was going to be forced to depend on a strange coachman to get her situated on the train. She had not realized how much she was depending on Jack's familiar face, disapproving or not, to send her on her way. Taking a deep breath, Lucille renewed her determination with a strong effort.

"All right. I suppose I'll have to depend on you to get me there. You do know the station I'm to leave from, the time of departure? . . ."

"Yes, ma'am. Jack gave me all the details. Don't you worry about a thing."

Lucille nodded, her frown tightening. Oh, she didn't like the way things were going at all.

The last of the cases had been secured atop the coach and the nimble young coachman was returning to the doorway, a large umbrella in hand. Lucille shot a short glance skyward and gave a small, annoyed sniff. A new, heavier cloud cover had managed to turn the morning even darker and the deluge was increasing. She made a silent observance that it was almost as dark as night, a far different day than she had envisioned when she had planned her gay excursion to Dodge.

Looking up as the coachman reached her side, Lucille stepped under the umbrella he held carefully over her head and began walking down the walk toward the waiting carriage. She was certain it had been Jack who had instructed the fellow to take the large closed-in coach on this occasion, and that Jack had probably been adamant about having the windows covered against the wind-driven rain that pelted it. She knew the depth of Jack's concern for her, and she was warmed by his obvious effort to see she was well cared for despite his own temporary disability.

But damn if this fellow wasn't walking too fast! His long-legged stride had her practically running! She darted the coachman at her side an annoyed glance, which went entirely unheeded as he continued his rapid pace down the walk. Biting her tongue against comment, Lucille struggled to keep up, realizing the fellow had probably been instructed to keep her as dry as possible.

Practically running as she reached the steps to the carriage, Lucille started with surprise as the coachman's hand closed firmly on her elbow, all but lifting her into the air at the same moment he dispensed with the umbrella and jerked open the carriage door. Within a moment she was helped inside in an effort that was just short of a thrust. Gasping, momentarily blinded by the darkened interior of the carriage, she turned an annoyed glance back toward the door, which had snapped tightly shut behind her. She was still attempting to settle herself so she might show the least amount of wear upon arrival at the station, when the carriage jerked unexpectedly into motion.

Knocked unceremoniously back against the seat by the sudden surge forward as the horses broke into a pace that was just short of a gallop, Lucille gave a small, unladylike grunt. That was it . . . all she was going to take from that ruffian Jack had so inconsiderately sent to replace him! Raising her hand, she was about to pound on the side of the carriage as a stern reminder to slow down, when an unexpected voice from the far corner of the carriage shocked her into rigid immobility.

"Don't waste your time, Lucy. Harvey has his orders, and no amount of pounding is going to slow him down. Besides, I think he's quite enjoying himself. . . ."

Her breath escaping her lips in a gasp, Lucille snapped her

311

head in the direction of the voice. She strained her eyes in the dimness of the carriage. A formerly unseen hand pulled back the window curtain a fraction, allowing a pale shaft of light to enter the darkened interior.

"Pat! What—what are you doing here?"

"Lucy, dear, you didn't expect I would allow you to travel alone, did you?"

Lucille lowered the hand she suddenly realized she was still holding over her head, using the moment to recuperate from her shock. She squinted tightly into the narrow face that had drawn suddenly closer to hers.

"I did not expect you would *allow* me to do anything, since what I do is none of your concern! And don't call me Lucy, damn it!"

Familiar green eyes were abruptly close. The peculiar light in their depths caused a strange fluttering in Lucille's stomach, and breathlessness assailed her. What in the world was wrong with her?

"Oh, come now, Lucy. You must have realized I had no intention of allowing you to take a train to Dodge by yourself, unprotected. . . ." Pat's warm, gentle hand had slid around her shoulder and was pulling her close enough to see the intensity of expression on his face. "You also didn't think I was going to let you go to a notorious cow town to throw yourself at a man who wants no part of you? . . ."

His words snapping her from the bemusement that had begun to overcome her senses, Lucille struggled to break free of the arm that now held her so securely.

"Damn you, Pat Patterson, I'll show you how much Rand Pierce *doesn't* want me! There's not a man I can't get if I want him! I'll make you a wager that I'll have him eating out of my hand within an hour of my arrival. He and I will be—"

His arm secure against her struggles, Pat corrected with a new edge to his voice, "There is no 'he and I' when it refers to you and Rand Pierce, Lucy. Just set your mind to it. That part of your life is over and done, whether you're presently willing to accept it or not. Even if Rand hadn't decided he had interests elsewhere, it would have been the same. Rand Pierce isn't the man for you, Lucy. . . ."

"He isn't, is he?" Her struggles increasing, Lucille gritted from between clenched teeth, "And I told you not to call me Lucy!"

"Stop. Stop struggling, damn it!" The sudden anger in Pat's voice more effective in halting her struggles than the short shake he employed to emphasize his words, Pat directed an unyielding glance into her flushed face.

"Look, Lucy, the time has come for plain words. No, Rand Pierce isn't the man for you. You don't have to go to Dodge to find the man you need. He's sitting right here alongside you. He's looking into your damned beautiful face, and he's telling you right now that he's not going to let your outraged pride ruin your life. Look close, Lucy. Whom do you see?"

Lucille blinked. What was he saying? Pat . . . the man for her? He was insane!

"You're crazy! We don't even *like* each other!"

"Oh, Lucy. . . ." A smile flickered at the corners of Pat's mouth. "*Liking* has nothing at all to do with the way I feel about you. You're a spoiled termagant of a woman, but you're more woman than I've ever known. If I'm crazy, you're the one who's made me that way. So you see, you have a responsibility toward me, darling. Your responsibility is to restore me to the man I was. And there's only one way you can do that. . . ."

Lucille's eyes were wide, incredulous saucers. Who was this tender Pat Patterson? He was a man she didn't know, a man she had never met! She had no idea how to handle the gentleness of his touch and the tumult it was raising inside her. It made her weak—weaker than she enjoyed feeling. She did not like this vulnerability, this feeling of being lost in the liquid green depths of his eyes. This feeling was foreign to her, frightening.

"Take your hands off me, Pat Patterson! I'm going to Dodge and you're not coming with me!"

The tenderness was slipping from Pat's expression. An emotion far more familiar was assuming its place.

"You're right in one half of that statement, Lucy." His arm slipping away from her shoulder, Pat reached behind him as

313

he continued to speak. The faint shaft of light coming through the window did not allow her clear sight of anything other than the determination evident on his face. "I'm not coming with you to Dodge. . . ."

What was the startling emotion she experienced at his unexpected statement? Was it regret, disappointment? No, it couldn't be. . . . Damn the man! He had her so confused. . . .

". . . I'm not coming with you to Dodge for a very simple reason. You're not *going* to Dodge. . . ."

"Not going! That's where you're wrong, Pat. Nothing or no one is going to stop me from meeting Rand in Dodge. And nothing or no one—"

But Pat was interrupting her. She smelled a sickening, cloying scent.

"Lucy, be quiet. You're not going to Dodge. You're going with me, but first you're going to sleep, darling. . . ."

Pat's arm was suddenly wrapped around her. She was crushed against his shoulder, her head forced back as he raised a cloth to her face.

"You're going to sleep, darling, not to Dodge. . . ."

Lucille was suddenly struggling wildly, fighting the heavy scent he held against her nose and mouth.

"Let me go, you bastard! Let me—me—"

She couldn't breathe. That smell was penetrating her mind, leaving it reeling. Her arms were losing their strength. . . . Reality was fading away. . . . What was he doing? . . . Oh, she'd get him for this. . . . She . . .

They had drawn straws for their position on watch. Truly uncertain whether she would have preferred the first watch instead of the second, Billie rode in silence. Willie, Stewart, Carlisle, Wond, Hall, and Johnson had all drawn the first trip into town along with her. The others had remained impatiently behind, in the knowledge that this first group would be returning sometime the following morning so they might ride off for their long awaited holiday. But Billie did not share the jubilation of the men in front of her. She remembered only too clearly the way Stewart had patted the pouch of money the men had contributed—and the twinkle in his eyes as he had muttered those two words with a small wink.

"Lotta McDevitt. . . ."

Billie shook her head and turned to survey the passing landscape. But it did not hold her interest. A dog in the manger, that's what she was. She had told Rand she didn't want him, and she was well aware of the pain he had suffered at her words, the pain he suffered still. Were she a more generous person she would not begrudge him the reduction of his tensions by a well-proved, age-old treatment. But the problem was, she supposed, that she was not as generous as she would like to believe herself to be.

The thought of Rand and the beautiful but yet unseen Lotta McDevitt made her sick. It had brought back more clearly than she dared to admit the sensation of Rand's lips against hers, his gentle touch against her flesh. She remembered the long length of his body pressed against hers, the glory when he moved within her. She remembered his grating whispers as his passion soared, the glow in his eyes as he gasped her name. She remembered the beauty that came to life inside her as their mutual passion had reached its summit, and she wished—oh how truly she wished—it need never have ended. She could not bear to think he would share that same beauty with another woman, that he would touch that other woman as he had touched her. . . .

Billie was beginning to tremble, and she closed her eyes briefly against her distress. Rand had gone into town ahead of them with a gruff statement that he had business to attend to. She was well aware that Dodge was the meeting point for buyers from every quarter. Often herds would sell at Dodge with a destination for delivery beyond the Yellowstone in Montana. She knew herds frequently changed owners without the buyer ever seeing the cattle. The same could be said for horses, and Billie knew Rand had yet to find a buyer for the remuda that was presently serving them so well. They were good horses and should bring him top dollar.

But it had occurred to Billie that perhaps his business had

been of another sort. Perhaps he hadn't needed Stewart's urging to ease his frustration. And perhaps, after all, it would be better if he took Lotta or someone like her now. Then, when she herself left Dodge, he would realize how easy she was to replace. There were so many willing women here, women who would not bring danger down upon him, who would not foster the threat against his life that his protection of her would.

Billie had come to a firm decision the previous night. She had decided she would take her first opportunity to sneak away from the men, and then she would find out which trains moved northward. . . .

The sudden animation in the conversation within their group snapped Billie's eyes forward. Dodge had just come into sight, and Willie and Stewart had responded by spurring their horses to a more rapid pace. Were she in a better frame of mind Billie knew she would have been amused by those two experienced drovers' reaction to the sight of that notorious haven for trail-weary cowboys. As it was, their rising spirits were picked up by the others in their group, and with a loud hoot and holler, Jeremy set the whole pack on the run.

Making no attempt to take up the new frantic pace, Billie was suddenly aware that Jeremy was dropping back. Grinning mischievously as he drew up alongside, he reached out unexpectedly and slapped Ginger's rump with a heavy hand. Shooting forward in a lunge that all but snapped her neck, Billie heard Jeremy's loud laughter echoing behind her. Within minutes she was up with the leaders as they entered Dodge.

His eyes on the group approaching, Rand made a supreme effort to hide his relief. Billie had not been put into the first watch. He had already decided that if she had remained behind, he would ride back to the herd to talk to her. He had gone over the situation between them in his mind again and again in the past weeks until it had all but driven him crazy. He needed to convince Billie that he needed her, that she

316

should give him another chance. And he had determined that this time it *would* be different. He would take each day they had together, one at a time, and not look to the future. He would convince her that he would be good to her and for her. He would . . . But he was getting ahead of himself. First he needed to get her to listen, and it was not going to be easy.

He had been extremely busy in Dodge. Immediately upon arriving, he had taken a room at the hotel and checked to see if Jess Williams might be registered. There was always the possibility that his telegram had not been received and the able foreman had come to Dodge with the full intention of taking the herd. His plan in that event had been to buy Jess a good meal and a few drinks and pay him in full for the drive he would not be leading. He had no intention of sacrificing the remaining time he had with Billie. He had the feeling he was going to need every minute before they reached Montana to convince her that she could depend on him to keep his word.

He had also visited the numerous saloons that lined the main street, making discreet inquiries to find out if anyone had been looking for Billie. He was not about to allow Carl Whitley and his bunch—or anyone like them—to sneak up on him. No. He intended to make full use of this time in Dodge to talk to Billie privately. He had been preparing his argument in his mind for weeks.

He had then visited the barber and gotten himself spruced up like a youth on his first date. A short trip to the local emporium had netted the fresh clothes he was presently wearing. On his way, he had passed a boutique with a bold display of women's nightwear, and he had been revisited by warm memories of Billie that had done little to relieve his growing agitation. Braving the stares of some of the passing womenfolk, he had gone inside. He had emerged a short time later with a package that contained a white Parisian negligee in a lace so delicate he had known instantly that only Billie's flawless skin could do it justice. He had been unable to resist the white satin slippers that had completed the outfit. Frowning, he recalled his reaction to the flirtatious saleswoman's offer to model the garments for him if he so

317

desired. The look in the buxom brunette's eyes had indicated only too clearly that she would have been even more accommodating if he had shown a desire.

He gave a low, disbelieving snort, still incredulous at the fact that he had done nothing more than pay for his purchases, tip his hat, and walk away. Only a few months before he would have followed her into the back room and taken full advantage of her willingness. He would have left the boutique whistling a while later, never giving the brunette another thought except for the ease she would have allowed his body. But those days were gone. If he had had any doubt before, that single incident had proved to him he wanted only one woman now, and that woman was presently riding toward him in the midst of a bunch of rowdy drovers.

Rand took a deep breath to still the rapid pounding of his heart. A quick glance assessed Billie's expression. She was unsmiling. What was she thinking? How soon would he be able to get her alone, to talk to her? Oh, God, did she want him as much as he wanted her?

A light tapping sound invaded the darkness that enveloped her. With a low moan, Lucille exerted a stringent effort to thrust off the heavy mantle that clouded her mind. Her ragged utterance was met with a gentle touch and a soft whisper against her ear.

"So, you're finally awaking, sleepyhead. Come on, open your eyes. I only gave you a little sniff of that chloroform, darling, and you've slept all morning."

The familiar voice stilled and a feathering softness moved against her cheek, her lips. Her first inclination was to enjoy to the fullest the warmth coming to life inside her, but a warning bell sounded loudly in her mind, effectively jarring her from her semi-sleep.

Abruptly, she was awake. Her eyes snapping wide, Lucille emitted a sharp gasp at the unexpected face that hovered over hers. Pat! What? . . . How? . . . Her eyes jerked to the window. The tapping of the steady downpour continued.

Her eyes darted around the unfamiliar, well-furnished bedroom, noting unconsciously the construction of the superb mahogany furniture, the fine silk fabric wall covering, the matching drapes and bed hangings that surrounded her. The bed on which she lay was broad and comfortable, but—but laying propped on his elbow beside her, a peculiar sparkle in his pale green eyes, was Pat Patterson!

She attempted to pull herself to a sitting position on the bed, only to have a dizziness assail her. Dropping back against the pillow, Lucille closed her eyes as Pat's concerned voice penetrated her spinning thoughts.

"No, lie still a little longer, darling."

The bed beside her moved, and within minutes she felt a strong arm raising her shoulders and a glass pressed against her lips.

"Drink this, Lucy."

The sound of the hated nickname snapped her eyes open once more, and within seconds Lucille was attempting to break free of Pat's supportive arm.

"Damn you, I don't want anything. I just want—"

But her anger was ineffective against the light-headedness that again assailed her, and she flopped back weakly against Pat's shoulder.

His voice holding a new note of irritation, Pat pressed the glass insistently against her lips.

"You're hardly conscious and you're fighting me already. Do what I say, damn it! Drink this and you'll feel better."

Realizing she had no recourse but to follow his instructions, Lucille parted her lips and swallowed the smooth, sweet liquid. Brandy. . . . She took another sip and then another, swallowing deeply. Her eyes opened at the sound of Pat's low chuckle.

"Take it easy, darling. You've emptied the glass. I don't want to give you any more now. I can't have you falling asleep on me again. . . ."

"Falling asleep? . . ."

A vague memory stirred in Lucille's mind: Pat's trailing

voice as she had struggled to escape him in the carriage. . . .

You're not going to Dodge, Lucy. You're going to sleep . . .

Sleep!

Lucille's eyes jerked again to the window.

"Where am I? What time is it? What day is it? How long have I been 'asleep'?"

"One question at a time, Lucy." Pat's expression was growing wary. He continued to support her with his arm, but his grip was growing more in the nature of a restraint as he responded carefully. "You're in my country house outside the city."

"Your house. . . ."

"You've only been asleep a few hours."

"A few hours! The train. . . . I'm supposed to be on my way to Dodge. . . ."

"It doesn't really matter, Lucy. . . ."

"It doesn't matter!" Aghast, Lucille was temporarily at a loss for words, allowing Pat the opportunity he awaited to continue.

"That's right. I told you Rand isn't the man for you."

Memory flickered again, and Lucille felt a flush rising to her cheeks.

"You're insane! Let go of me! You—you've kidnapped me, brought me here against my will! Do you realize what my father will do when he finds out about this? He'll—"

"Oh, do you really intend to tell him, Lucille? After all, if you do, you'll also have to tell him how you intended deceiving him."

"I did not intend to deceive him. I expected to tell him. . . ."

"After you returned? . . ."

Lucille lifted her face haughtily. "That is none of your concern."

"That's where you're wrong, Lucy."

Lucille took a deep, angry breath. "My name is Lucille. . . ."

"And you are a spoiled, determined little witch who is not going to get out of my clutches until I've had an opportunity

320

to show you how very wrong you are in attempting to pursue Rand Pierce."

"Your clutches? . . ."

"You are most definitely in my clutches right now, aren't you, darling?"

Taking the opportunity to impress her with the fact that she was still lying in the circle of his arms, Pat pressed a light kiss against her lips. The flood of warmth his unexpected action stimulated shocked Lucille into action. With a sudden thrust, she pushed herself free. Scrambling to the opposite side of the bed, she rolled off and onto her feet. Shaking off the temporary imbalance that ensued, she shot a glance toward the door, measuring the distance in her mind. She glanced back to Pat, her temper flaring at the amusement in his expression. She jerked herself suddenly erect.

"Don't you dare laugh at me, Pat Patterson! You are a beast and a lecher, and I do not expect to stay in this—this den of iniquity with you, no matter the force you intend to employ to hold me here."

Pat's smile broadened.

"Really, Lucy, don't you think you're overdoing the dramatics? I don't have any intention of chaining you to the bed to ravage you until my lust is satisfied, if that's what you're thinking." At the growing puzzlement on her face, he added with a raised brow. "I hope I'm not disappointing you. . . ."

"Ohhhhh. . . ." Barely able to contain her anger, Lucille turned and stamped toward the door, belatedly realizing she was walking in her stocking feet. She glanced down and jerked a slitted gaze in Pat's direction. "Where are my shoes? I'm leaving . . . now. . . ."

Making no attempt to impede her progress toward the door, Pat gave a small shrug. "Well, if that's what you really want, Lucy, but it's quite a long walk back to the city—especially in this inclement weather. And for the life of me, I can't imagine what you did with your shoes. . . ."

"What *I* did with my shoes? Oh, you—you—"

"On the other hand, if you'll be a good girl and remain my house guest for a few days—"

"A few days!"

"That's right, a few days. You did intend to spend at least that long in Dodge, didn't you?"

"I intended to remain in Dodge for as long as it took for Rand to arrive. I still intend to go."

The light in Pat's eyes dimmed despite his obvious determination to retain his smile. "I thought I had made myself very clear, Lucy. You're not going to Dodge. You're going to remain my house guest until there is no possibility of meeting Rand. During the time you spend here, I'll be your constant companion, but I have no intention of forcing myself upon you. Despite what you obviously think—or perhaps would like to think—I'm not a rapist."

Her face flaming, Lucille pulled herself up to her full petite height. "What would you call yourself then, Mr. Patterson?"

"I would call myself a man who is determined to stop you from making a very big mistake, a man who loves you— although I cannot imagine the reason why—and a man who is determined to make you realize that you love him in return."

Lucille was flabbergasted.

"I . . . love you? You *are* insane!"

"Oh, no, Lucy, quite the contrary. I am in absolute control of my senses, and when our allotted period together is over, I know you'll agree with everything I've said."

Her eyes fixed incredulously on his face, Lucille shook her head in a slow, bemused manner. Her only comment to his statement escaped her lips in a mumbled whisper.

"He is insane. . . ."

Pat's smile widened.

"I'm going to be leaving you for a while, but you needn't try to race me for the door, Lucy. I know you'll want to freshen up a bit before lunch, perhaps change into something more comfortable than that dress. It is still damp at the hem, is it not?"

Lucille darted a quick look down at the stained hem of her skirt. She sniffed. Did he notice everything? She raised her eyes haughtily back to his.

"You'll find most of your cases have been unpacked. Your

322

clothes are hanging in the wardrobe. The only things you'll find missing are your shoes—for obvious reasons, I might add. Do you think you can be ready for luncheon in thirty minutes or so? I'll have Mrs. Gunnerson prepare luncheon for that time. . . ."

Lucille strove to conceal the hope that flicked to life inside her. They were not alone. Surely she could persuade this Mrs. Gunnerson. . . .

"No, Lucy, don't get your hopes up. Mrs. Gunnerson is devoted to me. She is a lovely old woman and an excellent cook and housekeeper, but she's also deaf and dumb. And she does not read, I might add. I communicate with her entirely in sign language."

"Sign language?"

"Yes, I'm quite proficient in that manner of—"

Lucille could take no more.

"Oh, shut up!"

"Lucy, darling, you truly do have a way with words. . . ."

His effort to conceal his laughter decidedly inadequate, Pat turned and walked toward the door. His hand on the knob, he turned to toss over his shoulder, "Thirty minutes, Lucy. I'll be back for you then." His eyes meeting hers for the space of a moment turned abruptly serious. "We're going to have a fine time together, Lucy."

Lucille was standing staring solemnly at the closed door when the sound of the key turning in the lock snapped her from her incredulity-induced trance. Running to the door, she pounded on it, enraged.

"Pat Patterson, don't you dare lock me in!"

Pat's response was low and even.

"Thirty minutes, Lucy."

Music and raucous laughter punctuated the hum of conversation around the Long Branch bar. Adjusting the brim of her hat, Billie pulled it low onto her forehead. She took another sip of her drink and sauntered toward the faro table, intensely aware that Rand's eyes followed her covertly across the crowded saloon.

Billie stifled her growing anxiety with great effort. She had deemed it advisable to follow along with the rest of the men as they had headed straight for the nearest saloon for a drink to fortify them. She had been only too aware that she could not afford to show any inclination to go off on her own with Rand's close observance of her.

Rand had been waiting for the men and herself in front of Wright House when they had entered town. The men had greeted him with howling enthusiasm, and engrossed as they all had been, she had been free to allow herself the luxury of intense perusal of Rand. It occurred to her that she had seen Rand every day for the past two months, but the power that drew her unalterably to him had not lessened.

In his change of wardrobe, along with looking heart-stoppingly handsome, he had appeared more the successful cattle contractor he truly was than drover. Her eyes had traveled his impeccable appearance in dark trousers and vest, and a fine lawn shirt left open at the neck in deference to the heat of the day. He had disposed of his stained Stetson in favor of a broad-brimmed black hat, but Billie had noted unconsciously that the coal-black glow of his hair, freshly trimmmed, had put the color to shame. The broad planes of his face had been creased in a smile, startlingly blue eyes and white teeth in vivid contrast with skin darkened to a golden brown by the trail. The creases in mid-cheek had deepened into the incongruous dimples that accompanied his smile, and her heart had fluttered in response.

Billie had dismounted amongst the hearty enthusiasm of the men and walked past him, every nerve in her body calling out in memory of the last cow town they had entered together and the loving exchange that had followed. She had glanced back toward him, her eye inadvertently catching his as he had been trading jokes with a jovial Stewart, and she had read the same thoughts in his glance. Then she had turned away, knowing memories of that sort would only make it harder to do what she must.

Rand had directed the men across the railroad to the livery stable. There they had unsaddled their horses and turned them into a large corral before surrendering their guns in the office. When those necessities had been completed, Rand had handed each man twenty-five dollars in gold. She had followed the general stampede to the Long Branch Saloon, realizing the safety in numbers afforded against the sheer magnetism of Rand's presence. Rand had ordered drinks all around upon arrival, sliding into a spot beside her at the bar. In the time since, she had been avoiding his attempt to speak to her, and she was uncertain how much longer he would hold his patience.

Billie moved into a spot behind Willie at the faro table, her mind less on the game than on the man whose tight gaze had followed her. The sight of a familiar figure descending the staircase from the second floor caught her eye, and Billie felt her face drain of color. Jim Stewart's pleased expression was indicative of only one thing as he motioned to the men, signaling them toward the bar.

Trailing along as the last of the men gathered around Rand, Billie maintained her silence.

Stewart cleared his throat impressively.

"Now, Rand, the boys and me have been on the trail a long enough time to recognize a good boss when we got one, and you, fella, are he. But it's come to our notice that you've been a little tense on the trail these last weeks."

Pausing, Stewart assessed the suspicious light growing in Rand's eye before continuing soberly.

"It seemed to us that you've been alternatin' back and forth with this tenseness since the time we left Abilene. Concerned as we was with your physical comfort, we got together and discussed what we felt might be your problem. After eliminatin' all the petty annoyances we've all suffered this trip, we kinda arrived at what we figured was your problem—a woman."

Rand's expression tightened visibly, and Jim placed a conciliatory hand on his broad shoulder.

"Well, the fact is, Rand, that we've all suffered the pangs of unrequited love at one time or another in our lives, and we figure that pretty redhead was probably the first upset you've had in your long and illustrious contact with the feminine gender."

Billie was conscious of the fact that Rand relaxed visibly at the mention of the beautiful woman who had greeted him so enthusiastically in Abilene. It suddenly occurred to her that his growing stiffness had been at the thought that her secret had been discovered, and a new guilt assailed her. She watched as he replied with obvious impatience.

"Well, it's good to see you fellows are so concerned with my welfare, Jim, but I think I can handle my problems by myself."

Appearing unaware of Rand's resistance to his interference, Jim slapped his trail boss's shoulder heartily. The several drinks he had imbibed before taking his short walk up the staircase had obviously increased his enthusiasm for his plan.

"The thing is, Rand, we've decided to help you along, since we're the fellows who've been sufferin' your short temper in the last month."

Rand's brow raised with the first signs of annoyance.

"Oh, is that so? . . ."

"Yeah, that's so, Rand, old friend, and before you go gettin' yourself all hot and bothered, I want you to know me and the boys have settled your problem for you in two words."

Rand's expression was unsmiling, his voice flat.

"And what are those two words, Jim?"

Jim's grin turned just short of a leer.

"Lotta McDevitt."

"Lotta. . . ."

"That's right, friend. I just left Lotta's room. She remembered you real well, Rand. I'm thinkin' it's that memory of you just as much as the real generous amount I put in her hand that got her to agree to havin' you visit her a little later tonight."

"Visit? . . ."

"That's right, Rand. Now you know Lotta don't take just any old fella that staggers in off the trail. She's real particular like. The boys in this place so much as told me she'd turn me down flat. Why, she ain't taken in no more than four or five customers since she became part owner in this place. You can consider yourself real privileged, fella!"

Rand's shoulders stiffened along with his expression. It was obvious he was about to make a negative remark when Jim stopped him with a wink.

"Come on now, Rand. The boys and me chipped in our hard-earned money to see a smile back on your face. Don't let us down now." Turning unexpectedly as Rand was about to speak, Jim motioned in Billie's direction. "Even the kid chipped in. As a matter of fact, he was the first to ante up."

Her heart pounding, Billie held her breath as Rand turned slowly in her direction. His eyes blue ice, he directed a piercing look into her face.

"Is that so, Drucker?"

Aware that the eyes of the men were keen upon her, Billie nodded, her voice carrying to each of the men gathered.

"That's right, Mr. Pierce."

His intense gaze searing her for all its frigidness, Rand responded in a low, measured tone.

"Well, I suppose I can't let you down then, can I?"

"Well, that's what the boys and me wanted to hear! Now you just get ready, Rand. Lotta said she's goin' to fix herself up real pretty for you. She said she'll let you know when she's ready to see you." Jim winked again. "I'm thinkin' she'll be worth waitin' for."

"I'm sure she will be."

Rand's voice was cold, and Billie sensed he was about to turn back in her direction when a short, whiskered fellow appeared unexpectedly at his side.

Showing no hesitation in interrupting the conversation, the fellow tapped Rand briskly on the shoulder.

"You Mr. Rand Pierce?"

His frown darkening, Rand turned in his direction.

"Mr. Winthrop Collins told me to find you. He has a buyer for them horses you was offering for sale. The fella's waitin' back at the Wright House. He has to be leavin' town in a little while, and he wants to see you now."

"I'm busy now."

"Mr. Collins said it's now or never, Mr. Pierce. This fella is willin' to pay top dollar, but he's goin' to be seein' a couple of other fellas before he leaves."

Rand hesitated and finally nodded in assent. The short look he turned back toward the men stopped on Billie's face with intense deliberation.

"Tell Lotta I'll be back. I wouldn't miss enjoying your present for the world."

Striding away at a stiff, measured pace that demonstrated his anger far more clearly than words, Rand left the men at the bar exchanging puzzled glances.

"Hell, Jim, I think we made the boss mad. . . ."

"I'd say he's mad, all right. . . ."

"Well, he might be mad now, but he won't be mad for long after he steps through them doors upstairs." His leer more pronounced then ever, Jim lifted his bloodshot eyes to the ceiling. "That Lotta, she's all I remembered her to be and more. I tell you, boys, we're goin' to have us one happy boss when he leaves this town. As a matter of fact, I wouldn't be surprised if we all find ourselves gettin' a little bonus when we reach Montana—just for bein' so considerate of our boss' feelins'."

"Jim, you'd better stop drinkin'. It's goin' to your head. . . ."

"I'm tellin' you, boys, we're goin' to have us one happy man. . . ."

Unable to stand more, Billie put her glass down on the bar and turned away. She had taken only two steps toward the door when a hand closed on her shoulder.

"Where're you goin', Drucker?"

Billie turned to Jeremy's flushed face. Her response was instinctive.

"I don't see as how that's any of your concern."

"Maybe not, but I ain't goin' to let you slip away and have the boss come down on me like he did in Abilene. Hell, he was so mad. . . ."

"Abilene was a long time ago. . . ." Swallowing hard at the memories the name had raised in her mind, Billie shook off Jeremy's grip. "Besides, I don't see where you're going to have much choice unless you want to follow me to the baths and the barber shop and the emporium while I pick up some new neckerchiefs and—"

"All right, Drucker, you win. I ain't goin' to follow you around town like a puppy dog, no matter how mad the boss gets. Anyway"—his familiar grin creasing his pleasant face, Jeremy gave her a short wink—"if that Lotta lives up to half the things Stewart says about her, I'm thinkin' the boss will have other things on his mind. . . ."

The burning ache inside her growing stronger with every reference to the unseen woman, Billie gave a short grimace that passed for a smile. She nodded unconsciously to the voice that trailed on behind her as she walked toward the door.

"We'll be here when you get done, Drucker. Not a one of us is goin' to move until we see the boss walkin' up that staircase. . . ."

The mental image stimulated by Jeremy's remark almost more than she could bear, Billie pushed her way through the door and onto the street. The late afternoon sun glared in her eyes, and she took a deep breath against its sting. Rand would be angry at first when he found out she had left Dodge without saying good-bye, but Lotta or someone like her would always be there to soothe his temporary pain. She was acutely aware that it would not be so for her. Even now the thought of another woman lying in Rand's arms tore at her, tying her stomach into such knots that she feared she would retch.

But she could not afford to indulge this weakness that assailed her. She could not afford to think in terms of a future she did not have. McCulla's men had found her once. Sooner or later they would find her again. She needed to reach Montana first. This was her chance. . . . Twenty-five dollars would be more than enough to buy herself and Ginger space on a train going north. She knew she would be far more easily traced by buying a ticket north, especially traveling with Ginger. But she could not afford to be without a horse. And neither could she bear to be without Ginger. The small mare was her last link to the past. She had given up everything else and was about to give up even more.

Yes, she knew what she had to do. . . . She knew. . . .

*   *   *

329

Lucille's smile was slow and sultry as she flashed Pat a potent, under-eyed glance. Aware of the effect of long dark lashes rising gradually over the brilliant blue of her eyes, she gazed up into Pat's sober face as they walked down the hallway toward the sitting room. His light skin colored revealingly, and satisfaction combined with another unrecognized emotion fluttered across her senses. Oh yes, Pat Patterson, the tables would soon be turned. . . .

His response was low, slightly hoarse.

"Lucy, you scheming little twit, what are you up to?"

Realizing Pat's tone did not quite meet the sharpness of his words, Lucille felt victory within her grasp. Her thirty minutes up, Pat had appeared at her door only a few short hours before and escorted her down the rather impressive staircase of his home toward the breakfast room. There they had been served luncheon by a cheerful, pleasant woman who was indeed deaf and dumb as Pat had said. They had eaten an excellent well-prepared and served meal, and Pat had shown her politely around his stately country home.

The steady downpour continued, keeping them housebound, but Lucille could not be happier with the circumstances. She had determined only minutes after Pat's key had turned in the lock of her bedroom door that she would use the weather to her advantage, and things were working out exactly as she had planned. Her smile grew brighter.

"Scheming? Pat, dear, I don't know what you're talking about."

"Oh, you don't. . . ."

His green eyes intense, Pat hesitated in his step, and Lucille could not suppress a small laugh.

"Pat dear, only a few hours ago it was I who was poised in the upstairs bedroom, ready for flight, and somehow now I have the feeling you're the one who is preparing to retreat."

"I . . . retreat? No, you're wrong there. I'm just trying to give myself time to figure out what's going on in that devious little brain of yours."

"I . . . devious? I'd say that's the pot calling the kettle black, wouldn't you?"

"Not exactly. What I've done, I've done because you've

forced me into it. If I accomplish nothing else within the next few days, I'll have kept you from making a fool of yourself with Rand Pierce. . . ."

Lucille's smile dimmed, and she suppressed an urge to slap that all-knowing expression from Pat Patterson's face. Instead, she slipped her arm through his, urging him on toward the sitting room where a crackling fire burned in a truly elegant fireplace.

"Pat, you've been such an impressive host, and I'm trying to be a truly appreciative guest. Let's not spoil it, shall we?"

His hand closing over hers where it rested on her arm, Pat shook his head with a small laugh. "Now I know you're up to something. But if it suits you to be pleasant, I can only say I'm enjoying your new tactics immensely, even if I must warn you they'll win you no chance of a change in my plans. You're here for three days at least, darling. By my calculations, that will be long enough to allow you no opportunity of catching up with Rand Pierce in Dodge."

"I've already dismissed that possibility from my mind."

"Liar."

Lucille stiffened. "Pat, kindly do not provoke me."

"But you lie so beautifully."

Another potent, undereyed look accompanied her smile. "That's better."

They had arrived at the sitting room, and Lucille released Pat's arm to walk toward the fire. She was conscious of the manner in which the firelight picked up the colors in the copper-colored silk gown she wore. She had chosen it with great care, realizing that the neckline was modest enough not to be openly provocative, but was cut in a way that allowed a generous glimpse of her breasts if she positioned herself at just the right angle. She had found several opportunities to use that advantage to her purpose, and she knew Pat's awareness of her grew with each passing minute. She expected she would find numerous occasions to give him a tantalizing peek at the tempting swells while he entertained her in this quiet room, and she felt a short niggle of excitement touch her senses.

The sitting room door closed behind her, and Lucille

remained looking into the fire. She knew its soft glow was extremely flattering to her small, perfect features, and she turned slightly, allowing Pat a better view. Oh, yes, she had great plans for this afternoon. And before it was over, she would be well on her way back to St. Louis and the train station. She would soon be in Rand Pierce's welcoming arms.

But she had a very elaborate plan to accomplish first, the primary step of which she was about to commence.

"I am so glad you chose to close the doors, Pat." Turning, Lucille smiled sweetly as he approached. "When I awoke this morning, I admit to being extremely annoyed at the rain and unexpected chill, but there is a particular appeal to this weather when a fire is lit in the fireplace and it's so cozy and warm inside." Ignoring the suspicion rampant on Pat's face, she glanced toward the corner and the crystal decanter resting on the sideboard.

"I would so love a sip of brandy, Pat. If it is as good as the brandy you offered me upstairs, I know I'll enjoy it immensely."

"Of course, Lucy. I was just about to suggest the same thing."

Waiting until Pat had turned toward the sideboard, Lucille seated herself on the settee beside the fire, her shoulders artfully positioned to provide just the barest glimpse of the white flesh that swelled so warmly at her décolletage. Yes, just a small, teasing glimpse . . .

Raising her hand as Pat approached, Lucille accepted the glass gracefully and waved him to the seat beside her. "Do sit down, Pat. It occurs to me that in all the time we have known each other, we have never sat down to a simple conversation without ending up shouting at each other. Tonight I'm determined that shall not happen. Since you have gone to so much trouble to abduct me, I do believe you've earned a hearing."

"Oh, is that what this is?" The spark of amusement apparent in Pat's eyes was beginning to stoke familiar fires. "I thought this was more in the nature of a seduction scene."

"Seduction! Well, I never . . ."

"Not that I mind, you understand. Quite the contrary. I would be a most willing participant. But in truth, darling, I hate to see your obviously well-planned evening go awry."

"Pat, I told you I didn't want to argue. . . ."

"I don't want to argue either, Lucy."

Lucille gritted her perfectly shaped teeth. "If you really mean what you're saying, you'll stop calling me Lucy. . . ."

"That is your name, darling. . . ."

"Pat. . . ."

"All right. Compromise . . . temporarily. I'll call you Lucille if you'll tell me what you have on your mind."

"That will be fine with me, because what I have in mind is very simple. I intend to get to know you very well tonight."

The amusement was beginning to drop from Pat's glance. "Those were my intentions exactly, Lucy—Lucille."

"Then, that is what we'll do." Leaning forward, Lucille lifted her glass. "Shall we drink to knowledge. Knowledge is power, is it not?"

"I don't think that quote was intended for a situation exactly like this, but I'll drink to it."

Touching her glass to Pat's with an intimate glance, Lucille lifted it to her lips. She sipped the golden liquid, her eyes closing as it slid smoothly down her throat.

"Heavenly."

Unable to resist, she drained her glass, only to open her eyes to Pat's raised brow.

"Does part of this 'getting to know each other' include getting rip-roaring drunk?"

"Pat, don't be a boor." Glancing toward the decanter in the corner, Lucille smiled. "I really would like some more."

With a short shake of his head, Pat rose and walked to the corner. In the space of a few moments he had returned and placed the decanter on the table before them.

"This will make things easier, don't you agree?"

"Pat. . . ." Lucille's smile was beginning to stiffen. "I'm getting angry, and I told you—"

"You don't want to argue. But neither do I intend having you drunk and unconscious and thereby defeating my whole purpose. I told you, I don't intend to take advantage of you or take you by force or—"

"Pat, just pour me another brandy, will you? I think I'm a good enough judge of how much brandy I can consume without its affecting my senses."

Reaching over, Pat filled her glass without another word. He raised his glass to his lips and sipped with caution as she did the same.

"Now, tell me about yourself, Pat."

"What do you want to know, Lucille? You already have a sketch of my background: the only child of a hard-working servant and the town drunk, determined to succeed in life. The elaborate fireplaces in this house as well as those in my town residence reflect my childhood vow that I would sit in front of my own fireplace in my own house one day, and it would be bigger and better than any of those I'd been allowed to share in sufferance when I was a child."

Touched in spite of herself, Lucille was momentarily quiet at the picture of the lonely child he had presented.

"I do believe you're upset, Lucille." Pat looked genuinely surprised. He reached out to caress her cheek. "Well, you needn't be. I suppose I have my father's weakness and failure to thank for my own success, and I was blessed by a loving and thoughtful mother who managed to compensate quite well for my father's inadequacies. I was fortunate to come into contact with several businessmen who appreciated my own brand of fortitude and who sponsored my higher education. I have since paid them back for their original investment in me. It was through those gentlemen that I came to be introduced to your father. That was approximately six years ago, and I have enjoyed every minute of that association. Your father is a wonderful man, Lucille."

Lucille nodded. Why was it she had never noticed the golden specks that glittered so warmly in Pat's eyes when he spoke? Or the manner in which his mouth quirked so attractively at the corner with his witticisms? He really had the most excellent taste. . . . It was evidenced in his house, its furnishings, his manner of dress, even the brandy she was drinking. She raised the glass to her lips again. Her brows lifted in surprise. The glass was empty.

Not bothering to ask Pat to do the honors, Lucille picked up the glittering decanter and poured herself another measure. Taking a small sip, she leaned forward into the hand that had caressed her cheek. She truly did like the touch of his hand. It was gentle, quite lovely. She raised her hand to his shoulder and traced its line.

"Pat, what did you truly expect to accomplish with this short, enforced visit you maneuvered?"

"Expect to accomplish?" Pat's breathing was becoming affected, and he blinked in an obvious effort to retain a hold on his thoughts as her hand slipped up his shoulder to move sensuously in the hair at the back of his neck. "I suppose I hoped that you would come to realize you were wasting your time thinking of any other man but me, that you would begin to recognize your desire for me as I recognized my desire for you long ago. . . ."

"You desire me, Pat?" The golden flecks in Pat's eyes were dancing, glowing. They fascinated her and Lucille was unable to withdraw her gaze. They were drawing closer, closer, and she could see them no longer as Pat's lips began to move against her cheek.

"Oh, yes, I desire you, darling. I've desired you from the first moment I saw you. Aside from being the most beautiful woman I've ever met, you are by far the most unforgettable—in more ways than one."

Pat's lips were moving against her fluttering lids, the line of her cheek, circling her lips tantalizingly, driving her mad. She caught them with her own, her heartbeat rising to a roaring in her ears as Pat's mouth moved deeply into hers. She was clinging to him, holding him tight against her. She was returning kiss for kiss, caress for caress, when Pat suddenly pulled himself back.

"Lucille, I—I don't know what you're planning, but I warn you now, it's not going to work. There's only one place this kind of thing will lead, and it won't be out that door and onto a train to Dodge."

Feeling true annoyance, Lucille slipped her arms around

Pat's neck. A low moan escaped her lips at the delicious thrill that moved up her spine as she pressed herself full against him.

"Do stop talking. Whatever my intentions were, I have only one intention now. Kiss me, Pat. I do so enjoy your mouth. And your mustache, it feels so—"

But her thought went unexpressed as Pat's mouth closed over hers. He was kissing her deeply, fully. His kisses, passionate, stirring, covered her face, her neck, moving with breathtaking expertise to the warm white swells beneath. She was gasping, writhing in the throes of his tender assault, when Pat pulled back once more. His voice was hoarse with emotion as his eyes moved over her flushed face.

"Lucy, I don't want it to be this way for us. You've had too much to drink; your judgment is affected. When we make love, I want to you to be fully aware of what you're doing. I want your complete consent. I don't want our lovemaking to be accomplished in a flush of passion which you may regret. I want—"

"And what about what I want, Pat?"

"What you want?" His hand rising shakily to her face, Pat caressed her velvet cheek. He swallowed against the passion he controlled so tenuously. Her great azure eyes glowed into his, stealing what was left of his breath, and he swallowed again. "What do you want, Lucy?"

"Oh, Pat. . . ." Her voice trembling, Lucille closed the gap he had so firmly created between them only moments before. Her lips pressed against his, she mumbled almost inaudibly, "I want you. . . ."

With a low groan his arms were around her, crushing her close. His hands were moving in her hair as his mouth ravaged hers. Tearing his mouth from hers, Pat silenced her protest with a short, gasped response.

"Not here, darling."

Within minutes she was held high in his arms as he walked across the room. With a quick twist of his wrist he flicked open the door. Carrying her without the slightest strain, he ascended the steps and within moments he pushed open the door to his room. He closed the door behind them and was standing by the broad four-poster bed, his eyes glowing into hers when he spoke for the first time.

"This is your last chance, Lucy. If you don't want me to make love to you, tell me now."

"There's only one 'don't' left between us, Pat." Unable to control the trembling in her voice, Lucille whispered against his lips. "Don't call me Lucy. . . ."

The satin bedcovering was smooth against her skin as Pat slid her dress from her shoulders. But his lips were smoother, so warm and moist as they covered her flesh in loving adoration. He was removing the pins from her hair, winding his fingers in the silken length, running his hands in a loving sweep of her naked flesh. The curling golden brown hairs of his chest teased her sensitive nipples and she cried out in protest, only to feel the consolation of his lips as he worshipped the tortured flesh. His impassioned assault was complete, taking in all of her senses, raising a need inside her that drove her beyond the realm of sober thought. His slender, tightly muscled body moved to stretch out atop hers, and she gasped at the swell of his passion. She pulled him close, closer still, her hands moving warmly over his back, delighting in the muscles rippling beneath her palms.

He was probing her moistness with his throbbing manhood, and she gloried in his need. She opened herself to him, welcoming him, gasping as he thrust true and clean inside her. But he paused, and she uttered a soft sound of protest. Her lids rose in a questioning glance that met Pat's ardent gaze.

"Lucy darling, if this is some trick you're playing, it's too late to back out now. It was too late from the first moment my lips touched yours, that my mouth tasted your flesh. You're mine now, Lucy. Oh, God, you're mine. . . ."

His strong body trembling, Pat lifted himself in a last, searing thrust, plunging deep and full within her. Her soft cries echoing his, Lucille gloried in his possession, her emotions rising to join him in the soaring rapture of total consummation.

Moments later, motionless and spent as he lay intimately upon her, Pat whispered soft words of love that filled her

337

heart. Slipping to the bed beside her he drew her into the circle of his arms, his lips against her hair.

The rain was still drumming softly against the window, and Lucille heard the soft, even sound of Pat's breathing against her hair. Drawing herself away, she looked into his sleeping face. She whispered against his cheek, but he did not stir. Drawing herself away even farther, she carefully disengaged his hand from her hair, from her waist. She slid to the edge of the bed and moved quietly to her feet. She walked to the chair on which his trousers lay and quickly searched his pockets. Coming up with the key she sought, she dropped his trousers and turned to snatch up her clothes. Hesitating only a moment, she moved quickly to the wardrobe and opened it. Her shoes . . . neatly lined up beside his . . .

Slipping her feet into the nearest pair, she shot another look toward the bed. He was sleeping, unsuspecting. . . .

Making a quick sweep of the room with her eyes, Lucille turned quickly and with a few silent steps was outside in the hall. She pulled the bedroom door closed behind her. With great deliberation she inserted the key into the lock and turned it. The snap as the lock engaged echoed in the silent hallway and Lucille hesitated. Where was the flush of victory, the satisfaction of a game well played and won? Why the sinking feeling in her stomach, the thickness in her throat, the heat of tears in her eyes? She turned and took two steps toward the staircase, then came to an abrupt halt.

What was she doing? She glanced toward the window and the rain that blew in chilling gusts against its panes. It was cold and raw out there, and it had been so warm and lovely in Pat's arms. . . . It was late, too late to get to Dodge. She had missed Rand this time. There would be other days for Rand, but today . . . the next few days to come . . .

Turning back to the bedroom door, Lucille hesitated only a moment before reaching for the key and opening the lock with cautious stealth. She opened the door and peeked inside. Releasing a shaky breath as her eyes touched on Pat's sleeping form, she closed the door behind her and walked quickly to the wardrobe. With utmost haste, she slid the

338

door open and slipped the shoes from her feet. In light, fleeting steps she moved across the room toward the chair where his trousers lay. Sliding her hand into the pocket, she released the key. Turning, she dropped her clothes onto the floor where she had found them. Carefully, she slipped back onto the bed.

Lifting his hand with utmost caution, Lucille draped Pat's arm around her waist, a soft sigh escaping her as he spontaneously drew her near. His lips were again pressed against her temple, his fingers wound in her hair. A wave of pure contentment swept over her and she closed her eyes, at peace at last.

She did not see the cautious lifting of Pat's lids or the mixture of relief and joy that moved across his expression as she relaxed in his arms. She felt only the intimate touch of his flesh, the warmth of his embrace, and she slept.

Rand moved hastily up the crowded street. Unconsciously slipping his hand into his vest pocket, he removed his watch. He clicked open the catch, his eyes focusing in a swift glance on the face. An hour . . . He had been gone an hour. He had not expected to talk that long with that particular buyer, but the man had grown extremely cautious since the last time he had done business with him.

Dealing mostly on his excellent reputation, Rand was unaccustomed to being pressed for details. In this country, a yearling was a yearling and a two-year-old a two-year-old, and a man's word that the string of horses he was selling sight unseen was as good or better than the one he had sold last year was sufficient. But if he were to be completely truthful, his temperament on meeting the fellow had been testy at best, and he supposed it had been this quality that had instigated the man's caution.

Well, he had sold the herd in any case, with promised delivery in Montana when the drive had been completed and the cattle turned over to the Blackfoot agency. He realized he should feel extremely pleased, especially in view of the fact that McNulty at the livery stable had reported that over forty

339

herds had already passed this point on the trail. Rand gave a low, disgusted snort. Yes, that same accomplishment on another drive would have been cause for celebrating. After all, he was now not only guaranteed his original profit but the profit generated by the horses that would continue to serve him only too well. It was an accomplishment not usually guaranteed until much later in the drive, and at a much lower price. If things progressed in the way they had started, this particular drive would leave him considerably more wealthy than he had planned.

But somehow that thought gave him little consolation. He never had measured his happiness in monetary proportions. And at this point in time he was only too aware that his happiness lay in one place—in Billie's small, slender hands.

Rand frowned and increased his pace. He supposed it was best that he had been forced to step away from the Long Branch for a while. His patience had been all but expended. He still had not truly gotten over the shock of the men's "gift" to him. Lotta McDevitt. . . . Had this been any of his previous drives, he supposed he would have been flattered by the men's concern and as anxious to take advantage of their gift as he would have been to respond to the sultry brunette's invitation earlier. But that was most assuredly not the case now, and Billie's clear confirmation that she had been the first to contribute to the fund for his "gift" had been the last straw.

His first reaction upon her unwavering statement had been a rage he had been forced to conceal. He had realized Billie had doubtless been aware that Stewart had been upstairs making arrangements with Lotta all the while he had been trying to talk to her, that while his mind had been occupied with thoughts of Billie—only Billie—she had obviously been waiting for the time Lotta would take him off her hands.

In hindsight, he supposed it had been fortunate that the buyer's summons had reached him at that time. Feeling as he had been, he was certain to have revealed himself in one way or another. But he had had an opportunity to regain control of his shaken emotions. He was now determined to get Billie

340

out of that saloon and to a place where they could talk privately, even if he had to remove her physically. She valued her disguise, and he knew she would agree to go with him if he forced the issue. A ripple of distaste moved across his senses. He wanted nothing less than to force Billie to listen to him, but he was desperate. Oh, God, he was so desperate. A strong, instinctive feeling was growing within him. He was losing her past redemption.

Rand swallowed tightly and took a deep breath. The Long Branch was only a few steps away, and he felt a tremor of apprehension slip down his spine. He pushed open the doors of the saloon and stepped inside. His eyes searched the room, coming to rest on the familiar figures still leaning against the bar: Stewart, Carlisle, Willie . . . but Billie wasn't there.

He was only a few steps away when Carlisle spotted him.

"Well, Willie, you don't have to worry no more about Lotta gettin' tired of waitin' for him. Here he is!"

Nodding in greeting, Rand signaled the bartender for a drink. Still searching the room for Billie's slender form a few minutes later, he unconsciously downed his drink without blinking and turned to Willie's scrutinizing eye.

"You ain't lookin' too happy, Rand. From the look on your face I'd be guessin' that buyer didn't have too much to offer. . . ."

Rand attempted a smile.

"No, as a matter of fact, the remuda's sold, and at a good profit."

Willie shook his head in obvious bewilderment. "Well, if that don't beat all— Well, somethin's sourin' your disposition and I'm sure—"

At Rand's sharp glance, Willie raised his hands in mock surrender.

"All right, it ain't none of my business and I won't say no more."

His tension growing by the moment, Rand signaled the bartender for a refill. His voice was deceivingly casual as he turned back toward Willie.

"I can see you fellows haven't budged from this bar since I left. The only one who seems to be missing is the kid. . . ."

341

Willie swept the bar with his eyes. "Yeah, that's right, ain't it?" He turned back toward Carlisle automatically. "What do you say, boy? Where did Drucker take himself off to?"

Carlisle's face was flushed, and Rand gave a short mental note that the young fellow would probably have to be loaded on his horse and let out of town before the night was out if he kept up at the rate he was going. But he had little time for those considerations, and he felt a stab of annoyance as Carlisle hesitated before responding.

"Yeah, Drucker's been gone a long time, ain't he? He said he had some errands to do, but he was comin' back. I'm thinkin' he's not too fond of spendin' time at the bar. I guess he learned his lesson in Abilene. . . ."

"Errands?" Rand felt a touch of panic. Billie could be anywhere in town. It had never occurred to him she would leave the Long Branch, and he was suddenly grossly irritated with himself.

"Yeah, but he said he was comin' back. We're all planin' to go over to the Wright House for a good meal in a little while and I'm thinkin' he won't want to miss it. He'll be back. . . ."

Rand nodded, his tension rising. He supposed it would be best to wait a little while before running out to see if he could find her. Damn it! They had already wasted valuable hours. . . . He ached to hold her in his arms. He wanted . . .

Taking a deep breath, Rand deliberately dismissed his thoughts and ordered another drink. He'd wait, but the minute Billie stepped a foot back in this saloon, he was going to drag her out again. They had to talk. . . .

His hand a trifle unsteady, Rand raised the glass to his lips and took a sip of his drink. The level of noise in the crowded saloon had risen noticeably, punctuated with increasing frequency by the shrill feminine laughter and bawdy shouts that signaled a growing consumption of red-eye. He reached into his pocket and withdrew his watch. Another hour had passed, and Billie hadn't returned. Tension had grown into a tight knot inside him. He had left the Long Branch a half hour before and made a quick round of the stores, hotels, and saloons along the main street, but he hadn't found her. In a rush of panic, he had headed toward the livery stable at a pace that was almost a run, but Ginger had still been in the corral where Billie had left her. His relief had been profound. Knowing Billie's affection for the mare, he was certain she would not have left town without the animal. So he had returned to the Long Branch and waited some more.

In the time since he had returned, the suspicion that had nagged at him had slowly grown to reality in his mind. There could be only one reason Billie had disappeared so efficiently. How many times and in how many ways would she have to tell him the same thing before it sank into his brain? She wanted nothing to do with him, nothing at all. She had looked him straight in the eye when he had questioned her about Lotta. Her answer had been plain. She had been the first to ante up a portion of Lotta's fee. She had no desire to talk to him. She didn't want to give him another chance. She wanted him to go to another woman, any woman, as long as he left her alone.

That brief moment when their glances had met in the livery stable, when he had thought he had read fleeting memories in her eyes, had been a figment of his imagination, his own desire to see what he wished to see reflected there. As far as Billie was concerned, it was over, done. There was nothing between them but an employer-employee relationship and soon, after they reached Montana, they would not even have that. She would be gone. . . .

Rand gave a low laugh and raised his glass to drain it dry. He experienced a bitter stab of jealousy for the man she was running to in Montana, whoever he was. But Billie had given him her virginity. Perhaps she had considered it a necessary sacrifice in order to find a safe way to get to the man she loved. She had considered him a man of the world, had probably relied on his reputation, expecting him to tire of her once he had gotten his satisfaction. He supposed she wasn't far wrong. He had had countless meaningless encounters in the past, which he had walked away from without another thought.

No more, Rand. No more. . . .

Those softly spoken words had burned into his brain and heart in the past weeks. And now she was making it more clear than before that she had no intention of changing her mind.

The tight knot of tension inside him expanded into a searing ache, and Rand's mind cried out to the vision so vividly clear before it.

Billie, you never gave me a chance to tell you I love you. . . .

The realization that Billie had not wanted to hear the words had no effect on Rand's burning need to say them. He desperately wanted to hold Billie close, to feel her slenderness pressed against him, to breathe deeply of her scent as he whispered the words he had never before spoken to another woman.

But if he had learned anything in the last few months, he had learned that love could not be a selfish emotion. He loved Billie, but his love was not returned. She wanted to be free of him, and if he truly wanted her happiness, he knew he should let her go. But how did he let go of something he had unconsciously been searching for all his life? How did he go back to aimless self-gratification, the loveless fulfillment of bodily needs after he had experienced so much more? He had grown beyond that point. A new, pretty face, the lush rise of a breast, a sultry turn of the hip, no longer challenged him.

His thoughts were tied up with Billie in every respect of his life. He thought of the past only in relation to the time they had lost. He thought of the present in terms of the beauty they could share. And he could bring no clear vision of the future into his mind other than one in which Billie was beside him.

Rand stifled a short laugh. He was a man who had considered loving one woman for life unrealistic, an impossibility in his case. He was now faced with the realization that he had been wrong, drastically so. He was also faced with another painful reality: Having found that woman, having realized that love, he was going to have to let her go. Billie didn't want him. To cling to the hope that she would change her mind, to press her, would only cause her pain. And Billie had suffered enough.

Despite his determination of a short few minutes before, Rand signaled the bartender for another refill. Ignoring the curious glances he had been receiving from his men for the past hour, he emptied the glass with a well-practiced hand. Billie had bought him a present—a present she hoped he would enjoy and that she hoped would free both of them. Maybe it would—in her mind, at least.

His eyes rising toward the second floor, Rand took a deep breath. Lotta had sent down word a short time before that she was ready for him. He supposed the long delay in calling for him had been designed to raise his anticipation. He had no doubt it would be a great shock, indeed, if she knew he had needed every minute of that time to come to the decision to respond to her summons.

Without a word, Rand turned and walked briskly toward the staircase. It was time he accepted Billie's present to him and freed her of him once and for all. Yes, it was time. . . .

Rand was unconscious of the loud hoots and hollers that followed him as he mounted the steps and turned down the upstairs hallway. Stewart had painstakingly explained which room was Lotta's. His step slowed as he walked toward the third door.

Coming to a full stop, he raised his hand and knocked. The low, sultry tone that bid him enter raised an unexpected flush on his face. He turned the knob and stepped inside, closing the door behind him. His eyes flicked around a luxurious room protected from the afternoon light by drawn blinds, his gaze coming to rest on a feminine outline silhouetted against the muted light of the window. His gaze traced its proud carriage, the smooth lines of upswept hair piled high on a well-shaped head, a gracefully slender neck and shoulders, and womanly curves only too apparent through the diaphanous folds of the exotically sheer garment that covered them. As he stood in silence, her lithe arms reached out to welcome him, and despair grew to a living, palpable ache inside him.

No, this was all wrong. He didn't want this woman. . . . His mind and his body was rejecting her. He could not carry out this farce of lovemaking, not when his heart cried out so clearly for only one woman.

She took a step forward, only to be halted by the finality in Rand's tone as he reached into his pocket. Retrieving a few gold pieces, he laid them on the table beside him.

"I—I'm sorry, Lotta. I hate to disappoint the boys, but I guess I'm not in the mood today. Maybe some other time. . . ."

Rand turned. He was about to pull open the door when a soft voice met his ear.

"Rand. . . ."

His hand freezing on the knob, Rand stiffened, remaining motionless for the long space of a second before the voice sounded again.

"Rand, come back, please. . . ."

Turning abruptly, Rand stared at the slender outline with the afternoon sun at its back. He strained his eyes in an effort to penetrate the dim light of the room. His heart began pounding and a slow joy began to permeate his senses. He took one step forward and then another, finally moving to grasp the now familiar curve of womanly shoulders with his hands as he turned the shadowed face to the light.

The dark eyes that met his were bright with emotion; the delicate lips trembled in a smile. With a low groan, Rand slid his arms around her, crushing her tight against him.

"Billie, God, it's you. . . . And I almost walked away. . . ."

"I wouldn't have let you walk away, Rand."

Drawing back Rand stared into Billie's flushed face as if seeking to confirm what he already knew to be true. Billie . . . in his arms . . . at last.

With slow deliberation, Rand lowered his mouth to Billie's, his heartbeat rising to a thunder in his ears at the first touch of her lips. The sweet taste of her intoxicated him, and he pressed his kiss deeper, deeper. He ran his palms over the smooth line of her back, down her spine as he crushed her against him. He cupped her tempting flesh with one hand, pressing her softness against the firm rise of a passion that had been nil only a few short minutes before. He slid his other hand up to her neck, holding her still and close under

346

his marauding mouth.

Rand drew deeply of her sweetness, tasting and swallowing, his hunger a voracious need to consume her. He was trembling wildly and drew back abruptly in an attempt to rein his raging emotions under control. His chest heaving, he stared down into Billie's beautiful face, his love for her so intense that he dared not speak.

"You needn't pull back, Rand." Her eyes holding his intently, Billie whispered through trembling lips, "I—I've caused you pain, when you only sought to help me. I've regretted that, Rand. Arranging for Lotta wasn't my idea, but I have to thank her and the men for clarifying something in my mind. I finally realized that although our reasons were different, we both needed someone. But you've given yourself so much more generously than I. I have no valid excuses for my selfishness any longer, Rand. You've helped me, watched over me, whether I wanted it or not. And when my fear incapacitated me—would have defeated me—you protected me. You even cherished me for a while." In silence she conceded it was the cherishing that had been her undoing—of which she had been afraid.

Billie took a deep breath. "You've done everything for me, and I've done nothing in return but hurt you. I suddenly realized that if the men were right, if you needed a woman temporarily, I wanted that woman to be me. I'll be with you until we reach Montana, Rand, if you still want me. . . ."

"If I still want you? . . ."

A bittersweet joy rose inside Rand. Temporarily . . . Montana still loomed in the future, the time of separation. But Billie was here . . . now. . . .

In a facile movement, Rand scooped Billie up into his arms. He walked the two steps to the bed and lay her down. Within moments he was lying beside her, the only impediment between them the thin veil of her gown. Gently, Rand unfastened the gossamer fabric from Billie's shoulders.

Myriad emotions assaulting him, Rand indulged himself in Billie's naked beauty. This woman was more to him than his own life. He wanted to fill her with his love, to wipe the thought of every other man from her mind. She was young, inexperienced. She did not know what it was to feel the intensity of need he felt for her. She did not know how truly rare was this beauty they made with the blending of their bodies. He wanted to educate her, to awaken her. He wanted her to love him the way he loved her so when they reached Montana . . .

Refusing to allow himself completion of that thought, Rand cupped Billie's face with his palms. His lips left a searing trail across her cheek to whisper against her mouth.

"Oh, yes, I still want you, Billie. I've wanted you every moment since I last held you in my arms." His words blurring as he circled her mouth with hungry kisses, Rand drew back with a supreme effort. The words that followed were unmistakably clear. "But I have you back now, darling. You belong to me, here, now. . . ."

Rand's kisses were deepening, his involvement becoming more intense. Tearing his mouth from hers, he moved to the fragile shell of her ear to taste the silken hollows. He nibbled at the dainty lobe, his own heartbeat quickening as Billie emitted a low gasp. His lips followed the smooth line of her throat, drawing the delicate skin into his mouth, savoring its texture, worshipping it with his tongue.

He was losing himself in his loving, his hands fondling, caressing, traveling every inch of Billie's flesh. He was overwhelming her with his ardent ministrations, his love-making becoming more impassioned with each soft moan that escaped Billie's lips. He kissed her sweet, virgin breasts, drawing them in his mouth. He fondled the burgeoning crests with his tongue until Billie cried out in tormented ecstasy. He captured her writhing hips with his palms to press a spray of moist kisses against the flat expanse of her stomach. He kissed the pale curls below, irresistibly drawn to the intimate moistness beneath. He pressed his mouth to the delicate lips awaiting his kiss, his tongue finding the aching bud of her desire to assuage it with growing fervor. His kisses deepened, his senses rioting as Billie began to shudder under his touch.

He was no longer thinking but was reacting to his need to

348

love Billie completely, to make her his own totally, without restraint. He raised his eyes to Billie's face, his mouth still pressed intimately against her, his heart soaring at the passionate tremors that tore at her body. But it was not enough, not enough. . . .

Billie was trembling wildly beneath him as he drew away, and he felt her shock of loss. Her passion-drugged lids raised slowly, coming to focus on his face. Rand held her glance with his own, his surging need sounding in the hoarseness of his tone.

"Tell me you want me, Billie. Tell me you need me. Tell me you—"

But he could not make the final demand. He could not urge her to tell him she loved him, as much as he wished to hear those words from her lips.

Billie was trying to speak, her breath coming in short, labored gasps. He pressed his mouth to the fragrant mound once more, and her eyes flicked momentarily closed. Her voice was a breathless whisper.

"Rand, please. . . ."

"Tell me, Billie. I need to hear you say the words. . . ."

A light, fleeting kiss started Billie trembling anew, and Rand gloried in his power over her body. He would keep her with him. He would make her need him, love him. . . .

He urged again, "Tell me, darling. . . ."

"Rand, I—I do want you. I do. . . ."

Her shuddering was gaining control, and Rand pressed, "Tell me you need me. . . ."

"Oh, Rand, I do need you. . . ."

A supreme elation soaring to life inside him, Rand was unable to restrain himself any longer. Pressing his mouth passionately to Billie's intimate flesh, he drew from her lovingly, his searing kisses continuing until her quaking body gave forth in shuddering, breathless homage the full measure of her tribute to his loving assault.

Billie had stilled beneath him when Rand raised himself at last to cover her perspired flesh with his own. His eyes intent on her face, he lifted himself to probe the moistness he had loved so completely only moments before. With a smooth, quick thrust, he brought himself deeply and fully to rest inside her.

Billie's low gasp accompanied his entry. Her eyes flicking open, she held the clear azure heat of his gaze as his ardent whisper broke the prevailing silence between them.

"I'm home, Billie . . . where I should be . . . a part of you. Make me welcome, darling. Take me in. . . ."

Rand moved tentatively inside her, his heart expanding as Billie met his thrust with the fullness of her body. Abandoning himself to the driving need inside him, he plunged again, deeper, his breath catching as Billie picked up the rhythm of his lovemaking, taking it, returning it, rising with him on the waves of passion that soared to control his mind. Again and again he penetrated her softness, her slender body meeting and joining his strength until there was no longer a separation between them. They were one, totally, completely in each other as Rand raised Billie with him to the summit of their lovemaking. With one final plunge they soared high on the wings of their mutual passion, the glory of the moment coloring their world with the supreme vibrance of ecstasy . . . total fulfillment . . . theirs alone . . . together.

Billie was silent and still beneath him and Rand clutched her close. Surely she had to see, had to know that neither of them would ever need more than this. But no, he was getting ahead of himself. He had to take it slowly, with time. He had to allow her to come gradually to the realization his were the arms that brought her love; that nothing in the past mattered—and no one.

A fresh surge of jealousy swept over him, and Rand pulled Billie closer still. No one would take her from him, no one. Montana would come and go and they'd be together. That was the way it was meant to be. . . .

A pleasant warmth tickled her cheek and Billie stirred. It moved against her eyelids and she frowned. She did not want to awaken. It moved against her mouth and her lips parted. The warmth pressed deeper, and she abandoned herself to its sweet consolation. It was good, so good. . . .

The warmth abandoned her, and a low voice penetrated her twilight world with its familiar ring.

"Oh no you don't. I want your eyes open when we make love, Billie. . . ."

With a startling abruptness Billie was awake. Her eyes snapping wide came into contact with Rand's soft smile as he looked down into her face. She jerked her head toward the window, measuring the light against the drawn blinds before she turned back to Rand's growing frown.

"What time is it, Rand?"

Hesitating only briefly at her unexpected question, Rand rolled back against the bed and reached to the night table for his watch.

"A little past five."

Billie relaxed visibly. "Oh. We still have some time. . . ."

Rand made no comment. His eyes intent on hers, he turned back onto his side facing her, waiting for her to speak.

"I suppose you want to know what I—"

"No, Billie. . . ." His hand moving unexpectedly to cover her lips, Rand held her fast with his gaze. "I have no questions. . . . I've learned my lesson. Too many questions, and I almost lost you. I'm not going to make that same mistake again. I don't need to know anything that you don't want to tell me. I don't have to know where you come from if you're here with me now. It doesn't matter who you're running from or why when you're safe beside me. As for the man who hurt you"—Rand hesitated briefly—"I don't intend letting him or anyone hurt you again."

Obviously finding the words he spoke more difficult than he cared to let on, Rand took a deep breath before continuing.

"As for whatever Montana means to you, well, I don't need to know anything else besides the fact that you're in my arms now, and that's where you want to be. That's enough for me. . . ."

Billie raised her hand to Rand's cheek, her throat thickening at the soberness where a smile had reined only a short time before.

"Rand, I'm sorry. . . ."

"Don't be sorry, Billie, just let me love you. . . ."

His eyes intent on her face, Rand slowly lowered his mouth to hers. His words echoing in her mind, Billie closed her eyes against the beauty of his kiss, her arms moving around his neck, drawing him close. His naked flesh was tight against hers, and she felt again the rise of the searing emotion he evoked inside her. He was whispering soft, loving words against her lips, renewing her. She felt the firm rise of his passion against her softness, and she longed for its consolation. His strength gave her strength, his loving made her loving in return. . . . She had not known she . . .

A sound at the door alerted them to a presence outside the moment before a key scraped in the lock. Even as the sound rang in the semidarkness of the room, Rand rolled to his back, covering Billie's nakedness with the coverlet as he reached simultaneously to the night table beside him. He raised his gun at the same moment the door snapped open with startling abruptness.

An unexpected voice broke the tense stillness.

"Well, really, dear, I did tell you I would need the room back at five o'clock."

There was no mistaking Lotta McDevitt's statuesque figure silhouetted by the light from the hallway behind her, and a flush of embarrassment covered Billie's face. She darted a quick look toward Rand. He had lowered his gun and was replacing it on the table. A small smile curved his lips as he turned back, and Billie experienced a sharp stab of an emotion she chose to consider annoyance. It was obvious Rand was not uncomfortable being found naked in bed by this beautiful, bold woman. She snorted inwardly. That probably came from long exposure to women of Lotta's vocation.

Turning up the lamp beside her to its brightest illumination, Lotta smiled broadly and closed the door behind her. Her eyes assessed Rand openly as she approached the bed, touching on the dark shock of hair that spilled on his forehead, the clear brow and brilliant eyes that assessed her in return. Her gaze moved across the strong planes of his face, his bold profile, his full and smiling lips. Without embarrassment, she dropped her glance to the broad expanse of Rand's bared shoulders and chest, and the light coverlet at his waist where the obstructed view obviously intrigued her. She gave Billie a quick wink.

"I can see why you wouldn't want this fella to get away, Billie, dear. And I'll tell you true. If I'd had gotten this close a look before you made me your offer, I might not have let you take my place after all. . . ."

Rand's smiling, "Thank you, ma'am," flushed Billie's face even darker. Pulling herself to a sitting position in bed, Billie clutched the coverlet over her breasts.

"I'm sorry, Lotta. I thought you said I could have the room until six. . . ."

"'Fraid not, darlin', but I'm not opposed to givin' the two of you some extra time to get dressed in private. I've had a right pleasurable afternoon relaxing and knowing that my time was bein' paid double."

Turning back toward the doorway with a pleased expression, Lotta walked the few quick steps and paused with her hand on the knob.

"And don't forget, Billie dear, my offer still stands. If you're ever in need of a job, I'll find a good spot for you right here in my place. There aren't many men who wouldn't be wild for all that smooth white skin and silver-blond hair. Your angel face could get you far. Think it over. It's a sight easier work than trail drivin'. . . ."

The door clicked closed behind Lotta, and Rand turned stiffly toward Billie, his outraged senses reacting riotously to the full glory of her semi-naked appeal. A single strand of gleaming hair had escaped her upswept coiffure and lay raggedly against her slender neck, while small tendrils curled damply against her temple. Still clutching the coverlet against her, she unconsciously emphasized the smooth slope of her shoulders, the slender grace of her arms, the incredible delicacy of her small hands. His eyes moved over her face. Yes, her skin was white, flawless; her features perfect. No man would be able to resist those great doelike eyes or turn away from the giving warmth of her mouth. . . . The face of an angel . . . Unreasonable jealousy turned his voice sharp.

"What's Lotta been trying to talk you into? Has she been trying to convince you it's easier to earn your money on your back than on a horse?"

Billie's chin snapped up in silent anger.

"Lotta is a businesswoman and she likes her life. She and I had a good talk, and she promised to keep my confidence. She's very generous. She allowed me the use of the luxuries she's earned, had her servant prepare a bath for me and dress my hair. She even gave me the choice of any of her negligees to wear. She said she's a wealthy woman, that I could be just as successful as she if I—"

Rand's low groan halted Billie's recitation.

"Billie, please, don't say anything else."

Rand shook his head. His anger this time was obviously directed at himself. "I apologize for everything I said. I know I made you angry and defensive, but please, don't even pretend to consider that woman's proposition."

Reaching out for her, Rand drew Billie into his arms. Distress was evident in the startling blue of his eyes as he clutched her breathlessly close.

"Only my hands, Billie, only mine are going to touch that white skin she was talking about. Only my hands are going to stroke your hair. And I'm the only man who's going to hold your angel face close, to feel your mouth under his. . . ."

"Rand, I didn't say I considered for a minute . . ."

"I know, I know. . . ."

Rand continued to hold her tight against him, his hands smoothing her neck, the bared flesh of her back. With startling abruptness he separated himself from her.

"Let's get dressed and get out of here."

Suddenly as anxious as he to leave, Billie slipped quickly to the side of the bed and drew herself to her feet. She moved to the corner, unconscious of the fact that Rand's eyes followed her. Distaste flicked across her face as she reached for the breast-binding cloth.

"No, you won't need that. We're only going across the street. I have a room in the hotel. . . ."

Billie's eyes snapped back in Rand's direction. The flare of passion in his eyes sent a rush of color to her face.

Turning without response, Billie reached for her underwear and shirt. She was pulling on her trousers when she realized Rand was already dressed and observing her silently. Flustered at his intense scrutiny, she fumbled at the closure, only to have Rand close the distance between them and brush her inept hands from her waist. His eyes never leaving her face, he fastened the buttons with tantalizing slowness. When he spoke at last his voice was a hoarse whisper.

"It's inconceivable to me now that I could have believed, even for a moment that you were a boy. I must have been blind. . . ."

"You forget how I looked when I first walked into your camp. . . ."

"Even so—"

"And you were too angry at me most of the time to look any farther."

"You set me off into a rage faster than anyone I ever met; you still do. Half the time I can't think straight when you're near me."

Her face settling into sober lines, Billie shook her head. "Maybe I'm just no good for you, Rand. Maybe it would be best if I—"

"Don't say it, Billie. Don't say it, damn you!" His hands biting into her shoulders, Rand held her firm under his suddenly exasperated gaze. "We're going to leave this room now, walk down the back staircase, and go directly to my room in the hotel across the street. And I'm going to make love to you, Billie, until we're both too weak to move. Then we're going to sleep, and when we wake up, I'm going to make love to you again."

A familiar quaking began inside Billie at the warm flush that had transfused Rand's face, the desperate need he had inadvertently revealed. Her smile was tremulous.

"But—but I'm hungry, Rand."

Momentarily startled by her response, Rand suddenly smiled. His voice was deep with emotion as his hand slipped up to caress her cheek.

"We'll have some food brought up."

They were moving down the hallway toward the rear entrance a few moments later when Lotta emerged from the far doorway. She stopped in her tracks as she surveyed the slender boy in baggy clothes and oversized hat, his pale hair tied to the nape of his neck with a leather thong. Her eyes shot to the tall, handsome man walking beside him, dwarfing the boy with his size. Her expression was condemning.

"What a waste. . . ."

Rand stiffened, his hand sliding possessively across Billie's shoulders.

"No, Lotta, that's where you're wrong."

Drawing Billie a fraction closer, Rand tipped his hat formally in Lotta's direction.

"Thank you, ma'am, for the favor you did us and for agreeing to keep Billie's secret."

Her cornflower blue eyes assessed his possessive stance, and Lotta gave a short shrug.

"It's been my pleasure." Turning, she leaned forward unexpectedly and kissed Billie's cheek. "Remember what I said. If you ever need—"

Rand's hand tightened spasmodically on Billie's shoulder.

"Let's go, Billie."

Within minutes they were moving down the back steps.

Extremely pleased with herself, Lotta turned and walked toward her room. She raised her hand and tucked a straying wisp of golden hair into her upswept coiffure. She smiled. Lotta had heard a lot about Rand Pierce and his easy way with women. Love them and leave them. . . . Well, that was all right for her and women like her, but she had an idea that little girl wasn't one to play that kind of game. In any case, she had put a bee in Rand Pierce's bonnet that he wasn't goin' to forget for a while. And she had enjoyed herself—immensely.

Carl spurred his horse viciously in an effort to elicit a faster pace from the exhausted animal, but his efforts were to no avail. He shot the men riding beside him a tight look. They had been silent most of the day, and he was glad. He

356

had just about had it with their grumbling. It was easy for them to complain. They weren't the ones responsible for tryin' to trail a will-o'-the-wisp in a land where she could be lost so completely as to never be found again.

Carl shot a look at the sky above him, his eyes gauging the position of the sun as it dropped rapidly toward the horizon. It would soon be dark, and he wanted to make town before then. He was goin' to sleep in a bed tonight, and he was goin' to lay there until his body was good and ready to get up.

It had been a damned hot day . . . a damned hot week. They had been on the trail all that time with only the barest necessities: dried beef, coffee, beans. He was damned sick and tired of that meager fare. And he was damned sick and tired of the wild-goose chase them fellas with Rand Pierce's herd had sent him on. He had wasted precious time, and with every hour that had been wasted, his suspicions had grown. A pretty good picture was beginnin' to come together in his mind.

Them fellas in Rand Pierce's herd . . . He might've thought they was just havin' some fun with him, sendin' him off like that chasin' after the girl when she wasn't nowhere near where they said. But it seemed kinda strange that Rand Pierce's herd was the one waitin' just outside San Antonio whie the girl was there, and it was the same herd that was lookin' for drovers. In lookin' back, it also seemed kinda strange the way that big fella, Pierce, was anxious to get rid of him. He had been on the trail long enough to know that most cattle drovers were only too willin' to entertain a cowboy from back home in the hopes of gettin' some news.

In any case, he had backtracked, questioning every herd that he passed. Hell, he hadn't thought there were that many cows in the state of Texas—in the whole country, for that matter—as he had seen. And that much dust and heat and stringy dried beef . . .

So he had decided to have a second look at Rand Pierce's herd and the men drivin' it. He'd been a damned fool to ride off that way. It was worth another look.

It hadn't been difficult for him to find the herd a second time, settled and grazin' easy the way it was outside Dodge, and it hadn't taken him long to see that the girl wasn't with the men left to watch it. But he had a feelin' he was goin' to be a little more successful in Dodge. Pierce's drovers hadn't been too happy to see him show up again. They'd looked right anxious, as a matter of fact, and the more he thought about it, the better he felt.

Yep, he was goin' to be in Dodge tonight. And he was goin' to canvas every saloon in town before he hit that nice, clean bed. And he was goin' to find that damned little bitch, and when he did . . . Well, McCulla was goin' to be real appreciative. . . . Real appreciative . . .

Carl spurred his horse again, satisfied at last as the animal stretched out his legs into a steady gallop. Realizing he was leaving behind the two horsemen who had been riding beside him, he called back over his shoulder, "Get a move on, boys. We're almost there."

Oh, yes, they sure as hell almost was. . . .

Her eyes wide, Billie stared at her reflection in the small washstand mirror in Rand's room. She raised her hands to touch the exquisite garment she wore. Her fingers trailed over the incredibly delicate lace that covered her shoulders and swept to her wrists in full, voluminous sleeves. Her gaze followed the graceful lines of the magnificent negligee to the floor before moving to the exquisite gown beneath. An artful sweep of the bodice swathed her in the intricate beauty of the gauzy fabric, allowing the faintest outline of the tender thrust of her firm, rounded breasts. A wisp of the delicate material covered her rib cage and nipped in at her waist before flaring smoothly over the curve of her hips. The slender line of the skirt accented the delicate hollows of her body, allowing a pale shadow of the warm delta between her thighs as it clung erotically to the long length of her legs. She turned, fascinated by the manner in which the light, airy lace swirled about her, enveloping her in its glory.

A light, disbelieving laugh escaped her lips, and she raised her eyes to Rand's sober face.

"I—I've never worn anything as beautiful as this Rand."

358

Rand's eyes consumed her. "It's not the gown that's beautiful. . . ."

"Lotta would approve. . . ."

Rand stiffened. "I didn't buy it for Lotta. I bought it for you and for me." Reaching out, he drew Billie against his chest. He tilted her face up to his.

"Billie, I don't want to talk about Lotta or her propositions. I don't want to talk about the trail drive. I don't want to talk about the future or what we'll be doing in a few weeks. I want to talk about now, the way you make me feel, the way I want to make you feel. . . ."

Rand was kissing her, his lips moving against hers stirring a familiar heat inside her, and Billie sought to resist him. They had entered Rand's room only a few hours before, and the door had not closed behind them before Rand had taken her into his arms. He had made love to her with a tenderness that had touched her soul. She had been lost in him and him in her. They had slept and when they had awakened he had given her the lovely garment she now wore.

But she had not meant it to be this way . . . this loss of self when Rand took her into his arms. She did not want to be absorbed into Rand so completely that when the time came for them to part, she would not be whole without him. She would need a clear mind, all her strength. She could not be torn by memories of Rand. She didn't want that for her, and she didn't want that for him. A sudden panic assailed her and she tore her mouth from his.

"Rand, I— I think we should go downstairs for a while, maybe to the Long Branch to see the men. They'll be wondering where you are, where I am. . . ."

She was trying to disengage herself from his arms, but Rand held her fast. His expression was stiffening.

"It isn't the men you're worrying about, Billie. What's wrong? Did I do something that made you angry? Was it somethng I said or—"

"You didn't do anything, Rand. It's just—"

Rand tilted her chin up with his hand, forcing her to meet his gaze. His smile was a weak attempt at lightness that did not ring true.

"Are you tired of me already, Billie? Are you trying to get away from me?"

Rand's heart was pounding against her breast and Billie shared his anguish. He tried again.

"I know. You're hungry. We haven't eaten. I'll go downstairs right now and arrange to have someone bring up—"

Billie shook her head, desperation showing in her eyes.

"No, Rand. I'd—I'd rather get dressed and go down to Wright House to eat. It's almost time to go back to the herd."

"Billie, please, stop this." Rand's brilliant eyes raked her face. He gave a low, shaken laugh. "I'm overwhelming you, pressing you too hard. That's it, isn't it?" He raised an unsteady hand to her face. "I should've thought . . . realized . . . I've been wanting you, dreaming of you for so long that I didn't stop to think that you might not—" Rand paused and took a deep, steadying breath. "All right."

With great deliberation, Rand released her. "If you want to go downstairs to eat, or to Wright House, we'll go. I think the boys will be at least one meal and two bottles ahead of us by now. That, or they'll be so tied up in faro—"

His voice dwindling off in the face of Billie's discomfort, Rand offered softly, "Get dressed. It'll be any way you want it to be, Billie."

"Oh, Rand. . . ." Billie's hand moved out to touch Rand's cheek. "I don't want to make you think—"

Billie's voice dwindled off as Rand turned his mouth into her palm and held it for long moments against his lips. His chest was heaving with the heat of emotions held tightly in check. "I want you to be happy, Billie. . . ."

The flush of panic that had assailed her dissipated abruptly in the face of Rand's anguish. With a sudden clarity she realized it was already too late. The time of separation would not be any easier for the pain they suffered now.

She swallowed hard and attempted a smile.

"Then I guess we'll have to stay here after all so you can make love to me, because that's what really makes me happy. . . ."

Rand's eyes held hers for long, silent seconds. His voice

was low, cautious.

"You're sure, Billie? . . ."

"Yes, I'm sure. We only have a few more hours and—" Halting in mid-sentence, Billie shook her head as if to refute all that had recently passed between them.

"Rand, this is all so new to me. . . . I don't know how I'm supposed to act, how I'm supposed to feel. . . ."

But Rand was drawing her into his arms again, his voice tender.

"You're supposed to feel warm, loved, content, and safe in my arms, Billie. That's what I want you to feel. I'll make it that way for you, darling, you'll see."

Rand's mouth was moving on hers, his hand sliding beneath the delicate lace. Billie's eyes drifted closed. The last sight she saw was the brilliant sun spreading the final glory of day across a sky streaked magnificently with red and gold. Its splendor was reflected in her heart. Sunset . . . She abandoned herself to its colors, to Rand's touch, and to all that it entailed.

The steady drumming of rain had ceased, but the small patch of sky visible through the bedroom window was still leaden gray. It was late afternoon, but there would be no sunset tonight. How indeed could a sun, that for all intents and purposes had never risen, set? Suddenly amused by her own inventive riddle, Lucille turned toward the man whose face lay beside hers on the pillow. His eyes were closed, but she suspected he was not in a deep sleep. No, he was probably in a light doze, which had been the result of the rather vigorous, intimate activity they had indulged in most of the day.

Restraining an urge to reach out to stroke the wayward strands of pale hair back from his forehead, Lucille allowed her eyes to stray over Pat's sleeping face. She strained to remember her first impression of him, and she stifled a small laugh. Yes, it had been no impression at all. She had completely dismissed him as a colorless, anemic specimen of the male species, who held not the slightest appeal to her.

She had considered him average in every way—appearance, personality, intelligence—and she had *never* been drawn to the average male.

No. Rather, she had aspired to catch and hold a man like Rand Pierce: taller than most, certainly more handsome and virile than most, intelligent and successful, with a brilliant future of which she wanted to be a part. And a man who was a challenge. She was well aware that she had been outrageously indulged most of her life, and although she had enjoyed every moment of it, she did not wish to marry a man who would be a copy of her father—loving to a fault, and easy . . . too easy. . . .

No, Rand Pierce was the ideal she had been searching for, and if he didn't share her conviction that they were meant for each other, well, all the more incentive to capture him.

So, why was she lying in Pat Patterson's beautiful bed, naked and, oh, so sated? And how had she ever imagined Pat was *average* in any way? A slow flush suffused her body as memory returned their loving intimacies of the afternoon with breathless clarity. Reaching out, Lucille succumbed to the desire to brush back that fair lock of hair that lay against his brow. She trailed her eyes over his face.

Yes, she definitely had been in error when she had adjudged his face average. He was fair, yes, and she did prefer men of vibrant coloring as a general rule. But Pat's light wheat-colored hair and fair skin were contrasted so well by his dark brown brows and lashes. And his eyes . . . She truly had never seen eyes like his, a sober green with wild gold specks that flared to life with his more exuberant moods. When he made love to her they shone down into hers with a glowing heat that had almost melted her.

With a stringent effort, Lucille took hold of her straying mind and continued her perusal. His nose . . . Well, it was indeed average, not big, not small. He was certainly not possessed of the commanding profile of Rand Pierce. His lips? A now familiar flush began to transfuse her as Lucille remembered the touch of his lips against hers, their gentle caress of her skin, and the warmth of Pat's smile as they had stretched against his white, even teeth. She remembered the tickle of his neat mustache against her breasts and her eyes flicked temporarily closed in indulged memory. How had she ever considered that mustache ridiculous?

Opening her eyes once more, Lucille trailed her gaze across Pat's shoulders and chest. Perhaps he had not the size of some men, but his body was surely beautiful. Firm, compact, tightly muscled . . . She remembered the strength of those arms as they had clutched her close. . . .

Cautiously, she lifted the light coverlet that partially shielded his body and cast it carefully aside. She perused him more intimately, and a familiar heat rose inside her. No, he most definitely was *not* average . . .

Lucille reluctantly drew her gaze back to Pat's face, and a smile curved her lips. As for his personality and intelligence, well, she had long ago conceded that she had been wrong there. Pat had challenged her from the beginning with his wit and sarcasm, and she certainly admitted to being outsmarted by him in her aborted journey to Dodge. And to outsmart her was no easy task!

Yes, admittedly, she had been wrong about Pat Patterson. if he was not Rand Pierce, he was certainly worth her attention for a little while, at least. How long had he said he intended to keep her with him? Three days . . . ? Ummmm. . . .

Her heart beat rapidly in silent anticipation, and Lucille felt a new restlessness assail her.

Abruptly, Lucille was annoyed. How much longer was this man going to doze? Surely she could not have exhausted him so severely that he needed more than a half hour or so to nap. She was tired of waiting!

But even as her brows drew together in silent vexation, Pat turned toward her. His eyelids rose slowly and a smile spread across his lips. His arm snaked out unexpectedly, drawing her full against his naked length, and Lucille gasped as he tucked his head into her fiery locks and nipped her sharply on the ear. Her struggle to escape him was to no avail as he whispered softly, "Well, did you like what you saw?"

Pat allowed her to pull far enough away from him that she might look into his amused expression, and Lucille was outraged.

"You were awake all the time! I should have known you would not be that tired!"

"No, I was and am not 'that tired,' darling. As a matter of fact, it was extremely difficult for me to lie quietly still while you ogled me. I hope you've had your fill temporarily. . . ."

"Ohhhhh, you! . . ."

"Because I do have far more interesting plans in mind for us for the remainder of the evening."

Her pique not satisfactorily mollified, Lucille averted her face from Pat's smiling gaze.

"I'm not certain I'm of a mood to cooperate with your 'plans.'"

Submitting to the gentle hand that gripped her chin, Lucille allowed her face to be turned to Pat's. She was momentarily startled at the unexpected soberness of his expression and pensive darkness of his bright eyes.

"My dear Lucy, if I was only as sure of other things as I am that you'll cooperate with my plans for this evening, I would be a very relieved man. Darling, you're a very warm-blooded woman who has not been allowed to indulge her nature freely of late. I intend to allow you endless occasion toward that end in the next few days. Mrs. Gunnerson is very devoted to me. She is not only deaf and dumb, but she can also be conveniently blind if it is to my advantage, and I intend to take full advantage of her disabilities—with her blessings, I might add.

"So prepare to indulge yourself, Lucy. And prepare to indulge me, because I can think of no way I would more enjoy spending a dreary few days than in making my own sunshine with the woman I . . . find more attractive than any other."

"Attractive? . . ." Lucille wrinkled her nose. It was a decidedly inadequate adjective.

Pat's mouth turned up in a smile.

"All right, appealing."

"Appealing? . . ."

"Beautiful, intelligent, stimulating . . ."

But Pat was losing his trend of thought as he began to

punctuate his words with warm kisses on her face and throat.

" . . . desirable, loving . . ."

His ardent attentions moved to the full, tempting globes of her breasts and his mouth worshipped them lovingly. Withdrawing a few moments later, he glanced up into Lucille's passion-flushed face to continue softly between nibbling bites.

" . . . fascinating, charming, alluring . . ."

But Lucille was no longer listening.

Much later, their passion spent, Pat held Lucille in the circle of his arms. He moved his mouth against the warmth of her fiery curls, his mind completing the thought that had eluded him a short time before.

" . . . and the woman I love more than I have ever loved before. . . ."

The much abused lamp flickered dimly in the small hotel room as Billie drew herself to a standing position beside the bed. Her eyes moved to the window and she frowned at the darkness. A pale silver cast was slowly breaking through the night sky. It would soon be dawn.

She darted a quick glance toward the opposite side of the bed, her gaze catching and holding Rand's as he stood, staring pensively in her direction. In a few steps he closed the distance between them. Wrapping his arms around her, Rand strained her to him. His mouth was warm against her hair, his words muffled as he pulled her closer still.

"This is going to be harder than I thought. I don't think I'm ready to let you go."

Billie drew herself away. She flashed him a smile in an attempt at lightness.

"And I'm not ready to go back to the herd and face the men when I've missed my watch again. I have the feeling that lapse isn't going to be accepted too easily. . . ."

Unwilling to separate from her completely, Rand curved his hand around her slender neck, his mind unconsciously revelling in the silver-gold silk of her hair. He smiled.

"And you didn't even try to get away from me to return for your watch."

"I knew the boss wouldn't mind."

"He only would have minded if you had left him."

The sound of movement in the hall outside intruded into their quiet moment, and Rand turned a reluctant glance back toward the lightening sky. Without a word he released her and turned to his clothes.

Fully dressed a few minutes later, Billie walked to the door. Her hand was on the knob when Rand turned her unexpectedly back toward him. Annoyance flashing across his face, he jerked her hat from her head and threw it to the chair beside his own.

"I've gotten to hate that damned thing."

"Rand. . . ."

"I want to see your face without that brim blocking my view. I want to see your eyes when I talk to you. . . ."

"Talk about what?"

The molten blue of Rand's gaze burned into hers. The uncertainty reflected in its depths touched a chord deep inside her and she strove to control her spontaneous response to his silent need.

"You won't change your mind when you get back . . . and keep me from loving you? . . ."

Billie swallowed against the emotion choking her throat. "No, Rand. . . ."

"And you won't run off . . . leave me? . . ."

"I told you I'll be with you until the end of the drive."

"Montana? . . ."

"Yes."

"Billie. . . ."

She waited for Rand to continue, but he did not. Instead he shook his head and flashed her a smile. He reached over and picked up her hat, then his own. Stopping her as she began to raise it to her head, he dropped his mouth to hers and kissed her long and deep. Drawing away at last, he reached for the knob and pulled open the door. Within minutes they were walking down the hallway toward the first floor.

Carl adjusted his position on the uncomfortable chair and swore under his breath. He was supposed to have spent the past night in a nice, soft bed, but things had not worked out the way he planned. He shot a quick glance toward the lobby window. Damn that Pierce! It was almost dawn. What kind of trail boss was he?

Releasing a soft groan, Carl stretched out his legs in an attempt to relieve the crick he had developed in his back. What irked him even more was the fact that Marty and Larry were sleeping in comfort in rooms upstairs, and he had had to slip the desk clerk a few dollars just so the damned greedy bastard would let him stay in that particularly dark corner of the lobby where he could not be seen. Right now he was almost sorry he had run into Pierce's men at the Long Branch and found out that they were startin' the herd back on the trail this mornin'.

Of course the girl hadn't been with them—in her boy's getup or lookin' like herself—but those fellas had done too good a job of avoidin' his questions to alleviate his suspicions. He had decided then and there that since the girl hadn't been with the herd and she wasn't with the boys in town, there was only one other place she could be. He had checked every hotel on the main street, and when he had found the one that Rand Pierce was stayin' in, he had parked himself in the lobby where he was now.

One thing was certain. It wouldn't be much longer before he found out if he was wastin' his time. Pierce had to come down soon in order to start the herd on the trail. Them boys of his were expectin' to move on, and from the looks of things, Pierce was a hard boss who expected them to be movin' out on time. He didn't think . . .

The sound of steps on the staircase jerked Carl from his thoughts and he froze in mid-stretch. Lowering his hands slowly to his side he leaned forward, his eye on the two

367

figures that moved steadily closer. There was no mistakin'
the second fella. Rand Pierce . . . There weren't many men
around of his size and stature. And the way he carried
himself, so sure of himself, like he owned the world. But he
couldn't quite make out the first fella's face with that
damned hat pulled down like it was.

The first figure stepped down into the lobby and turned
toward the brightening light of morning. Carl stifled a gasp.
It was her! She had led him a merry chase, but he had found
the Winslow girl at last!

Almost unable to believe his eyes, Carl pulled himself to
his feet as the two figures walked to the door and stepped out
onto the street. Pierce and the girl had turned out of sight
when he started toward the door with extreme caution. A
quick glance revealed that Pierce and the girl were walking
rapidly toward the end of town. Careful to keep in the
shadows, he followed behind until they turned into the livery
stable.

He was still waiting in the shadows when they emerged
with their horses a short time later. He felt a flush of triumph
and the last of his doubts disappeared. The girl was leadin' a
familiar sorrel mare.

As he watched, Pierce slid his hand along the girl's
shoulder and pulled her into the shadows. The two figures
blended into one, and Carl scratched his whiskered face with
irritation. He had figured that was the way it was, Pierce and
her disappearin' like they did. He wasn't too happy about it,
either. It made for complications. It wasn't goin' to be too
easy to get to the girl with that Pierce standin' guard over
her. Well, the two of them were finally mountin' up and
ridin' off.

Scrambling out of the shadows, Carl moved quickly into
the livery stable and saddled his horse. Taking care to leave
a comfortable distance between them, he kept the two
mounted figures in sight as he followed behind.

Duck Creek was visible in the distance when Carl's spirits
suddenly lifted. Hell, his work was just about done! All he
had to do now was to send a telegram to McCulla and tell
him where the girl was, and keep his eye on her until his boss

arrived. He expected the boss would surely be travelin' with
enough men to take care of the situation, and the girl would
be McCulla's problem from there on in. All he and the boys
had to do was stand ready with their guns in case Pierce tried
to get in the way. That was no problem. He was used to that.

Waiting only until the two figures reached the campfire
and dismounted, Carl turned around and headed back
toward town. The rest of this job was goin' to be a piece of
cake, and he sure was goin' to enjoy his leisure until McCulla
showed up and took care of things. Yeah, he sure was.

A growing discomfort nudged Rand's senses. He shot
a quick look toward the figure riding at his side, and a fierce
possessiveness overwhelmed him. It had been all he could do
to keep to his resolutions when he had held Billie in his arms,
but he was determined not to drive her away with his
questioning again. Uneasiness again prickled up his spine,
and Rand's eyes shot spontaneously to the rapidly brightening horizon. It revealed no threat and he flicked a quick,
assessing glance behind them. Nothing . . .

Noticing his apparent unease, Billie looked sharply in his
direction.

"What's the matter, Rand?"

"Nothing. It's just instinctive caution, that's all."

Smiling a reassurance he did not feel, Rand resisted the
urge to say more. Instead, he turned his eyes determinedly
forward. Duck Creek would soon be coming into view, and
their silhouettes would be visible for miles against the
lightening sky. He could not afford to raise suspicion with
the men. It was going to be difficult enough to explain away
Billie's and his late arrival. And he had no desire to put any
more stress on Billie.

His eyes shooting once more in her direction, Rand
allowed his gaze to move over her profile, etched against the
growing light of day. Lotta had decried the waste of Billie's
beauty hidden from view in the clumsy disguise she wore. He
supposed it was true in a sense. He remembered his own
sense of loss when she had replaced the lace that had lain

369

against her exquisite skin with the coarse shirt and trousers she now wore. The binding of her beautiful body in that damned cloth had raised an instinctive protest inside him, which he had diligently suppressed, and his frustration had grown anew when she had bound her glorious hair into a tight queue and tied it with a rough piece of rawhide. He had wanted to tell her that she needn't hide anymore, that he would protect her against whatever threatened her. But he had not dared. Billie did not want to share that part of her life with him.

He was not about to question the pressure that had motivated Billie to allow him to love her, even temporarily. He had been successful in obtaining a commitment from Billie, even if it was limited at best. She would be with him for another two months. During that time he would prove to her that he loved her without saying the words. And he would make her love him. Whoever it was she was running to in Montana, whatever the reason that held her fast in her determination to reach that destination, he would change it with the sheer power of the loving force that drove him.

Turning to catch his eye, Billie shot him an inquisitive smile. Rand's heart gave a ragged leap. His silent response was instinctive, and he longed to say the words, "I love you, Billie."

Instead, he nodded toward the light of the campfire burning in the distance as they reached the outskirts of the herd.

"We're almost there. We're a little late. The boys have probably already eaten breakfast."

Billie frowned, and he wanted to tell her it didn't matter. Instead, he turned back toward the camp, growing ever clearer in the distance, and spurred his horse on.

Rand pulled up his horse beside a silent morning camp a few minutes later. The complete absence of sound accented the familiar sounds of a herd awakening to the new day, the shifting of heavy bodies, the soft lowing and answering calls. He slid his assessing glance around the camp and frowned. Sober faces; not a trace of the high spirits expected upon return from a successful night on the town.

370

The crackling campfire split the silence as Rand dismounted. He was intensely aware of the hesitation behind him before the creak of the saddle and Billie's step on the ground signaled she had done the same. So she sensed it too. . . .

Rand's eyes circled the fire once more. Averted glances . . . silence . . . He hardly recognized Carlisle in his newfound sobriety of expression. Rand's eyes touched on Nate's unwavering gaze, and he felt a moment's relief. Walking forward, Rand snatched up a cup and poured himself coffee. He glanced up with deliberate casualness.

"Looks like we're late for breakfast, Nate. Dish us up two plates, will you?"

"I'm thinkin' you might want to be talkin' to the boys first, Rand. You see, they've had quite a surprise thrown on them."

His eyes narrowing into cautious slits, Rand surveyed Nate's grizzled face. Nate nodded in silent confirmation of Rand's conclusion.

"That's right, Rand. They know. Seems like they ran into that Carl Whitley fella in Dodge."

The sharp gasp from behind him jerked Rand's eyes toward Billie's whitened face. He had taken a spontaneous step toward her before he stopped himself with supreme control. He forced his eyes back toward Nate. His tone was gruff.

"What do they know?"

"We know that Drucker ain't what he's supposed to be." His lined face pulled into a severe expression, Willie responded in Nate's stead. "That fella Carl told us somethin' he had neglected to mention the last time we seen him. Seems like Drucker ain't a boy at all, and I tell you, Rand, me and the fellas don't take kindly to bein' played for fools."

A surge of anger held Rand momentarily silent. He was well aware he owed the men explanations, but he didn't like the inference.

"Rand had no idea. . . ." Taking a deep breath, Billie broke into the intervening silence. She could not allow Rand to take the blame for a deception she had perpetrated. The

371

weakness that had struck her at the mention of Carl Whitley's name spread through her limbs, consuming her strength. She swayed, and Rand was immediately at her side.

His face flooded with color, Rand supported her with his arm. His voice was stiff with suppressed anger.

"You don't owe anybody explanations. You worked as a member of this crew and you did your job as well as any man here. If they choose to feel betrayed, that's their—"

Billie raised a shaky hand to Rand's sleeve. She attempted a smile.

"They have a right to feel betrayed. They stood behind me when Carl showed up in camp. I should've told them then. . . ."

Suddenly realizing the other men were listening intently to their soft exchange, Billie turned, her eyes touching on each of the faces around the fire.

"I—I'm sorry. I should've trusted you all enough to tell you, but—but I couldn't make myself do it." Despising the unexpected tears that filled her eyes, Billie took a deep, steadying breath. "I have no desire to cause dissension on this drive. I'll be leaving as soon as I can get my things together."

"Like hell, you will!" Rand's sharp expletive broke unexpectedly into Billie's soft dialogue.

"Rand. . . ."

"Wait a minute, ma'am. . . ."

Color flooding her face at Willie's unexpectedly polite form of address, Billie turned to his disturbed expression. Her silence afforded him the opportunity to continue.

"Me and the boys ain't askin' you to leave. Hell, we realize you're as good a drover as any one of us, and you're doin' a real fine job in the work you was hired to do. And I'm thinkin' the lot of us are suddenly seein' real clear the reason why Rand was as cranky and out of sorts as he was."

Billie's flush deepened and Willie dipped his graying head.

"Beggin' your pardon, ma'am, but it's clear to see old Rand here don't think of you as one of the boys. . . ." A small smile broke across Willie's narrow lips. "And I don't mind sayin' I ain't blamin' his reasonin' none. I always did think you was a mite too pretty for a boy."

The lump in Billie's throat thickened, and she swallowed hard to overcome it. But Willie had not finished his say.

"The thing is, the boys and me feel we should've been told sooner. A few of us feel like we didn't present ourselves the way we would've liked if we'd known there was a lady in camp. It was kind of humiliatin' to the lot of us to know that all the while we was tryin' to do our best to make a real man out of you, we didn't stand a chance in the world."

Billie could not suppress the smile that flicked across her mouth with her quiet response.

"Well, if I didn't make it, it wasn't because I didn't try, Willie."

Taking off his hat in a respectful gesture that all but undid her, Willie held her glance firmly.

"And now that we've had our say, ma'am, I know I'm speakin' for the boys as well as for myself when I say you may not be what we thought you was, but you're a bona fide member of this crew. And we'd take it right unkindly if we was to lose an able hand before this here drive was more than half through. As for them fellas that's chasin' you . . ." His face reverting to its former stiffness, Willie jerked a quick look behind him. His quick survey of the faces around the fire turned him back to her with new confidence. "Anybody'd that do to a pretty young thing like you what was done to make you show up in this camp in the condition you was deserves to get back more of the same. I'd say that Carl Whitley fella'd better not show his face around here no more."

Billie felt a stab of fear. She didn't want this. . . . They had no idea what she had done, what helping her would bring down on their heads.

"No, Willie. I don't want—" Biting down hard on her trembling lips, Billie paused. She turned to send Rand a plea for understanding before she spoke. "I—I think it would be better for all concerned if I left the drive. I can find my way north witho—"

A quick jerk on her arm turned her to Rand's whitened face the moment before he raised his head stiffly to the men's concerned faces. "Billie's upset, and she's sorry you found out the way you did, but she's not going anywhere but back on the trail with us."

"Rand. . . ."

Ignoring her interjection, Rand continued gruffly.

"Now, if you're done havin' your say, I'd say it's time to move this herd." Turning to the lean drover standing beside him, Rand ordered curtly, "Get them started, Willie. And keep them movin'. We don't have any time to waste."

"Sure thing, Rand."

Billie remained silent against the cutting bite of Rand's fingers on her arm as the men rode off into the herd. Soft hoots and calls raised the last, reluctant cattle to their feet as Rand turned to shoot her a furious glance. Her heart pounded wildly as he dragged her forcefully behind the protective screen of the wagon.

Jerking off her hat, he threw it to the ground with undisguised fury. The ache inside her so deep that she was uncertain she would be able to speak, Billie avoided his eyes.

"Look at me, damn it! Billie, look at me!"

Sliding his hand into the hair at the base of her neck, Rand forced her face up to his.

"You're not leaving. You gave me your word. You're staying until the end of the drive."

"I told you I'd stay until we reached Montana, but that was before—"

"There were no conditions attached to your promise, and I'm holding you to it."

"Rand, Carl Whitley must suspect. I'll only bring trouble down on you and the men. I don't want—"

"Right now I don't care what you want, Billie. I only care what's good for you and where you're going to be. The answer to those two things is the same. You're going to be here, with me. There's not a single man out there, Brothers and Hall included, who would want you going off on your own with that sleazy, good-for-nothing bounty hunter after you."

"He's not a bounty hunter, Rand."

"He's after you, isn't he?"

Billie nodded and Rand's arms tightened spasmodically.

"He's not going to get near you, Billie."

"I can't hide from him forever, Rand."

The torment in Rand's gaze almost more than she could stand, Billie whispered a soft plea.

"Let me go, Rand. It'll be better for everyone."

"No."

"Rand, I—"

"I'm holding you to your word, Billie, your promise. . . ."

Uncertain whether the emotion tearing at her was relief or despair, Billie whispered hoarsely, "It's wrong for me to stay, Rand."

Rand's arms sliding around her abruptly clutched her close, and Billie gasped at the passion in the azure blue of his eyes as he whispered against her lips, "Does it feel wrong for me to hold you like this, Billie?"

Her heart's response was spontaneous.

"No, Rand."

The lips only inches from hers closed the gap between, and Billie was lost in the depth of Rand's kiss.

Tearing his lips from hers, Rand grated hoarsely, "Does it feel wrong for you to be in my arms, Billie, for me to love you?"

Billie's voice was a breathless whisper.

"No, Rand, but—"

"That's all that matters. You're here, where you belong, with the drive, with me, and that's where you're going to stay."

The rattle of pans saved Billie the need of response, and Rand jerked his head toward Nate's approaching steps. Releasing her as Nate noisily continued his approach, Rand lowered his head for a last, fleeting kiss.

"Get mounted, Billie. We have a long day ahead of us."

Without a word, Billie picked up her hat and turned toward her horse. There was really nothing more she could say.

Chapter XII

TO:
DANIEL McCULLA,
SAN ANTONIO, TEXAS
PRIZE HEIFER LOCATED STOP AVAILABLE AT
   ANY TIME STOP
REMAINING AT DODGE TO AWAIT YOUR OR-
   DERS STOP
WILL NOT LET PRIZE GET AWAY STOP
CARL WHITLEY

Carl's lips stretched in a pleased smile. He rubbed his finger over his ragged mustache and darted a quick look around him. His eyes settling on the telegraph clerk's impatient stare, he strained for a more sober expression. His eyes darted back to the paper he held in his hand. He had been standing at the counter in the small office for over half an hour in an attempt to get the message right. Completed at last, his clever composition tickled him.

He really wished he could be there when McCulla received it. His smile stiffening, he remembered the boss's partin' words. He had taken real offense at McCulla's affront to his personal dignity. Hell, he had been on the trail for days because of the orders the big man had issued himself and had returned to report immediately as he had been told. He hadn't been sittin' behind a big desk, with all kinds of

377

servants waitin' on him hand and foot. No, he had been ridin' in the broilin' sun with two damned fool men beside him who had been no help at all in sharin' the load of the task McCulla had set for him.

Take a bath, huh? Well, it hadn't made no difference how pretty he smelled when he'd found that Billie Winslow. And it wouldn't make no difference whether he was wearin' a clean shirt or not when McCulla showed up to take care of everythin' once and for all. All that mattered then would be how well he backed up the big man with his gun.

His hot surge of temper leaving him just as quickly as it had come, Carl's lips picked up in a yellowed smile. Yeah, and he supposed it didn't make no difference what McCulla said, as long as McCulla put that bonus money into his hand like he promised.

Yeah, he really wished he could be there when Barney picked up the telegram in San Antonio and delivered it back to the big man. He sure enough would like to see his face. . . .

Looking up, Carl signaled to the balding clerk. He held out the much abused slip of paper.

"Here you are, fella, all ready to go. Send it right quick, will you? My boss won't want that prize heifer gettin' away." Carl laughed, enjoying his own joke. "No, he sure enough won't. . . ."

Billie lowered herself wearily to her usual spot beside the campfire, plate in hand. Almost self-consciously, she removed her hat and placed it on the ground beside her. It was a small luxury that Carl Whitley's revelation now allowed her, and a soft sigh escaped her lips.

It had been a grueling day's travel from Dodge. A small flush of heat suffused her. She had not envisioned this wearying result when Rand's intimate attentions had allowed her little sleep the night before. In truth, she knew that even had she realized, she would have been unable to turn away from his loving. Somehow, sleep and all other plans she had formulated in her mind had lost their importance in the face of the tumultuous emotions Rand raised inside her. And now, in the face of the danger that threatened her, their night together was an even more cherished memory.

But they had traveled a full day from Dodge without incident, and Billie was intensely relieved. Her perusal of the horizon had been constant and unrelenting until the mantle of night had dropped over the endless land surrounding them.

She had assumed her usual position within the herd after morning camp, maintaining her silence for the greater part of the day and noting absentmindedly that the men did nothing to interfere with her obvious preference for solitude. Rand had ridden out ahead of the herd in his usual manner immediately after they had been started on the trail, and he had returned for noon camp. She sensed that the news of Carl Whitley's presence in Dodge had stunned him as much as herself, and she had little doubt that part of his scouting would include a keen eye for the three men who had visited their herd once before.

But her mind had allowed her little respite. Ragged memories of pain, fear, and despair had assaulted her the day long. They had been so vivid that she had almost felt Wes McCulla's breath against her face, had almost heard his voice rasp in whispered threats. Her body had shuddered again and again as the sound of his pursuing step had resounded in her ear and the thundering pain of his heavy blows had rung again inside her brain. The gory memory of Wes McCulla's still, bloodstained body had flashed continually before her mind's eye, allowing her little peace.

Her edge of tension had been constant as they had made their way steadily northward, and she was relaxing for the first time that day in the temporary reprieve of night camp. A few hours while she need not look behind her . . . She knew that had Carl Whitley indeed discovered she was with the herd, he would not make a move against her now. No, Carl Whitley was no fool. He would choose his time, and it would not be when all the men in the crew were ringed around her.

A familiar fear tore at Billie's stomach and she resisted the trembling that assailed her. Carl Whitley. . . . He had been so close. . . . Had she not been with Rand, she would most likely have run into him in Dodge. She shuddered to think of the confrontation that would have resulted.

With startling abruptness, Carl Whitley's image returned clearly to her mind, and Billie fought the revulsion that ensued. There were no words that described Whitley more clearly than scrawny, unclean, harmless-looking. . . . But she knew only too well what was hidden behind that benign appearance. She remembered with utmost clarity the ease of his smile on the numerous occasions he had watched while Wes McCulla had taunted her. She remembered the speed of Carl Whitley's gun hand when her father had reacted violently to Wes's attempt to force himself upon her. It had only been a swift command from the young McCulla that had spared her father's life at that time, and Wes had made certain she had been aware of his generosity. He had also made certain she realized that Carl Whitley functioned on command and could be depended upon to do McCulla's bidding, whatever it entailed.

A small tremor of fear moved up her spine. The harmless joke that Whitley appeared to be, he was only too real and genuine a threat. In the hours that had passed since they had left Dodge, she had determined that no matter her promise to Rand, she would leave the herd at the first sight of Carl Whitley. She had already killed one man. She could not be responsible for any more loss of life.

Intensely aware of the uneasy silence that reigned around the campfire, Billie raised her head in covert perusal of the men seated nearby. She was fully aware that their obvious discomfort had nothing to do with the heat of the day, which still lingered, or the fine layer of dust that lay uncomfortably against their skins. A good meal and the solace of a few leisurely hours usually was sufficient to soothe those banes of the trail. Rand had not yet returned to camp from his check of the bedding ground. She had said little to the men since morning camp. The secret she still harbored inside her tied her tongue. She could not give them the explanation

380

they expected, which they indeed deserved.

Billie ran her eyes across the faces of the men present. Willie, Jim Stewart, and Russ Byrd had gravitated together as was their usual custom for night camp. Old trail buddies, they had much in common and had shared humorous memories with the crew countless times before the first watch began. But they ate in silence this night. Josh Hall and Seth Brothers, their companionship well established, sat a small distance away consuming Nate's hearty stew. The remuda settled for the night, Hank Casey had entered the soundless circle, plate in hand, seating himself beside Cal Johnson and Wyatt Wond. Fogarty and Cannon were with the herd.

A twinge of sadness jerked at Billie's senses as Jeremy Carlisle walked from the chuck wagon and settled himself a short distance from her. His eyes were stiffly fastened on his plate. It was almost amusing. The situation between Jeremy and herself was almost comically reversed. Where she had been the one who had formerly eaten in silence, her eyes glued to her plate, it had always been Jeremy who had sat beside her, forcing her into begrudging conversation with his unfailing humor and ready smile. But he was not smiling now. On the few occasions he had been forced by necessity to speak to her during the day, his smile had been noticeably absent. She did not have to study him closely to see that he was distinctly uncomfortable, even more so than the other men. A strong guilt assailed her, and unable to bear its weight a moment longer, Billie rose to her feet.

Within minutes she had replaced her almost untouched plate on the chuck wagon and, firmly ignoring Nate's reproving glance, had walked into the darkness behind the wagon. She needed some time to herself, some time to sort out her feelings. It was just as she had imagined it would be now that the men knew there was a woman in camp. They were uncomfortable and felt distinctly betrayed. She could not imagine this present level of discomfort being forced upon the men for the remainder of the time until they reached their destination. They deserved that no more than they deserved having a wanted woman being foisted upon them, a woman whom they would feel obliged to defend at the risk of their lives should the opportunity present itself.

Weary in mind and body, Billie headed instinctively toward the remuda. It was only now that she realized how rash had been her promises to Rand. If she were to be honest, she would have to admit that while Rand had held her in his arms, she had not been able to face the possibility of leaving him. The wonder he had raised inside her had been too fresh, the husky rasp of his voice too convincing, his touch too potent to be ignored. But the separation forced upon them by the trail had permitted the return of sanity.

She had made a mistake, indeed. Had she stayed to her original purpose, she would be on the train and traveling steadily northward. It had entered her mind that she might have been easily spotted by Carl Whitley had she approached the station. He was too familiar with Ginger's small proportions to miss her in a crowd of similar mounts, even if he had not recognized her as she was now dressed.

A slow feeling of inevitability began to overwhelm Billie and she stumbled on the shadowed terrain. Righting herself, she searched the darkness with her eyes in an attempt to identify one horse among the many who grazed in the faint light of a quarter moon. She needed the consolation of the small sorrel mare her father had presented to her so solemnly five years before. She remembered so clearly the halting note in her father's voice as he had led her to the spot where the mare had been saddled and waiting on her thirteenth birthday.

The minute I saw this mare, I knew she was made for my little girl. She's not big in size, darlin', but you can see her heart in her eyes. She won't ever let you down. I know horseflesh, and I can promise you that. And I'm thinkin' you're the girl she'd like to give that willin' heart to. Treat her well, darlin', 'cause she comes to you with my love.

A thickness choking her throat, Billie walked up to the outskirts of the silent horses. She gave a low whistle and waited. She whistled again, and the sound of movement within the herd tightened the lump in her throat. Within moments a soft whinny sounded in the stillness as a shadow worked its way through the herd.

The familiar velvet of Ginger's soft muzzle against her palm spread a bittersweet sadness through her veins, and despair struck her anew. It was obvious that Carl Whitley had received orders to continue searching for her. He would find her eventually, but she did not want that eventuality to be here, in this camp. And she did not want that eventuality to include senselessly endangering even one of these fine men. She leaned her forehead against Ginger's soft muzzle and stroked her gently. Her dilemma was such that she could not seem to think clearly. No, she did not want to think at all. . . . Not for now. . . .

Uncertain how long she had remained at Ginger's side, the mare's soft breathing and gentle devotion lulling her into a sense of calm that had eluded her the entire day, Billie was suddenly conscious of the shuffle of a step beside her in the darkness. Her heart jumping to a ragged pounding, she turned instinctively toward the sound at the same moment heavy hands closed on her shoulders. Her breath escaped in a gasp as an angry voice rent the silence.

"What in hell are you doing so far from camp? Damn it, Billie, don't you know it's dangerous to wander off at night?"

Spontaneous anger snapping her from her fear, Billie attempted to push Rand's hands from her shoulders.

"I don't need you to tell me where I should and should not walk Rand Pierce. Whatever you seem to think, you don't have the right to tell me what I—"

But Billie did not have the opportunity to say more as Rand's arms slipped around her unexpectedly, and he pulled her roughly to him. His fingers slid into her hair, stripping away the binding thong, and he clutched her close. His breath was warm against her temple as he gave a short laugh.

"Wait—wait, Billie. Let's start again." He drew just far enough away so that he might look into her shadowed face. "I'm sorry. I panicked when I came back to camp and the men told me you had just walked off. Willie said you had been gone for a while, but none of the men felt free to come after you, thinking you might just be wanting some privacy. Hell, I had visions of that Whitley fellow lying in wait for you. . . ." He paused, his concern slipping into a wry smile. "Anyway, I figured if you were after some privacy, I'd share it with you. . . ."

Billie could see the flash of Rand's repentant grin, and she felt a familiar tug in the pit of her stomach. She shook her head, refusing to relinquish her stubborn anger. She attempted unsuccessfully to release herself from his arms.

"The men were right, Rand. I was looking for some privacy. It's been a long day, and I have a lot of thinking to do."

"Billie, I'm sorry if I startled you." His head dropped unexpectedly, and Rand brushed her lips with his. Drawing his mouth from hers with obvious reluctance, Rand continued hoarsely, "I know we're both tired and I don't want to argue. . . ."

"Then please leave me alone for a little while, Rand."

"No."

"Rand. . . ."

"Wait. Give me a chance, Billie. If you want to walk at night, I'll walk with you. It's not safe out here for you; you know I'm right."

"Rand, you're worrying for nothing. Carl Whitley wouldn't risk—"

"I'm not going to attempt to anticipate that sneaky bastard. If he thinks you're with this herd, he's liable to try anything." His expression suddenly serious, Rand held her gaze with his. "Billie, I'm asking you to make this a little easier on all of us. Every damned one of the men was sitting on pins and needles in that camp waiting for you to come back."

"You're exaggerating, Rand."

"Oh, am I? Willie was all but twitching, and Carlisle looked like he was ready to jump out of his skin. And then there's me. . . ." His expression suddenly deeply earnest, he whispered hoarsely, "I don't want to lose you, Billie. You're mine, you know."

"Rand"—Billie fought the fluid weakness spreading through her veins—"I'm beginning to think that maybe—"

Anticipating her words, Rand cut her short, his tone gruff.

"Don't think. Just remember that you've given me your word, and a drover's word is as good as his bond."

"Oh, Rand."

"And I'm not about to let you get away from me, Billie." His mouth brushing her forehead, the fine line of her cheek, Rand continued hoarsely, "There wasn't a single minute today when you weren't on my mind in one way or another. If I wasn't worrying or planning, I was just indulging memories. When I got back to camp and saw you weren't there—" Rand swallowed hard, and Billie felt a tremor shake his strong frame. She could feel the swell of his passion hard against her, and a silent thrill shot up her spine. She longed, how she longed . . .

Rand's mouth was on hers, consuming her. His hands moved searchingly on her back, fingers splayed wide. The trail of his heated kisses moved across her chin, down the column of her throat. He was drawing the fragile skin into his mouth, biting and nipping, sucking deeply of its sweetness. She flinched at the tingling pain, only to hear Rand's low, self-deprecating curse. His hand slipped inside her shirt, a small sound of pleasure escaping his lips as he pushed aside the clumsy underwear to find her soft flesh. Within seconds he had bared the smooth skin of her breasts.

Rand was quaking with desire. Compulsion overcoming restraint, he stripped away the coarse cloth of Billie's shirt, his breath catching in his throat as the silver moonlight glinted on her flawless skin. He hushed her spontaneous protest with his kiss, his hands smoothing the bared flesh of her back, cupping her breast, caressing. He felt the brush of the burgeoning crest beneath his palm, heard Billie's soft murmur of passion, and he slid slowly to one knee to cover the aching bud with his mouth. Billie's arms slipped around his neck. She strained him against her and elation surged to life inside him. She was his. . . . His Billie. Whatever her previous doubts, she was again lost to the spell of his loving, and his heart sang.

He was kissing, tugging on the gentle swells, his attentions becoming more passionate as he drew the pink crests deeply into his mouth. Low gasps signaled Billie's rising ecstasy as

385

Rand continued his ardent ministrations, his hand working diligently at the buckle at her waist. Half his mind lost to the wonder that was Billie, Rand lowered her gunbelt to the ground. Within minutes he was slipping the rough trousers from her slender hips. Her feeble protests became nil as he followed the descending garment with his lips, tracing the line of her hips, the curve of her thighs. His parted lips trailed against the white skin of her stomach, nudging the warm mound nestling between her thighs. He cupped her firm, rounded buttocks in his palms, availing her more easily to his caress. His mouth moved amongst the damp ringlets of her womanhood, his tongue sliding full and true into the moist slit beneath.

Billie's low gasp of pleasure destroying the last of his restraint, Rand drew deeply from the sweetness of her body, the sound of her muffled cries driving all conscious thought from his mind. He caressed her with rising passion, worshipping the font of her womanhood with his searing touch. A sudden trembling besetting her slim frame, Billie attempted to withdraw from his touch, but Rand could not release her. He was lost to the ecstasy that was Billie, enthralled with the intimate taste of her body, drawing, seeking, longing for the giving proof of her complete subjugation to the loving bond between them.

Billie was shuddering wildly, her body quaking in short, jerking spasms. He tasted the sweet nectar of her passion and swallowed deeply, fully. When her trembling legs would support her no longer, he held her firm in his arms, his mouth pressed to the warm mound of her pleasure until she could give no more.

Still supporting her with his strength, Rand slid up the slender line of her body, holding her firm against him. Within moments his aching manhood was pressed against the moist mound. A low gasp escaped his lips as he lifted Billie to accommodate his entry and slid firm and true within her. His gaze on her face, Rand saw Billie's eyes flicker with renewed passion as he plunged deep inside her, saw the flutter of love-drugged lids as he renewed his claim with another searing thrust. His eyes sealing into memory each fleeting emotion registered on her flawless face, he increased the impetus of his claim until, with a final thrust, he carried her clear and through to the surging completion of their loving quest.

Drawing himself free of her at last, Rand clutched Billie's nakedness against him. Her trembling had ceased, but his hands continued to caress the smooth flesh of her back, the round curves of her derriere. He was covering her hair with light, fleeting kisses when she drew back from him. The vulnerability in the dark eyes raised to his stirred a deep wave of tenderness within him, and he crushed her close once more. The words he spoke came from the depths of his heart.

"I'm not going to let you get away from me, Billie. You're a part of me, darling . . . my heart, my breath. . . ."

Billie did not respond but remained silently pressed against him, her breathing slowing to a relaxed rhythm. Separating her from him at last, Rand picked up her discarded clothing from the ground. Gently, as he would a child, he helped her to dress. When she was done, he carefully stroked her hair back from her face. His mouth touched hers once more in a fleeting kiss before he turned her back toward camp.

A few minutes later they entered the circle of the campfire. Willie's gruff voice greeted them as they walked into the light.

"Well, I see you found her." Waiting only a second longer, he addressed Billie directly in an admonishing tone. "We'd all appreciate it, ma'am, if you'd let us know when you're anticipatin' an extended walk. The boys and me don't much care for worryin' whether you're all right or not."

Speaking for the first time, Billie looked directly into Willie's disturbed expression.

"You don't have to worry about me. . . ."

Not giving her the opportunity to finish, Willie responded tightly, "But the fact is, we do, ma'am. So if you'll be so kind as to give us that consideration. . . ."

This time it was Billie's turn to interrupt.

"I apologize, Willie. Of course, I'll do my best to cooperate in the future."

"We'd appreciate that, ma'am."

Following her intently with his eyes, Rand watched as Billie hastily prepared her bedroll and slipped beneath the blanket. He was still standing towering over her as her gaze rose to his. Suddenly uncaring of the reaction of the others, Rand walked to the other side of the fire and picked up his bedroll. Within minutes he had placed it a barely respectable distance from hers. He did not respond to the silent scrutiny of the men, but he flashed a quick smile at Billie's discomposure.

"Go to sleep, Billie. You need your rest."

Waiting only until her heavy lids had obediently dropped closed, he turned away and walked into the darkness.

Casting a parting look at the sleeping herd, Rand turned his bay back toward camp. He had been up for an hour, checking with the men on third watch. Everything appeared to be normal, but he could not seem to elude the strange sense of uneasiness that had urged him awake.

His eyes had snapped immediately to the spot where Billie had bedded down upon awakening, only to see that she still slept peacefully. A tenderness reserved for her alone had swept his senses. She was exhausted. A long day in the saddle, without much sleep, and a renewal of his loving attentions had all but depleted her remaining reserve of strength. He felt a short flash of guilt. Had he been more considerate, more in control of his emotions, he would have allowed a kiss to suffice when they had stood alone in the dark shadows of night. But he had sensed a separateness growing between them, and he had panicked. He had needed to renew his claim over her, to make her realize the bond that tied them together was stronger than either of them could sever. And, the truth was, once he had held her in his arms, he had been lost to his own emotions.

Rand knew he had made her distinctly uncomfortable by placing his bedroll so close to hers, but he had needed to lay immediate claim to her in the eyes of the men and had done it in the simplest way possible. Had Billie been in a different frame of mind, he knew she would have protested strongly.

His timing had been perfect to avoid another senseless confrontation with Billie—senseless because he had determined he would not take another backward step in his determination to make her his own.

Rand took a final look at the herd before dismounting. Well, if his uneasiness had not abated, he had at least satisfied himself that there was no immediate threat to Billie or their camp. It was time for the last watch. Rand turned toward the circle of men around the campfire. He would have to wake Billie.

A familiar warmth tightened a knot in his stomach. There was no time now for the emotions the thought of her raised inside him. Were they alone, he would take her in his arms and awaken her lovingly. Damn! That pleasure would be withheld for too long to satisfy his raging hunger for her. No, he would have to content himself with stolen moments. Vivid recall warmed him, and Rand felt the response of his body. No woman had ever stirred him, touched him like Billie. It was getting to the point where he dared not even think of her if he wanted to maintain a presentable appearance. He gave a low, disgusted snort, determined to hold himself in check.

His horse securely tied, Rand looked to the spot where he had left Billie sleeping. His heart leaping in his throat, he saw a figure crouched beside her as she slept. He started forward on a run, only to jerk to an unceremonious halt as he identified the crouching figure.

Carlisle . . . Not aware of the fact that he was being observed, Carlisle was peering down into Billie's sleeping face, seeming completely involved in his perusal. Memory returned to mind the camaraderie Jeremy had managed to establish with a reluctant Drucker since the beginning of the drive, and he felt a hot stab of jealousy. No, he wanted no one close to Billie but himself. He had no desire to share her, in any way.

His expression was stiff as he approached and stood beside Carlisle's still crouched form. Jeremy looked up, unperturbed by Rand's formidable countenance. His voice low, whispered in deference to Billie's peaceful slumber.

"She's sleeping like a baby. She's exhausted." Carlisle frowned, seeming hesitant to continue. "If you're agreeable, Wyatt and me won't mind one bit if you let Drucker sleep through the watch. She's been doin' more than her fair share of the work since she hired on. Me and the boys was talkin', and we all agreed that it's a wonder a frail little thing like her could've done all she did."

Touched by the young fellow's concern despite the nagging knot of jealousy that made him want to remove him forcibly from Billie's side, Rand shook his head.

"For all our good intentions, I think it would be a mistake, Carlisle." Rand could not suppress a smile. "She'd be furious when she woke up."

Carlisle's frown deepened. "You're the boss of this drive, Mr. Pierce. You make the decisions, and Drucker won't be able to say nothin' if you decide to take her off watch."

Rand's brows rose skeptically. "You have a short memory, Carlisle."

His familiar smile reappearing unexpectedly as he caught Rand's meaning, Jeremy nodded. "Yeah, I guess I do." Jeremy turned back toward Billie. The smile dropped from his face as quickly as it had appeared. He reached out a hand and gathered a handful of silver-gold hair into his fist. He shook his head.

"She sure is beautiful, ain't she, Mr. Pierce? I ain't never let myself look at her for too long before this. It didn't seem right, with her bein' so pretty for a boy." Jeremy moved his fingers in the silken strands, careful not to disturb her, and Rand restrained a growing desire to slap away his hand. But the young fellow had not finished his silent scrutiny. "I'm rememberin' how she looked when she first came into camp. . . ." His voice turning suddenly cold, Jeremy turned back to Rand. "And I'm thinkin' if them fellas had anythin' to do with it, they ain't goin' to show up here again without knowin' how me and the boys feel about it."

The sound of their whispered exchange seeming to penetrate her veil of sleep, Billie began to stir. Her heavily fringed lids began to flutter, and Jeremy released the silken strands, a light flush moving across his fair skin. Billie's eyes touched on his face with a start.

"What? . . . Is—is it time for watch?"

Jeremy nodded. "Yeah, almost. You have time for a cup of coffee. The boys ain't come back to camp yet."

Not waiting for her response, Jeremy turned and strode toward the fire. Billie's eyes followed Jeremy's strong, well-built form as he picked up the oversized pot and reached for a cup. There was concern in her gaze and Rand's jealousy deepened. He crouched down at her side as she uncovered herself and reached for her boots. He reached out and smoothed back a wayward strand of silver-gold.

"You don't have to get up yet, Billie. You—"

Billie's eyes snapped back in his direction. "You're up and Carlisle's up. You both worked as hard as I did." The intensity of Rand's gaze caused a light color to flood her face as she continued adamantly. "I said I could pull my weight on this drive when I hired on, and I don't intend letting anybody else take on my share of the load."

Barely restraining the desire to gather the irritating little witch into his arms, Rand shook his head. His voice was low. "When you signed on, you weren't expecting to take me on either. And I'm telling you now, I would much rather see you miss watch than be too tired to let me love you when I get the chance to put my arms around you. So I'm asking you, Billie, to stay in that bedroll for a few more hours."

A flush of anger brought a new heat to Billie's cheeks. "It sounds like you're offering to pay me just so I'll have the time and the inclination to let you make love to me." Drawing herself to her feet, Billie waited until Rand had done the same before she continued tightly, "If I wanted to adopt that vocation, I would've accepted Lotta McDevitt's offer."

Not allowing Rand a chance for reply, Billie turned and walked toward the fire. Unable to do else, Rand watched as Billie snatched up a cup and started to fill it with coffee.

The hot coffee splashed against her hand, and Billie muttered a low oath. Turning immediately in her direction, Jeremy ignored her protests and took the heavy pot from her hand to fill her cup. He had replaced the pot on the fire and turned to walk away when Billie reached out to stay him. His light eyes sober, he turned to face her.

Billie was suddenly at a loss for words. How could she tell him how she missed his friendly conversation, his limitless good humor? How could she tell him how she had appreciated his endless consideration, his warmth? Her eyes moved across his familiar face, realizing this was one of the few times she had not seen Jeremy smiling. She suffered the loss deeply. But he was still waiting for her to speak, and she began hesitantly.

"You've always been my friend, Carlisle. . . . I wanted to tell you that I'm sorry. I didn't mean to deceive you or any of the other men. I—I couldn't tell you or them. . . . And I'm sorry you had to find out the way you did that I'm not what I pretended to be. I hope you—all of you—will forgive me and continue to be my friend just as you were before."

His clear eyes holding hers intently for long moments, Jeremy did not respond. Finally appearing to have settled something in his mind, Jeremy shook his head.

"I don't see as how we can be the same friends as before, Druck—I mean, ma'am. Somehow, I can't see me slappin' you on the rump like I used to." Flushing, Jeremy added hastily, "And I do apologize for that, ma'am."

Billie could not suppress a fleeting smile. "I didn't really mind, Carlisle."

Obviously relieved, Jeremy nodded. His expression slowly softening, he finally smiled.

"And in that case, ma'am, I suppose I never mentioned that along with that younger brother I told you about, I also got a younger sister by the name of Sinda Lee. And I suppose I won't be able to stop myself from thinkin' of you just like I'd think of her if she was along on this drive. Not that she could do the job you're doin', ma'am."

"Thank you, Jeremy."

Flushing at Billie's use of his Christian name, Carlisle was about to respond when Rand appeared unexpectedly at their side. Frowning, he removed Billie's hand from Carlisle's arm with obvious deliberation.

"It's time to go to work, Carlisle."

His brows rising in surprise, Carlisle shot Billie a short

glance. His quick wink was unexpected, as was the return of his familiar grin.

"Anything you say, boss. Come on, ma'am. You heard the boss. It's time to get to work."

Within seconds Rand was staring at Billie's and Carlisle's departing backs. He bit back a soft curse as Jeremy leaned toward Billie with a smiling remark, his arm dropping casually around her shoulders. His frustration growing as Billie laughed up into his freckled face, Rand turned away.

Damn that Billie Drucker. . . . Damn her! . . .

With gracious formality and utmost care, Pat handed Lucille up into the waiting coach. Mounting the steps behind her, he shot his country home a last glance and pulled the door shut behind him. He signaled the coachman forward and turned with a smile.

"Four days . . . Four days of rain, Lucille. I do hope you weren't bored. I realize there is little to entertain guests at my country retreat when the weather doesn't cooperate."

The twinkle in his eye contradicting his modest statement, Pat waited for Lucille's reply. He was well aware that they had found no lack of amusement in the time they had spent together. There was a deep contentment inside him that he dared not reveal. But it had been exactly as he had known it would be. Lucille had been made for his arms, her body created specifically for his own.

The little whip that she was, she had not given him as much as a word of encouragement, but there was little need for words. The complete satisfaction of Lucille's body had glowed in her eyes. But had it been merely that which he had seen there, he knew he would have felt none of the elation that presently transfused him. Her awareness of him as a man had been a gradual awakening, which he had brought to full fruition on this enforced holiday.

He remembered with particular warmth the easy stream of conversation that had flowed between them, the fact that her sharp wit sparked his own. He also remembered the quiet moments when they had not needed to speak. He remembered the pleasure they had shared in their mutually pitiful assault on the piano and the hilarious results that had ensued.

But other memories were more fond, more dear. He remembered the breathtaking joy they had found in discovering each other intimately. He remembered with great warmth the appreciation Lucille had shown for the lean, compact power of his body, and his own overpowering addiction to her soft, white flesh. Admittedly, the manner in which Lucille had cast aside thoughts of Rand Pierce confused him. It was not like her to allow him an easy victory. But he knew with a deep certainty that she had not thought of the handsome entrepreneur since shortly after their arrival, because there had been no other man in her eyes after they had made love.

The host of warm thoughts assaulting his mind, Pat felt no irritation at the coquettish manner in which Lucille hesitated in responding to his question. If the truth were known, he was quite content to indulge himself in her beauty in silence. But she was not about to allow him that luxury.

Lucille raised her face to his. The first glimmer of the Lucille of old shone in her flirtatious, half-lidded eyes, and Pat felt a pang of apprehension. His newfound contentment slowly drained away as Lucille began to speak.

"Bored, Pat? No, I can't honestly say I was bored. You entertained me quite well. I can only say you must have a true gaggle of appreciative women at your heels if you treat them all as well as you treated me."

Pat attempted to ignore the warning glint in Lucille's eye. His response was filled with warmth. "I would hardly say I became as deeply involved in any previous affairs of the heart, Lucy."

"Are you trying to say I'm someone special, Pat dear?"

The warning signal in his brain was getting louder.

"Yes, I'd say that's true. . . ."

Raising her hand to Pat's cheek, Lucille smiled. She was stroking its smooth-shaven surface as she continued lightly.

"That is unfortunate. Because the truth is, I don't expect there will be a repetition of this rather unusual four days you arranged." At the tightening of his expression, Lucille smiled more brightly. "Oh, you mustn't think I didn't enjoy myself, Pat. Your home is lovely, and the accommodations excellent. And the entertainment, oh, it was more than satisfying. I recall it with particular warmth, actually. . . . But it is time to get back to our lives as before."

A flicker of concealed anger moved across Lucille's face. "You were successful in aborting my intended visit with Rand. Your plan was well formulated and carried through. I admit dear Jack would have been in for some rather bad times when I returned, had his failure to arrive with the coach been part of your plot, but you have saved him from me by explaining that you fooled the dear fellow as well as you did me. So, I have only you to settle with for interfering with my plans."

Her caress of his cheek concluding with a short, sharp slap, Lucille dropped her hand to her lap. Anger shone openly in her eyes.

"You see, Pat, I am not above enjoying a sensual romp with an attractive man, no matter my future plans. And whether you had intentions to the contrary or not, my plans for the future have not changed. I have had to come to terms with the realization that Rand probably indulged himself freely in the rather tawdry women of Dodge while you had me otherwise entertained. I have consoled myself that I probably enjoyed myself far better than he. There certainly must be an element lacking when dealing with practiced whores. And you are, indeed, an excellent lover, Pat."

"Lucy. . . ."

"Kindly do not interrupt. I have only a few more things to say and you may speak all you want." Her eyes slivered ice, Lucille stared into Pat's whitening face. "The fact is, you have delayed matters but not cancelled them. You have simply forced me to wait until September, when Rand returns to St. Louis, before resuming our affair."

His tone stiff, Pat interjected sharply, "Are you really so sure of yourself, Lucy? Rand is—"

"In answer to your question, I can only respond . . . you have sampled a taste of what I have to offer. Do you still think Rand can turn me away?"

The flush that colored Pat's whitened skin the only

response she needed, Lucille laughed with great enjoyment. Finally regaining her breath, the sparkle of laughter still in her eyes, Lucille turned again to Pat.

"So you see, dear boy, you've only put off the inevitable. I do thank you for entertaining me so well these past few days. . . ." Her voice trailing off as the shards of ice returned to her brilliant eyes, Lucille continued pointedly, "But I advise you not to try the same trick again. I will not be so gullible a second time."

Supreme satisfaction moving across her lovely face, Lucille turned toward the window and became completely engrossed in the passing countryside.

Taking a deep breath, Pat questioned softly, "Are you finished, Lucy?" There was no response, and the edge of anger concealed so carefully behind Pat's calm facade began to expand. "I asked you, *are you finished speaking?*"

Not bothering to turn in his direction, Lucille nodded. "Yes, I am finished."

"Well, since I've allowed you your opportunity to speak, it is time for you to listen. . . ."

Lucille's head snapped back toward his.

"No, it is *not* time for me to listen! You have no authority over me, Pat Patterson. I have not forgiven you for the trick you played on me, and I never will. So save your sermons. . . ."

"Lucy, you asked that I allow you to speak. I did. And now, according to your own words, it is my turn to talk to you. . . ."

"I said you could speak, say anything you want when I was done. I did not say I would listen!" Her eyes narrowing, Lucille continued viciously, "I have only one more thing to say to you. My name is *Lucille*. . . . I am not your Lucy. I will never be your Lucy. So speak on, if you so desire. I do not hear a word you say."

Turning her head firmly back toward the passing landscape, Lucille settled herself comfortably. For all intents and purposes, she was completely alone.

* * *

396

TO: CARL WHITLEY
    DODGE, KANSAS
PLEASED YOU HAVE LOCATED PRIZE HEIFER
  STOP
DO NOT LET HER OUT OF SIGHT STOP
DELAY ANTICIPATED IN COMING TO GET HER
  STOP
BONUS MONEY DOUBLED WHEN I ARRIVE STOP
WIRE LOCATION WHENEVER POSSIBLE STOP
WILL BE AWAITING WORD STOP
DAN McCULLA

His grimy hand tight on the small scrap of paper, Carl Whitley resisted the urge to rip the message into shreds. He jerked his head up to Marty's perspired face.

"What in hell kind of answer is this?"

His anger mounting, he continued heatedly, "That bastard is askin' us to follow that herd all the way to Montana!"

The relentless summer heat of the Kansas plains taking its toll, Marty reached for his canteen. He took the opportunity to shoot Larry a quick look where he sat in their makeshift camp nearby. They were both hesitant about venturing a comment. Being only too familiar with Carl's instant rage, neither one of them was stupid enough to get in his way until it was spent. They had learned long before that Carl Whitley allowed no considerations to interfere with the heat of the moment . . . and McCulla's orders.

Marty took a deep drink of the tepid water, using the time to avoid both Carl's comment and his gaze. He had left under Carl's orders at the first light of dawn the day before and ridden back to Dodge to wait for that wire from McCulla. As soon as the telegram had been placed in his hand, he had jumped on his horse without delay and headed back. Carl's patience had been all but nil when he had left camp, and he had hoped this wire would soothe his growing disgruntlement. And now all he got for his trouble was an angry growl and expectation of more of the same.

Marty's irritation was growing. Hell, Larry and he were a

part of this outfit, too. He was sick and tired of having to bow to Carl's moods. Besides, he and Larry weren't any happier than Carl about trailin' after that herd for time interminable until the big boss decided he could come to settle things with that girl. He had half a mind to tell Carl off and leave. The only trouble was his other half a mind told him he'd never make it out of camp on two feet. He had seen Carl in action before, and he was no match for the skinny bastard's gun hand or his temper. Still, it was time he put in his two cents. . . . He took a deep breath and started hesitantly.

"I don't know, Carl. That wire don't look too bad to me. . . ."

"Oh, yeah!" Carl's small eyes squinted into measuring slits and a fresh surge of fury colored his stubbled cheeks. "You mean to tell me you're fond of eatin' dust and sleepin' on the hard ground? I know you better than that, Marty! Hell, I couldn't hardly drag you out from between that whore's legs in Dodge! And you ain't tellin' me you don't wish you was back there now. . . ."

"No, I ain't tellin' you that Carl." Memories of that warm little brunette brought a lopsided grin to Marty's face despite himself. He continued carefully, "And I ain't fond of eatin' dust no more than you. But it seems to me if we play this game right, we can make it work out real well. . . ."

"What in hell you talkin' about, Marty? I ain't in the mood for games."

"Well, Carl, I was thinkin' . . ." Lifting his hat, Marty ran his stubby fingers through the black hair plastered to his head with sweat. He withdrew a stained handkerchief from his pocket and rubbed it against his scalp. He could not meet Carl's intense gaze as he continued. "It seems to me a real waste of time all three of us trailin' that girl. Hell, we've been crawlin' behind that herd for the past week, and the hardest work we done is workin' to stay out of sight. And it seems to me even that chore would be a sight easier if there was less of us kicking up dust. . . ."

When Carl made no attempt to interrupt, Marty glanced up. Carl was listening, even if his expression was somewhat mocking. He decided to continue. "I'm thinkin' that Winslow girl is goin' to stay with that herd right until Montana, especially with her and that hotshot beef contractor bein' so close. . . ."

"Yeah, so? . . ."

"Well, hell, it'll take this herd at least another month and a half to reach that Blackfoot Agency at this rate! I'm thinkin' we can take turns goin' back to the closest town sendin' wires to McCulla and spendin' free time. Hell, we don't have to worry about losin' that herd. We can travel three times as fast on horseback as that herd's travelin'. And we don't gotta worry that McCulla will come sneakin' up on us, 'cause he needs us to keep tellin' him where we're at."

"Go on. . . ."

Encouraged, Marty pulled himself up straight and pushed out his beefy chest. "Well, when McCulla wires us he's acomin', we'll just make sure we're together and workin' hard at our job. When he shows, we'll lead him to the girl and collect our bonuses."

There was a brief silence when Marty finished speaking. Carl's small eyes squinted in consideration. "Looks like you sure done a lot of thinkin', Marty. Of course, I'm goin' to do some thinkin', too. . . ."

Carl turned away abruptly to shoot a quick look up toward the cloudless sky, and Marty released a tense breath. He looked toward Larry, his mouth twitching at the obvious amusement on the man's face. Well, Larry could laugh. He didn't have the nerve to say nothin' to Carl. At least he had had his say.

Turning back toward him, Carl motioned toward the small, protected fire and the beans that bubbled over it.

"The sun'll be settin' in another couple of hours. It's too late to do anythin' tonight. I hope you brought back them cans of tomatoes like I told you. I'm tired of eatin' plain beans. The next time one of us goes into town, we're goin' to have to get us a pack mule so's we can carry some decent supplies."

Unexpectedly, Carl smiled. "You done real good, fella. Seems like this job is finally goin' to get down to some

399

honest-to-goodness fun. Hell, it's about time. . . ."

Turning, Carl reached for the coffee pot and poured himself another cup. "Yeah, it sure is about time. . . ."

The afternoon sun was warm on his head as Rand raised the cup to his lips again. Hot and strong . . . Nate's coffee was thoroughly dependable. He had needed its steadying power. Of its own volition, his gaze followed Billie's slight form amidst the men as they prepared to mount. Noon camp was over, and it was time to get back to the herd. His eyes assessed the stiffness of her posture as she walked, the determination evidenced in the firm tilt of her chin. But she wasn't fooling him. As she prepared to mount, the hand she raised to her saddle horn trembled. She was exhausted.

Another pang of guilt assailed him. Even now, realizing full well how he had contributed to her exhaustion with his loving demands of the night before, he could not take his eyes from her. She placed her foot in the stirrup, her arms stretching to pull herself up. His eyes followed the arch of her back, the graceful swing of one long leg as she threw it over her horse, the efficient manner in which she assessed her mount's momentary balking at her slight weight.

His eyes slid to her face, almost obscured by the brim of her hat. She was frowning slightly as she brought the animal under firm control. She turned and her profile was momentarily outlined against the backdrop of the sun-burned Kansas landscape. Her hair was tied to the back of her neck with yet another rawhide strip, allowing no obstruction in his view of the clear beauty displayed to his eye. His gaze traced its perfection from forehead to chin before slipping to the graceful arch of her neck. There it caught on the circular bruise so evident against her white skin, and he winced. It had been faint, barely visible when she had awakened, but had continued to darken as the morning had progressed. He had done that to her with his damned lack of control. But when he was kissing her, when he breathed in the scent of her skin, feeling its silk beneath his lips, everything—his good intentions, all his determinations—seemed to disappear in the wake of the longing that sang through him. Billie . . . in his arms. He could seem to think of nothing else. She was riding back to the herd, and his eyes trailed her back, the curve of her buttocks as she sat the saddle. He remembered the firmness of that flesh as it had rested in his palms, her low gasps as he had drawn her to him, tasted her intimately. . . .

His heart pounding, Rand raised his cup to his lips and drained it dry.

"I'd say that's a good idea, Rand, takin' a minute to yourself before goin' back to the herd."

Rand turned at the unexpected voice beside him. Willie's sober countenance met his gaze.

"Mind if I sit with you for a spell?"

But Rand was not taken in by Willie's casual tone. There was a severity to his features that indicated he had something to say, and Rand tensed spontaneously. It wasn't like Willie to skirt around a problem. . . .

"I was going to join the boys, but I have a few minutes if something's on your mind, Willie."

Willie's brown eyes were sober and direct.

"It ain't what's on my mind that's the problem, Rand. I'd say it's what's on yours that's causin' concern."

"On *my* mind?"

"Rand, there ain't a one of us here that can't see what's on your mind when you look at Drucker."

Rand stiffened spontaneously, and Willie's expression hardened. Anger glinted in his squinting gaze.

"You marked her, Rand, that bruise on her neck, and I don't mind tellin' you that me and the boys don't much like what we're thinkin'."

"I don't give a damn *what* you're thinking, Willie." Anger sending a heated flush to his face, Rand continued sharply, "Because it's none of your damned business how I look at Billie or what I do. . . ."

"That's where you're wrong!" His lean frame suddenly stiff, Willie did not allow the conclusion of Rand's heated response. "You may be the boss here, but it don't mean nothin' when it comes to that little girl. Speakin' for myself, I felt a real responsibility for Drucker from the first. Hell, a man would have to be hard as stone not to feel somethin' for the way that kid showed up here, all beat up and spunky and tough as could be. I don't have to tell you it shook me up pretty good when I found out the kid was a girl. I was kinda mad, thinkin' Drucker should've taken me into her confidence. It took me a little while to realize the poor child probably felt she couldn't trust nobody after what was done to her, and I don't mind admittin' I'm downright ashamed of my first reaction."

Willie's brow had tightened into a deep frown with his confession. He continued with new adamance.

"Well, all that's by the board now. Drucker's here and is a part of our crew, and I ain't intendin' to stand by and watch her get hurt no more."

Rand took a deep breath and a hold on his patience.

"I'm not going to hurt her, Willie. I'm just as concerned about her as you are."

"You marked her, damn it!" Unexpected rage flaring in his eyes, Willie clenched his fists. "Is that the way you show your concern?" Taking a minute to get his anger under control, Willie continued firmly. "I don't mind tellin' you, me and the boys don't like it . . . don't like it one bit!"

"Oh, the boys and you. . . ."

"That's right. Hell, that bruise on Drucker's neck is like a flag of warnin'. It didn't take me no time at all to see what Carlisle was thinkin' when he saw it. He was all for facin' you straight out, but I talked him out of it."

"Carlisle wanted to face me, huh?" Rand was starting to bristle.

"That's right. Stewart and Byrd was right hot under the collar, and Nate wasn't any too happy, either. Hell, even Hall and Brothers had their say. . . . There's only one kind of woman who walks around with marks like that on her neck, and the kid ain't one of them. I'd swear to that. . . ."

"You don't need to tell me that."

"And I ain't about to stand by and let you make her into one of your women."

"Wait a minute, Willie. I think you've said enough."

Rand's anger was beginning to mount.

"No, I ain't goin' to wait." Willie was facing Rand squarely when his expression abruptly changed. He shook his head and began anew. "Look, Rand, all of us boys know about how you been livin'. Hell, you got the world in the palm of your hand, and not a one of us blames you for livin' well and high. We seen that redheaded lady who was waitin' for you in Abilene, and we know you got women like that in just about every town up and down the line. Well, that's all fine and dandy with us. It's none of our business, and if the truth be known, we all kind of envy you a bit." Willie paused. His expression began to stiffen.

"But there ain't a one of us that's goin' to stand by while you play fast and loose with that little girl. You got too many years on her, Rand. You got too many women behind you to make the match even. That child don't stand a chance against you. . . ."

"That's where you're wrong, Willie."

"I ain't wrong. She's a spunky little kid, and she don't take nothin' from nobody. But she's a girl. She's scared of somethin'—real scared—and she's alone. We all seen what happened the first time that Carl Whitley fella showed up in camp. You took care of her then, and she's startin' to depend on you. And I'm tellin' you now, I ain't standin' by while you take advantage of that kid."

"Willie. . . ."

"I don't care if you are my boss."

"Willie, I'm not playing fast and loose with Billie. I'm not playing at all. . . ."

Stopped by the sobriety of Rand's tone, Willie squinted into his face, his eyes assessing.

"What're you sayin', Rand?"

"Do I have to make myself clearer than that?" Jerking off his hat, Rand ran his hand through his hair in an anxious gesture. "Hell, how do you think I felt when I saw that mark on Billie's neck? Christ, only a kid lets his feelings get out of hand like that. I should know better. . . . But the fact I've had to face is I don't have much control when it comes to her. It was like that from the beginning. You were here. You

403

know how she affected me. She set me off faster than anybody I ever knew with her cocky attitude. Hell, I couldn't get her out of my mind when I thought she was a boy, and when I found out she was a woman, well, nothing and everything changed. She still has the same affect on me, Willie, only now it's damned hard for me to keep my hands off her. She's got me wrapped around her little finger." Rand gave a short laugh. "And you want to know something? She doesn't know, and she doesn't care."

Willie shook his head. "I think you're wrong there, Rand. Drucker ain't the kind of kid to let you near enough to her to mark her the way you did if she didn't care."

Rand gave a small laugh. "All right, I'll modify that statement. She cares—I've seen to that—but not enough to make her tell me what she's hiding from, who's after her, where she's going, and to whom. . . ."

"The kid's just on the run . . ."

"No she isn't, damn it! She's running *to* somebody. . . ."

Willie's brows rose in open skepticism. "Rand, I'm thinkin' you're jumpin' to conclusions."

"She told me from the beginning, from the first time I touched her, that she's leaving at the end of the drive. . . . Montana."

Willie was obviously unconvinced.

"Well, if she's runnin' to somebody, why's she havin' anythin' to do with you at all?"

Rand averted his eyes. He replaced his hat on his head and stared into the distance for several silent seconds. He turned back slowly toward Willie.

"This is none of your business, you know that, don't you, Willie?"

Nodding his gray head, Willie smiled. "Maybe you're right, but you ain't answered my question."

"You want to know why Billie's having anything at all to do with me. Well, I'll tell you straight out. I think she feels she owes me that much."

The softness began to leave Willie's expression. "And how'd she get that kind of damned fool idea? Hell, that little girl works as hard on this drive as any one of us. She don't

404

owe you nothin' but a good day's work."

"I don't know how she got that idea, Willie, but I'm not about to tell her any different."

A flood of color rose to Willie's cheeks. "You're a goddamned bastard, Rand Pierce. . . ."

Rand's eyes turned cold as steel. "Maybe I am, but I'll tell you something, Willie. You and the whole damned crew can walk out on me right here and now before I'll do one thing to change anything between Billie and me. She's mine, Willie, do you understand that? She's mine until the end of the drive. You were right. She is beginning to depend on me, and I intend to get her to depend on me even more. I've got two months to make her feel she needs me the way I need her, and I'm not going to give them up for anybody."

"And if you succeed, what then?"

"What then?"

"Hell, man, that's what I said! What then? I want to know your intentions toward Drucker. She ain't got nobody to stand up for her, and I ain't lettin' that little girl go unprotected from the likes of you, even if you are my boss. Now, what in hell are your intentions toward that child?"

"My intentions?" Rand's laugh was filled with irony.

Willie gritted his teeth in an effort to control his fast waning patience.

"Your intentions . . ."

The brilliant blue of Rand's eyes burned into Willie's agitated gaze.

"If I get her to feel about me the way I feel about her, I'm going to snatch her up so fast that she won't know what hit her. I'm going to take her back to St. Louis with me and set her up in my house. I'm going to take her to church and put a ring on her finger and tie her to me so tight that she'll never get away. And I'm going to invite you to the christening of every one of our kids, Willie, from the first to the last."

Stunned, Willie was momentarily speechless. A smile slowly dawned on his face. He gave a short laugh, his hand coming down heavily on Rand's back in an appreciative slap.

"Well, Rand, old boy, looks like you finally been landed.

Hell's fires, I never thought to see the day!"

"I was landed a long time ago, Willie, but it doesn't look like Billie's willing to pull me in. As a matter of fact, it almost looks like she's going to walk away and leave me flapping in the dust."

Willie's smile faded abruptly.

"Do you mean that, Rand?"

Looking toward the herd, Rand sought out Billie's slight figure. His heart gave a little leap as she turned curiously in their direction. He turned back to Willie and nodded his head.

"I can almost feel the dust between my teeth right now."

Willie's thin, lined face turned pensive. When he spoke at last his voice was filled with regret.

"I want you to know somethin', Rand. Nothin' would please me more than to see you take that little girl into your heart and home. I'm thinkin', no matter the trouble that's followin' her, any man would be lucky to get her, and I don't like to see a little innocent like her travelin' the trail alone. But, if it's true what you say, Rand, if the girl don't want you, I'll be backin' up her right to her own choices every step of the way. She don't have nobody to stand up for her, and whether you like it or not, now she's got me."

Rand gave a short laugh.

"You and the rest of the boys. . . ."

"Well, I can't speak for the rest of the fellas, but I sure enough can speak for myself. And I just want you to know how I stand."

Rand's eyes hardened.

"Don't make the mistake of getting between us, Willie. She's mine. And whether she or anybody else knows it or not, what is mine I keep."

"I ain't the girl's keeper. I'm just her friend. And as far as the boys are concerned, they won't be doin' nothin' either, except—"

"Except? . . ."

"Just don't go marking the girl no more, Rand. I ain't goin' to stand for that, and neither are the boys. That little girl deserves all our respect, and she's goin' to get it, one way

406

or another."

Rand drew himself to his feet. He waited until Willie was standing beside him before responding in a solemn tone.

"I think it's time you got back to work, Willie."

Willie nodded, his gray brows drawing together in a small frown.

"All right, Rand. I appreciate your straight talk, and I want you to know nothin' you said will go any farther."

"Get to work, Willie. The boys are waiting for you to start them out."

"Sure enough."

Within seconds Willie was striding toward his horse. Mounting, he motioned the herd forward with a wave of his hand. Suddenly conscious of the weight of someone's stare, Rand turned to catch Nate's somber gaze. A sudden surge of temper stiffened his frame.

"Don't say a word, Nate. Not a damned word!"

Mumbling under his breath, Rand turned and strode toward his horse. Damn it, he had had enough!

Chapter XIII

Pat walked briskly along the St. Louis street. His eye on the stately bank building on the corner, he experienced no appreciation for the glorious summer sun that beat down on his shoulders or the pleasant breeze that stirred the humid air. He adjusted the narrow collar of his morning coat in an unconscious gesture and graciously stepped out of the way of a strolling couple who obviously had things on their mind other than returning to work after a midday meal.

He took a deep breath, his brown brows in a light frown, and adjusted the brim of his dark bowler hat. He had dressed extremely carefully that morning, taking great care in the adjustment of his high shirt collar and the selection of his necktie. He had paid particular attention to the fit of his coat and trousers, noting that the tailor had done an excellent job in fitting the trousers close to the leg and narrowed at the bottom as fashion demanded. He was aware that the dark blue fabric contrasted well with his fair hair and complexion and that the light blue of his tie was in excellent taste.

He gave a low, disgusted grunt. The cause for the particular care he had devoted to his appearance had not been excessive vanity on his part. The drive to present an impeccable appearance was the same drive that had given impetus to all his actions since he had returned from those idyllic four days at his country retreat almost a month before.

Lucille Bascombe. Damn the wicked little bitch! But he

had been no more successful when he had called upon her this morning than he had been in past weeks. Obviously having been given strict orders, the maid had not allowed him past the front door on his casual call. The reply to his inquiry as to Lucy had been the same.

"Miss Bascombe regrets that she is indisposed."

Indisposed! If he were to believe the negative replies he had received to his requests to see the haughty little witch since those glorious days they had spent together, he would have to conclude that she had contracted some dread disease, which fully incapacitated her. But he knew how truly inaccurate that assessment of the situation truly was. It had only been two days before that he had come upon the "sickly" Miss Bascombe at Katy Morrison's lively soiree. Actually, he had accepted the invitation only because Horace Bascombe had made the comment, intentional or not, that Lucy had bought a new dress for the occasion.

But as it had turned out, that evening had proved no more successful than this morning in granting him some time alone with the elusive Lucille Bascombe. After raising his hopes with a flirtatious fluttering of her lashes, she had dashed them to earth again as she had taken up with an extremely attentive beau. Each attempt to speak to her had been turned aside in a manner so practiced and perfect that he had the feeling he had effectively joined the ranks of an endless line of spurned suitors, who had been banished from the radiant light of Lucille Bascombe's presence forever.

Reacting to an abruptly uncomfortable feeling in his stomach, Pat slowed his step. The food he had consumed at a local tavern was sitting poorly, but he knew he could not hold the proprietor of the excellent establishment to account for his discomfort. Actually, he had been unable to escape this particular discomfort of late. It seemed the burning ache inside him that the thought of Lucille stimulated so easily affected every aspect of his life.

Inadvertently, Pat again reviewed the days he and Lucille had spent together. No, there had not been even the slightest clue that she would turn away from him so completely upon their return from his country retreat. His frown deepening,

Pat raised his hand to smooth his mustache in an anxious gesture. It was not as if he had forced himself upon her. It had been Lucille herself who had instigated the first intimacy between them. He had been aware of her attempted escape from him shortly afterward; indeed, he had allowed her to accomplish it in the hope that she would do exactly as she had done—return to him of her own accord. His hopes had soared when she had returned to his bed and pressed herself warmly against him.

He had searched his memory of the days that had followed and had been unable to find a single flaw in the perfection of the beauty they had shared. They had loved, laughed, enjoyed each other so completely that her dismissal of him in the carriage and her subsequent refusal to see him after she had returned home was totally incomprehensible.

A flood of anger inundated his incredulity. She was such a contrary little bitch! She . . .

His eyes snapping up to the corner, Pat stopped in his tracks. A familiar carriage had just turned the intersection and was moving cautiously down the street. He looked to the driver, his heart beginning an escalated beat as his glance settled on Jack's familiar figure. But the carriage was empty. His eyes darted to the boutique in front of which Jack drew up. Jack was obviously picking up . . .

The door of the boutique opened, and Pat moved immediately forward. Congratulating himself on his timing, he reached the carriage at the exact moment Lucille stepped onto the street. Smiling with considerable difficulty, he extended his hand in her direction.

"Lucy, how pleasant to run into you so unexpectedly! I'm happy to see that you've recovered from your discomfort of this morning. I hope it was nothing serious. You do look particularly well."

Particularly well. . . . The rank understatement echoed in Pat's mind. Dressed in a filmy green creation, which outlined the lush contours of her body and complimented her extraordinary coloring to perfection, Lucille was breathtakingly lovely. But facing her at last, Pat suddenly found himself inundated with insecurity. The only thing of which

411

he was totally sure was that he was approaching desperation in this situation—and Lucy was enjoying every moment of his despair.

Apparently not experiencing a moment of discomfiture, Lucille raised her eyes seductively to his.

"Pat! What a pleasant surprise! Yes, it is strange how quickly I became unwell this morning when you appeared at my door. And I know you will find it just as incredulous as I that my strange debility disappeared just as suddenly . . . when the door closed behind you. Unnatural, is it not? What do you suppose can be the reason for the onset and departure of such unexpected sickness?"

Pat's smile stiffened as the urge to wrap his hands around Lucille's white neck grew stronger.

"I'm sure you would like me to draw my own conclusion, wouldn't you, Lucy dear?"

"Pat darling"—her eyelashes fluttering gracefully, Lucille raised her flawless face fully to his—"I suppose those were my intentions."

"But since I am so dense . : ."

"Since you are so dense, Pat dear, I imagine I shall have to make myself a bit more plain, as much as I do despise repetition." Her eyes dropping to Pat's mouth, Lucille allowed her gaze to linger tantalizingly before she raised it once again to meet his. "You see, dear fellow, a month has already passed since our . . . charming . . . interlude. It was lovely, but it is in the past. I am extremely busy at present with a full social calendar and in readying a new, appropriate wardrobe with which to welcome Rand home. It includes the most charming of lingerie and sleeping garments. Rand does love luxurious fabrics, you know. And I do so enjoy pleasing him. . . ."

Conscious of the fact that he had played into Lucille's hands by presenting her with yet another opportunity to torment him, Pat restrained a violent urge to shake her into within an inch of her life. Damned, teasing little witch. He had taken enough. . . .

Lucille's smile widened with Pat's silence.

"Nothing to say, Pat dear? Well, that is unusual. So I

412

suppose our chance meeting has come to a conclusion." Lifting herself gracefully to her toes, Lucille pressed a light, lingering kiss against his cheek. "I suppose it is time to say adieu."

"No, Lucille. . . ." Exerting a stringent effort at control, Pat managed a full, truly engaging smile. "In view of everything you've just said, I've finally come to the conclusion that the more accurate word to use would be 'good-bye.'"

Taking Lucille's delicate hand in his, Pat raised it to his lips. "I have not been allowed the opportunity to adequately express my appreciation for your gracious behavior a month ago when you visited my home. You were so warm, so willing. As a matter of fact, I think the latter of those adjectives probably describes more perfectly the secret to your particular appeal. And now, dear girl, since you've decided to eliminate that element from our relationship, I think it would be more appropriate to say good-bye. It was lovely, Lucille."

Hesitating a moment, Pat smiled more brightly. "You did notice that I used the name Lucille. . . . I'm sure you'll be relieved to hear that I've decided the name does suit you after all."

Still holding her hand, Pat turned Lucille formally toward the carriage and opened the door. Assisting her as she mounted the steps, he waited until she was seated to raise his bowler politely. Aware that Lucille's smile had gone suddenly stiff, he turned toward Jack with a small salute.

"I believe Miss Bascombe would like to go home, Jack."

Not waiting until the carriage moved into motion, Pat turned and started briskly toward the impressive edifice on the corner. Yes, he could truly say he had had enough.

Rand's keen eyes searched the horizon, settling on a grove of timber beside a shady lake flickering in the distance. He dismissed the appealing scene without a second thought. With the exception of mornings and evenings, mirages had been constant and varied as they had traveled the last five

413

hundred miles of Kansas landscape. The strange optical illusions had been fascinating at first, distortions that lent an antelope half a mile distant the height of a giraffe, or horsemen and cattle in the lead of the herd the appearance of giants in a fairy tale to those in the rear. But the novelty of the phenomenon had long since ceased.

Now into late July, the length of the days had extended, pushing the cattle from the bed ground at dawn and urging them to graze as far forward as three miles before the men could breakfast, mount, and overtake them. The freshness of spring had passed, leaving the plain a natural monotony of sunburned color that went unbroken day after day. He could well understand the reason the part of Kansas through which they had passed had been declared a part of the Great American desert, for surely no land was more worthy of the name.

They had crossed the railroad at Grinnel, passing Beaver Creek and the Republican River. A waterless stretch of forty miles from the head of Stinking Water to the South Platte was behind them. Rand released a low sigh. Sixteen to eighteen hours in the saddle had been made more difficult by his own personal edge of anxiety and an unceasing surveillance of the horizon, which had little to do with concern for the herd.

Rand shot a quick, assessing glance to the rear. The cattle were moving at a moderate pace, strung out for nearly a mile. His eyes swept the mounted figures riding beside them, settling inevitably on Billie's slender form. She was slouched in the saddle, almost motionless as her horse moved from instinct beside the trailing beeves. He felt a rush of tenderness. She was such a determined little twit. . . .

In the days since they had left Duck Creek, Billie had steadfastly ignored all efforts toward preferential treatment offered by the men in deference to her sex, and she had earned their respect anew. But she was driving herself too hard, and Rand knew he was not alone in his concern. Nate's keen gaze accused him openly for his refusal to interfere with the pace Billie had set for herself. Only that morning Willie had approached him with an outspoken suggestion that he speak to her, tell her to slow down, tell her that the men weren't expecting her to better them in every effort, that she had proved herself to them long before they had had any suspicion that she was anyone other than Billie Drucker, fellow drover.

But he had already made his decision to maintain his silence in that respect with Billie. He knew instinctively what Billie's reaction would be, and he had no desire to stir up a renewal of friction between them. No, he could not afford a situation that would add to the considerable strain he labored under.

Rand's low, incredulous laugh was touched with irony. He had given the matter deep consideration and he was truly uncertain if he had been better off before Dodge, when Billie had been holding herself aloof from him. At least then he had not known the joy loving Billie on a daily basis could give and had not been faced with the prospect of it all coming to an abrupt and complete end once they reached Montana.

And he was distinctly aware that he was becoming possessive . . . too possessive. Sharp glances from Billie during the course of the day had revealed that her tender sensibilities had often been offended by his actions. But he could not seem to pass Billie without touching her. He could not seem to keep his eyes from her during their meal camps, while riding with the herd, even at times when her slender form was no more than an almost indistinguishable mounted figure within the sea of trailing beeves. The driving need was always with him to reassure himself that she was there, safe among his men, his cattle, his . . .

Damn it all, where was this going to lead? Almost a month had passed since Dodge, and the only satisfaction he had been able to receive in the situation was the realization that he had made Billie want him. The response that surged to life under his touch grew more instinctive each day. She gave herself to him with growing spontaneity in their stolen moments together, but it was not enough . . . not enough. While his thoughts ran the full range of loving, his unspoken, intimate plans spanning years to come, Billie spoke not a word of the future. It was as if she saw her life only in terms of the present, when he wanted, needed, so much greater a commitment from her.

And he had made no progress at all in breaking down the wall of secrecy that stood between them. It was inconceivable to him even now, loving her as he did, that he did not even know her true identity! The threatening ghosts of her past were still unnamed; the dream that continued to haunt her was still unexplained. His frustration grew more overwhelming each day, but he was well aware that he dared not break his word. No questions . . . It was that agreement which had given him the only part of Billie that she would allow him. Would it be that same agreement which would make him lose her forever?

Scanning the horizon one last time, Rand shot a quick glance upward toward the brilliant, unrelenting sun. It would soon be time for noon camp, and she would be close to him again, for a short while. In a few days they would reach Ogalalla. Nate would pull in for supplies, and the men would have a day in the notorious cow town. He had already determined how Billie and he would pass their time. His heart leaping in anticipation, Rand gave a low snort. He was completely at the mercy of his emotions when it came to Billie, and he was uncertain how much more of this he could stand.

Turning his horse with a heavy hand, Rand spurred him back toward the herd. Drawing up beside Willie a few minutes later, he nodded to the older man's curious stare and assumed his leisurely pace.

Sundown . . . He lived for sundown, when he would hold Billie in his arms again. For the time being, he would not allow himself to think past that point. He did not dare. . . .

The smoke of passing trains at their front had hung in the air for hours, signal clouds that had gradually raised the expectations of the men as they had scaled the last divide in their approach to Ogalalla. They had arrived early to find herds above and below them, and Billie had been aware that Rand had been faced with the choice to graze contrary to their course or to cross the South Platte. His decision had been unhesitant. His assessment of the wide, sandy river with numerous channels had proved accurate, and they had crossed it easily.

The valley on the north side of the river, beyond the railroad, had not been more than a half mile wide, and they had angled across it, skirting the graveyard on the first hill and passing within two hundred yards of town. Finding good grass a mile farther on, Rand had ordered the herd thrown off the trail, watered, and grazed. He then left. As moneyless as the rest of the group, he had gone ahead to cash a letter of credit, leaving Willie in charge of settling the herd and establishing the first watch. With a short glance in Billie's direction, Rand had informed the men before leaving that he would meet them at the outfitting store when he would advance them their twenty-five dollars each.

Now, a few hours later, with Rand's orders followed to the letter, the crew was mounted and headed toward town at last. Billie fought to suppress the strain of anxiety that had begun to penetrate her thoughts. Her eyes darted to the men at her sides, and she smiled absentmindedly at the anticipation evidenced on their faces. Willie had done a good job the night before in raising their expectations of the "Gomorrah of the cattle trail." She surveyed the fifty odd buildings stretched out before her, noting that not a single church spire pointed upward from their midst. From its reputation, she was already aware that three fourths of Ogalalla's business houses consisted of dance halls, gambling houses, and saloons.

Realizing her sense of anticipation was as keen as the others, if for another purpose, Billie released a deep sigh of relief as Willie spurred his horse to a faster pace. She joined the remainder of the crew to follow his lead. She was extremely grateful that she was not part of the first watch left with the herd at the river. Her silent agitation would have been too intense to bear if she had to wait to go into town.

Ogalalla, the first point in her quest . . . Anxiety tightened the knot that had formed in her stomach, and Billie took a deep, uncertain breath. If she was unsuccessful in getting the information she needed here . . .

Her heartbeat accelerating rapidly, Billie spurred her horse forward, unmindful of the difficulty of the trail. Her eyes scanning the tawdry town as they approached, Billie attempted to push her wandering thoughts to the back of her mind. She was well aware of the varied sport the men had in mind for this day. A hot knot tightened in her stomach and her slender brows knit in a frown. If things went as planned, she would not be with the herd much longer. Whatever entertainments Rand usually enjoyed in these trail towns he would enjoy again. She had already decided that she would accomplish her purpose in town and would immediately return to camp so that she would not inhibit the men's enjoyment. She did not expect Rand to accompany her.

It was time to begin a slow severing of the bond that had developed between Rand and herself. In truth, she had not expected that it would grow so strong. Unaccustomed to the demands of male appetite, she had not realized how consistent would be Rand's attentions, and she had not realized how complete would be his possession of her mind and body when he held her in his arms. But she had faced some very hard facts early on. Rand was a man accustomed to the pleasures a woman could bring him. Unlike her, he had doubtless also become accustomed to the loving responses of the opposite sex. The simple fact that he had reached his age and position in life without ever having married demonstrated only too well his success with women. She had faced the fact that he would have no difficulty replacing her when she was gone, and that knowledge had been a bitter pill, indeed.

She had no doubt his present feelings for her were sincere. She had read concern in his seeking gaze, seen the passion in his eyes when they had made love. She had heard it echoed in his husky tone when he held her in his arms. And she was content that the happiness she had given him had at least partially compensated for the worry she had seen in his constant perusal of the horizon. She owed him much. Only now, with her ultimate destination so close, did she realize how very poor would have been her chances of reaching it

418

had she been penniless and alone.

Unlike her, Rand had a promising life ahead of him, and she had determined she would not stand in the way of his brilliant future. Today she would take the first step that would separate them forever.

Conscious of the lump that had formed in her throat, Billie followed Willie's lead as he drew up before a rambling frame establishment. She turned her eyes to Jeremy's appreciative hoot.

"Here we are, boys! General Outfitters!"

Her eyes jerking to the boardwalk in front of the large emporium, Billie saw Rand step out of the shadows. As before, he had used his time in town to bathe and change his clothes, and Billie swallowed hard. She allowed her eyes a brief sweep of his tall, impressive frame, her eyes flicking back to his handsome, clean-shaven face and freshly trimmed hair. No, he would not have any difficulty replacing her. . . .

Rand's eyes caught and held hers. The creases in mid-cheek deepened unexpectedly with his smile, and Billie felt a slow flush color her face. Breaking contact with his knowing gaze, she dismounted and followed the other men as they walked around back to stable their horses.

Turning as she released her bay into the corral, Billie approached the spot where Rand had already started counting out the men's allotments. Jeremy's voice sounded in her ear as his brawny arm dropped around her shoulders.

"My hands are just itchin' to get at those cards, Drucker. I don't know if you know it or not, but I'm just about the best monte player in these parts. According to Willie, these houses have at least three monte layouts in each establishment, and I'm thinkin' if I can't make it big in at least one of them, I'm not the man I think I am." Jeremy hesitated, his freckled brow screwing up uncertainly. "Did you ever play monte, Drucker?"

"No. But I've watched while my father played. He used to say I brought him luck."

"Well! Maybe you'll bring me luck then!" His arm tightening, Jeremy gave her shoulders a friendly squeeze.

"You can stand behind me, and if I get a lucky streak, I'll split my winnin's with—"

Rand's broad hand closed unexpectedly on Jeremy's arm. His expression unsmiling, he lifted it firmly from Billie's shoulder.

"You're going to have to look elsewhere for your luck, Carlisle. Billie and I have other plans. . . ."

His eyes snapping to Billie's, Jeremy sent her a glance that brought a new flush of heat to her cheeks. Jeremy's lips tightened convulsively, and Billie did not have to stretch her mind to read his thoughts. He did not respond as Rand counted out the gold coins into his palm. Realizing she was the last to be paid, Billie held out her hand. Rand counted out the required amount with a small smile.

"You've earned your money, Billie, but you won't be needing any of it here." His voice dropped a notch. "I have everything arranged. . . ." Careless of possible onlookers, Rand dipped his head to brush her mouth with his. Sliding his arm possessively around her shoulders, he pulled her against his side and turned back briefly to the men.

"Just make sure you turn up on time for your watch, boys. I'm counting on you."

Embarrassment and panic flushed Billie's face with color, the latter of the two emotions assuming control. She could not spend all her time in Ogalalla with Rand, whatever intimate plans he had formulated without her knowledge. She needed time. . . . She had to . . .

"Rand, I'm sorry." Withdrawing herself from the circle of his arm, Billie shook her head. "I—I promised Jeremy . . ." Jerking her eyes to Jeremy's sudden frown, she continued, looking into his face in mute appeal, "I promised Jeremy I'd help him buy a gift for his sister. It's her sixteenth birthday next month, and he wanted to send her something special."

Picking up immediately on her lead, Jeremy nodded. "That's right, Mr. Pierce. Drucker kind of promised me she wouldn't give up until we found just the right present and sent it off to Sinda Lee." Taking her arm, Jeremy drew Billie to his side, his young face tightening with resolve. "So, if you don't mind, we're going to take care of first things first.

420

Right, Drucker?"

Billie nodded. Her heart pounded wildly as Rand stiffened and his easy smile dropped away to be replaced by an annoyed mask.

"Of course, if you've made other plans . . ." Turning abruptly toward Willie, Rand clamped his hand tightly on the older man's shoulder. "What do you say we show this town what it is to have a good time, Willie?" Not waiting for his response, Rand shot the other men a broad smile. "Come on, boys, the drinks are on me."

Turning his back without another word, Rand herded the men toward the street.

Waiting only until the men had turned the corner and were out of sight, Jeremy faced Billie soberly.

"What's wrong, Drucker?" His smile was tentative. "I'm thinkin' it might not be a bad idea at that to send Sinda Lee a present, but I know you had other reasons for comin' up with that excuse to get away from the boss." All trace of a smile slipping away, Jeremy continued quietly, "If—if he's been botherin' you too much, Drucker . . . If you don't want him to touch you no more, tell me. It don't make no difference to me that he's the boss. He ain't got no rights to you, and he—"

"No—no, Jeremy. It's not that." Her eyes filling with unexpected tears, Billie shook her head. "I—I have something I have to do, and I didn't want anyone with me."

Jeremy's brows drew into an unexpected frown.

"You ain't plannin' on runnin' out? . . . I wouldn't want to be no part of that, Drucker. I'm thinkin' the only fair thing to do would be to tell the boss if you're plannin'—"

"No. I just need some time to myself for a while, that's all."

"Then you don't want me with you, neither."

"I just need to talk to some people. If you want to come along, I don't mind, just as long as you let me talk in private."

"All right. I'm thinkin' it might be best if I go along with you. I got the feelin' the boss's eye is goin' to be on the street, followin' you, no matter how deep in red-eye he gets."

Gratitude obvious on her face, Billie nodded. "We can buy Sinda Lee that present, and then—"

"Anythin' you say, Drucker. I'm thinkin' it was a good

thing I mentioned Sinda Lee's birthday next month. I don't know why I didn't think of sendin' her somethin'. I do appreciate the suggestion, and I'll appreciate even more your help in pickin' out a present." Jeremy's smile flashed warmly into her eyes. "I knew from the beginnin' you was somethin' special, Drucker. I just didn't know how special. . . ."

Dropping his arm on her shoulders, Jeremy leaned down to whisper into her relieved expression. "Let's get goin'. That monte game is callin'. I'm losin' money every minute I spend away from them tables."

Emerging on the street a few minutes later, Billie walked briskly at Jeremy's side, unaware of the heated, light-eyed stare that followed her every step of the way.

"Where in hell's your sense, Rand?"

Willie took a moment to dart a quick glance around them to see if his sharp comment had been overheard by the men who stood beside them at the long, polished bar. Satisfied that the other men were deeply engrossed in other pursuits, Willie shook his head and squinted into Rand's angry face. His gray mustache ticked with annoyance. "What was you tryin' to prove back there with that little girl? That you had her in the palm of your hand? Was you tryin' to embarrass her, 'cause if that's what you was tryin' to do, you sure enough succeeded."

"I wasn't trying to . . . Oh, hell, I don't know what I was tryin' to do." Pausing to pick up his drink, Rand tossed it down in one swallow and signaled for another. He turned and shot a quick look around the crowded saloon. He had been standing at the bar for over a half hour, and he suddenly realized he hadn't done anything more than stare out the window watching for Billie to emerge from the stores across the street. It occurred to him that there was any number of available women present. He had shrugged off the two rather jaded beauties who had approached him without thought. Maybe he should try concentrating on them rather than . . .

Without his realization, his gaze slid back to the street.

Billie had not yet emerged from the last store she had gone into. Oh, hell, what was the use? He had no interest in any other woman.

"You ain't foolin' nobody, Rand Pierce. You ain't about to have a good time while Drucker's out there with Carlisle. But I'm tellin' you, if you're as crazy about that little girl as you seem to be, you sure didn't do yourself no favors with that display you put on for the boys. That girl ain't no tart, Rand. You can't go flauntin' things in front of the men without her feelings gettin'—"

"I know. . . . I know. . . ."

His frown deepening, Rand lifted his hat from his head and ran an anxious hand through his heavy dark hair. Replacing it a few minutes later, he turned back toward Willie's exasperated expression.

"Carlisle's always hanging around her, talking to her, laughing with her. I just wanted—"

"They were friends before Carlisle found out she was a girl, and he feels kinda responsible for her."

"He doesn't have to feel responsible for her. She's *my* responsibility."

"He don't see it that way, Rand. He's thinkin' what the rest of the fellas is thinkin' . . . that maybe you're takin' advantage of Drucker. . . ."

"You know better, Willie."

"Do I? I ain't so sure. . . ."

Rand's face tightened.

"What's that supposed to mean?"

"It means if the girl needs some space, you'll give it to her if you really care."

"I care, all right. . . ."

"Then? . . ."

"I care too much to lose her now. I'm not about to let her get away from me."

"Rand, you can't force her to stay with you."

"You know how things are with me, Willie. I've been real successful with this beef contracting, and this year's herds are going to make me richer yet. I can give her anything she wants . . . anything."

"The only trouble is, she's got to take you along with it, right?"

Rand's brilliant eyes held Willie's squinting gaze.

"I haven't been forcing myself on her, Willie."

"Then don't. Give her room."

"I only want to—"

Rand's voice drifted away as Billie's familiar figure emerged on the street. As he watched, Carlisle came out of the door behind her, a well-wrapped parcel in his hand. Laughing, Carlisle leaned down and whispered into Billie's ear. Billie flashed him a short smile in return, and jealousy stabbed Rand's vitals. No, this definitely was not the way he had envisioned Billie's and his stay in Ogalalla to be. He had not expected to be watching Billie from afar as she enjoyed herself in Carlisle's company. He had expected to use every minute of their time to spoil her, cajole her, love her. And when he held her in his arms, he had intended to talk to her, to attempt to gain her confidence. But it looked as if it were Carlisle who had her confidence now.

His stomach tying into tight knots, Rand followed Billie's slender figure with his glance. Moving closer to the window as she passed out of sight, he saw her turn toward the general store. They would be able to find a postal clerk in there to mail the damned package Carlisle was carrying. They'd be done soon.

Turning from the window, Rand moved back to the bar. Lifting his eyes briefly to Willie, Rand tossed down his drink. Hardly reacting to its sting, he ordered another.

Give her room. . . .

Billie turned away from Jeremy's grin and stepped through the doorway of Carter's General Store. The jingle of the bell drew the attention of the clerk in their direction, and Billie acknowledged his greeting with a short nod. The fragrance of freshly ground coffee beans was heavy on the air, and she inhaled the scent with keen appreciation. She ran her gaze over the crowded shelves of foodstuffs that lined the walls, the tables of yard goods where two women

424

browsed quietly, the small rack of ready-made clothes that stood in the corner. Her eyes touched on the scarred counter behind which the gray-haired clerk worked earnestly to fill a buxom matron's order. A smile lifted the corners of her lips as she slid her gaze to the glass containers of sweets at the end of the counter. Peppermint and cinnamon sticks . . . A bittersweet nostalgia assailed her. How well she remembered a similar store in her childhood. . . .

Firmly shrugging away her memories, Billie turned, her gaze touching on a small counter and desk in the corner, and she started in its direction. The small woman working behind it raised her eyes upon her approach, and Billie paused to glance over her shoulder. Jeremy was walking close behind her, the package with the elaborately embroidered shawl he had purchased for his sister in his hand. Stepping back as they neared the desk, Billie allowed Jeremy to precede her.

His irrepressible grin elicited a smile in return from the pleasant-looking woman.

"What can I do for you, young man?"

"I'd like to send this package to Louisiana, ma'am."

Her eyes moving to the hastily scrawled address on the wrapper, the woman smiled approvingly.

"Well. It does my heart good to see that there's at least one young fella who don't forget his sweetheart back home when he gets into this town. My husband and me been runnin' this store for many a year, and I can count on the fingers of my one hand the times I've sent packages to the girl waitin' back home."

Obviously unwilling to accept praise for a deed that was not his, Jeremy shook his head. "Sinda Lee ain't my sweetheart, ma'am. She's my sister, and she's goin' to be sweet sixteen. . . . And I can't take credit for the thought, neither. It's this fella here who give me the idea to send her a present." Shooting Billie a quick wink, Jeremy continued as the woman adjusted the weights on the scale. "Yeah, Drucker, he sure is a thoughtful fella. . . ."

"You show good sense in choosin' your friends well, boy." Holding out her hand for the stipulated price, the woman shot a quick glance in Billie's direction. Returning her gaze to Jeremy as he counted out his coins, the woman carefully placed the money in the drawer and the package in the leather mailbag nearby before turning toward Billie once again.

"Now, can I do anythin' for you, young fella?"

Taking a deep breath in an attempt to control the suddenly ragged beat of her heart, Billie stepped foward.

"As a matter of fact, I think you can, ma'am."

Pausing, Billie shot Jeremy a short look. Abruptly realizing its intent, Jeremy took a quick step backward.

"I—I got some things to look at over there, Drucker." Waving his hand vaguely toward the opposite side of the store, Jeremy took another backward step. "Just come and get me when you're done."

Nodding, Billie waited until Jeremy had moved out of hearing before turning back again to the waiting clerk. Tightening her small hands into fists in an attempt to still their trembling, she began hesitantly.

"Yes, ma'am, I'm hoping you'll be able to help me. . . ."

"Thank you, ma'am. You've been really helpful, and I do appreciate your kindness."

Turning away from the clerk's stare, Billie took a shaky step, and then another. Breathing deeply, she attempted to gain control of her rioting emotions. Frenchman's Creek . . . She needed only to go as far as Frenchman's Creek. . . .

Her pace taking up speed, Billie headed toward Jeremy where he stood browsing on the other side of the store. She shot a quick glance toward the doorway as she passed. The shock of an unexpected sight jerked her step to a sudden halt. Frozen with fear, Billie felt perspiration begin to mark her brow, a moistness dampen the palms of her hands. Unable to move even though the unexpected figure had moved on down the street and out of her sight, she stood staring stiffly at the door. She jumped with a start as a warm hand closed on her arm.

"What's the matter, Drucker? What happened? You look

like you seen a ghost."

Terror a hard knot in her throat, Billie jerked her glance up to Jeremy's concerned expression.

"Whitley . . . Carl Whitley . . . I saw him ride up the street. . . ."

Within seconds Jeremy was outside, his gaze sweeping the crowded street. Returning to her side after a few anxious moments, he took her gently by the arm.

"He ain't in sight, Drucker, but we ain't takin' no chances. Come on."

Slipping his arm protectively around her narrow waist, Jeremy urged Billie forward. A small smile turned up the corners of his mouth. "The fellas in this town are goin' to think I'm mighty fond of my little pal when we go walkin' into the Dew Drop Inn Dance Hall in this friendly posture. Well, the truth is, I am. So come on, darlin', let's give those boys somethin' to look at."

His patience almost expired, Rand turned to lean his back against the bar in a cautious stance that allowed him to view the street more clearly. He raised his glass to his lips and sipped the amber liquid carefully. He was fully aware that his incautious drinking earlier could lead him only in one direction, and he had no intention of spending the time remaining in Ogalalla in a drunken stupor. No, he would not sacrifice a minute more of the time he intended to spend with Billie. He had "given her room"—an hour's worth of room—and he had just about concluded if Billie and Carlisle didn't come out of that store soon, he was going to go in after them.

His concentration intense, Rand was not aware of the light step beside him the minute before a clinging arm slipped around his neck and a soft womanly body slid seductively against his. Glancing down, Rand looked into a young, brightly painted face. Full red lips spread in a wide smile, the sultry brunette rubbed her body expertly against his.

"I've been watching you, handsome. You're Rand Pierce,

427

ain't you? I heard about you, and I don't mind tellin' you that
you sure enough live up to your reputation. You are just
about the best lookin' man I ever seen. And I'm bettin' if you
live up to that part of your reputation, you're goin' to live up
to the rest, too. Anyways, I'm game to find out. My name's
Sarah Lou. . . ."

Reaching up, Rand unhooked the woman's clinging grip
from behind his neck with a patient smile.

"Sarah Lou, honey, I'm not looking for company today.
I've got other things on my mind. . . ."

"Well, darlin' . . ." Taking his hand in hers, Sarah Lou
raised it to her lips before sliding it down to press his palm
against the brilliant crimson satin that covered her full
breast. "It'll be my pleasure to take your mind off those
problems that are botherin' you right now. That's my
specialty, darlin', and I'm real good at it."

"I don't doubt it, but the fact is—"

His words coming to an abrupt halt, Rand watched
intently as Carlisle emerged from the store in a rapid step.
His expression tense, he glanced up and down the street
before turning back to disappear inside the store once more.

The edge of tension that had been with him the day long
intensified, and the hackles of apprehension moved up
Rand's spine. He was about to take a step forward when
Sarah Lou's arms slipped around his neck in a clinging grip.
She rubbed seductively against the length of his body, her
voice a low, purposeful purr.

"Rand, honey, I'm thinkin' you're not payin' much
attention to me. And I know I can give you a better time than
anybody walkin' on that street outside. As a matter of fact,
I—"

But Rand was no longer listening. The brilliant blue of his
eyes pinned on the doorway across the street, he drew
himself to rigid attention as Billie and Carlisle emerged. He
fought to control the flush of fury that suffused him as he
saw Carlisle's arm tucked firmly around Billie's waist, his
head bent solicitously toward her face. They were approaching at a rapid pace, and Rand took a step forward, unmindful of Sarah Lou's clinging posture. His eyes still on

428

the two approaching, he brushed her aside in silence and started toward the door.

Meeting them just as they came through the door, Rand slipped his arm around Billie's trembling shoulders, his eyes searching her white face. Seeing the fear there, he pulled her protectively against his chest. His scrutiny moved to Carlisle's concerned expression.

"What happened, Carlisle?"

"We were just about to come back when Billie spotted that Whitley fella ridin' up the street outside. I ran outside, but I didn't see nothin'. I figured it would be best if I brought her back here. . . ."

"Whitley! . . ."

Not realizing the men had come up behind him, Rand turned in time to see the lot of them stream past him onto the street. His eyes on their backs, he watched them split up, covering both sides as they moved up and down the street. Noting with a flush of irritation that Jeremy had not fully relinquished his hold on Billie, Rand turned her toward a table in the corner. He had seated her carefully when he raised his eyes to see Jeremy walking toward them with a glass in his hand.

"Here you go, Drucker. Drink this like a good girl."

Placing the drink on the table before her, Carlisle dropped to the seat on the opposite side of Billie.

Guiding her trembling hand as she attempted to raise the glass to her lips, Rand held the glass firm there until she had drained its contents. Replacing the glass on the table, he slid his arm across her back. The dark eyes she raised to his were bright with fear, and he fought the desire to draw her fully into his arms.

"Billie, tell me what happened. What did you see?"

His eyes intent on her face, Rand saw the rapid throbbing of the pulse in her temple, the wildness of panic still remaining in her eyes. Her color was slowly returning, but her lips still quivered intermittently. He longed to still their movement with the warmth of his mouth, to hold her close and safe against him.

"Billie, tell me. . . ."

429

"I—we were just about to leave Carter's store. I glanced outside as I passed the doorway. Carl Whitley was riding up the street. It *was* Whitley, Rand, it was. . . ."

"Was he alone, Billie? Or did he have the other men with him?"

"He was alone, but if he was here, the others weren't far away. He knows, Rand. He knows I'm with you. . . ."

"No, he doesn't know anything." Not at all certain if his reassuring words were true, Rand continued softly, his gaze intent on Billie's shaken face. "If he knew, he would've come after you by now, wouldn't he? No, it makes more sense that he's trailing all the herds that passed through San Antonio while you were there. Every one of them that's heading up this way will be passing through Ogalalla within the next few weeks. Anyway, you don't have to worry. If the boys catch up with him—"

"No! . . . No, Rand! You have to go after them . . . tell the boys to leave him alone! If you touch him, you'll only bring the whole lot of them down on you. I don't want—I don't want—"

"All right." Realizing her agitation was growing out of control, Rand raised his eyes to Jeremy's concerned expression. "Go after the boys, Carlisle. Tell them not to bother Whitley if they find him. We only want to find out what he's doing here . . . how many men he has with him."

"Rand, I have to get out of here. I have to get back to the herd, where Whitley can't find me. . . ."

"You're safer here right now, Billie. Whitley's not going to get within a hundred yards of this place without somebody spotting him. Come on, relax, darling. I won't let anything happen to you."

Her white face raised to his, Billie shook her head.

"Rand, I didn't want this to happen. . . ."

"Nothing will happen. You're safe, Billie, safe with me. . . ."

Nodding, Billie averted her gaze and Rand felt a flash of premonition. He was not going to let her out of his sight again . . . not again. . . .

* * *

430

His breathing short and labored, Carl Whitley jerked his horse roughly into the abandoned shed and closed the door behind him. Scrambling to the window, he peered cautiously out through the broken panes. Damn, that had been close! He had just been about to turn his horse into the Lone Star livery stable when he had spotted the girl and one of Pierce's men coming out of the general store. Startled to see them in town, he had watched from his hiding place as they had crossed the street and gone into the saloon. Minutes later Pierce's men had come streaming out of the Dew Drop Inn in a rush. There had been no doubt they were looking for somebody. Him. They were looking for him. The girl had probably spotted him when he had ridden down the street a few minutes earlier.

His hands tightening into angry fists, Carl growled low inside his throat. When he got his hands on Marty and Larry again, he was goin' to show them what it meant to put him in this spot!

Stupid, that's what they were. Stupid! And he was just as stupid for goin' along with Marty's scheme. But it had been so damned easy. He had left the two idiots following the herd a week before and come ahead to Ogalalla. Hell, he had followed the herd all by himself, keepin' his eyes on that damned girl from a distance like his life depended on it all the while them two wasters were ahead of the herd, enjoyin' themselves in town. He had earned a break, and when they had returned, he had left them watchin' the girl together and ridden straight ahead to Ogalalla.

It had been time to send McCulla another wire anyway. He had made his message short and sweet this time, including in it the fact that the drive would soon be coming to an end and it wouldn't be so easy to keep tabs on the girl. Hell, he didn't know what was holdin' McCulla up, anyway.

Catching his breath with a short gasp, Carl ducked his head down beneath the worm-eaten sill and held his breath. Those two burley drovers—the mean-lookin' ones, Brothers and Hall—had just passed within fifty feet of the shed. Hell, if he had to tangle with any of those fellas, he didn't want to

431

tangle with them. He had the feelin' they weren't the kind to spend time talkin'. He wasn't opposed to tradin' lead under certain circumstances, but not now, when he was so outnumbered.

His heart pounding, Carl slowly raised his head above the sill. He expelled a long, relieved breath. Both those drovers were almost past. Hell, they didn't even give this old shed a second glance.

A sudden scrambling in the corner and the scratching of tiny feet jerked Carl's head in its direction. His hand snapped to his gun as a fat, shiny rat scooted past his feet and out of sight into a hole just beyond him. Grimacing, Carl shot an assessing glance around the limited confines of the stuffy shed. Hell, he was stuck here for a while if he wanted to make sure he could leave without bein' seen. And he didn't fancy sharin' his quarters with them slimy creatures.

His eyes moving back to the street outside, Carl jerked his head down and swore under his breath. Two more of Pierce's men were walking past: that skinny gray-haired fella, Willie, and one of his sidekicks. What were they goin' to do, patrol the streets all day? Hell, he was lucky if he got out of this place before midnight at this rate.

Dropping himself roughly to his backside on the damp earthen floor, Carl turned at a familiar plopping sound and companion odor. He darted a swift look in his horse's direction. Damn the bastard! That was all he needed in these close quarters.

Jerking off his hat with disgust, Carl threw it on the floor beside him and wiped a grimy hand over his face. The light breeze had all but stopped. The heat and smell were beginning to rise, and perspiration was already running down his sides under his stained shirt. Damn! When he got his hands on Marty he was goin' to take great pleasure in enlargin' the spaces between his teeth. Oh, yes, he sure as hell was. . . .

Every muscle suffering the strain of long hours already spent in the saddle, Billie attempted to shake off the weight

432

of heavy air and a surprisingly hot morning sun. She pulled herself slowly erect and scanned the herd with a practiced eye before turning to survey the even terrain. Her instinctive surveillance had intensified since they had left Ogalalla with extreme caution almost a week before.

Carl Whitley . . . Even now thoughts of him raised familiar hackles on her spine. He had been so close. . . . She still could not understand how he had disappeared so completely without a trace. She suffered fresh pangs of guilt with the reminder that the men had sacrificed hours of well-earned entertainment to take turns in patrolling the busy main street long into the hours of night. But their surveillance had been to no avail.

In the days that had ensued, she had tried to convince herself that she had been mistaken when she had glimpsed Carl Whitley so briefly, but each time his image had returned so clearly to mind that she had had to struggle to fight her spontaneous revulsion.

Billie shot a swift glance to the man who rode in swing position to her rear. A quick smile creased Jeremy's freckled face, and Billie flashed him a short smile in return. Having served his shift in drag position, he had been replaced by Seth Brothers in that undesirable spot and had immediately assumed a position to her rear.

She gave a silent, disbelieving laugh. She had been stunned when Brothers and Hall had approached her individually and apologized for their treatment of her earlier in the drive. Their statements had been accompanied with a few choice words as to their feelings about the men who pursued her, and she had been sincerely touched.

She was well aware that Jeremy had allowed her little time out of his sight since Ogalalla. It was a precaution he and the rest of the men had seemed to take instinctively. It was also a precaution that had been extremely hard on Rand. She had seen the frustration in his eyes at the lack of privacy they had been afforded. His frustration had been echoed only too clearly in the shadows of her mind, which would give her no respite from the memory of his strong arms holding her close, his mouth against her skin. But she had grown too

433

accustomed to the consolation of his strength, too dependent on the security she experienced in his arms.

Three more weeks . . . The postal clerk had told her it was three weeks' travel by cattle trail to Frenchman's Ford. . . . It occurred to her she could make faster time traveling alone than with the herd, but Carl Whitley's image was too fresh in her mind. . . . She did not want to run into him on the trail or have him come upon her while she was camped in a lonely spot beside the road. She was still uncertain if he knew which herd she was traveling with or whether he was indeed still attempting to locate her in the cattle towns along the trail. She knew only of the fear that froze her into immobility each time she saw his face, and the painful, haunting memories that ensued.

And she needed that time—three weeks—to come to grips with the ambivalent feelings that assailed her at the thought of leaving. . . .

Suddenly aware of the sound of approaching hoofbeats, Billie raised her gaze with a frown. Rand. . . . Riding back toward the steadily progressing herd. He had ridden ahead at daybreak, a half hour before. It was not his usual practice to return until noon camp. Tension stiffening muscles already tense with fatigue, Billie trained her eyes on Rand's face. Reining up as he neared Willie, he spoke a few short words before spurring his horse in her direction. Within seconds he had reached her and turned his horse so that he rode alongside. His words were terse, his gaze brooking no argument.

"Follow me." Not allowing her time for response, Rand turned to shoot Jeremy a quick glance. "Fill in Billie's spot, Carlisle."

Avoiding Jeremy's glance, Billie turned her grulla to follow behind Rand's powerful bay. She did not like the tension that marked Rand's brow. Something was wrong. . . .

They had been riding at a considerable pace for an hour. Appearing almost unconscious of her presence beside him, Rand had continued a steady perusal of the terrain, his brilliant gaze touching on each speck of movement as the open range unfurled before them. Unexpectedly reining his horse to a slower pace, he turned toward her to point at a small strip of water glittering in the distance.

"That's Horse Creek, the last crossing before entering Wyoming."

Appearing not to expect a reply, Rand continued forward at a relaxed pace until they rode alongside the clear, fast-running strip of water. The concentration with which Rand's eyes swept the sparkling rapids was intense. Satisfaction slowly lifted the tight lines from his face. He spoke in a low tone, almost as if to himself, as he strained his eyes to see through the swirling rapids to the streambed below.

"We'll have no trouble fording this one. The bottom looks to be firm, free of bog." Dark brows furrowed over the startling blue of his eyes, Rand snapped in command.

"Wait here."

The strict posture of trail boss he had assumed the morning long demanded spontaneous compliance with his order, and Billie reined her horse to an abrupt halt. She watched intently as Rand spurred his bay into the stream. Riding cleanly across, he emerged on the other side minutes later. Obviously satisfied with the crossing he had chosen, he signaled Billie to follow.

Billie urged her grulla forward, grateful that the frightening episode the animal had experienced earlier on the drive had not caused a permanent fear of fast running water. Within minutes she was on the other side. Spurring her animal gently as they emerged onto the bank, she reined up beside Rand, aware of the growing intensity of his scrutiny as she neared.

Without warning, Rand leaned over, his arm hooking around her waist to lift her cleanly from her saddle. Within seconds she was seated on his horse in front of him. Removing her hat without a word, Rand tossed it to her saddle and gathered her close against him, fitting her back against his chest until she rested fully in the circle of his arms. His lips were warm against her hair, his words muffled by the pale, wispy silk.

"I need to hold you, Billie. It's been too long. . . ."

His lips moved hotly against her cheek, trailing down the side of her neck to spread a warm spray of fleeting kisses against the fragile skin. His arm tightened around her narrow waist, drawing her more closely against him. She could feel the ragged beat of Rand's heart against her back, the warm swell of his passion against her firm buttocks. She swallowed tightly as the beat of her own heart began a rapid escalation. A familiar lethargy swept over her as she leaned full into his strength.

With a low oath, Rand reached over for the grulla's reins. Affixing them to his saddle with a deft movement, he spurred his horse forward, trailing her mount behind.

Traveling tight against Rand's warmth, Billie was unconscious of the passage of time. Submitting to the myriad emotions he raised inside her, Billie was suddenly satisfied to feel the powerful wall of his body supporting her, holding her aloof from the fear and threat that followed her, if only for a short time.

But Rand was drawing his horse to a halt, releasing her to dismount inside the entrance to a clump of cottonwoods. Flipping his horse's reins over a low hanging branch, he reached up to sweep her from the saddle.

Still holding her high in his arms, Rand scanned the shaded interior of the small copse of trees until he found the exact spot he sought. In a rapid step he walked to the moss-covered base of a large tree and lowered her gently to the ground. Dropping down to lie beside her, he drew her full against his lean, muscular length. He wrapped his arms around her and held her breathtakingly close. His voice was low, throbbing with emotion.

"Billie, you feel so good lying in my arms. I need you darling, I need you in so many ways. . . ."

He was kissing her, his mouth moving against hers, and Billie gave herself up to the surging emotions he brought to life inside her. Rand had said he needed her. She knew it was true, as temporary as that need might be, and she longed to assuage it. She fought to escape the nagging voice that droned in the back of her mind. Frenchman's Creek . . .

Frenchman's Creek was no more than two weeks away, maybe less. . . . Rand did not know how very short their remaining time together would be.

But now, in Rand's arms, she would escape her uncertain future. She would let him love her, and she would love him in return. For in truth, she had no choice. She had lost the power to refuse him.

Separating her lips, Billie accepted the warmth of Rand's kiss. A low sigh escaped her throat as he tore his mouth from hers to trail a heated line of kisses to the fragile shell of her ear.

"You don't know what you do to me, Billie. . . . It's been hell being near you but always surrounded by others. Now that I'm certain we're not being followed, I promised myself that we'd have some time together this morning. I gave Willie and Nate their orders for the day. Noon camp will be a few miles south of here. The herd won't be catching up for at least a few hours after that."

A short flicker moved across Billie's expression, and she avoided his gaze. Rand frowned.

"Billie, it's not like that. I want to make love to you, but that isn't the only reason I wanted to get away with you for a while. The way I feel about you isn't simply a matter of physical need. If that was the case—"

But Billie was shaking her head in an attempt to negate his words. She did not want to talk. She was in too tenuous control of her feelings. If they talked, she would betray herself to him. And talking took time. There was so little time left for them.

Turning her face back to Rand, Billie slid her hand into the dark thickness of his hair and drew his mouth to hers. Stubbornly resisting her, he made an attempt to speak again, but his words were muffled by the light kisses she pressed against his full lips, by the gentle flick of her tongue against their warmth. Rand's words were becoming distracted as he fought to resist her seduction. His hands were tightening in her hair even as he turned his face from her kiss. Trailing her lips along the firm line of his jaw, Billie tasted his skin, felt his strong body shudder as she pressed sharp, nibbling bites

437

against the strong column of his throat. A thrill shot up her spine as he made one last attempt to speak.

"Billie, God . . . Let me talk to you, darling. . . ."

No, she would not talk, could not talk. . . .

Brushing his mouth with her parted lips, she coaxed him to deeper intimacy. In short, heated kisses, she tasted his tongue with hers, drawing him to her. With instinctive passion, Billie destroyed the last particle of his resistance until it was he who sought her mouth, he who clutched her close in wild abandon, he who no longer sought to talk but to love. Rand's low, helpless groan of submission echoed again and again in her brain, and elation flooded her mind.

The situation suddenly reversed, she was breathless under Rand's ardent assault, her senses reacting wildly to the hunger she had fanned to a blazing flame within him. She was returning kiss for kiss, caress for caress, when Rand shifted his weight unexpectedly, turning her until she lay atop him, her slenderness lying stretched out full on the firm pillow of his strength. Tearing his mouth from hers, Rand moved his trembling hands to the buckle of her gunbelt. Efficiently dispensing with hers as well as his own, he tossed them to the side and began working at the buttons of her shirt. Within moments he had bared the flesh of her breasts. His breathing rapid, he pressed his lips to the warm flesh, taking the smooth white swells lovingly into his mouth as he stripped away her shirt. A low gasp of ecstasy escaped Billie's lips, stirring him to greater heights of passion. Flinging her shirt aside, he pressed her full against him to pursue more ardently his loving quest.

Supporting herself above him, Billie shuddered under the onslaught of Rand's tender assault. Clutching his head to her breast, she closed her eyes to the brilliant hues, the kaleidoscoping colors endlessly assailing her mind. She was lost to the wonder of Rand's loving, floating in a brilliant void of ecstatic emotions. Her protest was instinctive as Rand drew his mouth from her aching flesh.

The translucent blue of his eyes intent on hers, he slid his hand to the closure of her trousers. The searing heat of his gaze held her transfixed as he succeeded in unsecuring the fastening, working the loose garment free enough to expose the soft mound of her passion. Raising his knees, his feet resting securely against the ground, Rand pressed Billie back against the support of his legs as he slid his hand into the moist crease below. Finding the bud of her desire, he stroked her. His eyes were fast on hers as he watched the play of emotions across her face, assessed the passion flooding the delicate planes of her face. Her breathing was growing rapid, her breath catching in her throat as his knowing touch sent her higher, higher into the breathless realm he had induced so zealously. Her heart was a pounding thunder in her ears, her mind lost to the ecstatic tumult that held her in its thrall. Her heavy, passion-drugged lids fluttered closed, and Rand's low whisper broke the silence of the wooded grove.

"Billie, open your eyes."

Responding to the need in his voice, a need closely mirroring her own, Billie lifted her lids to the burning indigo of Rand's gaze. Her eyes forged to his by the heat reflected there, Billie remained unmoving as Rand's fluid tones washed over her.

"Billie, do you feel the love swelling inside you? . . . It's growing, spreading, overwhelming you. It feels so good, doesn't it, darling, the fluid warmth that's moving through your veins, consuming you?" Her eyes were dropping closed, but Rand would not allow her that small retreat from the reality of his possession. His voice was more urgent than before.

"No, Billie, look at me." Satisfied that her gaze was once again intent on his, he whispered low in his throat, "Give. . . . Give to me, darling." His touch grew more lovingly relentless. The flower of passion was beginning to blossom inside her. It was growing, stretching out its petals, encompassing her in its dazzling wonder. She could see nothing but the loving hunger on Rand's face, could hear nothing but the throbbing need in his voice, could feel nothing but his intimate touch as it carried her to the threshold of ecstasy. She was quaking under the weight of its wonder, and with a short, breathless step she was thrust into its mindless, careening world. Leaning full back against the support of his legs, she gave to him lovingly, deeply, her body shuddering the full, loving tribute that he had so diligently sought.

Refusing to release her even as she sought to regain her breath, Rand drew her down upon him once again. Holding her securely, he allowed her sweet breath to fan his mouth as she sought to rein her ragged breathing under control. Finally able to wait no longer, he kissed her long and deep, his ardor profound and consuming. He relinquished her lips at last, his whisper warm against her ear.

"Billie, darling, you're a part of me, a part I can't do without. You're necessary to me. . . ."

Billie shook her head sharply in silent denial of his impassioned whisper.

Her wordlessly vehement refutation brought a sudden flush to Rand's face. His lips tightening with anger, he turned unexpectedly, pinning her against the moss-covered ground with his weight. Abruptly appearing to regain control of his emotions, he moved to straddle her with his knees and sat back on his haunches. Silent, his expression resolute, he began to remove his clothes. Not pausing until there were no further impediments to the meeting of their flesh, he covered her naked length with his own.

Meeting his frigid gaze with hers, Billie slid her arms around Rand's neck.

"Rand, don't be angry. . . ."

His expression sober, Rand searched her face. Appearing to recognize her silent despair, his hostility slowly dropped away.

"I can't be angry when you look at me that way, Billie." Running his hands up the slender arms wound tightly around his neck, he continued hoarsely, "And I can't be angry with you when you're in my arms and I'm loving you, especially when you're loving me back." Pausing to press fleeting kisses against her fragile lids and the bridge of her nose, to circle her lips, he continued softly against her mouth, "Right now there's only one thing that I feel, darling, and it isn't anger. . . ."

Raising himself in a swift, efficient movement, Rand thrust deep and full within her. Billie gasped at his unexpected entry, her eyes flicking momentarily closed as the moistness of her passion brought him fully to rest inside her. Cupping her chin in a firm but gentle grip, Rand raised her gaze to his. His voice was hoarse with the emotion coloring his handsome face.

"No, I'm not angry, darling, not when I'm deep inside you, where I belong. And I'm not angry when I see your eyes come to life with my loving." Moving slowly, his rhythm gradually increasing, he grated in a voice laced with passion, "Your eyes are coming to life now, Billie. I can see desire in their depths, a burning heat akin to the fire burning inside me." He paused, a tight smile curling his lips. "The flames are burning higher, aren't they, darling, the heat increasing? . . ."

His thrusts were growing strong and true, each plunge striking to the heart of her passion. A low laugh sounded in Rand's throat as Billie's body began to respond with growing impetus to the rhythm of his lovemaking. Abandoning herself to the throbbing need he had reawakened inside her, she offered herself wholly to him, meeting each thrust fully. Her heavily fringed lids dropping closed in silent ecstasy with each deepening of their joining, she raised her eyes again to allow Rand his full measure of satisfaction. She was teetering at the brink, ecstasy beginning its shower of radiance within her when she gasped through its glory, "Rand, I—I only want to make you happy. . . ."

Pausing, holding off the moment of culmination as long as he dared, Rand rasped against her lips, "Then ours is a mutual goal, Billie. So give to me, darling, now, the way I give to you, and we'll make it beautiful together . . . for each other. . . ."

His voice ending in a gasp as emotions held tightly in check soared out of control, Rand plunged deep and true within her. Moments later, their culmination complete, Rand lay intimately upon her soft flesh. His heart still beating erratically, he lifted his head to look into Billie's still face. Her eyes were closed, her lips parted as she sought to catch her breath. Her body had negated the denial of her words. It had spoken for itself, declared his silent victory. She belonged to him. He was more certain of it than ever. She was his. . . . His Billie. . . .

Separating himself from her at last, Rand rolled to his side beside Billie. Suddenly bereft, he slid his arm beneath her and pulled her against his chest. Her head was resting against his shoulder, her pale hair lying against his arm, spilling out in a shimmering halo against the ground.

A swell of love rose inside him. Tender words long suppressed came to his lips. But Billie was not yet ready to hear them, and he bit them back with a frown.

Billie's heavy lids lifted. Her dark eyes scanned his face, noting the furrowed brow and the tight line of his mouth. Her voice was a low whisper.

"You said you weren't angry anymore. . . ."

"I said I couldn't be angry when I was loving you. . . ."

Raising her hand, Billie pressed her palm against Rand's chest. Her slender fingers worked unconsciously in the dark, curling mat there, and Rand suppressed his spontaneous response to her touch.

"Then love me again, Rand. I don't want to waste our time in anger. . . ."

Rand's love a thick knot in his throat, he whispered hoarsely, "Billie, I—"

"I don't want you to be angry with me, Rand. . . ."

Closing his arms around her, Rand held her close. "Then I'm not, darling. I can't refuse you anything . . . anything at all."

A brilliant afternoon sun filtered through the lofty umbrella of gently swaying branches overhead. Rand watched the play of the dancing shadows on Billie's still face as she lay beside him. They had made love, rested, and made love again. They had then bathed in the small stream that

442

trickled through the glade, dressed, and consumed the food Nate had packed that morning. Making the most of the time remaining to them, they had stretched out again in the same mossy bower. Billie's eyes had slowly dropped closed, and he had been glad. She needed rest. She had been pushing herself too hard, and she had not been sleeping well. He was only too aware of the restless dreams that had interrupted her sleep with growing frequency in the past week. She was physically exhausted.

It occurred to him now that realization of her depleted physical state had not deterred his loving demands. But he was only too aware that he had not forced himself on Billie, that she had sought his loving attentions willingly, almost eagerly. Satisfaction visited his senses. Billie was not ready to hear the words—to hear him declare his love for her—but as strongly as her mind refuted him, her body called out its need. It was a need echoed strongly within him, a need that encompassed every facet of his life.

He wanted Billie. He wanted to love her, protect her, keep her safe. He wanted to share his life with her, his worldly goods, everything he had, everything he was. . . . He wanted to overcome the fears that shook her, to grant her serene, restful nights free of haunting dreams. He wanted to hold her safe in his arms, to declare his love openly for the world to see and know. He wanted her to take his name, bear his children. He wanted the challenge of her quick mind, her dedication, her tireless spirit to be his. He wanted her beside him for the rest of his life—a life that would be dull and empty without her.

But Billie was already his. She had already accepted the spontaneity of her loving response to him, although she sought to separate it in her mind from her independence of him. But he remembered only too clearly the moment when he had swept her from her horse earlier in the day. The stiff watchfulness, which had marked her manner of the morning, had disappeared the moment she had entered the circle of his arms. She had relaxed full against his chest, deferring to his strength, no longer suffering a distrust of the horizon when he held her. She had unconsciously sacrificed her independence to rely on him, had turned herself over completely to his care in the same manner in which she had turned herself over to his loving a short time later. The triumph of those victories had been sweet, sending his spirits soaring. If she would let him speak, he would gladly grant her a similar victory, for he had committed himself fully to her in his mind long before and only awaited the opportunity to say the words. The opportunity would come soon. He knew that instinctively. Billie was his. . . .

His elation dimming, Rand ran his eyes over Billie's still, parted lips. He did not fool himself that Billie's feelings for him presently reached the magnitude of his. She was too inexperienced to realize how rare was the depth of emotion they shared. But he was gaining ground with every day that passed. Another month, and Billie would be firmly entrenched in his love. She would be unable to leave him when they reached the Blackfoot Reservation, no matter her former commitment, no matter the men who pursued her, no matter the man to whom she ran. . . .

A hot stab of jealousy pierced Rand's vitals. Whoever he was, this phantom would not take Billie from him, not now. . . .

Billie was beginning to stir, her fragile, almost transparent lids flickering, her lush lashes, fully restored to their dark, luxurious length, fanning her cheeks. Propped on his elbow beside her, Rand allowed his eyes to caress her face. There was no longer the faintest trace of the brutal beating that had distorted her appearance on her arrival in camp. Even the faint red line of the jagged scratch that had marred her cheek had completely disappeared. His hand moved to tangle in the ragged silk of her hair, spilling against its verdant backdrop like a pool of liquid, moonlit gold. She had not bothered to trim her hair since joining the crew, preferring to keep it bound tightly with a simple leather thong. But he had released the thick, pale strands, unable to resist the desire to wind his fingers in their length. The result was a visual assault on his senses that all but stole his breath.

444

If you're as crazy about that little girl as you seem to be—

He remembered Willie's chance comment. Yes, he was crazy about Billie, crazy wild to love her, crazy wild to keep her. . . .

Unable to resist, Rand dropped his head to cover Billie's lips in a brief kiss. The last trace of sleep leaving her gaze, she smiled up into his face, and a familiar emotion came to life inside him. God, he loved her. . . .

Rand broke the silence between them with an unexpected question.

"Have you ever been to St. Louis, Billie?"

Startled, Billie shook her head. "No."

Enthusiasm widened Rand's smile. "You're going to like it, darling. It's an exciting town. It's growing by leaps and bounds. I gave the matter careful consideration before deciding to build a house there, before deciding to make St. Louis my home base. When I finally did build, I got kind of carried away with myself. It's a big house, Billie. Too big for me, but I intend to grow into it, especially now." He gave a small laugh. He had to watch himself. He was starting to weave his daydreams aloud. Billie wasn't ready for all those daydreams he held. He had to be more cautious.

"Maybe I'll see it some day."

His voice husky, Rand nodded. "Oh, yes, you will."

He wanted to tell her more, much more, but her expression was becoming strained. Even then, she was beautiful. He spoke his thoughts unconsciously.

"You're beautiful, Billie. . . ."

His words were unplanned, spontaneous. The short, negative shake of Billie's head was just as spontaneous. She gave a low laugh.

"You don't have to flatter me, Rand. I'm not beautiful, and I know it. I'm plain. I always have been. My features are plain. I have straight, colorless hair and dark eyes, instead of the more usual blue that ordinarily comes with its color. And I'm too tall and thin. I don't have enough of the appropriate female padding." Her expression darkened, her eyes trailing off to a point in the past. "That was one of the reasons I could

445

never understand why Wes—"

Billie stopped speaking abruptly. She attempted to rise, only to be held firm by the restricting pressure of Rand's hand on her shoulder.

"Wes?" Rand's expression tightened. "Who is . . . ?" Billie shook her head as he attempted to press her further.

"It's not important."

Noting the dawning of true agitation on Billie's face, Rand abandoned his question. He did not want to get onto uncomfortable ground today. Rather, he would store that name aside in his mind for another, more opportune time. Forcing a smile, he reverted back to the subject they had been discussing.

"Didn't it ever occur to you I might be a man who likes hair the color of moonlight . . . that I might actually prefer deep black eyes that I could lose myself in? And maybe I like tall, slender women. . . . As for your features being plain, let me see. . . ."

Taking the tip of his finger, Rand traced their fragile line. "Hmmmm . . . slender brows, just right. . . . Trailing his finger to brush the extravagant length of her lashes, he gave a short laugh. "They've grown in, you know. They're not short stubs anymore. As for your nose—" He trailed his finger to the delicate, narrow bone, tracing its perfection. He suppressed the slow flood of anger memory evoked. "I suppose you're fortunate it's still straight and perfect . . . that it wasn't broken when you were beaten."

Billie attempted to move from his intense scrutiny, but he held her fast. He suddenly realized he was amused with her refutation of her beauty.

"Are you uncomfortable with the thought of being beautiful, Billie? Because in spite of your denials, you are, you know."

"No, I'm not. You've been in male company too long, Rand. You're losing your objectivity."

"I lost my objectivity a long time ago when it came to you."

Billie ignored his husky comment, startling him with her

446

next words.

"You're the one who's beautiful, Rand."

Laughing spontaneously, Rand dropped another kiss against her lips.

"Leave it to you to turn the tables, Billie."

"You are." Her voice turning cooler with each word, Billie continued with low insistence, "You're the handsomest man I've ever seen, but I'm sure you've heard those words before. Women must tell you that all the time. I think the boys envy you your easy conquests."

Not liking the direction the conversation was taking, Rand frowned. "Is that what you think you are to me, Billie? A conquest?"

Billie considered his question thoughtfully, and Rand felt a flash of incredulity. It had never occurred to him that she thought . . .

"No, Rand. I don't believe you think of me as a conquest. I think you're more sincere than that."

Rand released a tight breath. He was inordinately grateful for that small expression of confidence on Billie's part.

"Thank you. I was beginning to think you thought I wasn't to be trusted. Hell, if I thought that, I'd—"

"No, I trust you, Rand. You've always kept your word to me. But I haven't allowed myself to manufacture any illusions, to pretend that this is anything more than a brief interlude for you. I'll be gone before long, and in a little while I'll be just another in a long line of women you've loved." Billie steeled herself against the knife of pain that cut into her heart with each word she uttered. "It won't take you long to replace me."

Rand stiffened. His hand on her shoulder cut sharply into her flesh.

"And if I don't want to replace you?"

Billie attempted a smile. "Some lovely young woman, maybe one with red hair and bright blue eyes, will talk you into it."

The fierce pain Billie's words inflicted struggled with Rand's growing rage. He waited long moments before responding harshly. "What are you trying to say, Billie? That I'm not worth taking seriously? Maybe you're the one who isn't worth taking seriously. Is this just a game you've been playing with me?"

"Rand, I told you what I—"

"What did you tell me? Nothing . . . I know you're being followed, and you're frightened half out of your mind each time that Whitley fellow appears. I also know you're running to someone, but I don't know who he is. . . . You challenged me, taunted me from the minute you appeared in camp. You drove me to the point where I could think of no one but you. You made me want you, need you. You let me love you. And then you loved me back. Why, Billie, when you knew you were going to someone else? Did you just want to give me a sample of what could have been? Or maybe you wanted someone to suffer the way you've suffered. Is that it? Did it give you some perverse satisfaction to see me turn myself inside out with wanting you, loving you, just so you could tell me to find someone else? I don't want someone else, Billie. . . ."

"Rand, please. A few weeks after I'm gone you'll hardly remember my face. . . ."

"Damn you!" Rand was shaking with the low rage building inside him. "Damn you for the cold little bitch you are! How did you manage to give to me so fully and not allow your emotions to be touched? Is everything about you a lie?"

"I've never lied to you, Rand."

Rand's harsh laugh did not reach his eyes.

"I suppose that's true. But you never told me the truth, either."

"I was honest with you from the beginning. I told you I was leaving as soon as—"

"All right!" Aware that he was on the brink of losing control, Rand drew himself rigidly to his feet. He took a quick backward step. "Then there's nothing else to say, is there? Get up, and let's get out of here. I've wasted enough of your time this morning."

Billie followed Rand's terse command, swallowing tightly as she drew herself to her feet. She glanced briefly in his

448

direction. The same eyes that had glowed with loving warmth only a short time before were cold blue agates, which froze her heart. Turning, Billie took a short step toward the horses, and then another. Within moments she was mounted. Not turning as Rand mounted behind her, she spurred her horse out of the small cluster of trees. It was over, and it was time to return to the herd.

Chapter XIV

Her slender shoulders erect, Lucille stepped through the doorway of the crowded room. Ignoring the admiring glances that snapped in her direction, she smiled fondly up toward the distinguished gentleman on whose arm her delicate hand rested. She was warmed by Horace Bascombe's smile.

Her eyes misted unexpectedly in the realization that her father's pride in her was profound. She experienced a moment of discomfort in the silent realization that she had not always been worthy of his unfailing pride.

Her brief discomfiture had not gone unnoticed. Lines of concern tightened her father's aristocratic brow, and Lucille shook off her momentary flash of melancholy. She did not quite know what to make of herself of late, but she had no intention of spoiling her father's evening because of her own annoying sense of unrest.

"Lucille, dear, are you all right?"

"Of course, Father." Favoring him with one of her brightest smiles, Lucille urged him forward into the room, forcing an enthusiasm into her expression, which rang hollow inside her. "It just occurred to me how fortunate I was to arrive at Laura Henderson's party on the arm of the most distinguished gentleman in the room."

"Lucille, dear, you are too generous."

His smile cautious, Horace continued to study her face. Lucille realized the malaise that had become her constant

451

companion in the last few weeks, affecting every facet of her life, had not escaped him. Touched by the love evidenced by his concern, Lucille reached up a hand and patted his cheek.

"Come now, Father. It is not like to cause yourself unnecessary worry. I'm quite well, and eager to—"

The rapid approach of Harvey Seager, trailed by a perspiring Bigelow Morse, afforded her the escape she sought, and Lucille permitted her statement to lapse. She need free her father of his concern so he might allow himself to seek out the demure Mrs. Lorrimer.

Surprised at her own generosity of spirit, Lucille realized that only a short few months before she would most steadfastly have resisted her father's recent interest in the quiet widow of his banking associate. But the passage of the last month had wrought a considerable change in her thinking. Somehow she was now able to fully empathize with her father's position. There was no doubt he suffered the loss of her mother still. Yes, that feeling of being lonesome for a specific someone, despite having everything and everyone around him, experiencing a void that took the joy out of life ... Yes, she could well understand his feelings. ... She was suddenly extremely happy he had finally found a woman who interested him. It was no reflection on his love for her mother that he had seemed to find someone with whom he wished to share his remaining years. In truth, she was happy for him. It was a mystery to her why she had not realized all this before.

"Ah, Lucille! How delightful to see you tonight!"

Harvey Seager's overly full lips were damp against her hand as he raised it to his mouth for a light kiss. Lucille suppressed her distaste. Why was it his annoying habit of licking his lips had never bothered her before? The sudden memory of the kiss she had allowed him to steal at a soiree a week ago before flashed before her mind, and Lucille swallowed at the quick surge of bile that rose to her throat. She must stop this!

"Harvey, how lovely! . . . I see Laura had the good taste to invite you and Bigelow as well to this lovely party."

Gritting her teeth as Bigelow Morse snatched at the hand

Harvey had relinquished, Lucille did her best to ignore his clammy touch. Bigelow was already perspiring profusely, great beads of perspiration covering his patrician forehead and dampening his mustached upper lip. A wave of revulsion swept over her. How had she considered these men interesting companions only a short time ago?

"Lucille, you are absolutely radiant tonight . . . the loveliest woman in the room. You must allow me to escort you to the buffet for some punch."

Chilled by the prospect of spending the next half hour or so watching Harvey moisten his lips at every third word and avoiding Bigelow's moist touch, Lucille exerted a stringent effort to widen her smile.

"That would be lovely, Harvey. You will excuse me, won't you, Father?"

Waiting only until her father had given a short nod of acquiescence, Lucille slipped her hand under Harvey's arm and reluctantly slipped the other onto Bigelow's already moist sleeve as she stepped in the direction of the sumptuously laden buffet table. Chatting brightly as she walked, she maintained a covert surveillance of her father as he turned, his line direct toward the distant corner in which Sylvia Lorrimer sat quietly. She breathed a hidden sigh of relief. At least her sacrifice was not in vain.

Gritting her teeth, she raised her glass to her lips as she nodded at Harvey's inane conversation. She scanned the room with her gaze, a flicker of disappointment moving across her mind. He was not here, damn him! Managing to offer an amused chuckle to encourage Harvey's boring recitation, Lucille controlled her growing annoyance.

Damn that Pat Patterson! It was as if he had disappeared from the face of the earth since their last meeting a month before. In truth, she had not expected him to give up his suit so easily. Admittedly, their last encounter on the street in front of Madame Boniel's boutique had been less than satisfactory. In fact, her triumph had fallen quite flat as Pat had bidden her a less than warm adieu. The manner of their parting had forced her to face the fact that she had truly been enjoying the cat and mouse game they had played, especially since the situation had been reversed and she had obtained the upper hand. She had abruptly realized that she had not truly intended to discourage Pat's interest. Not truly . . . She had become increasingly depressed as she had ridden home, and she had determined there and then that she would be home for his next visit.

But that visit had never materialized, and as far as she was concerned, Pat had dropped completely from sight. In the time since, she had languished in the doldrums from which she had not been able to shake herself, despite her frantic social activity. Even the realization that Rand would soon be returning to St. Louis had not been able to dismiss the peculiar depression that assailed her.

Her discomfort growing, Lucille adjusted the neckline of her gown. The dress, a pale pink, which was a departure from her usual choice of colors, dipped a bit more daringly in the bosom than she remembered at her last fitting. It exposed a bit more of the full swells of her breasts than she would have preferred, and she frowned. She had originally been quite pleased with madame's design. The pink bodice was decorated with white trim and nipped tightly in at the waist—too tightly, actually—and the skirt was white, trimmed with pink. Her gleaming curls were piled atop her head, scattered with pearls and pink bows, and she wore fine pearls at her ears and neck. Yes, she was an absolute confection for the eyes. She looked lovely, but Madame Boniel was certainly going to hear about her discomfort in the lovely garment, no matter how beautiful she looked.

Suddenly realizing Harvey had finished speaking and was awaiting her reaction to his tale, Lucille gave a short laugh and squeezed his arm playfully. Harvey licked his lips and smiled, and Lucille's stomach lurched. Turning away in the pretense of setting down her glass, Lucille caught a flurry of activity in the doorway just as Pat Patterson stepped into sight. Her heart giving a little leap, Lucille had taken a step forward when Marietta Healy's short, bosomy figure appeared at his side.

The bastard! He hadn't! . . . But he had. . . . A slow, angry heat building inside her, Lucille watched as Pat

454

lowered his head solicitously to the young woman's simpering smile and took her arm to escort her into the room. So it was true! She had dismissed as gossip the stories circulating about Pat and the sudden attentions he was paying the homely little heir to the Healy fortunes. And the girl *was* homely, despite the fact that others had referred to her as a "quiet" beauty. Quiet beauty! Humph! There was nothing quiet about those monstrous breasts, quaking with each step she took! Darting a short look downward, Lucille gave a little sniff. Pat probably considered her positively flat-chested in comparison with his little heiress.

Lucille took a deep breath and a firm hold on her temper. Pat Patterson, you are going to pay for this—this traitorous defection! Determined to bide her time until the right opportunity presented itself, Lucille turned to devote her full attention to Harvey's wet lips. Her stomach churned, but she smiled. Oh, how she smiled. . . .

Two hours had passed, and Lucille was almost at the point of twitching. Her smile stiff, her dress choking the breath from her lungs, she smiled into Samuel Archer's red face. Her smile had the effect of deepening the man's flush until she truly feared a stroke was imminent. She darted a quick look around her, only to catch Pat Patterson's amused glance. Her eyelids dropping haughtily, she glanced away and took the flushed young man's arm. Hoping desperately he would not expire as they walked, she directed him toward the punch bowl, her mind racing.

So, Mr. Patterson had finally condescended to acknowledge her presence! It had certainly taken him long enough! For two hours she had chatted brightly, expecting that the next step at her side, the next voice in her ear, would be his. She had been visited by every available bachelor present while Pat had not stirred from his tender consideration of the buxom little twit on his arm! The beast! The bastard! How dare he ignore her so!

The sudden heat of tears rising to her eyes, Lucille blinked them away with angry determination. Had he not held her lovingly in his arms at his retreat, made passionate love to her, whispered breathless endearments into her ear that had made her head swim? Had he not entertained her, cajoled her, thrilled her with his lovemaking until she had not spent a single night since free of the memories? It had in fact been her frustration with the persistent memories inundating her mind that had made her so stubbornly determined to regain the upper hand at their last confrontation.

She had fully intended to forgive him for tricking her into that loving interlude, for burning himself so indelibly into her mind. She had ony intended to make him suffer for a little while longer. . . . And as far as Rand Pierce was concerned, she had only taunted Pat with his name because Pat had irritated her so. In truth, she now had trouble evoking Rand's image. He had all but faded from her mind since those days in the country. . . .

Damn him! If Pat Patterson would not come to her, she would go to him! He would not be able to resist her when she turned on her charm. That pale "quiet" beauty with the huge breasts had little to offer him but a few more pounds of jiggling flesh!

Oh, you wait, Pat Patterson, you just wait!

Another half hour had passed, and Lucille was getting desperate. The room was stifling, her dress was choking her, and her stomach was tied into tight knots. The demure Marietta had left Pat's side several times, but on each occasion her own attempt to speak to Pat had been thwarted by the crowded room. She needed to get him alone, where she could assault him with her potent appeal, make him remember warm, intimate moments. . . .

Lucille's eyes shot to the clock on the mantel. Damn! Her father had expressed a desire to leave within the half hour. But she could not leave before she . . . before she . . .

Oh! He wasn't! The knots in her stomach tightening even further, Lucille watched as Pat took Marietta Healy's elbow and urged her toward the terrace. He couldn't be taking the top-heavy little witch out for some privacy! She was only too aware of the things that went on in the shadows of the lovely Henderson garden. She had spent some very entertaining moments there herself. But even as she watched, Pat ushered Marietta solicitously through the French doors and out of sight.

Lucille, are you all right? Your face is so red!"

Glancing up into Harvey Seager's concerned expression, Lucille flashed him a weak smile. He licked his lips. Oh, God, one more time and she would surely retch! She had to get away.

Raising her hand to her head, Lucille was about to plead a headache when, miraculously, Marietta's heavy bosom preceded her back into the room. But she was alone! Unwilling to allow her opportunity to pass, Lucille mumbled quietly, "Oh, it's nothing, Harvey. My—my father has just beckoned to me from the terrace. If you'll excuse me, I'll see what he wants." Taking a quick step away, Lucille jerked back around as Harvey made an attempt to follow her.

"No! You stay here!"

Braking to an abrupt halt, Harvey shot her a startled glance that was almost comical. But Lucille was presently in no mood for laughter.

Her breath short, she walked quickly onto the terrace. Her head jerked from side to side as she attempted to determine Pat's location in the dim light. Where was he, damn him! A true panic beginning to assail her, Lucille strained her eyes into the shadows. He was gone! She had missed him!

A thick lump choking her throat, Lucille was about to turn away when she heard a step in the darkness. Turning, she saw Pat step out of the shadows.

Stopping, surprise lifting his brows, Pat offered casually, "Oh, hello, Lucille." He glanced around. "Out here alone? You must be slipping."

The bastard!

Fury clearing the annoying lump from her throat, Lucille flashed a broad smile.

"Slipping? No, not I, Pat. As a matter of fact, I came out here specifically to escape the persistent regard of several young men at this party." She sighed. "They all but overwhelm me with their attentions."

"Oh, really? I hadn't noticed. Marietta and I were—"

"Oh, yes, Marietta . . ." Lucille's smile sweetened sickeningly. "A lovely girl. Her delicate health truly upsets me."

457

"Delicate health?"

"Pat . . ." Lucille shook her head solicitously. "She undoubtedly suffers from severe backaches with all that excess weight she carries. Certainly you've seen cows suffer from enlarged milk sacks like hers. . . . And weak kidneys, too? . . ."

"Weak kidneys?"

"I certainly would think so, considering the number of times she departed your side at a run in order to go off by herself.

The corner of Pat's mouth gave a strange little twitch.

"I hadn't realized you were counting."

"Merely sympathizing, Pat. The poor girl . . ."

"Oh, she's anything but poor, Lucille. As a matter of fact—"

Unwilling to allow Pat to recount the pale twit's overwhelming financial status, Lucille shook her head.

"Money isn't everything, Pat."

"No, I suppose not. There are beauty, intelligence, personality . . . countless things to consider when choosing a woman, aren't there?"

"Yes, and poor Marietta does fail so miserably in so many of them."

Pat choked unexpectedly. Withdrawing his handkerchief from his pocket, he covered his mouth as he coughed violently. Finally in control of his breathing, he carefully replaced his handkerchief in his pocket and took a deep breath. He turned a suspiciously sober expression in Lucille's direction.

Lucille's slender brows drew together with mistrust.

"It's a strange time of year for a cold, Pat."

"Yes, well, perhaps I've caught one of Marietta's numerous infirmities. . . ."

His gaze suddenly darting to a point behind Lucille at the entrance to the terrace, Pat smiled unexpectedly.

"Marietta, dear. Lucille and I were just talking about you."

Holding out his hand, Pat drew the silent young woman near and smiled fondly into her eyes. "You do know Lucille

Bascombe, don't you, dear? She's a very *old* friend."

Lucille's smile stiffened as Pat slid his arm around Marietta's waist. She nodded at the sound of Marietta's whining voice in greeting and frowned. Pat's eyes flicked upward in innocence when Lucille mumbled, "Hmmmm, she has a nasal condition, also. . . ." She directed her next comment directly into Pat's peculiarly flushed face.

"And I'm not really so *old* a friend as all that, Pat. But yes, Marietta and I do know one another. How are you, dear? I am so sorry to hear of your kidney problems. And if your backaches persist, dear, do give Dr. Stone a call." Lucille hesitated as her hand rose to her lips, and she smiled with innocent embarrassment. "Oh, no, I'm sorry . . . that's not. right." She shot Pat a short glance. "Dr. Stone is a veterinarian, isn't he, specializing in bovines? . . ."

Giving her delicate shoulders a little shrug, Lucille fluttered her lush lashes.

"In any case, you must excuse me. It is getting rather late. It was rather . . . pleasant . . . speaking to you both again." Lucille turned, took a few steps, and glanced back, as if in afterthought.

"Oh, Pat. I almost forgot to extend Rand's regards. I received a lengthy letter from him yesterday in which he apologized for his shortness with us when you and I were together in Abilene. It seems his men got into some trouble with the law, and he was unable to break free to rejoin us. He expressed his keen anticipation of returning to St. Louis and making up for lost time. He is such a virile brute. I find I can hardly wait, myself."

Raising her brow at Marietta's shocked expression, Lucille gave a short laugh. "Oh, dear, I've shocked you. . . . But then, dear, if you continue to travel in Pat's company, I'd say you have a few more surprises in store for you. You must ask him to tell you about his country retreat. I'm sure he'll be only too happy to show it to you. Of course, it's quite isolated. . . . But when one functions as Pat's guest, one finds one has to settle for a more . . . intimate . . . atmosphere. I know I did. . . . Ta ta, Marietta, Pat dear."

Pat's low monotone filled in the void as Lucille stopped speaking.

"Good-bye, Lucille."

"Oh, Pat, let's not be formal for Marietta's sake. Do call me Lucy, darling. . . ."

Turning on her heel, Lucille walked briskly back to the party. Her head held high, she signaled to Harvey and smiled as he hastened to her side. Aware of the fact that Pat and Marietta had followed her into the room, she raised her face toward Harvey's, swallowing with a gulp as his wet lips brushed her cheek. Her smile a grimace she was thankful Pat could not see, she slipped her arm under Harvey's and laughed in a voice calculated to be heard over the low rumble of voices.

"Oh, Harvey, you are such a charmer!"

Harvey licked his lips again and Lucille gritted her teeth. Damn you, Pat Patterson! Damn you!

Pat's eyes followed the provocative sway of Lucille's tantalizing curves. He suppressed a smile. He nodded absentmindedly as Marietta spoke, his expression tightening as Harvey Seager reached Lucille's side and brushed her cheek with a kiss. His stomach moved into familiar knots. With great determination, he adjusted his solicitous hold on Marietta's arm and urged her toward the buffet table. Firmly, with great finality, he turned his back and eliminated Lucille from his view.

Carl walked up the sun-drenched Ogalalla street. Ducking under the sagging overhang in front of the General Outfitters Store, he darted for the last vacant chair and sat down. Damn, he was sick and tired of waitin'. It had been over two weeks since Rand Pierce had left town and put his herd back on the trail. He was gettin' bored with the town and bored with the women in it. And he was runnin' out of money. He didn't like countin' his pennies when it came time to buy a drink.

Carl winced at the unpleasant memory of the hours he had spent in that stifling shed with his horse after being spotted on the street by that damned Winslow girl two weeks before. Pierce's drovers had patrolled the street well into the night, and he hadn't been able to escape until after sundown. He gave a low, unconscious grunt. By then, he had been twitchin' from his attempts to avoid the slimy creatures that had all but overrun the place. In addition, he had been thirsty, soaked with sweat, and almost suffocated by the smell of aging manure. He hadn't been able to look at his horse without gagging for days. . . .

Marty and Larry had appeared in town a short time later, full of excuses, and he had given them their just reward. His knuckles were still sore.

It had been that night that he had received the wire from McCulla.

McCulla was on his way at last, and he was damned glad this whole situation would soon be settled. As far as he was concerned, that wastrel son of McCulla's wasn't worth the trouble the boss was goin' to for revenge. But he supposed it wasn't up to him to say. McCulla paid him well and was goin' to be mighty grateful once that girl was taken care of. As far as he was concerned, he couldn't care less. All he wanted was that reward McCulla had promised him and time to spend it any way he wanted. Hell, he had never liked that Winslow girl anyway, with her and her high-and-mighty ways.

If he knew McCulla well enough, the man wouldn't be arrivin' alone. His wires to McCulla had carefully explained the fact that the girl was travelin' with a herd of over a dozen drovers. With that consideration in mind, he expected the greater part of McCulla's outfit would be travelin' with him with only a skeleton crew left at home. It would be a good thing, too, 'cause if the girl stayed put where she was, they were goin' to have a hard time with that Randall Pierce.

Frowning thoughtfully, Carl lifted his stained hat from his head and pushed back the sparse, graying strands of hair adhered to his scalp with pespiration. Hell, he had seen the way that fella had kissed that Winslow girl in Dodge. . . . He

461

had wrapped his arms around her and folded her against him like there wasn't nobody in the world who was goin' to come between them if he said not. And the girl hadn't budged in his arms, nothin' like the times when Wes had tried the same thing. Hell, she had fought Wes like a wildcat. Not so with Pierce. Pierce had her purrin' like a contented kitten.

Hell, she was smart, all right. The cold little bitch had sure warmed up when her life was at stake. And it looked like she had that whole damned crew of drovers eatin' out of the palm of her hand, too. They had patrolled the town with their hands on their guns and blood in their eyes. Yeah, it looked like it was goin' to be war if McCulla had to try to get the girl away from that crew.

His spirits rising unexpectedly, Carl grinned. Hell, it might not be bad at that. He sure as hell had been bored to death for the past week. Maybe that's what was needed to liven up things a little bit . . . a little action. He had no doubt that when it came down to the wire, Pierce's men would be no match for the men he worked with. He had chosen most of them himself, and he had kept an eye to a fast hand with a gun as well as with a steer. Pierce's men were nothin' more than hard-workin' yokels, headin' up trail.

He didn't fool himself that Pierce was of the same cut. That fella was cut from another bolt of cloth entirely. He was keen-witted, sharp, and he expected the fella was ruthless, too. No man got as far as that fella, startin' from scratch like he was rumored to have done, without havin' somethin' extra goin' for him. He expected that somethin' extra wasn't only them good looks that had women fallin' all over themselves to get to him. He had to admit that he had actually envied that Pierce for a while—that was, until he had shown he was no different from Wes or any other man in the end, fallin' prey to a woman just a little smarter than he was.

He had to give that Billie Winslow credit. She sure enough knew when she had a big fish on the line and how to play him. He had seen the expression on Pierce's face when the whole damned bunch had finally left Ogalalla. If ever a man was smitten, it was him. Pierce had walked her down the street, surrounded by his men, and had lifted her onto her horse like she was made of glass. He had followed the whole crew with his eyes until they had disappeared from sight, and that big black bay of Pierce's hadn't strayed one inch from the girl's side. The tense posture of Pierce's body as he had ridden protectively beside the girl had conveyed a clear message. It had said, "There's only one way you're goin' to get this girl away from me, and it's over my dead body."

Carl gave a small, unconscious shrug. He wouldn't have expected a man with Pierce's reputation with women to have fallen so hard. Well, if that was the way it was goin' to be, so be it. Just as long as McCulla came prepared. . . .

But hell, he was gettin' damned tired of waitin' for McCulla to arrive. He had dispatched Marty and Larry to follow Pierce's herd with strict orders. Stay with the girl. It wouldn't be no trouble at all catchin' up with the herd when McCulla finally did arrive, considerin' how slow cattle traveled on the trail. But he wanted to be sure the girl was with them when they finally did.

Suddenly warmed by a thought of another kind, Carl squinted in consideration. Yeah, it would be a damned shame if that Rand Pierce was to put up a fight to save the girl and ended up dead. Them of his men who was loyal to him would probably end up gettin' shot, too. And there'd be all them cattle on the trail—only a couple of weeks away from delivery to that Blackfoot Agency—with nobody to claim them. . . . Why, McCulla'd have no choice but to take them poor, dumb creatures under his wing and see that they was delivered on schedule . . . and collect the contracted price. And he knew damned well who McCulla would appoint trail boss of that fine herd. It wouldn't be no trouble at all to rake off a nice helpin' of the proceeds for himself. . . .

Carl was suddenly glad he had spent a few hours the previous night cleanin' his guns and makin' sure they were in good condition. Hell, this whole situation was goin' to turn out more profitable than he had thought. . . . All these hours he had spent waitin' would be . . .

His eyes snapping up toward the thunder of hooves in the

463

distance, Carl watched as a familiar cluster of horsemen turned the corner and rode down the main street. Immediately recognizing the man in lead, Carl gave a low snort. Well, I'll be damned. . . . His quick eye darted to the men behind him as he mentally calculated their number. Hell, McCulla had outdone himself. At least thirty men . . . This wasn't goin' to be no war. It was goin' to be a massacre!

Drawing himself to his feet, Carl walked casually to the edge of the boardwalk. Waiting a few seconds longer, he stepped down onto the street so he might be seen more clearly. His yellowed smile widened in greeting as he raised his hand.

Dust from the sun-parched street was thick in the air as the horsemen reined up, but Carl's smile did not falter.

"Mr. McCulla. . . . I sure am glad to see you, sir. . . ."

Billie looked to the horizon, her eyes taking in the clear blue of the sky, which dipped to touch the endless expanse of rugged terrain in the distance. She sent a quick glance around her. The herd continued steadfastly forward, a long, curling serpent of beeves, its length moving fluidly to her front and rear.

They had continued their direct northward course for the past week. For several days they had not been out of sight of a mountain range that ran to the left of their trail and the apparently limitless plain that had sloped off to the right. The air had gotten gradually cooler as they had gained altitude, and the warm hours of day had gradually shortened. The heat of summer was now confined to a few hours at noon, while the nights had grown almost too cool for comfort. A few days before, the mountains on the left had disappeared, and the country to their right had begun to take on its present rugged appearance. The change in terrain had elicited a comment within camp, which had only served to heighten her tension. The approach to the Black Hills . . .

Billie swallowed tightly, the sharp chill that passed over her frame unrelated to the chill that accompanied the gradual descent of the sun. Yesterday they had crossed the main stage road connecting the railroad on the south with the mining camps in the hills. They had followed the stage road for ten or fifteen miles before coming to a fork where one road led to the mining camp of Deadwood, while the other bore off to the Powder River and the Montana cattle trail. Another chill shook her frame. The grizzled old proprietor of the stage stand had been a friendly, talkative fellow. It had not been difficult to get the information she needed about Frenchman's Ford.

Her mind denying the emotion that choked her throat, Billie mentally reviewed his words. Frenchman's Ford was a cattle trail crossing point on the Yellowstone River, but it was the crossing point for the trail used by herds bound for the Musselshell and more remote points on the upper Missouri. Their herd would be branching off soon, taking the trail that would lead them in the opposite direction from Frenchman's Ford. She could no longer put off the inevitable. It was time to separate from the herd, and she need do it tonight, before the course of the herd began to run counter to her own. She could afford to lose no time. She was only too aware that Carl Whitley's presence in Ogalalla two weeks before was an indication that he would not be far behind. She need take the time left to her, using it well, before it was too late. . . .

Her eyes darted to forward position, settling inevitably on Rand's outline against the brilliant sky. A familiar ache twisted to life inside her. In strict control of his emotions, Rand had not spoken a personal word to her since that day beside the trail a week before. In the time since, she had gone over their conversation time and again in her mind. She had said what need be said, spoken her thoughts honestly, but in all truth, she had not expected the intensity of Rand's reaction. She had not meant to hurt him, to infer that he had taken advantage of her vulnerable position. She had not intended him to believe she considered him a callous womanizer. Such could not be farther from the truth.

A wave of guilt sweeping over her, Billie was faced with the sudden reality that it was indeed she who had taken advantage of Rand. She had unconsciously used his attraction to her to suit her purpose, to allow her a temporary reprieve from her fears, to afford her a security she could gain in no other way. She had given no thought to the possible outcome of her actions. In her inexperience, she had truly believed a loving situation, entered into with an outspoken declaration of its temporary measure, would remain so in her mind. She had not taken into account the heart-shaking potency of all that was Rand. She had not expected he would fill her heart and mind so completely with his tenderness, awaken her body so completely with his loving. She had not realized that the thought of leaving him could be so heart-wrenching as to make the pain inside her almost physical in intensity.

And she had not realized she would cause him pain. Her eyes unmoving from his broad-shouldered form, Billie allowed her gaze to move over its familiar proportions. Yes, the pain was still there, visible in the rigidity of his shoulders, the sternness of his expression. She had sensed Rand's eyes on her countless times in the past week. She had turned to have him meet her gaze with a frigidity that had turned her heart to stone. The loving warmth, which had formerly glowed in his eyes for her alone, had turned to glacial coldness.

The consolation she offered herself was indeed a double-edged blade. Yes, he would have no trouble replacing her. What woman could be left unaffected by Rand if he desired her? He was so blatantly and unaffectedly male. His spontaneous charm was too effective, his sincerity too touching, his tenderness too profound. He was too valuable, too loving to sacrifice to the specter from her past, which would follow her for the rest of her life.

Cutting most deeply of all was the realization that she could not say good-bye. No matter the present state of affairs between them, Billie knew Rand continued to feel responsible for her. His perusal of the horizon had been no less constant in the past week, his precautions for her safety no less stringent. She knew he would not allow her to leave, to take off by herself. She knew what she needed to do in order to allow him to put all thoughts of her aside in his mind. She would do what need be done. In truth, she had no choice.

Her eyes still intent on Rand as he moved steadily at the head of the herd, Billie felt a tremor of shock as he turned unexpectedly, catching her glance. An emotion akin to hatred, hot and searing, was reflected there. She took a sharp breath. She had not realized. . . .

Sorrow, regret, myriad emotions choked her throat. Yes, it was for the best that she leave tonight. Raising her chin, Billie faced Rand's accusing gaze for long moments before slowly, coolly turning away.

Her eyes were closed, but she was not sleeping. She heard familiar footsteps approach the spot where she lay in her bedroll in the quiet of night camp. She opened her eyes at Jeremy's light touch.

"Come on, Drucker. It's time for watch. The boys are already back in camp and ready to bed down."

Pausing, Jeremy studied her face a few moments longer. Momentary puzzlement mixed with concern flickered in his expression before he added in a softer tone, "I'm thinkin' you didn't do much sleepin' tonight. You don't have to put on an act for me. You ain't had a night this week without them thrashin' dreams, and it didn't take much to see you was full awake, waitin' for my call just now."

Aware that the entire crew was conscious of the estrangement between Rand and herself, Billie attempted to make light of Jeremy's intuitiveness. Her response was offered with a small smile.

"Nothing gets past you, does it, Jeremy? So I didn't sleep. So what? It won't be the first time." Noting that the lines of concern creasing his freckled brow had not loosened, Billie covered Jeremy's stubby hand with hers and gave it a small squeeze.

She was about to add a few more reassuring words when an unexpected step beside them raised her eyes to Rand as he appeared abruptly, towering over them. His tone was harsh, his words clipped.

"I don't pay you to hold hands, Carlisle. Get to work."

467

With a short glance in her direction, Jeremy drew himself to his feet. His eyes met Rand's tight stare for a few minutes before he turned in silence and walked toward his horse. Jeremy's retreating step echoing in her ears, Billie threw back her blanket. Making sure Jeremy had mounted and had turned away, Billie drew herself to her feet and faced Rand squarely.

"I know you have no use for me, Rand, but I don't want you to take out your hard feelings on Jeremy. He isn't—"

"He isn't doing his job if he's here, holding your hand, when he should be on watch!" Pausing, his mouth in a grim line, Rand continued stiffly, "And I don't need you to tell me how to handle my men."

Anger beginning to touch emotions, which had been floundering in regret only moments before, Billie taunted with a touch of her arrogance of old, "If you're so concerned about having your crew work for their pay, why don't you tell me to get on watch where I belong, too? Everybody else is already out there by now, and you haven't said a word to me."

A tight smile touched Rand's lips.

"I'm thinking I've already gotten my money's worth out of you, even if you don't do another day's work with the herd. So you can coast from now on or do whatever you damned well please on this drive, with the exception of interfering with the men's duties."

Her face draining of color at his deprecating remark, Billie took an instinctive step backward. Turning without another word, Rand walked to the horse he had saddled and waiting. Mounted within a moment, he rode from camp without another glance in her direction.

Choking back the sob that rose to her throat, Billie turned toward her bedroll. She hadn't realized how very much Rand hated her. God, she hadn't meant it to be this way. . . .

Working purely from instinct, Billie rolled her blankets and secured them to the saddle she used as a pillow. Swinging the saddle up in her arms, she walked blindly toward the temporary corral where Casey secured the day's mounts.

Turning as she swung the saddle on her back, Ginger nuzzled her head, and Billie reached out to stroke the velvet muzzle. The tears flooding her eyes making it all but impossible to see, Billie tightened the cinch and reached for the reins. Mounted and riding toward the herd, she took a deep breath and willed away her tears. Perhaps it was better this way. . . .

To his rear hung the mountains' great sentinel peaks, and to his front stretched the valley tributary to the Yellowstone. The air was cool, a rarefied atmosphere that was tonic to man and beast, and there was a primitive freshness to the country that rolled away on every hand. But Rand was unconscious of the beauty stretched out before him, the clarity of the air and the touch of the early morning sun that had risen only a few short hours before. Forcing his mind to adhere to the business at hand, he made a mental calculation. He would have to make the adjustment in the direction of their travel today. They would be traveling northwest from this point on. Rosebud, Sweet Grass . . . Countless small, clear rivers to cross in the time remaining before they reached their destination. The short time remaining . . .

A small quiver of panic touched his mind, and Rand dropped his eyes momentarily closed against the emotions assailing him. What had possessed him to say those things to Billie this morning? There were no more than two weeks left at most until the end of the drive, and Billie would leave him. With his behavior of the past week and his short angry exchange with her this morning, he had only seemed to ensure that she would. The realization of his own stupidity had forced him to ride out ahead of the herd immediately after his heated encounter with Billie. He had not stopped in this steady, forward push until this moment.

Jealous . . . He had been jealous. Unable to stand another day without talking to Billie, touching her, holding her in his arms, he had determined during the long hours of the night to make another attempt that morning to convince her she was wrong to leave him. He had intended to use every weapon at his command to keep her. He had turned toward Billie's bedroll, only to see Carlisle crouched beside her. They had been speaking in whispers and Billie's eyes had been tight on his. She had been smiling, and when she had reached out to take Carlisle's hand, Rand had been unable to restrain the jealous fury that had soared to life inside him.

Rand took a deep, steadying breath. He couldn't really blame Carlisle for his feelings. How could he blame anyone for loving Billie? And Billie had made no secret about her feelings as far as he himself was concerned. She no longer wanted anything to do with him, and Carlisle had taken the opportunity to make his move.

Yes, he was able to think rationally now and could understand Carlisle's thinking. But the fact was that understanding Carlisle's thinking and accepting it were not the same. If Carlisle so much as touched Billie in his presence . . . Rand took another deep breath in an effort to bring his emotions under control. Billie was his, damn it! He wasn't about to give her up, despite the damned long week that had passed. If anything, the passage of that time had only impressed more deeply upon his mind how much he loved her, needed her to make his life complete. He had thought he had seen a trace of that same longing in Billie's eyes and had actually begun to feel encouraged until this morning. . . .

Jealousy . . . Hot, raging jealousy had forced those words from his lips. His money's worth . . . The picture of Billie's white face was burned into his mind.

Then to top it off, he had ridden away, letting Billie out of his sight for the first time since Ogalalla. In the heat of the moment, he had reasoned that she would be safe with his men while he attempted to rein his rioting emotions under control. Another flash of jealousy had reasoned that Carlisle would not take his eyes off her for a moment while they were on watch. He knew Willie and Stewart would keep a watchful eye on her, as would Fogarty and Byrd, even Brothers and Hall. Oh, hell, Billie was safe against any and all enemies in his camp. The only one she was not safe against was himself.

Rand swallowed against the truth of his sober realization. Raising a shaky hand, he removed his hat to wipe a weary arm across his forehead. Oh, damn. . . . He had been riding from the early hours. He hadn't had a thing to eat since night camp, and he didn't expect he could possibly be back at the herd before noon. But in truth, his stomach was too tied up in knots to eat. What he needed was to go back, find Billie, take her away somewhere and beg her forgiveness. He'd agree to anything, just as long as she would stay with him. He had allowed himself a glimpse of a future without Billie that morning, and he knew it would be too much to bear. Far too much to bear . . .

His determination flushing him with resolve, Rand turned his horse and spurred him back in the direction from which he had come. He had waited long enough. . . .

Something was wrong! His eyes darting to the position of the sun as the herd drew into sight, Rand felt tension tighten the knots in his stomach. It was well past the hour of noon, and the herd was still grazing. Glancing toward the cook wagon, Rand saw the men were still seated around the campfire and only a skeleton crew rode beside the herd.

No, Willie would never allow the men to linger this long over the noon meal. Something was wrong. Rand spurred his horse forward.

Reining to a skidding halt, Rand jumped down from his bay and started toward the fire. Breathless, his heart pounding, he surveyed the faces around the fire. Billie . . . Where was she? His eyes darted to the riders with the herd. Fogarty . . . Johnson . . . Unwilling to believe his eyes he ran his glance around the campfire again.

"That's right, Rand, she's gone."

Willie's low drawl broke the silence, speaking the words Rand had so dreaded to hear. He shook his head, temporarily unable to speak, and Willie took the opportunity to continue.

471

"I figured you was due back any minute, and I wasn't goin' to take this herd a step farther without your say-so, Rand. I figured you might want us to—"

"Where is she? Where did she go?" Suddenly regaining his voice, Rand took an angry step forward. "You know she isn't safe out there alone. Why in hell did you let her leave?"

"They didn't know nothin' about it until a little while ago, Mr. Pierce."

His young face screwed into a tight frown, Jeremy spoke in a sober tone. "The cattle was restless, millin' and frettin', and we had to take turns comin' in for breakfast so the rest of us could stay with the herd. Nobody missed her until noon camp. Nobody but me. She told me she was leavin'."

"And you let her go? You damned fool!" Closing the ground between them in a few quick strides, Rand grabbed Jeremy by the shirtfront, all but lifting him off the ground as he growled heatedly into his face. "Tell me where she went, damn it! Tell me, or I'll beat it out of you. . . ."

"Wait a minute, Rand." Willie forced himself between them, his wiry frame an efficient buffer between the rage on Rand's flushed face and the growing heat of Jeremy's response.

"Wait? Every minute we wait exposes Billie to more danger."

"You should've thought about that before you spoke to her like you did this mornin'."

Jeremy's hotheaded response snapped Rand's attention again in his direction as the young man continued with growing anger, "She didn't say nothin', but I heard what you said."

Willie's callused hand restrained Rand's sudden lunge forward.

"I don't know what went on this mornin', but it's obvious you and Billie had words, Rand. Jeremy ain't talkin', but he said Billie made him promise not to let the men follow her. She left a letter for you."

"Letter?" His eyes darting to Jeremy's face, Rand demanded hotly, "She left me a letter? Where is it?"

His expression tight, Jeremy reached into his pocket and

withdrew two wrinkled, folded sheets. Snatching them from his hand, Rand stepped back from the group. Unfolding them, he devoured the neat, clear hand with his eyes.

Dear Rand,

I'm sorry to say good-bye like this, but I think you realize I had no other recourse. After our words this morning, it occurred to me you might consider yourself well rid of me, but I could not take the chance you still retained some sense of responsibility toward me. So I want to make myself very clear. I appreciate everything you and the men did for me, Rand. I appreciate your concern and the comfort you gave me, but I don't need you anymore. From this point on, I can easily find my way to my destination. You may rest assured I'll soon be as safe as I was in your care. I hope that will set your mind at rest. I also hope it will allow you to forgive me for what I am to say.

That last day we were together, you said you knew I was running to someone as well as running away from something. You were right, Rand. I'm going to find a man who is more important to me than my life. After I see him and am able to see my past more clearly, I'll be able to face those who pursue me and come to terms with my future. But however it turns out, Rand, there is no place for you in that future, either as my protector or my lover, if that thought should ever again enter your mind.

Your words this morning stung me, Rand. But I've since had time to consider them, and I realize I'm glad you feel adequately paid for your generosity. I had not realized how heavily I had come to rely on you, your strength, your protection, the consolation of your loving. I also know I could not possibly have gotten this far without you, and I thank you sincerely. You've enabled me to see the end of a dream. I'll never be able to thank you enough for that.

Don't be angry with Jeremy. He's my friend, as are the other men. I've imposed on that friendship to ask a difficult favor of him. Please, don't fault him for granting it to me.

I wish you much happiness, Rand. My only regret is that we parted in anger. I'll never forget you.

Sincere regard,
Billie Winslow

Sincere regard, Billie Winslow . . . Sincere regard . . . Sincere regard . . .

An absurd desire to laugh raced across Rand's mind. Sincere regard, not love. She had never mentioned the word love in regard to him. She loved someone else. What was it she had written? His eyes scanned the wrinkled sheets.

"I don't need you anymore. . . . But however it turns out, there is no place for you in that future, either as my protector or my lover . . ."

Had it never occurred to her that he loved her enough to want her as his wife? Maybe not. Perhaps that was the reason. . . . No, he was grasping at straws. She didn't want him. She wanted to strike the time they had spent together from her mind.

"My only regret is that we parted in anger. I'll never forget you. . . ."

He gave a low laugh. His only regret was that they had parted. . . . Maybe if he hadn't spoken so harshly to her this morning . . . Maybe if he had talked to her as he had originally intended, she would have confided in him. Maybe if he . . .

"Sincere regard, Billie Winslow."

A new thought clicked in his mind. Her name was Winslow. At least she had given him that.

Suddenly realizing he had the attention of the entire assembled crew, Rand raised his head. He frowned. When he finally spoke, his voice was strained with emotion.

"Willie, get those beeves moving. We've lost enough time here."

Incredulity moved across Willie's narrow face.

"Have you lost your senses, Rand? Damn it, I ain't doin' no such thing until you tell me what that little girl said in that letter!"

His frown darkening, Rand glanced down at the letter. He supposed he owed them that. Raising his eyes at last, he gave an unconscious shrug.

"She says she doesn't want anyone going after her. She says she considers all of you her friends and appreciates all you did for her." He hesitated, swallowing visibly. "She says she's going to the man she loves more than her own life." He hesitated again and took a deep breath. "And she signs the letter, 'Sincere regard, Billie Winslow.'"

Rand's short laugh was harsh.

"I suppose that says it all, doesn't it?"

It was Willie whose voice entered the void that met his words.

"She—she didn't say nothin' else? Hell, what about them men who was chasin' her? What if they run across her when she's alone? What if—"

"She said she'll be perfectly safe. She said she doesn't need us. . . ." Rand hesitated and shook his head. "No, that's not right. She said she doesn't need *me* anymore."

The silence that reigned after Rand's last statement was broken only by the last, dying crackle of the campfire. Suddenly inordinately tired, Rand allowed his hand to drop to his side. The wrinkled sheets brushed his thigh, and his hand tightened spontaneously.

"Get the herd moving, Willie. We've got a lot of ground to cover before sunset."

A short nod his only response, Willie turned stiffly toward the men. "Come on, boys. You heard the boss."

Slowly raising his hand, Rand stared down at the letter he still clutched so tightly. The sound of shuffling steps was moving past him, unheeded, when he abruptly looked up.

"Carlisle. . . ."

Jeremy paused as the other men continued toward their horses. His expression was stiff.

"Did you want somethin', Mr. Pierce?"

Taking the few steps that drew him to Jeremy's side, Rand nodded. "Yes. I want to apologize. I wanted to believe it was your fault Billie was gone, but the truth is, nobody could've

475

stopped her from leaving if she didn't want to stay." Rand's voice dropped a notch into huskiness. "And I want to thank you for being her friend when I let her down. I only wish she could have depended on me the way she depended on you."

Jeremy was silent for long seconds.

"Maybe she'll come back, Mr. Pierce."

"No, she won't come back."

If he knew anything, Rand knew that for sure.

Turning away, Rand walked toward the cook wagon and Nate's squinting stare. He signaled toward the coffee pot that still hung over the fire.

"Any left in there?"

"Think so."

Lifting the pot, Rand tilted it to drain the last remaining drops into his cup. And then it was empty. Just like him . . . Empty . . .

The station master had described Frenchman's Ford as a mushroom village on the Yellowstone. Riding at a casual pace up Front Street, Billie recognized the reasoning behind his apt description. At least two thirds of the buildings appeared to be of canvas, remarkably alike in color and shape to giant toadstools scattered carelessly along the irregular path of the street. Large bull trains were encamped on the outskirts of the village, receiving cargoes and discharging freight, and immense quantities of buffalo hides were drying or already baled and waiting transportation on the street. The drivers of the ox trains lounged in the streets, sauntering in and out of the saloons and gambling houses at their leisure.

Billie's eyes moved rapidly around her, her carefully concealed trepidation increasing. Buffalo hunters, freighters, plainsmen, immigrants . . . She had never seen such a mixed population in one place before. Having accompanied her father on cattle drives since early childhood, she had witnessed first hand the development of raw frontier, considering herself immune to the sights and sounds that accompanied it. But this town was something else again. She had only come a short distance down the street and had already seen scenes and heard languages that were completely foreign to her experience. Unknown specimens of northern Indians grunted their jargon amid the babel of other tongues, while groups of squaws wandered down the irregular street in gaudy blankets and red calico. The only civilized element present appeared to be a group of engineers, running a survey which, by the stenciling on their equipment, appeared to be for the Northern Pacific railroad.

Adjusting her hat so that it sat low on her forehead, Billie carefully scrutinized the busy area through which she rode. Her hand slid cautiously to her gunbelt and adjusted its position. Here, more than in any town she had entered, she was grateful for the comfort of the weapon that hung at her side.

Billie's eyes trailed the gaudily painted signs that hung over the storefronts. A shave, two bits . . . A drink the same price. General Store . . . Post Office . . . Her slender body going rigid, Billie inhaled sharply. Her heart beginning a thunderous beat, she turned her horse toward the hitch-rack to her left and dismounted. Her hands trembling, she secured Ginger's reins. Turning, she straightened and took the two steps up toward the doorway facing her. In a few minutes she would know if she had indeed reached her destination. . . .

Billie approached The Ragged Buffalo saloon in a measured step. The time had come, and she had never felt so completely alone. Her heartbeat beginning a rapid escalation, she hesitated a fraction of a moment at the scarred swinging doors before pushing through and entering the room in a deceptively casual manner.

Her mind racing the full gamut, Billie assessed her momentary fears. No, no one would see through her disguise. Her broad hat shielded the pale gold of her hair and her delicate features adequately from view. Her worn male clothing, hanging even more loosely on her slender frame than it had two days before when she had left the herd, was authentic and common enough in this setting not to stir curiosity in her direction. She had even made certain to cover her small hands with the rough leather gloves she had used while working. Yes, she was safe in her disguise.

Her hand unconsciously dropped to her belt, checking the position of her gun as she stepped up to the bar. A few moments later, drink in hand, she turned to survey the crowded premises. The room was small, the furnishings makeshift. There was an air of impermanence about the place, which stuck in Billie's mind. Her eyes moved to the tables in front of her where patrons sat, playing for drinks. Satisfied the person she sought was not present there, she turned her gaze to the rear of the room where games of chance were being conducted for those who wished to try their luck. Her observant gaze had not missed the fact that every man, employee, and customer alike wore a six-shooter at his hip, the only exceptions being those men who wore two.

As she watched, a chord was struck on an old piano in the corner of the room, and the heads of employee and patron alike rose and turned in its direction. An old fellow, his shiny pate bright with sweat, began playing a lusty ballad, and Billie felt a sudden air of expectation enter the room.

Abruptly, the faded curtain on the doorway beside him parted, and a tall woman, garbed in an extravagant dress of red and gold, stepped into the room. Her pale hair, piled high on her head, accented the unusual contours of her face, the long length of her graceful neck, and the enticing plunge of her daring neckline.

Billie assessed the woman with a slitted glance. She was not in the bloom of youth, despite the clear skin of her cheek and the splendid figure that filled the outlandish gown so perfectly. Instead, she was undoubtedly a woman who was of a more mature age than first glance would indicate. Her upswept hair was carefully combed to hide the fading of its natural color and to add an aura of youth to her maturing features. The low cut of her dress called attention to her full bosom, distracting the gaze from a waist that no longer measured girlish proportions. But the woman was nonetheless beautiful, able to capture the attention of the mixed assortment of customers who crowded closer as she rested her hand lightly on the piano and began to sing.

The woman's deep, rich voice burst forth with startling strength. Taking the riotous ballad in hand, she delivered a hearty version, which left her customers stamping their feet for more.

A shouted call was heard over the enthusiastic response of the crowd, and the woman raised her hand.

"All right, Harry. I'm happy to honor a request from one of my best customers." Turning, she gave the piano player a short wink. "You know that one, don't you, Charlie?"

His response was an immediate lapse into the haunting chorus of the requested song, and the woman nodded. Her dark eyes traveling the men who crowded around her, she paused. All sign of her previous levity leaving her face, the woman began to sing the soft lament of one who had loved and lost, who grieved the loss of his loved one still. The deep richness of her voice caressed the notes with masterful skill, holding them, stretching them, blending them. . . .

The soft shading of the woman's voice, its depth of tone, registered deep and hard within Billie. She closed her eyes briefly against the return of memory, hardening her heart against the fragmented pictures that assailed her mind. She turned away with great deliberation. She raised her glass to her lips and drained it dry. The fiery liquid burned her throat, scorching a path to her stomach, and she strained to regain her breath. Waiting only until her breathing had returned to normal, she signaled the bartender for another drink. Coolly, more in control of her emotions, Billie turned back toward the woman once more.

The song ended, and the woman could not be coaxed to sing another. Obviously pleased by the enthusiasm of her audience, she raised her well-tended hand for silence.

"If you want to hear me sing again, boys, make sure you're here tonight. I'll be singing all the requests you can make then."

With a small wave of her hand, the woman turned and disappeared back through the curtained doorway behind her.

Billie turned back to the bar. Pausing as the bartender poured her drink, she asked casually, "I suppose that's Lil Culver. . . ."

"It sure is, kid."

Nodding at the man's response, Billie picked up her glass and turned once more toward the doorway through which Lil Culver had disappeared. She took a short sip and carefully replaced her glass on the bar.

The man at the piano continued to play, and Billie stopped casually at his side as he beat out a bawdy tune. He glanced up, his wrinkled face covered with sweat, and Billie adjusted the brim of her hat lower on her forehead. She dropped a coin into the dish on the piano, and the fellow's face split in a toothless grin. A call from the side of the room snapped the musician's attention in its direction, and Billie took a cautious step. A moment later she slipped quietly and unobserved through the curtained doorway and was moving carefully up the staircase beyond.

Lucille raised a limp hand to her forehead and glanced helplessly at the lace-bedecked ruffles that hung from the canopy over her bed. Cautiously, she rotated her head to look toward the windows of her room. It was a brilliant, sunlight morning, but the air was still heavy with moisture, decidedly August in weight. She had slept poorly, as had been her plight of late, but she was beginning to believe that was not to be the worst of her fate.

Her eyelids dropped slowly closed over her clouded blue eyes. Ohhhh, would she never feel well again? Damn that Pat Patterson. . . . This was all his fault—her sleepless nights, her nervousness, her inability to enjoy as simple a pleasure as a good meal. Always having been a voracious eater and appreciative of all types of cuisine, she had suffered appreciably in recent weeks in finding her appetite had all but lapsed. And now it appeared she was about to suffer the final humiliation.

Swallowing with considerable difficulty, Lucille fought

the image that hovered at the borders of her mind. Another two weeks had passed. . . . Another two, and Pat still had not demonstrated even the slightest interest in seeking her company! The beast! She had tried everything! She had met Pat on two different occasions after Laura Henderson's boring party. Once had been in the park, when she was certain he would walk up beside her and attempt to stroll along. He hadn't. The second time had been when she had gone, out of sheer desperation, to visit her father at the bank. She had made certain to run into Pat, but the damned bastard had greeted her with the same enthusiasm and absentminded courtesy he would show a maiden aunt.

That afternoon had been almost a week ago, and it had been the first day of her horrid distress. In the time since, she had not spent a single day free of its rigors. A new, nauseating wave sweeping over her, Lucille squeaked aloud, "Pat, you monster! You're making me ill!"

But the vocalizing of her dilemma appeared to be the ultimate mistake. Her eyes bulging, Lucille suddenly thrust back the light coverlet and dashed for the washstand. Within seconds she was retching into the bowl, the sheer force of the heaving convulsions consuming the last of her remaining strength.

The violent spasms finally passed, Lucille slipped to the floor beside the stand, her breathing labored. Perspiration covered her forehead and her upper lip, running down the crevice between her full breasts. Slowly, laboriously, she crawled to her bed. With the most supreme effort she raised herself to her feet and collapsed upon its downy softness.

She was lying on her stomach, but that was a mistake. Her breasts, pressed against the surface of the mattress, screamed their abuse. She flipped over to her back, and the room reeled around her. A low sob rose to Lucille's lips.

"Oh, Lord, I'm dying! I'm dying, and I'll never have the opportunity to get Pat back!" Lucille curved a delicate hand over her pale face in true grief. "He—he'll never know that I love him. . . ."

Speaking aloud for the first time her own recent realization of her seemingly hopeless love, Lucille dropped

481

her hand to the bed in despair. Her tortured mind alluding to fantasy, Lucille found herself faced with an elaborate vision of herself lying in state. On view amidst a magnificent bower of flowers, she was beautiful, almost saintly in her defunct condition. A lone tear slipped out of the corner of her eye as Pat entered the vision, his face stricken with grief. He turned, shaken, to someone just out of her range of sight. But what was that, those huge mounds turning the corner of the doorway? No! The bastard! Suffused with rage, Lucille watched the play of her vision as Pat lowered his head against Marietta Healy's pendulous breasts, and Marietta closed her arms around his neck in ardent consolation. He was groaning his despair, but that look in his eye. . . . Was he grinning, damn him?

Ohhhh . . . ! He wasn't going to get away with that! Drawing herself abruptly to a sitting position on the bed, Lucille took a deep breath against the dizziness that assaulted her. Forcing her shoulders back, she lifted her chin and stepped down onto the floor. She paused, straining to maintain her balance. She took another deep breath. She would bathe and dress and go immediately to see Dr. Stevens. She would get a tonic or whatever was needed to overcome this daily horror, and then she would take care of Pat Patterson and his silly grin! She had had enough!

Her eyes huge blue saucers, her face flushed with suspicious color, Lucille stepped out of Dr. Steven's office and onto the street. Lost in her thoughts, she remained unmoving, staring into space for long moments before suddenly realizing her lapse. She darted a quick glance around her. No, no one seemed to have thought her actions peculiar. There were only the usual sweeping glances of admiration from the men who hurried by on the street and the usual jealous sniffs of their female companions. Lucille fluttered her lashes. Certainly she was not to blame for drawing men's eyes. She could not help being so beautiful.

But she had other, more important things on her mind right now. Raising an unconscious hand to her burnished,

482

upswept curls, Lucille turned and started down the crowded street. Jack would be waiting for her with the carriage at the corner, and she need go home.

No, on second thought, she would go shopping. She needed a new ensemble ... something different, elegant, breathtaking! Unconsciously moving her hand to her waist, Lucille attempted an unsuccessful adjustment to the band that squeezed her tender flesh unmercifully. No, she would amend that last stipulation. She had had her fill of "breathtaking" garments lately. . . .

A small, unexpected giggle escaped Lucille's lips. Yes, she would settle for an ensemble that was fabulously elegant, glorious, without being constricting. Yes indeed, extraordinary circumstances required extraordinary measures!

Her smile bright, Lucille walked briskly down the street. The white stuffed dove, perched so lightly atop her fashionable chapeau, appeared to flutter and dance in preparation for flight ... much alike her spirits, ready to take wing. . . .

"What do you mean, she ain't with the herd no more!"

The nostrils of his thin, hawklike nose flaring in anger, Carl Whitley glared into Marty's pale face. Darting a quick look at the man who stood immediately to his rear, cold fury burning in his eyes, Carl jerked his gaze back to Marty's nervous expression.

"It's just like I said, Carl! Me and Larry watched this damned herd, day after day, like you ordered. . . .

"All right, dammit! So you was watching it! So how'd that Winslow girl get away without you seein' her, and where'd she go?"

"How in hell do we know? We didn't even know she was gone at first."

Carl's presence of mind suddenly snapped. The reality of McCulla's almost rabid presence behind him and the fact that thirty of his men had ridden with them to the silent grove, ready to follow their boss's command to wreak vengeance, when there was presently no one on whom to wreak it, was more than Carl could stand. Grasping Marty roughly by the shirtfront, he raised the heavier man to his toes and shook him until his chipped teeth clattered noisily against each other.

"You listen to me, you stupid bastard. You already told me what you don't know, so now I want to know what you *do* know! You ain't tellin' me you stayed here, watchin' this herd after you realized the girl was gone, for nothin'! You must of had somethin' in mind. . . ."

A true fear flushed Marty's face with perspiration. Faced with sudden reality, he glanced around him. He was completely surrounded. This beautiful August day, with the sun shining so brightly on the rugged terrain outside the small wooded glade, would be the last day of his life if he didn't talk fast. Carl was furious enough to kill, and when he got this way, he knew Whitley acted first and thought later. He had to make it good. . . .

"That—that's right, Carl, we did. Me and Larry wasn't even sure when the girl got away. We hadn't seen her around the chuck fire for at least two meals. You know how it is sometimes, Carl. The dust gets so thick on the trail that you can't make out one rider from another, and we thought we was just missin' her at first. . . ."

"Marty. . . ." Carl's voice was a low growl. The muscle in his cheek ticked spasmodically. "You got just two more minutes. . . ."

"All right, all right. . . . So Larry and me took a chance when we realized she was gone. We waited for an opportunity and sneaked up behind the campfire at night, close enough so we could hear what they was sayin'. It didn't take long. That girl was all them drovers could seem to talk about when the boss stepped away."

His words beginning to tumble over themselves as Carl's patience began to slip visibly, Marty shuddered. "They—they said that they couldn't figure out where the girl went, that they was sure the boss didn't have no idea either, he was that upset. They did say that the girl left a letter that told them not to worry, that in a couple of days she'd be just as safe as she was with them."

When that statement did not seem to have any affect on Carl's growing fury, Marty added in a rush. "They—they said that to their mind that meant the girl was headin' somewhere that was about two days distance from the place where she left them. .. ."

Marty stopped talking. His eyes bulged with fear as Carl twisted his hand tighter in his shirt. Carl's fist pressed tight against his throat, effectively choking him.

"That's it? That's all you got to say, you stupid—"

"Yeah, Carl, but—but—" Struggling for breath, Marty attempted to shake himself free from Carl's hold. The cold muzzle of Carl's gun moved against his side, freezing his struggles, and a new tone of panic entered Marty's choked voice.

"But—but the spot where the girl left from, it was just about where the herd crossed the Montana state line, where Pierce changed direction to start travelin' northwest. Larry and me figured we couldn't go ahead and try to find her, 'cause we had to wait for you. But it wouldn't be no trouble at all findin' her if the men split up into groups, takin' different directions and searchin' the country within two days distance from that point. .. ."

His eyes almost popping from their sockets, Marty gasped for breath. Straining, he shot a quick, pleading glance to the man standing behind Carl.

"Mr. McCulla, this country ain't that populated that the girl could ride into a town without bein' noticed by somebody. She won't be hard to find. .. ."

The sudden click of the hammer on Carl's gun released a small whimper of fear from Marty's lips. He shot a short glance to his rear, only to see that Larry was being restrained by the other men, their guns drawn.

"Mr. McCulla, I—I can show you where the trail branched off, where the girl left the herd. You ain't goin' to have no problem findin' her. .. ."

Carl's eyes were cold. His gun jammed tighter into Marty's side.

"Mr. McCulla. .. ."

There was a brief silence, finally broken by McCulla's

low command.

"Let him go, Carl!"

The harsh whisper snapped like a whip in the clearing, jerking Carl's eyes to his rear.

"I had enough of this stupid bastard! I'm goin' to kill him. . . ."

"I said let him go!"

Releasing him so unexpectedly that Marty fell to the ground, Carl strained to catch his breath. He jammed his gun into his holster, his small eyes burning into Marty's perspired face.

"You sure as hell'd better be right! We'd better find that girl with no trouble or you and your stupid sidekick here are dead! Do you hear that, old buddy?"

McCulla's low, grating whisper from behind caught Carl's ear, snapping him back to the boss's livid face.

"That's right, Carl. We'd better find the girl. . . . We'd better find her. . . ."

His words more in the nature of an oath than a statement, Carl responded tightly, "Don't you worry. We will. . . .

Her breathing uneven, Billie stood in the dimly lit back hallway of The Ragged Buffalo saloon. She attempted to swallow against the lump that choked her throat, but she could not. She tried again, her breath catching on a short, choking sound. She closed her eyes and breathed deeply. Not now, she could not falter now.

With supreme strength of will, Billie forced away her debilitating weakness. She had waited too long, come too far. . . .

Raising a hand steady with purpose, Billie knocked on the scarred, wooden surface of the door. The sound echoed hollowly in her ears in the short moments before a feminine voice responded invitingly.

"Come on in."

Billie turned the knob, a rushing sound filling her brain as she pushed the door open and stepped over the threshold. She was inside an oversized room, which obviously served as

486

both living quarters and office for The Ragged Buffalo. A broad rumpled bed, visible behind a partially drawn curtain, dominated the far corner of the room. A small table, the remains of the noon meal still uncleared from its surface, occupied a cramped space nearby. A large desk, covered with papers, and an elaborate velvet settee and chairs occupied the opposite side of the room, in an obvious attempt to form a more formal area in which to discuss business. But the attempt was defeated by the multitude of gowns, similar in style and flamboyance to the one Lil Culver still wore, which hung around the room from every available nail and hook, adding a note of disorder and chaos to the already crowded room.

But Billie saw little of her surroundings. Her eyes focusing on the two figures who stood in the brilliant sunlight filtering through the corner windows of the room, she advanced slowly. Coming to a halt a few feet from them, she allowed her eyes to move over their intimate posture.

The sparkle of recent laughter still bright in her eyes, Lil rested her well-manicured hand against the younger man's chest. His gaze intent on her face, obviously waiting for a response that had not yet come, the fellow had not looked up at Billie's entrance. Billie's eyes moved over his tall, slender proportions. The angle at which he held his head as he looked down into Lil Culver's face was as warmly familiar as the broad stretch of his shoulders and the lean length of his body. Emotion choked her throat as her eyes followed his profile, boldly masculine and slightly harsh, held in dark relief against the light of the afternoon sun.

Lil turned in her direction.

"What can I do for you, boy?"

Unable to speak, Billie walked a few steps closer. Her heart hammering in her ears, she removed her hat and returned Lil Culver's stare.

Momentary puzzlement crossed Lil's fine features, followed by the dawning of recognition and a flash of incredulity. Her sharp gasp echoed in the silence of the room, snapping the eyes of the man beside her in Billie's direction.

His achingly familiar brown eyes touched her face. His expression was confused in the moment before shock registered on his rough, young features. He shook his head as if refuting her startling presence. His full lips quirked and parted, slowly spreading in a well-remembered smile.

The mellow timbre of his voice as he spoke struck a reminiscent chord within her, and Billie was filled with bittersweet pain.

"Billie? It's you, isn't it?" His momentary hesitation gone, he was beside her in a few quick strides. He reached out to grasp her shoulders, pausing for the permission of her response.

His craggy features blurred as tears sprang unbidden into Billie's eyes. Stepping forward with a low sob, she reached out unhesitantly to encircle his chest, clutching him tight. Her voice was a breathless whisper as his arms wrapped around her in return.

"Oh, Adam, at last. . . ."

The shoals of the Musselshell River lay stretched out before Rand's eyes as he paused in his position far in advance of the traveling herd. The gradual but steady climb of the past two days had brought the herd across a divide where buttes, like sentinels on duty, dotted the immense tableland between the Yellowstone and the mother Missouri. On their left had lain a thousand hills, and another half day's travel had brought them to this generations old crossing of buffalo and migrating elk.

Rand considered the winding course of the river, gauging its flow with a keen, assessing eye. He felt a sense of relief. The shallows, afforded by the numerous sandbars snaking its length, would make it an easy crossing. They were approximately twelve miles above Flatwillow Creek. They would camp that night at the junction of the Big Box Elder. The herd would travel the course of that river for several days and it would be there that they would quit the trail to intercept the military road running from Fort Maginnis to Fort Benton.

Once they reached Fort Benton, it would only be another six or seven days of easy trail until they reached the Blackfoot Agency. Two weeks travel at most, and his herd would be delivered and his contract filled. But two weeks were too long. . . . An unknown sense of urgency allowing him no rest, he had finally admitted to himself he could wait no longer before turning back.

His decision made, the course of the herd set in his mind, Rand turned his horse with a heavy hand and spurred him back in the direction of the approaching herd.

A short time later he was reining up beside Willie, where the gaunt Texan stood at a vantage point watching the progress of the herd over a particularly rough section of terrain. Willie's small eyes squinted into Rand's face.

"From the look of you, Rand, I'd say somethin's up in that mind of yours. Either that, or you got bit by somethin' poisonous. . . ."

The smile that glanced across Rand's lips was fleeting.

"You're right, Willie. I've been doing some heavy thinking these past few days, and I've come to the conclusion that I was a damned fool letting Billie go like that."

Willie's reaction was an immediate shake of his head. "Hell no, Rand. You couldn't force that little girl to stay. It was clear from the first that she had somethin' drivin' her, somethin' she didn't want to share with a one of us, even you. There was no way you was goin' to change somethin' that burned that strong inside her."

His expression tightening grimly, Rand stopped Willie's words with a quick wave of his hand.

"No, Willie, you got me all wrong. I—I know I couldn't make Billie return my feelings." He gave a short shrug that belied the pain in his eyes. "I had my chance. . . ." Taking a deep breath, Rand continued, his features hardening. "But that doesn't mean Billie doesn't still need me. Whitley and those other two men—"

"Rand, there ain't been no sign of those fellas since we left Ogalalla."

"I can't take the chance, Willie. I have to know she's safe. I'm leaving. . . ."

"Leavin'! We ain't goin' to reach them Blackfeet for another two weeks yet, maybe three! Who's goin' to? . . ."

"You are, Willie."

"Me!"

"Yes, you."

Startled speechless, Willie watched as Rand drew a folded sheet from his pocket. "Here it is, Willie. I've mapped the route out for you from this point on, and I've written down all the instructions as to how to handle the sale and payment."

"Now wait a minute, friend!" Wagging his head emphatically, Willie held up the flat of his hand. "I ain't takin' on the responsibility of this herd. I didn't sign on as no trail boss. I don't mind playin' segundo to a man like you, Rand, but I'm too old to—"

"Willie, you're not too old for anything, and we both know it." His brows knit in a tight frown, Rand stared hard into Willie's slitted gaze. "The responsibility for the herd will still be mine. I took it on at the outset, and I don't intend switching it off to you now. I'll back up any loss we might incur, and every man will get his full pay, whatever the outcome of the drive."

Willie remained adamant.

"That ain't the point, Rand."

"Maybe it isn't, Willie, but it's the best I can do, because I'm going. I'm going to find Billie and make sure she's all right. And if you won't take the herd, I'll turn it over to someone else."

"Rand, you're makin' a mistake. . . ."

"The only mistake I made was in not going after Billie the minute I found out she was gone."

"You don't even know where she went!"

"I'll find her."

"And when you do?"

"I just want to know that she's all right, Willie . . . and happy. I have to know that for sure. . . ."

"And then?"

"I'll let her be."

"You're sure of that?"

"Do I have a choice?"

Hesitating only a moment longer, Willie reached out and took the folded paper from Rand's hand. With a deliberation that signified a decision made, he opened it carefully and squinted down at the crude drawing.

"Looks like this spot here is the junction of the Big Box Elder. . . ."

Chapter XV

The hot afternoon sun still streamed through the window, bathing the cluttered room in its soft glow, but Lil Culver was no longer smiling. Her eyes unmoving from the two clasped in tight embrace, she waited only until they had drawn slightly apart to whisper into the silence, "So you finally know."

Billie's gaze jerked in her direction and she nodded.

"That's right, Mother, I know."

Steeling herself against the sudden flash that suffused Lil's face with color, Billie turned back toward the man who still held her in the comfort of his arms. She looked up, the heartwarmingly familiar lines of his face stirring her anew. He was the living image of her father. She would have known her brother anywhere. Her words were solely for him.

"Pa didn't tell me about you until just before he died, but I knew, Adam. I knew. A part of me was missing. You were a shadow in the back of my mind, a shadow always just out of my line of vision in a dream which had haunted me from childhood. I felt your loss, even though I didn't know you existed."

Adam nodded. "I knew about you, Billie. I've known since I was ten years old. Mama told me the whole story. . . ."

"And you never tried to contact me, write to me?"

"Mama said our father wanted it that way. She said he had made her promise when she left. . . ."

"No, Adam, please." Lil Culver's soft tone interrupted

493

Adam's explanation. "It's up to me to tell Billie the story, the entire story."

"You don't have to tell me anything. My father told me all I need to know."

Lil winced at the bitterness that had crept into Billie's tone. She shrugged her shoulders in a weary gesture of futility. "What's done is done, Billie. It'll do me no good to offer you my regrets. But I will tell you, I've had many. It isn't easy for a mother to leave her child, to separate twins as close as you and Adam were."

"No one forced you to leave. My father worshipped you! He loved you to the day he died! He—"

"And I loved him, Billie." Her eyes misting, Lil shook her head. "But I didn't love him in the same way he loved me. Rod Winslow was generous, patient, kind, loving—a wonderful man. But—" Lil paused. "You must forgive me for this, Billie, but I was in love with another man."

The resurgence of a hurt stored deep inside her turned Billie sharply away from her brother's arms. She took a step in her beautiful mother's direction, her expression accusing.

"If you loved another man, why did you marry *him*—my father? Why did you give him children—twins—only to split them up, take his son away, and break his heart? You must have realized what a son meant to a man like my father. He had worked hard all his life. He needed a son to work beside him. Even before I really knew the truth, I knew he suffered for the son he didn't have, needed him. I tried. I worked alongside him, giving him all I could, but I could sense his sorrow. I—I thought it was because my efforts fell short of his expectations. I tried harder, worked longer. Pa got angry. He told me he wanted me with him, but not for that reason. But I wanted to take away that hurt in his eyes.

"I didn't know until just before he died that my efforts were useless, that his sorrow ran too deep. I could never make him forget the loss of his son."

Unable to bear the weight of Billie's accusing gaze, Lil took a few nervous paces to the corner of the room before turning back in a swift motion that denoted sudden resolve. Her voice was low with emotion, holding a firm note of determination.

"You're right, Billie. Everything you've said is correct and honest. And everything you've said just now, I've said to myself a hundred times. But the truth is, if I had to make a choice again, I would do the same." Seeing the note of censure on Billie's face, Lil came to stand in front of her, her expression deeply earnest.

"So I think you deserve to know the whole story, Billie, from the beginning. Then you can make your judgment, if you think judgment is your province. Whatever, you deserve to know the full truth as I've told it to Adam. I want to tell it to you, also."

Not waiting for a response, Lil took a deep breath.

"My family—my mother, father, sister Jenny and I— came out west on a wagon train, Billie. We hadn't been settled on our homestead for more than nine months when a smallpox epidemic hit our area. We stood no chance against it. Within a month I was the only member of our family left alive.

"I was fifteen years old, Billie. I was alone, and I was afraid. I knew I couldn't work the homestead alone, so I took the wagon and horses and drove into Abilene. I sold them for the highest price I could get and went looking for a job. I got a job in a cafe, serving tables and cooking in the spare time, but that didn't last long. The proprietor's husband had an eye for a pretty face, and within a couple of weeks, I was fired. But the woman who owned the local saloon was a pretty steady customer, and she offered me a job. It turns out, I have a natural singing voice, and I was fortunate enough to have entertainment as the major part of my duties. I wasn't forced to service the back rooms in order to earn my money.

"I always was a frugal young girl, and singing in a saloon can bring in a pretty penny if a girl doesn't spend it right back on drinking and gambling. So, in a few years I had a pretty good sum saved. But I was still young, still green. . . . And I met Matt Carter. . . ."

Her face taking on an aura of youth that was startling, Lil smiled. "He was older than I was, and he was the most

495

beautiful man I had ever seen, Billie. He was tall, well-built, his features so fine that they were almost pretty. But he was all man. He swept me off my feet, and in a few weeks he was sharing my bed."

Her eyes darting to Adam's sober face, Lil blushed. "I'm thinking that I'm having an easier time talking to you, telling you this story, than I did when I told it to Adam. I'm hoping . . . I have a feeling you can understand the way I felt. I was eighteen years old and so completely alone. I had never loved a man before, never known how it could feel to become so completely a part of a man. . . ."

Lil's eyes searched Billie's gaze. Seeming to find what she wanted there, she paused for a moment before continuing.

"Matt was a gambler, and he did real well. It became our custom to spend our nights together in the saloon—me entertaining and him playing cards. When the place closed up at night, we went home together. Everything was beautiful—more wonderful than I had ever hoped it could be—and I was very happy.

"Matt and I started making plans. For the first time, I took my savings out of its hiding place and put my money in the bank. I put it under both our names because Matt and I were planning on being married. Everything was going well and we had made an appointment with the preacher, when Matt started on a run of bad luck. Night after night he lost, and his disposition suffered horribly. He started drinking more than was his custom, and I began leaving the saloon before him and going home by myself. One morning I awoke, and Matt wasn't lying beside me. I was fit to be tied. I figured he had gotten too drunk to come home, so I went to the saloon looking for him."

Lil's brows knit into a frown as dark memories clouded her eyes. "He was gone, Billie. And so was my money. Unknown to me, Matt had been steadily drawing my money out of the bank to cover his losses, and when he had gambled it all away, he left town. I couldn't believe he was gone. I waited for him to come back until I could no longer lie to myself that he had truly loved me. I made myself admit that he had used me, and then my despair was overwhelming.

496

"It was then that Rod Winslow came into my life, Billie. He was passing through Abilene on the way back from a cattle drive, but after he met me, he stayed on. It didn't take me long to realize that your father loved me. I was so alone, Billie, more alone than I had ever been. Rod Winslow was so good, so kind, so understanding. I needed him, Billie, and when he asked me to marry him, I said yes.

"Rod took me back to his homestead in Texas. It was more than a homestead by that time. It was a working ranch, quite successful. We had a good life, and when I found out I was pregnant with you and Adam, I was more happy than I thought I ever could be again.

"When you and Adam were three years old, your pa took me into town shopping one day. I was in the General Store when I felt a touch on my shoulder and turned around to see Matt Carter standing beside me. All the hurt and years between slipped away, Billie. He had me in his arms and was kissing me like I was still his Lil, and I was letting him. He told me he had run off from Abilene because he had been ashamed of what he had done. He told me he had come back to find me as soon as he had been able to get the entire sum together which he had taken from me. But I had been gone. He said he wanted me back, but I told him it was too late, that I was married and had children. Matt told me he would never give up. . . .

"He didn't, Billie, and in the end I left Rod to go with him. I told Rod I was going. I won't tell you what passed between us when I did. The memory is too painful for me to even bring it back to my mind, much less tell either of you. But I knew I could no more leave the both of you than I could take both of you from your father and leave him with nothing. We struck a bargain, and I took my son with me. To your father's and my mind, it was better for him to raise a girl on his ranch, where her reputation would not be stained by having a saloon woman and a gambler for a father, for I had recognized at that point that my life would go that way if I left with Matt. I also knew it would be easier raising a boy under those conditions. It was.

"Billie, I want you to know something." Her dark eyes

497

heavy with sorrow, Lil searched Billie's stiff face. A call for understanding was written in their depths as she reached out and took Billie's hands into hers. "There's not been a day that has passed since that time fifteen years ago that I've not thought about you, wondered how you've fared. I started to write to you a hundred times, but each time I could not make myself break that promise I had made to your father not to see you again. At the time I had thought that cruel of him—to make such a demand—but I know now his pain was too strong to have been able to bear it any other way."

Her words drawing to a halt, Lil continued to hold Billie's hands, her eyes intent on her face. Unable to shake off in minutes the resentment that had festered so long inside her, Billie carefully withdrew from her mother's grip. The flicker of pain in Lil's eyes caused a similar stirring in her. Unwilling to allow her mother to see her weakness, Billie broached the silence.

"This Matt Carter, where is he now?"

Lil gave a rueful laugh. "I wasn't the same green girl I was when it came to the second time around, Billie. When I left your father, I told Matt I wanted to put all my money into a saloon of my own. We became partners, Billie—Matt and I—and we still are. Right now he's off inspecting some investments we have in nearby mines. We're married, and Matt's been the best father to Adam that he's known how to be."

Billie's eyes shot to Adam's sober face for confirmation of Lil's statement.

"Matt and I are partners, too, Billie. He backed me financially so I could start the Flying A brand. My herd is small now, but I'm thinking it'll be growing fast." A familiar light sparked in Adam's eyes, and a smile began to grow on his lips. "I've got big plans for the herd. . . ."

A small, choked laugh escaped Billie's lips.

"You've got cattle in your blood, Adam—Pa's blood—and the same gleam in your eye that Pa had when he talked about his brand. You know something, Adam? Pa's proud of you. Wherever he is, I know he's proud of the man you turned out to be."

His expression sobering, Adam slid a strong arm around Billie's shoulder and a long sought quest came to rest inside her. Yes, it had been worth it, the long journey, the exhaustion, even the pain of knowing a love that could not be. . . .

Rand's image returned abruptly to her mind, strong and clear, calling out to her, and Billie struggled against her need. Forcing her mind back to the present, she realized Adam was speaking.

". . . because I've been looking for someone I could trust to work with me. You'd be perfect, Billie. I don't mean woman's work, either." He gave her a quick smile that tore at her heart. "I need somebody who can think cattle. I know you can. And I need somebody who can take over on some of the paperwork."

Adam's enthusiasm fading, he stared at Billie uncomprehendingly as she shook her head in adamant refusal.

"No, Adam. I can't."

"Why not? I need someone to work with, Billie. I was in here today, talking to Ma about hiring another man. You can ask her. . . ."

"No, I can't. I have some—some unfinished business to take care of."

"Unfinished business . . . ?" Adam scrutinized Billie's face. The evasive shift of her eyes, the trembling that had beset her hands, the defiant lift to her chin . . .

"What are you talking about?"

"I'm wanted by the law, Adam." Her face suddenly void of expression, Billie turned to look directly into her brother's eyes. "I killed a man."

Billie's low, whispered statement lay on the air in the silent room, refusing to be absorbed by the two standing before her. She took a deep breath and continued speaking, voicing the decision she had reached so firmly in her mind only a few days before. "And I'm going back—back to Texas to turn myself in."

"Back? No. . . ."

A rain of protests shattered the silence. Billie made no response.

Lucille glanced warmly into Jack's lined face. Accepting his hand, she stepped down from the carriage, pausing briefly on the sidewalk before the Merchant Bank and breathing deeply. Glorious! The mid-morning sun beat warmly on her head and shoulders, and the air was fresh with the scent of the new day. The light breeze that lifted her brilliant fiery curls had been successful in drying the humidity of the past week from the air, and the result was a summer day beyond compare.

Turning back to Jack, Lucille caught the relief in his observant gaze. Poor fellow. He had been more than disturbed by her melancholy of late. She had seen it in his eyes, in the deepened furrows of his brow, but in her despondent condition, she had not had the strength to hide her distress. It had been all she could do to maintain a cheerful facade for Father. Had it not been for the admission she had finally made to herself that this whole mess—her unhappiness, Pat's painful defection to another woman, his reluctance to reassume their loving relationship—was all her fault, she most certainly would have cried out her despair onto her father's strong shoulder. But the truth was, she had outsmarted herself, and pride would not allow her to reveal to her father what a fool his daughter truly was.

No, she had gotten herself into this predicament, and she would get herself out. Dear Pat . . . He had provided her with her strongest weapon and she, Lucille Elizabeth Bascombe, intended to use it skillfully to achieve her purpose. A happy sigh escaped her lips. Oh, Pat, my dearest darling, you don't stand a chance against me!

Lucille's confident smile softened.

"Jack dear, do find a shady spot to wait for me. I may be a little while in the bank. It may take some time to come to terms with Mr. Patterson about my . . . business affairs."

The curious glint in his eye Jack's only indication that he

suspected Lucille was up to something, he nodded his assent.

"I'll be waiting for you, Miss Lucille."

Taking only a moment to shake out the folds in her skirt, Lucille turned toward the bank in a brisk step. Brushing through the entrance and taking only a moment to smile warmly at the young man who held the door, Lucille paused briefly. She did, after all, owe it to the poor clerks who labored so steadfastly behind their desks and windows to bring some brightness into their day. She was at her lovely best today, and she knew it. She had fussed endlessly in front of her mirror to make certain of it, and in her brilliant walking out dress of buttercup yellow, she was a veritable beam of sunlight within the somber confines of the sober establishment.

She had put considerable pressure on Madame Boniel and had been adamant that her dress be ready within two days' time. In truth, she would have been unable to wait any longer to speak to Pat. But she was now absurdly happy that she had. Long hours before the mirror had assured her that the sheer batiste of her dress added just the right aura of delicacy to her dainty stature, and the deep neckline and the narrow waist, which was still a bit too tight for complete comfort, had just the right touch of wanton appeal. The pert straw chapeau, decorated with yellow flowers and a gracefully poised butterfly, balanced jauntily on her glowing curls, adding the right note of propriety. Her matching parasol and gloves were a touch of the demure, which she used to great advantage.

Satisfied that her entrance was a true success, Lucille strode confidently toward the offices at the rear, her eye on a specific door. Sweeping past the awestruck clerks, she breathed throatily, "Don't bother to announce me, gentlemen. I believe Mr. Patterson is expecting me."

Her hand on the knob, Lucille suddenly felt a tremor of trepidation. Annoyed with her own momentary weakness, she gritted her teeth and took a deep breath. Pat Patterson, you will not put me at the disadvantage of making me nervous to face you! You will not!

Giving a sharp little rap on the door to Pat's office, Lucille pushed it open slowly. Seated at his desk, Pat snapped his head up in her direction. An enigmatic flicker crossed his expression in the moment before he rose to his feet and walked around his desk. He extended his hand toward her, drawing her courteously into the room in greeting as he closed the door behind her. His smile was cautious.

"Lucille, I must say this is a surprise. To what do I owe the honor of your visit?"

Managing to hide the fact that her heart started racing the moment her eyes touched on his face, Lucille shot Pat an impatient glance. "Really, Pat, not that old chestnut. . . . You disappoint me. I should think you'd have something more original to say to me than that."

"Oh, really?" His mouth giving a short quirk, Pat raised his brow in mock surprise. "What would you consider a more appropriate greeting to your unexpected call, Lucille?"

Choosing to ignore his question, Lucille smiled. "Well, if the truth be known, I've decided, dear Pat, that if the mountain will not come to Mohammed, then Mohammed most certainly will have to make the first move. . . ."

"Dear Lucille, am I to understand that you are now classifying yourself in the same category as the prophets?"

Lucille gritted her teeth. "No. Do me the favor of not pretending to be obtuse, Pat. It doesn't become you."

His narrow face lapsing into a smile for the first time, Pat gave a short laugh. "All right. If we're going to be straightforward, then I'll come right out with what I'm thinking. What do you want? You didn't come here to make a social call."

"Are you so sure of that?"

"Yes, I am. What do you want from me, Lucille?"

Taking a step forward, Lucille raised her eyes slowly to Pat's. They were standing so close that they were almost touching, and Lucille could feel the heat emanating from Pat's body.

"Actually, Pat dear, I wanted to ask how Marietta is feeling. I was truly concerned about her backaches, her weak

502

bladder, her annoying nasal condition. . . ."

"All infirmities that seem to exist merely in your mind, I assure you. Marietta is an extremely healthy young woman. I have no doubt she will make an excellent wife and mother for—"

"Wife and mother!"

Her eyes snapping wide, Lucille felt a hot flush suffuse her face.

"Wife and mother! You cannot be serious, Pat!"

"I most certainly am serious." His expression reinforcing his statement, Pat continued quietly, "Marietta is a very sincere young woman. She has reaffirmed her desire for just that status in life many times, and I have—"

"You have *what?*" A searing, jealous fury suddenly burning through her veins, Lucille raised her voice angrily. "You have decided to afford her that opportunity?"

A sudden thought striking her mind, Lucille took a step backward, her hand rising to her lips as the recent surge of color drained abruptly away to leave her a ghastly white. She swayed, and true concern swept Pat's face.

"Lucille, are you all right? Come—come over here and sit down."

Drawing her with him to a couch at the side of the room, Pat seated her carefully. Allowing him to assist her only because she was truly uncertain her trembling limbs would support her, Lucille turned stiffly to Pat's anxious gaze as he sat beside her.

"Lucille, what's wrong?"

Her voice a harsh rasp, Lucille shook her head.

"Oh, Pat, you haven't—haven't—"

Impatience gaining control at her uncharacteristic hesitation, Pat urged tightly, "I haven't what, Lucille?"

"You know. . . . You know what I mean, damn you!" Unable to make herself actually put her fear into words, Lucille felt a true horror fill her mind. The result was the glazing over of the brilliant blue of her eyes with hot tears. Despising their presence, Lucille was suddenly filled with a rage that added a new firmness to her shaken tone.

"No, you *cannot!* I won't stand for it! You will not marry that woman!"

His expression suddenly guarded, Pat drew back. The pale green of his eyes reflected a trace of anger.

"Oh, I cannot marry Marietta. . . . Pray, tell me why I may not, Lucille? Is it because my marriage would interfere with the little games you like to play with men's emotions? Is it because my marriage would deprive you of a playmate with whom you have already become bored but only wish to cling to because he is with another woman?"

"No. That isn't the reason. The reason is—is—" Lucille took a deep breath. She was trembling so badly that she was uncertain she would be able to hold herself erect. But Pat's expression showed no sign of sympathy for her shaken condition, and taking a deep breath, Lucille forced the words past her trembling lips. "You cannot marry Marietta because I'm pregnant with your child."

A frightening stillness came over Pat. His face suddenly almost as white as her own, he finally broke the silence that reigned between them.

"And how am I to be sure that this child of yours is also mine, that I am not merely the most convenient man on whom to—"

A pain so severe that it all but stole her breath pierced Lucille's vitals, pushing her to her feet. Releasing a low gasp, she turned and had taken a frantic step toward the door when Pat's hands closed on her shoulders. Jerking her back toward him, he turned her to a face suddenly torn with the emotions rampant in his voice.

"No, you can't run away this time, Lucille. And you can't evade or flirt your way out of this, either. The truth! I want the truth from you. How do I know this child is mine?"

No longer bothering to hide the pain that shattered her, Lucille shook her head. "Pat, how can you doubt me? I never thought you would think—"

"Answer me, Lucille. I have to know!"

Taking a deep breath, Lucille raised her chin. "The child is yours because I've not been with another man since we were

504

together at your country retreat! I have not been able to think of another man in that way since that time, not a single one. That nonsense about Rand . . . I've not heard from him and, in truth, have not wasted a single hour in thinking about him or any other man. But I have spent countless hours in the time since thinking of you. I resented those hours, Pat, and the ties you had fostered on me. I wanted to make you pay for insinuating yourself so deeply into my life, for the freedom I was beginning to feel seep away. I wanted to show myself and you that I didn't want you or need you." Her voice breaking unexpectedly, Lucille continued, "Oh, Pat, I didn't know, didn't realize—" She swallowed against the tears that choked her throat. "I didn't know how much I love you. . . ."

Lucille's low whispered statement hung on the air between them as Pat stared into her eyes. He made no response. Her hopes and dreams collapsing, Lucille gave a low sob and attempted to break from Pat's hold.

His grip on her shoulders tightening almost to the point of pain, Pat held her fast. His verdant stare bore unrelentingly into hers.

"Say that again, Lucille."

"What? No, I—"

"Say it again, damn you!" Giving her a hard shake, Pat whispered hoarsely, "I have to be sure. . . ."

"Sure of what? That I love you? If it will make you let me go, I'll say it again. Yes, I love you, you damned arrogant bas "

"Shut up, Lucy. Shut up, darling, and kiss me."

Abruptly drawing her into his arms, Pat covered Lucille's protesting lips with his, his arms tightening around her to crush her full and tight against him. He drew his mouth reluctantly from hers a few moments later, a glorious smile gradually growing on his lips. Lucille opened her mouth to speak, but he silenced her with a quick kiss.

"No, it's my turn to talk now, and I want to say the words. I've been aching to say them since those days we spent together. You're spoiled, conceited, arrogant, selfish. . . ."

505

Lucille's soft glow dimmed, and he added with a widening smile, "And you're beautiful, intelligent, witty, and so intensely desirable. . . . I love you, darling. I've loved you since that first day you walked through the doorway of your father's study in your wrapper and dismissed me with a haughty glance. You challenge me, stir me, make me want you more than any woman I've ever known. It's been a damned hard pull, getting you to love me back. . . ."

The tears brimming in Lucille's eyes suddenly overflowed in abundance, and she wiped them away with annoyance. "Pat, you bastard! How you made me suffer. . . ."

"Did I, darling? I'm glad."

"Glad! Ohhhh. . . ."

"Just like you made me suffer. But you're mine now, and you won't get away again."

"Not much chance of that in the next seven months or so. . . ."

"Not ever!"

Lucille smiled at the supreme finality in his tone, gaining tremendous satisfaction as Pat pressed tightly, "You're going to marry me, Lucy. That'll be the end to your 'sensual romps with attractive men,' do you understand?"

"Yes, darling, unless that attractive man is you. . . ."

"And you're going to be a good wife to me. . . ."

"Of course, darling, but what about Marietta?"

"She's going to be a good wife to Willis Ramsey."

"Willis Ramsey?"

"Yes, Willis Ramsey, one of the clerks in her father's office. They've been in love for months." Pat hesitated. "Willis is—uh—rather fond of bovines. . . ."

"Oh, Pat! And you made me think—"

"Made you think what? That I was fond of bovines?" Pat gave a short laugh. "No, you're the only woman I love. . . . And I do love you, Lucy. I love you with all my heart."

His arms sliding around her, Pat crushed her against him in a deep, shattering kiss. Drawing away, breathless, he whispered against her lips, "Say it again you little witch."

"Say what? I don't know what you mean. . . ."

"Lucy. . . ."

"I love you, Pat, cruel bastard that you are. I love you."

Pat's laughing response was low, supremely happy.

"I knew you did, you know."

"Pat, you—"

But Pat's mouth cut off Lucille's angry retort, a flame growing inside him as her anger turned to an emotion of a far deeper hue. This was what he wanted, what he had always wanted, and now his joy was supreme because Lucy wanted it, too. It would always be this way between them. Always. His arms tightened spontaneously around her and Pat deepened his kiss. He'd see to it, that was for sure. That was for damned sure. . . .

The sweet, heavy fragrance of berries filled the air as Rand urged his bay steadily down the trail he had climbed only days before. Upland huckleberry bordered its winding length for miles, its ragged branches reaching out to him with tempting display, its scent overwhelming. But he was unconscious of all but his driven haste. The sense of urgency deep inside him would not allow consideration of the enticing fragrance.

His eyes intently scanning the endless expanse of land around him in vain hope of sighting a slim mounted figure, Rand's mind reviewed over and again the last day Billie and he had spent together.

Blind . . . He must have been blind. Billie's loving hunger for him, which had made him forget his resolve to settle things between them . . . She had sought his mouth in order to induce him to forget his questions. She had given him her body so he might forget all else—and he had. So filled with love for her, he had chosen to ignore the desperation in her response, wanting to believe she merely wanted him as much as he wanted her. He knew better now. That last day when Billie had loved him so completely she had been saying good-bye.

A resurgence of the pain ever present inside him tightened Rand's watchful scrutiny of the sun-swept trail. He had been a fool. He had allowed himself to be led, handled exactly as

Billie had planned. And in falling into her hands, he had allowed her to leave without a single clue as to where she had run.

He strained his mind, searching backward in time. Ogalalla . . . The thought suddenly occurred to him that Whitley's unexpected appearance had pushed completely from his mind the angry frustration he had been nourishing while waiting for Billie in the saloon. He had been angry because Billie had spent so much time with Jeremy, going from store to store. Why had it not occurred to him that she had been looking for someone or searching for information?

Rand shook his head in an attempt to clarify his thoughts. It was when the herd had reached the main stage road and he had turned northwest that he had begun to notice a re-surgence of Billie's tension. The station master had been an easy talker. He remembered Billie had spent some time in conversation with the man while he had tended to the affairs of the herd. He remembered because he had watched the fellow carefully. Jealous . . . He had been jealous of that friendly old man. . . . And now he had lost Billie completely. For all he knew, she was now in her lover's arms. . . .

No, he could not afford to waste time in regret. He had to think. . . . Think. What was it he had heard the old man mention to Billie? The jealous eavesdropping he had done could come to some good now if he could remember. The old fellow had been talking about a new town, which had sprung up as a result of the heavy buffalo hide trade waiting for transportation to navigable points on the Missouri. He had said it was an enterprising little town. . . . Frenchman's Ford . . . That was it!

Rand's heart pounding, he sought to recall more of the old man's comments. How far had he said Frenchman's Ford was from the station? Had he said forty miles, fifty?

However far it was, Rand was suddenly certain that was where he was going. And if Billie were not there, he would continue looking. He would not, could not stop until he had found her, seen her safe, even if that meant seeing Billie in the arms of the man she loved.

Rand spurred his horse forward. An aching desire was

strong in his mind, even as he silently acknowledged its futility. He wished desperately, so very desperately, that the man Billie loved could have been he.

". . . I shot him again and again . . . couldn't make myself stop until he fell. I killed him, and then I felt nothing. . . . Nothing. I covered his body and went in the next room to bathe and dress. I left that night. . . ."

Billie was hardly aware her brother sat beside her on the velvet settee in Lil Culver's room, was barely conscious of her mother's sober stare. Still caught in the horror of memory, she experienced again the numbness that had allowed her to function after Wes McCulla's attack, after she had taken his life.

A low voice penetrated her semiconscious state. Its warmth of tone drew her back to the present, turning her to Adam's concerned expression.

"You had no choice, Billie. You were defending yourself. . . ."

"He—he's dead, Adam. I killed him. I have to go back. I can't spend the rest of my life wondering, looking over my shoulder. . . ."

Billie saw the quick, helpless look her brother shot in Lil's direction. She felt a flash of regret.

"I didn't come here to bring you my problems, either of you. I just had to know you, Adam, to discover the part of me that was missing before I could face—"

"Face what? You said yourself the fellow's father owns the whole county! It makes no sense to go back. . . ."

"They'll find me sooner or later, Adam. I told you about Carl Whitley. . . ."

"We can handle Carl Whitley." Lil's hushed tone interrupted the exchange with a low note of finality. "Matt, Adam, and I aren't without friends here. Matt will be back from the mines in a day or so, and if Whitley should show up—"

"No! I don't want it that way." Billie turned to her brother. "Try to understand, Adam. I saw life leave Wes McCulla's body. It was a life I took, was responsible for ending, no matter the reasoning involved. I don't want to see another life lost to a useless purpose. And most especially, I don't want it to be the life of someone I love. I— It's a decision I've made, to which I'm committed. Whether you understand it or not and whether or not you agree, I'm leaving here. I'm going to the nearest railroad and I'm going to buy a ticket to Texas. . . ."

"Billie, don't be a damned fool!"

Billie's head jerked in Lil's direction.

"Maybe I *am* a fool, Mother. Maybe I'm making a mistake. But it's my conscience I must live with, not yours. You made your decision fifteen years ago, and you've lived with it. I made a similar decision several days ago, and this is all part of it. I have to bring all this uncertainty to an end, this fear of bringing death down on someone I love."

The silence that followed Billie's earnest declaration reigned unbroken for long moments before Adam's reassuring arm pulled her against him for support.

"All right, Billie. I think Mama and I can understand how you feel. . . ."

"All right?" Lil's voice was incredulous. "Adam, are you crazy?" If she goes back—"

"Wait, Mama, let me finish." Turning back to Billie, Adam shook his head. "It's not that we don't understand, Billie, because we do. As much as she protests, Mama and I both know you've suffered with the knowledge that you killed Wes McCulla, and you want to have it settled once and for all. But it doesn't make sense to go back until you're certain you'll get fair treatment when you return. This is all new to us, Mama and me. Give us some time to find out what's going on back in Texas. We can send a wire to San Antonio. The sheriff there can make the necessary inquiries and find out how things stand. You've waited this long. A little while longer can't make that much difference."

Adam raised Billie's chin with the tip of his finger. His gaze was earnest, the soft plea in its depths touching Billie deeply.

"We're only asking that you wait until we get a reply.

510

We're not asking you to change your mind. Just give us time to see if we can help you."

A little while longer . . . Billie debated the thought in her mind. With reluctance she submitted to his reasoning. Adam was right. She had waited this long. If a few weeks more would give her brother peace of mind, she would wait. She had not come all this way to cause Adam distress.

"All right, Adam. But if we don't get an answer soon—"

"We will, Billie."

Obviously vastly relieved, Adam shot Lil a quick smile before turning back in her direction. "Since I don't have decent accommodations to offer you, Mama will make room for you."

"No!"

"Don't be ridiculous, Billie!" As if reading her mind, Lil continued tightly, "I don't expect to put you up in this room. You can see how crowded it is, and I know you don't look forward to meeting Matt, much less sharing a room with him when he returns in a day or so. Matt and I own the hotel across the street. . . ."

Relieved, Billie grudgingly nodded her head.

"All right, Mother. That'll be fine. Then I can pay my own way."

A stiffness entering her manner at Billie's last remark, Lil continued quietly, "But as your mother, I'm going to ask you to do something for me, Billie." Noting Billie's immediate tensing, Lil gave a short laugh. "I know what you're thinking. I haven't earned the right to ask anything of you. Well, I guess you're right, but I'm going to ask anyway. If not for my sake, I ask for Adam's. Frenchman's Ford is a wild town. People are coming and going all the time and you said some men are pursuing you. They could get by us unnoticed until it's too late if you stray too far from here."

Billie was already frowning, but Lil continued. "I'm asking that you stay within sight, Billie. Adam has a room at the hotel, too, and he'll be spending most of his time in town for the next week or so. You can get to know each other better. As for the rest of the time, you can stay here, upstairs."

511

"I can take care of myself."

"Ma's right, Billie." His earnest plea adding to Lil's, Adam smiled. "We've only just found you. We don't want to take a chance on losing you to these fellas. . . ."

"I don't expect to ask permission every time I make a move, Adam."

"All right, not every time. . . ."

"I'm not joking, Adam."

"And neither am I." Adam released a short sigh, his smile fading. "Billie, give us a chance to—"

"All right." Regretting her sharpness, Billie nodded. "I didn't come here to be a burden. I'll do my best to cooperate."

Intensely aware that Billie's agreement had hinged entirely on her brother's plea, Lil was suddenly weary.

"Take your sister across the street and get her a room, Adam. I'll see you both later."

Billie turned away and moved instinctively toward the door at her mother's abrupt dismissal. Her mother's instincts were keen. It was time for Billie to get away by herself so she might absorb all that had been so recently disclosed to her. She needed to come to terms in her mind with the beautiful woman whom her father had loved and lost to another man . . . the beautiful woman who had broken his heart.

A hand curled unexpectedly around Billie's shoulder, and she raised her eyes to Adam's gaze. A deep warmth suffused her. It stayed with her as he opened the door and ushered her out. She had found the part of her she had been seeking. But the price she had paid was exorbitant. Rand's handsome image flashed before her eyes and a familiar thickness choked her throat. She continued to pay it still.

Ignoring the chill of early morning, Carl scanned the passing landscape with an assessing eye. The heavy pounding of hoofbeats immediately to his rear was a reminder that he could allow no further foul-ups in his bid to locate the Winslow girl. He had no desire to look any more the fool than he had already appeared to McCulla and

512

his men.

Carl frowned and spurred his horse to a faster pace. He darted a short glance to the man who rode silently to his right as they moved over the uneven terrain. McCulla's expression was stiff, and Carl was only too conscious of the man's silence. It boded poorly for him. He knew he had only one more chance to redeem himself in McCulla's eyes. And redeem himself he would. . . . He had determined that the moment he had arrived at the herd to find the Winslow girl gone.

A hot surge of rage snapped Carl's head to his other side and the two men who rode just slightly to his rear. Oh, yes, Larry and Marty were making sure to stay as far out of his range of vision as they dared. Carl's thin lips pulled back in a grim smile. His ragged mustache twitched as he fought to suppress the fury that surged through him.

Frenchman's Ford . . . The girl would be there, he was certain of it. He could feel it in his bones, and his instincts were never wrong. And he'd be damned if he'd let her get away this time. . . .

An unexpected tremor moved down Carl's spine. No, he could not afford to let her get away. McCulla's eyes . . . There was death in them, and he knew with a deep certainty it would be either the girl's or his own. But he intended to live for a long time, and he was going to make sure McCulla got what he wanted. That Winslow bitch had made a big mistake when she had turned down a McCulla.

It was a mistake that was going to prove fatal.

Billie cast a quick glance into the mirror in her hotel room, her eyes catching on her own reflection with curiosity. She had worn the trail clothes of a drover for so long that she had almost forgotten how she looked in female attire. But she had little interest in the pale blue batiste gown she wore or the manner in which her mother had dressed her hair a few hours before. Rather, she had donned the clothes her mother had provided and allowed her to trim her hair and dress it, only because to do otherwise would have indicated a hostility she no longer felt toward the still beautiful Lil Culver.

In truth, Billie realized that a few months earlier she would not have had the faintest idea of the depth of torment her mother had suffered in making the choice between Rod Winslow and Matt Carter so many years before. She would not have realized that to suffer separation from the man you loved was a knife of pain driven so deep inside as to steal the life from your soul. She was now certain that no matter how unsure her future with Rand would have been, nothing could have induced her to leave him except the threat on his life his closeness to her ensured. That realization had allowed her new insight into the decision her mother had made. And if she could not truly forgive her mother for leaving her father and herself, she could surely understand the overwhelming love that had forced her to that ultimate decision. In any case, she now realized only too clearly that it was not in her province to attempt to judge her mother.

Although she chafed sorely under the restrictions requested of her by her newfound family, Billie had allowed Adam to settle her in the hotel several days before. She had forced her natural independence aside to allow them peace of mind, realizing the limited time they would have together. In the time since, the vague shadows that had been so long beyond her range of vision had taken on flesh, and balm had been added to raw emotional wounds.

Shooting a quick glance toward the window, Billie caught sight of the setting sun in all its glory. Another day on the wane . . . She would not remain in Frenchman's Ford much longer, whether a response had been received to her mother's wire or not. She felt a deep, innate desire to settle her life, to return to Texas and the justice that awaited her. And when all was settled, when threat no longer pursued her, perhaps she would see Rand again. . . .

Her throat suddenly filled with emotion, Billie turned abruptly toward the door. She could wait no longer for Adam. Waiting allowed her too much time for thought, too much time to become morose. . . . And tonight she would tell them, tell them both that she would leave Frenchman's

Ford at the end of the week.

Taking the few steps to the doorway, Billie turned the lock and pulled the door open. She gasped at the unexpected shadowed figure standing there. Her parted lips suddenly moving into a smile, she stepped into the hallway and took Adam's arm. She indulged his short reprimand, grateful for the love it evidenced and knowing she would be subjected to it for only a short time longer.

Twilight . . . The setting sun had disappeared behind the distant peak, dropping the world around him into the first shadows of night as Rand moved through the winding streets of Frenchman's Ford. But the exhaustion he felt deep inside had dulled neither his mind nor his senses as his slitted gaze moved around the crowded streets. Frenchman's Ford was obviously a town in transition, blooming on the trade in buffalo hides that were piled in the streets awaiting transportation. The setting was raw, ripe for violence, with the primitive law of nature known as self-preservation as much in evidence in the swagger of men with six-shooters buckled securely to their hips, while they made their festive rounds, as it was in the wild drunken shouts of others who staggered in and out of the saloons that lined the main street.

A deep frustration setting his nerves on edge, Rand searched the streets for the sign of a familiar slender figure. He had been pushing himself and his mount hard for two days in his conviction that Billie had headed in this direction when she had left. But in truth, he had not expected Frenchman's Ford to be such a booming town. Attempting to find someone who saw Billie was going to be more time-consuming than he thought, if indeed she had come to this place.

A deep, gnawing sensation in his stomach brought Rand to another realization. He had eaten very little for the past two days on the trail, and he had dispensed with all but the barest necessities of physical comfort. Raising his hand to his chin, he rubbed his palm against the stubble there. Yes, he needed a good meal, a bath, and a shave. He would take

515

care of those necessities first, before he started making his rounds and asking questions. He gave no thought at all to the possibility of rest. That would come later.

A familiar ache tightening deep inside, Rand could not suppress the hope that sprang to life in his mind. Later, if luck were with him and if Billie were still here, he might hold her in his arms again. But the sudden, cold thrust of reality invaded his thoughts, and Rand shook his head. No, he was only indulging in fantasy, torturing himself with something that could not be. Billie had left him to go to another man . . . the man she loved. She could not have been more open, more honest in the letter she had left behind. He would have to obtain his satisfaction in seeing her once more, making certain she was safe and happy. That was the only reason he had come after her, wasn't it? Wasn't it? . . .

Unwilling to face his own silent question, Rand turned his horse toward the well-lit livery stable a few yards ahead. Dismounting a few moments later, he removed his saddlebags and turned his horse over to the bearded attendant. His hands moved automatically to his hips to settle his gun more comfortably before he turned toward the building to which he had been directed. Yes, a bath, a shave, and a quick meal, and he'd be fresh enough to start his round of inquiries.

The unexpected visitation of a pale-haired vision before his mind's eye quickened the beat of his heart, and Rand's step hastened spontaneously. Yes, if he were lucky, he might find out where Billie had gone tonight. He might see her, touch her. . . . God, he needed to know she was safe. He needed at least to set that demon at rest within his mind. He needed . . .

Unwilling to indulge his thoughts any longer, Rand consumed the last few feet to the bathhouse in a lengthened stride and walked through the doorway. He would take things one step at a time from here on in. One difficult step at a time . . .

Billie pushed her way through the flimsy curtain in the doorway and stepped into The Ragged Buffalo proper. She turned toward Adam as he stepped into the room beside her, shaking her head at his frown.

"Adam, I truly cannot understand your thinking! Mother owns this saloon. She sings here several times daily and has done the same in this saloon or one like it since the time of your first recollection. Yet, you say you don't want me in here. Adam, saloons are nothing new to me. On the trail drive up here I went with the men. . . ."

"On the trail drive up here you were dressed like a boy."

Adam's heavy features were pulled into a scowl strongly reminiscent of her father, but Billie was determined not to allow the similarity between them to influence her. She had submitted to enough coddling in the past few days. It was time she attempted to stand up on her own two feet again.

"That makes little difference. . . ."

Firmly gripping her arm, Adam steered Billie toward a vacant table in the corner. Seating her carefully with her back to the wall, he signaled for a drink before turning back to face her. His scowl had darkened.

"That's where you're wrong, Billie, and I think you know it. Tell me something. Have you looked at yourself in the mirror recently?"

"Of course I have! I—"

"But you obviously haven't paid much attention to what you saw."

"What are you trying to say, Adam?"

Adam took a deep breath and an obvious hold on his patience.

"Billie, we may be twins, but sometimes I think we couldn't be farther apart in thinking. . . . You're beautiful, Billie."

Billie shook her head. Her eyes misted as similar words, spoken in Rand's soft whisper, returned to haunt her mind.

"You're the second man who's said that to me, Adam. And I'll tell you what I told him. I'm not beautiful. . . ."

"Then maybe the both of us are blind, Billie, but the truth is, we aren't. And another truth is, I didn't know my father, but I know the kind of man he was. Both Mama and I know he wouldn't have wanted you in here. . . ."

517

Unable to dispute that statement, Billie averted her gaze momentarily. The dark eyes she turned back to her brother's face were suspiciously bright. She attempted a smile.

"Adam, try to understand. I'll only be here a few more days. I don't know when I'll return, if ever. I'm storing up memories, Adam. . . ."

"Don't be ridiculous." Adam's arm slipped around her shoulder, and his face softened. "You're wasting time if you're storing up memories. You won't be getting far enough away from us to need to employ them. You don't really think Mama and I are going to let you—"

"I told you, I'm leaving at the end of the week, Adam. Nothing you and Mama said are going to change that."

"Billie. . . ." Adam's arm tightened, drawing her closer as he attempted to speak more confidentially. "We're bound to have an answer to our wire before then, and when we do—"

"And when you do get an answer, nothing will change. I'll still have to return to Texas." Feeling true distress at the pain in Adam's expression, Billie raised a hand to stroke his cheek.

"Oh, Adam, don't you understand? I want to go back. I have to, to put my life in order before everything falls down on those I love. But I'm ahead of the game, Adam. A few months ago, after Pa was killed, I had nobody left to love and no one left to love me. That's changed now, and I've grown because of that change."

"But you haven't grown enough to realize you owe it to the ones you love to let them love you in return, to let them help you."

"Even when I could be bringing disaster down upon them?"

"Even then. . . ."

"I can't, Adam. I can't do that."

His expression hardening, Adam responded in a subdued voice. "We'll see, Billie. We'll see. . . ."

His heart beating an uneven tattoo in his chest, Rand

strode toward the entrance to The Ragged Buffalo. Minutes before he had returned to the livery stable for a few last-minute instructions as to his mount. He had turned, almost disbelieving, to see a small sorrel mare being led from an end stall. Ginger. . . .

A few seconds of inquiry had sent him rapidly in the direction of the saloon he was now approaching. Billie had arrived in town a few days before. She was staying with the woman who owned the saloon, Lil Culver. The stableman had made no reference to a man. . . . Elation lifted Rand's spirits. Obviously, something had gone wrong with Billie's plans. The man she had been seeking was not here.

He had been given another chance. Breathing deeply against the new raging tempo of his heart, Rand attempted to draw his emotions under control. The other fellow's loss was his gain. He had allowed Billie to slip away from him before. He would not allow it to happen again. He'd go to this Lil Culver, make her tell him where Billie was. Then he'd convince Billie that she needn't wait for this man, whoever he was. He'd tell Billie that he'd be everything she ever wanted, ever needed in a man. He'd tell her that he'd make her forget this other fellow and whatever they were to each other. He'd promise to spend the rest of his life making certain she never regretted allowing him to love her.

And then he would love her. His love for Billie an aching need inside him, Rand clenched his fists against the trembling the thought elicited. Billie. . . . His Billie. . . . He had been given a second chance. God, he could not lose her this time, not again. . . .

Taking the steps up onto the boardwalk in front of The Ragged Buffalo in a quick leap, Rand strode to the doorway and pushed through. He hesitated, his eyes scanning the crowded room. The sound of raucous laughter that met his ears, the rapid tempo of voices went unnoticed as he strained his eyes through the blue cloud of smoke that hung over the room. His gaze was moving systematically along the bar and the surrounding tables when it jarred to a sudden halt. His body abruptly draining of his newfound hope, Rand stood stock-still, unwilling to believe the sight that met his eyes.

Billie. . . . Looking more beautiful than he had ever seen her, sitting close in the circle of a dark-haired man's arm. Their faces were close in intimate conversation, their gazes tightly held. Billie's hand rested against the fellow's cheek. She caressed it lightly as she spoke, her expression reflecting both love and pleading earnest. The fellow nodded, his arm tightening to draw her closer, and Rand could stand no more.

A jealous rage overwhelming him, Rand was beside the table in minutes. Billie jerked her eyes upward, catching his, and Rand's breath caught sharply in his throat. The love evidenced in the sober depths of her eyes in the moment before she realized his presence was a devastating blow.

Billie drew herself to her feet, her slender body going rigid. She darted a quick glance to the man who rose immediately at her side in a guarded stance. The fellow's right hand slid to his gunbelt, his features darkening. His voice held a menacing tone.

"Who is this fellow, Billie? What does he want?"

Aware that Rand's hand had also snapped to his gun, Billie immediately reached out to stay her companion's hand. She shook her head.

"No, Adam. . . ."

The fellow's hand dropped slowly back to his side, and Rand was shocked by the realization that he would have welcomed the opportunity to use his gun on this man—the man Billie loved more than she loved him.

Instead, Rand managed a tight smile.

"I turned the herd over to Willie. I couldn't go on until I was certain you were all right." He forced a short glance toward the man who still stood protectively at her side. "He's the one, isn't he, the man you came looking for. . . ."

Billie responded with a short nod, and Rand swallowed hard at the knot that began to tighten in his throat. His eyes held hers intently.

"In the back of my mind I knew you'd find him. You were always so determined when you set your mind on something. . . ."

Billie's dark eyes were reading the torment in his, but

Rand could not tear away his gaze. She was his Billie, more beautiful than he had ever dreamed, and none the less his in his heart, despite the distance she had forced between them. And he loved her. . . . He loved her so much.

"I had to make sure you were safe . . . and happy. . . ."

"You don't have to worry about me anymore, Rand. Yes, I'm safe . . . and happy." Billie attempted a smile, but the effort fell flat. "Adam—Adam is determined to take care of me."

As if to emphasize the truth of her statement, Billie took a step closer to the dark-haired fellow's side. His reaction immediate, the fellow slid his arm supportively around her waist, and Rand steeled himself against his desire to jerk Billie free of his hold. Unable to trust his waning restraint, Rand took a step backward.

"That's what I want for you, Billie—happiness." He gave a short laugh. "Only, I wanted you to find it with me. . . ." Finding it suddenly difficult to say more, Rand raised his hand in a short salute.

"You know where to find me if you should ever need me, Billie. That big house in St. Louis that I told you about . . ." Rand's mind finished silently, "That big, empty house . . ."

The memory of Billie's stiff white face burned into his mind, Rand turned and strode from the saloon. Stopping only long enough to pick up his saddlebags, he went directly to the livery stable. A desperate need drove him to get out of town quickly, before the pain became too great, before he did something he would regret. If he pressed hard, he could catch up with the herd and begin to put all this behind him where it belonged, in the past.

Mounted within minutes, Rand turned his horse back in the direction from which he had come only a short time before. He spurred his mount hard, not stopping to look back. . . .

His arm around her waist Adam all but lifted Billie up the final three steps and onto the second floor of the hotel. His expression intense, he guided her toward her room. Pausing

521

as he reached the door, he frowned down into her white face.

"Billie, don't be stubborn. That fellow shook you up more than you admit, and you know it. I realize you have a right to your privacy, but I have the feeling you shouldn't have let him think that we—"

"I answered his questions, didn't I, Adam? Rand wanted to know if you were the man I had come looking for. You are. He wanted to know if I was happy that I had found you. I am."

Adam's frown darkened. "You know damned well he got the wrong impression. He left his herd in somone else's care just to come looking for you. He deserved to be told the truth. He—"

"What truth would you have me tell him, Adam? That I'm being hunted for taking a man's life? That I'm a fugitive from the law, who is about to return to face what she's done? Would you have me tie him to me under those circumstances? Or would you have me attempt to evade everything by running away with him? That wouldn't work, you know. Rand is a wealthy man, Adam. He's well-known. I could never hope to elude the law or the men who are following me if we were together. No, Adam, I have no other choice but to leave Frenchman's Ford tomorrow."

"Tomorrow! You said you'd wait until the end of the week, at least until Mama and I have had a chance to—"

Adamant, Billie shook her head. "No, my plans have changed. I'm leaving tomorrow."

Adam took a deep breath. He had been attempting to make Billie see reason for the past hour since that Pierce fellow had walked out of The Ragged Buffalo. It was now clearer than ever that his sister was a very determined woman.

"It's plain to see there's no use talking to you tonight." Taking the key from her hand, Adam unlocked the door to her room and pushed it open. "Get a good night's sleep. I'll pick you up for breakfast, and you, Mama, and I can discuss this whole thing then."

Unwilling to prolong the agony of their discussion any longer, Billie nodded and turned into her room. Pausing to

522

light the lamp on the table near the door, she shot Adam a parting smile as she closed the door. She locked it from the inside. Her smile flickered again in the realization that Adam had waited to hear the click of the lock before turning back to the staircase.

A deep sadness permeating her senses as Adam's step faded from her hearing, Billie turned toward the bed. She had taken two steps in its direction when an arm closed unexpectedly around her waist from behind, jerking her backward against a hard male body. A rough hand clamped simultaneously across her mouth, stifling her gasp as it cut cruelly into her lips. Her eyes wide with fear, her heart pounding, Billie attempted to turn to see the face of her captor.

But her effort was to no avail. For long, terrifying minutes Billie was aware of nothing but the hot breath fanning her cheek, the low grunting sound that accompanied a tightening of the grip that all but crushed her breath from her body. A low snicker sounded against her ear, and Billie's blood turned cold. A deep shuddering beset her as incredulity struggled with reality within her mind. A sudden weakness turned her knees to water.

She was struggling to maintain consciousness as a low voice whispered hotly into her ear.

"Yes, it's me, darlin'. . . . You're surprised, aren't you? I knew you would be. You thought I was dead, didn't you? But I wouldn't let myself die. I promised you somethin' special, and you should know by now that I always finish what I start. Let me see, I was teachin' you a lesson, wasn't I?"

Abruptly, Billie was jerked around to face her captor. Soul-chilling terror kept her voiceless and immobile in his grasp as Wes McCulla slid his hand into her upswept hair, twisting the gleaming strands cruelly.

"Do you remember your teacher, little bitch? Here, let me refresh your memory."

Without warning, Wes McCulla's mouth closed over hers, its cruel pressure cutting her lips, robbing her of breath, causing a soft cry to escape her as McCulla ground his mouth deeper into hers. Drawing away at last, Wes breathed raggedly into her white face.

"You almost killed me, little bitch, but you didn't. No, I wasn't goin' to die and let you get away, no matter how many bullets you pumped into me. I laid there in that bed for almost three months, thinkin' of nobody but you: how you made me look like a fool to my pa and my men, how I was goin' to get even, how I was goin' to make you pay for what you did to me. And I planned it all, darlin', how I was goin' to enjoy it, right to the end. . . .

"You almost got away. . . . You even found that whore of a mother of yours. It's her hot blood you got runnin' in your veins, ain't it? You found your long lost brother, too. You even managed to pick yourself up a lover. . . ."

A hot rage setting his pale eyes afire, Wes McCulla twisted his hand tighter in her hair, causing Billie to gasp in pain.

"You gave yourself to him real easy, didn't you? The rich, handsome Rand Pierce . . . Did you know Carl was watchin' you all the time you was playin' around with that dandy? I hope you enjoyed yourself, darlin', and I hope he taught you a few things, 'cause you're goin' to show me all you learned. But not here. . . ."

Suddenly regaining her voice, Billie gritted from between teeth clenched with pain, "I—I should've killed you the first time. If I get the chance again—"

"You won't get a chance, bitch! But *I* will. . . . I'll have the chance to take you as slow as I want, to teach you all the lessons I wanted to teach you months ago. But it's goin' to be all the better for the waitin', you'll see."

Her strength suddenly returning, Billie began to struggle violently, her arms flailing in wild punches that landed with surprising strength against McCulla's face. A low grunt of pain preceded a quick movement in which McCulla twisted Billie's arms tightly behind her with one hand. His words were short with anger.

"I'm tired of talkin', and I'm tired of your strugglin'. And for now, I'm tired of you."

Her eyes widening, Billie was unable to avoid McCulla's fist as it descended unexpectedly. A flash of blinding color was simultaneous with the pain that crashed against her cheek and her own spontaneous outcry before she saw no more.

The low voice penetrated the dark, silent world in which she floundered. It spoke Billie's name, called to her, but its sound drove her deeper into the shadows she sought to avoid. A harsh grip took her shoulder, shook her, but still she avoided the light of consciousness that accosted her mind.

"Come on, little bitch, wake up. . . ."

A new shuddering besetting her frame, Billie was unable to resist dawning reality. Her eyes slowly opening, she felt the rough hand tighten as her vision met a familiar pale-eyed gaze. Panic assailed her senses, and Billie made an abrupt effort to rise. The weight of Wes McCulla's hand held her down against the bed on which she lay. Helpless against it, Billie darted a quick glance around her, only to have McCulla's low laughter snap her attention back to his face.

"Don't know where you are, do you? Well, I'll tell you, I'll tell you anythin' you want to know. . . . You're at a cabin just outside Frenchman's Ford. The boys and I discovered it on the way in. Seems like the prospector that lives here is out in the hills right now, and he ain't expected to be back for at least a month. Hell, I figure I'll be done with you by then, and then he can have you and the place all to himself if he wants. . . ."

Wes's hand was moving in her hair, and Billie's flesh began to crawl. In a quick movement, she attempted to roll to the far side of the bed, only to have her move stopped by McCulla's sudden weight as he threw himself atop her.

"Oh no you don't, little bitch!"

Peculiarly dim pin-points of light shining in his pale eyes, Wes McCulla groaned as his heavy body made first contact with Billie's supple softness. His low voice grated on the silence of the room.

"Damn you, bitch. . . . I laid in that bed for almost three months. You left me for dead, and I almost bled myself dry of blood before the men found me in the mornin'. I swore I'd

525

get you for that. . . . I don't think I hated nobody or nothin' as much as I hated you.

"When I rode into Frenchman's Ford and saw you goin' into that saloon your mother runs, I was all for chargin' up the street then and there to take you. But Carl stopped me. He's a right smart fella, that Carl, even if he did lose you for a while. He was smart enough to figure out he was goin' to have to find you again for me, or he was goin' to die in the attempt. I knew I could count on Carl. He has a real lust for life, that fella.

"Carl held me back, little bitch, and you can thank him for your bein' so nice and comfy on this bed here, with me layin' on top of you. But that ain't all you can thank him for. You can thank him for makin' me keep my promise to you. I don't like breakin' promises, bitch, especially the kind I made to you. So I'm tellin' you again. You got a lesson comin' that's long overdue. I'm goin' to teach you how a real man takes a woman. I'm goin' to fill you, spill my seed inside you, and fill you again. And you know somethin', little bitch? I'm goin' to enjoy every minute of it. I'm goin' to like makin' you cry out my name, makin' you beg me for more. . . . I'm goin' to like usin' you until I'm used up, and then makin' you pleasure me some more. . . ."

Wes McCulla's heavy body was beginning to move subtly atop hers, and Billie stifled the low protests that choked her throat. No, it would do no good to attempt to squirm free of him. If anything, his long confinement had added poundage to McCulla's powerful frame. She would have to await her opportunity. . . .

"That's right, darlin'. . . ." Mistaking the revulsion that forced her heavy lids partially closed for the dawning of desire, McCulla tightened his hand in Billie's hair. He dropped his head to move his mouth wetly over hers. His tongue invaded her mouth delving deeply, and Billie gagged.

Drawing back, his expression enraged, McCulla raised his hand to deliver a quick blow to her jaw that snapped Billie's head sharply to the side. The bitter taste of blood filled her mouth as Billie turned her blurred vision back to the fury in McCulla's gaze.

"My kisses make you sick, do they? I'm tellin' you now, you'll be beggin' for them in a little while, and I'll be enjoyin' every minute of it. You know why? Because the truth is, all the while I was layin' there in that bed, hatin' you, I was wantin' you more and more. And you're goin' to want me too, you know that, Miss High-and-Mighty Winslow? Because I'm goin' to drive thoughts of any other man out of your head, even if I have to beat them out. But first things first, little bitch. . . ."

Unexpectedly, Wes lifted himself slightly from the cushion of Billie's body. Seeing her chance, Billie scrambled wildly to be free, only to have Wes McCulla's grip on her hair jerk her cruelly backward until she was once again pressed helplessly against the bed. In a quick, unexpected movement, Wes straddled her with his knees and jerked Billie's hands above her head, pinning them there with one hand. With a low laugh he dug his other hand into the neckline of her gown and ripped it savagely down the center. Her loathing rising out of control as Wes took the soft flesh of her breast and began to knead it painfully, Billie hissed with obvious venom.

"You low, vile beast! You think you can use pain and fear to make me say I want you? You're a fool! There's only one man I want, and you're not the one. Yes, I let Rand Pierce love me, and I loved him back. I took him willingly inside me. You may force yourself into that same place, but the only joy you'll receive will be from the violence you inflict on me."

A wild rage flushing his face, Wes McCulla raised his hand again to strike her. The shrill laugh that escaped Billie's lips froze his hand in the very act of descending.

"That's the only victory you'll have over me. . . ."

Wes's hand was again descending when a sharp knock sounded on the door, once more freezing his blow.

His eyes snapping toward the sound, Wes leaped from the bed and scrambled for the far chair and the holster hanging on the back. His gun in hand, his expression rabid, he turned back toward the door.

"Who is it?"

Carl's anxious voice sounded quickly in response.

"It's me, boss, Carl. There's at least a dozen riders comin' over the hill. It looks to me like it might be that brother of the girl's and a posse. I'm thinkin' we'd better get ready to fight if you expect to keep her. . . ."

Wes's expression going livid, he covered the few steps to the doorway in a rush and jerked the door open. Clutching her torn gown closed, Billie pulled herself to her feet beside the bed in time to see Carl's perspired face in the opening. His small eyes on the gun Wes held in his hand, Carl began to stammer as Wes stepped closer.

"Carl, what in hell—"

In a sudden lurch Carl was thrust forward into the room. Barely missing crashing into Wes, he hit the floor at the same moment Rand appeared in the opening behind him. Wes's pale eyes taking on a maniacal gleam, he gave a low growl and jerked his gun in Billie's direction. Within seconds the sound of gunfire shattered the silence of the room, freezing the dramatic tableau: the two men, guns smoking, staring at Billie as she clutched her chest.

The sound of human weight crashing against the floor turned Rand's eyes briefly toward the spot where Wes McCulla had fallen motionless, dead.

Billie's eyes were riveted on McCulla's unmoving form. She was shuddering so wildly that she was unable to move or speak. Her gaze snapped upward at a familiar touch just as Rand's arms closed around her, crushing her close. Rand's voice was husky in her ear. His heart pounded raggedly against her breast.

"Damn you, Billie, you stubborn, hardheaded—" Breathing heavily, Rand forced himself to relinquish his breathtaking embrace so he might look into her face. She saw the flicker of pain in his eyes as he saw her cut lip, the bruises on her cheeks. His voice was low with promise.

"He'll never hurt you again, Billie. I'd kill him again for what he did to you, what he wanted to do. . . . But you're safe now. You don't have to be afraid anymore."

Oblivious to the men who had moved swiftly into the room, pulling Carl up from the floor to take him into custody, bending low over Wes McCulla's prostrate form to confirm his death, Billie felt only the warmth of Rand's arms around her, the gentle touch of his lips against the bruised skin of her cheeks. Rand's voice came to her through the haze of terror and disbelief that was only just clearing.

"Why didn't you tell me what you were running from? Did you think I wouldn't understand, wouldn't want you? Don't you know I've loved you, Billie, from the first day I saw your battered face?"

Billie's eyes were trained on his, and Rand continued softly, "You almost made me lose you. . . . I was so determined to allow you the happiness you sought with the man I thought you loved. If Adam hadn't come after me, explained—"

Her eyes snapping toward her brother where he observed their loving reunion from the doorway, Billie heard his quiet confirmation.

"That's right, Billie. I rode after him and told him the truth. You're not the only hardheaded Winslow left, you know. . . ."

Still clutching her torn dress over her breast, Billie allowed Rand to urge her from the room. Darting a last look behind her, she paused as the tall man with the star on his vest dropped a blanket over Wes's still form. She swayed weakly. Her voice was a harsh rasp as she forced her thoughts into words.

"He died twice, Rand. . . . I killed him the first time. . . ."

"He won't be coming back for you again, Billie—or for me. As for the law—"

"You ain't goin' to have no problem with the law, Mr. Pierce." His bushy brows furrowed, the man with the badge turned from his completed task. "I seen it all. If it wasn't for you, this lady here would be layin' dead on the floor instead of this fella. And if anybody gives you any trouble, you just tell them to look to Federal Marshal Jim Hawkes's report on the matter, which I'll be filin' just as soon as I reach my office. It'll be a cold day in hell when a man goes to jail for savin' somebody's life."

His statement made, the husky marshal turned back to

the men who awaited his orders. Still trembling, Billie leaned against Rand's side as he urged her through the outer door into the yard. In a moment she was astride Rand's horse, and he was mounted behind her. Not waiting to see who followed them, Rand wrapped his arms tightly around Billie. He hesitated as Billie raised her eyes to his.

"I didn't want you to get involved in all this, Rand. I was going back, to Texas, to face the law. . . ."

"For killing a man who wasn't dead, a man who almost killed you. . . ." Anger hardened the strong planes of Rand's face. "You damned stubborn little twit. I tried to tell you that last day on the trail, but you wouldn't listen. I love you, Billie. Nothing you've done or ever will do can change that. You gave me a hell of a scare. . . . I've waited for you all my life , and I thought I was going to lose you. So I'm giving you fair warning now. You're not going to get away from me again. We're going to fill that big, empty house in St. Louis. We're going to start our own dynasty, darling, and you're going to spend the rest of your life in my arms, in my bed, and in my heart."

Rand hesitated when Billie did not respond. His eyes moved over her sober expression, the first glimmer of uncertainty sparking in their crystal brightness.

"Billie, did you hear what I said?"

"I heard."

"And? . . ."

"And I love you too, Rand. But if I wasn't so tired, if I wasn't so happy, I'd tell you I don't like you calling me names, even if they are true. And I'd tell you that I don't intend taking orders from you for the rest of my life, unless you deliver them all with your arms wrapped around me. I'd tell you that I know I'm a hardheaded, stubborn twit who doesn't like taking orders, who's too independent for her own good sometimes. But I'd also say that nothing short of fear for your life could have driven me from your side, Rand, and nothing ever will again."

Rand's eyes were suspiciously bright.

"And that big house in St. Louis? . . ."

"Big house or small house, as long as it's ours . . .

Sliding his hand up to cup her cheek, Rand gave a low, husky laugh. He pressed a light kiss against her bruised lips, chafing at the need for caution. Elation spread a warm golden glow through his veins, which threatened to consume him.

"Ours, darling . . ."

"Ours, Rand."

Epilogue

Billie's fair hair was no longer confined by a coarse leather thong. Instead, it glowed a moonlight gold, piled high atop her head in smooth, curving swirls. She did not wear the rough garments of a drover. Instead, fragile silk in a shade of the palest pink lay against her skin, baring her smooth shoulders, the gentle rise of her bosom, fitting softly to her slender curves. Rough, ill-fitting trousers and heavy boots no longer covered the long length of her legs. Instead, the draped and trained skirt of the exquisite garment she wore flared out dramatically to feet encased in soft leather slippers. Diamonds suspended from a fragile chain encircled her neck and hung from her ears. Another diamond, far larger in size, winked from her finger as she raised her hand uncertainly to her hair.

From his position to the far side of the room, Rand observed Billie in silence. His impressive stature was clothed in a well-fitting dark evening suit and white linen shirt, which emphasized his overpowering breadth of shoulder and chest and the dark lights in his heavy, well-groomed black hair. His chiseled features were cast in a thoughtful expression, the penetrating, crystal blue of his eyes reflecting a fiercely possessive pride.

In the three months of their marriage, Rand had told Billie countless times how very beautiful she was, but he knew she still did not believe him. It utterly amazed him that she could look into the mirror without seeing the perfection reflected

533

there: in the exquisite planes of a face in which small, fine features now shone with a loving peace; in the slant of mysteriously dark eyes in which a tender glow only partially obscured the inborn, tempestuous spirit and determination so much a part of her; and in the long, fluid line of the body he had loved so well and would continue to love for the rest of his life. It was a total beauty of body and spirit. Standing still as she was now, she put Rand in mind of an extravagant porcelain figurine, frighteningly fragile, immensely rare. But priceless, indeed, because she was truly flesh and blood, ardently loving, intricately a part of him . . . his alone. . . .

Feeling the rise of a seldom dormant passion, Rand took the few steps that brought him up behind her. His arms encircling Billie's waist, he pressed light kisses against the line of her neck and shoulder, his heartbeat escalating anew as Billie turned in his embrace, her arms sliding around his neck to offer her parted lips. Rand's mouth moved warmly against hers. The taste of Billie, the sweetness, the excitement of her indefinable flavor, sent a familiar hunger burning through his veins. He was becoming lost to a rising tide of feelings, which had grown so large in scope as to appear infinite to his continually startled mind. Tearing his mouth from hers, aware that he was physically as well as mentally aroused, Rand shook his head.

"You know it's a mistake kissing me that way, Billie. You know I lack control when it comes to you."

Her expression sober, Billie responded in a hushed voice, "And what makes you think I'm any more in control than you are, Rand?"

Rand gave a low, pleased laugh. "Then we're in sorry shape, with a whole house full of guests waiting for us downstairs."

The first trace of disquiet entering her expression, Billie avoided his gaze.

"I don't know, Rand. . . . I don't know if I'm cut out to be the hostess you expect of me. St. Louis society . . . I'm more at home in old clothes and boots, sitting astride a horse and working cattle."

"It's only a little dinner party, Billie, a welcome to St.

534

Louis. It's balm to my conscience for rushing you into such a quick wedding in Montana." His smile dimming, he offered with a hint of apology in his tone, "If I hadn't been so afraid of losing you again if we waited—"

"And are you still afraid?"

Realizing Billie had posed the question merely in jest, Rand evaded answering. How could he make her understand how he felt? He was only too aware it was a mere caprice of fate that had brought her to his herd outside San Antonio instead of one of the many others passing through. And fate was fickle indeed. How could he explain to her that those few, brief days after she had left him in Montana had given him all too clear a picture of how barren and empty his life would be without her? Oh, yes, he believed she loved him, but he truly doubted she could comprehend the total scope of his feelings for her. She was his life, his future, his immortality. She was the best of him, the worst of him, his anger and his joy. She was his love. She had added a new, sparkling facet to his life, the glory of which overshadowed all the others. Content before to live a day at a time, he now had a greater purpose in life. He was building for the future—for her, for the children they would share, the home they would fill with love and laughter.

But Billie was frowning.

"Rand, you didn't answer me."

An evasive smile curved Rand's lips.

"What if I'm tired of answering your questions?"

"What if I'm tired of answering yours?"

"You know my answer to that, Billie. . . ."

The sly rise of Rand's brow brought a quick smile to Billie's face.

"Oh no you don't! We have guests, remember?"

"That's what I've been telling you for the past half hour."

Laughing at the trapped expression that flitted across her face, Rand took Billie firmly by the arm.

"And you've been avoiding them long enough."

Ushering her purposely the few steps to the doorway, Rand pulled open the door. In a few minutes they were walking down the staircase toward the twinkling lights and the babble of voices that came from the rooms below.

Poised in the doorway to the spacious living room of their St. Louis home a few seconds later, Billie flicked her eyes around the room with incredulity. Dear faces—well-loved faces—met her startled gaze. A few steps to her right, immaculately dressed in spanking new clothes, their hair slicked unnaturally smooth, stood Willie, Jim, Nate, Casey, even Brothers and Hall—the whole crew of drovers. And Jeremy, dear Jeremy. Billie opened up her arms to him, and in moments she heard Jeremy's familiar, affected voice in her ear as he enclosed her in a breathtaking hug.

"Billie, you near take my breath away. I hate to admit it, but you're a hell of a lot prettier than Sinda Lee."

Billie turned her gaze to the group that stood a few feet farther away. A tall woman stood in misty-eyed silence, her pale hair only a shade softer than her own, for the gray intermingled with gold, her face startlingly similar to Billie's except for the subtle differences painted by the gentle hand of maturity. At her one side was a mature, handsome man who gazed at her soberly. On her other side was a younger man who matched him in height, whose harsh profile and rough features awoke a familiar, bittersweet pain inside her. She took a few quick steps to their side and embraced each one, lingering in Adam's arms a few moments longer, for the sheer happiness they provided.

A buffer of love surrounding her, a proud Rand tall and strong at her side, Billie faced the sea of new faces, experiencing an unexpected pleasure at the warmth extended to her. She was radiant with its glow when yet another couple approached. Momentarily startled, Billie caught her breath. The man was only faintly familiar, but the red-haired woman at his side, still beautiful despite her advanced stage of pregnancy, revived an unpleasant memory. The vivid picture of that blazing red mane resting against Rand's shoulder, those white arms encircling his neck as Rand's mouth moved to cover hers, turned her stiffly in Rand's direction.

"Billie, I'm not certain whether you've met Pat and Lucille Patterson. They're old friends. . . ."

Her great blue eyes bright, Lucille extended her hand warmly in Billie's direction as she reproved Rand lightly.

"Actually, it's *Lucille* and *Pat* Patterson, Rand." Turning to Billie, Lucille gave her a short wink. "I do so resent the propensity of the male to put the man's name first when introducing couples. You see, I do agree that we women have our definite place in life. It's just that I've not yet decided if that place is, indeed, where the male would most happily put us."

Flicking his eyes openly over Lucille's extended abdomen, Rand shook his head with a laugh. "Well, I would expect Pat has made a good start with you in establishing a foothold in that direction."

Lucille laughed good-naturedly. "It would appear that way at first glance, wouldn't it, Rand? But I would ask you to consider how well you know my determined nature." Shooting Pat a startlingly loving look as she slid her arm through his, she turned back toward Rand once more. "Does it make sense to you I would find myself in this ungainly state if I had no desire to have it so?"

Momentarily at a loss for words, Rand gave a short laugh. "Lucille, you never cease to amaze me."

"Funny, those were the exact words Pat said to me this morning when we— Oh, well. . . ." Pausing as a slight flush colored her husband's face, Lucille patted his arm. "I guess I won't go into that any farther."

"No, darling, I should think you shouldn't." His smile widening, Pat shook Rand's hand warmly. Stepping forward, he pressed a light kiss on Billie's cheek. "I do congratulate you on your marriage. Lucy and I are most happy to help you celebrate tonight."

Her gaze free of malice, Lucille appraised Billie openly. "I've heard so much about you, Billie. The story of your unorthodox travel with Rand's cattle drive has almost become legend since your marriage, and as much as I am unable to fathom how you managed to put up with the hardships involved, I admit the rumors of your adventures

537

intrigue me. So exciting . . . Flooded rivers, Indians, especially that particular fellow—I think White Hand was his name—who has since stirred up quite a furor near the border. He is quite a handsome savage, I am told. . . . You two were fairly close from what I understand. Oh, yes, I do admire your courage, your audacity. . . . I'm considered a bit of an audacious woman, myself. Of course"—pausing to pat affectionately the great protrusion in front of her, Lucille continued—"I find that aspect of my personality considerably curtailed at present. But in a few months, I expect I will—"

"You will what, dear?" Pat's soft interruption of Lucille's rambling speech deepened the color of his already green eyes. His tone held a gentle threat. "If you continue to talk this way, Lucy, you'll force me to adhere to an old adage in order to feel safe. You know the one I'm referring to, about keeping a wife 'barefoot and pregnant'. . . ."

"Yes I do, dear Pat, and the work involved in keeping me that way does sound delicious to contemplate." Turning Pat expertly toward the buffet, Lucille continued sweetly, "But we've taken up enough of Billie and Rand's time right now." With a short glance in Billie's direction, Lucille winked again. "We must get together soon, Billie. We have our audacity in common, you know. And when I'm free of my lovely encumbrance, we may find some truly daring schemes to hatch up."

Watching as Lucille waddled into the line at the crowded buffet, her husband maintaining a tight, proprietary hold on her arm, Billie gave a small laugh. Looking down, she was startled to see Rand's hold on her arm had become just as tight and proprietary. Realizing Lucille had skillfully maneuvered two strongly possessive men into just the position she desired, Billie gave a short laugh.

"I wasn't prepared to like that woman, Rand, but I do. Maybe she's right. We probably could be great friends once she—"

"No, I don't think so."

Billie jerked her gaze to Rand's flushed face. Was she wrong, or had his blue eyes taken on a slightly green tinge at the mention of White Hand and audacious adventures? Suddenly amused, Billie pressed in her drover's tone of the past.

"You may be my husband, Mr. Pierce, but that doesn't mean you can run my life any which way you want."

"Maybe it doesn't, Mrs. Pierce, but that doesn't mean I'm going to stop trying."

Abruptly, Rand's eyes were intensely blue again with sweet promise of all his love entailed, and a familiar warmth stirred inside Billie.

"Oh, no, Mr. Pierce, never stop trying. . . ."

Rand didn't need to say the words his eyes silently spoke to hers. He knew he never would. . . .

MORE HISTORICAL ROMANCES
from Zebra Books

PASSION'S FLAME   (1716, $3.95)
by Casey Stuart

Kathleen was playing with fire when she infiltrated Union circles to spy for the Confederacy. Then she met handsome Captain Matthew Donovan and had to choose between succumbing to his sensuous magic or using him to avenge the South!

MOONLIGHT ANGEL   (1599, $3.75)
by Casey Stuart

When voluptuous Angelique answered the door, Captain Damian Legare was surprised at how the skinny girl he remembered had grown into a passionate woman—one who had worshipped him as a child and would surrender to him as a woman.

WAVES OF PASSION   (1322, $3.50)
by Casey Stuart

Falling in love with a pirate was Alaina's last thought after being accused of killing her father. But once Justin caressed her luscious curves, there was no turning back from desire. They were swept into the endless WAVES OF PASSION.

SURRENDER TO ECSTASY   (1307, $3.95)
by Rochelle Wayne

A tall, handsome Confederate came into Amelia's unhappy life, stole her heart and would find a way to make her his own. She had no idea that he was her enemy. James Henry longed to reveal his identity. Would the truth destroy their love?

RECKLESS PASSION   (1601, $3.75)
by Rochelle Wayne

No one hated Yankees as much as Leanna Weston. But as she met the Major kiss for kiss and touch for touch, Leanna forgot the war that made them enemies and surrendered to breathless RECKLESS PASSION.

Available wherever paperbacks are sold, or order direct from the Publisher. Send cover price plus 50¢ per copy for mailing and handling to Zebra Books, Dept. 1964, 475 Park Avenue South, New York, N.Y. 10016. Residents of New York, New Jersey and Pennsylvania must include sales tax. DO NOT SEND CASH.

BESTSELLERS BY SYLVIE F. SOMMERFIELD ARE BACK IN STOCK!

SWEET MEDICINE'S PROPHECY
by Karen A. Bale

#1: SUNDANCER'S PASSION (1778, $3.95)

Stalking Horse was the strongest and most desirable of the tribe, and Sun Dancer surrounded him with her spell-binding radiance. But the innocence of their love gave way to passion — and passion, to betrayal. Would their relationship ever survive the ultimate sin?

#2: LITTLE FLOWER'S DESIRE (1779, $3.95)

Taken captive by savage Crows, Little Flower fell in love with the enemy, handsome brave Young Eagle. Though their hearts spoke what they could not say, they could only dream of what could never be. . . .

#3: WINTER'S LOVE SONG (1780, $3.95)

The dark, willowy Anaeva had always desired just one man: the half-breed Trenton Hawkins. But Trenton belonged to two worlds — and was torn between two women. She had never failed on the fields of war; now she was determined to win on the battle-ground of love!

#4: SAVAGE FURY (1768, $3.95)

Aeneva's rage knew no bounds when her handsome mate Trent commanded her to tend their tepee as he rode into danger. But under cover of night, she stole away to be with Trent and share whatever perils fate dealt them.

#5: SUN DANCER'S LEGACY (1878, $3.95)

Aeneva's and Trenton's adopted daughter Anna becomes the light of their lives. As she grows into womanhood, she falls in love with blond Steven Randall. Together they discover the secrets of their passion, the bitterness of betrayal — and fight to fulfill the prophecy that is Anna's birthright.